Sons and Daughters
&
The Tulip Girl

Born in Gainsborough, Lincolnshire, Margaret Dickinson moved to the coast at the age of seven and so began her love for the sea and the Lincolnshire landscape.

Her ambition to be a writer began early and she had her first novel published at the age of twenty-five. This was followed by twenty further titles including *Plough the Furrow*, *Sow the Seed* and *Reap the Harvest*, which make up her Lincolnshire Fleethaven trilogy. Many of her novels are set in the heart of her home county, but in *Tangled Threads* and *Twisted Strands* the stories included not only Lincolnshire but also the framework knitting and lace industries of Nottingham.

Margaret's latest novels – *Wish Me Luck*, *Sing as We Go*, *Suffragette Girl* and *Sons and Daughters* – have all been set in her native Lincolnshire, known in World War II as 'bomber country'.

www.margaret-dickinson.co.uk

ALSO BY MARGARET DICKINSON

Margaret Dickinson

Sons and Daughters
&
The Tulip Girl

PAN BOOKS

Sons and Daughters first published 2010 by Pan Books
The Tulip Girl first published 2000 by Pan Books

This omnibus first published 2011 by Pan Books
an imprint of Pan Macmillan, a division of Macmillan Publishers Limited
Pan Macmillan, 20 New Wharf Road, London N1 9RR
Basingstoke and Oxford
Associated companies throughout the world
www.panmacmillan.com

ISBN 978-0-330-54545-7

A CIP catalogue record for this book is available from
the British Library.

Typeset by SetSystems Ltd, Saffron Walden, Essex
Printed in the UK by CPI Mackays, Chatham ME5 8TD

Sons and Daughters

For Mandi

Acknowledgements

My grateful thanks to Eric and Mervyn Griggs for a lovely day out around Wainfleet All Saints and district. Thank you for sharing all your memories with me.

Many thanks to David Henson, Chairman at the Magdalen College Museum, Wainfleet All Saints, for a warm welcome at the museum and to David Turner for his kind interest and knowledge of the area in times past.

And as always my love and thanks to my family and friends for their continuing support and encouragement, especially to those who read the typescript: Fred Hill, David Dickinson and Pauline Griggs.

One

'Is that the – the coffin?'

'Yes, Charlotte dear.'

'And is – is Mama lying inside it?'

Mary, standing beside the child and holding her hand tightly, gasped and covered her mouth with her handkerchief, her eyes brimming with tears. She could not answer.

From an upstairs window of the farmhouse, Charlotte watched the cortège move away from the front door with sadness in her dark, violet eyes. But she did not weep. The coffin, smothered with wreaths of white lilies, lay in a glass hearse drawn by four black horses. Behind it walked her father, Osbert Crawford, and behind him were the men who worked for him. Charlotte – even at five – knew them all. First there was Edward Morgan. He was their household manservant. His wife, Mary, was their housekeeper and cook with only a young girl, Sarah, who came in daily to help her. Between the three of them they took care of everything and everyone in the household. Papa, Mama and Charlotte.

Only now there would just be Charlotte and her father.

1

Harry Warren, Osbert Crawford's farm foreman, walked beside Edward. Though still only in his mid-fifties, he suffered from arthritis and needed a stick. Usually he rode his chestnut horse around the fields and lanes overseeing the farm workers. But today he was obliged to walk with the rest of the mourners and every step looked painful. Just behind him and ready to help if he was needed was Harry's son, Joe. He'd worked on the land since leaving school and even before that he'd worked during the holidays, at weekends and most evenings, always ready to do his father's bidding, always eager to learn the ways of Buckthorn Farm and to please its master, Osbert Crawford. No doubt, Joe would take over his father's job when the older man retired. The Warren family lived in one of the two semi-detached cottages two hundred yards down the lane from the farm. Charlotte wondered where they all slept, for now there were not only Mr and Mrs Warren and their son Joe, but also Joe's wife, Peggy, their two sons and a little baby girl, Lily, who'd been born two weeks ago.

Charlotte bit her lip. Was it really only such a short time ago that she'd walked down the lane to the cottage holding her mama's hand and taking a large basket of food for the family and gifts for the new baby?

So how, the child puzzled, could her mama have got so poorly so quickly that she'd died?

Mary had tried to explain it gently. 'Your mama's gone away, sweetheart.'

Mama never went away. Charlotte had never known a night when her mother had not been there to tuck her into bed. She'd been there a few days before, had bent to kiss Charlotte gently and whisper 'My darling daughter' before tiptoeing from the bedroom. The last sound

Charlotte remembered had been the rustle of her mama's silk gown and the soft closing of the door. Even after she'd gone, Alice's perfume still lingered, enveloping the child in her mama's reassuring presence. But in the cold light of morning, Charlotte's world had fallen apart

'When is she coming back?' Charlotte had asked.

Mary had dabbed her eyes with the corner of her apron. 'She won't be coming back, lovey.'

'Not – ever?'

The woman had shaken her head and glanced up at her husband, Edward, standing solemnly beside her. 'No,' she'd whispered. 'Not ever.'

The child had asked no more. Despite Mary trying to break the news gently, Charlotte knew her mother was dead. Living on a farm, she'd seen dead animals. She'd sat on a stool at Mary's kitchen table often enough, watching the cook pluck a chicken, skin a rabbit or a hare. She'd seen the pheasants hanging in the barn – row upon row of them – after one of her father's shooting parties. She knew full well what 'dead' meant. And now – though she couldn't see her – she knew her mother was lying silent and still in that coffin disappearing down the lane on its way to the churchyard.

'No women,' Osbert Crawford had instructed harshly. 'I don't want unseemly weeping and wailing. My wife's funeral will be conducted with dignity.'

So even the faithful Mary, who'd come to Buckthorn Farm ten years earlier when Osbert had brought his bride home, was not allowed to attend her mistress's funeral.

Two years after Mary's arrival, Edward Morgan, already employed at the farm, had asked her to marry him. At first, Osbert had forbidden the match, but when both had threatened to leave, he'd been forced to capitulate, aware that good and loyal servants were hard to find for the lonely farm set amidst the flat Lincolnshire marshland near the Wash.

So, Edward and Mary had married and continued to live at Buckthorn Farm, serving their strict master and caring for his lovely, dutiful bride. And so it was Mary Morgan's hand that Charlotte now grasped as she watched her mother leaving home for the last time.

All the other men and boys who worked on the farm lined up behind Harry and Joe Warren. Charlotte knew them all and they all knew her. They always smiled and waved and raised their caps to her when they saw her. But today, they were not smiling or waving. They were walking with their caps in their hands and their heads bowed. Today, they didn't even look up at the window.

'Come, child,' Mary said, trying to pull her away from the scene below, but Charlotte stayed, obstinately watching until she could no longer see the procession. Only then did she allow the woman to lead her downstairs to the comforting warmth of the huge kitchen.

And through all her growing years it was the only place she was ever to find warmth and comfort and affection.

Two

LADY DAY, 1926

'I hear the kitchen maid's gone from the farmhouse, then?'

Peggy Warren straightened up from bending over the range and turned towards her husband as he sat down heavily at the table. As she placed his dinner in front of him she sighed. 'Not another one!'

'Aye.' Joe picked up his knife and fork. 'But who can blame 'em, eh?'

Peggy sat down before her own meal. 'Not me, for one.'

Joe chuckled. 'Don't fancy havin' a go yarsen, then? Earn yarsen a bit o' pin money?'

Peggy stared at him. 'Joe Warren, have you taken leave of your senses? Haven't I enough to do looking after you and your two strapping sons who refuse to find themselves wives and leave home? To say nothing of your poor old dad, who can hardly get out of his bed these days. And then there's Lily, who still comes home now and again from her job at the manor, and as for our Tommy – ' Peggy cast a despairing glance to the whitewashed ceiling. 'Always in some scrape or other.'

At seven, Tommy was the youngest of the Warren family. His arrival had been a 'surprise' to the 44-year-old Peggy, who'd thought her childbearing days were over. Indulged by his parents and three older siblings, the boy ran wild.

Joe's smile widened. 'I was only teasing, lass. I wouldn't want you working in that miserable place.'

Peggy was thoughtful. 'If things were different, I wouldn't mind. Me an' Mary Morgan have been friends ever since she came here. We'd work well together, I know. And Edward's a lovely feller. Still,' she sighed, 'I can't and that's that. Has his lordship – ' this was Peggy's scathing nickname for Osbert Crawford – 'gone into town today to hire someone else?'

Joe glanced at her briefly. When he'd swallowed a mouthful, he said shortly, 'No. Rumour has it, he's expecting Miss Charlotte to do the work.'

Peggy's fork clattered on to her plate as she gaped at him. 'Miss Charlotte? You're joking.'

'I only wish I was.'

'His own daughter? Working as a kitchen maid as well as all the work she does on the farm?'

'Daughter, you say? Huh! Now tell me, Peg – ' he waved his fork at her – 'has that man ever – *ever* – treated that lass of his as a daughter? A *proper* daughter?'

Peggy sighed. 'No, he hasn't. But that's just it, isn't it, Joe? It's because she *is* a daughter . . .' She paused and, as she met his gaze, whispered, 'And not a son.'

Joe placed his knife and fork neatly together on the empty plate and leaned back in his chair. 'Aye,' he said softly. 'That's the tragedy of it. Poor Mrs Crawford miscarrying three bairns, all boys, and the first two in the same years as our lads were born.' He shook his head. 'That must have hurt. Seein' his farm worker the proud father of two healthy lads and him havin' to bury his sons in the churchyard. You've got to feel sorry for the feller, Peg.'

'I suppose so. The last one – two years after Charlotte was born – went full term, but he was stillborn. Poor little mite. Mary told me once, he was a bonny baby – just perfect. But he never even drew breath.'

'Aye, the master was distraught, they said. Locked himself in his room for days and wouldn't come out.'

Peggy rose and gathered the plates, clattering them together with swift, angry movements. 'But he's got a daughter. A lovely girl, if only he'd see it. But d'you know summat, Joe.' She stood very still for a moment as she added quietly, 'I reckon he'd willingly sacrifice her if it'd give him just one of his sons back.'

'Poor lass,' Joe sighed. 'She hasn't got a lot going for her. Plain little thing, isn't she?'

'Not so little now, Joe. She's twenty-six next month. But she doesn't make the best of herself, I'll grant you. Shapeless, drab clothes; round, steel-rimmed spectacles; and her shining black hair always scraped back into a plait and covered with an old-fashioned bonnet. And have you seen the shoes she wears? They're like a man's.'

Joe grinned. 'Well, not all lasses can be as pretty as you, my love.' His tender glance roamed over Peggy's face, as lovely to him as the day he'd married her despite the fact that she had borne him four children and led such a busy life. There were only a few strands of grey in the curly brown hair and her figure was as slim and lithe as a young girl's.

'But he treats her like a boy,' Peggy was still preoccupied with thoughts of Charlotte. 'Worse than a lad, if you think about it. He never lets her out to enjoy herself. She's never even been to the annual Harvest Supper at the manor, now has she?'

After her mother's death, Mary and Edward had cared for Charlotte. She'd been kept firmly within the confines of Buckthorn Farm, not even allowed to attend the local village school. A governess, Miss Helen Proudley, had taken care of her education. Living in, even sleeping in the same large bedroom, she'd become a companion to the girl too, but it'd always been Mary who'd mothered Charlotte and she who was the constant in the girl's life. At fifteen, Charlotte's formal education had ended.

'You're old enough to work now,' her father had said, dismissing the governess at the end of July 1915. 'With all the young men off to war, you'd better help about the farm.'

From that day forward, Charlotte had spent most of her waking hours out of doors working alongside Joe and his two sons. Now her education was the farming way of life. In her bedroom at night, she would write in a journal all that she had learned that day from old Harry. Though retired through ill health by that time, Harry still lived with his family in the cottage at the end of the track where it joined the long lane running from the sea to the small town of Ravensfleet. Before long, Joe, who as expected had taken his father's position as foreman, could be heard telling anyone who'd listen that Miss Charlotte knew as much as he did about the workings of the farm. 'Though mebbe not quite as much as me dad,' he would add in deference to the man who'd taught him, 'but, you mark my words, she'll be as good as any lad when her turn comes to tek over the farm.'

It was the greatest compliment Joe could pay Charlotte and he said it again now as he rose and kissed Peggy, adding, 'I'd best be off. Doesn't do for the foreman to be seen slacking.'

Peggy laughed. 'That'll be the day any of us on Buckthorn Farm is seen slacking. Not even Miss Charlotte. Poor lass.'

'Aye, poor lass indeed.'

At that moment, the 'poor lass' was laughing her head off in the farmhouse kitchen.

'Stop it, Jackson Warren. You're making my sides ache.' She took off her glasses and wiped her eyes. 'I've got work to do in the dairy. Butter won't churn itself.'

Rolling pastry at the table, Mary Morgan chuckled too. It was good to see the girl laughing and her kitchen was the only room in the house where merriment was ever to be found. The older woman watched as the young man stood by the table looking down at Charlotte.

'You know, you've got pretty eyes, miss. Violet, they are. Shame you have to wear them specs. They hide them.'

'Go on with you, you and your flirting.' Charlotte perched the spectacles back on the end of her nose and looked at him over them like a severe school marm. 'I've heard about you and all the village girls. And I've seen you after church on a Sunday, walking with your arm round the waist of some unsuspecting lass.' She chuckled and glanced at Mary. 'I think we should put up a warning notice to all the town's maidens, don't you, Mary?'

'Oh, I think they all know about Jackson Warren. That's why he can't find himself a nice girl to settle down with. Not like his brother.'

Jackson threw back his head and laughed heartily. 'Our John? Get married? He's been walking out with Grace Whitehead for years. Why she dun't give him the boot, I don't know.'

'They'll marry when they're good an' ready.' Mary nodded wisely. 'It dun't do to rush into things.'

'I don't call five years courting rushing,' Jackson countered. 'He's thirty next month and Grace must be twenty-six if she's a day. She'll be an old maid if she dun't watch out.'

Charlotte's smile faltered.

'You mind your tongue, Jackson Warren,' Mary said tartly. 'And you'd best be off about your work. If the master hears all this noise—'

'I'm goin', I'm goin'.' He pulled on his cap and touched it in farewell to both women. 'Thanks for the tea, missus. And you, Miss Charlotte.'

They both nodded acknowledgement at him, Mary with pursed lips and Charlotte with the ghost of a smile.

After the back door had banged behind him, there was silence in the kitchen except for the thumping of Mary's rolling pin.

'That boy,' she declared, 'will be the death of his poor mam! Unless, of course, their Tommy gets there first.' She laughed wryly. 'And that wouldn't surprise me one bit.'

'Jackson's all right,' Charlotte said softly. 'He's a lot of spirit about him. I like to see that. And young Tommy has, too. He's very like Jackson.'

'Aye well, mebbe so. He's a little scallywag, that Tommy. But then, so was Jackson at the same age. But now it's spirit that's mostly out of a bottle on a Saturday night in Jackson's case, so I've heard tell.'

'He's only young.'

'Twenty-eight. He's ready to call others, but he doesn't take a look at himself and realize it's high time he settled down an' all.'

Now Charlotte laughed. 'Peggy looks after him far too well for him to leave home. And as for settling down, I doubt he ever will. He's having too much fun.'

'And whose fault is that, might I ask? Them silly girls who let themselves be charmed by his flirting ways. I just hope none of 'em gets themselves into trouble 'cos it'd break poor Peggy's heart if her lad were to be chased with a shotgun by an angry father.'

She glanced at Charlotte, who was still sitting pensively at the table, lost in thought, scarcely listening to the housekeeper's chatter.

'Don't you mind now, lovey. What he said. He dun't mean no harm. He didn't stop to think what he was saying.' She sniffed disapprovingly. 'He never does.'

Charlotte sighed. 'I know. I'm quite resigned to the thought that I'll never get married. I'll be here in this dusty old house, dreaming of a wedding day that never happened and was never going to.' She chuckled suddenly. 'Another Miss Havisham – that's what I'll be. No, it's not that. It's just – it's just that when Jackson talks about all the *fun* he has, I – well – it's only then I feel the loneliness.'

'But you've a busy life. All the kiddies at the Sunday school love you. And you're always out an' about the farm – you laugh and joke with the hands, now, don't you?'

'I know, I know. Everyone's very kind, but there's always this sort of – barrier, you know. I'm their

11

master's daughter. They're always so polite. *Too* polite, if you know what I mean. And—'

There was a pause before Mary prompted quietly, 'Go on. What is it?'

The words came out in a rush. 'I think they feel sorry for me.'

'Oh lovey, no!' Mary dropped her rolling pin with a clatter and moved to put her arm round the girl's shoulders, leaving a floury smudge on Charlotte's grey dress. 'That's not true.'

Charlotte turned slowly to look at the woman who'd brought her up from the age of five. It was a kind face; round, with soft, smooth skin, though there were a few wrinkles there now and grey strands in the once dark hair. Her hazel eyes were honest and direct – and Charlotte trusted her with her life. Now she smiled. 'Mary Morgan, you are one terrible liar.'

Mary swallowed hard. Oh my dear girl, she was thinking, if only you knew the terrible lie I've been forced to live all these years.

Three

Buckthorn Farm lay in Fleet Marsh, a flat, fertile land on the edge of the Wash. The nearest small town, Ravensfleet, had a long history, a close-knit community, and was the centre of the surrounding farmland. Though several farms and cottages were some miles from the town, they still came within the parish boundary. Most farmers and their workers made the effort, whatever the weather, to attend church every week travelling on foot, by farm cart or pony and trap. It was a chance to meet their neighbours and the townsfolk – the blacksmith, the wheelwright and all those who were a vital part of their own lives. Most of the farms around the town were part of the Ravensfleet Estate, owned by the acknowledged squire of the district, who lived at the manor. A large, rambling house on the outskirts of the town, its windows overlooked the land belonging to its owner. By tradition, Home Farm was farmed by the squire, whilst the rest of the estate was divided up into tenanted farms. Only Buckthorn Farm had been owned outright by the Crawford family for four generations. The farmhouse, with outbuildings clustered around it, faced towards the coast. To the north was the growing seaside resort of Lynthorpe; to the south, the historic town of Boston.

Mary had been right when she said that all the village children loved their Sunday school teacher and Sunday was Charlotte's favourite day.

Come rain or shine, she and Mary walked along the straight track westwards through the fields to the church near the railway station in Ravensfleet, whilst Edward drove Osbert Crawford in the pony and trap. They aimed to reach the church gate as Edward drew the conveyance to a halt. Then they'd wait until Osbert had descended and, without a word or even a glance at his daughter, walked up the path between the lines of his farm workers, their wives and families. Again, without a word to anyone, or even a glance, he'd enter the church and make his way to the front pew on the left-hand side whilst the rest trooped in to take up the pews behind him. Charlotte, with Edward and Mary Morgan, sat in the seat directly behind him. No one, not even his own daughter, sat with Osbert.

The squire from Ravensfleet Manor had always occupied the right-hand-side front pew. But on this last Sunday in March the pew was empty. Old Mr Davenport had died some months before without close relatives and his heir – a second cousin once removed – lived abroad and had no intention of taking up occupancy. So, the manor, along with the whole of the Ravensfleet Estate, had been sold and a new family was expected. Indeed, the whispers running amongst the congregation said that the new owner had arrived and taken up residence on Lady Day, three days ago. So now they all waited, craning their necks, to see if anyone would arrive for the service.

As the vicar, Cuthbert Iveson, young, eager and newly ordained and inducted into the parish of Ravensfleet, moved forward to begin the service, there was a disturbance at the back of the church. The door opened and a blast of the cold wind from the sea swept into the church skittering around the ankles of the worshippers, so that they all frowned and turned to see who had caused their discomfort.

A man – tall and broad shouldered, with dark brown hair smoothed back and dressed in a smart three-piece suit – walked down the aisle. He nodded to either side and then gave a little bow towards the vicar as he took up his place in the right-hand side front pew. Three boys followed him. The first – who perhaps by now considered himself a young man – was about sixteen. Tall and thin, with straight fair hair and cold blue eyes, his fine, handsome young face was spoilt by a petulant pout to his mouth. The middle boy – about twelve or so – walked with his head bent, his shy gaze upon the floor. But the youngest of the trio skipped down the aisle, grinning up at the people on either side.

'Hello,' he said, his piping voice echoing to the rafters. 'How do you do? I'm Georgie. I'm six and we've come to live at the manor.'

Smothered laughter rippled amongst the congregation and all eyes turned towards the little chap and his round, cherubic face to return his friendly smile. Blond, unruly curls and bright blue inquisitive eyes brought soft 'Ahs' from the women.

'Come along, Georgie,' his brother murmured, ushering the younger boy with a little push into the pew to sit between himself and the eldest boy.

Whispering broke out until Mr Iveson cleared his throat and his parishioners settled down. But their curiosity had been aroused and, throughout the service, necks craned to catch sight of the new arrivals. Charlotte was entranced. She could hardly concentrate on her hymn book. The little boy in a smart little sailor suit fascinated her. The middle boy, with dark colouring like his father and soft, dark brown eyes, was having

15

difficulty in keeping a straight face himself. But the eldest boy, now he was a different kettle of fish altogether, Charlotte thought. He frowned down at Georgie and once bent to whisper in his ear. The little boy was immediately subdued, but only for a few minutes before he began to twist round in his seat and smile at those sitting behind him. His gaze wandered all around the church and at last came to rest upon the pale face of the vicar in his pulpit. The little boy swung his legs, his heels drumming on the pew until, once again, the eldest brother frowned at him.

Charlotte tore her eyes away and tried to concentrate on what Mr Iveson was saying. As she brought her gaze to the front again, she saw with surprise – indeed, with a sense of shock – that her father, sitting directly in front of her, was not paying attention to the vicar either.

He was watching the man with his family of sons.

As the service ended, the congregation filed out from the back with the occupants of the two front pews leaving last. Just outside the porch, Mr Iveson stood shaking each and every hand, but his flock was in no hurry to depart. Not this morning. They hung about in little groups, spilling out on to the road, pretending to talk to one another, whilst their children chased each other amongst the gravestones. But their glances kept coming back to the church door watching for the newcomers to emerge.

'That must be our new squire and his family, then.'

'Where've they come from?'

'Why is there no woman with him? Where's his wife?'

'He's a widower, I've heard tell.'

'Are those three boys his sons, d'you suppose? Aren't they handsome young fellers?'

''Cept that oldest one. He looks a mardy 'un.'

'Snooty, if you ask me.'

'But the master looks nice. Not uppity. He was pleasant enough, now, wasn't he? Nodding and smiling to us all.'

'And the youngest – what a little cherub he is.'

Charlotte, Mary and Edward walked down the aisle towards the door, where Charlotte paused and glanced back over her shoulder to see her father hovering at the end of his pew and holding out his hand.

'Osbert Crawford, sir, of Buckthorn Farm. And, by what your young son said, you must be the new owner of the Ravensfleet Estate?'

The dark-haired man smiled. Laughter lines crinkled his eyes. 'There are no secrets when Georgie is around,' he said in a deep voice. 'And yes, we moved into the manor on Lady Day.' He shook Osbert's hand and introduced himself. 'Miles Thornton.'

Osbert inclined his head. 'And these' – he waved his hand towards the three boys already walking – or, in Georgie's case, skipping – down the aisle – 'are your sons?'

'Yes, they are.'

There was a slight pause before Osbert, with undeniable envy in his tone, murmured, 'You are indeed a fortunate fellow.'

There was a fleeting bleakness on the other man's face as if he carried some secret sorrow. Then he seemed to force a small smile but, to Charlotte's surprise, he made no comment, no murmur of agreement with her father's statement.

17

She smiled at the three boys moving towards her. The eldest, leading the way, looked her up and down with such disdain that Charlotte almost felt the urge to curtsy under his superior glance. He passed her by without a word, put on his hat and marched out of the church. The second son smiled before following his brother, but did not speak. Georgie, however, stopped and beamed up at her.

'Hello. What's your name?'

Charlotte smiled, her eyes sparkling behind her spectacles. 'Miss Charlotte.'

The young boy put his head on one side. '*Miss* Charlotte?' His smooth forehead puckered in a puzzled frown. 'Who d'you work for?'

Now Charlotte was puzzled. 'Work for? How – how do you mean?'

'You're a maid, aren't you? So, who d'you work for? The gentleman you were sitting behind?'

Charlotte almost gasped aloud and then she realized. In the young boy's mind, she had every appearance of a maid. In her dowdy clothes and seated behind her father alongside his household staff, she appeared to be a servant too. For a brief moment, she was hurt, but then her natural sense of humour and the realization of how she must look to anyone who did not know her – and her circumstances – came to her rescue. She chuckled and bent down towards him.

'The gentleman talking to your father – the one I was sitting behind – is my father.'

Georgie blinked and for a brief moment seemed lost for words. 'Oh,' was all he said.

Charlotte straightened up and put her head on one side, regarding the boy with wry amusement. 'But I suppose you're right. I do work for someone. I work for my father on his farm and about the house. And I suppose I work for the church, too. I teach at the Sunday school. Would you like to come?'

'Ooh, yes please. When is it?'

'Well, right now, after Morning Service, but—'

Georgie held up his hand and, almost without realizing how it had happened, Charlotte found his warm little hand grasping hers. 'I'll come now.'

The two men were walking towards them and Charlotte turned anxious eyes to the stranger. 'I'm sorry, I—'

'Georgie,' his father said easily, 'are you misbehaving?'

The child turned his blue eyes and his beatific smile on his father. 'No, Papa. This nice lady's called Miss Charlotte and she's the Sunday school teacher. And I'm going with her to Sunday school.' He turned back to Charlotte. 'What time do we finish, Miss Charlotte, so that Brewster may come back in the motor to fetch me?'

'Well – I – er – ' Again she cast an anxious, questioning gaze at the boy's father. He was watching her with amusement.

'This, Mr Thornton,' Osbert said grudgingly, 'to my eternal disappointment, is my daughter.' He waved his hand towards her. 'So now that you see her in all her *glory* – ' his mouth curled with sarcasm – 'dithering like some halfwit, perhaps you can understand why I called you "a fortunate fellow".'

Mr Thornton seemed startled and a small frown deepened the creases in his forehead. Then he gave a courteous little bow towards her and said quietly, 'I'm happy for Georgie to come with you, Miss Charlotte. Shall I send my man back for him at twelve?'

'That – that would be fine,' Charlotte found herself

stammering and blushing, not only from embarrassment at her father's cruel words, but also as, under the soft brown gaze of the stranger, she found the colour rising in her face and her pulse racing.

As she led the little boy to the room at the back of the church where the Sunday school was held, Charlotte heard her father say, 'I was not blessed with sons like you, sir, and, as you can see for yourself, with her looks, it's most unlikely she'll marry and present me with a grandson.'

To Charlotte's surprise, the little chap walking sedately beside her now, suddenly squeezed her hand, looked up at her and smiled, and her father's words – true though they undoubtedly were – lost some of their sting.

Four

The children came running from all directions into the schoolroom. Georgie had seated himself in the centre of the front row. He sat on the small chair swinging his legs and smiling up at Charlotte. The others jostled each other to sit beside him. They all wanted to know about the newcomers. Charlotte sighed inwardly. She could see she was going to have a battle this morning to keep order and gain their attention.

She opened the children's book of Bible stories that formed the basis of her Sunday school teaching and stood in front of them, waiting patiently until the shuffling stopped and silence reigned. She had to wait quite a while, for there was a lot of nudging and whispering.

At last she said, 'Quiet now, children, please. We must begin. Today, as it's Palm Sunday, I'm going to read you the story of how Jesus rode on a donkey into Jerusalem.'

For the next half an hour she read the story of Palm Sunday to them and then asked questions, but the children were still inattentive and fidgeting.

Then, in the second row, a hand shot into the air. 'Please, miss,' Tommy Warren – with a cheeky grin so like Jackson's – asked, 'can we do a play? Like we did last week with the loaves and fishes?'

Charlotte smiled. The children loved to act out whatever story she'd read. They got rather excited and noisy, but Mr Iveson didn't seem to mind. He encouraged it. Sometimes, if he arrived to visit the class, he joined in and took one of the parts. Not like the previous vicar – old, crusty and certainly of the 'children should be seen and not heard' brigade. He'd heartily disapproved of her even reading anything that was not straight out of the Bible itself. He hadn't liked her reading the simplified stories, but Charlotte knew the children could understand them so much better and that performing them brought the tales to life. They really remembered them.

'So, you want to act out the story of Jesus riding into—?'

'No, miss. Can we do the story you read us last week? About the Good Samaritan. It were brilliant, miss.'

'Well . . .' Charlotte said, but, glancing around the class, she saw that all the scuffling and the chatter had ceased and they were sitting up straight, their innocent eyes turned towards her. 'Very well, then.'

She was organizing who was to play which part when Tommy piped up again. 'A' ya goin' to let Georgie have a part, miss?' Two other boys beside him giggled and clapped their hands to their mouths to stifle the sound.

How thoughtful they are, Charlotte thought, to include the new little boy so soon. 'That's a very good idea, Tommy. Now – ' she turned towards Georgie – 'what part would you like to play?'

'He could be the chap who gets set upon by thieves, miss,' Sammy Barker, one of Tommy's friends, suggested.

The golden-haired little boy nodded eagerly and slid off his chair. When all the parts had been arranged, Georgie and Tommy and his two friends, who were to be the robbers, took their places at the front of the room.

'Now,' Charlotte directed, 'you go over there, Georgie, and you three go to the opposite side of the room. Now, you're travelling along a road, Georgie, and these three robbers jump out and attack you. We're just pretending, of course . . .'

Scarcely had the words left her mouth, before the three boys launched themselves at Georgie, punching and kicking him. Fists flailed as the small boy fought back. He landed a punch in Tommy's eye but he was no match for the three of them. They wrestled him to the ground as Charlotte rushed forward. 'No, no!'

Horrified, Charlotte dragged them away. It had all happened so quickly. 'Sit down at once,' she cried. The three boys returned to their seats with Tommy holding his eye. But they were all grinning.

'That'll show the "little cherub",' she heard Sammy mutter. She'd deal with the three of them in a minute, but first she bent down in front of Georgie. A cut on his lip was oozing blood. Charlotte's heart missed a beat. Oh, dear Lord, the child was hurt, but to her surprise, Georgie was grinning. 'What did you stop us for, Miss Charlotte? They were robbing me like the story said.'

'Yes, I know, but they were only supposed to *act* it, Georgie, not do it really.' She took a clean hanky from her pocket and dabbed at his lip. 'Whatever will your father say?' she murmured, mortified to think what a bad impression the locals would have made on their new squire.

At that moment, Mr Iveson chose to appear. He entered at the back of the room and strode to the front. Charlotte looked up at him with worried eyes. She hated telling tales, but it would be obvious to him at once that all was not well in her class this morning. She gave her handkerchief to Georgie. 'Keep pressing that on your lip, dear. It'll stop the bleeding.'

The little boy shrugged. 'It's nothing, Miss Charlotte. Honest. I'm always in the wars. Father says I'm –' he paused, his smooth brow wrinkling in thought – 'I'm accident prone.'

The child was nonchalant about the whole incident and comical too, but Charlotte didn't feel like laughing. The naughty boys had attacked the newcomer deliberately and she was very angry with them.

She sighed as she stood up and turned towards the vicar.

'What happened?' Cuthbert asked.

Before she could speak, Georgie piped up. 'We were doing a play, sir. The Good Samaritan. Please may we carry on now?'

'But you've hurt your mouth,' Mr Iveson began, but Georgie ignored him and beckoned the three boys to come to the front again. 'Let's show the vicar.'

Tommy, Sammy and Michael sidled out of their seats once more, glancing at one another uncomfortably. What was the new boy playing at? Now the vicar had arrived, they were going to be in such trouble.

'Right –' Now it was Georgie directing. 'Let's start again and –' Charlotte saw him glare at the other three boys in turn – 'let's do it properly.'

She almost gasped aloud. His fierce look was warning them. She couldn't believe a boy of six could act with such maturity. But the three miscreants were meekly taking up their places again. Georgie turned to her. 'Tell us what to do, Miss Charlotte.'

Charlotte swallowed, embarrassed under Mr Iveson's

watchful eye. 'Er – well,' she stammered, her usual composure quite deserting her. She took a deep breath to calm her jangling nerves. 'You're walking along the road when three robbers jump out at you and' – Charlotte turned what she hoped was a stern gaze on the other three boys – 'you three attack him but you're only *pretending*.'

Out of the corner of her eye, she saw Cuthbert raise his eyebrows, but he said nothing and the three urchins looked suitably chastised.

This time they threw mock punches at Georgie but not one of them touched him, though the younger boy cried out with realistic terror as Tommy pulled his off his sailor jacket. Georgie fell to the ground, but intentionally now. Michael pulled off Georgie's boots.

'That's enough,' Charlotte cried, suddenly afraid that the three boys were going to strip the child naked in the interests of authenticity. The three 'robbers' ran to the back of the room, whilst Charlotte beckoned the two children who were to act out the roles of the priest and the Levite, who 'passed by on the other side'.

Georgie lay on the floor, moaning and reaching out with pleading hands. 'Help me, oh please help me.'

'He's a good little actor, isn't he?' Cuthbert murmured, coming to stand beside Charlotte.

'Now you, Phoebe,' Charlotte instructed. 'You're the Good Samaritan . . .'

The girl walked shyly towards Georgie and held out her hand to help him up. Then she put her own shawl round him and led him off to the side of the room.

All the other children clapped.

Cuthbert moved to the front of the class and began to ask questions about what they had all learned from the story. The children glanced at each other and then one or two hands were raised tentatively. Then, with growing enthusiasm, the answers and comments came thick and fast, with the vicar nodding and smiling, pleased at such a good response.

As the hands on the clock on the wall reached twelve, Mr Iveson dismissed the class, but Charlotte raised her voice above the scraping chairs and scuffling boots. 'Tommy, Sammy and Michael – I want a word with you. Stay here until I come back.' She held out her hand towards Georgie. 'We'll see if your father's motor car has come back for you.'

They went outside to see Brewster leaning against the vehicle, reading a newspaper whilst he waited for his young master.

'I'm so sorry about what happened,' Charlotte said to the boy. 'I – I'll come and see your father later to explain.'

Georgie grinned up at her. 'There's no need really, Miss Charlotte. Father always says we must stick up for ourselves and fight our own battles. And not be a telltale,' he added.

'You're certainly not that. But I feel I must explain to your father. I'm responsible for all the children while they're in Sunday school.'

Georgie was thoughtful for a moment. Then he nodded. 'Just so long as you promise not to tell him their names.'

Charlotte sighed. It would be a difficult interview with the new squire but she felt duty bound to see him. She felt it was all her fault.

'Very well,' she promised and the little boy's grin widened.

As the motor drew away, Charlotte returned to the schoolroom. Cuthbert had disappeared back into the

26

church, but the three boys were waiting for her looking ill at ease. Sammy – not so brave now – looked as if he might cry at any moment. His father would give him a beating if he found out what had happened. And what on earth Joe would do to his son, Charlotte dared not think.

'Now,' Charlotte said severely, 'what you did was very naughty. You know very well when we do our little plays about the Bible stories, we are pretending. So why did you all hit Georgie?'

Even as the question came out of her lips, Charlotte already half guessed the answer herself. Their action had been a kind of primeval instinctive reaction against someone who was different. Georgie was from a privileged home. He wore a smart suit. He was articulate and bright and outgoing. And hearing their mothers gushing over the angelic-looking little chap, the local boys had taken an instant dislike to him. Luckily, Charlotte thought, it was most unlikely that Georgie would be attending the village school. And he probably wouldn't want to attend Sunday school again.

She turned towards the one she knew had been the ringleader. 'Tommy Warren, I'm surprised at you. Whatever were you thinking of?'

Tommy went red and hung his head, afraid that Miss Charlotte would tell his father. 'I'm sorry, miss. I didn't think.'

'And you, Sammy. Your father is now Mr Thornton's tenant.' Saltwort Farm, where the Barkers lived, was part of the Ravensfleet Estate.

Tears were running down Sammy's face now. 'Please don't tell me dad, Miss Charlotte. He'll whip me.'

'So'll mine when he finds out,' Tommy muttered.

Charlotte bit her lip. She so wanted to tell them that

27

she thought it unlikely that their fathers would get to know of their escapade. But a few hours, days maybe, of fear would be an apt punishment.

'Well, I hope you've learned your lesson. And the next time you see young Georgie Thornton, you apologize to him. D'you hear me?'

Three heads nodded vigorously. 'We're sorry, Miss Charlotte.'

'Just mind you tell that to Georgie, too. You may go now.'

She watched them walk out of the schoolroom and down the path through the churchyard. There was no running and whooping and yelling. They were suitably subdued, their heads together, no doubt swapping stories of what punishment awaited them. She felt mean but was determined to stick to her resolve.

Besides, the little rascals had put her in an unenviable position. Feeling responsible for what had happened to his son, she felt obliged to face Miles Thornton.

Five

As Charlotte walked up the long lane leading to the manor on the edge of the town the following morning, she was trembling all over. Her palms were sweaty and her stomach churned.

Knowing some of the servants there, she went round to the back door.

'Miss Charlotte,' Lily Warren cried, 'whatever are you doing here?' The girl's welcoming smile faded suddenly. 'Oh!' She clapped her hand to her mouth. 'Nothing's wrong at home, is it? Don't say it's me grandad!'

'No, no, Lily,' Charlotte reassured her swiftly. 'Nothing's wrong. I'm so sorry – I never thought.'

Lily breathed a sigh of relief. 'It's all right, miss. It's just me being silly. But you know how bad me grandad gets.'

'I do and I'm sorry. I'll call at the cottage on my way home and see your mother. See how things are.'

'Would you, miss? Oh, that is kind. We've been so busy just lately with the new family arriving.' But Lily was smiling as she said it, as if the changes in their lives were very welcome. Lily had worked at the manor since the age of fourteen, starting as a scullery maid and working up to become first housemaid. Now she wore a black dress, a frilly white apron and cap. Servants were fast becoming a dying breed since the end

29

of the Great War. Women had begun to look for work in offices, shops and even factories. Menial housework was beneath them, they felt, but Lily liked her life at the manor. She loved living in the grand house and she could see her family often. Any other employment would have meant her leaving the countryside she loved.

There was a pause before the girl asked again, 'So – what are you doing here?'

Charlotte pulled in a deep breath. 'I've come to see Mr Thornton.'

'Oh – right. Come away in, then. I'll introduce you to Cook. Mr Thornton brought his own cook.'

'What's happened to Mrs Overton? Has she been dismissed?'

Lily laughed. 'No, no, nothing like that. When old Mr Davenport died, Mrs Overton left to go an' live with her widowed sister in Bognor. She was getting on a bit anyway and her legs were bad. So it all worked out well.'

'What about the rest of you?'

'We've all been kept on, miss. 'Course, when the old man died it was a bit worrying, like. Not knowing who might buy the place and if we'd all still have jobs. But the master only brought Cook and his chauffeur with him and a tutor for the two younger boys. But of course we hadn't got one of them anyway.'

Charlotte was relieved. The manor had a large household of servants, some of whom would have been hard pressed to find new employment locally either because of their age or the scarcity of jobs available.

'And the oldest son – ' Lily went on. Did Charlotte fancy it, or did the girl's tone of voice alter? She glanced at the housemaid to see a pink tinge in the girl's cheeks.

'Goes to boarding school, but he's home for Easter just now.'

Lily opened the kitchen door and ushered Charlotte inside. Cook was standing in front of the huge range but she turned at the sound of the door opening and smiled a welcome.

'Cook, this is Miss Charlotte Crawford from Buckthorn Farm. This is Mrs Beddows, Miss Charlotte.'

The cook wiped her hands on her apron and came forward. 'I'm pleased to meet you, Miss Crawford.'

Charlotte took the plump hand. 'Please call me Miss Charlotte. Everybody does.'

Mrs Beddows smiled, invited her to sit down at the table and take a cup of tea and a slice of her chocolate cake, but all the while Charlotte was uncomfortable under the woman's scrutiny. Not that the cook was being impolite, just curious. Charlotte wondered what she'd been told. She could imagine what might have been said. 'Miss Charlotte's plain as a pikestaff. She'll die an old maid at the beck and call of that miserable old devil of a father.'

It was not how she would have chosen to be described, but Charlotte was honest enough to realize that it was the truth.

'You go an' get on with your work, Lily, whilst me an' Miss Charlotte here have a nice little chat.'

When the girl had left the room, Mrs Beddows said, 'I didn't know how they'd all accept me, to tell you the truth. But since the last cook left of her own accord, it's been easy. They're a nice bunch what works here.' She leaned forward, confiding. 'And they can't get enough of my chocolate cake – it's a speciality of mine.' She nodded towards the half-eaten piece in Charlotte's fingers. 'All right, is it?'

'All right? It's delicious.'

Mrs Beddows smiled and sat back. 'So, what brings you to the manor?'

'I've come to apologize to Mr Thornton.'

'Apologize? Whatever for?'

Charlotte sighed. 'Georgie stayed on yesterday after Morning Service to attend my Sunday school. We were acting out the Good Samaritan and the three "robbers" got a little – well – shall we say over enthusiastic.'

'Ah, so that's how he got a cut lip?'

'I'm afraid so.' There was a moment's pause before Charlotte asked, 'He didn't say?'

'Little Georgie wouldn't tell tales and his father wouldn't encourage it, I assure you. In fact, my dear, if you'll take my advice, you'll not give the master any names either.'

'I wasn't going to. Georgie asked me not to and I admire him for that. I'm just here to apologize for not keeping better control of my class.'

Mrs Beddows laughed. 'Boys will be boys. It's not the first time Master Georgie's been in a scrape and it'll not be the last.'

Charlotte began to feel a little easier, but she was still determined to see the boy's father. 'Is Mr Thornton at home?'

'I believe so. He'll be in the room he's had fitted out as his study.' Her face clouded. 'He spends a lot of his time on his own since his poor wife died.'

'You've been with him a long time?'

'Ever since they were married. Mrs Thornton appointed me when she set up house. Lovely lady, she was. So sad.'

'What – I mean – when did she die?'

32

'Three days after little Georgie was born. She got the childbed fever.'

'How dreadful.'

'The master's never got over it and I don't think he ever will.'

'He must have loved her very much,' Charlotte said huskily.

'Oh he did, he did.' The cook sat a moment, lost in memories in which Charlotte could have no part. Then she shook herself and heaved herself to her feet as Lily came back into the room.

'I've told the master you're here, miss, and he says to take you up.'

Suddenly, the churning stomach and the sweaty palms were back, but Charlotte rose, thanked the cook for her hospitality, and followed Lily up the back stairs and into the hallway. The housemaid led the way to a door on the right-hand side and knocked. She opened the door and announced, 'Miss Charlotte Crawford, sir.'

Charlotte stepped into the room and the door closed behind her.

Miles Thornton was seated behind a large mahogany desk, with his back to the long windows overlooking the front lawns. The room was more like a small library than a study, for most of the wall space was lined from floor to ceiling with shelves of books. There was a large marble fireplace on one wall. Above it hung a huge oil painting of a beautiful woman. Charlotte couldn't help staring at the lovely face framed by blond curling hair. The woman's mouth curved in a sweet smile and her blue eyes seemed to follow everyone in the room. This was Miles Thornton's late wife and Georgie's likeness to her was unmistakable.

Charlotte tore her gaze away and let her glance rest on the big dog stretched full length on the rug. It raised its head and growled softly, but at a word from its master it was silent, though it remained watchful and wary.

Miles rose, came around the desk and held out his hand. His face creased in a smile, but Charlotte noticed that the sadness deep in his brown eyes didn't quite disappear. Now she knew why. This man was still mourning the loss of his beloved wife six years earlier.

'Good morning, Miss Crawford. Please come and sit down – if you can find your way around Duke.' Miles gestured towards one of the two wing chairs that were placed one on either side of the hearth.

Charlotte smiled nervously and went towards one of the chairs. It was not the dog of whom she was afraid, but the man. She bent and held out her hand towards the animal.

'I wouldn't. He's not very friendly towards strangers. He's—' Miles stopped mid-sentence and stared in astonishment. His temperamental guard dog was actually licking the hand of this woman.

'Well, I'll be damned,' he muttered. 'I'd never have believed it if I hadn't seen it with my own eyes.'

Mesmerized, he sat down in the other chair, still staring at his dog. Now, Charlotte was scratching Duke's head and the animal was gazing up at her with a bemused expression.

Miles chuckled suddenly; a deep, infectious sound. 'Are you a witch?'

Charlotte relaxed a little. 'No. I just seem to have an affinity with animals.' She forbore to add that she felt more at ease with animals and children than she did with adults. Especially strangers and, even more particularly, men. The thought reminded her of the reason for her visit and nerves gripped her once more.

'I've come to apologize,' she began, never one to put off doing whatever had to be done. 'Georgie got into a fight yesterday at Sunday school and I feel responsible.'

'You? How come?'

She repeated what she had said to Mrs Beddows.

'Ah, so that's why three urchins presented themselves at my front door this morning asking to see Georgie?'

Charlotte gasped in surprise. 'They – they did?'

'They did indeed. In fact, they're still here somewhere – outside in the grounds, I think – playing with him.'

'Oh!' Charlotte could not hide her surprise and a sliver of anxiety. Was little Georgie safe? What if . . . ?

As if reading her thoughts, Miles said quietly, 'Have no fear for my son, Miss Crawford. Though I didn't interfere, I heard them apologizing to Georgie and he invited them to play with him in the orchard. Cowboys and Indians, I think he suggested. So I'm sure all is well.'

'I – do hope so,' Charlotte said fervently.

'And you have no need to feel guilty any more. They're just being what they are. Boys.'

Charlotte smiled wanly. 'Yes,' she whispered. 'I suppose so.'

He watched the pain in her face and knew from his brief conversation with her father that he was approaching delicate ground. Charlotte gave the dog a final pat and stood up. 'I mustn't take up any more of your time. You must be very busy. Thank you for seeing me.'

Miles rose too. 'It's been a pleasure.' His deep tone was warm and genuine. He opened the door for her.

'And I'll be seeing you again very soon. Tomorrow evening, in fact.'

Charlotte stared up at him. 'T-tomorrow?'

'Hasn't your father told you? He's invited us all – even Georgie – to dinner.'

Six

'I don't believe it. I *can't* believe it.'

Charlotte had still not recovered from the shock by
the time she reached home and went straight to the
kitchen. Mary was in a blind panic.

'He's just told me,' she said. 'It's more than twenty
years since I cooked for a dinner party. Not since – ' She
paused and glanced at Charlotte. 'Well – not for a long
time. Dear, oh dear. I'll have to get Joe to take me on
the cart into town. We've nothing in but the plain fare
we normally have. "The best, Mary." That's what he
said. "The best." Whatever's he thinking of? And with
such short notice, an' all. I'll have to have some help,
Miss Charlotte.'

'Yes, yes, of course. I'll help you.'

'Oh, more'n that. I'll have to ask Peggy Warren to
come. That'll be all right, won't it?'

'Of course. If she can leave the old man.'

'She'll just have to – for once,' Mary said firmly. She
stopped her agitated pacing and sat down at the table.
'But why? Why now and why them?'

Charlotte was silent for a moment. Then she said in
a flat voice, 'Because Mr Thornton has three sons, Mary,
that's why.'

Mary gaped at her and couldn't think of a word to say.

*

By the time Mary and Edward were in their own bedroom that night, however, Mary could think of plenty to say.

'All these years he's been a recluse and kept that lovely girl away from any kind of society 'cept his farm workers and their families,' she whispered angrily, to avoid being overheard. There were three large bedrooms on the first floor of the farmhouse. Osbert slept in the biggest, reached by the main staircase, and Charlotte in the one on the opposite side of the landing. The third room, beyond Charlotte's, was where Mary and Edward slept and it was reached by a narrow back staircase from the corner of the huge kitchen. 'So why does he suddenly want to start entertaining now?' Mary was still ranting. 'Miss Charlotte reckons it's because of the boys. Mr Thornton's sons. But I don't see why he wants to befriend them?'

'Wouldn't put owt past that old devil,' Edward muttered. 'He's got a devious mind. I wouldn't like to even try to guess what be goin' on in his head.'

'So why've we stayed here all these years?'

'You know as well as I do, love. We've only put up with him for Miss Charlotte's sake. If it hadn't been for her, I'd've been long gone.'

Mary smiled. 'Aye, me an' all.' She sighed. 'But we've stayed and now we're too old to move on. Who'd want us now?'

The two glanced at each other. What Mary said was true. They were probably too old now to find domestic work elsewhere, but not for one moment did they regret their decision to stay here. For it was Miss Charlotte who would own the farm one day, and she would see them all right.

Of that, they had no doubt.

*

'I don't want you at the dinner party,' Osbert told Charlotte the following morning. 'I shall inform our guests that you have a headache and have begged to be excused. You can either stay in your room or help Mary in the kitchen.' He gave a snort of derision. 'Yes, you'd better do that. She's going to need all the help she can get. I hope she's up to the task. I don't want to be shamed in front of our new squire and his sons.'

Charlotte stared at her father. Had his disappointment in her festered for so long that it was now akin to hatred? She'd no choice but to obey him, but, once over the initial surprise, she'd been looking forward to the dinner party. Now, it seemed, she was to be kept in the background like some mad woman in the attic.

Her father was ashamed of her. She sighed inwardly as she left the sitting room. If you could call it that for *she* never sat in it. Her father had made it his own sanctuary, surrounding himself with his books. He spent most of his days in the room now, scarcely venturing out except to church and the occasional visit to the market. Once he had been a regular public figure, had attended shooting parties and had even hosted such events on his own land. But after his wife had died, he'd ceased to socialize.

Back in the kitchen, Charlotte found Edward opening the door to Joe Warren.

Seeing her, Joe pulled off his cap. ''Morning, miss. Could I have a word?'

'Of course.' She led the way from the back door to the outbuildings running at right angles to the house and to the former tool shed that had been converted into a farm office.

'Sit down, Joe.'

'No, 'tis all right, miss. I mun't stay long. I just

wondered if you'd come and have a look at one of the 'osses, miss. He seems lame and old Matty said to ask you afore we call the vet.'

Living alone in the cottage next door to the Warrens, Matty Whitehead had worked for the Crawfords all his life, working his way up to become a waggoner. What he didn't know about horses wasn't worth knowing.

Charlotte nodded as she sat down behind the desk. For the last seven years, this room had been her domain. As she'd grown up, Osbert had passed more and more of the running of the farm to his daughter. The foreman now came to Charlotte for instruction and advice. But very few people knew the truth; Mary and Edward, of course, and Joe and Harry Warren. But no one else. Not even Peggy and the rest of the Warren family. Some of the farmhands might have guessed if they'd stopped to think about it. But few did. They'd been so used to seeing the young miss about the place all her life and took her interest and involvement as natural. What they did not realize was that the farm was hers now – in all but name. And her father did nothing to disillusion them. In his twisted mind, he still ran things and his daughter was less than useless.

'I'll meet you at the stables in ten minutes,' Charlotte said.

'There's nothing in his hoof. I think he's pulled a muscle or a tendon. Rest him for a few days and I'll come and massage it twice a day. Can you manage with the other two until he's better?' There were four horses on Buckthorn Farm – three shires and a pony that pulled Osbert's trap.

'Oh-ar, miss.' Matty nodded.

'There, there old boy.' Charlotte ran her gentle fingers down the horse's right front leg. The animal flinched and moved restlessly but seemed to sense that she was trying to help him. 'There doesn't seem to be anything out of place,' she murmured. 'Just a strain.' She straightened up. 'But we'll get the vet if you think it best, Matty.'

'Aw no, miss.' He grinned toothlessly at her. 'You're as good as any vet I've seen. You should have been one.'

Charlotte smiled sadly, reminded once more that if only she'd been a man, she could have done or become anything she liked.

But the truth was, she wasn't even thought enough of by her own father to sit at his table when he entertained.

'That's an absolute disgrace.'

Edward didn't think he'd ever heard his wife so angry. 'I've a good mind to go on strike just like them miners are threatening.'

The newspapers had been full of the coal crisis and rumours were spreading that if the miners went on strike, the whole country would soon come out in support of them. Edward had followed the news avidly, reading snippets out to Mary.

'Wouldn't do you any good, love,' he said mildly now. 'You'd just get the sack. And me along with you.'

Mary's eyes glittered. 'And right this minute, I wouldn't mind if I did.'

'Aye well, it wouldn't help Miss Charlotte, now, would it?'

'But have you ever heard the like? Banning his own daughter from a dinner party and suggesting she work like some skivvy in the kitchen!'

41

'Likely she'll be happier down here with us than up there.'

'Mebbe so, but it's the principle of the thing. What on earth will Mr Thornton think?'

'I doubt he'll ever know. He'll have no reason to doubt the master's word and he's not likely to venture down into the kitchen. Unless, of course, he comes to compliment the cook.'

Mary gave him a wry glance and continued to beat the batter for Yorkshire puddings. The back door opened and Peggy Warren came in with the breeze.

'By, but it's blowy today, Mary. Nearly lost my wig on the way here.' She laughed. 'That's if I'd got one.' She hung her coat and scarf on the peg behind the door and tied a white apron round her waist. Washing her hands at the kitchen sink, she asked, 'Now, Mary love, what can I do to help?'

'Mek us a cuppa, there's a dear. Edward's tongue's hanging out and I haven't a moment to stop. Then you can start on the veg over there on the draining board.'

'Where's Miss Charlotte? Prettying hersen' for tonight?'

Husband and wife exchanged a glance that was not lost on Peggy. 'What? What have I said?'

Mary explained.

'Not being allowed to join the dinner party?' Peggy's voice was high-pitched with indignation. 'Well, I've heard it all now. Wait till I tell our Joe. He'll never believe it. Not this, he won't.'

Peggy and Mary carried on grumbling to each other about the unfairness of Charlotte's life long after Edward had escaped upstairs to lay the dining table. There was no separate dining room at Buckthorn Farm, but the long sitting room was spacious enough for a seating area around the fireplace and for the dining table and chairs and a sideboard to be placed near the front window overlooking the lawn.

He found Charlotte, a scarf around her hair and a copious apron covering her dress, dusting and polishing the furniture. Any stranger arriving at that moment could certainly be forgiven for taking her for a house-maid.

'Father's gone upstairs for a rest, so I thought I'd give the whole room a good going over before he comes down again.' She stood back and surveyed the whole room. 'There, what do you think, Edward?'

'Looks grand, Miss Charlotte.'

'What about the china and the glassware?'

'All done, miss. And the cutlery. Everything fair sparkles. I'll lay the table now, if you've finished kicking up a dust.'

Charlotte laughed. 'I have. I'll go and see if I can help Mary.'

'Peggy's here, so they're fine if there's anything else you need to be doing.' Edward bit his tongue, longing to add, 'Like getting yourself ready for the dinner party.' But he didn't want to hurt the girl's feelings any more than they had already been wounded.

'If everything's under control, then, I'll just nip down to the stables and check on Tobias,' she added, referring to the lame horse.

She left the house by the back door, wearing a long trench coat, wellingtons and her headscarf. She lifted her head to the breeze and tasted the salt air blowing in from the sea. It was surprisingly warm for early April and promised fine weather for Easter weekend.

Charlotte would have loved a walk to the sea, but with Father's unexpected dinner party, there was no time today. Perhaps tomorrow.

Turning to the left, she crossed the path that ran down the side of the house and the farm buildings, walked past the greenhouse and entered the paddock, where Joe was watching Matty leading the horse in gentle circles.

'Hello, Miss Charlotte.' Joe touched his cap and Matty nodded to her.

'How is he?'

They stood side by side watching the horse.

'Improving already we think, miss. What d'you say?'

Slowly, Charlotte nodded. 'Yes, he's definitely not limping as much as he was this morning. But I think you should rest him for at least a week.'

He grinned at her. 'Better'n a vet, you are. It's them healing hands you've got.'

Charlotte laughed aloud, the sound carrying on the breeze so that the horse pricked up his ears and whinnied softly. Matty brought the animal to a standstill and Charlotte moved forward to pat the horse's neck and feed him a carrot from her pocket. 'Good boy,' she soothed. 'You'll soon be better. What about Jacob and Lightning?' Charlotte was referring to the other two shires.

'They're fine.'

'Another day or so and I'll take Tobias for a short walk, Matty. Then later on, maybe as far as the beach before we let him on the land again.'

When there was little work on the farm for the horses – which wasn't often throughout the farming year – Charlotte took them to the beach further north near the seaside resort where the sand was safer and firmer for the horses. In the warmer weather, they loved a paddle. It would have done the horse good now, she thought, and today would have been warm enough, but she daren't risk the horse on the soft sand yet and it was too far away, anyway, and there was no time.

She bent and ran her hand down the animal's leg. Tobias whinnied again, but he did not flinch or move away from her touch. 'There, boy, there.'

She straightened up. 'I'd best get back to the house. There's a lot to do.' She turned to Joe. 'Peggy's come to help. I expect you know?'

Joe nodded, his mouth tight. He'd called into the farmhouse kitchen only minutes before and heard that Charlotte was to be kept out of sight that evening. His anger threatened to spill over and he literally bit down on his lower lip to stop the words coming out of his mouth. It was a disgrace. An absolute disgrace. A travesty. Charlotte was speaking again and he dragged his angry thoughts back to what she was saying.

'But are you sure your father's all right, Joe? Is he well enough to be left?'

'Our Tommy's there, Miss Charlotte. He's to stay in all day. The little scamp's been fightin' again. He's sporting a shiner of a black eye.'

Charlotte glanced away, avoiding his gaze as Joe went on, 'So I've told him he's to stay at home and watch over his grandad. He'll run and fetch me if there's owt wrong.'

Charlotte turned away, her heart thumping in fear lest Joe should say more about the 'fight'. But, rationally, she knew there was no earthly reason why he should think she'd know anything about it.

As she began to walk away, Joe called after her. 'I'll be up to see you in the morning, miss, if that's convenient. There're one or two matters I need your say-so on.'

'That'll be fine, Joe. About ten. See you then.'

But before that, she thought as she walked back to the house, there's this dinner party to get through.

I'll be glad when it's all over.

Seven

'Where's Miss Charlotte? I want to see Miss Charlotte.'

From the kitchen, Charlotte heard the little boy's piping voice in the hallway as the Thornton family arrived and, then, her father's answer.

'I'm very sorry, young man, but Miss Charlotte has a headache and has begged to be excused.'

'But I've brought her some flowers. Father said I might.'

'And magnificent they are, too. I'll see that they're taken to her room. Morgan,' Osbert addressed Edward, 'see to it at once. Now, if you'll come this way, dinner is about to be served.'

The voices died away as Osbert and his guests moved into the room and Edward pushed his way through the door from the hall, carrying the biggest bouquet of flowers Charlotte had ever seen in her life.

'I expect they're from the greenhouses at the manor, miss.'

With trembling fingers, she touched the lovely blooms – daffodils, tulips, iris and even roses.

'No one's ever given me flowers before,' she murmured. 'How thoughtful. How kind.'

And how sad, Edward was thinking, that they come from a six-year-old!

*

The dinner party was going well. Osbert sat at the head of the table looking around with deep satisfaction. Three sons. How lucky the man was. And he didn't even seem to appreciate it. If only . . . Osbert's attention was drawn, not to the little chatterbox, whom his father made no attempt to quieten, but to the eldest of the three boys.

Philip Thornton was everything that Osbert looked for in a young man and everything that he'd desired in a son of his own. At sixteen, the youth was tall and slim, with handsome, even features. His blond hair – so fair it was almost white – was smoothed back from his broad forehead. His blue eyes were intelligent, if a trifle cold and calculating. But even that was a quality Osbert esteemed. He liked the steely look of determination. The young man would go far in life.

Osbert felt an unaccustomed thrill and his heart quickened its beat as an idea began to form in his mind. A preposterous idea, but a wonderful one. He continued to regard Philip through narrowed eyes, assessing him, judging him. The boy caught his gaze and held it with a haughty arrogance that further increased the older man's admiration.

What a splendid young man! What a son!

He leaned towards him. 'And what do you hope to do, Philip? I understand that you're at boarding school at present?'

Philip smiled stiffly. 'Yes, sir.' He answered politely enough, but he was not enjoying the evening. He'd been aware of their host's gaze upon him and had found it disconcerting.

'And after school?' Osbert prompted. 'What then?'

'I'd like to read law at university.'

Osbert felt a flash of disappointment. 'Indeed? So you do not intend to take over the running of the

Ravenfleet Estate from your father?' He smiled, though the smile did not reach his eyes. For many years Osbert's smile had been a mere stretching of the lips. No humour or kindliness ever reached his eyes. 'Though, of course, that should be many years off.'

Philip glanced across the table at his father. There was a slight sneer to his mouth as he said, 'I don't think farming is for me. Besides, as you say, that's many years off. And there are two more sons – ' he gestured towards his siblings – 'who are probably more suited to – ' he paused and added sarcastically, 'more suited to the bucolic life.'

Osbert's eyes narrowed. It was a blow to his idea, but merely a setback. Far from being put off by the young man's arrogance, he liked him even more.

'I – see,' he said slowly. 'But you wouldn't – surely – be averse to being a land*owner*, would you? Even if you didn't want to till the soil with your own bare hands, as it were, you'd like to be a man of property?'

Philip shrugged nonchalantly, not quite sure what their host was driving at. 'I suppose so. But the estate my father's just bought is hardly vast. Certainly not large enough to divide amongst three sons.'

'Precisely so,' Osbert murmured, his gaze still on Philip. His glance went next to the middle son, sitting so quietly. He'd hardly spoken the whole evening and then only when directly addressed. He did not attract Osbert's admiration like his elder brother did.

Benjamin Thornton was the quiet one of the three. At twelve, he was still a little shy and would have been far happier visiting the stables at Buckthorn Farm and seeing all the animals than sitting in this stranger's shadowy front room with its heavy, dark furniture.

'And you, my boy?'

Benjamin started as he realized their host was addressing him directly. 'What do you hope to do when you leave school?'

The boy ran his tongue nervously around his lips and glanced at his father. Miles Thornton smiled and came to his son's rescue. 'Ben is the one who is most likely to take over the running of the estate. His ambition is to go to a good agricultural college when he leaves school. It's one of the reasons we've come to Lincolnshire. The move doesn't affect Philip, of course. He'll still attend the same boarding school and as for Georgie – ' His smile was indulgent. 'Well, he's a little young to worry about what he'll do when he's grown.'

'I shall be a soldier,' the little boy piped up. 'Like you, Papa.'

Osbert raised his eyebrows as his gaze now shifted to the man sitting at the opposite end of the table.

'Is that what you were, Mr Thornton?'

Before his father could reply, Georgie spoke up again. 'He was a colonel in the war, weren't you, Papa?'

For a moment, Miles's eyes clouded as he remembered the terrible days of the Great War. He did nothing – at present – to discourage the little boy's dreams, but he fervently hoped that no son of his would ever have to fight in another war.

'Yes,' he replied heavily, 'I was. But it's not a time I care to remember.'

'Quite so,' Osbert replied stiffly. 'But now you are the country gentleman? Have you any experience of running a large estate?'

Miles smiled and his eyes crinkled merrily. Like his sons, he hadn't quite worked out why the invitation to dine at Buckthorn Farm had been so swiftly forthcoming. He'd suspected – though with her absence from the dinner table perhaps he'd been wrong – that the man had designs on him as suitable marriage material for his spinster daughter. Unless, of course, that *was* the case and the girl herself had made her excuses out of embarrassment. If so, Charlotte Crawford went up in his estimation.

Having been devoted to his beautiful and vivacious wife, Miles had no desire to even think of remarrying. Already he'd fended off several designing females and had no wish to be the object of Osbert Crawford's plans for his daughter.

Answering the older man's question, Miles shook his head. 'I come from a family of soldiers and that's what was expected of both my brother and me.' For a moment, his face was suddenly bleak. 'My brother was killed at Ypres in 1915.'

There was a moment's pause before Osbert asked, 'But you've finished with the army now?'

Now there was a bitter tone to Miles's voice. 'Most definitely.'

'So,' Osbert leaned back and steepled his fingers together as Edward began to serve the pudding, 'how do you expect to run the Ravensfleet Estate with little – er – training or knowledge?'

'Well, as you will know, most of my land is divided up into four farms, three of which are run by tenants, with only Home Farm attached to the manor and left to my tender mercies.'

'Pah! You can't trust tenants to farm properly. You should oversee everything they do. Keep your eye on them – all the time. My own foreman – Joe Warren – is a good man. His father, who preceded him in the job, trained him from a young age. I can confidently leave everything to him. Of course, he consults me, but I have great faith in his abilities.' He waved his hand benevolently. 'If you have any problems, speak to Warren.'

Miles inclined his head politely but said nothing. Only the tightening of his mouth told his sons of his outrage at Osbert's superior attitude.

Georgie, spooning pineapple pudding into his eager mouth, broke the tension. 'I say, this is jolly stuff. We must get Mrs Beddows to make this, Papa.'

Miles Thornton's mood lifted and he chuckled. 'You should know, Georgie, that a lot of cooks guard their secrets very jealously. Perhaps Mr Crawford's cook wouldn't want to hand out her family recipes.'

Osbert laughed, but it was a humourless sound, sarcastic and with a bitter note. 'Cook? Mary Morgan?' Again he laughed but then nodded towards Georgie. 'But if you like her pudding, my boy, I'll see she sends the recipe to the manor.'

The boy scraped the spoon on the plate, criss-crossing it until every drop was gone. He stood up and turned towards their host. 'Thank you for my dinner. Please may I leave the table?'

At least the little rascal has manners, Osbert thought, as he inclined his head giving permission.

Georgie pushed back his chair and marched towards the door, which was opened for him by Edward hovering close by. The young boy beamed up at him. 'Thank you, Mr Morgan. Which way is it to the kitchen? I want to see Mrs Morgan.'

A perverse pleasure shot through Edward Morgan as he pointed across the hall. Let them find out, he was thinking, just how their precious host treats his own daughter.

'Now, Georgie,' his father began, 'you mustn't go wandering about the house. It isn't polite.'

But the child was already skipping across the polished floor of the hall.

'Stop him, Morgan,' Osbert bellowed, suddenly realizing that Charlotte was probably still in the kitchen, dressed in her skivvy's clothes. But the boy paid no heed, and pushed open the door leading directly into the huge kitchen that ran the full width of the house.

Behind him, Edward hid his smile.

Georgie stepped into the kitchen, a ready smile on his face. He glanced around at the three shocked faces. Mary Morgan, Peggy Warren – and Charlotte.

For a brief moment the young boy's smile wavered. Then it broadened again. 'Miss Charlotte! You're feeling better. I'm so glad.' He went to her and took her hand, gazing up at her. 'Why didn't you come to see us? Even if you didn't feel like eating.' He grimaced. 'Headaches can make you feel you don't want to eat, can't they? I had one once and I was sick, too. Were you sick, Miss Charlotte?'

Lost for words, Charlotte shook her head. But she put trembling fingers to her forehead. She was about to get a headache for real any moment now.

Eight

By the time Georgie had finished chattering to the three women in the kitchen, Osbert had led his guests to the chairs and settee around the fire. Though he was agitated by the young boy's action – behaviour he firmly believed should have been checked by the over-indulgent father – he managed to steer the conversation towards the news of the day.

Once again, he addressed his remarks to Philip. 'And what do you make of this threat of a miners' strike and the call for other unions to follow suit in support?'

'If it happens, I think they should send the army in to break it up,' the young man replied at once. 'They'd be holding the whole country to ransom.'

Osbert's eyes gleamed. The boy talked sense. Good sense, in his opinion. But it seemed the father was softer.

'I think,' Miles said, 'that you should consider what is being done to the miners and their families before you make such a statement, Philip. They're trying to reduce their wages and increase their hours of working. Now that doesn't seem fair to me.'

Philip shrugged as if the folk affected by such an action were of no consequence. Miles frowned, disappointed by his eldest son's lack of thought for others. It was not how he and his beloved Louisa had brought up their boys. But, as he glanced across at their host, he could see that Osbert delighted in Philip's reply and said as much.

'Well said, my boy. Well said.' He even patted Philip's shoulder.

At that moment, Georgie returned and sat beside his father. His cheeks were pink, his eyes bright and he was strangely subdued.

Miles rose. 'I think it's high time this young man was in his bed. Thank you for a most enjoyable evening,' he said evenly. 'And for your hospitality. You – and your daughter – must dine with us some time.'

In the motor car on the way home, Georgie sat in the front seat beside his father who was driving.

'Papa – ' Georgie was the only one to still call their father by that name. The older boy's now addressed him as 'Father'.

'Yes, Georgie,' Miles shouted above the noisy engine.

'You know when I went to the kitchen . . . ?'

Miles tried to hide his amused smile. He knew he should reprimand the boy for having gone there without their host's permission. But he felt a perverse devilment and said nothing.

'And you know he told us that Miss Charlotte had a headache . . . ?'

'Ye-es,' Miles said slowly, wondering what was coming.

'Well, she was in the kitchen. Dressed like a maid and doing the washing-up. Now, why do you think that was, Papa?'

'I don't know, Georgie,' Miles said thoughtfully. 'I really don't know.'

As he drew the car to a halt in front of the manor, the two boys in the back seat got out. Just before he shut the door with a slam, Philip answered his little brother's question. 'Because she's drab, uninteresting and no better than a maid. No wonder he didn't want her "gracing" his dinner table.'

Miles and his youngest son stayed where they were, gazing out of the windscreen into the darkness, a thoughtful silence between them.

'Joe, ya dad's taken a turn for the worse. Ya'd best fetch the doctor.'

Joe stared at Peggy, his eyes widening. Over Easter his father had seemed much better. He'd even struggled downstairs to join the rest of the family for their Easter Sunday dinner. During the week since then, the old man had stayed in his bedroom. That was nothing unusual so Joe had thought nothing of it. But now, for Peggy to ask for the doctor to be called, it had to be serious.

'I'll send our Jackson. He'll ride like the wind on his bike. D'ya think . . . ?' His voice trailed away but they continued to stare at each other with serious faces.

Slowly, Peggy nodded and said huskily, ''Fraid so, love. He's got steadily worse this last week.'

The doctor confirmed their fears. 'His heart's giving out.' He put his hand on Joe's shoulder. 'I'm sorry, lad.'

Dr Markham had been in Ravensfleet since arriving as a newly qualified young doctor. He'd served the small town and the nearby villages, to say nothing of the outlying farms and cottages, for over thirty years. Sprightly and energetic in his mid-fifties, he showed no sign of wanting to retire. A widower for the past five years and his family grown and flown, his patients were his life.

'What would I do with myself?' he'd say, spreading

his hands in a gesture of helplessness to the unanswerable question of impending retirement.

He knew all the families around here, had delivered their babies, watched them grow, and seen them leave the world, too. And now one of his oldest friends was about to depart.

'Something seems to be bothering him.' Dr Markham eyed both Joe and Peggy quizzically. 'Do you know what it could be? He's asking for the vicar.'

Joe and Peggy glanced at each other. 'I'd guess,' Joe said slowly, 'it's about where he's to be buried.'

'Ah, yes. I remember now. Your mother's not buried here, is she? Taken to – Lincoln, was it?'

Joe nodded slowly, his brow creasing. 'He – wouldn't let – any of us go,' he said haltingly. 'He reckoned Ma wanted to be with her own folks. She was from near Lincoln. He insisted that only he accompanied her coffin to the interment there.'

'You had a service in the church here, though, didn't you? I seem to remember it was somewhere around the same time that poor Alice Crawford died. Didn't we have two funerals within a couple of days of each other?'

'That's right. Mam died two days before Mrs Crawford.'

'I wasn't called to Buckthorn Farm when she died so suddenly.'

Joe detected the note of bewilderment, even hurt, in the devoted doctor's tone, even after all these years. 'I'd always been the family's doctor, yet Osbert Crawford chose to call a doctor from Lynthorpe. I never did understand why.'

'Aye, he's an odd one, doctor, I don't mind telling

you, even though I work for him. I could never understand why he wouldn't let any women go to his wife's
funeral. Poor Mary Morgan was heartbroken, so my
Peg said at the time.'

'Ah well,' Dr Markham shrugged philosophically,
'ours not to reason why, eh, Joe? Long time ago now.
What we've to do now is to find out what's troubling
your poor old dad. I'd like to see him go peacefully. Go
in and have a word. If it's Iveson he needs to see, then
send for him. But' – his voice dropped – 'don't delay,
lad. Don't delay.'

As the doctor left, Joe and Peggy went upstairs to
Harry Warren's bedroom. The old man had suffered
cruelly over several years with arthritis and he was a
shrunken, pain-racked shadow of his former self. Now
Harry clutched Peggy's apron with a skeletal hand. 'Get
the vicar,' he rasped. 'I need – to speak to him.'

'I'll go, Dad,' Joe answered him. 'I'll go this minute.
Don't fret. Lie quietly. I'll get him.'

Reminded of his mother's passing by his conversation
with the doctor, Joe realized that Harry's health had
deteriorated from that time. Only five years after her
death Harry had handed the foreman's reins to Joe and
for the last sixteen years he'd lived the life of an invalid,
sitting hunched in his chair by the fire or lying in bed.
The only person able to raise a smile, apart from his
own grandchildren, had been Miss Charlotte. He'd rel-
ished her visits, transported back to happier times in his
reminiscing.

Joe touched Peggy's shoulder lightly as he hurried
from the room, murmuring, 'I won't be long, love.'

*

Mr Iveson arrived, his pale, round face solemn, ready to take the dying man's confession. Though neither he nor many of the locals were of the Catholic faith, he'd already found during his short ministry that the dying often wished to confide in him in their last, frightening moments.

As he sat down beside the bed, Harry, calling on his last reserves of strength, pulled himself up. He waved Joe and Peggy away. 'Go. This is – private.'

Joe shrugged. 'We'll be just downstairs, Vicar, if you need us.'

Cuthbert Iveson nodded and took the old man's hand in his.

Joe closed the door and he and Peggy went down the narrow stairs.

'We should get Jackson to fetch Lily home. And find John too?' Peggy said. 'They'd never forgive us if—'

'You're right. I'll call him. He's digging the vegetable patch as if there's no tomorrow.'

'He likes to keep busy when there's trouble,' Peggy murmured. 'It's his way of coping.'

'Me an' all. I'd like nothing better than to get on me horse and gallop round the farm. But I know me duty's to stay here. I wouldn't leave ya on yar own, lass, to cope with . . .' His voice faltered. Peggy squeezed his arm comfortingly.

She mashed a pot of tea and they sat either side of the range waiting for what seemed a long time before they heard the vicar's footsteps on the stairs. Cuthbert came into the room looking white faced and slightly dazed. Peggy rose at once and poured him a cup of tea. He sank down into a chair at the table and gulped it gratefully. Then he sat, staring into the middle distance, almost as if he was unaware of the other two people in the room.

'So, Vicar,' Joe prompted at last. 'Where's he want to be buried, then? Lincoln, with me mam?'

Cuthbert jumped visibly and blinked rapidly. 'Er – well – no,' he stuttered, avoiding meeting their eyes. 'Er – it seems he has a plot already purchased in the churchyard. Next to Mrs Crawford.'

'Next to Mrs Crawford?' Joe was shocked. 'A' ya sure?'

Cuthbert pursed his mouth. 'Oh yes. He was adamant. I must look it up in the records, he said. It was all done properly over twenty years ago.'

'But surely, Mr Crawford must have reserved a plot next to his wife? I mean . . .' Peggy faltered.

Cuthbert shrugged, but still he avoided meeting their gaze. 'I presume he's reserved one on the other side, perhaps. I – don't know. I'll need to look it up.' He rose hurriedly, took his leave and was gone.

Through the window, Joe watched him go. 'Ya know summat, our Peg. I'd say yon vicar couldn't get out of here fast enough.'

'He's only young. Mebbe he's not got used to attending the dying yet.'

'Mm,' Joe said, but the sound expressed his doubt.

The Warren family gathered around old Harry's bed as he slipped away. Lily cried openly and there were tears in the boys' eyes, though they fought hard not to let them fall. Young Tommy was dry eyed but solemn faced. It was the first time someone close to him had died, but he couldn't remember his grandfather as anything other than a grumpy, bedridden invalid. He had no memories of happier times as had John and Jackson, and even Lily. Peggy and Joe, though sad, couldn't help but feel a sense of relief, too. The old man had suffered dreadfully, but now he was at peace.

'You know, love,' Joe said later that night, 'if you want to help Mary Morgan out now and again, I wouldn't mind.'

'What about Tommy? He needs a firm hand. He runs wild as it is.'

Joe smiled. 'He's all right. He can't get up to much mischief that one of us won't hear about.' He lowered his voice. 'Lily was telling me that he arrived at the manor the other week with two other lads, looking very sheepish. She reckons they'd got into a fight with young Georgie Thornton.'

Peggy gasped. 'Oh no! We don't want to make an enemy of the new squire.'

Joe chuckled softly. 'Seems the boys all ended up playing together, so no harm done, eh?'

'Not this time, mebbe. But we'd better keep our eye on him. He's Jackson all over again. Allus in trouble.'

'Well, Jackson's not turned out so bad, now, has he?'

'No,' Peggy agreed. 'But even so . . .' She said no more, but Joe's approval of her helping out at Buckthorn Farm had made her think. If it gave that poor lass a bit more freedom, then she'd do it willingly. The thing was, would that miserly old devil agree to it?

Nine

The church was packed for Harry Warren's funeral. Foreman for Buckthorn Farm for much of his adult life, he'd been well known and liked in the district. Farmers whom he'd met at the weekly markets years before in Ravensfleet, and even from farther afield, attended. Miles Thornton was there as a mark of respect for the family, even though he'd never known Harry.

Osbert Crawford did not attend. His absence was whispered about, but when they surrounded the newly dug grave, many thought that perhaps he couldn't bear to see his wife's grave right next to the yawning hole.

The headstone bore the wording: *Alice, beloved wife of Osbert Crawford. Born 1 August 1876, died 6 June 1905.*

'Two days after our mam,' Joe murmured, standing with Peggy and his family as they lowered Harry's coffin into the ground. He glanced across at Charlotte, who, white faced, couldn't help glancing at the place where her mother lay. She'd not attended that burial but the fleeting images of watching the cortège leaving the farmyard still haunted her.

It was something she knew she'd never forget.

The committal, spoken by an obviously nervous Cuthbert Iveson, was over. Once the earth had been scattered by members of old Harry's family on to the coffin, the mourners began to move away.

'A grand feller.' One burly farmer put his hand on Joe's shoulder. 'But you'm following in his footsteps and meking a good job on it, by all accounts. Funny your boss hasn't come,' he added, looking round. 'Old Harry served him well. I'd've thought the least he could do was to come to his funeral.'

Joe gave a wan smile. 'Well, Miss Charlotte's here and it's her that . . .' He stopped, not wanting to give away the truth about the running of Buckthorn Farm nowadays. Charlotte had always made it very clear to him that no one was to know. Swiftly, Joe altered what he'd been going to say. 'She's here to represent them both. Mebbe her father isn't too well,' he added, making an excuse.

The farmer eyed him speculatively, but said no more. He went away muttering, 'There's summat funny there. Still, none o' my business, an' I'd best be on me way. Me cows'll be burstin' to be milked.'

Charlotte was still standing near her mother's grave when Peggy touched her arm. 'We'd like you to come back to the cottage, Miss Charlotte. We can't ask everyone, but we've put a bit of a spread on. Just for the family, old Matty, the Morgans and you.'

Charlotte turned to her and smiled. 'I'd love to, Peggy. Thank you.' She glanced down at the coffin now lying deep in the hole. 'Your father-in-law was always so kind to me. I'll miss him too. I used to love our little chats. He taught me so much about farming and country ways.'

'He always said you should've been a boy, that you—' Peggy stopped, appalled at her own thoughtlessness. 'Oh, miss, I'm so sorry. I wasn't thinking. Me an' my mouth. Joe allus ses it'll get me into trouble one of these days.'

Charlotte smiled and patted Peggy's arm. 'Don't worry, Peggy. It was what Harry used to say to me, though I don't think he realized just how very true his words were.'

'What he meant, miss, was that you'd be as capable as any man to run the farm. And one day – you will.'

Charlotte glanced at her briefly and then looked away. So, she thought, Joe had kept his promise. Not even his wife knew that Charlotte already ran the farm.

Peggy's voice butted into her thoughts again. 'Dad was a good man and your visits to the cottage, even after he'd given up work, always brightened his day. But there was something troubling him at the end, and we've no idea what it was. He told the vicar that last day, but he wouldn't tell us.'

Charlotte glanced again at her mother's grave. 'Perhaps it was because he couldn't be buried beside his wife, d'you think?'

Peggy sighed. 'Maybe so, but he could've been if he'd asked. At least, we could've found out if it was possible, but he never asked. He never asked,' she repeated, the unspoken question hanging between them. Why?

Far from being a sad occasion, the little gathering at the Warrens' cottage drank a toast to Harry and reminisced about the years they'd all worked alongside him. Charlotte recalled him teaching her to ride and instilling in her a love for all the animals in their care.

'He always said,' she reminded those present, 'that it was a funny mixture being a farmer. We breed and raise animals sometimes to be slaughtered, but we should always respect and care for them. He couldn't abide cruelty to animals in any form and he would travel miles to find the best slaughterhouse.'

'He always told us you had a gift with animals, miss,' Matty told her. 'Healing hands, he said you'd got. And he was right.'

Charlotte's cheeks were pink with a quiet pleasure. She wasn't used to compliments or praise.

Peggy touched her arm and drew her a little aside. 'Mebbe I shouldn't say this so soon, miss, but – well – now poor old Harry's gone and my boys are old enough to fend for themselves a bit ... I mean, even young Tommy's always out with his pals. What I'm trying to say, Miss Charlotte, is that if ever you need any help at the house, I'll be only too glad.'

'That'd be wonderful, Peggy. I must ask Mary, of course. I wouldn't like her to think I felt she wasn't coping.'

'She'd not think that, miss, I promise you. Why, she said—' Peggy stopped and bit her lip. Perhaps she was betraying a confidence by repeating what the older woman had said on the night of the dinner party.

'It's not fair,' Mary had muttered to Peggy when she'd thought Charlotte was out of earshot. 'That lass should be in there sitting in a pretty frock and playing the hostess. But no, he's ordered that she's here in the kitchen working like a scullery maid.'

Charlotte smiled, patted Peggy's hand and said softly, 'I know exactly what Mary thinks. In fact, let's go and ask her now.'

'Shouldn't you talk about it without me there? I mean ...'

Now Charlotte chuckled. 'No, no, Mary Morgan has never been afraid to speak her mind. If she doesn't want you there, she'll say. Have no fear.'

But Mary was delighted, as Charlotte had known she would be. 'That's a lovely idea, Peggy. And it'll give you more time, Miss Charlotte, to keep up with the books and such.'

Charlotte actually giggled and put her finger to her lips. 'Shush, Mary, no one's supposed to know.' Until a few moments ago, Charlotte had presumed that Joe would have confided in his wife about the unusual set-up at the farm. Obviously, he had not.

Peggy blinked and glanced from one to another. 'Know? Know what?'

Charlotte and Mary exchanged a glance. 'Well, if you're coming to work at Buckthorn Farm, you'll soon find out. But you're sworn to secrecy. Isn't she, Mary?'

Mary shrugged as if she didn't agree, but she murmured, 'Aye well, if it keeps his lordship happy . . .'

Peggy almost laughed aloud to hear that Mary Morgan had the very same nickname for Osbert Crawford as she did.

What Peggy found out after working a few days at the farmhouse was that Osbert Crawford idled away his days reading and smoking in the sitting room.

'I can't believe it, Joe. Why did you never tell me that it's Miss Charlotte who runs the farm?'

'Not allowed, love. There's only me an' the Morgans know.'

'What about John and Jackson?'

Joe shook his head. 'No, they haven't guessed. An' as far as I know, neither's Matty, for all that he's worked there for years. Me dad knew, 'cos he was the one who taught her the most when she was a young lass growing up and taking on more and more. She's always asked his advice right up until he got so ill. When he was still foreman, of course, Miss Charlotte wasn't old enough, but since I took over, Mr Crawford has left more and more to her and now she's running the whole place.'

'With your help, of course,' Peggy said proudly.

'Well, yes, that's what his lordship tells everyone. He doesn't give her an ounce of credit. Not for anything. But it's her I go to now for advice. And when we go to market, although I do the bidding, it's always been talked over between us afore the sale starts. She's done the picking and choosing *and* she tells me what price I'm to go to.'

'Really? Well, I never!'

'And I'll tell you summat else not many know. She's a very good little artist.'

'An artist?'

Joe nodded. 'Sometimes when she's riding around the farm, she brings her sketchpad with her and her Brownie Box camera.'

'What does she paint?'

'Scenery mostly, I reckon. The fields, the marsh, the farmhouse – but I caught her one day in the stable yard doing a lovely sketch of one of the shires. I'd love to know if she ever did a proper painting.' He sighed. 'It's another little secret she's got. I asked Mary about it once and you should have seen her face.'

'Why? What d'you mean?'

'Frightened to death, she was, that I was going to let the cat out of the bag.'

'I don't understand.'

Joe sighed. 'Evidently, the old man doesn't approve. Ses Charlotte's wasting her time. A *woman* will never become a famous painter. So, the lass has to keep her drawing books and paints in her bedroom.'

Peggy shook her head slowly. 'That man's not right in the head, if you ask me. Fancy denying the poor girl a bit of pleasure. I don't expect she even thinks about being famous. She just does it as a hobby. Like I do me knitting.'

'True, but your hobby keeps us warm in winter with all the lovely jumpers you knit. I suppose he thinks painting pretty pictures doesn't produce anything useful.'

Peggy glanced around the rather bare walls of their cottage. 'Well, I wouldn't mind one of her pretty pictures on my wall if she's as good as you say she is, and that's a fact.'

'She's good all right,' Joe said firmly. 'Just a pity her father doesn't appreciate her a bit more. And not just for her painting, either.'

Ten

The return invitation to dine at the manor came towards the end of May. And this time, because Miles had insisted on Charlotte being present, Osbert could not avoid taking her.

Charlotte had no choice of fine gowns to wear. Her one good dress – a deep purple, plain, shapeless garment that reached to her ankles and had not a scrap of likeness to the fashionable shorter skirts that were all the rage of the mid-twenties – would have to suffice. She scraped her shining black hair back from her face and plaited it, coiling it up into the nape of her neck. She did not possess even one item of jewellery to brighten the drab garment and what she thought of as her one good feature was masked by her round, steel-framed spectacles. No wonder, she thought as she regarded herself solemnly in the mirror, her father didn't want to take her anywhere. She was a sad disappointment, as he never tired of telling her. Not only was she not the son he so obviously desired, but she was also plain and had inherited none of her mother's beauty. With a sigh, she left her room and went down the stairs to find him waiting impatiently in the hall.

'I don't know why it takes you so long to get ready,' he grumbled. 'However long you spend in front of the mirror you're not going to make a silk purse out of a sow's ear. Come on, we don't want to be late. It's impolite. And I don't want to offend the Thorntons.'

Charlotte handled the reins of the pony and trap, whilst her father clung on to the sides.

'Not so fast, girl. Are you trying to have me thrown out?'

Charlotte pulled the horse to a slower speed as they entered the gates of the manor and trotted up the drive. Coming to a halt outside the front door, Osbert clambered down.

'Take it round to the stables,' he ordered. 'You can come in the back way.'

Grousing under his breath, he mounted the steps up to the front door and rang the bell. As Charlotte manoeuvred the vehicle round the side of the house to the stable yard, Miles Thornton's manservant, Wilkins, opened the door.

As Osbert stepped inside, Georgie ran towards him across the wide hallway. 'Good evening, Mr Crawford,' the boy began, smiling a welcome. Then his face fell. 'Where's Miss Charlotte? Hasn't she come?'

'Yes, yes,' the older man said irritably. 'She's taken the pony and trap round to the stables.'

Georgie beamed once more. 'That's all right, then. I'll go and meet her.' He skipped towards the front door, which Wilkins began to open for him. But Osbert's next words stopped the boy in his tracks. With a growl he said, 'I've told her to come in the back way.'

Georgie turned and stared at the man for a moment before marching purposefully back across the hall towards the door leading to the kitchens.

'Wilkins, please show Mr Crawford into the drawing room,' the young boy said with a maturity exceeding his tender years, 'whilst I find Miss Charlotte.'

70

'Certainly, Master Georgie. May I take your hat and coat, sir, and then if you'd come this way . . . ?'

When Georgie burst into the kitchen, he found Charlotte already there talking to Mrs Beddows and Lily Warren.

'*There* you are. I've come to find you,' Georgie said. 'I thought you might get lost.'

The cook turned to smile at him. 'Master Georgie, Miss Charlotte has brought the recipe for that pineapple pudding you liked so much.'

The boy clapped his hands together. 'Oh thank you. Please thank Mrs Morgan, too, won't you?'

'Of course, I will.' Charlotte held out her hand. 'And now we'd better go up.' She glanced at Mrs Beddows and Lily and they were in no doubt that she'd be much happier down there with them in the kitchen than facing the ordeal of a formal dinner party upstairs.

But with the excitable Georgie at the table there was little formality. He'd arranged the seating to his own liking. He'd seated Charlotte at one end of the polished mahogany dining table, with his father at the opposite end. Georgie sat on Charlotte's right-hand side and opposite him, was his brother, Ben. Osbert and Philip sat on either side of their host.

Miles smiled. 'I'm not sure my son has complied with the rules of etiquette.'

But Osbert was not going to criticize. He was where he wanted to be – sitting opposite the eldest son.

As they sat down, Charlotte glanced around her. The dining room was spacious, with gleaming mahogany furniture, lovingly polished by Lily, no doubt. The table sparkled with cut glassware and silver cutlery. A square of thick, luxurious carpet covered the floor and over the fireplace was another portrait of Louisa. This one, unlike the one in Miles's study, showed an older woman with her children. Leaning against her knee was a golden-haired child of five or so, and sitting on her lap was a baby. Seeing her staring at the picture, Ben leaned forward and whispered. 'That's our mother – with Philip and me.'

'She's lovely,' Charlotte said, smiling at him. She could see the sadness in Ben's eyes. He would have been about six, she reckoned, when Louisa died and he would have only fleeting, disjointed memories of her. Just as Charlotte had of her own mother. She glanced down the table towards Philip and saw that his gaze, too, lingered on the portrait every so often. Aged ten or so when she died, he would have much sharper memories of the beautiful woman. Perhaps that was the reason for his abrasive manner; he still missed her dreadfully.

'So, the General Strike didn't last long, then, Philip,' Osbert opened the conversation.

Philip actually smiled. 'No, sir. It did not. Just as you predicted.'

'But the miners are carrying on their strike, aren't they?' Before she'd stopped to think, Charlotte, who'd followed the news avidly during the strike, which had affected the whole country for nine days at the beginning of May, spoke up.

There was a moment's awkward silence. The girl held her breath, expecting to be banished from the table for her impudence in daring to join in the conversation. She heard her father's sharp intake of breath and waited for his wrath to descend. But before he could speak, Miles said softly in his deep voice, 'You're quite right, Miss Charlotte, and I can't say I blame them. It seems hardly fair to dock their pay and then expect them to work longer hours, too. And it's one of the most dangerous and unhealthy jobs I can think of.'

Charlotte cast him a grateful glance down the table.

'I wouldn't want to be a miner,' Ben said quietly at her side. 'I'd hate to have to work in total blackness like that.' He shuddered.

'Do you know,' Georgie piped up, 'they take a canary down there just to make sure the air's good. If it isn't, the poor bird might die. Don't you think that's cruel, Miss Charlotte? To the canary, I mean.'

Osbert and Philip laughed, but Ben and Charlotte – and even Miles – took Georgie's comment seriously.

After that, whilst the meal was served and eaten, the table seemed to divide into two. The two adults and Philip at one end talked politics, whilst Charlotte, Ben and Georgie talked about the local countryside.

'I haven't seen the sea yet,' Georgie said. 'And we've been here two months already.'

'Then perhaps your papa would allow me to take you one day,' Charlotte offered. 'Do you ride a pony?'

'Papa's just bought one for me to ride. She's called Gypsy. Philip has a big horse called Midnight, but he's rather wild at the moment. Phil can't ride him yet.'

'I'd love to see them.'

'Why don't you come over tomorrow after Sunday school?' Georgie suggested excitedly. 'You could come back in the motor car with Brewster and me.'

'Well, I . . .' Charlotte hesitated and glanced down the table to their host, but Miles was listening intently to something Osbert was saying and she couldn't catch his eye.

'That's settled then,' Georgie said firmly and there seemed no point in arguing with the determined little chap. Charlotte hid her smile.

As the meal ended, Georgie raised his voice again. 'Papa, thank you for my dinner. Please may I leave the table?'

'You may, Georgie.'

'And may Miss Charlotte and Ben come up to the playroom?'

'I'm not sure that Miss Charlotte—' Miles began, but she interrupted swiftly.

'I'd be happy to, Mr Thornton.'

The three made their escape from the solemn talk at the opposite end of the table, giggling as Georgie led the way to the second floor of the big house.

'Oh my!' Charlotte gasped as the boy flung open the door of what had once been the nursery. 'I've never seen so many toys.'

In pride of place in the centre of the room stood a huge rocking horse, looking very much the worse for wear. It had obviously been ridden and played with so often that its mane was shaggy, its paint peeling.

'This is Starlight,' Georgie said, patting the horse's neck. 'He was father's when he was a little boy, but now he's ours.'

Charlotte stroked the toy's nose just as if it was a real animal.

'And this is Georgie's new toy,' Ben said softly. 'He got it for his birthday recently.'

Charlotte turned to see a motor car that Georgie was able to sit in and pedal.

'He frightens us all to death tearing up and down the landings.'

'I bet!' Charlotte laughed.

74

There were teddies, mechanical toys and games galore. Georgie ran around picking up one thing after another. At last he said, 'What shall we play, Miss Charlotte? Snakes and ladders? Ludo?'

'I . . .' Charlotte faltered. She wasn't very good at games. She had never had any playmates during her childhood – only her governess and Mary. Her upbringing had been severe. Miss Proudley had been told that her sole purpose was to instruct the child, whilst poor Mary was kept fully occupied running the house. So games and play had not figured very much in Charlotte's childhood. Only at Sunday school had she learned how to act out the Bible stories, as she did now with her own class. Though sometimes, she remembered ruefully, even that went wrong.

But now she smiled. 'We'll play whatever you want. You can teach me.'

'Ludo, then,' Georgie said promptly. 'Me 'n' Ben play it, but it's better with three or four.'

'Phil won't play now,' Ben whispered. 'He says he's too old for puerile games.'

Charlotte chuckled inwardly, not in the least surprised that the superior young man had abandoned such childish pursuits. As for herself, she couldn't wait to play.

They were in the middle of a second noisy game of Ludo, Charlotte having surprisingly won the first, when Lily came to say that her father was ready to leave.

Charlotte scrambled up from the floor at once, but Georgie cried, 'Do let's finish the game first. Your papa won't mind, will he?' Without waiting for Charlotte's reply he addressed the maid. 'Please tell Mr Crawford we're just finishing a game. We won't be long.' He grinned. 'Because I'm winning.'

'I really don't think . . .' Charlotte began but Lily had already disappeared.

Five minutes later, Georgie whooped with glee as his last counter arrived 'home'.

'Now, I must go,' Charlotte said standing up. 'Thank you so much for a lovely evening, I—' Georgie launched himself at her, flinging his arms round her and pressing his cheek against her waist. 'You'll come tomorrow and see Gypsy and Midnight, won't you?'

'Yes, yes,' she said, stroking the child's hair with gentle fingers. She was touched by his affectionate gesture. 'I promise.'

As she turned towards the door, her glance caught sight of a magnificent dolls' house sitting in the corner of the room. Her eyes widened and she stopped. 'What a beautiful dolls' house. I – I always wanted one.' She forgot her father waiting impatiently below. She forgot that their host might want them to leave. She forgot that it was perhaps way past George's bedtime. She forgot everything except the sight of the magnificent toy. She crossed the floor, drawn to it against her will.

Georgie got there first. 'We don't play with this,' he said, opening the front of the house to reveal the tiny, perfectly replicated furniture and the family of dolls in residence. He laughed delightedly. 'Father was so sure I was going to be a girl that he bought this in readiness. I think he really wanted a girl, didn't he, Ben?' Gleefully, almost as if he had engineered it personally, he added, 'But I was a boy.'

Charlotte glanced at him but the child had no sense of being a disappointment to his father. He knew himself dearly loved. Not like . . . Charlotte pushed away the unwelcome thoughts. Enchanted, she fell to her knees in front of the house and touched the furniture and the dolls with gentle fingers.

'You can come and play with it, Miss Charlotte, if you like,' Georgie offered generously, but Ben nudged him.

'Miss Charlotte's too old to play with toys,' he said, but fell silent as he watched her rearranging the furniture and putting one of the dolls into the bed in one of the upstairs rooms. 'Or maybe not,' he murmured under his breath.

The two boys watched as Charlotte continued to kneel in front of the house, taking in every little detail.

'It's lovely,' she whispered at last, 'but I really should go.'

But for several more minutes she made no move to leave.

As they hurried down the stairs at last, Charlotte could see her father waiting impatiently in the hallway. He scowled up at her, but Georgie explained guilelessly, 'It was my fault. I made Miss Charlotte stay to finish the game of Ludo. You see – ' He spread his hands and widened his eyes as if it explained – and excused – everything. 'I was winning.'

Charlotte saw Miles hide his smile, but her father merely transferred his glare to the boy.

As Wilkins opened the front door, they saw that it was raining hard.

'You can't drive home in the pony and trap in this,' Miles insisted. 'You'll get soaked. I'll get Brewster to drive you home in the motor car. Your pony will be fine in our stables and I won't take "no" for an answer.'

The Thorntons' chauffeur drove them home but once inside his own door, Osbert still complained. 'Noisy contraptions. Don't you go getting ideas we shall ever have a motor car, girl.'

'No, Father,' Charlotte said obediently. But it was not something that worried her. She much preferred riding a horse anyway, even if it was only the pony or one of the huge, cumbersome shires.

And tomorrow, on Georgie's invitation, she was to visit the manor again.

Her heart lifted with excitement, anticipating the pleasure in store.

Eleven

'I won't be in for lunch today, Mary,' Charlotte said as they got ready for church the following morning. 'I'm going over to the manor straight after Sunday school.'

Mary cast her a quizzical look but didn't ask questions. Charlotte smiled. 'On Georgie's invitation. He wants me to see his pony.'

Mary smiled and nodded. 'That'll be nice.' There was a pause before she added, 'Are you telling your father?'

Charlotte shrugged. 'I don't think he'll notice.' The remark was made without self-pity, which, to Mary, was remarkable. She couldn't understand why the girl couldn't see that she was treated like a servant. Less than a servant, Mary thought bitterly. At least employees got paid, pittance though it was.

Charlotte never took meals with her father but always ate in the kitchen with Mary, Edward and the kitchen maid if there was one. It had always been so. Osbert had never wanted the child at his table and the practice had not changed even now that his daughter was an adult.

Mary sighed. She supposed Charlotte accepted it because she'd never known any different.

'Right, are we ready?' Charlotte asked, pulling on her coat and jamming her hat on to her head. 'Where's Edward?'

'He fetched the pony and trap back from the manor first thing this morning, so they've gone already.'

'Oh heck! We'll be late.'

As usual, the women walked down the long lane together to the church in Ravensfleet. On a normal Sunday, the pews were comfortably full and the Sunday school in the little room at the back of the church was well attended. But at Christmas, Easter and especially at harvest time when the congregation swelled, it threatened to burst at the seams.

'Your father's already there,' Mary panted as they came in sight of the gate.

Charlotte bit her lip but said nothing. Father didn't like them to be late. He was waiting in the porch, scowling. He opened his mouth to say something, no doubt to berate them, but then his gaze moved beyond them. To her surprise, Charlotte saw him begin to smile as she heard the sound of the motor car from the manor pulling up at the gate.

Briefly, his gaze came back to his daughter. 'Get inside,' he snarled. 'And don't let this happen again.'

Charlotte's mouth dropped open. Her father always demanded that she and his servants enter church following meekly in his wake. Yet now he was sending them in ahead whilst he waited to greet the Thornton family.

She glanced at Mary, but she was already marching through the door, a grim expression on her face. As she made to follow, Charlotte looked back over her shoulder to see Georgie wave and begin to run towards her. She hesitated.

'Get in!' her father hissed and, raising his stick, hit her across the shoulders. Mortified that the young boy had witnessed his action, Charlotte hurried into the church, her back smarting. Red faced with shame, she sat beside Mary, and bowed her head. She heard quick footsteps coming down the tiled aisle. They stopped beside her and Georgie's small hand crept into hers.

'Miss Charlotte,' he whispered anxiously. 'Are you all right?'

She took a deep breath. 'Yes, dear. I'm fine.'

'Can I sit with you?'

'Well, yes, but won't your father – ?'

'Papa won't mind.' He grinned mischievously. 'And you'll keep me in order, won't you?'

Despite her humiliation, Charlotte smiled down at him. He was such a dear little imp. Her golden boy. How she wished he really was hers.

He slid in beside her and bowed his head in prayer as he'd been taught to do on taking his place in the church. Charlotte watched him, longing to stroke his blond curls. As the rest of his family passed her and entered their own pew, she caught Miles Thornton's eyes and raised her eyebrows in a silent question. His glance rested briefly on his small son. He smiled and nodded his approval. But when her father sat down in front of them, Osbert glared round at her and muttered, 'I'll see you at home, miss.'

Just as before, Georgie's tiny hand crept into Charlotte's and held it tightly all through the service.

'Papa, Papa.'

Georgie ran down the church path to his father and brothers as they were leaving after the service.

Miles turned. 'What is it? Aren't you staying for Sunday school this morning?'

'Yes, Papa, but last night I invited Miss Charlotte to come back with me afterwards to see my pony. And

81

she'd like to see Midnight, too,' he said beaming up at Philip. 'She likes horses.' He turned back to Miles. 'May she stay to luncheon, too, Papa?'

'Of course.' Miles nodded.

'Thank you, Papa,' the boy shouted back over his shoulder as he ran back to Charlotte.

'Did you really have to invite that dreary creature again, Father?' Philip muttered. 'Wasn't last night enough?'

'Now, now, Philip,' Miles admonished gently. 'Don't be unkind.'

'Philip's always unkind, Father,' Ben said. Shocked, his father and brother stared at him. 'Haven't you noticed?' He turned away. 'I think I'll go to Sunday school too.'

'Well, well, well,' Miles murmured, his gaze still on his middle son as he walked away. So, the quiet, shy one of the trio did have some spirit after all. The man felt a warm glow.

'Huh,' Philip muttered, his mouth twisting cruelly. 'The worm turns, does it? He'd better watch it.'

The glow in Miles Thornton's heart died instantly.

'So, Ben, have you got a pony or a horse?'

They were sitting in the motor car on their way to the manor after Sunday school had ended.

'I did have a pony.' The boy's eyes were bleak. 'But he had to be put down just before we moved here.'

'He was very old and got sick,' Georgie put in. 'Father said we shouldn't let him suffer.'

'That's quite right,' Charlotte said gently. 'But it doesn't make it any easier, does it?'

Ben smiled at her.

'Father promised to get Ben a bigger horse when we moved.'

'There's a horse fair at Horncastle. It's not until August, but that's only ten weeks or so away.' Charlotte said. 'Would you like me to have a word with your father? Tell him about it?'

'Would you?' Ben looked up eagerly.

'Of course.'

The car chugged up the drive and around the side of the house, coming to a halt in the yard.

The boys scrambled out.

'This way, Miss Charlotte. The stables are this way,' Georgie said excitedly. 'Look, Philip's got Midnight in the training ring.'

They walked through the yard lined with stables on either side to where, beyond it, was an area of open ground. A huge circle was fenced off. In the centre of the circle stood Philip, with a whip in his hand. Near the fence was a magnificent black stallion. Charlotte gasped in horror. The animal was sweating, his eyes wild and frightened. He was snorting and stamping his feet. Every so often he whinnied and reared up on his hind legs.

Philip approached the animal slowly, menace in every step. 'I'll teach you to obey me, if it's the last thing I do,' he yelled. The horse whinnied again and cantered away. But there was no escape from the circle and the young man, whip in hand at the ready, followed.

Appalled, Charlotte, Ben and Georgie watched as Philip raised his whip and lunged towards Midnight, beating him once, twice, three times on his flank.

'No – no, Philip. Not like that.' Lifting her skirt, Charlotte climbed the fence, threw her leg over the top and jumped down inside the ring. She had begun to run towards them when the horse turned towards his attacker and reared, his front hooves pedalling the air. He came down heavily, his left hoof catching Philip on the shoulder and knocking him to the ground.

Charlotte reached the horse and, unafraid, caught hold of the bridle and led him away to the side of the ring, throwing the reins over the top bar of the fence to tether him there. Then she ran back to the inert figure on the ground and fell to her knees beside him. Philip opened his eyes and his face twisted, with both pain and anger. 'See what you've done? Get away from me and mind your own business – ah!' His words ended in a cry of pain as he tried to raise himself from the ground.

'Lie still,' Charlotte commanded and began to feel around the young man's shoulder.

'I said, get away from me—'

'And I told you to lie still and let me help you. I think you've dislocated your shoulder.'

'Oho, a doctor are we now?' Despite the pain he could still raise a sneer.

A shadow fell across them and Charlotte glanced up to see Eddie Norton, the stable lad at the manor, standing there. 'You'd do well to listen to her, Master Philip. Miss Charlotte's clever like that. Knows about animals and bones and such. Not much of a jump to a human.' His face darkened as he added, 'At least – not in your case.'

'Why, you impudent young – ah!' Again, whatever Philip had been going to say was lost in a pain-ridden yelp.

'For goodness' sake, lie still,' Charlotte said sharply. 'Eddie – get something to use as a stretcher. We must get him to the house quickly.'

'Is he all right?' Georgie's voice, quavering with

fright, called from the other side of the fence as Eddie hurried away. 'Ben's gone to fetch Papa.'

'He'll be fine,' Charlotte called back. 'Don't worry.'

'This is all your fault. If you hadn't come into the ring shouting your head off, he'd never have reared.'

'Nonsense,' Charlotte countered sharply. 'That's no way to train a horse. Cruelty will get you nowhere with any animal.'

'He needs to be broken.'

'But not like that.'

'What's happened?' Miles Thornton vaulted the fence with the agility of a man half his age and ran towards them.

'That horse is a vicious beast, Father. I want him shot.'

'No – no,' Charlotte cried in dismay. 'It was Philip's treatment of him, Mr Thornton. He whipped him. That's no way to break a young horse in. He's a magnificent animal – '

'I want him shot,' Philip repeated through clenched teeth.

'Never mind about that now. What about you? Are you hurt?'

'It's his shoulder. It's dislocated.'

'Thinks she's a bloody doctor,' Philip muttered then groaned in agony, his face white.

Eddie returned with an old door and set it down beside the injured young man. He went to Philip's head and bent as if to lift him on to it.

'Wait, Eddie. We should bind his arm to his side first. Any movement will be very painful. Here, we'll use my scarf.'

Charlotte unwound the cotton scarf from her neck. 'Just raise him gently.'

Though Philip cried out again, Charlotte managed to get the scarf beneath his shoulders and tie it across his chest, fastening his arm to his side.

'Now, lift him gently on to the door.'

'Let me,' Miles said, moving to his son's feet.

Eddie pushed his arm under Philip's shoulders whilst Charlotte supported his back as the three of them slid him on to the door.

'Father – look out,' Ben called. 'Midnight's pulled free.'

Startled, Charlotte, Miles and Eddie looked round. The horse had somehow pulled and pulled until the reins had slid off the fence.

'You carry him to the house. I'll see to Midnight.'

'Don't go anywhere near him, Miss Charlotte,' Miles said at once. 'I'll get the vet to come and put him down. I—'

'No, you will not!' Charlotte rounded on him, forgetting in her anger just to whom she was talking.

'I think,' Miles said stiffly, 'I can be allowed to make my own decision on that matter. For the moment, my son is my concern.' He bent and grasped the end of the door. At the opposite end, Eddie did the same.

'Lift,' Miles ordered.

As they carried Philip away, Charlotte moved slowly towards the horse. As she neared him, she spoke quietly and soothingly. At last she was able to grasp the bridle and lead him out of the ring. There was no one about now – they'd all gone up to the house – so she led the animal to the nearest empty stable, settled him as best she could and closed the door on him.

She paused a moment, watching him. He was calmer now, but there was still terror in his eyes.

'Poor old fellow,' she murmured. 'I'll not let them hurt you.' Then she turned and made her way to the back door of the house.

Entering the kitchen, she found the servants in turmoil and Lily in floods of tears.

'Oh, Miss Charlotte. What's happened? Is he badly hurt?'

Despite her anxiety, Charlotte blinked in surprise. She glanced around. Cook's face was anxious, the little kitchen maid's fearful, but Lily's agitation was excessive. But it was Eddie's grim expression that startled Charlotte the most as he watched Lily's weeping and wailing.

'Calm down, girl,' Cook snapped at last. 'Miss Charlotte – tell us what happened. Please.'

Swiftly, she explained and then added, 'I should go upstairs and see how he is.'

'The master's told me to fetch Dr Markham,' Eddie muttered.

Lily gasped and cried out. 'Then what are you waiting for?' She ran to him and dragged him by the arm towards the door. 'Go on, go on – fetch him.'

'I'm going,' the young man said morosely, his furious gaze still on Lily's face. 'But there's nowt wrong wi' him that Miss Charlotte couldn't put right in a jiffy.'

'Go *on*,' Lily cried again, pushing him out of the door.

'I'll go up,' Charlotte murmured and turned towards the door leading upstairs, amazed to find that Lily was following her.

'You stay here, girl,' Cook snapped.

'But—'

'No "buts".'

Crestfallen, Lily turned away, wiping the tears from

her eyes. Charlotte glanced at the cook, but Mrs Beddows avoided meeting her gaze.

Thoughtfully, Charlotte made her way upstairs.

'Keep her away from me. I don't want her anywhere near me,' Philip spat as Charlotte entered the morning room where the young man lay on the couch. 'She's done quite enough damage for one day.'

'You brought it on yourself,' Charlotte said quietly. 'Like I said before, whipping a horse is no way to break him in. You'll make him wilder.'

'Father, just get her out of here, will you?'

Miles frowned. 'That's enough, Philip.' Now he could see his son was not seriously hurt, he would no longer tolerate the boy's rudeness to Charlotte. He turned towards Ben. 'Will you tell me what happened?'

For once Georgie was silent, standing white faced beside his father, his gaze on his brother lying on the couch.

'We were taking Miss Charlotte to see the horses. Phil was in the training ring with Midnight.' Ben paused and bit his lip. 'We stood by the rail to watch. The horse was – ' again he paused briefly – 'very agitated. It was sweating and snorting and – and trying to get away from Phil.'

'That's a lie. It's a disobedient beast that needs disciplining,' Philip spat out, but his words ended in groan. He winced and closed his eyes.

'Phil went after him – with the whip. He hit him three times on his flank. Then – then – ' The boy glanced at Charlotte with an apologetic look. 'Miss Charlotte shouted "no – no" and climbed over the fence. She was running towards them both when Midnight reared. His hoof caught Phil on the shoulder and he fell down.'

Georgie slipped his hand into Miles's. Tears filled his eyes and his voice trembled as he said, 'It wasn't Miss Charlotte's fault. It was Phil's. He shouldn't have hit Midnight, Papa.'

Philip opened his eyes again. 'It was all her fault. If she hadn't shouted—'

At that moment, Wilkins opened the door and ushered the doctor into the room. 'Dr Markham, sir.'

'Now, what have we here?' The portly, bewhiskered man's eyes twinkled through his spectacles. 'Nothing too serious, I trust. Ah,' he said, spying Philip on the sofa. 'This is the patient, I presume.'

Swiftly, Miles explained what had happened and the doctor examined the young man gently. 'Dislocated shoulder,' he pronounced. He glanced around the room and spotted Charlotte. 'Ah, the very person. Charlotte, if you'd assist me, we'll soon have—'

'I don't want her anywhere near me. Get – her – out – of – here.'

'My dear boy,' Dr Markham regarded him benignly over his spectacles, 'there is no one better to help me put your shoulder back in place than Miss Crawford, I can assure you. And unless you want a very uncomfortable half-hour ride in your father's motor car to the nearest hospital and a possible wait of anything up to an hour, then I suggest you let us help you.'

'Father – are you going to stand there and let these – these *yokels* pull me limb from limb?'

Before Miles could answer, Dr Markham laughed. 'Come now, my boy, that's a trifle harsh. Country folk we may be, but we know a thing or two when it comes to dislocated bones, now don't we, Charlotte? Now – ' a note of firmness crept into the man's tone as he beckoned Charlotte to his side – 'this may hurt a bit . . .'

They heard Philip's scream down in the kitchens as between them the doctor and Charlotte clicked his dislocated shoulder back into place.

'Now – we need to bind it to keep it in place. See he takes two of these . . .' Dr Markham pulled a bottle of tablets from his bag and handed it to Miles – 'every four hours. That'll ease the pain. Rest and quiet for a day or two. I'll call in again.'

When the doctor had departed, Charlotte faced Miles. 'Mr Thornton, if you are seriously contemplating getting rid of Midnight, then let me have him. I'll buy him from you.'

Miles stared at her. 'You know someone who can tame him?'

Charlotte hid her smile. 'I do,' was all she said quietly.

'The damned animal needs putting down,' Philip muttered.

'Papa,' Georgie tugged on Miles's hand, 'don't have Midnight killed. He's not old and ill like Ben's pony was. Let Miss Charlotte have him. Please, Papa. Or – ' his face brightened as another idea came to him – 'sell him at the horse fair.'

'The – the what?'

'The horse fair. Miss Charlotte told me about it. She said you might be able to get a horse from there for Ben. You promised he could have another when we got settled in here.'

'And you can get me another. I don't want that devil,' Philip muttered.

'Where is this horse fair?' Miles asked.

'It's at Horncastle at the beginning of August,' Charlotte said.

Miles appeared to consider. 'I only bought Midnight recently,' he murmured. 'Perhaps I should sell him and get Philip something more – suitable.'

'I'd still like to buy Midnight from you. I'll give you whatever you paid for him.' She held out her right hand to him. After a moment's hesitation, Miles took it and she felt his firm, warm grasp.

'Very well,' he said. 'If you're sure.'

'Oh, I am. In fact, I'll take him home with me now.'

'Don't you have to ask your father first?' Now Miles was puzzled. The girl had seemed so downtrodden, so meek and subservient. And yet, here she was giving her word to buy the unbroken animal without even conferring with her father. And she'd taken charge over Philip, telling everyone – even him – what to do. And, it seemed, she'd been right about the dislocated shoulder too.

He was even more puzzled when she said quietly, 'Not on this occasion – no.'

Twelve

A week later, on the last day of May, Joe came to the farm office.

Charlotte was seated behind the desk and looked up as he entered. 'Good morning, Joe. Please sit down.' She waved towards the chair in front of the desk. They talked for a while about the farm.

'It'll be haymaking before we know it,' Charlotte said. 'And then harvest.'

'Aye, and talking of August time, there's something else I'd like to ask you, Miss Charlotte. Mr Thornton drove over yesterday to ask my advice about buying a couple of horses for his sons.' Joe smiled. 'To replace the one you brought back from there and another for the middle boy – Benjamin, is it?'

'That's right. But everyone calls him Ben.'

'He said you'd mentioned the horse fair at Horncastle in August. I was wondering if we could take Mr Thornton. I mean, you could look over the horses there and then . . .' His voice petered out.

Charlotte was thoughtful before she said, 'Can we do it without him guessing?'

'Would it really matter, miss, if he did find out?'

She sighed. 'My father . . .' she murmured and needed to say no more.

Joe's mouth tightened. 'It's high time you got the

credit, Miss Charlotte, for everything you do, if you'll forgive me saying so.'

Charlotte's smile was pensive. 'It's kind of you to say so, Joe, but you know that's not possible. There's only you and the Morgans who know the truth.' She sighed. 'And that's the way it's got to stay.'

'Miss Charlotte, it's 1926 for heaven's sake. You're living the life of a daughter in the Victorian age.' He bit back the words, 'And dressing like one too.'

'I can't see a way out, Joe. Unless I pack my bags and leave. And where would I go? I've no money of my own. No relatives. No – ' There was a catch in her voice as she realized just what an isolated, lonely life she led. 'No friends.' Then she added swiftly, 'Apart from everyone around here, of course. And besides,' she added with wry amusement, 'who'd care for my father? Mary and Edward only stay here because of me. If I went, they'd go too. They've told me so.'

'I know that,' Joe said boldly. 'And my Peg only comes to help out here because of you, an' all. By heck, I'm opening me mouth and letting me tongue run away with itsen'. I don't mean no disrespect, miss, but all of us don't like to see you treated the way you are. And him hitting you last week at morning service, well, it riled us all.' He leaned forward. 'Don't think it wasn't noticed, 'cos it was. Does he often hit you, Miss Charlotte?'

'Not – often. Not now, anyway. Only when I anger him. His punishment when I was younger was to lock me in my room for hours on end. If it hadn't been for Mary and Edward . . .'

Joe's face was grim.

'Please, Joe, not a word to anyone. I've said more than I should. Promise me.'

Reluctantly, Joe nodded, hoping that his promise didn't include keeping secrets from his Peggy, because he had no intention of doing that. Not any more. Now she, too, worked at Buckthorn Farm occasionally, she was seeing for herself how things were.

'So,' Charlotte went on, briskly bringing them back to the topic that had caused the shared confidences, 'Mr Thornton and the Horncastle horse fair. I suggest you offer to go with him and just ask, casually, if he minds if I come along. He knows of my fondness for horses – ' she grimaced comically, 'so I don't think he'll be surprised to see me amongst them. And, somehow, I will communicate to you which animals I think might be suitable. It's worth a try. I'd like to see Ben with a nice mount.' Her mouth tightened. 'But as for Philip, I'm not sure he deserves to be in charge of a horse. Still, perhaps I can find him a nice docile one.'

Joe laughed. 'There's nothing docile about that young man. Anyway, we can but try.'

June was a busy month for haymaking and all the farmers in the district helped each other not only with machinery and horses, but also with manpower. It was a time of the year that Charlotte loved, for it gave her an excuse to work alongside the farm labourers each day, spreading the cut grass out to dry and then, just before nightfall, raking it into long rows down the fields.

Eddie Norton and two other workers from Home Farm, the farm attached to the manor, came to help at Buckthorn Farm and, in turn, the Warren family and old Matty went to work on Miles Thornton's fields. Even her father had not been able to stop Charlotte mixing with the workers on neighbouring farms at haymaking and, later, at harvest time. Her help was needed.

'The new master dun't know the first thing about farming, Joe,' Charlotte overheard Eddie say as she raked the cut grass into windrows alongside Peggy. 'But Master Thornton's such a nice feller. We all like him. And we know how lucky we are to've been kept on. And I'll tell you summat else an' all, that second son of his – Ben, is it? He'll mek a grand farmer one day. He listens and learns and he's been working out in the fields as good as any man.'

As they worked, Georgie and his three friends scampered about the field, playing.

'Now, Master Georgie,' Jackson warned, 'don't you go trampling down the grass before the mower comes, else it won't get cut proper.' He frowned at his own brother and the other two local lads. 'You should 'a known better, our Tommy. Don't go leading this little lad into bother. He dun't know country ways. Not yet.'

Georgie stood still and regarded Jackson solemnly. 'Why mustn't we trample it?'

Jackson leaned on the wide rake he was using and smiled at the boy, whose golden curls glinted in the sunlight.

'Because,' Jackson explained patiently, 'if the grass is lying flat, the mower can't cut it. You go and watch it, Master Georgie, then you'll see what I mean. But don't get in the way of the cutter bar.'

The boys ran to where the mower was cutting the grass on the far side of the field, drawn by two of the farm's shires. A little later the boys returned and now, Charlotte noticed, they were skirting carefully round the uncut grass. The workers had all been at Buckthorn Farm for several days and today, by mid afternoon, they were almost finished here. Charlotte stood up and eased her aching back. She glanced across the flat fields and smiled with satisfaction at the long rows of cut grass. Then, suddenly, she felt a little hand creep into hers.

'Are you tired, Miss Charlotte?' Georgie asked.

'A little. We all work very hard at this time of the year. And soon it will be the corn harvest. That's an even busier time.'

The boy's face fell.

'Why do you ask?'

'I – I just wondered if we could go to the beach. You – you did promise to take me.'

Charlotte's smile broadened. 'So I did. Then we'll go.'

'Now?'

'Yes, now. But first, we must ask Eddie to take a message to your father that—'

'Papa's over there. We can ask him.' And before she could say another word, he was capering across the field towards his father, but still, she noticed with a smile, avoiding the grass that was yet to be cut. Georgie was hopping up and down excitedly in front of Miles as Charlotte walked towards them.

'Please may I go, Papa? Miss Charlotte will bring me home before bedtime.'

Miles looked up. 'I'm sure Miss Charlotte's tired. Another day perhaps . . .'

'I don't mind. Any excuse to go to the shore.'

'Then of course he may go with you.' He paused and she felt his brown gaze upon her. 'Would you mind if I came too?'

'Of course not. And if we can find a sack, we can collect samphire.'

'Samphire? What's that?'

Charlotte laughed. 'Poor man's asparagus. It grows on the saltmarsh, even where the tide covers it. You should try it.'

Miles laughed. 'I doubt Mrs Beddows would know how to cook it. You do cook it, I take it?'

She nodded. 'I'll get Mary to send you the recipe.'

Moments later, when they'd collected a sack, the three walked along the lane towards the sea.

'Oh look, Papa. The sea!' The boy stood on top of the bank, his eyes wide in wonder as he took in the vast expanse of marshland, mudflats, sand and the North Sea beyond.

'Now,' Charlotte said, bending down, 'you must never come here on your own, Georgie. The tides can be very treacherous. It's coming in now and you see how the water is swirling round and forming creeks—'

'What's a creek?'

Charlotte pointed. 'There, that water that looks like a pond just now, but watch, you see the strip of marshland beyond it – between it and the sea?'

'Yes.'

'Now see how the water starts to cover the land?'

They watched for several minutes until the piece of marsh disappeared beneath the encroaching waves and the creek became one with the sea.

'I think I understand what you mean, Miss Charlotte,' Miles said. 'You see, Georgie, if you'd been standing on that bit of marsh and the sea had come swirling in around you, perhaps by the time you'd realized you were getting cut off, the water in the creek would have been too deep for you to get across. Do you understand?'

The boy nodded solemnly.

'I've always been told that if you walk that way,'

Charlotte gestured to the left, 'towards the north, you can beat the water coming in from the right, but it'd be safer not to risk it. I never go beyond the creeks when the tide's coming in. Now, will you remember what I've said, Georgie?'

'Do Tommy and the others know?'

'All the children living here are told as soon as they're old enough to understand. And another thing – ' she turned and pointed inland – 'you see that windmill over there? That's Webster's Mill. You can see it from the marsh, but as soon as it disappears from view we mark our path across the mudflats with thakking pegs, so that when the tide starts to come in you can see your way back. We won't need to do that today, but you will remember what I've said, won't you? And you must be wary of sea frets, too. A sea mist. They roll in very quickly sometimes.'

'I'll tell Ben – and Phil,' Georgie promised solemnly.

'What on earth is a thakking peg?' Miles asked, amused.

'It's something that thatchers use to hold the thatch in place whilst they're working.'

'Ah.' Miles chuckled. 'Maybe one day I'll learn all these Lincolnshire words.'

'Now can we collect samphire?' Georgie demanded.

For the next hour or so, until the sun began to sink behind the sandbank, streaking the sky with red and gold and the tide crept nearer, the three of them picked the fleshy-leafed plant to carry back to the farm. As they left, they paused at the top of the bank to look back across the marsh, listening to the soft sound of the sea.

'In a month or so,' Charlotte told Georgie, 'the marsh will be covered with lilac sea lavender, and later yellow and mauve sea asters. There are all sort of plants that grow on the marsh. It's really very pretty. I'll bring you again. We'll look for crabs or just watch the birds feeding on the mudflats when the tide's out. That's if – ' she paused and glanced at Miles – 'your father doesn't mind.'

'Any time, Miss Charlotte.' She heard his low chuckle. 'Just so long as I can come too.'

'We wondered where you were, Miss Charlotte,' Mary greeted them at the back door. 'Good evening, sir – Master Georgie. Would you care for something to drink before you go home? A nice glass of my elderflower wine, perhaps? And lemonade for Master Georgie?'

'That'd be very nice,' Miles said, stepping over the threshold.

'Mrs Morgan,' Georgie piped up, 'we've collected some samphire. Will you cook it for us?'

'I will indeed, Master Georgie. I'll show you what to do and then you can tell Mrs Beddows. It's very easy, but she might not have heard of it, not being from these parts. First you wash it well, then boil or steam it for about ten minutes. Serve it with a knob of butter and season it with black pepper and vinegar. Now, Master Georgie, can you remember that?'

Solemnly, Georgie nodded whilst Miles looked on with an amused smile.

'It goes nicely with fish or meat,' Mary went on. 'And you can pickle it, too, so you've got supplies through the winter.'

It was a very tired, but happy little boy who travelled home in the pony and trap driven by Edward, tightly clutching the tureen of samphire Mary had shown him how to cook.

Thirteen

August arrived and, with it, Georgie's excitement reached fever pitch at the anticipated trip to the horse fair.

It was arranged that Mr Thornton, his two younger sons, Joe and Charlotte should all travel to Horncastle in Mr Thornton's motor car.

'Would you like to go on the Sunday?' Charlotte asked Miles. 'A lot of the dealers and their horses start arriving immediately after Bank Holiday Monday. There'll have been some buying and selling even in that first week, but the following Sunday is what they call show day and the fair starts in earnest on Monday, the ninth. The boys would love it.'

'You've been before?' There was a surprised note in his tone.

'Joe's father, Harry Warren, used to take me. I was only ten the first time I went.' She bit her lip, resisting the urge to confide in him that trips to the horse fair had been the only outings she'd ever known, except for the occasional visit to the optician in Lincoln. For some reason, her father had never stopped her going to the annual fair. No doubt it had been because it all added to her farming knowledge.

So the trip was arranged for the second Sunday in August, with another visit to buy two horses the next day.

'A lot more arrive then and the best 'osses are snapped up quickly,' Joe explained, winking at Georgie. 'So we need to go again.'

He was rewarded by a beaming smile from the excited little boy.

'I hope you don't mind squashing in the back seat with the two boys, Miss Charlotte.' Miles Thornton smiled as he held open the car door for her.

'Of course not.' She'd been looking forward to this day ever since it had been suggested and her heart lifted even further when she saw that Philip was not joining the outing. There was only one thing that might prove difficult. She was worried that Georgie – and possibly Ben too – would stay with her and she wouldn't have the chance to look over the horses and indicate her choices to Joe. But, unwittingly, Miles came to her rescue. 'If you need to go off on personal matters, Miss Charlotte, just say so. We don't want to spoil your plans.'

But then Charlotte thought that having the two boys alongside her might be a good idea. Perhaps she could glean which animals took Ben's eye, since one of them was to be for him. She would have plenty of time that evening to talk to Joe before their buying trip the next day. She'd already primed Joe that he should ask Miles how much he wanted to pay. As they travelled, she heard snatches of the conversation from the front seats and knew they were discussing the details.

'I thought it'd be an auction,' she heard Miles say. 'But Miss Charlotte mentioned "dealing". What actually happens?'

'The fair's not so big now as it used to be. Years ago,

the town was packed, but it's still a good place to buy a horse; that's if you watch out for the scams.'

'Scams?'

'Oh aye, not all dealers are honest, Mr Thornton, but don't you worry, we can usually spot 'em. When me dad first brought me here,' Joe went on, 'there used to be a couple of fellers held auctions in the yard of the Reindeer and used the paddock to put their 'osses through their paces. We allus went to them. Honest as the day is long, they were. They're not there now, more's the pity, 'cos I'm talking twenty years or more ago. Still, we'll have a good look around for you.'

Charlotte caught her breath, wanting to say, 'Don't say "we", Joe.'

Innocently, Georgie came to her rescue by interrupting. 'Ben doesn't mind what colour 'oss he has. But he doesn't want a big one like Midnight, do you, Ben?'

Charlotte felt the urge to giggle at Georgie copying Joe's Lincolnshire dialect, but Ben, seeming not to notice, shuddered and shook his head. 'No – nor one so wild.' He glanced sideways at Charlotte. 'Where's Midnight now, Miss Charlotte?'

'Still in our stables at Buckthorn Farm. He's being schooled,' she added. It was the truth, but not the whole truth. The horse had indeed been broken in – and was making good progress – by Charlotte herself with old Matty's help. But again, this was one of the secrets of Buckthorn Farm. In the summer evenings, when all but perhaps Joe had left work, Charlotte worked with the horse.

Sunday was, as Charlotte had said, show day. Stalls had been set up in the inn yards in readiness for the days ahead and dealers were already showing off their horses, running them up and down the street or on the nearest piece of grass, hoping to secure early interest in their animals.

'Oh look – do look!' Georgie exclaimed as Miles parked the car and they all scrambled out. 'I've never seen so many horses. How are you ever going to choose one, Ben? You'll have to come with us, Miss Charlotte, and help us.'

Charlotte and Joe exchanged a swift glance. It couldn't have worked out better. She held out her hand to him. 'Come, let's see if we can find a horse Ben might like.'

They wandered through the Bull Ring, where the main concentration of business would be, but the dealing spilled over into the surrounding streets and inn yards. There were more public houses than normal for the size of the town, but these stabled the horses and provided accommodation, food and drink for the dealers and buyers. August was a busy month and usually a profitable one for the town even though, as Joe had said, the heyday of the fair had been years earlier. But there was still much business to be done and many of the local residents relied on the fair. Even the surrounding farms grew oats especially to provide feed for the horses at this time of the year.

They all enjoyed the day; even Ben forgot to be a sedate twelve-year-old and ran around excitedly with Georgie.

'Mind where you're stepping,' Joe warned them both. 'I dun't reckon your Pa'd like 'oss muck in his car.'

'Have you seen anything you like?' Charlotte asked Ben. 'Because if you have, Joe could have a word with the owner.'

'He likes them all!' Georgie piped up before his brother could answer. They laughed and Miles said, 'I don't think I could afford to buy *all* of them, Georgie.'

'Couldn't you, Papa?' the young boy asked innocently. Then, suddenly, his attention was caught by the sound of music. 'What's that?'

'That'll be the Methodists,' Joe said. 'They hold an open-air service in the Bull Ring after the normal evening service. They have speakers and singers and—'

Georgie caught hold of Charlotte's hand and began to drag her along the street towards the sound. 'Let's go and listen.'

Laughingly, they all followed his lead.

Charlotte couldn't remember such a perfect day and it was almost dark by the time Miles left them at the gateway to Buckthorn Farm, promising, 'We'll be here bright and early in the morning.' He nodded to the back seat, where Georgie had been asleep against Charlotte's shoulder. 'If we can get Georgie to wake up, that is.'

The following day, Charlotte and Joe were waiting by the gate, almost as if they'd never left it, when the car bowled into view. Georgie was wide awake bouncing up and down on the back seat. 'Are we going to deal, Joe, or go to an auction?'

'We might do both, Master Georgie. It depends on what we see.'

They wandered through the streets that were even more crowded than the day before. There were men in suits and bowler hats or caps, but few women.

'Joe – the one over there.' Charlotte touched his arm and whispered. 'The bay.'

'Master Ben,' Joe said at once, taking the hint. 'Let's

go and have a look at this one.' As the five of them wove their way through the throng, Georgie asked, 'Is this one for Ben or Phil? Isn't it a lovely colour?'

'He is,' Charlotte said and, forgetting for a moment to hide her interest, she stepped forward and ran her hand over the horse's back. Then she patted his nose and murmured soothingly, 'Now, feller, now then.'

The dark-haired man holding the reins greeted her, 'Hello, Miss Crawford. Nice to see you again. Looking for a mount for yarsen, a' ya?'

Charlotte smiled and blushed. Her secret could be out any minute. 'Not today, Ned, but Mr Thornton here is looking for two horses for his sons.' She turned quickly before the man could say more. 'Joe – what do you think?'

Joe was pretending to examine the animal closely, but he knew that Miss Charlotte approved of this horse, otherwise she would already have moved away.

'He looks all right,' Joe said carefully.

'He's a good trotter,' the man said. 'Like to see?'

Joe nodded and Charlotte stepped back as Ned ran with the horse up and down the short stretch of available street.

Charlotte and Joe exchanged a glance and, when everyone else was watching the horse, she gave Joe a slight nod. As the dealer slowed the animal to a walk and came back to them, Joe said, 'Are you putting him through the auction?'

'Nah,' Ned said dismissively. 'I know there's not the dealing done in the streets now like there used to be.' He sniffed. 'More's the pity, I reckon. But I like to do me own selling, see who me 'osses are going to. And strike a fair bargain.'

'How much?' Joe asked bluntly.

'Sixteen guineas.' The man held out his hand as if to strike a deal, but Joe only grinned. 'Now, Ned, you know you'll never get that for this 'oss. Not these days, you won't. 'Tis not like the old days. Prices have gone down since the war.'

Ned laughed, took off his cap, scratched his head and then replaced it. 'Fourteen, then; I can't go no lower, Joe. Not even for you.'

Joe pretended to consider and then slowly shook his head again.

'Papa – Papa.' Georgie tugged at his father's sleeve. 'Can't you buy him? Ben likes this one.'

'Shush, Georgie. Leave it to Joe,' Miles whispered.

But Joe seemed lost and could do no other than look to Charlotte. With an inward sigh, she was obliged to take the risk. 'Twelve guineas, Ned,' she said firmly. 'You know that's a fair price.'

The man grinned, spat on his hand and held it out to her. 'I'll not argue with a lady. 'Specially not you, Miss Crawford. I could never fool you, now, could I?'

Charlotte took his hand and the deal was made.

Leaving Joe to make the arrangements, the others walked away.

'Ugh, he spat on his hand, Miss Charlotte. And you shook it.'

'That's the way Ned makes his deals, Georgie. It means he gives his promise to sell the horse to us. Even if he got a better offer, he won't break his word. That horse is Ben's now.'

After a few moments Joe caught them up. 'Ned says there's an auction in one of the inn yards at two o'clock. He reckons we might find a good mount there for Master Philip.'

Charlotte glanced at Miles to find him watching her. 'Is that all right?' she asked him.

'Whatever you say, Miss Charlotte.' He smiled and she had the uncomfortable feeling that he was beginning to guess just exactly who was choosing the horses – and striking the deals.

When the auction began, Georgie got very excited. 'I can't see, I can't see. I want to see when our horse come up.'

They'd already viewed all the horses due to go through the auction and had picked out one they liked for Philip. A grey, docile-looking animal.

'Sh,' Charlotte whispered, hiding her laughter. 'You mustn't say which one you like.'

He turned his innocent blue eyes on her. 'Why?'

'Because,' she explained softly, 'it lets other people know the one you're interested in and it might make someone bid against your father and drive the price up. You don't want your papa to have to pay more than he needs to, do you?'

Georgie shook his head and pressed his lips together as if to stop himself speaking. Then unable to help himself he said, 'But I still want to see.'

'All right, then. I'll lift you on to the wall, but you mustn't say anything or wave your hands because the auctioneer might think you're making a bid.'

Charlotte sat on the wall beside Georgie and Ben climbed up beside her. Miles and Joe were standing close by. Miles, under Joe's guidance, was to do the bidding. The two boys were lost in the proceedings, whispering every now and again to Charlotte, asking

107

her questions. Then Georgie wriggled with excitement and squeezed Charlotte's hand. 'This is Phil's.'

The horse was paraded in front of the crowd and the bidding began. As Miles watched and waited but made no move, Georgie became agitated.

'It's all right,' she murmured to the boys. 'Just wait and see.'

The bidding slowed and two of the men, who'd been making bids, shook their heads. Now there was only one man left who'd made the last bid. The auctioneer raised his gavel, his gaze travelling around the faces in front of him. Georgie, his eyes wide and fearful, drew in a deep breath, just as, close by, they heard Joe mutter, 'Now, sir. Raise your hand . . .' And Miles's hand shot high in the air. The gavel was lowered as the auctioneer nodded towards Miles in acknowledgement. Now bidding between Miles and the other man continued backwards and forwards until, at last, the other man shook his head. The gavel fell and Joe turned with a wide grin to Georgie and Ben. 'And he's a fine mount, but gentle. I think he'll suit your brother.'

Ben nodded and Georgie clapped his hands in glee. 'What shall we call him, Ben?'

'I don't know. Maybe he's got a name already – like Ned said mine's called Blaze. Besides, Phil should decide.'

'It's Prince,' Charlotte said, quite forgetting in the excitement, that she was not supposed to know. But having looked around at all the horses together, the boys didn't seem to notice her slip and question how she came to know the name of the horse.

Only Miles glanced over his shoulder and regarded her curiously yet again.

'I just hope Philip's going to take better care of him

than he did of Midnight,' Charlotte said later to Joe, as they waved the family off outside Buckthorn Farm.

'I had a word with the master. He's going make sure he does.'

'Mm.' Charlotte was doubtful. Miles couldn't supervise his eldest son every minute of the day. There were bound to be times when the young man was riding alone, and what would happen then?

Fourteen

Two days after the horse fair, Charlotte took Midnight to the beach further north to avoid the treacherous marsh. It was the first time she'd ridden him any distance from the farm. Gentle patience coupled with a firm hand had earned the animal's trust. Old Matty had always been on hand to offer his advice, but he'd hardly been needed. He'd merely nodded his approval. It had been a few weeks before she could put a saddle on the horse's back and another week or so before he would let her ride him.

'You've worked wonders with that 'oss, miss,' Joe marvelled. 'And in such a short time an' all. It takes some o' them so-called experts months sometimes.'

Charlotte smiled and glowed inwardly at his praise as she stroked Midnight's face. 'He's a beautiful animal. All he needed was to be treated with kindness and he responded. That's all, Joe.'

She made it sound so simple, but all Joe could think was that it was a pity she didn't receive that same kindness from a certain person. But he held his tongue.

Now Charlotte felt confident enough to take Midnight to the sea. 'A good canter along the beach will do him the world of good. He's a big horse and could do with the exercise.' And it would do her good, too, she couldn't help thinking, to get away from the gloomy house.

'Want me to come with you, Miss Charlotte?'

'I'll be fine, Joe.'

He nodded. 'If you say so, miss, but if you're not back in – let's say three hours – I'll come looking for you. I know where you're going.'

She smiled down at him from her lofty seat on the horse's back, but she was touched by the man's concern. At walking pace, she and Midnight left the stable yard, but she could feel Joe's anxious eyes watching her a long way into the distance.

She turned north, along the lanes, until she came to the area near the seaside town's golf course where there was no marsh between the sea bank and the beach. The stretch of hard sand left by the receding tide was firm enough for the horse to feel surefooted. As she urged him up the sand hill and on to the beach, Midnight whinnied, unused to the softness beneath his hooves. But she soothed him gently and, trusting her, he obeyed her commands. Gaining the top of the rise, Charlotte lifted her face to the sea breeze and breathed in deeply. How she loved the sea! She loved it in all its moods. Calm, like today, when the waves seemed almost too lazy to lap the shoreline, or ferocious, when the gales whipped the waves into a raging frenzy, crashing on to the beach in fury. But she loved it best when its mood was somewhere between the two extremes; when the waters seemed playful, the waves bowling to the shore, trying to catch anyone unawares who dared to step too close.

Charlotte encouraged Midnight down the slope. When they gained the firmer sand near the water's edge, she urged him into a brisk trot, then a canter and, finally, a gallop.

Breathless but exhilarated she reined the horse in and slowed him to a walk again.

She saw three horses in the distance coming towards her. As they drew nearer, she could see the little figure on the smallest mount, waving excitedly. Georgie, she thought, and then recognized Ben and Miles Thornton alongside him.

'Did you see, Miss Charlotte? Did you see me riding, Gypsy?'

Charlotte laughed, her face pink from the fresh air. 'I did indeed, Georgie. And very well you ride, too. Good afternoon, Mr Thornton – Ben.'

They were staring at her, but both of them touched their caps with their riding crops, which Charlotte fervently hoped were more for show than use.

'You're not wearing your spectacles,' Georgie said suddenly.

'Now, son, don't make personal remarks,' his father rebuked gently. 'It's not gentlemanly.' But the young boy only grinned.

'Then is it gentlemanly, Papa, to tell her she looks so much prettier without them?'

'Well . . .'

'I take it as a lovely compliment,' Charlotte put in swiftly to save them any further embarrassment. 'Thank you.' She forbore to say that this was the only time she was sure her father wouldn't find out that she'd taken them off. She hoped fervently that the little chatterbox would not let her secret slip out.

'I say,' Ben said, 'I've just realized. You're riding Midnight. Father – she's riding Phil's horse.'

'So I see,' Miles said quietly. 'But it's no longer Philip's horse. It's Miss Charlotte's.'

'Except that you haven't let me pay you for it yet.' She laughed, then turned to ask Ben, 'How are you getting along with Blaze?'

112

She turned Midnight round and they began to walk alongside each other back the way Charlotte had come.

'He's great,' Ben said.

'And the horse you got for Philip?' She wanted to ask if the young man was treating the animal kindly. She hesitated and bit her lip. But Georgie came to her rescue.

'He's being good with him, Miss Charlotte,' he giggled, 'but he calls him an old nag and doesn't ride him much. He wanted Ben's horse instead, but Papa said no.'

'He's decided he wants a motorcycle or a car,' Miles put in. 'But I shall hold out against that as long as I can. I don't think he'd be safe with either.'

They rode together companionably until they came to the end of the short lane where Charlotte turned for home.

'I must get back or Joe will be worried. This is the first time I've brought Midnight away from the farm.' She leaned forward and patted his neck. 'But he's done very well, haven't you, old feller?'

Having bade them goodbye, Charlotte rode towards Buckthorn Farm, unaware of Miles's thoughtful gaze following her.

'But she *was* prettier without her glasses,' Georgie said to no one in particular.

The wheat was ready for cutting and the extra hands arrived at Buckthorn Farm. Mary and Peggy had been baking for a week to provide food for the workers, but on the days when the corn was cut even they went out into the fields to help put the sheaves into stooks. Then, when all the fields at Buckthorn Farm had been cut, everyone moved on to the other farms to help out where needed.

On the following Monday morning, Joe knocked on the door of Charlotte's office and then poked his head round it. 'Could I have a word, miss?'

She smiled a welcome and gestured towards the chair he always sat in.

'It's about Dan Bailey at Purslane Farm, Miss Charlotte. He's not well again and he'll be struggling to get his harvest in. I was wondering if you'd mind us helping him out. A bit more than usual, I mean.'

'Of course not, Joe. Have you told Mr Thornton?'

Joe shrugged. 'I don't like to. It'd seem like telling tales. I'm not one to kick a man when he's down. Dan Bailey's a good man. He's just hit a bad patch of illness and his farm's suffering, that's all.'

Charlotte smiled. 'I'll let Mr Thornton know we'll all be helping out there now that we've finished here. He needn't know it's any different from normal.'

'We'll need the threshing tackle from Home Farm,' Joe warned. 'Dan's let his gear get into bad repair, so his farmhand, Jim, was telling me in the pub last night.'

Home Farm had its own traction engine and threshing drum that the estate's tenant farmers had the use of if they needed them. Buckthorn Farm, too, had always hired the gear but Dan Bailey, although a tenant of the estate, had his own. Until now, it seemed.

'And can me and the lads lend a hand with his threshing through the winter? We're used to the squire's engine.'

'Of course. We'll all help whenever it's needed. Just one thing, Joe,' she added as he got up to leave. 'Don't forget to save me some of the last sheaf of wheat from our fields when it's brought to the stack yard. I must make a corn dolly for the Harvest Supper as usual.'

Joe nodded, unable to speak for the lump in his

throat. This poor lass, he was thinking. Ever since she'd learned how to make a corn dolly as a little girl, she'd made one to be carried to the Harvest Supper celebrations at the manor. The irony of it was that the girl had never been allowed to join in the festivities.

Her father had seen to that!

Harvest time in the rural area around Ravensfleet had always been a big celebration. Almost as big as Christmas. Until recently, when the largest landowner in the district, Mr Davenport of Ravensfleet Manor, had fallen ill and died, the festivities had always been held in one of his huge barns and people had travelled for miles to attend the Harvest Supper. Farmers and labourers mingled freely, forgetting, for one night, their 'place'. Landowner served his tenants and, in turn, tenant farmers served their workers. All the workers on Buckthorn Farm attended, even though they were not part of the Ravensfleet Estate, for Osbert Crawford owned his farm. But Osbert himself never joined in the revelry.

Only Charlotte Crawford had never been allowed to attend a Harvest Supper.

'It'll be different this year.' Mary nodded sagely to Peggy. 'You'll see, that owd beezum'll go to the manor this year. You mark my words.'

'Thing is,' Peggy remarked thoughtfully, 'does Mr Thornton know what's expected of him? I mean, it's obvious to us – me 'n Joe – that he's new to this game. He's always asking my Joe for advice.'

'Is he?'

The two women exchanged a look of understanding, but it was Mary, greatly daring, who murmured softly so that only Peggy might hear. 'And your Joe asks Miss Charlotte, I suppose?'

Peggy nodded, her mouth a tight line. 'But Mr Thornton dun't know that.'

'Of course not,' Mary said on a sigh. There was a pause before she added, 'And is Joe going to tell him?'

Peggy sighed. 'I expect he'll have to be the one to say summat. About what's expected of him as regards the harvest celebrations. We can't expect Miss Charlotte to do it.' Again there was a hard edge to her tone as she added, 'Seein' as the poor lass never even gets the chance to go.'

Fifteen

The only place where Charlotte did have some say in the celebrations for a harvest safely gathered in was in Sunday school. And Cuthbert Iveson also relied upon her to explain to him what was expected of him in the church services, this being his first year.

'I don't know what I'd do without you, Miss Crawford. Your advice ever since I came here has been an enormous help to me. And your work with the children – well – I've never seen anyone so universally loved by the little ones.'

Charlotte blushed under the unexpected compliment. 'Well, I love them all dearly,' she said and added impishly, 'even the naughty ones.'

Cuthbert smiled too. 'And there are certainly one or two of those in your class. But you do seem to have a wonderful way of handling them. I hear you have an amazing affinity with animals, too. It must be a gift.'

She blinked behind her spectacles. 'I – I'd never thought of it like that.'

'Then I think you should,' Cuthbert said solemnly. 'It's not something given to everyone.'

He paused and then added. 'You're well liked in the community. Have you – I mean – would you ever consider becoming – ' he paused again and ran his tongue nervously round his lips – 'more involved with parish work.'

Suddenly Charlotte felt uncomfortable. How could she be involved in church work more than she already was, unless . . . ? She forced a laugh and hoped he wouldn't notice the blush creeping up her face. 'I'm sorry, Mr Iveson, but I really couldn't. My father would never allow it.'

There, she thought, that should put a stop to whatever he might have been about to say.

'But what am I going to say to Mr Thornton, Peg?' Joe asked his wife worriedly. 'You've got to spend a lot of money throwing a party for a lot of people you don't even know?'

Peggy laughed at Joe's worried expression. 'I'm sure – from what you've told me about the new squire – that he'd be more than willing to do it. It'll be a way for him to meet all his tenants in a friendly atmosphere and to get to know a lot of the other landowners and farmers around here, too.'

Joe wasn't so sure. 'Don't forget half the folk from the village come an' all.'

'I hadn't forgotten. But they're all part of this community. They may not actually work on the land themselves, but they're involved. Where would the greengrocer be without his supply of fresh vegetables straight off the land? Where would all the little shops be without the custom of all the farm workers and their families? I don't think you need worry about Mr Thornton, Joe. But,' she added, putting her head on one side and smiling mischievously at him, 'you could always get Miss Charlotte to speak to him herself.'

Joe shook his head vehemently. 'Oh no. Any advice

Mr Thornton asks for has to seem to come from me. She made that quite clear at the horse fair.' He chuckled. 'You should have seen us. Never knew I could be so – what's the word? – furtive.'

'Well, well, I shall have to watch you, Joe Warren.'

'It's only to protect Miss Charlotte, love. I'm an honest sort of bloke most of the time. But I wouldn't want to bring more trouble on her head, poor lass.'

When he'd finished work that evening, Joe walked the mile or so to the manor. It was growing dusk when he reached the back door. He'd already raised his hand to knock, when he heard a scuffling in one of the outhouses nearby. He paused, listening. Then he heard girlish laughter. He stiffened. *That's our Lily's laugh*, he thought. *I'd know it anywhere*. He'd already turned, ready to stride towards the outhouse, when the girl herself appeared, straightening her apron and smoothing her hair. At the sight of her father, even through the gloom, her eyes widened and colour suffused her face.

'Dad! What are you doing here?'

'I might ask you the same question, girl.' He nodded to the door behind her. 'What are you up to in there? One of the farm lads, is it? If it's young Eddie Norton, I'll—' He took a step forward.

'No, Dad. No, it isn't,' Lily said quickly, linking her arm through his and urging him away from the outhouse and towards the back door leading into the kitchen.

'But I heard you laughing. There's someone in there.'

Lily laughed, still a little nervously, Joe thought. 'It's – it's only the farm cat. She's got some kittens. I – I was playing with them, that's all.'

Joe's eyes narrowed. He didn't like to think that his

daughter would lie to him, but somehow he couldn't quite believe her. When he said nothing, Lily asked again, 'What are you doing here?'

'I've come to see the master. Is he in?'

'I'll see. But it's almost dinner time.'

'Dinner?'

'Oh aye, we're posh here, Dad. Dinner's in the evening, not midday.'

Joe grinned ruefully. 'Aye, well, 'tis tea or supper in our house, now, ain't it? And I'm ready for mine. But I need to see Mr Thornton and I can't come in the day.'

He didn't need to explain to his daughter what would happen if Osbert Crawford found out he'd been visiting the manor in working hours.

'I'll see if he's free, Dad. Come on in . . .' She skirted round him, opened the back door and held it for him to enter.

Just before the door closed behind him, Joe heard the squeak of the door across the yard. That's no cat, he thought grimly. He said no more for the moment, but he'd tell Peg about what he'd heard. Lily was of age, but she was still his little girl. However, maybe such matters were best spoken of between mother and daughter.

A few minutes later he was standing in Mr Thornton's study and the man was leading him to a chair by the fire and bidding him to sit down. It was a courtesy that was never extended to him on the rare occasions he saw Osbert, though Charlotte always treated him with this same respect.

'A drink, Joe? You've no doubt finished for the day?'

'Aye, well, I have an' I haven't, Mr Thornton.' He chuckled. 'I suppose I'm a bit like our local bobby. I'm never really off-duty.'

'You're a good man, Joe.' Miles wrinkled his forehead. 'D'you think I should employ a foreman here? Obviously, my predecessor didn't find it necessary, as most of the land is worked by the tenant farmers, but – just sometimes – I feel a bit at a loss to know what to do, especially around Home Farm which I'm *supposed* to manage.' He grinned ruefully. 'As I think you know by the number of occasions on which I've sought your advice.'

Gently, Joe said, 'Well, the old squire's family had lived here a long time. So he was brought up to it.'

'Mm,' Miles said thoughtfully and Joe put in, 'But I'm sure we – that is, Mr Crawford – would always be willing to help you out.'

Miles nodded. 'He's said as much, but . . .' He stopped and held Joe's gaze steadily. 'Is it *really* Mr Crawford who runs Buckthorn Farm?' Joe held his breath, fearing the end to the question. 'Or you?'

Joe breathed again and smiled lopsidedly. 'Well, without wanting to sound conceited, Mr Thornton, I suppose it's me. Though I always ask for advice when I need it,' he added, choosing his words carefully.

'Mm.' The other man was still thoughtful. 'You took over the position from your late father, didn't you?'

Now Joe was on more comfortable ground. 'That's right, sir. I was born in the cottage where we still live.'

'So, he taught you everything you know, eh?'

Again, Joe was cautious. 'Something like that, sir.'

Miles crossed the room to the sideboard, poured generous measures of whisky into two glasses and brought them back to the fire. Handing one to Joe, he sat down opposite him.

'Now, what is it you've come to see me about?'

'I'm not keeping you from your – dinner, sir, am I?'

121

'No, no. Another half an hour or so yet. We dine a little earlier, perhaps, than most households. I like all the family to be present and Georgie is only young. You have a young son too, I believe. He and Georgie have become friends. Young Tommy often comes to play here.'

'Does he?' Joe couldn't hide his surprise. 'I hope he's no trouble.'

'Good heavens, no. My boys are free to make their own friends and anyone they choose is always welcome here.'

There was a moment's pause before Joe began, haltingly, to explain the reason for his visit. 'Except for the past two years, sir, when old Mr Davenport was too ill, it's always been the tradition that the squire – and that's really what you're thought of, living at the manor – has held the harvest supper in the big barn at the back of the house.'

'Really?' Miles's eyes lit up. 'That sounds a splendid idea. What do I have to do?'

Joe breathed a silent sigh of relief. He hadn't expected it to be so easy. The two men spent the next half-hour happily discussing plans for the festivities. As the gong sounded, Joe said, 'I should be going and let you get to your dinner, sir.' They both stood up as Miles said, 'Won't you stay and eat with us?'

'That's very kind of you, sir.' Joe was touched by the man's magnanimity. 'But Peg – my wife – will have my supper all ready and waiting.'

'Of course.' Miles held out his hand. 'Thank you so much for coming to see me. We must talk again. I'll be very grateful for your guidance. Perhaps I could see Miss Charlotte, too—'

'Oh no, sir,' Joe said swiftly. 'Miss Charlotte isn't allowed to attend the harvest supper.'

'Isn't *allowed*?'

The two men stared at each other, both realizing that perhaps they had said – or implied – too much already.

'Good night, sir. I'll see mesen out the back way.'

Joe almost hurried from the room, still afraid that Miles Thornton would voice the question that was in his eyes.

Sixteen

The preparations for the harvest supper were well underway by the day that Miles rode over on horseback to Buckthorn Farm to invite Osbert and his daughter to attend. All the sheaves of wheat had stood in the fields to dry for three weeks and then had been brought to the stack yard. Threshing would go on through the winter months, a little at a time on each farm in turn, but now it was time to think of celebrating a harvest safely gathered in.

'I understand it's a tradition that the squire should host the harvest supper in the big barn at the manor.'

'Huh!' Osbert grunted. 'A waste of good money, if you ask me. We never go.'

'But I'd very much like you and Miss Charlotte to come this year. I believe all your workers attend.'

'Aye, they do,' Osbert said bitterly. 'And a fat lot of use they are for work the next day after all that free beer.'

Miles sighed, thinking the man had a very Scrooge-like attitude, even though it wasn't Christmas. But maybe he had the same outlook on those festivities, too. 'Well, I'm sorry you feel that way,' he began, but, suddenly, Osbert smiled.

'Your sons will all be there, I take it?'

'I hope so.'

'Hmm.' There was a pause before Osbert said, 'In that case, I'll be glad to come.'

'And Miss Charlotte?'

'No.' His mouth was a hard line. 'Not her.'

'I – see,' Miles said, though he didn't see at all. Instead, he added firmly, 'Well, I hope very much that she will come. I'd like to see her there and,' he added pointedly, 'I'm sure my sons would too.'

With that, he gave a curt but polite bow and strode from the room.

The harvest festival service took place in September. Under Charlotte's guidance, the children brought vegetables, fruit and two sheaves of wheat. On the previous Sunday, Charlotte had worked on her corn dolly at Sunday school, showing the children how to plait and weave the straw into the shape of a doll. Now this sat in the centre of the display on the altar steps. The service was a joyous occasion with everyone singing lustily the hymns they knew so well.

During the next week, several of Miles's workers readied the barn for the celebrations on the following Friday evening. They decorated it with flowers and replicated the display of produce that had been in the church. Mrs Beddows, Lily and the kitchen maid were run off their feet cooking and baking and Brewster was dispatched to the town to buy ale from the local brewery.

To everyone's surprise, Osbert Crawford was one of the first guests to arrive at the supper and, to their shock but enormous delight, walking in behind him, came Charlotte, shyly carrying the corn dolly she'd made to take pride of place in the celebrations.

Sadly, she was still dressed in her drab Sunday purple with a long dark coat over her dress, but before many minutes had passed Jackson had grabbed her hand and whisked her away from her father.

'Here, let me take your coat, Miss Charlotte. Biddy!' he called to one of the villages lasses. 'Take care of Miss Charlotte's coat, will you?'

The girl smiled, dimpling prettily. 'Hello, Miss Charlotte. Nice you could come,' she said diplomatically.

The villagers were whispering to each other.

'He's let her come.'

'Fancy, after all these years.'

'Why now, d'you suppose?'

'He's all over the new feller at the manor like a rash, that's why. An' Mary Morgan says the squire rode over to Buckthorn Farm last week and invited them both to come, an' he wouldn't take "no" for an answer.'

'Well, good for 'im then, I say. I'll raise me glass to Mr Thornton and drink 'is health. 'Specially as it's 'is beer I'm drinking!' The blacksmith from Ravensfleet laughed raucously and drank the squire's health. Those nearby joined him. 'Good health, Squire.'

'And hers,' someone else added. 'Let's drink to the lass, an' all.' With one accord they all raised the tankards or glasses they held and turned towards Charlotte.

'Good health, miss, and happiness to you.'

Hearing them, Jackson touched her arm and nodded towards the four or five men. 'They're toasting you, Miss Charlotte.'

She turned and smiled and bobbed a little curtsy of thanks.

'Aye,' muttered one of the drinkers. 'An' no one deserves it more'n you, lass.' But he didn't speak aloud the words that were in everyone's mind: 'But you'll not find happiness whilst yon miserable devil you call "Father" still has you in his clutches.'

Miles had seen the Crawfords arrive and noticed how Jackson went at once to Charlotte's side and drew her into the gathering of the younger folk at one end of the barn. He'd heard the toast to her and seen her smile and the pink tinge of pleasure – and perhaps a little embarrassment – touch her cheeks. And now Georgie, too, had seen her and was running across the barn towards her. Then he noticed that Osbert Crawford was standing alone near the door, leaning heavily on his walking stick and glaring around him with a morose frown on his face. No one had gone to him to take his coat or welcome him to the proceedings. Always aware of his position as host, Miles moved towards him and held out his hand.

'I'm so glad to see you both. Come, this way. I'm sure you'll know most of the men here . . .' He led Osbert to the corner where other farmers from the district were gathered. They nodded towards him, but not one of them made any effort to engage him in conversation. Miles felt a distinct chill in the atmosphere now that Osbert had arrived which had nothing to do with the autumnal evening. But he pressed on, offering him a drink and something to eat. The man and his daughter were here at his express invitation and it was his duty to see that they had a pleasant evening.

It was not until Philip appeared that Osbert smiled, excused himself from the gathering and moved towards the young man.

'Thank God for that,' muttered Roland Thompson into his beer. 'Can't abide the man. No offence, Squire, but as you've mebbe gathered, Osbert Crawford in't exactly popular round here.'

'No,' Miles said thoughtfully, his gaze still on the older man now talking to Philip. 'So it would seem.'

127

But, even though he waited, no one volunteered any further information.

When the dancing started, Jackson drew Charlotte into the throng.

'Oh, but I can't dance.'

'Neither can I, miss,' he grinned, 'but all we've got to do is jig about a bit.'

She laughed and put her hands into his.

It was all right whilst the merry dances were playing, but when it came to a slow waltz, after treading on her toes three times, Jackson said, 'This has got me beat an' all. I reckon we'd best sit this one out.'

Charlotte, fanning her hot face, agreed. But she'd not been sitting down for many seconds when a diffident Cuthbert Iveson approached her and asked if he 'might have the pleasure of this dance'.

'Go on, miss,' Jackson urged. 'Mebbe Vicar can mek a better fist of it than I can.'

Charlotte rose and put her hand shyly into Cuthbert's. Together they stepped in amongst the dancers. Cuthbert put his arm about her waist and whispered, 'Just relax and let me lead you.'

Now he was holding her firmly against him. Her body moulded to his so that when he moved, she automatically followed his steps.

'One, two, three. One, two, three,' he murmured in her ear and smiled down at her.

The other dancers, seeing Charlotte and the vicar together, smiled and nodded. Gradually, couple by couple, they stopped dancing and stepped to the side. At last, only Cuthbert and Charlotte were left in the centre of the floor. As the music came to an end, applause burst out spontaneously. Cuthbert bowed and Charlotte curtsied. They were laughing and moving to the side, when there was an angry roar as Osbert pushed his way through the throng, brandishing his walking stick. He stopped in front of his daughter and the vicar.

'How dare you disgrace yourself, girl? And you, sir.' He turned his venom on the timid man. 'Cavorting in public in such a manner. You dishonour your cloth. I shall report you to the bishop.'

'But, sir . . .'

'Father . . .' Charlotte began, but Osbert grasped her arm roughly and dragged her after him towards the door. In disbelief, the revellers parted to let them through, too stunned to move to help her. He pushed her through the door into the dark night. 'Get yourself home, this instant. I should never have let you come. I knew it was a mistake. You can't be trusted.' His raised his stick and struck her viciously on the side of her face.

There was a cry from the women watching and one or two men moved forward, but before anyone had time to come to her aid, Charlotte picked up her long skirt and ran out into the night.

Jackson pushed his way through the throng and ran outside, Georgie beside him. But already Charlotte had fled into the darkness.

'He hit her,' the little boy said, tears choking his throat. 'He hit her again.'

Jackson looked down at the young boy. 'Again? What do you mean "again"?'

'I saw him hit her with his walking stick once before. At church. Why, Jackson? What's she done wrong?'

Jackson put his hand on the boy's shoulder, his mouth a grim line as he muttered, 'God only knows, Master Georgie. God only knows.'

Seventeen

After the incident, the merriment seemed to die. Even though the musicians – locals who played an instrument and got together to entertain at such gatherings – struck up once more, no one had the heart for dancing now. Georgie was in tears and was carried off to bed by the housekeeper at the manor, Mrs Harkness. Ben soon followed of his own accord and only Miles and Philip were left of the Thorntons. Miles would have liked to escape too, but seeing as he was the host, he knew his departure would be seen as a signal for the party to break up.

'Come on, Lily,' Philip said, grabbing her hand and pulling her towards the empty space which served as a dance floor. 'Let's liven things up a bit. Let's get their tongues wagging. We'll do the Charleston. D'you know it?'

'Well, a bit, Master Philip. Someone tried to teach us it at the Valentine's Dance in Ravensfleet village hall, but I—'

'Let's give it a go then. Now, I wonder if this motley crew can play the music.'

'Eddie Norton on the fiddle can, Master Philip.'

'Right, I'll ask him. But stop all this "master" stuff. It's Philip.'

Lily blushed but as the music began, she kicked her legs in a pretty fair go at the dance that was sweeping the aristocratic parties of the 'flappers'.

From the sidelines, Miles watched with amusement, but in Joe's eyes there was a wary, anxious look.

'She's only having a bit of fun, love,' Peggy whispered at his side. 'She's a good girl.'

Joe said nothing. He buried his nose in his beer, but his gaze never left the gyrating couple.

As the festivities came to their natural end just after midnight, Jackson said, 'Miss Charlotte left her coat and hat. Shall I take them to the farm tomorrow, Dad?'

Miles, overhearing, butted in before Joe could reply. 'It's all right, Jackson. I'll see they're returned to Miss Charlotte first thing in the morning.'

A swift look of disappointment crossed the young man's face, but, dutifully, he nodded. 'Right you are, sir.'

The following morning Miles mounted his horse and took the package his groom handed up to him. He lifted his face and breathed in the autumn air. He loved September and never more so now that he had been introduced to the traditional harvest celebrations. There was a special smell to autumn and the colours were so glorious, though here on the flat open land there were few trees. That was the only thing he missed about his previous home in Derbyshire, the abundance of tree-laden slopes in all their wonderful greens and browns and golds. But in compensation, he revelled in the magnificent Lincolnshire sunsets. Never had he seen such skies. The glowing pinks, mauves and bright oranges of the setting sun. He was so thankful that he and his family had been accepted into the community and he felt a moment's sadness when he thought how his dear wife would have loved it all too.

131

At Buckthorn Farm, Edward opened the front door.

'Is Miss Charlotte at home?' Miles asked. 'I've come to return her hat and coat.'

'Yes, sir, but she's – er – indisposed this morning.'

A concerned frown furrowed Miles's forehead. 'She's ill?'

'Not – exactly, sir.'

The man said no more, but from his grim expression Miles deduced that she was perhaps suffering the ill effects of the incident the previous evening. Perhaps her problem was more emotional than physical harm.

'And Mr Crawford? Would he see me?'

Edward inclined his head in his best butler manner. 'If you'd care to step inside, sir, I will enquire.'

Edward took the package from his hands. A few moments later, Miles was being shown into the sitting room; not, as he had expected, into a study.

Osbert was sitting by the fire, a book in his lap. He rose as Miles entered and waved him towards a chair on the opposite side of the fireplace. 'I'm glad you've called, Mr Thornton. I planned to call upon you later today myself.'

Miles sat down whilst Osbert instructed Edward to bring coffee. When the door closed behind the man-servant, Osbert said, 'I must apologize for my daughter's disgraceful behaviour last evening. As for the vicar, I shall take steps to get him removed from his post. Dancing, indeed!'

'I saw no harm in Mr Iveson enjoying himself amongst his parishioners. Surely, it helps him get to know them and vice versa.'

Osbert glared at him. 'You think so. I'm afraid I cannot agree. A man of the cloth should keep himself aloof – be an example – not be cavorting like a village lad. And I shall have to have words with Joe about his son, Jackson, too, I can see.'

Miles stared at the bitter, twisted man and couldn't stop the question. 'Why?'

'Why?' Osbert barked. 'Do you really need to ask?'

'Yes, I do.'

'Making a fool of my daughter.'

Miles shook his head. 'He did no such thing. He danced with her, that's all.'

'Well, she made a fool of herself, then. I won't have it.'

There was no persuading the man that it had been harmless enjoyment.

'There's one good thing come out of it, though,' Osbert went on, his mouth a hard, bitter, unforgiving line. 'It's made me come to a decision. That's what I was coming to see you about.'

Miles waited.

'I have realized that I am getting on in years and I need to make a will if I am to safeguard the future of Buckthorn Farm. Since I have no son of my own to carry on the family farm, I intend to bequeath my farm and all my possessions to your eldest son, Philip. I've taken a liking to the young man and he will be a worthy landowner and employer, I've no doubt.'

Miles's jaw dropped open. 'But – but what about your daughter?' he spluttered. 'It's her inheritance.'

Osbert glared at him but offered no explanation. 'What I want to do with my farm – and the reasons for it – is my business,' he said tartly.

'But you hardly know us.'

Osbert shrugged. 'That's of no consequence. As I say, I've taken a liking to your boy. If it should come about that he proves unworthy of my confidence in him, then

I can always change my will.' He stared at Miles with cold, hard eyes that defied contradiction.

'But – but Philip made it clear that he has no interest in the land. He wants to become a lawyer and I intend to help him achieve it if that's his ambition.'

'You don't wish to hand your estate on to your eldest son?' Osbert was surprised and it showed.

'I – ' Miles hesitated. He'd been going to say that he had two other sons, both of whom might prefer to be gentleman farmers. But it seemed a cruel remark to make to the man who had no son and was so obviously disappointed. He altered what he'd been about to say. 'Ben seems more interested in the land than his brother.'

'Hmm.' Osbert frowned. 'He seems a sensible young fellow, I grant you. Quiet and well mannered, but as for your youngest boy, God knows what will become of him.'

The note of disparagement in Osbert's tone was not lost on Miles, but he smiled quietly to himself at the thought of Georgie. Then he brought his wandering thoughts back to the amazing – and to his mind ridiculous – suggestion.

As if sensing the other man's doubts, Osbert leaned forward to press home his point of view. 'Even if Philip doesn't want to manage the farm himself, I'm sure his brother would oversee it for him. Just think how the addition of Buckthorn Farm would enhance the Ravensfleet Estate. Between them, your sons would be the biggest landowners for miles.'

'But – your daughter . . . ?'

Osbert leaned back. 'Ah, now there is a proviso. As you can see for yourself, she is unlikely ever to attract a suitable marriage partner. She is plain, dull and useless. But I suppose I must make provision for her in some way.' His eyes narrowed. 'In return for me leaving my farm to a member of your family – most likely Philip – I would expect you to marry her.'

Miles stared at him. Was he in a dream? Or rather a nightmare? The man must be crazy to think up such a preposterous scheme. It was tantamount to being back to the days of arranged marriages amongst the landed gentry, when unions were sought for reasons of wealth, possessions or power. Well, he would have none of it. He stood up suddenly, the coffee cup he still held clattering in its saucer.

'I'm sorry. I cannot agree to such a suggestion. It is totally unacceptable to me, my family and, I'm sure, to Miss Charlotte, whom I presume you have not even consulted.' He gave a small bow. 'I wish you good-day, sir.'

As he turned away, Osbert said in a silky tone, 'I beg you not to be so hasty. You are throwing away a superb opportunity for your son.'

But Miles, incensed by the man's arrogance, marched towards the door, flung it open and left the house, passing a surprised Edward in the hallway without a word.

Eighteen

That evening, after work had finished for the day, Miles again rode over towards Buckthorn Farm. He would have enjoyed the gentle ride through the dusk of the balmy September evening, but his mind was still reeling. This time he did not go to the farmhouse, but stopped at the farm workers' cottages. The two semi-detached cottages each had a piece of ground at the back culti-vated as a vegetable garden and room at the far end for chickens and a pig.

Horse and rider came to a halt outside the Warrens' cottage. Through the lighted window Miles could see the five members of the family sitting down to their evening meal. Only Lily was missing. Whilst he had no wish to interrupt them, the matter he wished to discuss with Joe – and possibly with Peggy too – was gnawing at him. As he watched, he saw John, the eldest son, come to the window and peer out. Then the young man turned back towards those still sitting around the table, presumably to say something, for Joe got up. Moments later, he was opening the front door and coming down the short path. Miles sighed and dismounted.

'Mr Thornton?' Joe's tone was worried. 'Is owt wrong?'

'No, no, man. It's just – well, I'd like a private word with you and your wife, but I see you are eating. I didn't want to interrupt—'

'Think nowt of that. Come away in. We've almost finished and Peg will make us all a cup of tea. That is—' Joe hesitated as he realized he was speaking to this man as if he were an equal. Miles Thornton – and his family – were so friendly, it was easy to forget the differences between them. 'If – if you'd like one, sir?'

Miles smiled. 'That would be most welcome. Thank you.'

He tethered his horse to the fence and followed Joe up the path, to be greeted a little anxiously by Peg and her two sons.

John and Jackson exchanged a glance and raised their eyebrows. Jackson could contain the question no longer. 'Is it our Lily? Is summat wrong?'

Miles blinked and then said swiftly, 'Good heavens, no. Oh dear, I never thought my coming here might make you think that. No, no, Lily is fine.'

The tension in the room relaxed and Peggy bade her surprise visitor sit down in Joe's chair by the range whilst she made tea.

'Away to your bed, Tommy,' Joe said to the youngest boy.

'Aw, Dad,' he began to protest, but Jackson put his hand on his young brother's shoulder and, without another word being spoken, steered him towards the door leading to the staircase. As the door closed behind him and they heard his footsteps thumping up the stairs, they all exchanged a smile.

'Boys!' Peggy said and raised her eyes to the ceiling.

'Now, Ma,' Jackson teased. 'You'd not be without any one of us.'

When they had all been served with tea, the four remaining members of the family looked towards Mr Thornton expectantly. Under their scrutiny his resolve wavered. He glanced at John and Jackson, a little unsure whether he could trust them. But they were grown men, one thirty already and the other in his mid-twenties.

'I would be very grateful if you would keep this conversation confidential.' His gaze swept them all. Joe turned towards his boys and seemed to be about to ask them to leave, too, but Miles held up his hand. 'No, I'd like you all to hear what I've got to say – or rather to ask.' The family members glanced at each other but their gaze came back to the squire.

Miles took a deep breath and smiled a little sheepishly. 'This is difficult. If you don't wish to answer my questions, please say so. I shall quite understand.'

Joe frowned, growing more mystified by the minute. He felt like saying, 'Get on with it, man,' but of course he said nothing.

'Joe, just what is going on at Buckthorn Farm?'

Joe blinked. Whatever he'd thought the purpose of Miles's visit might be, it wasn't this. 'I – er – don't understand what you mean?'

'Mr Crawford's treatment of his daughter doesn't seem – well, normal.'

Now Joe understood and his face was grim. For a moment the man sitting opposite him believed he was about to get short shrift and asked – politely, no doubt – to leave. But to his surprise, the four all spoke at once.

'No, sir, it isn't—'

'You're right there—'

'That poor lass—'

'It's a bloody disgrace—'

This last remark from Jackson earned him a glare from his mother. The young man apologized at once. 'Beggin' your pardon, sir, but it is. She's a lovely girl

138

and she's been held down and used – yes, used – all her life. He treats her like a skivvy—'

'That'll do, Jackson,' Joe said quietly. For a long moment, he looked into Miles's face, wondering if he dare trust the man. He was still a stranger to them. If Joe spoke out of turn and it got back to Osbert Crawford, the whole family could find themselves in serious trouble. And not even Miss Charlotte would be able to save them.

He glanced at Peggy and, seeing her silent nod of agreement, he cleared his throat. 'I'd better explain it as I see it, sir, but it's only as I see it, mind.'

'We, Dad,' Jackson put in. 'As we all see it.' And his brother nodded agreement.

'Our family have lived in this cottage and worked on Buckthorn Farm for four generations now, if you count the boys.' He nodded towards his sons. 'It started with my grandfather who came to work for Mr Osbert's grandfather. I reckon it was *his* father who bought the farm. Now, grandfather came here in the late forties, because my father, Harry, was born here just after they arrived. His father died when he was about twenty, I think, and he stepped into his dad's position.' Here Joe paused and smiled. 'Didn't go down too well with some of the older workers, so he used to tell me. Him being made up to foreman at such a young age. But there you are; he was, and he made a damned good job of it.'

Miles nodded. 'If your expertise and knowledge come from him, then he certainly did.'

Joe's smile faded. 'Ah well, I'm coming to that in a bit, Mr Thornton. I'm sorry it's taking a while to tell you it all, but I want you to understand everything.'

'That's quite all right. I *want* to hear it all.'

'More tea?' Peggy asked, taking the chance of the pause in Joe's tale.

'Thank you,' Miles murmured, but his attention was still wholly on Joe. Whilst Peggy moved about quietly, pouring them all more tea, Joe went on.

'Mr Hubert Crawford – that's Mr Osbert's father – took over the farm when *his* father died in – let's see – ' Joe wrinkled his forehead.

'In 1870,' Peggy put in helpfully, 'because it was the same year as Mr Osbert was born. I remember your mam telling me, Joe.' She turned to Miles. 'Joe's mam loved relating family history. Not only her own family, but everybody else's as well. And I suppose it was natural she should take an interest in the Crawfords. Their two families had been – what's the word – entwined, is that it? – for so long.'

'That's right, love. And then Mr Hubert died fairly young really. Only forty-eight, he was. I remember that. I was about sixteen and Mr Osbert was only twenty and, of course, he had to take over the farm there and then. That was in 1890. Five years later he brought home a bride.'

'Alice Hall.' Peggy took up the tale briefly. 'But where she came from and how he met her and courted her, none of us ever knew and never have known.' She glanced at Joe and murmured, 'That's when it all began to get a bit mysterious. They were married the same year as us – '95. She had a baby boy same year as John was born and another the same year as our Jackson. But she miscarried them both at about seven months. I felt dreadful, I don't mind admitting, that there I was with two healthy strapping lads and that poor lass couldn't give her husband the sons he craved. And I mean *craved*.'

'She had another boy, didn't she, Ma, before Miss Charlotte came along?' Jackson said.

'No, that was after, but poor little mite was stillborn.'

'But they had a daughter by then?' Miles looked around the faces before him, seeing the family glance at each other, their expressions a mixture of sadness and anger.

Quietly, Joe took up the tale once more. 'And that was the tragedy of it. All Osbert Crawford wanted was a son to carry on the farm and the family name. That's all he's ever wanted and he treats that lass – well, I don't rightly know how to say he treats her, but it's not like a daughter. If it hadn't been for Mary and Edward Morgan looking out for her, I don't know what might have happened to the little lass, 'specially after her mam died. Charlotte was only five.'

'But she seems – well – all right. I mean, she doesn't have pretty clothes, I grant you, and those glasses—'

'She doesn't need no glasses,' Jackson burst out. 'They're made out of plain glass. He makes her wear 'em because – because it makes her look even more plain and – and unattractive.'

Miles stared at him, unable to believe that a man would do such a cruel thing. He remembered now how, when they'd met her riding on the beach, sharp-eyed little Georgie had said with the guileless candour of the young that she was prettier without her spectacles.

'And now we come to the crux of it all, sir,' Joe went on. 'And here I must ask you in return, most sincerely and respectfully, to keep what I am about to say to yourself, else my family could all find themselves thrown out of their jobs and home.'

'Of course,' Miles said quietly. 'You have my word.'

Joe met and held the other man's steady gaze and

then gave a small, satisfied nod. He believed he could trust him. 'As you've seen for yourself, sir, Miss Charlotte is kept downtrodden. It's as if he's punishing her for not being a boy. Thing is – ' Even now he hesitated in telling the secret he'd held for years. He glanced once more at Peggy for her reassurance, but then, taking a deep breath, said, 'The thing is, it's Miss Charlotte who runs Buckthorn Farm. You say I'm knowledgeable, well yes, I've learned a bit about running the farm from me dad, like you say, but I still go to her for a lot of help and advice about things. And it was her that chose them 'osses for you at the fair. We 'ad to be careful you didn't see.'

'I didn't, not really, and yet there was something about that day I didn't quite understand,' Miles murmured, amused and yet appalled at what he was hearing. 'Now I do.' If the girl was clever enough to run the large farm, knowledgeable about horseflesh, then why . . . ?

'The master does nothing, sir, not a thing now. He did in the early days, of course, but for the last – oh, almost ten years – he's done nowt. It's her sits in the office at the back of the house, her does all the books, pays the wages, buys everything we need. Together – her and me – we plan the crops, buy and sell beast, sheep and pigs at market. And yet he treats her as if she's worth nothing.'

'And she works out on the farm alongside us, an' not just at harvest,' John said. 'She's first up in a morning to do the milking and last to bed at night when she's shut up the chickens.'

'And I'll tell you summat else, an' all,' Jackson put in. 'She's a clever artist. I've seen her out with her sketchbook, drawing. Painting too, sometimes. But she has to keep it all hidden – secret.'

There was silence before Peggy spoke. Now it was she who was a little hesitant and she glanced towards Joe for support. 'There's another bit of a mystery, Mr Thornton, that we don't understand. You know that Joe's dad died in April – just after you came to live at the manor?'

Miles nodded.

'Well, he was very agitated just before he passed away. Had us send for the vicar and insisted on speaking to him alone.' A flicker of a smile crossed her face. 'God only knows what he said to the poor chap, 'cos the young feller came out white as a sheet and scuttled off.'

'Dad died without telling us owt,' Joe added. 'And we can't expect the vicar to break a confidence, now, can we?'

Miles shook his head.

'We did find out a bit, though, and that was what was odd, you see.' Jackson now took up the tale. 'Me grandad had bought a plot in the churchyard – a grave – next to Mrs Crawford.'

'Osbert's wife,' Peggy put in, 'died two days after Joe's mother back in '05.'

Miles frowned in puzzlement. 'I don't understand . . .'

'Me mother was buried in Lincoln,' Joe explained. 'Dad said at the time that she wanted to be buried with her own folk and that's where she'd come from.'

'Was that true? I mean – did her folks come from Lincoln?'

'Oh yes. We used to go there to see me grandad and grandma. And Mam had brothers and sisters there too, though we've lost touch now.'

'So what are you saying, exactly?'

'It just seemed odd that me dad didn't want to be

buried alongside her. They were a loving couple, none closer, but he bought a plot here in the churchyard at Ravensfleet.'

'Presumably you went to your mother's funeral in Lincoln, so you know—'

'No, sir, that's just it. None of the family went from here. Dad insisted he went alone. After Jack Layton, the undertaker in Ravensfleet, took her from here, we never saw her again.'

'And when was Mrs Crawford buried?'

'Two days after Mother.'

'It does sound a little odd, as you say. And maybe Reverend Iveson knows more, but like you say, we can't expect him to divulge whatever it was your father confided in him.'

Miles stared round at them, biting his lip. Slowly, he said, 'Thank you for your confidence in me. And now, it's only fair that I explain the reason for my visit.'

Nineteen

All four members of the Warren family sat waiting expectantly. But now it was Miles who sought their reassurance that they would not betray his trust. 'I went to Buckthorn Farm this morning, mainly to enquire after Miss Charlotte.' He glanced at Jackson. 'And to return her hat and coat. Edward said that she was indisposed, so I asked to see Mr Crawford.' Miles shook his head wonderingly, still unable to believe it had not all been a dream. 'He was obviously still very angry with Miss Charlotte for her "unseemly behaviour", as he called it. And then – ' he glanced round at them all – 'he came out with the most preposterous suggestion I've ever heard in my life. It seems' – he ran his tongue nervously round his lips – 'that he's taken a fancy to my sons, especially my eldest, Philip.' He paused a moment, overcome by the enormity of what he was about to tell them. 'Mr Crawford tells me that he plans to make a will leaving everything he possesses – land, buildings, livestock, everything – to Philip.'

There were shocked gasps from each and every member of the Warren family. They stared at him in disbelief.

'Can he do that?' Jackson blurted out.

Miles shrugged. 'I think a man may do anything he wants in his will.'

'Would she be able to contest it?' John asked thoughtfully.

'She could. But it would take money to do that and – as far as I see it – he intends to leave her penniless. I know,' he said simply, as if reading their minds, 'it's outrageous, isn't it? But that's not all. In return for my son being left such an inheritance, I have to marry Miss Charlotte.'

Now their mouths dropped open.

'That's – that's blackmail,' Jackson burst out. Then he blinked and glanced around him, seeking confirmation. 'Isn't it?'

Miles sighed. 'I agree with you. It *is* a sort of blackmail.'

'But – but – ' Even Joe was spluttering with indignation. 'I mean – do you *want* to marry Miss Charlotte? Does she want to marry you?'

Miles's face was suddenly grey with sadness. 'I – I'd never looked to marry again. I lost my beloved wife, Louisa, when Georgie was born. I adored her and I still miss her every day.' He bit his lower lip. 'I'd never even thought about it.'

'Then you don't love Miss Charlotte,' Jackson burst out. 'It'd be a marriage of – of – what is it they call it, Mam?'

'A marriage of convenience,' Peggy said quietly, her gaze on the squire. Surely, he wouldn't think of doing such a thing, just to gain land and property for his son? He would plummet in her estimation if he were seriously to contemplate it.

'Jackson,' Joe said warningly and the young man apologized swiftly.

'Begging your pardon, sir. I meant no disrespect. But I'm fond of Miss Charlotte. We're friends. I'd not like to see her forced to marry someone who doesn't love her.'

146

'Your defence of her does you credit, young man. And no offence taken, I assure you. And I have no intention of agreeing to his absurd suggestion.'

Peggy breathed a sigh of relief. She'd not been wrong in her estimation of the new squire. He was, as she'd thought, a man of honour.

'According to her father,' Miles murmured, musing aloud, 'she's never had any suitors and,' his tone hardened, 'in his opinion, is never likely to have.'

Jackson sprang to his feet. 'That's a cruel thing to say.'

'His words, not mine, I assure you.'

'Sit down, son,' Joe said softly and Jackson sank back into his seat.

'Her father has never allowed her to have a young man,' Peggy put in quietly. 'She's never had the chance to meet anyone other than the young fellows who work on the farm.' She nodded towards her own son. 'Like Jackson says, Mr Thornton, him and Miss Charlotte are friends – have been since they were little – but if the old man got wind of it, he'd sack Jackson on the spot and likely throw us out an' all.'

'We don't want him to hear about it,' Jackson said shortly and glared at Miles almost warningly.

Miles grimaced. 'He's none too pleased about you dancing with her last night,' he warned. 'He'll be having a word with your father, he said.'

Jackson groaned and muttered, 'Oh, heck! I didn't mean to get her into more trouble. I was just so pleased to see her there.'

'So,' Miles said slowly, his gaze still on the hotheaded young man, 'would you *like* to court Miss Charlotte? Are you fond enough of her to want to propose to her?'

147

Jackson stared at him. The thought had quite obviously never crossed his mind. 'Um – er – well, I am fond of her,' he stuttered, forced suddenly to examine his feelings for Charlotte. 'Very fond, but I don't think I'd call it the sort of love you should feel for the girl you want to marry.' Now he shook his head in a swift decision. 'No – no, I don't think of her like that.'

'So – is there anyone else who's shown an interest in her?'

The Warrens glanced at each other.

'What about the vicar?' John suggested. 'He was dancing with her last night.'

Miles laughed wryly. 'Her father noticed that, too. I think that's what incensed him. He's threatening to have him removed from his living here. But, as it happens –' he smiled at them – 'I know the bishop. I can put in a good word for him if necessary.'

There was silence for a moment. Joe shook his head in disbelief. 'I've never heard the like. Really I haven't.'

'Of course,' Miles said, thinking aloud, 'years ago marriages were arranged amongst the gentry to unite families for money, possessions or power. And widowers often married again to give their children a mother.' He sighed. 'Just between ourselves, I get lonely. I thought it might be better when we moved here, away from the house that held all the poignant memories. But it isn't. It's worse, if anything.'

'But you have your boys,' Peggy said softly. 'You seem to have a wonderful relationship with them.'

'Oh I do, I do. But it's not the same, is it? They'll grow up and lead their own lives. I hope we'll always be close, but it's not like having a – a wife.'

Peggy and Joe glanced at each other. They understood – even if their sons didn't at this moment. They couldn't imagine what it would be like for either them if something happened and one of them was left alone. They couldn't even bear to think about it.

Miles said no more. Though he felt that Joe and Peggy perhaps understood, he could see from their faces that the two young men thought it incredible that anyone should marry other than for love. He smiled sadly to himself, thinking of all the arranged marriages that had taken place through all the different cultures – and were still taking place in some parts of the world. Even here in Britain, particularly amongst the aristocracy, he was sure that parents still decreed that their offspring should marry 'suitably'.

'I mustn't keep you good folk any longer. Thank you for your time.'

They all rose and Joe held out his hand. 'And thank you for your trust in us, Mr Thornton. That means a lot.'

Miles took his hand and shook it warmly. 'If there's anything I can ever do, you'll let me know, now, won't you?'

'Thank you, sir.'

'And now I must go home and break the news to my eldest son that I have just refused a handsome inheritance.'

'You're going to tell him about it?' Joe was surprised.

Miles nodded. 'I try to instil honesty and trust in all my boys and therefore I always try to be open and truthful with them. I know Philip's still only young, but when his mother died, being the eldest, he had to grow up quickly.' He sighed and murmured, more to himself, 'Maybe too quickly.'

*

'You mean you said "no"?' Philip spluttered. 'You'd no right to do that. It's me he wants to have his farm. What right have you got to deny me an inheritance?'

He'd listened to his father's explanation with growing excitement, but Miles's final words had shattered his hopes. Philip faced him angrily across the broad surface of the leather-topped desk. Outside the door of their father's study, Ben and Georgie crept closer to listen. Seeing them, Wilkins smiled and tiptoed away, wishing he could eavesdrop too.

'I've every right,' Miles said mildly, not rising to anger like his son. 'For several reasons.'

'Name them,' Philip snapped.

'One,' Miles ticked them off on his fingers, 'the farm should go to Charlotte, his daughter.'

'But he doesn't want her to have it. You've just said so yourself.'

Ignoring him, Miles went on. 'Two, part of this – this bargain is that I should marry Charlotte. Do you want me to do that?'

Philip glared at him, hesitating. His glance strayed to the portrait of his mother, which had hung over the fireplace in his father's study in whatever house they'd lived in for as long as he could remember. He stared at the lovely face. The portrait had been painted at the time of her engagement to his father. She'd been eighteen then, young and lovely, and her sweet smile, captured for ever on the canvas, was like no other he'd ever seen. And it wasn't just the portrait that reminded him of his mother, for Philip, being the eldest, could remember her well. He could remember her voice, her laughter and, if he closed his eyes, he could almost feel her love for him reaching out even from beyond the grave.

Seeing the torment on his son's face, Miles said softly. 'Do you really want me to marry Charlotte Crawford?'

The fight and the anger drained out of the young man and he sought the armchair behind him and sank down into it. 'No,' he said huskily. 'No, I don't.' He saw his dream of becoming a landowner fading into the distance.

There was silence and Miles heard a scuffle outside the door. He raised his voice and called, 'Come in, you two scallywags. I know you're there.'

Sheepishly, the two boys entered the room.

Georgie, the bolder of the two, approached his father's desk. '*I* wouldn't mind if you married Miss Charlotte, Papa. I think she's lovely.'

Miles noticed Philip's lip curl disdainfully. 'That's only because you don't remember our mother. But then, you wouldn't, would you? Seeing as she died having you.'

'Philip!' his father roared, for once roused to swift anger. 'That's enough.'

He glanced at his little son and saw Georgie's mouth quivering. 'Come here,' he said gently. The boy moved round the desk and clambered on to his father's knee. Miles stroked the boy's fair curls. 'You should all know, but especially you, Georgie, that each of you was a much-wanted child. You all were. And yes, your mother did die just after giving birth to you, Georgie, but she was willing to sacrifice her own life to bring you – to bring *any* of you – into the world.' He glanced at her portrait. 'See, she's smiling down at us. She's watching over us. All of us.'

'But,' Georgie's eyes were still brimming with tears, 'you wanted a girl, didn't you? Not another boy?'

151

Miles smiled sadly. 'I'll not lie to you, Georgie. I hope I'll never have cause to lie to my sons. It would've been nice to have had a daughter, yes. I think all men dream of the day they'll walk their daughter down the aisle. But no, you're very precious to us all, Georgie, and I wouldn't change a hair of your head.'

Now the little boy beamed as he said, 'But you could walk me down the aisle, Papa, because when I'm grown up, I'm going to marry Miss Charlotte.'

There was a moment's stillness before they all burst out laughing.

The following morning neither Osbert nor Charlotte was at church. Nor were Edward and Mary.

Cuthbert Iveson, his pale faced blotched with patches of pink, conducted a nervous service and then dismissed the children.

'Papa, Papa!' Georgie cried, running after the rest of the family as the Thorntons climbed into their car. 'Miss Charlotte's not here to take the Sunday school. Mr Iveson says we're all to go home.'

He scrambled into the front seat beside his father. 'Papa, could we drive to Buckthorn Farm and see if she's all right?'

'I don't think that would be a very good idea, Georgie. Not today.'

The boy's face fell. 'Oh.'

Miles smiled gently at him. He was proud that Georgie cared so much about others. It was a trait that seemed to be sadly lacking in his eldest son. As for Ben, the boy was so quiet and reserved that Miles hardly knew what he was thinking most of the time.

'I'll have a word with the vicar,' Miles murmured,

climbing out of the vehicle again. 'Perhaps he'll know something.'

'Oh, for heaven's sake!' he heard Philip mutter impatiently, but chose to ignore the remark. As the last member of the congregation shook Cuthbert's hand and left, Miles approached him.

'Mr Iveson – a word, if you please.'

The vicar, about to turn away to go back into the church, hesitated. 'Mr Thornton . . .' He ran his tongue nervously around his lips.

'Have you heard anything from Buckthorn Farm? I'm concerned for Miss Charlotte.'

For a moment, Cuthbert stared at him before saying hesitantly, 'Would you step into the church a moment? There is something I would like to tell you.'

Together they stepped into the dim interior once more. Sitting down in one of the pews, they faced each other.

'I had a hand-delivered note from Mr Crawford this morning,' Cuthbert began, his already high colour deepening yet further, 'informing me that he intends to write to the bishop about my disreputable behaviour at the Harvest Supper and asking – no, demanding – my dismissal from this living.'

'Then I will also write to the bishop and tell him that your behaviour was perfectly correct. You were merely joining in the harvest celebrations. And even dancing with Miss Charlotte – ' Miles spread his hands. 'Well, that's perfectly in order. I mean, you're not married, engaged or anything, are you?'

Cuthbert shook his head. 'No – no. There's no one.'

There was a slight pause before Miles asked, 'But are you – shall we say – interested in Miss Charlotte?'

Cuthbert sighed. 'In a way. It's best if a young vicar

153

is married, you see. And I thought she might make a suitable wife for me.'

Poor Charlotte, Miles thought with compassion. No declaration of love or even affection. Just that she would make a 'suitable' wife for him. How cold and calculating. The man was almost as bad as the girl's father. Miles bit back a retort and, instead, asked, 'And was there any indication in his letter as to how Miss Charlotte is?'

Cuthbert shook his head. 'No, none. I suppose we'll just have to wait and see what happens,' he murmured, but Miles had the distinct feeling that the young man was more concerned for his own future than for Charlotte's. He almost regretted his promise to write to the bishop on his behalf, but his innate sense of fair play came to the fore once again. The vicar had done nothing wrong and it was only right that the bishop should hear the truth.

Miles rose. 'I'll visit Buckthorn Farm again. See what I can find out.'

Cuthbert rose too. 'He's a manipulative and dangerous man,' he burst out suddenly. 'He seems to think he can run the lives of all those around him. Certainly, the lives of the people who work for him.'

Miles stared at him. 'What d'you mean?'

Cuthbert turned away. 'I'm sorry,' he muttered. 'I've said too much already.'

Miles watched him as he hurried up the aisle towards the altar steps where he knelt and bowed his head in prayer.

Twenty

In the afternoon, Philip was missing.

'I think he's gone to Buckthorn Farm, Papa. I saw him riding in that direction.'

'Has he indeed?' Miles said grimly. He suspected his son had gone to plead with his benefactor to lift the condition attached to his inheritance. Miles had to admit, with sadness in his heart, that his eldest son was utterly selfish. Ruthless, even. After a moment's hesitation, he left the room. Minutes later, Georgie, watching from the window, saw his father galloping in the same direction.

'Oh, Georgie,' Ben murmured, 'now what have you done?'

Miles was shown into the sitting room at the farm to find his son and Osbert sitting opposite each other on either side of the fireplace. They both turned to look at him as he strode towards them. 'This nonsense has to stop. I shall not allow you to make Philip your heir.'

Philip sprang to his feet, 'Father . . .' he began, but Miles held up his hand to silence him, his gaze on the older man.

Osbert merely smiled. 'I don't think there's anything you can do to stop me, Thornton. A man can will his possessions where he wishes. That is the law and, hopefully, by the time I meet my Maker, the boy will be of age and you will no longer have any say in the matter.'

'But your daughter – ' Miles began.

Osbert's eyes narrowed. 'If you're so concerned about the girl, then do as I suggest.'

Miles let out a breath and shook his head. 'I don't believe you,' he muttered. 'I really don't. What sort of a father are you?' When Osbert did not answer, Miles asked huskily, 'Where is she? Where is Charlotte?'

Osbert raised his eyebrows. 'Coming round to it, are we?'

'Most certainly not,' Miles snapped. 'I just want to see for myself that she's all right.'

'She's all right,' Osbert said dismissively. 'Locked herself in her bedroom, that's all.'

Miles stared at him as he asked icily, 'And why would she need to do that?'

'Who knows what foolish girls will do or why they do it?' He glared at Miles as he added bitterly, 'But then you wouldn't know that, would you, being blessed with *sons*?'

Miles grunted and marched from the room, across the hall and through the door leading to the kitchen. As he entered the room, Mary threw up her hands in surprise, flour from the bowl in which she was mixing pastry scattering everywhere. 'Oh, Mr Thornton!'

With wide eyes, Peggy turned from the sink where she was peeling apples, but Edward, carrying logs in through the back door, merely nodded and greeted him as if it was the most natural thing in the world to see him there. 'Good afternoon, sir.'

Miles took a deep breath, wondering if he'd over-stepped the line of propriety. But for once, he didn't care. He was encouraged when Peggy dried her hands and indicated a Windsor chair set near the range. 'Please – sit down, sir. I'll make a cup of tea.'

'It would be very welcome, Mrs Warren, but please don't go to any trouble.'

'No trouble, sir.' She smiled. 'Edward and Mary never say no to a cuppa.'

As he sat down he said, 'I just wanted to know how Miss Charlotte is. I can't seem to get any kind of answer from her father.'

The other three in the room glanced at each other uncomfortably. Mary spoke up. 'To tell you the truth, sir, we don't rightly know ourselves and we're worried about her.'

Shocked, Miles glanced from one to the other. 'You – you don't know?'

Edward dropped the logs into the hearth. 'When she got home from the harvest supper on Friday night, she ran upstairs and locked herself in her bedroom. We haven't seen her since.'

'We've left trays outside her room,' Mary said. 'But she's touched nothing.'

'Only a jug of water I took up – and a glass. She's taken that in,' Peggy put in. 'But she's eaten nothing.'

'But you've spoken to her?'

'We've tried, sir, but she won't answer.'

'But – but she might be ill. Have you a key for the door?'

Edward shook his head. 'We've knocked and called, but there's no answer. We've all tried.'

'Her father too?'

Mary snorted. 'Not him! No. He wouldn't care if she were alive or dead. An' he's up to summat. I know he is.'

'Mary,' Edward said softly, warningly. Miles and

157

Peggy exchanged a glance and he knew she'd done as he'd asked. She'd kept the conversation he'd shared with her family to herself. But perhaps it was time that these good people – the Morgans – who obviously had Charlotte's welfare at heart, knew, too, just how devious their master was.

Mary covered her face with her apron and sobbed. 'I'm out of me mind wi' worry, sir. We don't know what to do.'

Peggy handed a cup of tea to Miles and turned to Mary. Gently she pushed her into a chair at the table and placed a cup of tea in front of her. 'Here, Mary love, drink this. It'll be all right now Mr Thornton's here. He'll help us. He'll tell us what to do.'

There was a long silence in the kitchen whilst they all drank their tea.

'We must do something,' Miles said. 'She might be ill.'

'That's what I'm afraid of, sir,' Mary said, recovering a little. 'She walked all the way home from the manor on Friday night with no coat or hat. I'm so afraid she might have taken a chill.'

Miles stood up and set his empty cup down on the table. He glanced round at the three anxious faces. 'I'm willing to do whatever it takes, but you do realize, don't you, that this could cause trouble for you? All of you. Because if I get involved, he'll know it's come from you.'

Edward nodded. 'We know that, sir, and we're not bothered for ourselves. Just Miss Charlotte. Though mebbe Peggy should go home. Keep out of it. She's her family to think of.'

But Peggy shook her head adamantly. 'No, Joe would back me up. And so would the boys. If he turns us all out, then so be it. We've that poor lass to think of.'

Miles nodded grimly. 'Very well. First of all, Mrs Morgan, you go upstairs and have one last try to get her to open the door. If only she would, it would make things a lot easier.'

Mary got up eagerly. 'You come an' all, Peggy.'

'Shall we tell her you're here, sir, and want to see her?'

'Of course, if you think it'll help.'

The two women disappeared and the two men were left to wait anxiously in the kitchen. Several minutes passed before Mary and Peggy returned, shaking their heads.

'No sound, sir. We can't hear a thing.'

Miles smacked his fist into the palm of his other hand. 'Then we must take drastic action.' He looked at Edward again. 'You really haven't got a key?'

'As far as I know, there's only the one and she's got that.'

Miles turned on his heel. 'I'll ask her father.'

'Sir, I wouldn't . . .' Edward began, but Miles had already gone and was striding through the house back to the sitting room. Edward gave a helpless shrug and followed him.

Without even knocking, Miles marched into the room. Osbert and Philip were still seated as he had left them, leaning towards each other, deep in conversation. They both looked up in surprise as the door was flung open and Miles entered like a whirlwind.

'It seems, Mr Crawford, that Charlotte might be ill. She's locked herself in her room and won't answer. Have you another key?'

'Let her be.' The man waved his hand. 'She'll come out when she's hungry.'

'It's been two days. If she was all right, she'd surely have come out by now.' He glared at the man who was

159

lying back in his chair. Anger boiled up inside him. 'Have you a key, sir?' he shouted.

Slowly, Osbert turned his head. 'No, I have not. And even if I had, I wouldn't give it to you.'

'Then you have two choices,' Miles burst out. 'Either I break the door down or I call the police.'

'Father—' Philip was on his feet.

'Be quiet, boy! You're partly the cause of all this. If you were man enough, you'd refuse his ridiculous suggestion, but no, you're too selfish and greedy.' There, it was said, and whilst he was sorry, it had needed saying, he didn't regret it for it was the truth.

White-faced with shock, Philip sank back into his chair. He couldn't remember his father ever speaking to him so harshly.

Miles's attention turned back to Osbert Crawford. 'Very well. You leave me no alternative.' He turned and left the room once more, taking the stairs two at a time. Mary, Peggy and even Edward were waiting for him at the top.

'This is her door, sir,' Mary said, gesturing to her right.

He knocked gently on the door and called out. 'Miss Charlotte. It's Miles Thornton. We are all anxious about you. If you can, please open the door.'

There was silence, not even the sound of movement from within the room.

Miles turned the doorknob, though he knew it was futile. 'Charlotte,' he called now with more firmness in his tone. 'If you don't open the door, I shall break it down. Can you hear me?'

Still, there was no response.

Mary moved close to the door and cried, 'Please,

160

Miss Charlotte, open the door. Mr Thornton means what he says.'

Silence.

Miles turned and nodded towards Edward. 'Right, let's give it a go.'

Edward looked at the door doubtfully. 'I don't reckon we can brek it open wi' just our shoulders, sir. 'Tis a solid door and the lock's sturdy.'

'We'll try. If we can't we'll have to fetch something to use as a battering ram. Right,' Miles said, putting his shoulder to the door. 'Are you ready?'

But as Edward stood beside him, they all heard the key turn in the lock. They glanced at each other in surprise and relief. Miles stood aside and motioned for Mary to go in first. 'See if she's all right first, before we all troop in,' Miles said, though in his growing anxiety for the girl, he would readily have charged in first.

Entering, Mary stood a moment, glancing round the room. Miles saw her eyes widen and her mouth fall open. 'What is it?' he demanded urgently. 'What's the matter?' Unable to contain his impatience any longer, Miles pushed the door wider and stepped into the room. With like urgency, Edward and Peggy were close behind him.

Charlotte was sitting in the far corner at a small table, a paintbrush in her hand, her head bowed in concentration.

'Miss Charlotte,' Mary said tentatively, 'why didn't you open the door? It's been two whole days. We've been that worried . . .' Now a note of reproach crept into the woman's tone. The girl seemed in perfect health, calmly pursuing her hobby as if nothing was wrong. And yet . . .

Miles touched Mary's arm. 'Gently, Mrs Morgan. There must be something . . .'

'Charlotte?' Mary tried again, but it was Peggy who pushed the others aside and crossed the room towards Charlotte.

'Now, miss,' she began gently, but with a note of firmness, 'you've had us all worried and here's Mr Thornton – oh!' Her words ended on a startled cry and her hand flew to cover her mouth. She glanced back at the others still standing near the door. Then she turned back to the young woman, knelt down beside her and put her arms round her waist.

'Oh, Miss Charlotte. Whatever happened?'

Now Mary rushed forward and she, too, stood staring down at Charlotte, her hand to her mouth. Miles and Edward glanced at each other before also moving towards her.

With a sigh, Charlotte laid down her brush and turned to face them all. Down the left-hand side of her face was an ugly weal and her eye was swollen until it was all but closed, the bruise blackening the tender area around her eye.

'My God!' Miles muttered. 'When did that happen? And how?' He already guessed the answer, but he had to be sure. He'd heard Georgie saying that Mr Crawford had hit Charlotte. He'd thought his son must have been mistaken, but now the evidence was before him.

Charlotte bowed her head. 'I – I'm sorry to have worried you all, but I didn't want anyone to see. I – I'm so ashamed.'

Peggy, still kneeling beside her and looking up into her face, said, 'Ashamed? Why should you be ashamed?'

'I – I made a fool of myself at the Harvest Supper. I—'

162

Four voices spoke at once, refuting her.

'Nonsense!' Miles Thornton's voice rose above the rest and then asked the question, the answer to which they had all guessed already. 'Did he do that to you? Your father? Did it happen as you were leaving the other night?'

Miserably, Charlotte nodded. Silently, Miles made a vow never to disregard anything Georgie said again.

'Mary, pack her clothes. I'm taking her back to the manor with me. I'll have the doctor look at her and then—'

Charlotte looked up in fear. 'No – no, I can't do that. I can't leave here. Who would—?' She stopped whatever she had been going to say and bit her lip, lowering her head again. 'It's very kind of you, but I can't leave. It's not possible.'

Anger surged through Miles. The girl's loyalty to her father and to Buckthorn Farm was admirable – but sadly misplaced. He was sure that she was totally unaware of her father's schemes. She could have no idea that he intended to leave her penniless when he died. He ran his fingers through his hair. So many underhand goings-on. And for the moment, he didn't know how to handle it. He needed time to think. And he needed to tell Philip just what sort of a man his benefactor was.

Twenty-One

Miles returned home deep in thought. He tried to tell himself it was none of his business. He was a newcomer to the district; he had no right to interfere. Yet his conscience would not let the matter rest. He could not stand by and let that poor girl be cheated out of her rightful inheritance, nor see his selfish son benefit from such an absurd and vengeful action by a man who was obviously unbalanced. Osbert Crawford's desire for a son was out of all proportion. It had been an obsession and his only issue – a daughter – was being made to pay the price for something that was not her fault.

Miles called his three sons into his study. They stood before him as he gazed at each one. Philip, the eldest, tall and slim, golden haired and handsome. But his angelic looks hid a selfish, ambitious streak. Ben – the quiet one. Dark haired with brown eyes – solemn and deep-thinking. He was perhaps the cleverest of the three, and it was to him that Miles would turn to run his affairs when he was no longer capable. He knew that already, even though the boy was still so young. There was something dependable about Ben.

And then there was Georgie. The adorable scamp. Still so young, but already showing the ebullient character he would always be. He would always – always, Miles knew – put others before himself. Everyone loved

Georgie – even Philip, albeit grudgingly, in spite of himself. And throughout his life, Georgie would always be loved. Miles cherished all three of his boys – he'd give his life for them, just as his beloved Louisa had given hers to bring their youngest child into the world. But there was still a tiny corner in his heart – a special place – that had always been reserved for a daughter. A little girl whom he could dote on and spoil. But it had always remained just that: a wish which had not been fulfilled, but which would never, ever, become an obsession that would overshadow and eat away his love for his sons.

Miles sighed. 'Sit down, boys. This may take a little time.' He paused whilst they settled themselves. Georgie wriggled to get himself comfortable, his legs swinging. He had a wide grin on his face; he felt important at being included in a family discussion. But Ben looked apprehensive and Philip mutinous.

Miles leaned back in his chair and linked his fingers together. 'I've seen Miss Charlotte.'

'Is she all right, Papa?' Georgie couldn't help interrupting.

'Yes – and no.' He paused, wondering how best to explain. 'She'd locked herself in her room since Friday night because she's got a nasty bruise on the left side of her face. She was ashamed to let anyone see it.'

'Why? I mean, why was she ashamed?' Georgie asked innocently.

'Because of how she got it, stupid,' Philip muttered.

Unperturbed by his brother's insult, Georgie was still anxious about Charlotte.

Ben said nothing, but he regarded his father steadily. He was taking in and digesting every word.

'I know he hit her on Friday night. I saw it,' Georgie

said, tears starting in his eyes at the memory. 'What I don't understand is – why?'

Georgie, who'd never been hit by his father in his life, not even spanked, had been horrified. He'd had bad dreams about it each night since.

'It seems he thinks she misbehaved at the Harvest Supper.'

Misbehaved? The little boy frowned. That was a word that was applied to him if he was naughty, not to a grown-up like Miss Charlotte.

'He didn't like to see her dancing with the vicar,' Miles tried to explain. 'In fact, he didn't even want her to come to the festivities. He's never allowed her to attend in the past.' Now he must admit his own part in the incident. 'I'm afraid it was I who persuaded him to let her come.' He glanced uncomfortably at Philip. 'You were the bait.'

'The bait?'

Miles sighed. 'Mr Crawford wanted all three of you to be present, but especially you, Philip. I sort of implied that you would be there as long as he allowed Miss Charlotte to come too.'

'Why's he never let her go before?' Georgie asked.

'Because he's ashamed of her,' Philip said scathingly. 'She's drab and plain and never likely to find a husband. I expect he thinks everyone will ridicule her, snigger about her behind her back.'

'But they *don't* laugh at her, do they?' Ben put in quietly. His father and brothers all turned to look at him. Such was the rarity of Ben putting forward his opinion that, when he did, everyone listened. 'At church all the villagers greet her and talk to her. They're fond of her. You can see they are. And the children – her Sunday school class – they all love her.' It was a long speech for Ben and by the time he'd finished, he lowered his head, his face red.

'That's right,' Georgie said excitedly. 'He's right, Papa. They do. Everyone was disappointed when she wasn't there this morning.'

'So,' Miles said slowly, 'what d'you think we should do to help her?'

'You could always marry her,' Philip said sarcastically. 'As the old man suggested.'

Miles glared at him, a jolt of anger running through him suddenly. 'I thought you said you didn't want that. Not even if it robs you of your inheritance?'

Philip smiled smugly. 'He's dropped that condition. He's promised to leave me his entire estate anyway. He told me so this morning. And yes, since you're all so concerned, he is ashamed of his daughter. She's neither use nor ornament. That's what he said.'

Miles sat forward in his chair. 'I think you'll find—' He stopped and bit back the words that, in his fury, he'd been about to unleash; the truth about Charlotte that he'd been told in confidence by the Warrens. It was a trust that he could not betray, however much he wanted to wipe the self-satisfied look off his son's face.

'What?' Philip snapped.

Miles sighed, his anger dying to be replaced by a great sadness. He'd hoped never to see such greed and self-interest in any of his sons. For the first time in six years he was glad that his dear wife was not here to witness the man their eldest son was becoming. She would have been heartbroken. He leaned back in his chair and merely made a gesture with his hand, dismissing what he'd been about to say as if it was of no consequence.

'Miss Charlotte could always come here, Papa,' Georgie suggested. 'You wouldn't need to marry her. She could live with us as a friend. And she could play with me.'

Once more, it was Georgie who brought laughter back into the room.

The following morning, Miles went again to Buckthorn Farm. This time, he entered by the back door and was greeted by Edward, Mary and Peggy like an old friend.

'So,' he asked, 'how is she this morning?'

'Better, sir, thank you. She's had some breakfast and – ' Mary glanced at Edward – 'she's going about her daily routine as normal.' Miles hid his smile as he interpreted her words as meaning Charlotte was at her desk in the farm office. But he gave no indication that he knew and Peggy turned away lest her face should betray her.

'We don't know how to thank you, sir, for helping us yesterday,' Mary went on. 'If you hadn't come, goodness knows how long she might have stayed locked in her room.'

'Would she see me, d'you think?'

'Best not try today, sir, if you don't mind. She's still embarrassed about it all.'

'Mm. Very well, then, but will you tell her from me that if she needs any help – any help at all – she's only to ask?'

'I will indeed, sir.' Mary smiled. 'And thank you once again.'

There was nothing more he could do and Miles drove home feeling disconsolate that he'd not been able give Charlotte some practical help. He was the sort of man who, faced with a problem, was happiest if he could take some positive action to solve it. If he couldn't, the matter lay heavily on his mind. And the thought of Charlotte was beginning to fill his waking thoughts and trouble his restless nights.

Twenty-Two

The matter of the vicar's dismissal was more easily remedied. As he'd promised, Miles wrote to the bishop and received a friendly letter in return:

Every incumbent of the parish of Ravensfleet
seems to displease Mr Crawford eventually. He had
a previous one removed, I believe, in the days of
my predecessor. Despite his complaints I shall
not be taking any further action in the case of
Mr Iveson – as indeed I have not on two previous
occasions!

Miles folded the letter away and put it in his drawer. Later he would ride over and give the good news to the young man.

Perhaps, after all, Charlotte could do worse than become a vicar's wife.

Charlotte attended church the following week and took up her Sunday school duties once more. During the week no one, except the household staff and Joe, had seen her. The bruise had faded and was scarcely noticeable and it was to the credit of those closest to her that no one else knew the cause of her absence.

The Thornton boys – as they were becoming known throughout the neighbourhood – had been sworn to

170

silence by their father. Even little Georgie had said nothing to his playmates. So, on the morning of her return, the villagers were fulsome in their concern for her.

'Have you been ill, Miss Charlotte?'

'We've missed you – and so have the children.'

If they'd looked closely beneath the brim of her close-fitting cloche hat, they might have seen the telltale yellowing mark. But no one did. The hat – borrowed from Peggy – was the closest Charlotte had ever come to wearing something remotely fashionable. But the plain, single plait down her back looked absurd beneath it, though the villagers made no remark upon it. Only the local dressmaker with her eye for fashion noted it and felt a rush of pity for the girl.

Charlotte smiled and thanked them all for their concern and assured them she was quite well, thank you. As she sat in the pew behind her father with Mary and Edward beside her, she kept her head bowed, her gaze fixed on the floor, and never once did she meet the vicar's gaze. He, too, it seemed, was at pains to avoid her. After the service, having said his goodbyes to his parishioners in the porch, Cuthbert scurried back to the vestry and then to the vicarage.

He did not, for the first time ever, visit the Sunday school to inspect its progress and take part.

On his return home Georgie couldn't wait to tell Miles.

'Did you see, Papa, that Mr Crawford walked straight past the vicar after the service? He didn't even shake his hand. And *then*,' he added dramatically, 'he – Mr Iveson, I mean – didn't come into the Sunday school class at *all*. And he *always* does.'

Miles laid a hand on the boy's shoulder. 'Now, you

mustn't speak of it to anyone else, Georgie, there's a good boy.'

The boy shook his head. 'I won't, Papa. I wouldn't do anything to hurt Miss Charlotte. Not for the world.'

Miles smiled to himself. Well, he thought, Charlotte has one champion, even if he is only six years old.

'D'you know, Miss Charlotte,' Georgie told her solemnly after Sunday school the following week, 'Tommy, Sam and Mikey can't play with me this week.'

'Oh dear! Why not?' she asked, suddenly afraid that there'd been yet another falling out.

'Because they're going 'tatie picking.' Charlotte hid her smile as the boy added, 'D'you think Papa would let me go, too?'

'I don't know, darling,' she replied as seriously as she could. 'You'll have to ask him.'

The following day, Charlotte was amused to see the four boys, wearing warm coats, with a piece of string tied round their waists, Wellingtons and flat caps that were several sizes too big, solemnly marching into the fields at Buckthorn Farm, armed with baskets and buckets.

'Where d'you want us to start, Miss Charlotte?' Tommy, taking the lead, asked.

'You can all work a row each near me.' She smiled.

By midday, Georgie was white-faced with tiredness and wincing with backache. As Mary and Edward appeared at the gate into the field carrying baskets of food and drink for the workers, Charlotte called a halt to the work. She turned to the boys. 'That's enough work for you boys today. Thank you for coming. Now, go back with Mary and Edward and they'll find you some scones and lemonade.'

'Oh but, Miss Charlotte . . .'

Forestalling the argument, she said firmly, 'See you in the morning. Eight o'clock sharp, mind.'

She watched them cross the field, trailing wearily after each other, and marvelled at how the youngsters had stuck doggedly to the backbreaking task, not wanting to be the first to give in. But she'd seen the relief on all their little faces when she'd called a halt.

'Can I go an' all, miss?' Jackson mimicked a child's high-pitched tone. 'I like lemonade and scones.'

'You most certainly cannot, Jackson Warren.' She laughed and bent again to her own labours.

As the last load of potatoes trundled its way from Buckthorn Farm to the railway station in Ravensfleet, Joe said, 'That were a good 'tatie harvest this year, miss. For us, any road.'

'Mm. We've been lucky. And now we'll have to start planning what we're going to plant for next year.'

'I was talking to some of the farmers in the Mucky Duck last night . . .'

'The Mucky Duck' was the local nickname for the White Swan pub in Ravensfleet.

'. . . And some of 'em are thinking of growing sugar beet. There's a new sugar beet factory planned for Bardney. All being well, construction'll start next spring and they reckon it'll be operatin' by October for next year's crop. Now if we—' Joe broke off as he saw the smile spreading across Charlotte's face. 'What, miss?'

'Funnily enough, I've been reading up about sugar

beet. It seems it's a very good crop to rotate with wheat, barley, potatoes – all the things we grow. It helps the soil, so' – she linked her fingers together – 'how about we grow a few acres for next year? And even if the Bardney factory isn't ready, there's one at Spalding, isn't there?'

'There is, miss, but the others reckon we could send our crop by train from here to Bardney.'

'Really? That'd be excellent.' She thought a moment then said, 'What do you think about five acres as a trial the first year?' When Joe nodded, she added, 'I must check up when's the best time to plant sugar beet.'

'Er – ought you to run the idea past his lordship? Oh, begging your pardon, miss.' Joe coloured at his slip of the tongue, but Charlotte only chuckled.

'No, let's just do it.'

On Christmas Eve, an unexpected visitor arrived at the manor on foot, but leading a horse. There'd been a light scattering of snow and the ground was icy.

'It's Miss Charlotte,' Georgie cried excitedly, seeing her coming up the drive. He ran to the front door before Wilkins could reach it and flung it open, rushing to meet her, slipping and sliding down the steps.

'Miss Charlotte, Miss Charlotte! You've brought Midnight.'

The horse shied a little and Georgie stopped abruptly, aware that he was frightening the animal. Charlotte patted the horse's neck and quietened him with a soothing word. She smiled down at the excited boy. 'Come and stroke him.'

Though the animal was still a little restless, and there was wariness in his eyes, Georgie approached him fear-

174

lessly. He reached up and stroked his neck. 'There, boy, there,' he murmured.

'That's good, Georgie. Very good. Now, is your father at home?'

'Yes, I'll fetch him.' He turned away and walked a little distance before he began to run. Charlotte smiled, watching him go. At least one of the Thornton boys was learning how to treat a nervous animal.

Only a moment later, Miles was coming down the steps, his feet crunching on the snow, Georgie skipping beside him. He held out his hands towards her. 'Miss Charlotte – this is a pleasant surprise. You must come in and have some mulled wine. We were just trying it out ready for the party tonight. You are coming, I hope.'

Charlotte blinked at him.

'Ah,' Miles said, understanding at once. 'You didn't receive my invitation?'

She shook her head. 'No. I – I'm sorry, we – we can't have. It must have got lost in all the Christmas mail.'

If only that was the explanation, Miles thought grimly. He'd had the invitation delivered by hand but, he realized now, he'd made the mistake of addressing it to Mr Crawford. Hence, the girl knew nothing of it.

'Then if you are free this evening, I do hope you will come.'

Now he'd embarrassed her, for she blushed and avoided his gaze. 'I – I'm sorry, I don't think we'll be able to.'

'No matter.' Miles smiled, trying to ease her discomfort. 'Perhaps at New Year?'

She smiled weakly and nodded. 'Perhaps.'

'Don't let's stand here getting chilled. And you, Georgie, out here without a coat. Dear me, Lily will have a ducky fit, as she calls it.'

175

'I'll take Midnight round to the stable yard, shall I?' Charlotte said.

'Yes, yes.'

Whilst Mr Thornton and Georgie returned inside, Charlotte led the horse round the side of the house. As she rounded the corner, she almost bumped into Philip and Lily, hurrying, hand in hand, in the opposite direction.

'Oh!' Lily cried and snatched her hand from Philip's, blushing a bright pink. 'Oh, miss. I—'

But, smoothly, Philip covered her embarrassment. 'Lily is going home for the afternoon as we're having a party tonight and she'll be here over Christmas too.' His eyes challenged Charlotte. 'I was just making sure she doesn't slip and fall.' Now he turned to Lily. 'You'll be all right now. I really should get one of the men to clear the path from the back door round to the front.'

'Yes – I – er – thank you, Master Philip.'

With her hat pulled down low and her scarf covering the lower half of her face, Lilly hurried away.

'Take care, now,' Philip called after her before turning his attention back to Charlotte and to the horse she was leading. His face darkened. 'So, you've brought that creature back, have you?'

Charlotte regarded him with her head on one side. 'He's rightfully still yours. Your father wouldn't let me pay for him, so, I thought now that he's had a little training, it's only right that you should have him back. He'll be fine now – if he's treated properly.'

Philip's face was thunderous. 'How dare you speak to me like that? Who do you think you are?' His mouth curled. 'I suppose,' he drawled sarcastically, 'you think that one day you'll be a woman of property because Buckthorn Farm will be yours when the old man dies.

Well, let me tell you, Miss Charlotte Crawford' – he thrust his face close to hers – 'you won't inherit a penny. Not – one – penny. Not one blade of grass. The whole lot's coming to me.' He struck his chest. 'Me!'

Charlotte's face was white and she clung to Midnight's reins to keep upright. 'I – don't understand,' she whispered at last. The boy must be unhinged. She feared for his sanity. He was given to uncontrolled fits of temper. She'd seen that with his treatment of Midnight. And now she wished fervently that she'd not brought the horse back. Her sense of fairness had made her make the offer. But now she regretted it heartily. The horse might have been tamed, but she doubted the boy ever would be. The preposterous idea that he – a comparative stranger – was to be her father's heir, astounded her. Was it really possible that her father would do such a thing?

Philip's next words confirmed her worst fears. He'd plunged the knife into her heart and now he twisted it with vicious delight. 'He's taken a liking to me. He looks upon me as the son he's never had. And – ' he sneered, 'you are, as he says himself, "neither use nor ornament".'

Charlotte stared at him, at the young, handsome face that was at the same time ugly with malice. With a strength and resilience that she hadn't known she possessed, she straightened her shoulders and said tightly, 'If you will let me pass, I will ask one of your men to stable Midnight. I must see your father.'

A flicker of fear crossed the boy's face. His hand shot out and he gripped her arm, his fingers biting into her flesh. 'Don't you say a word to him about this. Don't you dare. You're not supposed to know.'

'Oh, I'm sure I'm not.' She shook herself free of his

grasp. 'No doubt my father was saving this little piece of information for an appropriate moment.' She forced a smile. 'But I'm very grateful to you for telling me, Philip. Very grateful indeed. At least it allows me to make my own plans. I can leave now without any guilt, without any shred of filial duty left. And as for the farm, I hope you're up to running it because, unless you take over right now, by the time you inherit it, it won't be worth the paper his precious will is written on.'

'Me? Run a farm? I've no intention of running a farm.' Once more his mouth curled disdainfully. 'I'm no country yokel. But my brother, Ben, now, Father has him earmarked to take over running our lands one day.' He shrugged nonchalantly. 'Buckthorn Farm will just become part of the estate and he can pay me a fair rent.'

'You really are despicable, Philip. How you come to be the son of such a kind and caring man as your father I don't know. Now, if you'll kindly let me pass, your father is waiting for me to sample his mulled wine.'

Twenty-Three

'Come in, come in,' Miles cried when Charlotte found her way through the kitchens to the morning room. 'We thought you'd got lost.'

'I ran into Philip,' she said, taking the glass of steaming mulled wine gratefully. She'd become chilled, standing talking in the cold, but that was nothing compared to the bleakness in her heart. 'I'd come to offer you Midnight back, now he's broken in. He's a wonderful animal, but he still needs careful handling – gentle treatment. The horse is ready, but I'm not sure – now – that Philip is.'

'I give you my word—' Miles began, but at that moment Philip entered the room, a look of apprehension on his face when he saw Charlotte and his father deep in conversation. Georgie followed close behind him.

Before anyone else could say a word, Georgie piped up, 'Miss Charlotte's trained Midnight for you. She's brought him back.' Then he frowned and added as sternly as a little boy of six could manage, 'But you've got to promise not to whip him any more.'

Philip glanced from Charlotte to his father and back again. He bit his lip and muttered morosely, 'I promise.'

Miles smiled and said benignly, 'Good, good.'

But Charlotte was not so sure as she watched the boy turn and leave the room. Philip had just proved, to her at least, that he was not capable of keeping confidences.

179

It did not bode well for his chosen profession in the law, Charlotte thought, with a surprising hint of silent amusement, considering the disastrous news she'd just heard.

'Now, we're having a party for all the staff here tonight in the big room they tell me used to be used as a ballroom, but on New Year's Eve I'm planning a quiet dinner party. Just the family, you and your father, Mr Iveson and an artist friend of mine. He lives in London now and although we've always kept in touch, we haven't seen one another for several years. He's on his own, so I've invited him to come here for New Year. It's Ben's birthday that day and it's what he's chosen.' He smiled. 'No big birthday party for the quiet one of the family. Now, do say you'll come?'

With a defiant sparkle in her eyes, Charlotte said, 'I can't answer for my father, but yes, I'd be delighted to come to your dinner party. Thank you.'

She raised her glass to him and they smiled at each other.

'Papa,' Georgie said, 'Brewster and Wilkins have put the tree up in the hall. Please can we decorate it now?' He came to Charlotte's side and slipped his hand into hers, beaming up at her. 'And may Miss Charlotte stay and help us?'

For a brief moment, Miles hesitated, his expression suddenly melancholy, but then he forced a smile and said quietly, 'Of course.'

They went out into the hall where Philip and Ben were coming down the stairs, carrying down the boxes of Christmas decorations for the tree. Georgie hopped excitedly from one foot to the other. 'Where's the fairy for the top? Papa always puts the fairy on last. We'll do the bottom branches, Miss Charlotte, and Philip and Ben—'

As Charlotte touched the paper decorations in the box, gently lifting the first one out, Philip said harshly, 'What d'you think you're doing?'

She looked up to see him glaring at her, his face thunderous.

'I—'

'Miss Charlotte's going to help us decorate the tree,' Georgie said, rummaging in each box, trying to find his favourite ornaments.

'Oh no, she isn't,' Philip snapped. 'That was always Mother's job and no one – *no one* – is ever going to take her place.'

As he glared at her, Charlotte could see that he was not just referring to the decorating of the family Christmas tree. She dropped the paper chain as if it was burning her fingers. Huskily, she said, 'I'm so sorry.'

'Phil, please—' Georgie began, but his brother rounded on him.

'You can't remember. How could you? But *I* do. And Ben does.'

Charlotte saw Ben's head drop and he said nothing. Then she saw tears start in Georgie's eyes. She squatted down in front of him. Taking a deep breath, she smiled and said as brightly as she could manage, 'I ought to go, anyway. I've so much to do at home.'

It was a lie; there was nothing to do at home. Christmas was not celebrated at Buckthorn Farm.

'I'll come and see your tree when you've got it done. I promise.'

She stood up, turned away and walked quickly to the front door and all the while she was acutely aware of

Miles watching her with troubled eyes. She pulled open the door and paused, just a moment, to look back. Georgie was delving into the boxes, his excitement overcoming his brief disappointment. Ben now avoided her glance, but Philip caught and held her gaze, a smile of triumph curving his mouth. It was a double victory for the scheming young man.

The news Philip had given her stunned Charlotte and, as she walked home, she was proud of herself that she'd managed to carry off her conversation with the rest of the family without giving away the fact that she was in a state of shock. Who else knew about this? Did Mary or Edward? And how could she find out anything more without causing embarrassment to them? If nothing else, the knowledge that her father intended to leave her quite penniless strengthened her resolve. She would indeed, she told herself, need to plan her future carefully. But how – and where – to start? That was the problem.

Apart from a slight change in the usual food, Christmas at Buckthorn Farm was a dull affair. Mary cooked a goose with all the trimmings and proudly presented a plum pudding she'd made weeks earlier. Charlotte, Mary and Edward exchanged small gifts but their dinner was eaten, as always, in the kitchen whilst Osbert ate alone in the gloomy room across the hallway.

Charlotte couldn't help her thoughts returning to the manor. How she'd love to have seen Georgie opening his Christmas presents. She could imagine his excitement and his indulgent father and brothers watching. They'd make the day special for the little boy. Even Philip would unbend a little, she was sure. There'd be warmth and laughter and love in that household. How she longed to be a part of it.

But, despite the shattering news about her inheritance, Charlotte carried on as normal. She was as courteous and obedient as ever to her father, affectionate as always to Mary and Edward – and to Peggy, who'd now become a part of the household. She wondered if Joe knew about it.

And then, the day after Boxing Day, she suddenly realized that there was someone she could confide in. Someone she could trust with her life. Jackson. She could talk to him. He would tell her, if he knew anything. And if he didn't, then he was the very person to find out.

But that same morning, Peggy came with news that halted Charlotte's plan – at least for the moment.

'Our Jackson's got the influenza. He's ever so poorly.' Peggy bit her lip. 'We even had to get the doctor.'

If that was the case, Charlotte realized, then the young man must be very ill. People like the Warrens didn't often call the doctor in, if they could help it. Doctors needed paying and country folk, knowledgeable in the ways of Nature's remedies, seldom called upon Dr Markham's services.

'Jackson must stay off work as long as he needs to,' Charlotte reassured her.

'Thank you, miss. I'll tell him what you've said.'

Later that day, Charlotte inspected the contents of her wardrobe. It was dismally inadequate. There was nothing there that was suitable for another dinner party. She fingered the dress she'd worn the last time she and

183

her father had dined at the Manor. She allowed herself a wry smile; it was the *only* dinner party she'd ever attended. She turned away with a sigh and sat down at her dressing table and regarded her reflection critically. She had a well-proportioned face, with smooth skin that was lightly tanned from being out doors in all weathers. Removing her spectacles, she leaned closer to the mirror. Her eyes were violet, with thick, black lashes. Her nose was the right size and shape for her face and her mouth generous and turned up at the corners as if she were ready to smile at any moment. And, despite the harshness of her life, she was. Until now, she'd never really stopped to compare her life with that of others. She'd always been housed, clothed and fed. She'd always had the affection of Mary and Edward, the friendship of the men and boys who worked on the nearby farms – and in some cases, that of their wives too. And as for the lack of love from her father, well, she'd never known any different. So how was she to know that her life was unduly harsh, very different to what it would have been as the daughter of a loving father? But now she was becoming painfully aware of the differences. She remembered all the times she'd visited the Warrens' cottage home. How there was affection between each and every member of the family for one another. How Joe treated his daughter, Lily, with the same love he had for his boys. If anything, Charlotte thought wistfully, it was a love that was even more tender and protective. And Lily's brothers looked out for her too. Charlotte smiled at herself in the mirror. And that was how she thought of Jackson. He was like a brother to her.

Lost in thought, she didn't hear the quick footsteps on the stairs and she jumped when an urgent knock sounded on her bedroom door.

'Miss Charlotte, Miss Charlotte. Come quickly.'

Charlotte rose at once and hurried to the door, flinging it open. 'What is it? What's the matter? Is it my father?'

'No – well – yes, in a manner of speaking.' Mary was standing there, twisting her fingers together agitatedly.

'Is he ill?' Charlotte hurried to the head of the stairs and began to run down.

Mary, following close behind, said, 'No, but he will be if he carries on like he is doing.'

As they reached the hall, Charlotte heard raised voices in the sitting room, her father's voice loud and angry above another, female, voice. It was not a voice she recognized. She hurried into the room.

There were two visitors in the room with her father, but it was immediately apparent that they were not welcome. Osbert was standing in front of the fireplace, holding on to the mantelpiece as if for support. But he was shaking his fist at the woman standing straight-backed before him and shouting, 'Get out! Get out of my house.'

The woman was middle-aged. Tall – stately, Charlotte thought irrationally – and elegantly dressed. Tiny curls of brown hair escaped from beneath her tight-fitting felt cloche hat and she wore a knee-length cross-over coat trimmed with fur at the collar and cuffs and fashionable, pointed-toe T-bar shoes. Behind her, a man was standing near the window, keeping out of the altercation. Of medium build – neither fat nor thin – balding and sporting a moustache.

As Charlotte entered the room, they all turned to look at her – the man and the woman with interest, her father with anger. 'And you can keep out of this, girl. Go to your room and stay there.'

185

The woman was smiling and coming towards her, her arms stretched wide to embrace Charlotte. 'My dear, dear girl. We meet at last! Come, kiss your Aunt Euphemia.'

Twenty-Four

In a trance, Charlotte submitted to the woman's embrace and kiss on her cheek. Then the stranger stood back and held Charlotte at arm's length. 'Let me look at you. My, my, such a pretty little thing . . .'

Charlotte smiled weakly, more at the misplaced compliment than anything else. 'Did you say *aunt*?'

'I did indeed. I am your father's sister.'

Charlotte gasped in surprise. 'Father's – sister? I didn't know he had a sister.'

The woman threw back her head and laughed. 'Dear me, am I such a black sheep that he hasn't even mentioned me in all these years? I hoped you might remember us, but then you were only four – or was it five? – when we were last here.'

'Euphemia . . .' The warning note in Osbert's voice was unmistakable, but the woman carried on smoothly, as if she hadn't heard him and certainly as if she intended to take no notice.

'I'm the older by four years. And this is my husband, Percy. Percy Bell.' She waved her hand vaguely in the direction of the man standing near the window. He smiled towards Charlotte and gave a courteous little bow. But he made no attempt to approach her, to kiss her cheek or even to shake her hand.

'We've been abroad for many years. Percy worked for the Foreign Office, so we've been all over the world.

But we've come back home to England now Percy's retired.' Euphemia linked her arm through Charlotte's and drew her further into the room. 'Your father and I had a silly quarrel when—'

'Euphemia!' Osbert roared, this time successfully cutting off whatever she had been going to say. 'That matter is never spoken of in this house. I'll thank you to hold your tongue.'

She stared at him for a long moment, before saying, with surprising meekness, 'Very well, Osbert. If you say so.'

'I do. And you will speak to no one about it. *No one*, do you hear?'

Charlotte watched the change on the woman's face. She was staring at her brother, frowning, as if trying to read the reason behind his words – his demand. She gave a slight nod, but this time she made no promise.

Euphemia turned back to Charlotte with a bright, rather forced smile. 'We've taken rooms in Ravensfleet. At the White Swan.' She patted Charlotte's hand. 'You must come and see us there. We can go to Lincoln on a shopping spree and—'

'She'll do no such thing,' Osbert spat. 'I don't want her looking like some – ' he gestured towards his sister – 'some woman of the streets.'

'Oh I say, old boy, steady on,' Percy murmured and began to move towards his wife, as if in support. But Euphemia waved him away, 'Don't worry, my dear; I'm used to my brother's insults.'

Osbert moved stiffly from his stance near the fireplace to sit in his chair. He made no offer of refreshment for them nor did he even invite them to sit down. 'I wish you good day, Euphemia. You are not welcome in this house.'

For a moment there was stunned silence. But then the woman laughed gaily. 'Nonsense, Osbert. You are my only living relative. I want us to put the past behind us.' She released her hold on Charlotte and moved to stand on the hearthrug in front of her brother. Charlotte glanced at her uncle. He was watching the proceedings, but taking no part now.

'We were close once, Osbert,' Euphemia said softly.

'We were never close,' Osbert barked, his frown deepening. He nodded towards Percy. 'You married *him* against Father's wishes and ran off to Timbuktu or wherever it was.'

'India, actually, old boy.' Percy spoke for the first time. 'And we didn't run off, as you put it. My work was out there already, as you very well know.' He spoke with a well-bred, superior tone of voice, but his eyes twinkled merrily when he glanced at Charlotte. She watched him stroke his moustache and heard a low chuckle.

He's enjoying this, Charlotte thought. I wonder why?

Osbert was scowling at them both now. 'Nevertheless, you were out there when Father died and I was left to run this place on my own. At twenty.'

Euphemia laughed, a merry sound that was at once infectious. 'And you're trying to tell me you wanted it any other way? What could I have done? A mere *girl*?'

Charlotte caught her breath. So, she thought, her father's antagonism against girls went even further back. It sounded as if his attitude towards his sister had been the same as it was now towards his daughter. But at her aunt's next words, Charlotte realized that the feeling went back a generation further.

'Father always made it perfectly clear that I – as a daughter – would inherit nothing.'

'That's why he wanted you to marry well. So that

189

you'd be provided for and not be a burden on me.' He glanced with a sneer at Percy, who was still smiling benevolently. Charlotte doubted the man could be offended, however hard one tried. And it seemed her father was trying to do just that.

Osbert sniffed. 'He didn't think a junior in the Foreign Office would ever amount to much.'

'Well, he was wrong,' Euphemia said tartly. 'Percy did amount to something. He rose to an important position, as a matter of fact. We've had a wonderful life and he's retired on a very nice pension which allows us to do just what we like. But I would have married him anyway. We, Osbert dear, married for love, but of course you wouldn't know anything about that, would you? When I think of poor, dear Alice—'

Osbert sprang to his feet with an agility that Charlotte had not seen for years. He thrust his face close to Euphemia's and spat out the words, his spittle showering her face. 'Her name – is – not – to be spoken – in – this – house. Do – you – hear – me?'

Euphemia blinked, but remarkably she kept her composure. 'I can hardly fail to, Osbert,' she said calmly.

'No need for that, old boy,' Percy put in mildly.

Osbert turned his venom on his brother-in-law. 'I am not your "old boy". I believe I am a good ten years younger than you, if I remember rightly. And now I'd be obliged if you would leave my house. As I said, you are not welcome here.'

'But Father, surely – ?' Charlotte took a step forwards, but her father flung out his hand towards her, pointing his forefinger threateningly. 'And you can hold your tongue, girl. This is no concern of yours.'

'Oh, but I think it is, Osbert. Surely even *you* would

not stop me becoming acquainted with my own niece? Especially if, in view of Percy having done so very well in his career, I give you my word, brother dear, that I shall never become a burden on you or your daughter when she inherits. That's if I outlive you, of course.'

Osbert's eyes gleamed. 'There's no fear of that.' His voice was silky with malice.

Euphemia laughed. 'What? That I shall outlive you?'

Osbert shook his head. 'No, not that.' His eyes narrowed as he said, 'Of my daughter' – he said the word as if the very feel of it on his tongue was abhorrent to him – 'inheriting Buckthorn Farm.'

Euphemia gaped at him and Charlotte couldn't prevent a startled gasp.

'I don't understand – ' Euphemia's glance went from one to the other.

'It's not for you *to* understand,' Osbert snapped. 'It's none of your business.'

'But she's your only child, isn't she? And she's not married, is she?' She turned to Charlotte. 'Are you?'

Wordlessly, Charlotte shook her head.

There was silence in the room. Everyone seemed like a statue, stunned into stillness. Osbert, having delivered the bombshell, calmly sat back down in his chair.

'You mean to tell me,' Euphemia said, her own temper rising now, 'that you are not going to leave the farm to your daughter? Your only child?'

'That's correct.'

Charlotte, her eyes wide, stared at her father and put out her hand to the nearest chair to steady herself. Her legs felt weak and her head was swimming. So it was true. She was hearing it now from his own mouth. He was not going to leave the farm to her. She knew only

191

too well that her being a daughter had disappointed him deeply, but she'd never thought that his bitterness was quite so vindictive.

'My dear girl.' Percy moved solicitously towards her. 'Are you all right? You look as if you've had a shock. D'you mean to tell me that you'd no idea?'

'Not – not really.'

'Appalling,' the kindly man said. 'Absolutely appalling!' But whether he meant the fact that she was to be left penniless or that she hadn't known her fate was unclear. Probably he meant both, Charlotte thought.

Her aunt was still locked in a battle of wills with Osbert.

'You're quite right, as always, Percy dear,' she murmured, though her gaze was still on her brother. 'That is exactly the word for it.' She paused and, with her head on one side, added, 'Then who, if I might be so bold, is to inherit?'

'Philip Thornton.'

As her legs finally gave way beneath her, Charlotte sank into a chair.

'And who's he when he's at home?' Euphemia demanded.

'None of your business,' Osbert snapped again.

At last, summoning all her strength, Charlotte said quietly, 'The Thorntons have just come to live at the manor.'

Euphemia turned towards her. 'Where Jeremy Davenport lived?'

'That's right.'

'What happened to him? Oh, don't tell me he's dead.' Her hand fluttered to her mouth and her eyes were wide.

Charlotte regarded her aunt. She must have known him, she thought. 'I'm afraid so,' she said gently. 'His heir was a second cousin once removed who lived abroad and didn't wish to take up occupancy. The manor and the whole estate were sold to Mr Thornton and – and – ' her voice faded to a whisper, 'his three sons.'

Euphemia stared at her for a long moment, absorbing the news and beginning to realize what the arrival of the new family had meant for Charlotte.

Osbert leaned towards his sister. 'It was Davenport whom Father had lined up for you. So you see, if you'd been obedient and married him, you would now be a very wealthy woman.'

Pulled back to the present, Euphemia started and then, in a very unladylike manner, snorted with laughter. Despite the shocking confirmation that what Philip had told her was true, Charlotte smiled. She was beginning to like her new-found relative very much.

'Me! Marry Jeremy Davenport?' Euphemia almost squeaked. 'Don't be ridiculous, Osbert. He was a philanderer. A womanizer. No girl in her right mind would have *married* him.'

Osbert put his head on one side as he said slyly, 'Maybe it was Davenport who had the lucky escape. He did marry late in life – someone much younger than him – and had two sons. Sadly, they were both killed in the war and his wife – still young enough to have borne more children, mark you – died in 'eighteen of the influenza.' He paused and then smiled maliciously at Euphemia. '*You* haven't been able to give your husband any children at all, let alone sons.'

All through the exchange of heated words, Euphemia had remained in control, but now her brother had touched a raw nerve. Her hand fluttered to her mouth and tears filled her eyes. At once, Percy was at her side. 'There, there, old girl. Don't take on.' He turned towards Osbert. 'And you, sir, mind your tongue. Even if she is your sister, it doesn't give you the right to be so cruel.'

'Huh, we're in the same boat. I've no son, only a useless, good-for-nothing daughter, who can't even catch a husband. I tried to arrange a marriage with Miles Thornton, but even he won't have her. Not even to secure his son's inheritance.'

'Father!' Charlotte gasped. 'What are you saying? What d'you mean?' This she did not know.

He turned to her now. 'I intend to leave all my lands and possessions to Philip Thornton, but I tried to make provision for you. As a condition, I proposed that his father – Miles – should agree to marry you. But he refused.' His lip curled disdainfully. 'But who can blame him? Look at you. Just look at you! Drab, colourless and spineless. Who on earth would ever want you for a wife?'

Hurt and humiliated more than ever before, Charlotte pulled herself up and ran from the room. As she dragged herself up the stairs, the racking sobs built in her chest, but not until she reached the sanctuary of her own room, did she throw herself on her bed and give way to a storm of weeping.

Twenty-Five

She must have fallen asleep for it was dusk when she woke. Her face was blotchy, her eyes swollen. She splashed cold water from the ewer into the bowl and washed her face. Then she unwound her plait, brushed her long, shining black hair and replaited it. She looked at herself in the mirror. Her violet eyes stared back at her. She picked up the spectacles she had worn since the age of seven. She remembered her father taking her to Lincoln. It had been such a rare occasion that he took her anywhere that the day was still clear in her memory.

They'd gone to an optician where her father had insisted the man test her eyesight. When she'd done reading all the letters and he'd looked into her eyes, the man declared that she had perfect eyesight.

'She needs glasses,' her father had said abruptly. 'You will make her a pair of spectacles with round, plain steel frames.'

The man had spread his hands helplessly. 'But she doesn't need spectacles. She—'

Slowly and clearly, Osbert had repeated the words, 'You will make her a pair of spectacles to my specification with plain glass.'

The man had gaped in surprise. He'd tried to argue once more, but to no avail. Osbert had been adamant and the man, only an employee who dared not turn away a customer for fear of his superior's wrath, duly obliged. On completion, the spectacles were posted to Buckthorn Farm and from that day Charlotte had worn them. They had been replaced twice more, but still they were the same style of round, steel-framed glasses that she had worn as a child.

Staring at herself in the mirror, Charlotte felt an overwhelming rebellion. The spectacles slipped from her fingers to the floor and before she had scarcely stopped to think what she was doing, she had ground them into the worn linoleum with the heel of her sturdy shoe.

Then she left her room and went down to the hall. She paused a moment. There was no sound now from the sitting room, so she turned towards the door to the kitchen.

Mary and Edward were seated either side of the range. The remains of their meal still lay on the kitchen table and a plate of food, which had obviously been taken on a tray to her father, had been returned untouched.

At the sound of her entry, they both stood up and Mary came hurrying towards her, arms outstretched. 'Miss Charlotte – there you are. I came up, but you were sleeping, so I left you.'

Charlotte smiled weakly. 'Is there any tea? I could drink a horse trough.'

'Of course, of course. There's still some in the pot, but I'll make you a fresh one.'

'No need. That'll be fine.'

'Are you hungry?'

Charlotte shook her head. 'Not really.' She sat down at the table and, when Mary poured a cup of tea out, she drank it gratefully.

'So,' she began, 'have our visitors gone?'

A glance passed between husband and wife. 'They've

gone, but they left you a message, miss,' Edward said. 'They're staying at the White Swan in Ravensfleet and they'd like you to contact them there.'

Charlotte placed her cup back in its saucer with deliberate care. 'D'you know them, Mary?'

Again Mary and Edward exchanged a swift look. When they didn't answer, Charlotte said, 'It was my aunt and uncle. It seems – ' she paused with a wry smile – 'that my father has a sister I've never known about.'

Mary was twisting her apron between nervous fingers. Charlotte eyed her suspiciously. Softly, she said, 'You *do* know her, don't you?'

Mary's eyes filled with tears and she put her apron up to them, half covering her face.

Edward touched his wife's arm comfortingly and then turned to face Charlotte. 'Miss Charlotte, we saw her once or twice, years ago, before – before – ' he gulped nervously, 'before your mother went. But since then – nothing. I swear, miss.'

'It's all right, Edward. Mary, please don't distress yourself,' Charlotte tried to reassure them both, though secretly she was puzzled over their reaction to what seemed to her a simple question.

'Euphemia!' She smiled, trying to lighten the tension. 'It seems my paternal grandparents had a penchant for ridiculous names for their children.' She chuckled and repeated, 'Euphemia.' Then she went on, 'From what I can gather, my father and his sister fell out some years ago and the feud has lasted all this time. So like my father, don't you think?' she added dryly. 'And they've been abroad for many years. Uncle was with the Foreign Office. Did you know that? But now he's retired and they've come back to England.' She shrugged. 'And I suppose my aunt wanted to see her only living relative – well, relatives, if you count me too.'

Mary nodded and whispered, 'Yes, miss.' Then she seemed to pull herself together. 'I must get on, Miss Charlotte. I've a lot of work to do. Peggy's not coming today. Joe came in to tell me. I think she's going down with the flu that Jackson's got.'

'Oh dear,' Charlotte said, at once concerned for the Warren family. 'Look, pack some food into a basket, Mary, and I'll take it over later. I want to see Jackson anyway.'

'Now don't you go running into infection, miss,' Edward warned. 'We don't want you going down with the flu. It's the very devil. Let's hope it doesn't get as bad as at the end of the war.'

'I'll be fine,' Charlotte said airily. She'd always been blessed with robust health and never feared catching anything. She'd had all the usual childish ailments, but wasn't a martyr to winter coughs and colds or even the dreaded influenza that everyone feared so. She rose. 'And I suppose I'd better get on as well. Now all the excitement's over.'

It wasn't until she was halfway along the passage leading to the farm office at the back of the house that she realized she hadn't asked Mary and Edward if they knew about the will her father intended to make.

Later that afternoon as the dusk of a winter's afternoon settled over the marsh, Charlotte took the basket of food and walked down the lane to the Warrens' cottage. She hadn't been able to concentrate properly on her paperwork today. Plans for spring planting had been pushed aside not only because of the sudden appearance of relatives she'd known nothing about, but also because, obliterating everything else, of the revelation about her father's intentions towards her.

She'd always known that she was a bitter disappointment to him, but it was only recently that she'd realized she was not treated as a daughter should be treated. She'd been naïve, ignorant, but she'd never known any different. How could she? The realization had come only very slowly. Subconsciously, she realized now, she'd seen the contrast between her own life and that of the Warrens. But she'd thought that their happy family life was because there was a mother in the household; a mother around whom the home and family life revolved.

She'd had no such good fortune.

But now that she'd seen Miles Thornton's affection for his sons and how he managed to make a happy home life for them even without his wife at his side, it had dawned on her that her father had not a scrap of paternal affection for her. Indeed, it could be said that he hated her and her very existence. This last callous act proved it.

The thought saddened her. She'd tried to be a good and dutiful daughter. She'd done everything he'd demanded of her. She'd dressed in the drab garments, worn the clear-glass spectacles. Tied her long, glossy hair into an unbecoming plait. All as he'd dictated. She'd taken over the day-to-day running of the farm – with Joe's help and advice, of course. She'd even hidden her one pleasure – her hobby of drawing and painting – because he ridiculed it.

She sighed as she reached the cottage and raised her hand to knock. John opened the door.

'Please don't come in, Miss Charlotte. Me ma's gone

199

down with it now. Jackson's on the mend, but she's real bad.'

'Have you had the doctor?'

He shook his head and smiled wryly. 'No, miss. She fetched him for Jackson, but she won't have him for hersen. She sticks to all the old-fashioned remedies. Swears by 'em.'

Charlotte smiled. 'She is very knowledgeable about such things, I know. But just promise me, John, that if you're worried about her, you'll call the doctor. You needn't worry about the bill. I'll see to that.'

'You're very kind, miss.'

'Mary's sent this. Just to help out.'

John took the basket and smiled his thanks.

'I really wanted to see Jackson, but—'

'He's on the mend and he'll be out and about in a day or so, I shouldn't wonder. Will it wait till then?'

Charlotte bit her lip. 'Of course,' she said, but was bitterly disappointed.

As she left the cottage, she took the path across the fields to the manor. She was shown at once into Miles's study. At once Duke lumbered towards her, wagging his tail and pushing his head into her skirt to be patted. 'Now then, boy,' she said softly.

'Miss Charlotte – what a lovely surprise. Please, sit down,' Miles invited, gesturing towards one of the leather winged chairs near the fire. 'Wilkins, would you bring us tea, please?'

The manservant gave a little bow and left the room.

Miles didn't return to his seat behind the desk, but sat down in the chair opposite. 'What brings you here?'

Charlotte took a deep breath. 'Several reasons. First, the Warren family has influenza. At least, Jackson and Peggy have and I wondered if you'd allow Lily to go home to help them. I know it's an imposition of me to ask, especially as you have a guest coming and the dinner party on Friday evening—'

'Of course, she must go at once.' He made as if to stand up that instant to send for her, but Charlotte put up her hand to stop him.

'Would you mind if I told her myself? I want to impress upon her that they must call Dr Markham in.' She smiled. 'Peggy is just like most of the country folk – they try their own remedies first when they get sick, but sometimes . . .' She shrugged and spread her hands in a helpless gesture.

Miles nodded. 'I understand. Of course, you must see Lily yourself.' There was silence before he prompted, 'And what else?'

Putting off the real reason for her visit for as long as possible, she said, 'How is Philip getting along with Midnight?'

'Ah.' Miles smiled ruefully. 'Well, now – I hope you won't mind, but I've taken Midnight as my mount for the moment. Philip is still wary of him and the animal gets restless every time he goes near him. And as Philip is away at school for several weeks at a time, and Midnight is a big animal who needs his exercise, I'm riding him. He's too big and still a little difficult for Ben, and certainly for Georgie.' He laughed and suddenly his face seemed much younger. 'Though that little rascal would have a go, if I let him.'

Charlotte smiled at the thought of her daring 'golden boy'.

'But he's fine with me,' Miles went on. 'So, I hope you don't mind.'

'Of course I don't. He's your horse.'

'But you trained him for Philip.'

'I know.' Her eyes twinkled merrily as she added, 'But, to tell you the truth, I'm relieved.'

'Because it's not Philip riding him?'

'Well – ' She hesitated to criticize his son yet again, but Miles only laughed.

'Perhaps you're right. I think my eldest son has some growing up to do, and learning the right way to treat animals – and people, if it comes to that – is part of it. Anyway, you need have no worries for the present whilst I'm riding him. We're getting along fine. He's a beautiful animal. Still a little wilful, but we respect each other, I think.'

'I'm glad.'

He waited a moment before saying softly, 'But there's something else, isn't there?'

Charlotte took a deep breath, but at that moment Wilkins returned with a tray of tea, freshly baked scones, jam and cream.

'Thank you, Wilkins. We'll see to it.'

As the butler left the room, Miles said, 'Will you pour?'

'Of course,' Charlotte said, but as she reached for the teapot she was trembling so noticeably that Miles touched her hand and said gently, 'Allow me . . .'

As he handed her a cup her hands were still shaking so that the cup rattled in its saucer.

'My dear girl, whatever's the matter?'

Charlotte set her teacup down. 'I scarcely know where to begin.'

He sat back in his chair, waiting patiently until she regained her composure sufficiently to explain. 'You can tell me whatever you like, you know. It will be in the strictest confidence, I promise.'

'I've had two shocks recently. One was that – out of

202

the blue – an aunt and uncle I never knew existed arrived at Buckthorn Farm. She's my father's sister and they've – they've not seen each other for years. Some sort of family feud, it seems. She's trying to make it up, but my father . . .' Her voice trailed away.

'And the second surprise?'

Charlotte bit her lip, not wanting to tell tales on his son. Although it had been Philip who'd first told her, now she'd learned the same fact from another source. The horse's mouth.

'You probably know about it.' She took another deep breath. 'I'm sorry, I find this very embarrassing. It seems that my father wishes to make Philip his heir.'

Miles rubbed his hand across his eyes and groaned. 'Oh, that ridiculous nonsense. I'd hoped you'd never hear of that. We've refused, of course.'

Charlotte smiled a little sadly as she added quietly, 'Because of the condition he made? That you should marry me?'

'No – no – ' Miles started forward, spilling his tea into the saucer. 'What he's suggesting is not right. *You* should inherit everything. The farm shouldn't go to a comparative stranger.'

'But what does Philip say? Doesn't he want it?'

'To my eternal shame – yes, he does. But as I say, he has some growing up to do.'

'Don't be too hard on him. It's not his fault. He's only young. And let's be honest, who wouldn't want to be left a thriving farm?'

'Well, we won't accept it. *He* won't accept it. I'll make sure of that.'

'I don't think he – or you – will have any choice. I think my father can will his estate and his possessions to whomsoever he pleases. Can't he?'

'No doubt,' Miles said curtly, 'but I'm taking legal advice from my solicitor. He's looking into the matter. There may be some way round it.'

'And if there isn't?' she asked softly.

'You will always have a home – I promise you. I would see that you were provided for.'

'I don't want charity,' she snapped and then added swiftly, 'I'm sorry. That came out all wrong. I know you meant it kindly, but—'

'Don't apologize. I'd feel exactly the same in your place.'

There was silence between them before he asked tentatively, 'Charlotte, is there anyone in your life – a young man? What I mean is, is there any possibility that you could get married?'

She pursed her lips and glanced down at her lap as she twisted her fingers together nervously. She shook her head and said huskily, 'No one. He – he's never let anyone get close. And if there's ever been the slightest sign – well, he gets rid of them.'

Miles knew that was true because of Cuthbert Iveson.

'It's strange,' she mused, thinking aloud. 'You'd think he'd be just the opposite, wouldn't you? That if he doesn't want me to inherit, he'd want to encourage suitors to get me off his hands.'

Miles laughed wryly. 'Huh! You're too useful to him. You run the farm, don't you?' He raised his hand as she began to refute the suggestion. 'Don't deny it. I have it from a good source. A very good source – but one which I'm not about to reveal.'

Charlotte smiled. 'Joe, I suppose.'

'Now, now.' He wagged his finger at her playfully.

She sighed. 'Yes, it's true. Father does very little

nowadays. Even when I try to talk over any problems with him, he just waves me away and says, "Ask Joe."'

'This aunt and uncle of yours who have suddenly appeared – are they staying with you?'

Charlotte laughed. 'No. They got short shrift when they came to Buckthorn Farm. Father more or less ordered them out. They're staying at the White Swan in Ravensfleet, so I intend to go and see them.'

There was mischief in Miles's eyes as he said slowly, 'We-ell, invite them to dinner on Friday night.'

'Oh, I couldn't – I mean – ' She blinked. 'Why on earth would you want to do that?'

'Because sometimes I find life a little – shall we say, quiet – in the countryside.' He chuckled, a deep, rumbling, infectious sound. 'It might liven things up a bit.'

Charlotte gaped at him and then started to laugh too. 'D'you know, I think you have a wicked streak in you. Now I know where Georgie gets his mischievous ways from.'

'Most certainly it's from me.' But there was pride in his tone when speaking of his youngest son.

'Well then, I will. I will invite them,' she said, surprising herself with her sudden daring. She got up and held out her hand. 'Thank you for listening to me. And for being so understanding.'

He rose, too, and took her outstretched hand. Looking down into her eyes, he said, 'I hope you know you can always count on me as a friend, Charlotte.'

As she looked up into his kindly face and read the concern in his dark eyes, Charlotte felt a tremor run through her. She caught her breath and her heart began to race. Her hand trembled a little in his warm grasp, but she managed to say levelly, 'Thank you. You're very kind.'

Then she turned and walked out of the room in search of Lily, marvelling at the strange trembling in her legs that his touch had caused.

Twenty-Six

'She's in there, miss,' Mrs Beddows said, nodding towards the back scullery situated off the main kitchen. 'Though what you'll mek of her, I don't know. She's upset about summat, but I can't get a word of sense out of her.'

'Oh dear,' Charlotte said. 'Perhaps she already knows that her mother's ill.'

But Mrs Beddows shook her head. 'She might, but I dun't reckon it's that.' The woman cast an anxious glance at Charlotte. 'I'd be grateful if you could find out what's ailing her, miss. And that's the truth, 'cos she's neither use nor ornament to me like she is.'

Charlotte hid her smile. The words, spoken lightly by the cook, bore none of the malice they held when issuing from her father's mouth.

She went into the scullery to find Lily with her arms in the deep sink washing clothes. The girl was scrubbing vigorously at a shirt collar, sobbing as she worked, her tears falling on to the garment.

She jumped as Charlotte put her arm round the girl's shoulders. 'Lily dear, don't take on so. Your mam'll be all right and Mr Thornton's given permission for you to go home and take care of the family until she's better. And Jackson's on the mend now and—'

Lily turned red-rimmed eyes to face her. 'What – what are you talkin' about, miss?'

Charlotte stared at her. 'I – I thought that's why you were crying. Because your mam and Jackson have the flu.'

Lily shook her head and mumbled, 'I didn't know.'

'Oh.' For a moment, Charlotte was dumbfounded. 'I'm sorry – I thought that's what was upsetting you.'

Lily sniffed and dried her hands on a towel. She was still hiccuping miserably.

'What is the matter, then?'

Lily looked frightened and shook her head violently. 'Nothing, miss. Honest. Does Mrs Beddows know about me mam and about Mr Thornton saying I can go home?'

'I don't think so, but I'll tell her.'

'How long can I go for?'

'You'd better talk to Mrs Beddows, but I'll wait for you and walk back with you, if you like.'

'No, no, miss. Don't wait.' Again the girl seemed fearful. 'I'll be a bit finishing up here and then getting me things together. I'll be home later tonight, though.'

'All right. Would you like me to call as I go home and tell them you'll be coming?'

'If – if you like, miss.'

Charlotte frowned. The girl seemed distracted and as she walked home, it was now thoughts of Lily that troubled Charlotte. There was something very wrong with the girl. Was she not happy working at the manor any more? Was Mrs Beddows too strict? Had someone been unkind to her? Perhaps she had a young man and they'd had a tiff. Yes, Charlotte thought, that would be it. Oh well, no doubt it would all come out in the wash, as Mary was fond of saying. Charlotte felt a pang of envy for Lily. Not because she was upset – of course not. But she doubted she would ever know the pangs of love and all its vicarious emotions. What was the phrase? 'Better to have loved and lost than never to have loved at all.' Well, right at this moment, Charlotte would give anything to love and be loved. Even if it all ended in heartache, she'd just like the opportunity to experience it.

But whilst her father still held sway over her life there was no chance of that.

'My dear child, how wonderful to see you again.' Euphemia held out her arms in welcome. 'Do come up to our room. Percy has gone out for a stroll. He loves quaint old places like Ravensfleet. They say it was a Roman settlement. Is that true?' Without waiting for an answer, she linked her arm through Charlotte's. 'I'll get them to bring some coffee up.'

The bedroom was quite small, but there were two easy chairs set near the window.

'Now,' Euphemia said, sitting down, 'we can have a nice little chat.'

'Before I forget,' Charlotte said, 'you are both invited to a dinner party at the manor on Friday evening.'

Euphemia's eyes gleamed. 'How kind of Mr Thornton. I must send a note at once, thanking and telling him we'll be delighted.' She leaned forward as if sharing a confidence. 'Might one of his three sons be paying court to you, dear child?'

Charlotte almost laughed aloud at the innocent irony of her aunt's words.

'No. The eldest boy is only sixteen.' Then, in spite of the bitter pill she was being forced to swallow where

Philip was concerned, her innate sense of humour reasserted itself when she thought of Georgie. 'Though the six-year-old is a little charmer.'

'What about the father, then? Do you like him? He's a widower, isn't he?'

Embarrassed now, Charlotte said, 'That's the man my father was trying to marry me off to.'

'Yes, I know, but do you like him?'

'He's a very nice, kind man, but – ' Charlotte smiled wistfully – 'I don't think he'd even look at someone like me. Not in that way.' She sighed inwardly, but smiled brightly at her aunt. 'If you accept his invitation, you'll see the portrait of his beautiful wife hanging over the fireplace in the dining room. He has another in his study. I – I think he's still in love with her. After all, it's only been six years since she died.'

'Six years! My dear girl, in my day a widower would be married again within six *months*. Especially if he had young children.' Euphemia put her head on one side and regarded her niece. 'You're not wearing your glasses today, my dear. You look so much better without them. You've got lovely eyes. Just like your mother's.'

Charlotte's heart leapt. 'You – you knew my mother?' Perhaps here was someone who'd be willing to talk to her about the shadowy figure from the past. Mary always seemed reluctant to talk about Alice Crawford. Charlotte believed it was because the woman was afraid that Osbert would find out that she'd been speaking about the forbidden subject.

Euphemia regarded her for a long moment before choosing her words very carefully. 'I – knew your mother. Not at first, of course. As I told you, we were abroad, and by the time your parents married, Osbert and I had fallen out – well, we'll talk about all that some other time.' It was obvious she was anxious to change the subject. Charlotte sighed inwardly. She'd so hoped her aunt would be willing to answer some of the questions that had troubled her for years. 'You know, my dear,' Euphemia had turned her attention back to Charlotte's appearance. 'You could be quite pretty if you had a new hairstyle, some fashionable clothes and, with a very discreet use of cosmetics—'

Now laughter bubbled up inside Charlotte. 'Cosmetics! Father would have a seizure at the mere thought.'

Euphemia's mouth tightened. 'Mm,' was all she said.

'So, you will accept Mr Thornton's invitation?'

'Just try and keep us away!'

Osbert was incensed when he heard. 'What on earth is the man thinking of? Inviting those two. You should have put a stop to it, girl. How did he know anything about them?'

Charlotte answered him calmly. 'I mentioned their arrival to him and he said he'd like to invite them.'

'You'd no right to mention private matters to strangers.'

Greatly daring, Charlotte snapped back, 'They're hardly strangers now, since you intend to leave Buckthorn Farm to Philip.'

He glared at her. 'Well, you'd better undo your meddling, miss. I won't have them anywhere near me.' His eyes narrowed. 'Have you seen them again? Answer me.' His tone was a whip crack.

Charlotte lifted her chin with a defiance she'd never realized she possessed. 'Yes, I went to the White Swan.'

He took a step towards her. 'You deliberately disobeyed me, girl. I won't have it.' He was shouting now, enough to bring Edward to the other side of the door, bending so that he could listen, and poised to enter if the row got any uglier than it already was.

'You keep away from them, do you hear me? I don't know what my sister's been telling you, but you're not to believe a word of it. It's all lies to discredit me. She wants to get her hands on my farm. Well, she won't. Not now. Not ever. And nor will you. And the sooner they go back abroad, the better. Out of my way.'

'They're not going abroad again. They're going to settle in England now.'

'Well, they needn't think they're going to stay around here. I won't have it.'

For the first time in her life, Charlotte retorted, 'I don't think you'll have any say in the matter.'

Osbert stepped close and, for a moment, Charlotte thought he was about to strike her. Instead, he shook his fist in her face. 'Don't you back-answer me, girl, else you, for one, won't be going to any dinner party. Or staying in this house for much longer. I'll throw you out, without a penny to your name or clothes on your back. You hear me?'

Charlotte turned away and headed for the sanctuary of the farm office. Her father's threats no longer frightened her. She'd heard them all before. He wouldn't throw her out. Not yet. He needed her to run the farm. But she did believe that he intended to leave Buckthorn Farm to Philip Thornton. Oh yes, that she did believe.

She sighed as she sat down at her desk and tried to concentrate on the paperwork in front of her. Joe would be calling in soon and she was anxious to know how the family fared.

But Joe didn't come and by mid-morning, Charlotte was worried. Perhaps he, too, had flu now. She went down to the kitchen. 'Edward, I'm very concerned about the Warrens. Joe hasn't arrived and he always comes in on Monday and Thursday mornings, as you know. I don't want to go down to the cottage again myself, however; it might look as if I'm – well, implying he shouldn't be off work. D'you think you could go there or maybe find John and ask him? If they've all fallen victim to the influenza, we must do something to help.'

'Of course, Miss Charlotte. I'll go at once.'

Edward was gone a long time and he returned with bad news. 'You were right, miss. Joe's got it now, and John too. Lily's looking after them all, but she looks very peaky. She's sickening for it an' all, I reckon.'

'We must call the doctor.'

'I've already done that, miss. That's why I've been a long time getting back. I went into Ravensfleet and left a message for Dr Markham to call to see them all. I thought it'd be what you'd want.'

'Shall I pack another basket of food, miss? Edward can take it down.'

'I think you'd better make it a hamper, Mary,' Charlotte said wryly. 'Poor Lily won't have much time for cooking and baking with all of them ill. And I'd better see if Matty's managed all the milking.'

Mary nodded and bustled into her pantry. 'Soup,' she murmured. 'That's what they all need. Nourishing soup. That'll not cause Lily too much trouble just to heat it up.'

Later in the day, Edward brought more news. The doctor had called and pronounced Jackson and Peggy 'on the mend'. They'd soon be up and about again. Joe and John were still in bed.

'And Lily?' Charlotte asked. 'Is she coping?' She saw Edward and Mary exchange a glance.

'She'll be all right, miss,' Mary said, but Charlotte had the strange feeling that she was not just referring to caring for the rest of the family.

Charlotte frowned but asked no more questions. 'Let me know if there's anything else we can do. Anything they need.'

'We will, miss.'

Twenty-Seven

'I've a good mind not to go. And I certainly shouldn't be letting you go. You're not used to civilized company,' Osbert grumbled as he and Charlotte climbed into the motor car that Miles Thornton had sent to fetch them on New Year's Eve. 'And where are your glasses? You should be wearing your glasses. You're as blind as a bat without them.'

Charlotte said nothing. She'd known her father would not stay away from the dinner party – not when Philip was home from school. And he couldn't leave her at the farm; Miles had been adamant that his invitation included her. As for the remark about her spectacles, she chose to ignore that.

Euphemia and Percy were already there when Charlotte and her father arrived.

'Dear me,' Euphemia murmured in her ear as she kissed Charlotte's cheek. 'I really must take you in hand, child. That dress is like something out of the ragbag.'

Far from being insulted, Charlotte felt an overwhelming desire to giggle. It was a perfect description for her shabby, purple dress. Euphemia was dressed in a lovely silk, low-waisted pale-blue dress and dainty high-heeled satin shoes.

'Miss Charlotte, Miss Charlotte . . .' Georgie was at her side, taking her hand and dragging her across the room. 'Come and meet Uncle Felix. He's a friend of

Papa's. They were in the war together. He's an artist.
He painted the portraits of Mama.'

'I'd love to, Georgie dear, but first I must give Ben
his birthday present.'

'Ooh, what have you got for him? Ben – Ben, come
here. Charlotte's brought you a present.'

Shyly, Ben unwrapped the leather hunting whip with
a staghorn handle and silver collar. 'It's wonderful,' he
stammered, taken aback by her generous gift. 'Thank
you.'

'You're most welcome.' Charlotte smiled. 'I know
you will use it properly.'

There was the merest accent on the word 'you', but
Ben met her steady gaze and, understanding, nodded.
'I will, Miss Charlotte, I promise you.'

Georgie was tugging at her hand. '*Now* come and
meet Uncle Felix.'

The man held out his right hand, but Charlotte
noticed, with a shock, that the sleeve of his left arm was
empty and tucked into the pocket of his jacket.

'Felix Kerr.' The man smiled at her.

'Charlotte Crawford,' she murmured.

He was small and thin, but his bearing was upright,
his back straight. He had a small, goatee beard, once
brown but now liberally flecked with grey. His hair was
thinning a little, but his dark eyes looked boldly into
hers as if he would read her very soul.

With a jolt, Charlotte realized. 'Felix Kerr. Not *the*
Felix Kerr?'

The man laughed.

'I'm so sorry.' She blushed, feeling foolish. 'You must
get inane remarks like that all the time.' Perhaps her
father was right; she wasn't used to polite society. She
shouldn't have come. She'd be embarrassing Miles and

216

she'd no wish to do that. She tried desperately to repair the damage. 'I've read about your work, but I'm sorry, I've never been able to see any of it – except, of course, the portraits of Mrs Thornton.'

But his eyes were twinkling with amusement. 'Don't apologize. Of course, the last portrait I did of dear Louisa – the one with her two children that we'll see in a moment in the dining room – was done at the beginning of the war just before I volunteered.' He sighed. 'My style has changed a little since.'

'Oh? Why?' The direct question was out before she thought to stop it, and once more she found herself apologizing.

But Felix was happy to explain. 'Not because of my injury. Luckily, I'm right-handed. It would have been devastating if I'd lost my right arm, I don't mind admitting. But no, it's because of what I went through – what all of us went through.'

Charlotte glanced across the room towards Miles. 'Mr Thornton too? Was he wounded?'

'Twice, I think, but fortunately not seriously, though the last injury ended the war early for him. I had to wait until the very last month of the war, would you believe, before I got myself a Blighty wound. Still, we should be grateful. We're both still here. So many of our fellow soldiers aren't.'

'It was a dreadful time,' Charlotte murmured. 'The papers were full of casualty lists every day and almost every family had someone involved. And waiting for the dreaded telegram . . .'

'I know. And then the influenza that swept the country at the end of 'eighteen. I lost my wife and child in that epidemic.'

'I'm sorry.'

He shrugged and sighed. 'I wasn't the only one who'd lost loved ones. All those mothers and wives losing their men in the war. And Miles, too, losing poor Louisa in childbirth.'

'What – what was she like?'

'Louisa? A lady in the very best sense of the word. Beautiful, charming, but with a deliciously wicked sense of humour. I can see a lot of her in Georgie. He's a charmer, isn't he, but in a nice way?'

Charlotte laughed. 'He most certainly is. He's adorable.'

She saw Felix glance down at her left hand. 'You're not married, Charlotte?' She was startled, but pleasantly surprised, at the use of her Christian name after such a short acquaintance, but perhaps, she thought, that's how things were done in the artistic world. She felt a sudden pang of longing; not, for once, to be married, but to be part of the exciting world of artists.

'No – no, I'm not.' She was stuck now for a topic of conversation and suddenly felt her inadequacy in socializing. But, like the perfect host, Miles arrived at her shoulder. 'I'm so glad you and Felix are getting to know one another. I've heard a whisper that you are an artist too, Miss Charlotte.'

Now Charlotte blushed. 'No – oh no,' she protested. 'Please – I don't deserve such a title.'

Miles chuckled. 'That's not what I've heard. You're being modest.'

'No, no, really I'm not. I love drawing and painting – that's true. But I've no talent. It's just a hobby.' She glanced across at her father as she added, 'A *secret* hobby.'

'A secret?' Felix was scandalized. 'You should never keep a talent hidden, my dear. You should be proud of it.' He linked his arm through hers as dinner was announced and the guests moved through to the dining room. 'Now, I shall insist I see your work. *I* will tell you – truthfully – if you have any talent.'

Charlotte smiled, but said no more as Georgie appeared at her other side and took her hand. 'You're sitting by me, Miss Charlotte. I arranged all the places especially.'

'I see you have an admirer, my dear,' Felix whispered. 'But I do hope I'm placed on your other side.'

Indeed he was, and by the end of the evening, Charlotte could not remember ever having enjoyed herself so much. She'd even managed to ignore her father's glowering looks from the other end of the table. She'd been monopolized by Felix and Georgie, so there'd been only a brief exchange of words between herself and Cuthbert Iveson. And she had the feeling that he was avoiding being seen talking to her. Besides, at the dinner table it was Euphemia who held sway, regaling them all with tales from their days of living abroad. As for Osbert, his attention was taken up by Philip sitting opposite him.

Miles sat at the head of the table, surveying his guests and making sure they were looked after and entertained. He watched Charlotte and Felix talking and was fascinated by how the girl's face came alive as she talked and listened to Felix. But she was attentive to Georgie, too, turning every so often to make sure he was not left out.

She's a kindly soul, he thought, who deserves a better life than the one she's got.

As the party broke up at about eleven, Felix squeezed her hand. 'I don't know when I last enjoyed myself so much.'

219

'Nor me,' Charlotte said with guileless honesty.

'And you must let me see your work. I'm staying the weekend with Miles. Perhaps you could come over tomorrow and bring some of your drawings and paintings. I—'

'What's that?' Her father was at her side. He had his hat and coat on and was carrying his walking stick.

'I was just asking your daughter—'

'Oh please,' Charlotte whispered, suddenly frantic. 'Don't—'

'You're the artist fellow, aren't you?' Without waiting for a response, Osbert turned on Charlotte. 'What have you been saying? Making a fool of yourself again, I don't doubt.'

He grasped her arm and began to pull her towards the door. 'Get yourself home. You're a disgrace. I wish you'd never been born. I'd rather be childless than saddled with you.'

The other guests stood rooted to the spot, shocked to the core by the vicious words spilling from his mouth. Miles stepped forward, but Osbert was already pushing her down the steps and into the waiting motor car. Though Miles hurried after them, Osbert slammed the door and the vehicle moved off before he could reach it. He returned to his other guests, still standing where he'd left them.

Euphemia found her voice at last. 'I see my dear brother hasn't changed in all these years. That poor girl.'

It was a sentiment echoed by all of them, except one. Philip Thornton turned away with a smirk on his face.

*

When they arrived back at Buckthorn Farm, Osbert hustled her into the house through the door Edward was holding open.

'Stay here,' Osbert commanded. 'Morgan – see that she does, else it'll be the worse for you.'

White-faced, Charlotte watched her father mount the stairs.

'What's wrong? What's happened?' Edward whispered urgently as soon as Osbert was out of earshot.

'There was an artist there. Felix Kerr. And Miles – Mr Thornton' – she had begun to think of him as 'Miles' in her head – 'told him that – that I painted.'

'Oh dear!' Edward murmured.

'Yes,' Charlotte said flatly. 'Oh dear.'

Osbert had reached the top of the stairs, had turned to the left and disappeared. They both heard the door of Charlotte's room being flung open, crashing back against the wardrobe that stood behind it. Then the sound of crashing, things being swept off a table, pots and paints scattered and, finally, whilst Charlotte closed her eyes and cringed, the sound of tearing paper.

'Come on, love.' Edward put his arm about her shoulders. 'Let's go to the kitchen.'

Dumbly, she allowed him to lead her, stumbling, through the door and into the warm, comforting kitchen. She was shaking. Mary, knitting by the range, let her work fall to the floor as she got up. Her worried eyes went to her husband.

'It's him,' Edward said shortly. 'He's upstairs in her room, destroying everything, by the sounds of it.'

'Destroying?'

'Her paintings. Just because some chap at the dinner party – an artist – took an interest.'

'In her,' Mary asked shrewdly, 'or in her paintings?'

'Both, I expect.'

'Come on, lovey. Sit down. I'll make us some cocoa. Edward can go up in a bit and see if the coast's clear.'

Mary was pouring hot milk into a mug, when they all heard footsteps in the passage and the door was flung open. Osbert came in, brandishing his stick. Bravely, Edward leapt up and stood in front of Charlotte.

'Out of my way, man. This is between me and my hussy of a – *daughter*.' He spat out the last word with venom.

He raised his stick, but Edward stood firm. 'You'll not hit her again. Not ever, not whilst I'm in this house.'

'Then you can pack your bags and go. The pair of you. You and your good-for-nothing wife.'

'Gladly, but if we do,' Edward said with surprising calm, 'Miss Charlotte goes with us. We'll not leave her here to your tender mercies,' he added with sarcasm.

'And where d'you think you'll go, eh? The work-house – the three of you.'

'Mebbe that'd be preferable to staying here. Aye, I reckon it would, an' all. But dun't you forget, *sir*,' Edward grabbed the stick and twisted it out of Osbert's hand, 'that me an' my missis know a few secrets, now, don't we? We've only stayed here all these years and kept silent for *her* sake. Not yourn. Never yourn.'

'You wouldn't.' Osbert's voice was a whisper now – a menacing, terrifying whisper. 'You wouldn't dare!'

'Oh we would. Believe me, we would. Because she's old enough now to know the truth. And now that Miss Charlotte's aunt has come back, well, she's someone of her own flesh and blood to turn to, hasn't she?'

'My sister will keep her nose out of my affairs, if she knows what's good for her.'

'I doubt you have any hold over her now – that is, if you ever had.'

'Oh, I had. I still have, because I doubt she's ever told that milksop of a husband of hers the truth about herself. She was a whore, that's what my dear sister was. Still is, by the look of the way she dresses. I won't have her corrupting *her*.' He stabbed his finger towards Charlotte. Irrationally, at such a moment of drama, Charlotte realized that she couldn't remember when her father had ever called her by her name. She had always been 'girl', 'her', 'she' or even, on occasions, 'it'.

Seeing that he was not going to get beyond the stronger, fitter Edward, Osbert turned away. 'Go on, then. Get out. Do your worst. See if I care. There's plenty more to take your place. And you can take her with you – and welcome. I never wanted her in the first place.'

As the door swung to behind him, the three in the kitchen were left staring at it.

Twenty-Eight

The following morning Charlotte rose with bleary eyes and a heavy heart. Whilst she'd never been really overwhelmingly happy, she'd never been sad. She'd never realized that her life should, and could, be very different. But now the misery lay like a heavy weight on her chest.

I'll go and see Jackson, she thought. Maybe he's well enough to talk to me. But it was Peggy who opened the door of their cottage and when Charlotte saw her face, her own worries were forgotten.

'Whatever's the matter, Peggy?'

The woman's face was pale and drawn – no doubt from the illness. But the anguish it showed could have nothing to do with a bout of influenza. For a moment Peggy stared at her, almost as if she didn't recognize her. The older woman was locked in some private grief that obliterated everything else.

'Is it Joe?'

Mutely, Peggy shook her head.

'One of the others, then? Are they worse? Have you called the doctor again? You must—'

'No, miss.' Peggy's voice was husky with weariness following a sleepless night. Her eyes were dark hollows and her mouth quivered. She was close to tears. 'Please, miss. I can't say. Just leave us.'

'No, I won't. There's something obviously very wrong. And I want to help.'

'You can't help. Nobody can.' Peggy's voice was flat, drained of emotion. For some reason her world was in tatters.

'Don't shut me out, Peggy.' Charlotte touched her hand. 'You're like my family. You, Joe, the boys – ' She forced a smile, trying to cheer Peggy somehow. 'Even that little rapscallion, Tommy. And Lily, too.'

At the mention of her daughter's name, Peggy's mouth trembled. Tears welled in her eyes and trickled down her cheeks. 'Oh, Miss Charlotte . . .' She covered her face with her hands and as Charlotte stepped forward to put her arms round her, Peggy wept against her shoulder.

'You can tell me,' Charlotte murmured against her ear. 'Whatever it is. You know it will go no further.'

Peggy sniffed, raised her head and scrubbed at her face with the corner of her apron. 'It'll get round eventually, miss. Bound to. You can't keep summat like this secret for long. Everyone'll know soon enough.'

'Then—?'

'But we're so ashamed, miss. We never thought summat like this'd happen to our little family. We've tried to bring the bairns up proper. To know right from wrong. But this – it's destroying my Joe. Lily was the apple of his eye and now she's brought shame on all the family.'

Realization began to dawn in Charlotte's mind. 'She's – she's not – ?'

Peggy nodded. 'She's got 'ersen into trouble.'

'Who's the – the father?'

'She won't say. We thought it might be Eddie Norton. You know, the stable lad at the manor. Seems he's always been sweet on our Lily. But Jackson went to see him. Gave him a bit of a leathering, I reckon, but the lad still denied it. When they'd both calmed down, Jackson says Eddie was genuinely shocked.'

'She really won't tell you? But – but surely – I mean, perhaps they could get married.'

'She's shut up like a clam and barricaded herself in her bedroom. Well, I say *her* bedroom. It's Tommy's room now, 'cept when she comes home for a night or two. Then he moves in with the boys. They've got Grandad's old room.' She sobbed afresh. 'All Joe can say is, "Thank God me poor ol' dad's not here to see this."'

Charlotte caught her breath. When Lily comes home, Peggy had said. Of course, the girl spent most of the time at the manor now as a live-in maid. A shudder ran through her as brief images flashed into her memory. Lily emerging from one of the outbuildings and Philip appearing moments later; Lily and Philip holding hands in the icy weather. Lily and Philip . . . Oh, surely not.

Charlotte hugged Peggy again, feeling tears stinging her own eyes too. Then she stood back and said briskly, 'Now, come along, let's see what we can do to sort this out. May I come in?'

'I don't know, miss, Joe won't—'

'Never mind Joe. I'll deal with him.'

With a sigh Peggy gave way. She was obviously troubled about her husband's reaction as she led Charlotte through the back scullery and into the kitchen, but Joe didn't even look up. He was sitting hunched in front of the range, as if the weight of the world rested on his shoulders. And, at this moment, Charlotte thought, no doubt it felt as if it did.

'Joe?' She sat down opposite him and reached across the hearth to touch his hand. 'Joe, don't be angry with Peggy. I want to help. What can I do?'

Slowly, he raised his head and stared at her for a

moment. In a low, defeated tone, he said, 'There's nowt can be done, Miss Charlotte. If she won't even tell us who the – the bastard is, who's—' For a brief moment he was roused out of lethargy by the anger surging through him.

Peggy stood between them, wringing her hands. 'She – we ought to tell them at the manor. She – won't be going back.'

'Leave it!' Joe snapped and then said more calmly, 'leave it for now. They'll think she's still looking after us. It can wait a day or two. Till I've got me head round it.' He paused and added heavily, 'If I ever do.' He covered his face with his hands. 'Oh Lily. My Lily. My little girl,' he moaned, his shoulders shaking, whilst Peggy looked helplessly at Charlotte.

Charlotte waited patiently, until Joe became calmer. 'Joe, I promise I won't do anything behind your back – without your permission, but I really believe I could help you. Will you trust me?'

Slowly, he raised his head. 'Miss Charlotte, I'd trust you wi' me life. I know you'd never knowingly do anything to hurt me and mine. But, I beg you, don't tell anyone. Not yet.'

Charlotte bit her lip. 'I understand how you feel, Joe, but I may not have much time.'

'I don't understand.'

Charlotte sighed. 'There's been trouble at home. My father's more or less told me to leave. Mary and Edward too. At the moment, I don't know if he was serious or whether it was just said in a fit of temper. All I know is my own future is uncertain.' She took a deep breath. 'It seems my father intends to leave all his worldly goods to someone else, leaving me penniless. Even I never thought his bitterness went quite so deep.'

She saw the glance that passed between husband and wife and a gasp of surprise escaped her lips. 'You – you *knew*?'

Joe looked guilty and Peggy wouldn't meet her eyes.

'I'm sorry, miss. Mr Thornton told us in confidence.'

'And did he tell you too,' Charlotte added bitterly, 'that my father tried to – to blackmail him into marrying me to ensure his son's future?'

Joe nodded and Charlotte felt the flush of embarrassed shame creep into her face. But then she sighed. It wasn't the fault of these good people. They'd been put in an invidious position. Again, she reached across and touched Joe's hand. 'It's all right. I understand and respect you keeping the man's confidence. But, Joe, I'm begging you to let me help you now. Lily's – condition – is bound to be obvious very soon. What difference would a few weeks make when we may be able to sort something out?'

Joe sighed and glanced up at his wife. Peggy gave a little nod.

'I suppose you're right, miss. Do whatever you think best. I know you'll have our best interests at heart. And Lily's.'

'You can be sure of that, Joe. Very sure.' There was a moment's silence before she asked gently, 'So, do you want to know what I intend to do?'

Joe shook his head. 'No, miss. I can't take any more. Not just now. Just – leave me be. Leave me be.' The last was said in a whisper as he buried his face in his hands again.

Twenty-Nine

It took all Charlotte's courage to saddle a horse and ride to the manor. Leaving her horse with the stable lad, she entered through the kitchen door. Mrs Beddows greeted her.

'Am I glad to see you, Miss Charlotte. D'you know when we can expect Lily back? We're run off our feet here. She's such a good little worker. I never realized just how much work that lass gets through until she's not here, if you know what I mean.'

Charlotte smiled weakly. 'It – it might be a little while yet, Mrs Beddows.'

The cook's face fell. 'I'm sorry to hear that. Mebbe I'd best get someone from the village in temporary, like. That's if the master doesn't mind.'

'Perhaps it would be best, Mrs Beddows.' She paused and then, trying to make her question sound casual, she asked, 'Is Mr Thornton in?'

'I think so. I'd get Lily to take you up if she was here, but—'

'Don't trouble, please. I can find my own way.'

'But Wilkins should announce you, miss.'

Charlotte hid her smile. Mrs Beddows liked things to be done properly. 'I'll see if I can find Wilkins,' she promised the cook.

But as she emerged from the door leading from the

kitchens into the main hall, Charlotte saw Miles running down the stairs, heading for his study.

Hearing the sound of the door, he turned.

'Charlotte,' he said in surprise. Irrationally, her heart lifted as she noticed he'd dropped the 'miss' when addressing her. But her pleasure was lost in an instant as she thought about the reason for her unannounced visit. 'Come in, come in. Shall we go into the morning room? I'll ring for coffee.'

'No, no, your study will be fine. I – I like your study.'

Miles laughed. 'So do I. It's my favourite room in the house.'

When they were comfortably seated and Wilkins had been summoned and instructed to bring coffee, Miles said, 'I'm so relieved to see you. I was so worried after last night. We all were. Georgie couldn't sleep. He came into my room twice in the night because he was so worried about you. Your aunt too – she said she'd be going to Buckthorn Farm first thing this morning. And Felix – he felt responsible. *Are* you all right?' he ended, concern etched on his face.

Charlotte took a deep breath. 'Well, there was some trouble at home. I'm not quite sure what will happen yet, but that's not what I've come to see you about.' She bit her lip.

Wilkins brought the coffee in and they were obliged to wait whilst he poured them both a cup. As the door closed behind him, Miles said gently, 'You can tell me anything, you know.'

'It's – very difficult. It's about Lily.'

'Has she caught the flu too?'

Charlotte shook her head. 'No – it's worse than that.'

There was a pause but now Miles asked no more questions.

'She – she's in trouble.'

Miles frowned for a moment and then understood. 'Lily? *Lily?* She's pregnant?'

Charlotte nodded miserably.

'Bless my soul. I can hardly believe it. Lily – of all people. She seemed such a good, sensible girl.'

'She is – usually.'

'Poor Joe – and Peggy. They must be devastated.'

'They are.'

'Is there anything I can do?'

'Yes. Help me find the father of her child.'

'I don't understand.'

'Lily is refusing to name him.'

He eyed her shrewdly. 'But you think you have an idea who it might be?'

Charlotte set her cup down. This was where it got very difficult.

'Had she any – ' she almost smiled at the use of the old-fashioned term, but it seemed to sum up the situation – 'any followers?'

'Not that I know of, but then, I'm afraid I don't know everything that goes on below stairs.' His face clouded for a moment as he murmured, 'Perhaps if Louisa was still here . . .'

'I understand,' Charlotte said gently. She paused a moment before adding, 'Would you give me your permission to talk to the staff? They might know something.'

Miles ran his hand across his face. 'Of course. Oh dear, I feel so responsible. She's been in my care, so to speak, and now – this.'

'It's not your fault. It happens. But I did think,' she added sadly, 'that Lily had more sense.'

'Do you think whoever is the father might marry her?'

Charlotte shrugged. 'That rather depends on who it is.' She avoided meeting his gaze. A suspicion had begun to grow and take root, but it was one which, until she knew more, she could not share with Miles. Especially not with Miles.

She finished her coffee, set the cup down and stood up. 'If you'll excuse me, the sooner I start, the sooner I can find out, and we might be able to – to arrange something.' She was praying silently that her misgivings were not true. What trouble it would cause if they were.

Miles rose too. He took her hands in his and looked down into her face. 'Promise me that you'll come to me if there's anything – anything at all – that I can do.'

Charlotte nodded, whilst hoping fervently that it had nothing at all to do with Miles Thornton and his family.

Moments later, she was back in the kitchen talking to Mrs Beddows and the kitchen maid – a young girl of fourteen from the village who lived in too. For the moment, Charlotte confided in the cook, keeping her voice low so that Jane should not hear.

'Mrs Beddows – I'm so sorry, but I don't think Lily will be coming back. She's – she's in trouble.'

The woman's mouth dropped open, not because she didn't understand at once what Charlotte meant, but because she was shocked to hear such a thing about the girl she liked so much. '*Lily* is?' Her surprise was as great as Miles's had been.

'Do you know if she'd been walking out with anyone?'

Mrs Beddows pursed her lips. 'I don't encourage it, Miss Charlotte. Oh, I know you can't stop it like you could in the old days, but – ' she sighed – 'look where it leads.'

Silently, Charlotte thought, Maybe it wouldn't have if you'd allowed her to meet her young man openly.

'It'll be that Eddie Norton,' Mrs Beddows said grimly, nodding her head as if agreeing with her own statement. 'He's always hanging about the kitchen when she's about. I've had to clear him off many a time.'

Charlotte sighed. 'Apparently not. Jackson's already spoken to him and he's denied it.'

'Well, he would, wouldn't he?' Mrs Beddows pursed her lips. 'That's what they all do. Have their fun and then leave the poor girl to cope. The silly, silly girl!'

'Is there anyone else who works here other than Eddie who—?'

But the cook was shaking her head. 'No, not that I can think of. No one of her own age, certainly.' Then she nodded towards the girl washing dishes at the deep sink in the scullery. 'You'd better talk to Jane. She sleeps in the same bedroom. Mebbe she knows summat.'

'Thank you, Mrs Beddows.' As she went towards the scullery, she heard the woman muttering beneath her breath. 'Wretched girl! Now I've got to train another one to my ways.'

'Jane?'

The girl, singing softly to herself as she worked, gave a startled cry and almost dropped the wet plate she was holding. 'Oh, miss, you gave me a fright.'

'I'm sorry. Could you spare me a moment?'

'Of course, miss.' The girl dried her hands on a rough piece of towelling.

'Lily's in trouble. You – you know what I mean, don't you?'

The girl's eyes widened. 'You mean she's going to have a bairn?'

233

Charlotte nodded. 'But she won't tell us who the father of her child is. And if we could find out, then maybe we could help her. Help them both.'

Jane was biting her lip anxiously and looking away. Quietly, Charlotte said gently, 'I think you know, don't you?'

'I – I daresunt tell, miss. She'd never forgive me.'

'Your loyalty does you credit, Jane, but we all need to be able to help Lily, and the only way we can do that is to find out whom she's been seeing.'

Now tears were running down the young girl's cheeks. She twisted her fingers together agitatedly.

'Is it one of the stable lads? Eddie – or someone else?'

Jane shook her head.

'One of the farm workers, then?'

Again, a shake of the head.

Charlotte took a deep breath and plunged in, forced into voicing her own fears. 'Is it – is it someone who lives here? In this house?'

'Please don't ask me,' Jane wailed.

Charlotte took hold of the girl's shoulders and shook her gently. 'You must tell me. Is it?'

The girl's tears flowed freely and she pressed her lips together as if to stop the words bursting out. She closed her eyes, trying to shut out Charlotte and her troublesome questions.

'Is it – Philip?'

Jane's eyes flew open, staring and frightened. Then, slowly, she nodded.

Thirty

Charlotte now believed she knew the truth. What she couldn't decide was how best to deal with it. She didn't feel able to tell Miles until she was absolutely sure; until Lily had admitted it. So, the only thing to do, she decided, was to confront the girl herself.

She remounted her horse and rode slowly back towards the Warrens' cottage. The family were seated much as she'd left them, except that John had now got up out of his sick bed and was sitting huddled in a blanket near the range. He still looked pale and ill. Joe was sitting just as Charlotte had last seen him, but Jackson was pacing the floor of the small room.

'Peggy, could I speak to Lily, please? Alone?'

'If you can make her open her door, miss. She's put summat against it and none of us can open it from this side. Not even Jackson, an' he's as strong as an ox. Usually. Reckon the flu's taken more out of us all than we realized. And now this.' Charlotte went up the dark, narrow staircase. How ironic, she thought, that only a few months ago she, too, had locked herself in her room and refused to come out. She sympathized with Lily; she knew just how she felt.

Only one bedroom door was closed. She knocked and called out softly, 'Lily, it's me – Charlotte. Please open the door. I need to talk to you. I want to help.'

Silence.

She tried again. 'Lily – ' Her voice was firmer now and she was aware that Jackson was listening at the bottom of the stairs. 'You've got to come out some time, so why not now? Let's talk about it and see what can be done.'

Still – silence.

Charlotte sighed. There was nothing else for it except to be cruel to be kind. 'Lily – I believe I know who the father of your baby is and if you don't come out, then I'm going to tell your family – and his father.'

There was a scrambling sound inside the room, the scraping of something heavy being pulled away from the door and then the door itself was flung open. Wild-eyed, her face swollen and ravaged by tears, Lily faced her. 'Don't you dare say anything, miss. It's nowt to do wi' you. Leave me alone. I'll sort it out mesen. I'll go away – '

'Now, now, don't be silly. There's no need for all this. Your family's shocked and hurt, but if I know them – and I think I do – they'll stand by you. *I'll* stand by you.' She wasn't sure how she was to do it when her own future was so precarious, but somehow she'd see the girl cared for.

Suddenly, the girl was crying heart-wrenching tears. She sobbed against Charlotte's shoulder. Charlotte put her arms round Lily and held her close. 'There, there,' she soothed. 'We'll see what's to be done. Come along downstairs now.'

She led the weeping girl to the head of the stairs to see both Peggy and Jackson staring up at them. Lily gave a sob and tried to flee back to the sanctuary of her bedroom, but Charlotte held her firm. 'It has to be faced, Lily.'

Downstairs in the crowded kitchen, the atmosphere was tense. Even Tommy, the only one to escape the influenza, had come indoors from playing outside and was staring wide-eyed at his sister, not understanding what was happening.

'Tommy, love, go out and play, there's a good lad,' Peggy said.

'But, Mam—' he began to protest but seeing the look on his mother's face, his father hunched by the fire and Jackson looking like thunder, the boy went meekly, even closing the back door quietly behind him.

Lily flew into her mother's arms. 'Oh, Mam, I'm so sorry. I thought he really loved me. He said he knew how to – to be careful. He *promised* me . . .'

Seeing her genuine distress, the tension in the room eased. The Warren family came together in their love for this daughter, this sister, who'd been so hurt.

'Who is it, Lil?' Jackson demanded. 'Just tell us who it is? I'll bloody kill him.'

'Aye, well,' Peggy said, holding her daughter close. 'You're not the first lass to be taken in by promises, an' I don't expect you'll be the last.'

'Come here, love,' Joe said huskily, standing up and holding out his arms. 'Come to your ol' dad.'

As Lily went into his embrace, Charlotte couldn't help feeling tears prickle her eyes. How wonderful to have a father who loved his daughter enough to forgive her anything.

'Don't worry, Lily.' John spoke up too. 'If he can't or won't marry you, we'll take care of you and your bairn. Fancy,' he smiled round at the rest of the family, trying to lighten the tension even further, 'our Tommy is going to be an uncle. Whatever will he say?'

'Sit down, lass,' Joe urged at last. He pushed her gently into the chair and sat down opposite her, taking her hands in his. 'Now, you've got to tell us who it is.'

'I can't, Dad.'

'Why not, lass? Whoever he is, he ought to know.'

'Is he married?' Jackson asked bluntly.

Lily's head shot up. 'No – no. I'd never . . .' She began to deny it hotly, then subsided into fresh tears.

'Then tell us.'

Lily glanced at Charlotte, who asked, 'You want me to tell them?'

The girl bit her lip but nodded.

'Of course, if I'm wrong—'

'I'll say if you are, miss. I won't let someone else take the blame, I promise you that.'

All eyes turned upon Charlotte now, Lily's almost imploring her to be wrong, so that she could deny it. How desperately she wanted to keep her secret.

'I've seen you with him twice,' Charlotte said quietly. 'Once coming from one of the outbuildings at the back of the manor. The other time was in the icy weather on Christmas Eve. He was holding your hand, saying he was helping you . . .'

Lily gasped, her eyes wide, her hand flying to cover her open mouth and everyone in the room knew that Charlotte was right.

'It *is* Eddie Norton! The little liar,' Jackson shouted, thumping his fist into the palm of his other hand.

'No, Jackson,' Charlotte said softly. 'It isn't Eddie, though—' She stopped herself mid-sentence. She'd been going to say that if the father of Lily's baby had been Eddie, then she'd no doubt the lad would marry her willingly. Charlotte pulled in a deep breath before she said, 'It's Philip, isn't it, Lily? Philip Thornton.'

There was a stunned silence in the room, but seeing Lily hang her head and make no denial, they all knew it was the truth.

'Philip Thornton!' Joe was incredulous. 'But – but he's only a boy. He's – he's still at school, for heaven's sake.'

'Huh!' Jackson spat through gritted teeth. 'Not such a *boy*.'

Lily clutched at her father. 'Please, Dad, don't make trouble for him. I'm as much to blame. I – I love him and he loves me. I'm sure he does.'

'Aw, lass,' Joe said heavily. 'But he'll never marry you. Not the likes of him with – with *us*.'

Now Peggy turned to Charlotte. 'Thank you for your help, miss. We appreciate it. At least we know the truth now. We know what we've got to deal with.'

Already Peggy was stronger. The whole family was rallying round, taking strength from their love for each other and determining to protect Lily. They'd be all right now, Charlotte was sure.

'If there's anything I can do to help, you let me know.' She looked straight at Joe. 'Promise me?'

Joe nodded. 'Aye, an' thank you again, miss.'

She left the cottage and walked her horse back up the lane towards Buckthorn Farm. They'd be all right. They'd come through this trouble, she knew. They'd pull together as a family.

As she neared her home, she lifted her head and let her glance roam over the house, the buildings and the surrounding fields.

But what about her? What was to become of her?

The only two people in the world who had any affection for her were no blood relation: Mary and Edward. And by nightfall, if her father had meant what he'd said, they could all find themselves homeless.

She smiled wryly to herself. Never mind trying to help others in trouble – who was going to help her?

Thirty-One

Charlotte entered the farmhouse by the back door to find the kitchen alive with chatter. Euphemia and Percy were sitting in the Windsor chairs on either side of the range whilst Mary was busy making tea and handing round her home-made biscuits. Edward stood to one side, listening as Euphemia held court.

As Charlotte opened the door, they all looked up.

Euphemia flung her arms wide. 'My dear child, we were so worried about you after last night. We just had to come and see if you're all right. Come here and kiss your old aunt.'

Charlotte was enfolded in a perfumed embrace. 'Now, sit down, dear girl. Your uncle and I want to talk to you.'

Edward placed a chair for Charlotte to sit beside her aunt, who didn't let go of the young woman's hand.

'We've seen your father – briefly – but he's made it quite clear we're not wanted in this house, but' – she glanced up – 'we found a welcome with Mary and Edward. From what I can glean, it's these two good people who've been the mainstays in your life. Am I right?'

'You are, Aunt,' Charlotte said huskily, realizing just how very much she owed these loyal people. She couldn't and wouldn't call them servants. They were more than that. So much more.

'Well, now,' Euphemia went on, patting Charlotte's hand. 'We've come to ask you to come and live with us when we find a place and get settled. We're hoping to buy a house somewhere near Lincoln.' She looked up at the couple standing nearby, a question in her eyes. 'I don't know, though, what Mary and Edward want to do. I mean, we'll be needing a cook, so . . .'

Edward was shaking his head. ''Tis very kind of you, ma'am, but as long as Miss Charlotte's settled and cared for, then maybe it's time me an' Mary thought about retiring.' He smiled ruefully. 'We're not getting any younger, as the saying goes.'

There was silence as they all looked towards Charlotte. It was for her to make the momentous decision. She took a deep breath. 'Aunt Euphemia – Uncle Percy. I am touched by your kindness. Really I am. We've only just met and yet here you are offering me a home.' Tears filled her eyes. She'd rarely known such thoughtfulness. And from comparative strangers, too, even though they were blood relatives. She bit her lip, not quite knowing how to phrase her next words. 'At the moment, everything here is in turmoil. I really don't know what's going to happen. If my father didn't really mean what he said yesterday, then I must stay here and – and run the farm.'

'Run the farm?' Euphemia almost squeaked. '*You* run the farm?'

Charlotte lowered her gaze. It had been kept a secret for so many years that she found it hard even now to break her silence. But Edward had no such qualms – not now.

'Miss Charlotte has run things since she was about eighteen. When she was growing up, she helped around the farm all the time. The labourers and their families have been her friends, ma'am. As she got older, your brother passed more and more responsibility on to her shoulders. "You see to it, girl," he'd say, waving his hand and disappearing into the sitting room. D'you know, ma'am, except for church on a Sunday, he's spent the last few years shut away in that room. I mean, if he'd been off out to the city or going to shooting parties or to market, like he used to, I could've understood it. But no, he's done nothing 'cept sit in that room ever since – ' he paused abruptly, cleared his throat and then went on, 'well, for years. He's had no life, ma'am, and, if you'll excuse me saying so, he's made sure his daughter hasn't had either.'

'Yes,' Euphemia said slowly. 'I can see that.' She turned back to Charlotte. 'But you still feel – duty-bound, I suppose – to stay here?'

Charlotte sighed. 'At least until things sort themselves out a little. Then I'll know. But I must see that Mary and Edward are all right.' She held out her hand and reached for Mary. 'But for them' – her voice was husky with emotion – 'I don't know what would have happened to me.'

'Oh, Miss Charlotte,' Mary wept.

'I do understand,' Euphemia said. 'We just want you to know that you'll always have a place to come to if ever you should need it.'

'Thank you, Aunt.'

'And now, I'll brave the lion in his den one last time. I still don't like being at loggerheads with my brother, but there you are. There's nothing more I can do. I've tried.'

In the sitting room Osbert was as truculent and determined as ever. 'I don't want to see you again, Euphemia. You're nothing to me. And if you think

242

you've a right to the farm when I'm gone, then you can think again. I shall be making a will that cannot be broken. Philip Thornton will get everything.'

Euphemia, for once in her life lost for words, turned away and, with her husband, stalked from the house.

In the farmhouse kitchen, Charlotte, Mary and Edward sat around the table.

'There's something you'll have to know,' Charlotte began. 'I don't usually break confidences, but I know I can trust you both.' Quickly, she told them of the misfortune that had befallen the Warren family. To her surprise, they both took the news calmly and philosophically.

'We knew summat was wrong, but not what.' Mary sighed and shrugged. 'It happens, Miss Charlotte. I could tell you about one or two folks round here whose marriages were hastily arranged and then their bairns appeared less than six or seven months afterwards.' She smiled. 'But I won't.'

'The Warrens took it hard at first, but I think they're coming to terms with it now. They'll all stand by her.'

'Of course they will,' Mary said firmly. She wouldn't have expected anything less.

The two young men, crouching in the long grass near a copse to the south of Ravensfleet, watched as the rider on horseback approached.

'Is it him?' John whispered. 'We don't want to get the wrong one.'

'I don't much care as long as 'tis a Thornton,' Jackson muttered.

243

'It could be the master. Philip's horse is that big black one that Miss Charlotte brought home to break in. That's a grey.'

Jackson squinted through the grass. 'Aye, but it's him right, enough. It's Philip.'

'Are you sure he ain't gone back to school? All the kids round here have gone back.'

'Nah – his fancy school don't start back till next week. It's him, right enough. Look sharp – he's coming this way.'

'I'm not sure we ought to be doing this,' John murmured.

'He needs teaching a lesson. He's brought our sister down. He's going to pay.'

As the horse neared the shadow of the trees, its pace slowed. The brothers stretched a rope across the pathway – and waited.

Thirty-Two

In the afternoon, Charlotte went into Ravensfleet to do some shopping. Walking across the market place, she heard shouting coming from the direction of the school.

It was 'home time' and the cries of joy as the children were let out for the day always made her smile. But then her smile faded. The cries she was hearing today were not the joyful sounds of laughter she'd expected. She glanced down the side road leading out of the market place where the school was situated. A group of boys – and even a few girls – were standing in a circle on the pathway and spilling out on to the road. They were shouting and yelling encouragement to two boys fighting in the centre of the ring.

Charlotte hurried towards the mêlée, glancing around for a teacher who might put a stop to the trouble. But there was no one.

'Never someone in authority when you want them,' she muttered to herself and quickened her step. Placing her shopping basket on the ground, she waded in amongst the crowd of children.

'Stop it! Stop it at once,' she shouted. As she pushed her way through, she saw to her horror that the two boys fighting were Tommy Warren and Georgie Thornton. 'Not you two again,' she said, grasping them strongly, one in each hand. 'Stop it – the pair of you.' As she pulled the two boys apart, they stood glaring at

245

each other, gasping for breath. Georgie had a bleeding nose and Tommy's eye was beginning to swell alarmingly. His lip was cut and bleeding too.

Still holding them, Charlotte turned back to the other children. 'Away home with you. The fight's over.'

'No, it ain't, miss. Not till I've knocked 'im flat.'

'Tommy! I thought you two were friends now.'

'Friends?' the boy spat. 'After what his precious brother's done to me sister?'

Charlotte gasped. 'Tommy! How – how d'you know about such things?'

'I heard,' the young boy muttered.

'And what good do you think fighting with little Georgie is going to do, eh?' She bent closer. 'Tommy, I shouldn't think he even understands what it's all about.'

'He does now.' With a sudden twist, Tommy pulled himself free of her grasp and, before she could stop him, landed another vicious punch to Georgie's tender chin. Then he turned and began to run, shouting as a parting shot, 'You wait, Georgie Thornton. I'll get you. You won't allus be able to hide behind Miss Charlotte's skirt.'

When Charlotte looked down at him, she saw that Georgie was crying, but she had the feeling that his tears were not so much for his injuries as for the broken friendship.

She bent down in front of him and gathered him into her arms. 'Don't cry, darling. Please don't cry. It's not your fault. Tommy is upset about something and he's taken it out on you, I'm afraid.'

'I – I don't know what he meant, Miss Charlotte. What has Philip done to Lily? Has he hurt her? I thought he liked her. They're always laughing and talking. I've seen them.'

Charlotte straightened up and took his hand. She picked up her basket and began to lead him back towards the market place where she'd tethered the pony and trap. 'Come, you shall ride home with me.'

'But what's Philip done?' the boy persisted.

'It's not for me to explain, Georgie. You must ask your father.'

And now, she realized, as she helped the boy into the back of the pony and trap and prepared to take him home, she would have to be the one to break the news to Miles.

She pulled up in front of the manor and helped Georgie down, leading him by the hand up the front steps. She rang the bell. Miles himself flung the door open. He stared at them for a moment as if it didn't register who they were. But as he glanced down and saw the battered face of his son, he sighed heavily and pulled the door open wider. 'Now what?' he muttered, but he seemed preoccupied, almost irritated that there was yet another problem to deal with.

As she and Georgie stepped into the hall, Charlotte's heart missed a beat. He must know, she thought. His distracted air was shock.

'Take him through to Mrs Beddows. She'll clean him up.'

'I'll see to him,' Charlotte said softly. 'Come along, Georgie.' But as she tried to lead him away, Georgie looked up and asked, 'Papa, what has Philip done to Lily?'

Charlotte saw Miles blink and stare at his young son. 'What? What are you talking about, Georgie?'

'Tommy said Philip had hurt Lily.' He wiped the back of his hand across his nose and blood smeared his sleeve. 'He hit me, Papa.' Fresh tears welled in his eyes.

'He says he's not my friend any more because Philip's hurt Lily.'

'Come along, Georgie,' Charlotte urged, pushing him gently towards the door leading to the kitchen. 'You can talk to your papa when we've got something on those cuts and bruises.'

'But—'

'Come along,' she said firmly and, at last, he allowed her to lead him away. But with every step, Charlotte was aware of Miles watching them with a worried frown on his face.

Half an hour later, Charlotte prescribed a mug of hot milk and rest on the nursery couch.

'But I want to talk to Papa,' the little boy insisted, though his eyes were drooping. The long school day and then the distressing fight had taken its toll even on the stalwart Georgie.

'Can Jane take him up and stay with him, Mrs Beddows? I must speak to Mr Thornton.'

'She can, miss, but I don't think the master'll want to be bothered about a playground fight just at the moment. He's worried out of his mind.'

'So he does know?'

The cook stared at her. 'Know what, miss?'

Charlotte blinked. 'Er – I just thought – er – ' She took a deep breath and asked, 'What is he worried about?'

'Master Philip. He's missing. Been gone since early morning when he went out riding.'

'Oh no!' Charlotte breathed, and she turned and hurried back towards Miles's study. She found him pacing the floor.

'Mrs Beddows has just told me that Philip's not come home since early morning. Have you got people out looking for him?'

'I sent two of my men out a couple of hours ago, but there's been no word. I'm about to ring the police.'

'Give me half an hour, Miles. I'll be back . . .' Once more she turned and ran out of the room, out of the house, climbed into her pony and trap, and drove off at speed. It wasn't until she was halfway down the long lane that she realized she'd addressed the man to his face by his Christian name – the name she always used in her own thoughts.

Charlotte banged on the door of the Warrens' cottage and then, without waiting for it to be answered, opened it and went in.

The family was in the kitchen. Peggy was bending over Tommy, tending to his black eye. They all looked round, startled, as she entered like a whirlwind. Charlotte's glance sought Jackson.

'Where is he? What have you done to him?'

Jackson refused to meet her gaze but she saw the glance that passed between him and John. She took a step closer. 'Jackson – Mr Thornton is about to call the police. If you value your freedom you'll tell me now what you've done. Where is Philip?'

'Philip?' Lily cried before anyone else could answer. 'What about Philip?' Her wild glance went to her brothers. 'Have you hurt him? If you have, I'll never forgive you. Never!'

Joe and Peggy looked anxious but mystified. Joe had had no part in whatever had happened, Charlotte could see that.

'Come on, you'll have to tell me. He's not been home since he went out early this morning. Mr Thornton has sent two men out, but he's about to take matters further.'

Again the brothers exchanged a mutinous glance, but it was John who said, 'We – we brought his horse down and then—'

'We gave him a bloody good hiding,' Jackson spat out. 'One he won't forget in a hurry.'

Charlotte turned from them. She'd have more to say to the pair of them later, but for now she must find Philip.

'Where is he? Where did you leave him?'

Reluctantly, Jackson muttered the answer. 'The copse south of the town.'

Charlotte turned to their father. 'Joe – you'd better come back with me.'

'But he ain't well enough yet—' Peggy began.

'He'll have to be. And as for you two – ' she nodded towards the brothers, 'if you're fit enough to give a boy a hiding, you're fit enough to be back at your work. I'll expect you first thing in the morning. In fact, you can go and do the evening milking right now. It looks like I'm going to be too busy.'

With that she stalked out of the house, Joe following reluctantly in her wake.

Thirty-Three

Back at Buckthorn Farm, they saddled two horses and rode towards the town, then veered to the left. Neither spoke, each busy with their own thoughts and trying to keep an overwhelming fear in check.

They found him lying motionless in the long grass at the edge of the copse as if he'd been thrown there and callously abandoned.

'My God!' Joe breathed, as they both dismounted and ran towards him. 'What have they done to him?'

'He's alive,' Charlotte said, feeling for the boy's pulse. She took off her coat and laid it over Philip. 'You'll have to fetch something to carry him home on, and a farm cart. If he's been thrown from his horse and then set upon, there's no knowing what injuries he's suffered. Go to the manor, Joe, it's nearer.'

'Can't we—?'

'No,' she said firmly. 'We might cause more damage.' Beneath her breath she added, 'If that's possible.'

They both glanced across at Philip's horse. It was writhing in agony, trying to stand and falling again.

'Bring Eddie back with you and tell him to bring a gun. That poor creature's not going to make it.' She forbore to add the word 'either'.

*

It took a while, longer than the half-hour she'd promised Miles, but at least Philip had been found and carried home and upstairs into his own bed. His father had not called the police. At least, not yet.

Now it was the doctor they called.

Whilst they waited, Miles said, 'If – if he lives, it will be thanks to you, Charlotte.' His glance rested upon her as he added quietly, 'But you seem to know what's happened. Will you tell me?'

'Of course. When the doctor's been, I'll tell you everything.'

'He'll have to go into hospital for observation. None of his limbs are broken, but he's concussed and I'm worried about his spine. I can't tell if there's damage there.'

'My God,' Miles muttered, running his hand through his hair.

Within an hour, Philip was on his way to the cottage hospital in Lynthorpe. When Miles returned from accompanying his son and seeing him admitted, Charlotte was still waiting anxiously.

'I need a drink,' Miles said, leading the way back to his study. 'And I don't mean coffee. Brandy, Charlotte?'

'I don't usually, but on this occasion,' she muttered grimly, knowing the task that lay before her, 'I need it too.'

They sat down and sipped the liquor but Charlotte knew he was anxious to hear what she had to say.

'I'm so sorry to have to tell you this, but you have to know. I – I should have told you before, but' – she sighed, wishing she'd not delayed even the few days – 'Miles – Philip is the father of Lily's child.'

He sat forward in his chair, his hand shaking so suddenly he almost spilt what was still in the glass he held. 'Philip!' he said hoarsely. 'My son – my seventeen-year-old son has – has seduced a girl who was living in my house – under my *protection*?' He groaned, closed his eyes and fell back in the chair. The glass slipped from his hand and fell to the floor, spilling the brandy on to the carpet.

Charlotte bent and picked up the glass, mopping the spillage with her handkerchief. She glanced up at him anxiously, fearing she was going to have to send for the doctor yet again. He sat slumped in the chair with his hand covering his eyes. She poured another brandy and took it to him.

'Here – drink this.'

He pulled himself up like a man rousing himself from a nightmare. He took the glass, but his hand was still shaking. Charlotte remained standing close by. At last, he took in a deep, calming breath. 'Thank you,' he murmured.

She moved across the hearth and sat down again. 'I'm sorry.'

Slowly, he raised his head to look at her. 'Sorry? What have you got to be sorry about, my dear?' He smiled wryly. 'I'm not one to blame the bearer of bad news.' He sighed, groaned and swept his hand across his forehead again. 'What a mess!'

'Joe and Peggy were very shocked, of course, but they're standing by her.'

'They know about Philip?'

Charlotte nodded and bit her lip. 'Yes,' she admitted huskily, 'and I'm afraid that's my fault. At first she refused to name the father, but of course her family wanted to know. They thought there might be a chance of whoever it was marrying her. But they realize that's impossible now.'

Miles's head shot up. 'Why? Why do they think that's impossible?'

'Well – they wouldn't expect – I mean—'

Bitterly, he said, 'They wouldn't expect the squire's son to marry the maid he's seduced, eh? Well, that's not what happens in my family. At least – ' he closed his eyes and groaned again. 'At least, I didn't think it was.'

'I have to tell you that Jackson and John went out looking for him. They brought him down off his horse and attacked him.'

For a long moment, Miles stared at her, a blank, unreadable expression on his face. Then, to her surprise, he muttered, 'It's no more than he deserves. If it'd been *my* daughter – if I'd been blessed with a daughter – ' His voice broke with such an unexpected depth of longing, almost loss, that Charlotte was shocked. 'I would have done exactly the same. I – I hope Philip's not permanently injured, of course I do. But I can't blame those lads, even though I know I should.'

'You really are a most extraordinary man.' She'd spoken the words aloud without meaning to, but now it was said, she went on, 'You're so kind and considerate of others' feelings. And *very* understanding.'

'I must go and see the Warrens at once,' he said.

'Do you want me to come with you?'

He shook his head. 'No. I must face the music myself.'

Charlotte smiled sadly. 'I think they'll be thinking they've "music to face" now too. But just one thing, Miles.' The name came naturally from her lips. She didn't even stop to think about it now. 'Just remember it's not *all* Philip's fault. It takes two, because I am sure of one thing. Philip didn't force himself upon her. She was a willing – a willing – ' She couldn't think of an appropriate word, but Miles understood and nodded.

'And you,' he said huskily, 'are very generous to be so fair-minded. My eldest son hasn't exactly treated you with the courtesy and respect you deserve.'

'He's young.'

Miles's face clouded again. 'But not too young to sire a child, it seems.'

Charlotte returned to Buckthorn Farm to face her own particular music, whilst Miles saddled Midnight himself and rode over to the Warrens' cottage.

Joe, grey-faced, opened the door and held it silently for the man to enter. Miles removed his hat and bent his head as he passed through the door. As he went into the kitchen, he saw that the whole family were gathered there, even Lily, almost as if they were waiting for him. Young Tommy was standing in the corner, his eyes fearful.

Miles glanced round at them all and then spread his hands. 'I don't know what to say to you. I'm so very sorry.'

He saw glances pass between them. Surprise, shock and the beginning of relief. Joe spoke first. 'We expected the constable, sir.'

'The constable? Whatever for?'

Joe gestured towards his sons. 'We knew Miss Charlotte would tell you. Oh, she had to – don't get me wrong. But we thought – when you found out what my – my boys had done . . . Is he badly hurt, sir?'

'He's in hospital and his back may be damaged. I don't know yet.'

Lily let out a wail and buried her head against her mother's shoulder, sobbing and distraught.

'He shouldn't have brought our Lily down,' Jackson burst out. 'We didn't mean to injure him, sir. Not like that, not permanent like, but . . .'

'I know,' Miles said gently. 'Like I said to Miss Charlotte, in your place I'd've done the same. Maybe not brought him off his horse, perhaps, but I'd have given him a good thrashing. In fact,' he added grimly, 'if he wasn't lying in a hospital bed right now, I probably still would.'

'So – you're not bringing charges against them?' Joe still couldn't quite believe what he was hearing.

Miles shook his head and his glance went to Lily. 'No – it's Lily and her child we must think of now.'

Joe stuck out his hand awkwardly. 'You're very generous-spirited, sir. The lads shouldn't have done what they did, but I'm sorry to say I can understand *why* they did it. And they've lost you a valuable horse an' all.'

Miles shrugged. He was a kind man and the harm that had befallen the animal distressed him, but the welfare of his son was what mattered most.

Solemnly, he took Joe's outstretched hand. 'There is just one more thing . . .' As he released Joe's hand, his eyes sought Tommy, skulking in the corner. The young boy had been listening to every word, yet taking no part. Miles crooked his forefinger, beckoning the boy towards him. Tommy came, dragging his feet and hanging his head.

Miles put his hand gently on the boy's shoulder. 'It's all right. I'm not angry with you, but I just want your promise that you will not fight little Georgie again. At least, not over Lily. He's too young to understand what it was about and he's in tears at home – not because of his bloodied nose and black eye –' Miles heard Peggy's gasp, but he carried on, saying gently – 'but because you've fallen out with him. What's happened is not Georgie's fault. And he shouldn't have to bear any retaliation. Do you see that, Tommy?'

The boy nodded. 'I'm sorry, sir. It was just – it was just –'

Miles squeezed his shoulder. 'I know, I know. And sticking up for your sister does you credit. But—'

'What happened?' Joe interrupted sternly.

Tears streamed down the boy's face now. 'I'm sorry, Dad. I – I thumped Georgie because I heard you saying Philip had hurt our Lily.'

'Oh Tommy,' Peggy cried. 'You shouldn't have done that. Poor little boy. It's not *his* fault.'

'Miss Charlotte saw us and stopped us. She – she took Georgie home.'

Joe's face paled. He glanced round his family. 'Miss Charlotte knows it all. Everything you've done.' There was a veiled threat in his tone. His sons, all three of them, had brought more trouble on the family than Lily had caused. She might have brought shame upon them, but her trouble would not see them dismissed and turned out of their home. But the action of his sons might well do so when Osbert Crawford got to hear about all this. Even Charlotte would not be able to save them then.

Miles cleared his throat.

'I'll talk to Philip. We must arrange a marriage as soon as we can.'

Now the whole family was dumbstruck. They'd not expected this. Even Lily's sobs subsided and she looked up at him, her eyes swimming in tears.

257

'Marriage?' Peggy said. 'You – you'd *want* them to get married?'

'I presume they must love each other, else – ' He waved his hand unable to find the words, though everyone knew what he meant.

'Oh we do, we do,' Lily burst out and, wrenching herself from her mother's arms, she went to Miles and caught hold of his arms. 'I do love him, sir, with all my heart and – and he loves me. I know he does.'

Miles put his arms round her. 'There, there, Lily. Don't cry, my dear. We'll sort it all out. Your parents and I. Everything will be all right, I promise.'

'Where's Warren? And those idle sons of his? They're not at their work.'

When Charlotte stepped back in through the front door of Buckthorn Farm, she was startled to find her father standing in the middle of the hall, thumping his stick on the floor. 'I want to see him. Good for nothing layabout.'

She sighed. Today of all days he would have to decide to take a sudden interest in the workings of the farm again.

'Joe and his sons have all had the influenza. The boys have done the evening milking and they'll all be back at work full time tomorrow.'

Osbert scowled at her. 'Mind they are. And you can stop their wages for the days they didn't work.'

Charlotte didn't reply. She'd no intention of doing any such thing. But he'd never know that. One thing he never did now was look at the paperwork in the farm office any more. That had become her domain.

He turned away, heading once more for his sanctum.

She watched him go, biting her lip. It seemed he'd forgotten all about ordering her and the Morgans to leave his house. Or, more likely, he'd chosen to forget it.

But what would happen, she wondered, when he learned the latest news of his protégé, Philip Thornton? What then?

Thirty-Four

It was four days before Osbert found out. Four days in which Charlotte had learned that Philip had been moved to a hospital in the Midlands for tests on his spine.

'He – can't feel anything,' Miles had told her distractedly when they'd met accidentally whilst riding on the beach. 'They think his spine might be broken.'

'Oh, dear Lord,' Charlotte had breathed. 'No!'

'And there's another thing,' he said, his eyes dark with anxiety and something that Charlotte couldn't quite define. Disappointment? Shame? At his next words, she understood.

'I've talked to Philip about Lily. But he flatly refuses to marry her. He says she was only a bit of fun to him. Nothing more. Charlotte, I'm so ashamed of my own son.'

'I'm sure the Warrens hadn't expected you to suggest such a thing. Servant girls don't expect their masters to marry them. I'm sorry to say it, but Lily, being four years older than Philip, should have known the score.'

Miles sighed. 'I don't blame the girl. My son' – a note of bitterness crept into his tone – 'can be very charming and very persuasive when he wants to be.'

Miles was right, Charlotte thought, the young man had certainly charmed her own father.

When she returned to Buckthorn Farm, an agitated Edward met her at the door.

'Your father wants to see you in the sitting room, miss. He's in a high old dudgeon.'

Charlotte pulled a face. 'Now what?'

'He's found out about Master Philip being injured. Evidently, the boy was due to visit here before returning to school tomorrow and when he didn't arrive, the master made enquiries.'

'Who told him?' Charlotte asked sharply. She knew it wouldn't have been Edward.

'I believe he sent a note to the manor and word came back saying the boy was in hospital. That sent him into a panic, I can tell you. He had the pony and trap harnessed and he rode over to the manor. Mr Thornton was out, it seems – '

Charlotte nodded.

'One of the servants – Wilkins, I believe – told your father that the Jackson brothers had set upon Master Philip and injured him so badly that he'd been taken to hospital.' He paused, then added, 'But from what I can make out, miss, the man didn't tell the master the reason behind the lads' attack.'

'No,' Charlotte said grimly. 'I don't suppose he did. And even if he had, I doubt my father would have believed it. Not about Philip.'

She took off her riding jacket and hat, smoothed her hair back, and went towards the sitting room. Edward hovered in the hallway, and Charlotte was glad to know he was close by.

'What's this I hear?' Osbert demanded almost before she had stepped into the room.

There was no point in prevaricating, so Charlotte said, 'Lily Warren is pregnant with Philip's child, that's what. And her brothers – well, they gave him a good hiding because of it. They didn't intend to cause such serious injury, but sadly, they have.'

Osbert stared at her. 'Don't talk ridiculous, girl. Philip's only a boy. No – no, I won't believe it. The little slut's laying it at his door to get money out of the family.'

'I've seen them together, Father, holding hands, and Philip had admitted it to his father. Mr Thornton is trying to persuade Philip to marry her, but he's refusing.'

'I should think so too. The very idea. My boy being forced to marry that little trollop.'

Charlotte stared at him. My boy, he'd said. My boy, as if he'd taken ownership of someone else's son. His disappointment and bitterness had coloured the whole of his life and now was turning his mind. Osbert thumped his stick on the floor, frowning angrily. 'The very idea,' he muttered again. And then he seemed lost in thought.

Quietly, Charlotte left the room.

'All right?' Edward whispered as she emerged.

She shrugged. 'I'm not sure, Edward. He refuses to believe that Philip is the father of Lily's child.' She smiled wryly as she added with heavy sarcasm, 'He can't believe such a thing of "his boy", as he called him.'

Edward made a noise in his throat that sounded suspiciously like a growl, before saying, 'Jackson's in the kitchen, miss, asking to see you.'

Charlotte sighed and followed him along the passageway.

Jackson was standing nervously by the table, turning his cap through agitated fingers. 'We're back at work, Miss Charlotte. All of us. That's if – that's if – you want us.'

'Of course I do, Jackson. This trouble has nothing to do with your work on Buckthorn Farm.'

Relief flooded across his face. He pulled on his cap, gave her a quick grin and almost ran from the house to prove his eagerness to resume his work. Charlotte watched him go, a heavy feeling in her heart.

She had no wish to dismiss any of the Warren family. But she wasn't so sure what was in her father's devious mind.

She didn't have long to wait to find out. The following morning, she rose to find that her father had already left to catch the train to the city where Philip was hospitalized. For the rest of the day, Charlotte was on edge and her anxiety was only lifted slightly by a letter addressed to her from her aunt:

> *We have found the loveliest little house near*
> *Lincoln, my dear. You must come and visit very*
> *soon. And don't forget, Charlotte, there is always*
> *a home with us should you ever need it.*

Now Charlotte did not feel so alone.

Her father returned late that night, tired but jubilant. Even as Edward helped him remove his coat, he was saying, 'He's standing firm. He's not going to agree to marry the little slut.' And then he added the words that Charlotte had been dreading. 'And as for those Warrens, they're to be dismissed and turned out of their cottage. Do you hear me, girl? They're to be given notice.' His pronouncement delivered, he glanced at Edward. 'You may serve my dinner now.'

Charlotte sat in the kitchen, her elbows resting on the table, her head in her hands.

263

'What am I to do, Mary? What *am* I to do?'

'Nothing – for the moment, love.' Mary placed her dinner in front of her. 'Now eat up.'

Charlotte pushed the plate away. 'I can't eat a thing.'

Edward and Mary sat down to their own meal.

'He'll not want to lose Joe Warren. Where would the farm be without him and his sons? That'd only leave old Matty and you'd be in a pretty pickle, miss.'

Charlotte sighed. 'He'll only say there's plenty of folks looking for work to take their place.'

'Aye, mebbe so, but not half as good.'

'But he'll do it. I know he will.'

Thirty-Five

For the first time in her life Charlotte stood up to her dictatorial father. She refused to issue the notices to the Warren family.

At church on the following Sunday morning, there was tension in the air. Everyone felt it. Miles and Ben were subdued. Even little Georgie's merry smile was gone. He walked down the aisle behind his father and brother without even glancing to left or right as he usually did, greeting everyone in his cheery, high-pitched voice. Instead, he ignored everyone and especially Tommy Warren. Only when he reached the front of the church and was about to step into his family's pew, did he glance up to his left and give Charlotte a watery smile. She smiled down at him and touched his shoulder.

Cuthbert Iveson seemed even more nervous than usual. When it came to the part in the service where he made special prayers for any parishioner who was ill, he said in a halting voice, 'We pray for the recovery of Philip Thornton and for his family in their time of trouble. And we ask you to forgive those who perpetrated the – the attack upon his person. Lead them to repentance, Lord . . .' Cuthbert mumbled on but his words were lost to Charlotte. She glanced up to see that Miles had raised his head and was staring angrily at the vicar. Then suddenly, he stood up. 'Come,' he said to his sons. 'We're leaving. This is a mockery.'

A shocked gasp rippled through the congregation as, prayers forgotten, they watched Miles lead his two sons out. The door banged behind them and, as Charlotte turned back to face the front, she saw Cuthbert glance down at her father. Osbert was smiling and nodding.

He'd arranged that, she thought. Not Miles. Miles wouldn't do something like that.

But her father would. And his reaction to the vicar's words proved it.

When the service ended, the members of the congregation trooped out, their faces solemn or puzzled. They stood in small groups, those who knew what had happened whispering the tale to those who did not.

Charlotte glanced around for Miles. He was pacing up and down the narrow path leading round the side of the church. Ben was standing close by amongst the gravestones, his hands pushed deep into his pockets. Georgie stood beside him, watching his father's agitated pacing with anxious eyes.

The Warren family, without Lily, stood together but a little apart from their neighbours and friends. No one, it seemed, knew quite how to deal with the news they were hearing. They didn't know what to say.

Charlotte plastered a smile on her face and walked across the long grass between the gravestones towards Peggy and her family. She stretched out her hands and took Peggy's.

'How are you? And how's Lily?'

'Oh you know, miss. Still crying. Still heartbroken. You know the young master has refused to marry her?'

Charlotte nodded.

Peggy went on in a flat, emotionless voice. 'We didn't expect it, but it was good of Mr Thornton to try. We – we appreciate that.'

'He's a good man,' Charlotte said softly. 'I'm sure—'

Charlotte was interrupted by her father's strident voice. 'Warren. You there, Warren.'

Charlotte turned to see him a few yards away, leaning on his stick and shouting so that all the world might hear. 'You're fired. The lot of you. And you're to leave the cottage at once, d'you hear me? At once. You'll be packed and gone by daybreak tomorrow.'

Charlotte turned and ran towards her father. 'No, Father, no. You can't do this. I won't let you.'

As she met his glare, she stopped, shocked by the vehement hatred in his eyes.

'You'll hold your tongue, girl, if you know what's good for you. Else you'll be gone an' all . . .' In a swift movement, he raised his stick and brought it down against her shoulder in a vicious blow. Charlotte reeled and fell to the ground. She heard everyone's cries of shock and alarm, but before anyone could reach her, Miles's strong arms were round her and he was lifting her up. Before he carried her away, he glanced just once at her father.

'You'll rue this day, Crawford. Mark you well. You'll rue this day.'

'You're coming home with us,' Miles said. 'And I won't hear any arguments. You're not staying with him a moment longer.'

Charlotte was too shocked to argue. She felt foolish, but her shoulder was hurting so much, and her legs felt so weak, that she had no choice but to allow him to carry her to his motor car and place her gently inside.

He straightened up and looked around for his sons.

'Ben,' he called. 'Come along. We're going home. Where's Georgie?'

Ben came running up. 'He's with the Warren family. I think he and Tommy are making up.' He climbed into the front seat. 'They're all smiles, anyway. He didn't see what happened. How are you, Miss Charlotte?'

She touched her shoulder and winced. 'I'll be all right, I think. I don't think it's broken.' She glanced out of the window to see Edward wrenching her father's stick out of his hand and flinging it as far away as he could. Then he grasped the older man by the arm and hustled him towards the pony and trap. She didn't think she had ever seen Edward look so angry or stand up so defiantly to his master.

'Now he'll sack Edward and Mary for real. It won't be just one of his threats this time.' She leaned her head back against the leather seat and closed her eyes. 'Oh dear!'

Georgie came running across the grass to the car. He made no attempt to get in but, instead, stood near the driver's door, his face upturned towards his father. 'Me 'n Tommy is friends again, Papa,' he said, the wide beam back on his face. 'Can I stay to Sunday school?'

'I don't think there'll be Sunday school today, Georgie. Come along, climb in.'

As he clambered in, he saw Charlotte. 'Oh! You're here! Are you coming to luncheon?'

'I—'

Ben turned round in the front seat. 'Didn't you see? Mr Crawford hit her and Father rescued her. We're taking her home with us, aren't we, Father?'

'Indeed we are, Ben.'

268

As Miles got out of the car again to crank the starting handle, Georgie slipped his hand into Charlotte's.

'Wilkins, show Miss Charlotte to one of the spare bedrooms. See she has everything she needs. Then I need to see you and Mrs Beddows in my study. Boys, amuse yourselves until luncheon.'

A short while later, a rather nervous Wilkins and Mrs Beddows tapped on the study door.

'Wilkins – Mrs Beddows – please sit down.'

The servants glanced anxiously at each other. They were not used to being treated with such courtesy by an employer. But then Mr Thornton had already proved himself to be an unusual master. They sat down nervously on the edge of their seats.

'There may have to be some changes here and I want to – well – consult and include you in any decision I make. But let me make it quite clear from the outset that, although it might affect you, your employment with me is quite safe and your home is here for as long as you want it. Now, I'm not sure yet what is going to happen, but it may mean that Miss Charlotte and Mr and Mrs Morgan, too, will be coming to live at the manor . . .'

For the next half an hour, the two servants listened in amazement, nodding their ready agreement when Miles finished by saying, 'Can I rely on you both to keep everything I've said confidential for the moment?'

'Most certainly, sir, and thank you for your trust in us. I think Mrs Beddows would join me in saying that.'

Mrs Beddows smiled and bobbed a curtsy. As they left the room, it was Miles who was left with a small smile on his face. What good people there were in these parts. At least, some of them were. His face sobered as his thoughts returned to all the problems that faced him.

There was a small tap at the door and Wilkins entered again with a letter on a silver tray. 'This was delivered by hand, sir, whilst you were at church. I do apologize for not handing it to you sooner.'

'No matter, Wilkins,' Miles said mildly. 'I don't expect it's anything important.'

But he was wrong. It was important. Very important. He sat for a long time in his study, the single sheet of paper in his hand, thinking. It didn't alter any of the plans he'd discussed with both Wilkins and Mrs Beddows. But there were things it could alter.

As he rose to go to the dining room for luncheon, he was smiling. Despite his concern for Philip, the unexpected letter had brought news that could make his other problems easier to resolve.

Perhaps, after all, there was some truth in Cuthbert Iveson's sermons. For, at this very moment, it seemed as if some, if not quite all, his prayers had been answered.

But for now he must make his unexpected guest feel welcome in his home.

That evening Miles rode over to the Warrens' cottage once more.

'I'm sorry to disturb your evening,' he began, but Joe held the door wide, inviting him in.

''Tis already disturbed, Mr Thornton. We're in the throes of packing up our belongings. Please excuse the chaos,' Joe said apologetically, adding, 'and don't mind the wife. She's been crying ever since we got home from church.'

'I do mind, Joe, I mind very much. About all of you.'

'Here's Mr Thornton, Peggy love. Boys, mek room for the master.'

Jackson leapt up at once and placed a chair near the fire.

'Please excuse me, Mr Thornton.' Peggy was still dabbing her eyes with the corner of her white apron. 'I must look a sight, but I just don't know where we're all goin' to go, and given a moment's notice like that. By daybreak, he said.'

'I know,' Miles said grimly. 'But I wouldn't take that too literally, if I were you. He can't turn you out physically.'

Joe and Peggy gaped at him. 'Can't he? I mean, won't he get the constable – the bailiffs – if we don't go?'

'I doubt it.'

Peggy sank into a chair. 'And then there's Miss Charlotte. I can't stop thinking about that poor girl.' Fresh tears welled in her eyes. 'How is she, Mr Thornton?'

'Well enough. The doctor's been this afternoon and there's nothing broken. She's just badly bruised and shocked.'

Joe snorted. 'Who wouldn't be? Her own father striking her like that. And it's not the first time, is it?'

'She's going to stay at the manor for a day or two until things calm down,' Miles told them. 'But she's insisting on going home. She says the farm won't run itself and she – ' he paused, his final words coming out on a sigh – 'she still feels she has a duty to her father.'

'I wouldn't go back, if I was her,' Jackson muttered.

'What about Edward and Mary?' Peggy asked.

'I'm going to see them when I leave here.'

'Edward and Mary'll look out for her.' Joe tried to soothe his wife's worries.

271

'They won't be able to stop him hitting her, though, will they?'

Joe was silent, unable to argue the facts.

'Maybe when things have settled down a bit, Miss Charlotte will get the old man to change his mind. I mean, about sacking us and turning us out,' John put in. 'It was all done and said in a fit of temper. You could see that. Let's face it, Jackson. It's because of you an' me. Because of what we did to Master Philip.'

Miles waited, looking round at their anxious faces.

'Well, I'm not bothered about me job,' Jackson muttered stubbornly. 'I can get work anywhere.'

'I don't know that you can,' John said. 'The state the country's in at the moment, jobs are going to be hard to come by.'

'Then I'll emigrate,' Jackson muttered, but this only brought a wail of desolation and fresh tears from his mother.

'But the real worry is Dad getting a job.' John was still the one speaking what was on all their minds. 'And somewhere for them to live with Tommy and Lily and her bairn. We'd be all right, Jackson. We can go anywhere, but what about them?'

Miles cleared his throat and, from his pocket, brought out the letter he had received that morning.

'Perhaps there is something I can do to help in that respect. I had notice this morning from Mr and Mrs Bailey, who – ' he smiled – 'as you probably know even better than I do, are my tenants in Purslane Farm, the other side of Ravensfleet.'

'Aye, we do, sir. Poor old Dan Bailey's not been well for some time and his farm – if you'll forgive me saying so – has not been run as well as it once was.'

Miles chuckled. 'If you say so, Joe, if you say so. But

here's the thing. Mr and Mrs Bailey are moving down south to live near their married daughter, it seems.'

'That'd be Elsie, their eldest. She married – oh, must be ten years back – and moved away,' Peggy put in, always ready with a bit of family history. She perked up a little now her thoughts had been distracted for the moment from their problems.

Mr Thornton fingered the letter, turning it round and round. 'The thing is, I'll be needing new tenants, won't I?' Joe stared at him and Miles returned his gaze steadily. 'I'm not sure what acreage it is, but is it big enough to support you and all your family, Joe?'

Joe stared at him open mouthed. 'You mean – you mean . . . ?' He was overcome and couldn't get the words out, but Jackson could.

'You're giving us first chance of the tenancy, Mr Thornton?'

'If you want it, yes.'

Jackson gave a whoop of delight, jumped to his feet and slapped first his father and then his brother on the back. 'Our own farm. Our very own farm.'

'Wait a bit, our Jackson. Just hold yar 'osses.' Joe faced Miles. 'Is this 'cos of our Lily?'

Miles nodded. 'Yes, Joe. I'll not deny that. I feel – very responsible. I'm ashamed to say that Philip is still refusing point-blank to marry Lily. But she is, after all, carrying my grandchild. But besides that, I like your whole family, Joe. You're good people. You don't deserve the way that bitter old man is treating you any more than his daughter does. I don't know if there's anything I can do to help her – not yet – but I *can* help you. And I want to – if you'll let me.' He held out his hand to Joe. Slowly, not quite knowing how this good fortune had befallen him, Joe took his hand and shook

273

it firmly. After all the heartache and tragedy of the past few days, Joe felt humbled by this man's goodness.

'We'll not let you down, master,' he said huskily. 'We'll mek a go of it and turn that farm around, back to what it used to be.'

'I've no doubt of that, Joe. No doubt at all. The only thing that does worry me is, what's going to happen to Buckthorn Farm?'

But to that, no one had an answer.

Thirty-Six

'I have to go back, Miles,' Charlotte insisted two days later. 'You've been so kind – incredibly kind. And your offer to take in not only me but also Edward and Mary is so, so generous. But my duty is at Buckthorn Farm. Now Joe and the boys are leaving, I must seek more workers. And Edward and Mary – I must find out what is happening to them.'

'They're fine,' Miles insisted. 'I saw them yesterday and their only concern is for you. Your father seems to have conveniently ignored Edward's actions. I expect it suits him to do so,' he added wryly.

Charlotte smiled weakly. 'Father can be very perverse.' She leaned forward across the breakfast table. 'I don't want to go. You – and the boys – have made me so welcome. Despite your worries over Philip, this is still a happy household. I've loved being here, playing with Georgie' – she put her head on one side and her eyes twinkled mischievously – 'and with the dolls' house.'

But Miles didn't smile. His expression was wistful. 'I bought that when my wife was expecting Georgie. We so longed for a daughter, you see.'

She shook her head. 'It's amazing,' she murmured.

'What is?'

'That you should have wanted a daughter so much, when my father . . .' She stopped, but there was no need for her to say more. She sighed. 'And talking of my father, I really must go home. You do see that, don't you, Miles?'

He sighed heavily. 'I suppose so, but I want you to promise me that you'll come back here at the very first sign of trouble.'

'I will. I can promise you that.'

'Very well, then. I'll drive you over this morning.'

'No need,' she said getting up from the table. 'The walk will do me good.'

He rose too and laughed wryly. 'There's just one thing – I think you're going to have a much harder job persuading Georgie to let you go.'

Laughing together, they left the breakfast room to go in search of the little boy.

Charlotte entered Buckthorn Farm by the front door. This is my home, she told herself. No skulking in by the back door any more. She went at once to the sitting room. Osbert looked up as she entered.

'Oh, it's you. Come to beg forgiveness, have you?'

'I most certainly have not,' Charlotte said quietly, but with a firmness that had never before been in her tone when addressing her father. Until this moment, she'd always felt downtrodden in his presence. But now she'd found a self-confidence she'd never thought she possessed or could possess.

'Where are your glasses, girl?'

'They're broken, Father.'

'Then you must get a new pair at once.'

'There's no need, Father. My eyesight is perfect.' Her mouth twitched with mischief as she added mildly, 'I don't know what optician it was who told you all those

276

years ago that I needed spectacles, but he certainly conned you into buying something I do not need.'

Her father glared at her, but said nothing.

'And as for the Warrens, Father, they will be staying for another month. I don't know if you know or not, but the Baileys are moving out of Purslane Farm and Mr Thornton has offered Joe the tenancy.'

Osbert's face turned purple and, for a moment, Charlotte thought she had gone too far. She took a step towards him. 'Father?'

'Get out,' he spat. 'Get out of my sight.'

Charlotte turned on her heel and left the room, heading towards the farm office. Her hands were trembling, but there was a small smile of triumph on her lips.

Today, she thought, my new life begins. From today, things are going to be very different around here.

After Sunday school the following week, Georgie slipped his hand into hers. His mouth quivered and his eyes were full of tears.

She squatted down so that her face was on a level with his. 'What is it, darling? What's the matter? Has Tommy been nasty to you again?'

The boy shook his head. 'No, no. It's just – we miss you. Won't you come and live with us?'

'Oh Georgie – '

'And Philip has come home.'

'But that's wonderful! How is he?'

'Horrible. He's in bed all the time. He can't walk and he's bad tempered. He shouts at everyone and throws things.'

'Oh dear.'

'Papa is so upset. He doesn't know what to do.'

'I'll come over this afternoon and see you all.'

Georgie nodded and allowed her to lead him to where Brewster was waiting to drive him home.

That afternoon, Charlotte found Miles sitting in one of the deep leather wing chairs beside the fire in his study. He looked tired and defeated. She sat down opposite him and poured the tea Wilkins brought into the room without being asked.

Miles had greeted her perfunctorily when she'd come in, but now he sat slumped in the chair, his long legs outstretched, his gaze on the flames in the fireplace almost as if he was unaware of her presence.

'Here,' she said gently. 'Drink this and tell me what's the matter. Is it Philip?'

With a deep sigh, he roused himself, took the cup she held out to him and stirred the liquid. 'Yes,' he said heavily.

'It's – it's bad news?'

'The doctors say,' he said slowly, 'there's nothing wrong with his back. Nothing's broken – badly bruised, of course – but not broken.'

'But that's wonderful news—' she began, then stopped. From the look on Miles's face, it didn't seem to be. 'Isn't it?'

'You'd think so, wouldn't you? But Philip says he can't move – can't feel his legs. He's not even trying. He's just lying there letting everyone wait on him. And his behaviour's – well, there's no other word for it – it's disgraceful. He shouts and screams at the servants. He throws anything he can lay his hands on. He threw his dinner last night at poor Lucy – that's the new girl

278

Mrs Beddows took on to replace Lily. She's from Ravensfleet. She's a good little thing, but I doubt she'll stay long if she's treated like that. And as for Georgie, he's in tears every time he comes out of Philip's room. Do you know what Philip said to him yesterday?'

Charlotte shook her head.

'He said, "It's your fault Mother died. She'd have looked after me. She'd have taken care of me, but she died because of you." It took me two hours to get the poor little chap to calm down and make him believe he was not to blame. And I'm not sure if I succeeded even then. He still seems – subdued.'

'He was tearful at Sunday school – that's why I'm here. He said Philip was home.' She omitted to tell him what else Georgie had said, but she felt that Miles probably guessed. 'Is there anything I can do?' she added.

'I don't know what anyone can do. I'm at my wit's end, Charlotte, I don't mind telling you. Ben seems to be the only one he'll tolerate.' He gave a wry laugh, 'Mind you, that's probably because Ben doesn't let Philip rile him.' He paused then added, 'I'm getting a second opinion. A doctor from London is coming on Wednesday. Perhaps we'll know more then.'

'Well, if there's anything I can do, let me know. And after Wednesday perhaps we'll have a better idea as to how to handle it. If he really has nothing physically wrong, then it sounds to me rather like a case of very bad temper.' She chuckled, trying to raise Miles's spirits. 'Rather like Midnight was when you first bought him. Bad tempered and stubborn.'

He gazed across the hearth at her as he murmured, 'Maybe you're right.'

*

When he heard that Philip was home, Osbert insisted that Edward harness the pony and trap and drive him to the manor. On arrival, Edward told Charlotte later, Osbert demanded to be allowed to see the boy. What passed behind the closed door, no one knew, only that Osbert emerged with a satisfied smirk on his face and – for a while – Philip was more amenable.

But that all changed once more after the visit of the specialist on the Wednesday. He was a bluff, no-nonsense man. He was clever and knowledgeable and Miles had no need to doubt his opinion.

'He confirms what the other doctors said,' he told Charlotte when he drove to Buckthorn Farm to see her. 'There's nothing physically wrong. It's more – now what was the word he used? – psychological. It's all in his mind. But he did ask me if there was anything troubling the boy. Was there any reason why staying put was more attractive than getting up?'

'Is he worried Jackson and John might attack him again? Is that it, d'you think?'

'Possibly.'

'Well, he can be reassured on that point.'

'Yes, but . . .'

'But – what?'

'Surely he doesn't think that's going to happen again. I would call the police then. I can forgive – and understand – the first time, but I wouldn't tolerate any more attacks.'

'It's not going to happen. The Warren family have every reason to be grateful to you for what you've tried to do to make amends.'

'Short of Philip marrying Lily, you mean?'

Charlotte regarded him with her head on one side. 'Are you still pressing him to "do the decent thing"?'

Miles sighed. 'It's not been mentioned since he was injured, but I think he still knows that's what I think he *should* do.'

'Then I think that's the problem. It may not even be a conscious thought, but if he lies there, a helpless cripple, he can't be made to walk up the aisle with a girl he doesn't want to marry.'

'Do you think so?'

'It's possible.' She paused then asked, 'Would you let me see him?'

'Of course, but I doubt he'll want to see you. And I wouldn't like him to be rude to you.'

Charlotte laughed. 'He won't be able to throw me out physically, will he? And if he did,' she chuckled again, 'problem solved.'

Miles spread his hands. 'You can but try.'

She stood up. 'And have I your permission to tell him he's not going to be forced into marriage?'

Miles sighed once more. 'Sick or well, he's never going to agree to it. I rather gather that's what your father was telling him when he visited the other day – that he had no need to marry the—' He glanced at her. 'Well, I won't use the words he did.'

'I can guess,' Charlotte said wryly. 'Did he tell you what had been said?'

Now Miles chuckled. 'No, but Georgie – the little imp – was listening at the keyhole.'

'Good for him!' Charlotte smiled delightedly.

'What do you want? Come to gloat, have you? Think Buckthorn Farm will be yours if I'm a cripple? Well, it won't. Your father has been here and he's promised he'll draw up a watertight will. There'll be nothing you can do.'

281

'I don't think I particularly want to. Not now.'

'What d'you mean, "Not now"? My father's not been stupid enough to propose to you, has he?'

Charlotte threw back her head and laughed. 'No. What I mean is I have plans.'

'Plans?' he sneered. 'What plans can you have? You've no money. Nowhere to go. And who in their right mind is ever going to marry a drab, plain creature like you?'

'Very true.' To his utter surprise, Charlotte agreed. 'But you're wrong about one thing. I do have somewhere to go. My aunt has offered me a home with her. And I may well take her up on it.'

'Typical. You'd sponge off relatives for the rest of your life. I expect you hope they'll leave you all their money now your father's cut you out of his will?'

'No. I shall train to be a teacher. Women can go to college now, get proper qualifications.'

Without thinking what he was doing, Philip pressed his fists into the bed to lever himself upright. Charlotte noticed, but made no comment. 'And who's going to look after Buckthorn Farm if you go?'

Charlotte shrugged and turned towards the door. 'Buckthorn Farm? Why should I care about Buckthorn Farm?'

'Because it's my inheritance, that's why.'

'Really? Then you'd better get out of that bed and start learning how to run a farm, hadn't you?'

As she reached for the doorknob, she saw, out of the corner of her eye, the teacup come sailing through the air towards her. She ducked just in time and it smashed against the door panel.

She wagged her forefinger at him as she opened the door to leave the room. 'Temper, temper!'

Thirty-Seven

'Did you tell him about Lily?'

'Not this time,' Charlotte told Miles. He was waiting for her in the hallway when she came down the stairs. She smiled. 'We got on to other things. He sat up to throw a cup at me, so that's a start.'

'Charlotte—' Miles began to apologize, but she held up her hand to stop him.

'It roused him – made him move. It's a good sign. He's still in a filthy temper. though. Anyway, I'll come again tomorrow.'

'Well,' Miles was still doubtful, but felt obliged to say, 'the specialist from London did say we're not to pamper him.'

'We won't do that, I promise you. He needs breaking in – just like Midnight. And, sometimes, you have to be cruel to be kind. You have to let them know just who's the boss.'

'I thought you trained your horses with gentleness and kindness?' He couldn't hide the surprise and the amusement in his voice.

'Sometimes. It depends on the nature of the animal you're dealing with. If it's a nervous creature, it needs soft handling, but a bad-tempered, brutish beast needs taming. Anyway, I must go. Joe's coming to see me this afternoon. He has someone in mind to take over as farm foreman when he leaves.'

'I'm sorry if my offering Joe the tenancy of Purslane Farm will cause you problems.'

'I shall miss them all, but I'm happy for them.' She looked at him, her violet eyes softening. 'I expect you're doing it for your future grandchild, aren't you?'

He nodded. 'That more than anything, I suppose. But Joe – and his sons – deserve a chance. Besides, they made it quite clear that if you were likely to leave, they didn't want to stay at Buckthorn Farm anyway.'

'Really?' Charlotte was startled.

He regarded her thoughtfully. 'You know, my dear, I don't think you know how loved you are by the people around here.'

At that Charlotte blushed and turned away. 'It's time I went,' she said over her shoulder but he heard the catch in her throat and knew his words had touched her.

As she walked home, Charlotte thought, *But there's only one person around here that I want to love me, Miles Thornton, really love me, but I don't suppose you ever will.*

Charlotte was quite happy to hire the new farm foreman and two young lads whom Joe had recommended to take the place of the departing Warrens. But before she made her final decision, she felt obliged to consult Miles once more.

Any excuse to see him, she castigated herself as she went again to the manor.

'It's Eddie Norton, Miles. Joe says he's the makings of a good foreman. He'll need some guidance for a while but Joe is sure he's the right one. But I'd be taking one of your best workers from here on Home Farm.'

Miles waved aside her doubts. 'No matter, Charlotte.

Like John Warren rightly said, there are a lot of young men looking for work in these difficult times. There'll be dozens after the vacancy here, I've no doubt. No, no, you take Eddie.'

Eddie Norton had worked on the Ravensfleet Estate since leaving school. And, better still, he was the son of Peggy's cousin. Charlotte felt she would still have a member of the Warren family on Buckthorn Farm. And she felt he deserved a piece of good luck after being suspected of bringing Lily down.

'You'll be wanting to move into their old cottage, I take it?'

The young man stood nervously in front of her desk in the farm office.

'Oh no, miss. I'll still live with me ma near Ravensfleet, if that's all right with you.'

'I'm surprised you're not married,' she said candidly. He was a good-looking young man and he'd already told her he was twenty-six years old. The same age as she was and just the right age to train up as a foreman, she'd thought.

At her question, Eddie's face fell. 'No, miss. I was walking out with a lass from Ravensfleet way but she caught the influenza, when it was so bad, miss, if you remember. Just at the end of the war. We was only eighteen, but we was both serious, if you get my meaning. We'd talked about marrying, but then she got ill and – and she died, miss.'

'I'm so sorry, Eddie. I wouldn't have asked you if . . .'

''S'all right, miss. I suppose one day I might meet someone else. Me mam's allus on at me to find a nice girl and get wed. I had thought that me and Lily might – ' He shrugged his strong shoulders and sighed, 'but you know all about that.'

'So, you won't be needing the Warrens' cottage, then?'

Eddie shook his head. 'Me mam's settled where she is. She moved in there as a young bride and she dun't want to leave all her memories. She – she still feels me dad's close.' He smiled, embarrassed. 'You know how some folks are, miss.'

'Of course,' Charlotte hastened to reassure him. 'I wouldn't dream of asking your mother to leave her home.'

'I'll mek sure it dun't interfere with me work here, miss. I mean, I know I won't be as close at hand as Joe's been, but—'

Charlotte raised her hand. 'It's not that. I just thought you might need a home of your own, that's all.'

At the end of the month the Warren family moved into Purslane Farm.

'It's the end of an era, Joe,' Charlotte said as she stood watching them load all their belongings on to the farm cart. There'd be one or two more trips before everything was moved.

'Eddie's here helping. His ma and Peggy have never been what you'd call close, but they're making up for lost time now. Edith and Eddie live just down the lane from Purslane Farm, so we'll be seeing more of them. It'll be nice for Peg. She's going to miss you – and Mary.'

'She's welcome here any time. She should know that.'

'She does, miss, but' – he puffed his chest out proudly – 'she'll not have much time, I'm thinking. She's a farmer's wife now.'

'She is, Joe, and you're a farmer.' She handed him the brown paper parcel she carried. 'And I've brought you a present to start you off.'

'That's very kind of you.'

Charlotte laughed. 'You might not think so when you see what it is. It's a set of ledgers to keep your accounts.'

Joe's face was a picture. 'Ah, but I'm not so good with the paperwork side of it, miss. I'm a hands-on type of a chap.'

'I know that, Joe, but I think your John is the ideal man to keep the books for you. And tell him not to be too proud to come and ask for a bit of help if he needs it.'

'I will, miss. And thank you.'

She stood watching as the cart swayed down the lane, Jackson driving with Lily sitting beside him. Walking behind and keeping an eye on the precariously balanced belongings were Joe, Peggy, John, young Tommy and Eddie. Charlotte felt a lump in her throat. She was so glad for them; they deserved this chance, but she was going to miss them dreadfully.

And there was someone else who was going to miss Peggy, too. Charlotte retraced her steps back to the kitchen of Buckthorn Farm. As she stepped through the door, she said, 'A cup of tea and a little chat, I think, Mary.'

With the departure of the Warren family and the removal of Lily from the immediate vicinity, Charlotte fully expected that Philip would make a miraculous recovery. Both she and his father had told him – more than once – that he was not going to be pressed into marrying the girl.

But still, he languished in bed, insisting that those louts had irreparably damaged his spine and that he'd never walk again. He'd not be able to return to school or go on to university as he'd hoped and his dreams of a career as a lawyer lay in tatters.

'Nonsense,' Charlotte had told him briskly. 'You could still be a lawyer from a wheelchair, if needs be.'

'Get out! I don't know why you keep visiting. Nobody wants you here, least of all me.'

Things might have continued thus if it hadn't been for another visit from Aunt Euphemia and her husband. She swept into Buckthorn Farm kitchen dressed in furs and in a cloud of expensive perfume.

'I want you to come on a little holiday with us, Charlotte dear,' Euphemia announced in a tone that brooked no argument. 'We're going to Derbyshire for a week at the end of February. Bakewell. It's a charming little place and so quiet at this time of year. You'll love it, I'm sure. Your father can manage without you for a week or two.'

Charlotte chewed her bottom lip thoughtfully.

'You go, miss,' Mary encouraged. 'You deserve it. You've never had the chance before. We'll look after your father and the farm'll be all right. Eddie can always go over and ask Joe if he's worried about anything.'

'D'you know, Mary,' Charlotte said slowly, her eyes sparkling with sudden excitement. 'I'll go.' She turned to her aunt. 'Thank you, Aunt Euphemia, I'd love to come. But – not a word to Father, mind, until everything is settled.'

Euphemia wriggled her plump shoulders. 'Oh, I do love a secret.'

Charlotte and Mary did not dare to catch each other's glance. They didn't think the loquacious Euphemia would be very good at keeping secrets.

*

Everything was ready; her suitcase packed with the meagre few pieces of clothing she possessed. Edward had the pony and trap waiting in the yard as Charlotte, in her best hat and coat, went into the sitting room to tell her father that she was going away for a week or so with his sister.

'You're what?'

For a moment, Charlotte felt a shaft of fear. Her father's face drained of its colour and then flushed a fiery red. His hands shook and when he tried to rise out of his chair, he fell back, panting. His eyes glazed over and Charlotte thought he was suffering a seizure.

'Father . . .' She stepped towards him, her hand outstretched.

'Get away,' he spat. 'You – you Jezebel! Leave me too, would you? Go, then, go and never come back. I never want to set eyes on you again.'

Seeing that he was not ill, Charlotte fled, but she was trembling and distressed when she returned to the kitchen. 'He – he was so angry, Mary. He said, "Leave me too, would you?" I don't know what he meant.'

She was so preoccupied that she didn't notice Mary turn pale and cast frightened eyes towards Edward, standing near the open door with Charlotte's suitcase in his hand.

But Charlotte, thinking aloud, answered her own question. 'I expect he meant the Warrens going. Perhaps he feels everyone's deserting him. But he dismissed them – he was going to turn them out. And who can blame them for taking the chance Mr Thornton offered? Anyone would have done the same, wouldn't they, Mary?'

Mary swallowed her panic and said shakily, 'Yes, of course, miss. That's what he does. He makes people leave. He—'

'Mary . . .' There was a warning note in Edward's voice, but Charlotte thought no more of it when he added, 'Tis time Miss Charlotte was leaving, if she's not to miss the train.'

Charlotte hugged her quickly and followed Edward out of the door. She was unaware of Mary, her hand to her throat and something akin to terror in her eyes, watching her go.

Thirty-Eight

'We shall have the most marvellous time and I have a lovely surprise for you when we get to Derbyshire,' Euphemia burbled, clapping her hands like a small child at the thought of a special treat.

'Now, now, Euphemia,' Percy said, smiling benignly. 'You promised.'

'I know I did, but I can hardly keep it to myself. But I must – I must. I mustn't spoil it. She'd be so cross with me if I did.'

'She?' Charlotte asked. 'Who, Aunt? Who are we going to meet?'

Euphemia pressed her lips together to stop the words escaping. 'My lips are sealed. In fact, I'll get Percy to put sticking plaster across them if I don't keep quiet.'

Charlotte laughed. She couldn't imagine what the great secret was or what wonderful surprise was in store for her. But she was content to wait. There were so many other things to interest and delight her.

For a start, her aunt insisted on a trip to Lincoln, where she swept her into one of the main department stores in the city. There she bought dresses, coats, hats, shoes and even two handbags.

'Now, you really should have your hair cut into an Eton crop. It's the very latest fashion for the young. And you have such a well-shaped head, it would suit you to perfection.'

But here Charlotte stood firm. 'Aunt, it's very kind of you, but I really don't want my hair cut short.' Not to seem ungrateful, she added, 'But what I would like is for a hairdresser to show me how to put my hair up into an elegant style.'

'If that's what you want, my dear, then that's what we'll do.'

The hairdresser was delighted. 'It's a while since I had the chance to put up long hair. And yours is lovely, Miss Crawford. You've kept it in wonderful condition. Now . . .'

For the next hour or so, Charlotte's hair was washed, trimmed and styled into the most elegant chignon she had ever seen and the hairdresser was kind enough to give her tips as to how she could achieve it for herself.

'My dear, you look wonderful,' Euphemia enthused.

'Whatever will Father say?' Charlotte murmured as she regarded her new self in the mirror. But Euphemia brushed her fears aside and led her eagerly to the next department. 'And now you must learn to use cosmetics. Discreetly, of course, my dear. Ah, now, here's the lovely April, who's going to show you what to do. April, this is my niece – the one I was telling you about.'

So, Charlotte thought, amused but not offended. This has all been planned.

When, at last, Charlotte emerged from the store, she didn't recognize the reflection of herself in the plate-glass window. The fashionable, pretty young woman, who stared back at her, was a stranger.

'My dear girl, you look adorable. Doesn't she, Percy?'

Her uncle nodded and smiled benignly. 'Adorable, my dear. Absolutely adorable. She'll have young men queueing at the door of Buckthorn Farm now.'

Charlotte laughed and pulled a face. 'I hope not.

Father would have a seizure.' Her expression sobered. She knew he was going to be very angry with her for what she'd already done. She had no wish to make her father ill, but at almost twenty-seven, it was high time she stood on her own two feet.

'And tonight we're staying in a hotel here in the city and going to the theatre,' Euphemia went on. 'Then tomorrow, we must go home and pack all these lovely new clothes for our trip to Derbyshire.'

'You have been so generous, Aunt, but I can't let you pay for all this. You must let me—'

Euphemia flapped her hands. 'Nonsense, my dear. Besides, if I'm not mistaken, it's your birthday next week, isn't it? Just call it an early birthday present. It's wonderful to have someone to spoil, isn't it, Percy?' Her face clouded as she added sorrowfully, 'We've never had the chance before, have we?'

Percy shook his head. 'Sadly, no, my dear. We were not blessed with children, you see. And my darling Euphemia would have loved a daughter to spoil.'

'A daughter? You'd've liked a daughter?' Charlotte couldn't keep the surprise from her tone.

'Most certainly,' Percy said.

'But – but wouldn't *you* have wanted a son?' she asked him.

He wrinkled his forehead as he considered the question. 'Not particularly. You know the old saying, "A son is a son till he takes him a wife; a daughter is a daughter all of her life."'

'I – I've never heard that.'

'Har-humph,' Percy said, stroking his moustache. 'Haven't you, my dear? But more to the point, neither has your father, I suspect. More's the pity.' He turned to his wife. 'And now, let's book into the hotel and then

I'll leave you two ladies to try on all these fripperies.'
But his eyes were twinkling as he said it. 'I shall go for
a walk up the hill to have a look at that magnificent
cathedral.'

Charlotte had never been to the theatre, had never seen
people acting out a story on stage. She'd read all her
life; it had always been one of her greatest pleasures to
lose herself in another world and escape from the loneliness of her own life shut away from all society at
Buckthorn Farm except for Mary and Edward. But now,
a whole new world was opening up to her. But with it
came the bitter knowledge of just how deep her father's
cruelty had been.

The following morning they returned home to pack
for their trip to Derbyshire, which began the following
day.

They stayed at a hotel in the centre of Bakewell.
Charlotte sat at the window of her room looking out on
the streets below. At this time of the year, the town was
quiet, but she imagined it would be a popular place for
visitors during the summer months.

At dinner that evening, Euphemia seemed unsettled.
But it was a kind of scarcely suppressed excitement. She
toyed with her food and kept glancing at the long-case
clock standing in the corner, solemnly ticking away the
hours. After a while her glances were directed towards
the door, as if she was expecting someone.

As they left the dining room, she linked her arm
through Charlotte's. 'My dear, do you remember that
when I proposed this visit to Derbyshire, I promised a
surprise for you? A nice surprise, of course.'

'I do, Aunt. But I thought that it was perhaps all the

beautiful clothes you've bought for me. I can't begin to thank you—'

'No, no, child, that wasn't it.' Euphemia chafed her bottom lip nervously.

'Then – what?' Charlotte asked.

'Let's go into the lounge and then I'll explain.'

There were one or two other guests there, but they found a quiet corner where they wouldn't be overheard. Percy hovered in the hallway, pretending, Charlotte was sure, to find a painting hanging there fascinating.

'Now, I must have your solemn promise that you will never, ever, tell your father.'

Charlotte stared at her. 'What about? The – the clothes, you mean?'

'No – no, not all that. That's not it at all.' Euphemia flapped her hands and glanced nervously at the door leading into the hall.

Charlotte followed her gaze and saw Percy greeting a woman who'd just come into the hotel by the main entrance. He was kissing her on both cheeks. A tall, dark-haired woman, dressed fashionably, with a lovely face and . . . As the woman turned and began to walk towards the lounge, Charlotte felt the room spin. She reached out and clutched at Euphemia for support.

No, no, it couldn't be . . .

But the woman was coming towards her, her arms outstretched, tears in her fine violet eyes. 'My darling girl . . .'

Charlotte stared at her, her head whirling and then everything went black.

Thirty-Nine

She thought she was in her own bed, at home at Buckthorn Farm, yet there were people bending over her, someone was cradling her head and trying to get her to drink something. She groaned and heard a strange voice say, 'She's coming round. Oh, thank goodness! We shouldn't have sprung such a surprise on her, Euphemia.'

'She'll be all right. She'll be fine and so happy to see you. She must have so longed all these years to find you.' Euphemia patted Charlotte's hand. 'Now, come along my dear.'

Charlotte opened her eyes and slowly pulled herself up. The stranger was still holding her, her arm about Charlotte's shoulders. Slowly, Charlotte turned to look into the woman's face and found it was like looking into an older version of her own. But this woman was beautiful; she was skilfully made up, wore lovely clothes, and had her hair professionally cut and styled.

'But – but you're dead!' Charlotte blurted out. She was still not thinking rationally. 'I must be dreaming.' She closed her eyes momentarily and then opened them again, but the woman – her mother – was still there, in the flesh, smiling at her.

'No, my love, I'm here. I'm really here.' Her eyes clouded with concern. 'Are you all right? I'm so sorry, we shouldn't have done that. Euphemia should have told you gently before I arrived.'

'You know me, Alice.' Euphemia flapped her hands. 'I would have blurted it out and it would have been just as much of a shock for the poor girl. I'm like a bull at a gate – Percy always says so.' She peered at Charlotte. 'The colour's coming back to her cheeks. She'll be all right in a moment.' She turned and summoned a hovering waiter. 'Another brandy, if you please?'

'No – no, Aunt, I'll be all right now.'

'Oh, it's not for you. It's for me!' Euphemia said comically and patted her chest dramatically.

Charlotte turned towards her mother. 'I – can't believe it. Is it really you? All these years, I thought you were dead.'

'Dead!' Euphemia and Alice spoke together and Percy, standing close by, frowned. Charlotte's earlier words had not registered with any of them.

'Your – your grave's in the churchyard at Ravensfleet. I put flowers on it every week. But father doesn't know,' she added swiftly.

'Well, I don't know whose grave you've been tending all these years, but it isn't mine, my darling.'

Slowly, Charlotte shook her head, completely mystified. 'I don't understand.'

Euphemia and Alice exchanged a glance. 'No,' the latter murmured. 'And neither do we.'

When Charlotte was feeling quite well again, though her mind was still reeling from the shock, they began to talk.

'What happened?' she asked. 'I want to know. Tell me everything. Right from the beginning.'

'The beginning? You mean, how I met your father and married him?'

'Yes, everything.'

Alice's eyes darkened as she was forced to relive her

memories, memories that perhaps she would rather forget. 'I – I don't know how much you know already.'

'I know nothing. My only memories of you are fleeting, just vague pictures and – and then the day of your funeral.' Charlotte shook her head in total bewilderment. 'I still can't believe all this. I mean – I know I was only five, but I watched the funeral procession leave the house – my father and all the men walking behind the horse-drawn hearse. I was watching from an upstairs window with Mary—'

'Mary,' Alice cried, 'is she still with you? She promised she would always take care of you. She and Edward – oh my dear, what is it?'

'Mary,' Charlotte whispered. 'Mary – and Edward? They *knew* that you were still alive?'

Alice took hold of her cold hands and held them tightly, chafing them to warm them. 'Darling, you must believe me, I know nothing of what happened after I left.'

'Left? You left Father and – and me?'

At this, Alice's face crumpled. 'My darling, you don't know how difficult it was. It was the hardest thing I've ever had to do in my whole life. To leave you – my precious daughter, but I—' She closed her eyes and swayed slightly. When she opened them again, they were brimming with tears.

'Your father,' Euphemia stepped in, 'my dear brother,' her tone was hard and bitter, suddenly totally unlike the gregarious, generous-spirited and jolly person Charlotte had come to know, 'was Cruelty personified. Alice had no choice but to leave him. He'd probably have killed her if she'd stayed.'

Charlotte drew in a sharp breath. 'He – he hit you?'

Alice bit her lip and nodded. 'Has he ever hit you?'

Charlotte nodded. 'A few times, but Mary or Edward stepped in whenever they could. When he got in a temper, I'd lock myself in my bedroom until he'd calmed down. I learned to see when one of his black moods was coming.' She didn't tell them about the recent whacks with his stick that, to her shame, everyone knew about.

Alice groaned. 'I'm so sorry. I never thought he'd beat you. I – I thought it was just me. Because – because I couldn't bear him a son.'

Charlotte smiled wryly. 'I expect it was because I'm the daughter he never wanted,' she said matter-of-factly without self-pity.

Alice was still shaking her head in disbelief, guilt etched on her face.

'But why?' Euphemia couldn't believe what she was hearing either, even though she thought she knew her brother better than anyone. 'Even I didn't think he'd stoop so low. I mean, how's he kept it secret all these years?'

'Easily,' Alice said flatly. 'When I left, he threatened me that if I ever tried to contact Charlotte he'd kill me. I was frightened enough of him by that time to believe him. And besides, I thought it was perhaps best for you, darling, if I went out of your life for good. I thought the dreadful rows would stop and that perhaps he'd be kind to you.'

Euphemia snorted but it was Charlotte who said thoughtfully, 'To be honest, until recently, I never questioned my life. There were times, of course, when I wondered why I was never allowed to have friends, never allowed to attend school. I had a governess until I was fifteen. The only people I knew were on the farm, but even then I was never allowed to mix socially with them.' She gave a wry laugh. 'I only attended my first harvest supper last year because – ' She paused. She couldn't explain all that now, so she ended with the words, 'And *that* caused a lot of trouble.'

Charlotte looked into her mother's troubled face and said softly, 'Don't look like that. I just want to know what happened. I'm not *blaming* you, I promise.'

'Perhaps you should,' Alice said quietly. 'I should have been braver, stood up for myself more, but his cruelty had worn me down. I'd had three miscarriages – all boys. And when I lost the last one, when you were two, it just seemed to tip him over the edge. The mental cruelty was worse – far worse – than the physical abuse. I stayed for three more years, but I could bear no more. I was ill and desperate, but I should have taken you with me. I see that now. I should have run away in the night without him knowing, but I always thought he'd hunt me down and snatch you back.'

'I'm sure he would have done,' Charlotte agreed. 'Not because he wanted me, but out of spite.' She paused then asked, 'So where did you go?'

Alice took a deep breath. 'Let me tell you it all from the beginning. I met your father Osbert through our fathers. We lived in Boston – my father was a potato merchant. He came into contact with the Crawford family through business and I suppose it was what you would call an arranged marriage. My father was very strict – a real Victorian father – and he chose Osbert for me.'

Euphemia snorted and said dryly, 'Just like my father tried to do for me, only it didn't work.' She reached out and took Percy's hand, glancing up at him. He smiled benignly and patted her hand. Then he sat down beside her, making himself comfortable.

'Osbert was charming when he was paying court to

me, generous and attentive. And – if I'm to be fair and I do want to be – in the first years of our marriage, everything was fine. But after the miscarriages, when I couldn't give him a boy, he changed. He blamed me and became obsessed with wanting a son.' Her voice quavered as she gripped Charlotte's hand tightly. 'He hardly took any notice of you. He resented you, I could see that. I suggested to him that he should divorce me and marry someone who could give him a son. I promised we – you and I – would live quietly and be no trouble to him. But he was vitriolic. "But you'll want keeping," he said. "You'll want my money. You'll drain all my future son's inheritance."' Tears ran down Alice's face and gently Charlotte wiped them away with her handkerchief.

'Don't cry, Mama.' The name she had called her mother in childhood came back to her and, hearing it, Alice cried all the more. She held out her arms and after so many years of separation mother and daughter hugged each other. After a few moments, Alice continued her tale.

'So – I thought that if I left him, he'd have grounds for divorce and he'd know that I'd make no demands on him, except that he should look after you. I always made sure his solicitor had my address, but no word ever came.' She looked questioningly at Charlotte, who shrugged and said, 'As far as I know, there's never been anyone else. For the first few years, he ran the farm but as soon as I was old enough, I had to work outside. Then as I got older, gradually he handed over more and more of the day-to-day running of the farm to me. Now I do everything.'

'You run the farm?' Alice was surprised but then, suddenly, she smiled. 'So, he's training you up to take it over one day. He does intend—' She stopped abruptly as she saw Charlotte shaking her head.

'Oh no, I'm not to inherit Buckthorn Farm. He's going to make a will and name Philip Thornton as his heir. He intends to leave me penniless.'

Forty

'Who is Philip Thornton?'

Swiftly, Charlotte explained.

'Your father intends to leave everything to complete strangers?' Percy asked. 'The man's lost his reason.'

'And all because I couldn't give him a son,' Alice said tremulously.

There was silence between them until Charlotte asked her mother, 'But where have you been all these years? Did you go home to your family? Your parents?'

Alice smiled wryly and shook her head. 'My father would have sent me back. No.' She glanced at Euphemia and Percy. 'Strange as it may seem, I went to my sister-in-law for help.'

'She's been with us ever since. She's been everywhere with us. My dear, dear friend and confidante all these years.' Euphemia smiled at Alice. 'Percy was very ill a few years ago and I don't think we'd have got through it without your mother's help.'

'Strange, isn't it?' Alice said. 'You'd think the one person in the world who wouldn't want to know me would be the sister of the man I was leaving.'

'Huh! I knew my brother. I knew what he's capable of. At least,' Euphemia hesitated, 'I thought I did, but this last – leaving Buckthorn Farm to strangers, out of the Crawford family, just because you're a *girl* ... well, that shocks even me.'

'Indeed it does, my dear,' murmured Percy. 'And if only we'd known how your father was treating you, well, we'd have come for you too. We'd have taken care of both of you.' He chuckled. 'We could have shared in your daughter, Alice.'

Charlotte smiled at the dear man. She believed him. Then she turned back to her mother. 'I still can't believe that he would deceive everyone into thinking you were dead. Hold a mock funeral – ' Then she remembered what her mother had said earlier. She looked into Alice's eyes as she said softly, still not quite able to believe it, 'You – you said Mary knew that you hadn't died.'

Alice nodded. 'We worked it all out between us. She and Edward would stay and look after you, but even I never thought for one moment that Osbert would stoop so low. I expect poor Mary felt trapped. She and Edward would have to obey him or be turned out. And she'd given her promise to me. Besides, she loved you dearly. They both did.'

'But she's deceived me all these years,' Charlotte murmured. 'She could have told me when I was old enough to understand.'

'She was probably too frightened of Osbert,' Euphemia said tartly. 'It takes a lot of courage to stand up to him. He's like our father. A bully. Your poor mother endured years of misery before she dared to walk away. Her only regret is leaving you. But you must understand, my dear, that, at the time, she thought she was doing the right thing for you.' The two women exchanged a glance. 'She wasn't to know,' Euphemia went on softly, 'that the old tyrant would wreak his bitterness on an innocent child.'

With a supreme effort, Charlotte summoned a smile. Whilst she truly understood the nightmare her mother's life must have been, whilst, rationally, she couldn't blame her for going, there was still a tiny corner of her heart that questioned it. Why didn't she take her daughter with her? Why did she leave her?

But she buried her thoughts and said gently, 'Well, we've found each other now. That's all that matters.' Then she turned to Euphemia, 'But, Aunt, there's just one thing. I have to break my promise to you. I intend to have this out with my father.'

Euphemia laughed. 'Well, after what you've just told us, Charlotte dear, I release you from that promise with the greatest of pleasure. My word, Alice, what a girl to be proud of. What spirit she has.'

Now Charlotte threw back her head and laughed. 'And if the folks who know me back home heard you say that, Aunt, they'd laugh. They think I'm this downtrodden, good little daughter. But they're all about to find out that the worm has turned.'

At the end of the week – a week in which she had got to know her mother and her aunt and uncle so much better – Charlotte returned home. Her uncle had been generous in the extreme. He insisted on opening a bank account for her and pressed more cash upon her than she'd ever had for her personal use in her life before this moment.

'My dear girl, you'll be coming to live with us soon, now, won't you?'

'Uncle Percy, you're a dear and you don't know what it means for me to know I have somewhere to run to. But—'

He patted her hand understandingly. 'You still have responsibilities at home and I can see that you're not the sort of person to walk away from them. Not that I blame your poor mother,' he added swiftly, lest it should sound as if he was criticizing Alice. 'The poor woman had no choice. Things are very different now for women than they were in '05. Very soon, all women will have the vote. You can have careers and – thank God – you can marry whomsoever you choose. It's a very different world now compared with then. And in most ways, a better one.'

Charlotte smiled as she said softly, 'I certainly mean to change my world. Whether or not it means leaving home, I don't know yet. But I thank you from the bottom of my heart, Uncle, for your generosity, because it means I can decide for myself exactly what I do. You have given me my freedom.' She kissed him on both cheeks and then boarded the train. Her goodbyes to her mother and her aunt had been said at the hotel. Only her uncle had come with her to the station to wave her off. She could have stayed with them longer, but she needed – and wanted – to go home.

There was so much she must do. And there was one person she wanted to see and to talk to before anyone else.

Miles Thornton.

'Miss Charlotte, Miss—' Georgie was running down the drive to meet her, but he stopped suddenly and stood quite still, staring at her. 'Oh – I thought it was Miss Charlotte.' Then he squealed with delight. 'It *is* you.'

He ran towards her and took her hand, skipping beside her the rest of the way to the front door.

'You've got your hair so different, and you look so

pretty. Papa – Papa – come and see,' he called as he bounded up the steps and in through the front door. 'Miss Charlotte's home and just *look* at her.'

Miles appeared from his study and Ben, halfway up the stairs, paused and turned to look down at her, his mouth gaping open.

Blushing a little, Charlotte submitted herself to their scrutiny. Dressed now in a fashionable coat and hat, she knew she looked very different from the drab creature they had known before.

'My dear, you look wonderful. What a transformation! Oh, I'm so sorry,' Miles added at once. 'That's sounds dreadfully rude.'

Charlotte threw back her head and laughed out loud. 'But true. You can't offend me, Miles. I'm too busy basking in your compliments.'

'Where've you been?' Georgie was tugging at her hand. 'We've missed you, haven't we, Papa? Even Philip. He says he's no one who'll answer him back now.'

Charlotte sobered and her glance went to Miles. 'How is he?'

Miles shrugged. 'No improvement, I afraid. Physically – or in his temper. I've had to ban Georgie from going in to see him. The little chap comes out crying.' He ruffled the boy's curls affectionately. 'And Ben only pokes his head in now and again. He tried to read to him, but Philip only snatched the book out of his hands and flung it across the room.'

'I'm sorry to hear that. I'll see what I can do later, but first, could I talk to you, Miles? I – I need your advice.'

Miles blinked. 'My advice? It's usually me coming to see you for advice about farming matters.'

'This has nothing to do with farming.'

'Ah well, in that case, please come into the study. Georgie – run and play, there's a good boy.'

'Please may I ask Brewster to drive me to see Tommy?'

'After luncheon.'

The little boy beamed and looked up at Charlotte. 'And will you come and play with me in the playroom after you've finished talking to Papa?' Artfully, he added, 'You can play with the dolls' house.'

'Maybe I'll come tomorrow, Georgie. I've only just come back from my holiday. I haven't even been home yet. But I'll come and see you and Philip tomorrow.'

Releasing herself from his hold, she waved her hand at both Georgie and Ben, who was still standing on the stairs gazing at her, and followed Miles into his study.

'So,' he said as they both sat down either side of the fireplace. 'How can I help you, Charlotte?' Just like his son, he was still gazing at her as if he couldn't quite believe his eyes.

She took a deep breath and relayed to him all that she'd learned. 'I still can't believe that my father could be quite so devious. And how he managed to arrange a funeral without a body, I just don't know.'

Miles's mind was working fast. He was remembering his conversations with the Warren family, how they had been mystified as to why old Harry had insisted on seeing the vicar before he died and how he'd been buried next to Alice Crawford's grave. A woman, who, Miles now learned, was not dead at all.

'Leave it with me, Charlotte. I have a suspicion as to how it was done, but will you trust me to find out for you?'

She nodded. 'Of course,' she said simply. 'I can hardly ask my father, can I?'

'What do you plan to do?'

She sighed. 'I really don't know. I have Mary and Edward to think of. They've devoted their lives to me, even though they've hidden this secret all that time.'

'Don't blame them. I expect your father put an intolerable pressure on them.'

'No, I don't.'

'But?'

'But I don't know if I want to go on living at Buckthorn Farm, running the place when it isn't even going to be mine eventually. I'm sorry,' she added swiftly, 'to sound so blunt.'

Miles grimaced. 'It's the truth, and I think you know I don't like it any more than you do.'

'If I could find a position for Mary and Edward, then I would leave.' She'd already told him that her aunt and uncle had offered her a home.

'They could come here and they would be welcome,' Miles said at once and then asked gently, 'but what of your father? I know you're angry with him and you have every right to be, but would you really leave him?'

She shrugged. 'He can employ people to do everything I do.'

'But they wouldn't be a daughter to him.'

Charlotte looked him straight in the eyes and her words broke his heart.

'He'll not miss me. He's never wanted me. All he's ever wanted was a son.'

Forty-One

It was getting late when she entered Buckthorn Farm
and went straight to the kitchen. Mary and Edward,
seated at the table eating their evening meal, looked up.
Mary's spoon clattered on to her plate and she threw up
her hands, giving a little scream. 'Oh, Miss Charlotte,
whatever will he say? You look lovely, but – but whatever will the master say?'

Charlotte peeled off her new gloves and smiled at
Mary. These two people were very dear to her. They'd
been like parents to her – better than either of her own.
For she had to face the reality that, whatever her reasons
and however good those reasons were, her own mother
had abandoned her. She hoped that she could persuade
Mary and Edward that she didn't blame either of them,
even though they'd kept such a dreadful secret for over
twenty years.

Mary bustled about the kitchen, spooning food on to
a plate.

'I'm not hungry, Mary, truly, though I'd love a cup of
tea. Then, please, sit down. I want to talk to you both.'

Husband and wife exchanged a glance but neither of
them could foresee the bombshell that Charlotte was
about to drop.

She told them everything that had happened over the
past week. When she got to the part about meeting

her mother, finding out at last that she was still alive, Mary's eyes widened and she burst into noisy tears. Edward hung his head and refused to look at her.

Charlotte clasped Mary's hands across the table. 'I don't blame you – either of you. You've always cared for me. You're the only people in this house who've shown me any love.'

'The master made us promise never to tell you,' Mary sobbed. 'He'd've sent us packing if we hadn't agreed. And I'd promised your mama that we'd look after you. Besides,' she added, as if it explained everything – and it did – 'we do love you, miss, like you was our own. We always have.'

'And do you know how he managed to arrange that travesty of a funeral? Because that's what it was.'

Again, Mary and Edward exchanged a glance.

'No, we don't, miss,' Edward said. 'We never did know. That I promise you. When we got to the church gates that day, he sent us all packing. Said he wanted to be on his own. Just him and the vicar. None of us knew what happened after that.' He glanced at his wife. 'Of course, me an' Mary knew it wasn't really your mama in the coffin.'

'Then who was it? Or was it empty? Was it all just a charade?'

'I don't know, miss,' Edward said, looking harassed. 'Truly I don't.'

Slowly, Charlotte rose. Mary looked up at her nervously. 'What are you going to do?'

'I'm not sure yet.' Charlotte grinned impishly. 'Maybe the shock at the sight of the new me is going to be quite enough for the moment, don't you think?'

*

'You Jezebel! You whore! You – you wicked, ungrateful girl. When I think of all I've done for you and this is how you repay me.'

'All you've done for me, Father?' Charlotte repeated. 'Tell me – exactly what have you done for your *daughter*?'

'I've fed you and clothed you – kept a roof over your head. What more do you want? To be pampered and cosseted and spoiled, I suppose.'

'There's been no fear of that,' she retorted.

His eyes narrowed to spiteful slits as he looked at her. 'You're getting very cheeky, miss. I can see Euphemia has been a bad influence on you. I might have known. She always was a flighty piece. Ran off to marry that good-for-nothing against our father's wishes. Thought herself better than the rest of us. We Crawfords have always worked for our living and worked hard.'

'And you think I haven't?' Charlotte said, deceptively softly.

He gave a low growl and his disdainful glance raked her from head to toe. 'You've been useful, I'll grant you that.' It was the closest he'd come – or was ever likely to – to giving her praise. 'So, you can take off those fripperies and get back to your work.'

'You told me to leave, not so long ago.'

'You'll do as you're told, miss.'

'Why should I work to keep this farm going for someone else?'

His lip curled. 'You'll be taken care of. D'you think his father won't make an offer soon? His son's a cripple now. He'll never walk again. His fancy notions of a career in the law are gone. And Thornton – if he's any sense, which I sometimes doubt – will want to secure his son's future. It's too good an offer to turn down.'

'And your will is made, is it? In favour of Philip Thornton.'

'It will be. I'll see to that.'

'I see,' she said quietly. For a long moment she was silent. She'd entered this room determined to face him with the news that she'd found out his dreadful secret; that, despite all his efforts to hide from her the fact that her mother was alive, she'd met her and talked to her. Moreover, she had the offer of a home with her aunt and uncle – and her mother.

But something held back the words. She saw him hunched before the fire, an old man before his time, his shoulders rounded, his back bent, his face lined with bitterness and his eyes joyless, and the words would not come. She had the uncomfortable feeling that such news would cause a seizure – one from which he might not recover. Oh, she would tell him – eventually. One day she would demand an explanation, but perhaps the sight of her transformation from the drab, docile creature he'd always demanded she be, was enough for one day.

'Get out of those clothes,' he said again. 'Burn them, d'you hear me? And find another pair of spectacles to wear. You must have an old pair somewhere. You look like a woman of the streets, dressed like that.'

As she turned to leave the room, devilment made her deliver her last remark. 'Well, if you're turning me out, that's what I may have to become.'

'I couldn't do it, Mary,' Charlotte laughed ruefully. 'There I was coming home dressed in all my finery, thinking I was this changed woman who would stand up to my bully of a father and, at the last minute, I couldn't do it.'

313

'Maybe now's not the right time, Miss Charlotte.' Mary's relief was obvious. 'I mean, do you really need to tell him at all? Isn't it enough that you know? That you can keep in touch with your mother in secret? Maybe see her from time to time?'

Charlotte took the older woman's hands into hers. 'Mary – darling Mary – what are you so frightened of?'

'Him. I've always been frightened of him.' Tears spilled down her face again. 'The times I've had to stop Edward from squaring up to him. And, sometimes, I haven't been able to stop him and I thought we'd be thrown out on the spot. But – but I think the master knows that he'd be hard pressed to find anyone to take our place.'

Charlotte laughed wryly. 'It would be impossible, I'd say.'

'He's hopping mad that the Warrens have left.'

'But he gave them notice. He said it in front of half the village.'

'I know, I know. But your father says these things and he doesn't mean them. They're all threats to keep people under his thumb.' She smiled wistfully. 'But he threatened your mama once too often – and she went.'

'Leaving me,' Charlotte whispered.

'That was the last thing she wanted,' Mary cried at once. 'It broke her heart. But she knew that if she took you, he'd hunt her down.'

'I don't know why, when he obviously didn't want me anyway. Because I'm a girl. Why didn't he just let me go – let us both go?'

Mary bit her lip, knowing what she was going to say was going to be painful for Charlotte. 'Because – because you were better than – than – '

'Than what?'

314

'Than nothing,' Mary whispered. 'And besides, you don't take anything from Osbert Crawford whether he really wants it or not. He's a vicious, cruel, self-centred man, who doesn't know the meaning of the word "love". I doubt he ever loved your mother. He just wanted someone to bear him a son. There now, I've said it – even though he's your father.'

Charlotte shrugged. 'My mother said as much herself. She said it was a marriage arranged by their fathers.' She gave a wry smile. 'My two grandfathers, weren't they?'

'I never knew anything about all that,' Mary said. 'I only came to work here when your mother and father were married, and Edward only a few months before me. But I loved your mother. She was a sweet, innocent creature – and very young – who was cruelly used. I never blamed her for running away. She suffered cruelly.' Mary paused and looked at Charlotte. 'I hope you can find it in your heart to understand and forgive her.'

Charlotte nodded, but at the moment could not make that promise wholeheartedly – not yet.

'What happened to her when she left here?' Mary wanted to know. 'Did she tell you? Has she been all right all these years?'

Charlotte stared at her, realizing for the first time that Mary had never known what had become of Alice from the moment she'd 'died'. She began to smile and shook her head slowly. 'You're not going to believe this, Mary, but she went to my Aunt Euphemia for help. My father's own sister. They – Euphemia and Percy – took her in and cared for her – even took her abroad with them.'

Mary's mouth dropped open and then they both began to laugh.

Forty-Two

'So,' Charlotte said brightly, entering Philip's bedroom the following afternoon, 'isn't it time you made an effort to get up out of that bed and stop playing the fool?'

He glared at her. 'So you're back, are you? I was hoping you'd gone for good. But I suppose', he sneered, 'you can't let go of what you consider to be your rightful inheritance.' Suddenly, he became aware of her changed appearance and he laughed. 'Ugly duckling turned into swan, is it? Well, allow me to tell you, it hasn't worked. Father still won't propose. He'll never forget my mother. Never.'

Quietly, she said, 'I don't expect your father to propose to me, Philip. My father was being vile in even suggesting such a thing.'

'Georgie'd love it. He'd like you as a stepmother. Ben too, probably. But not me.' Philip pulled himself up off the pillows. He was scowling at her and, in his anger, he was completely unaware of what he was doing. 'I'll never see the day you ensnare my father.'

But Charlotte was not looking at his face; she was staring at the bedclothes covering his legs. Slowly, she raised her eyes to look at him. 'Philip, how long are you going to go on with this charade?'

He lay back, as if exhausted. Covering his eyes with his arm, he muttered, 'I don't know what you're talking about.'

She moved closer to the bed and leaned over him. 'Just now, when you were shouting at me, your legs moved. Are you, for some devious reason, *pretending* to be crippled?'

Slowly, he lowered his arm and she could see there were tears in his eyes. His mouth quivered as he said, 'No, I'm not. How could you even think that?'

'I don't *like* to think it of you, but you're not making any effort to help your recovery.'

'Those bastards broke my back. I'll – I'll never walk again.'

'No, they didn't,' she countered softly, but firmly. 'The doctors say your back was badly bruised and, yes, for a time maybe you couldn't move. But now they say there's no reason at all why you can't get up out of that bed.'

'What do they know? They're fools – all of them. They're not the ones lying here with their life in ruins.'

She stared down at him, chewing her lip thoughtfully. He was like a young, stubborn horse who needed firmness and gentleness in equal measure. And just like a horse needing to be broken, he had to know who was boss. 'Philip, please be truthful with me. Can you really not walk?'

His eyes were haunted and hopeless and tears shimmered in them.

'I – can't.'

She believed him.

Softly, she said, 'Will you trust me to help you?'

'You can't. No one can.'

'I think I can, but I need you to believe in me.'

'Why should you bother with me?' he whispered. 'When I'm the one taking everything that should rightfully be yours?'

317

'I don't blame you for that. What young man of seventeen would turn his back on such a gift?'

'My father thinks I should be "man enough" to do just that.'

'Is that what he said?'

Philip nodded and she saw fresh tears well in his eyes. She sat down on the edge of the bed, but she made no attempt to take his hand as she would have done with Georgie or perhaps even with Ben.

'What else is worrying you?'

Again, he covered his eyes with his arm. 'Nothing,' he muttered at last.

'I think there is,' she said softly and this time he was silent. After a pause, she murmured, 'Is it Lily?'

When he still didn't answer, she went on softly. 'You don't have to marry Lily.'

Now he burst out, 'Father thinks I should. I should take responsibility for my – my – '

'The Warrens don't expect you to marry her. They never did. Philip, unless you raped her—'

'I didn't,' he shouted, raising himself off the pillows again. 'I swear I didn't.'

'No – I know that. Just listen to me. Lily was as much to blame as you. More so, in a way. She's older than you and should have known better. She's not ignorant of the facts of life. How could she be, brought up on a farm? But she is, perhaps, a naïve country lass, who believed the words of a charmer. Oh yes, I've no doubt you whispered many a sweet nothing into her willing ears. She would believe everything you said to her. Did you say you'd marry her?'

There was a long pause before he muttered, 'I – might have done.'

'But you didn't mean it?'

He shook his head.

'Then that's what you've done wrong. Making a promise that you had no intention of keeping.'

'I know.' His whispered admission touched her heart and for the first time, since she'd known him, she felt a stab of affection for him. He was, after all, little more than a boy. A boy who'd acted like a man and was having to live with the consequences. And now, for the first time she could see that, deep down, he felt shame. A shame and anxiety that was keeping him from making the effort to get up out of his bed and face the world. Shut away in his room, he was safe. And he'd turned any blame on to his attackers. Crippled for the rest of his life, he would provoke sympathy, not censure.

Now Charlotte dared to touch his hand. 'I'll talk to your father and then we're going to get you well again.'

Philip stared at her saying nothing. But she was worried to see the fear in his eyes.

'I need to talk to you.'

She found Miles in his study where he seemed to spend most of his time. He smiled and laid aside the book he was reading. But the deep sadness in his eyes was still there.

'More trouble?' he asked gently, seeing her anxious face.

'I hope not.'

She told him of her conversation with Philip and ended by saying, 'I expect there's some fancy medical name for his condition. All I can say is, he's not getting up out of that bed because he doesn't want to.'

'Doesn't want to?' Miles was scandalized and disbelieving. 'Surely not.'

'Miles, he needs your reassurance and support. He needs to hear it from you that you are not going to try to force him to marry Lily. I know you've already told him time and again,' she added swiftly as he opened his mouth to protest. 'But you've got to make him believe it. Also, you must tell him that you'll allow him to accept Buckthorn Farm and – ' she hesitated over the final words, for her heart contracted as she spoke them – 'and that you are not going to propose to me.'

'Propose to you? Why should he think that?'

'He thinks you'll comply with my father's demands to secure his inheritance.'

Miles spread his hands. 'But that's contradictory. He knows I don't want him to accept your father's preposterous idea. So, how can he think I'd marry you to bring it about?'

Charlotte shrugged. 'I don't know. But that's what seems to be in his mind. One of the things, anyway.'

'I'll talk to him. If you – and the doctors – are right and there's nothing physically wrong with him, then we must get him back on his feet.'

'It'll take time. His muscles must be wasted with all these weeks in bed. And he'll have missed so much schooling. What'll happen about that?'

'I've been in touch with his headmaster. His place is still there for him, though he may have to drop back a year, start the Lower Sixth Form again. But that won't matter. He did well in his recent examinations and the headmaster said all the staff expect him to be a certain candidate for university.'

'Then you should tell him that, Miles. No more talk of marrying Lily or becoming a farmer. My father will probably live for years anyway – just to spite everybody. Philip should get on with his life – the life *he* wants.'

He sat gazing at her before asking softly, 'But what about you? Do you intend to carry on as before – running Buckthorn Farm just to hand it over to someone else?'

She shrugged. 'Perhaps Philip would let me see out my days there. Run it for him or even become his tenant.'

'That would be very unfair. What if you should marry and have children? What about their inheritance, never mind yours?'

Charlotte laughed wryly. 'I don't think that's likely, do you?'

The conversation was getting too personal for comfort, so she got up quickly, saying, 'And now I must find Georgie. He's promised I may see the dolls' house.'

As she reached the door, Miles said, 'By the way, it's Georgie's birthday tomorrow. He's seven.' He sighed. 'He says he doesn't want a party, not whilst Philip – ' he gestured helplessly.

But Charlotte smiled. 'Perfect,' she said. 'We'll have a party in Philip's room.'

Philip's recovery took many weeks, but, with encouragement from his father and brothers and firmness from Charlotte, he made progress, albeit slowly. Charlotte was the one he shouted and raved at. It was she who could answer him back and fire him to anger. But it was intentional. She knew that was the only way to make him try. Tempered with understanding and gentleness when it was needed, she roused him back to a life worth living.

The day, in early June, when Philip walked outside on to the terrace at the side of the house caused great rejoicing. Georgie hopped up and down, whilst Ben walked beside him, giving Philip his shoulder to lean on. Miles watched with quiet thankfulness, and as for Charlotte, she turned away with tears in her eyes. Her job here was done and she could make a decision about her own future. But she was devastated that she now had no excuse to come to the manor most days. No more excuse to see and be near Miles.

Life at Buckthorn Farm had settled down into its old routine. In some ways little had changed, but in others nothing was the same. She still had Mary and Edward, as before, and her father had slipped back into his domineering ways. For the moment, she went along with it, but she missed the Warren family. Eddie Norton was a good worker and willing, but he hadn't got Joe's knowledge or devotion to Buckthorn Farm. And she missed Jackson's teasing and John's solid, dependable presence. She went often to Purslane Farm to see them, but it was not the same as seeing them every day, working with them and laughing with them.

And now she missed the Thorntons. All of them, but especially Miles.

'But nothing will ever come of it,' she murmured as she sat alone in the corner of her bedroom where she did her watercolour painting. 'I'd do better to resign myself to spinsterhood than waste my life yearning for something that will never be.'

Letters came frequently from her mother, but were always addressed to Mary. Her father would not open those addressed to their servants but he'd always opened any with his daughter's name on the envelope.

'And who's writing to you?' he'd say. 'That curate or some other schemer who has his eyes on my fortune?'

Euphemia wrote too, reminding Charlotte that there

was always a home with them. But something held her here and it was not just her desire to see Philip well again. No, Miles filled her mind and her heart and that, more than anything else, kept her at Buckthorn Farm. Even though she now had a gateway to freedom and a new life, she no longer wanted it.

Forty-Three

'Could I have a word with you, Miss Charlotte?' Eddie was standing before her desk in the farm office, twisting his cap round and round between nervous fingers.

'Of course, Eddie. What is it? Something wrong?'

'Not – not really, miss. At least, I hope you won't think so.' He paused, bit his lip and then burst out. 'Me an' Lily want to get wed, miss, and quick, like, afore the babby comes. 'Tis due at the end of June.'

'Eddie, that's wonderful news. But you'll have to be quick.' She laughed. 'Lily's the size of an elephant now.' Then her face sobered. 'Are you sure – both of you? It's a big step and – and to take on another man's child . . .'

'I'm sure, miss. Lily took a bit of persuading, like. And her mam and dad, but they're all happy about it. Even me ma. She dun't mind. Ses she'll like havin' a little 'un to spoil and she's not the sort to mek a difference because it's not mine. She loves kids.'

'I think that's wonderful news. So what's the problem?'

'There's a couple, really. One is that although Lily's mam and dad say there's plenty of room at Purslane Farm for us to live with them – ' He paused and twisted the cap faster and faster. Taking pity on him, Charlotte said, 'You'd like to start married life as you mean to go on? In a place of your own?'

'That's about the size of it, miss, yes.'

'That's easily solved. Since you're employed on Buckthorn Farm, you can have the Warrens' cottage. I did
offer it to you before and it's still empty.'

Eddie beamed. 'And would you mind me mam living
with us?'

'Of course not. But I thought she wanted to stay in
the house where she's always lived?'

The young man shrugged. 'She ses she'll not know
what to do wi' 'ersen. Never lived on her own, see. But
she'd be willing to do jobs around Buckthorn Farm and
here – in the farmhouse – if Mrs Morgan ever wanted
any help.'

'I'm sure Mary'd be delighted. I know she's missed
Peggy's help. So, that's settled then. You can move in
whenever you like. So, what was the other problem?'

Eddie's face sobered again. 'Telling Mr Thornton,
miss. After all, Lily's bairn *is* his grandchild.'

Charlotte stared at him, unsure where this conversation was leading. 'You mean – you expect him to help
support the child?'

'Oh no, miss.' Eddie looked hurt. 'I wouldn't want
anyone to think that of us. We don't want money. We
want nothing from them except – approval, I suppose.
And I'd like to know what they want us to tell the little
'un as it grows up, like. Mesen, I'd believe in being
honest and telling it the truth, but mebbe the Thorntons
wouldn't like that. I want the kiddie to have my name,
an' all. Just so it doesn't get called horrible names as it's
growin' up.' He shrugged. 'See, folks round here have
got long memories. If we're not honest with it, poor
little thing'll likely be told in the playground, don't you
think?'

'Eddie Norton, you are a remarkable young man,'
Charlotte said. 'And I'm sorry if you think I thought

badly of you. I didn't and I don't. The reason I said what I did was because Miles Thornton himself said he'd always see that Lily and her child were provided for.'

'I see, miss. Well, there's no need. I'll look after it as if it were me own. I promise you – an' him – that, and mebbe, if we'm blessed,' the young man twisted his cap even faster in embarrassment, 'we'll have some little brothers and sisters for him or her one day.'

'I hope you will, Eddie.'

Charlotte pondered for a couple of days on how best to broach the subject with Miles, but she knew she couldn't put it off for long. The quiet marriage ceremony was to take place at eight o'clock the following Saturday, for Lily's baby was due any time and Eddie was determined that the child, in the eyes of the world at least, should not be born illegitimate. Not many folks knew the identity of the natural father and Eddie was more than happy to take the responsibility. To outsiders, he'd be seen to be 'doing the right thing' by the girl he'd got pregnant.

They met by accident on an early morning ride on the beach. Charlotte's heart turned over as she saw the familiar figures of Miles and Midnight cantering along the firm sand at the water's edge. He saw her and rode towards her. After greeting each other, they rode for a while in companionable silence.

It was Miles who opened the subject she was finding difficult to broach by asking, 'What's this I hear about Lily and Eddie Norton getting married? Is it true?'

She glanced at him, trying to read his expression. Was he pleased or angry? But his face told her nothing.

'Yes, it's true. On Saturday at eight in the morning.'

He nodded. 'I suppose it's just family, is it?'

'Mm.' There was a pause before she said, 'Actually, I wanted to come and talk to you about it, but I've been putting it off.'

'Oh? Why?'

'Well – I wasn't sure how you'd feel.'

He sighed. 'I'm pleased for her.' His voice hardened a little. 'Since my own son refused to do the honourable thing.'

Charlotte smiled weakly, anxious not to get into that particular discussion again. 'Eddie wants the child to have his name but he wants to know if you'd have any objection to it being told the truth, when it's old enough of course. He promises he'll bring the child up as his own and no difference will ever be made between it and any more children they might have together. It's just that he doesn't want the child to hear playground gossip when it's older. He believes in honesty from the start.'

Miles was thoughtful for so long that she began to grow agitated, thinking that he disapproved in some way.

'He's a remarkable young man,' he murmured at last.

'Yes – I told him that. But he wanted your approval. That's what he said. Your approval.'

'Charlotte, would you ask him to come and see me? I'd like to talk to him, but reassure him, he has my blessing on everything he is planning.'

'There's just one thing I ought to mention. He's not looking for financial help. In fact, when I half suggested it, he was most indignant.'

'Then my admiration for him is growing by the minute. I'll tread carefully, Charlotte, I promise. I'll not offend him. But it *is* still my grandchild and I'd like to see if he would let me do something. Set up a trust fund, perhaps, for when the child comes of age.'

'Perhaps. But he might see that as being unfair on any other children, as he said, if they're blessed.'

'If they're blessed,' Miles repeated the words softly and then sighed. 'My grandchild . . .' And then he added words which brought a lump to Charlotte's throat and a twinge of envy. 'I hope it's a girl. Oh, I do hope it's a girl.'

Forty-Four

Miles's hopes were not realized. Lily's baby, born on the last day in June only five days after her marriage to Eddie, was a boy. He was named Alfred Joseph, but would always be known as Alfie.

Osbert almost danced with glee. 'There, my boy has proved he can sire a son. Now he only has to find someone worthy to bear him an heir. Someone better than that little trollop. Still –' his eyes gleamed with excitement – 'a young feller has to sow a few wild oats. But now he should choose more carefully, and next time—'

'I don't think Master Philip will be siring any more children – boys or girls – for a while yet,' Charlotte reminded him tartly. 'He's seventeen and is to return to school and his studies now he's recovering so well.'

'Yes, yes, but one day – one day he will marry well and have a family. I wonder,' the devious man mused aloud, 'if he would change his surname by deed poll to Crawford.'

'Father!' Charlotte was appalled. 'That would be grossly unfair on his own father. Think what you're saying.'

He regarded her through narrowed eyes. 'I know *exactly* what I'm saying.' He was thoughtful for a moment. 'Mm, yes, that's a good idea. Now, why didn't I think of that before? If the father won't marry you,' he looked her up and down, sniffed and then muttered, 'and I can't say I blame him – then the boy could take my name. He reckons he's going to be a lawyer, so he'll know how to go about it.'

Charlotte was so angry – not for herself, but for Miles Thornton – that she almost spilled out the news that she'd found her mother alive and well and had met her. But something held back the words. Was it still fear of this man? No – she didn't believe that. Not now. At least, not for herself. But perhaps she was afraid, deep down, of what he might try to do to her mother if he knew where to find her. Or was it pity? She looked at the man, wizened by bitterness and grown old before his time because of it. He looked seventy or even older – so much older than his fifty-seven years. She'd not had much of a life – but she still had a chance to make something of it. He'd wasted his. Of his own choice, he whiled away the years sitting wrapped in discontent and resentment, manipulating the lives of others for his own insidious schemes. And he was still trying to do it. No, she wouldn't tell him about her mother, but her decision was more to protect Alice than for any other reason.

Life settled back into a routine. The weeks passed – another haymaking and another harvest were over. Philip went back to boarding school at the start of the autumn term and, this time, Ben went too, so there was only Georgie left at home in the great rambling house to keep his father company. The little boy – though growing rapidly now – still attended the village school, continued to play with Tommy Warren and the other boys, and never ceased to charm the locals with his cheeky grin.

'Perhaps he ought to go to boarding school soon too,' Miles confided in Charlotte. 'But I can't bring myself to let him go.'

'I can understand that,' she said quietly. She didn't add that she wouldn't be able to let her children out of her sight – if she were fortunate enough to have any. But she kept silent. Things were different for boys. They had to have the best education that could be found – or afforded. She'd have given her eye teeth to have been sent to boarding school, she mused, but that would have meant her father loosening his domination over her. And he'd never have done that. She sighed. Despite his threats, she knew he'd never let her go, even now. If she were ever to escape, the decision would have to be hers.

But something still held her here at Buckthorn Farm amidst the bleak, windswept marshland. Was it loyalty and duty to her father? Or was it the presence of the handsome man on the big black horse riding beside her along the beach? They met often and Charlotte no longer rode one of the shire horses now. At the August horse fair that year, she'd bought herself a more suitable horse for her outings to the beach where she hoped to encounter Miles.

One morning in October, when Charlotte took a well-earned break from work, they met on the beach. It was the first time in several days she'd had the chance to slip away, for she and all her workers had been fully occupied with the lifting of their first harvest of sugar beet. The crop had been good – better than they'd dared to hope for. But now it was safely on its way to Bardney, Charlotte allowed herself a brief respite. She'd also given Eddie and the other workers on Buckthorn Farm the day off. 'As long as the milking gets done and the animals are fed,' she'd warned.

After greeting each other, Miles asked, 'Have you ever told your father that you've met your mother?'

Charlotte shook her head. 'No,' she said hoarsely. 'I – I couldn't.'

'Mm. So,' he added slowly, 'you've never solved the mystery of the grave in the churchyard, then?'

She shook her head and murmured, 'I'm not sure I want to.'

'Ah,' was all Miles said and they rode on in silence. They parted in the lane, he to canter towards the manor, Charlotte to ride slowly back to Buckthorn Farm, her gaze holding sight of him until the very last moment when he disappeared from her view.

'Miss Charlotte – ' Cuthbert Iveson had visited the Sunday school class as usual, but today he lingered until all the children had gone. This was the first time he'd deliberately sought her out since her father's threats to have him removed from his living.

She looked up at him and smiled, but her smile faded when she noticed how thin and pale he'd become. His hands were shaking and he chewed nervously on his bottom lip.

'Miss Charlotte – I have to tell you – I'm leaving.'

'Oh, Mr Iveson – no!' She paused and then asked, 'Has this anything to do with my father?'

'Well – in a way, but—'

'But I thought Mr Thornton wrote to the bishop and explained—'

'He did, he did,' Cuthbert said quickly. 'And I was

grateful – most grateful. No, I'm leaving of my own free will.'

But his eyes were haunted and she was sure that this was not the truth – or at least, not the whole truth.

'Why?' she asked candidly.

'I am no longer comfortable here.'

'But I don't understand. Your services are well attended. The church is almost full – well, most of the time. And always on special occasions like Harvest and Christmas and Easter. So why?'

He avoided meeting her gaze. In anyone else, she would have described his manner as shifty. But in a vicar – Heaven forbid! she thought.

'There are things I can't tell you about. Confidences, you know.'

'Like confessions, you mean?'

'Well – sort of. Look, I'm sorry. I just have to go. Make a fresh start. I had hoped . . .' He looked at her now, meeting her gaze. 'There was a time I'd hoped that you and I . . .'

She touched his hand and said gently, 'I know.' But there was no regret, at least, not on her part. Now she knew how it felt to fall in love, she knew she could never have felt about Cuthbert the way she felt about Miles. 'When do you go?'

'The bishop has found me another living. My last services here will be next Sunday.'

'So soon? Who will take the services until a replacement has been found?'

'Mr Knoakes from Lynthorpe will take one service a day here. Matins, I think.'

'And the Sunday school?'

Now he actually smiled. 'I hope that will continue as it always has – under your expert tuition.'

Charlotte laughed. 'I don't know about the expert bit, but I'll certainly do my best.'

'I'm hoping the next person to come here will be older. And a married man. I said as much to the bishop. I – I think he understood.'

Charlotte nodded and said quietly, 'I think it would be for the best. But I'm so sorry if it's my father who's caused you to leave.'

Cuthbert became agitated again. 'It wasn't because of you and me. It was something else.'

'Oh? What?'

He pressed his lips together. 'That's what I can't tell you. I'm sorry. It – it was a deathbed confession and must remain so. But it troubles my conscience.'

'Have you discussed this with the bishop?'

'Yes.'

'And?'

'He advised me to move away. It – it was none of my making, you understand. Something that happened years ago, but I'm finding it hard to cope with the knowledge.'

'I – see,' she said slowly, but of course she didn't understand at all. And yet, as they parted company, there was something nagging at the back of her mind, but she couldn't quite think what it was.

As she walked back towards the farm, she was deep in thought. Then suddenly, in the middle of the lane, she stopped and said aloud, 'A deathbed confession? Why, that'd be old Harry Warren. It must be.' She remembered suddenly that Peggy had told her of old Harry's agitation shortly before he died. And – he'd asked to see the vicar.

During the eighteen months since Harry had died, there'd been only two deaths of people Charlotte knew, which had also involved Cuthbert's church. One, Flora Brown, had been a non-believer ever since she'd lost her husband and two sons in the Great War. She'd raged at a God who could let that happen – and not only to her. Another had been a young man killed in a horrific accident with a traction engine. There'd been two or three old people in Ravensfleet who'd died, and whom Charlotte had known slightly, but she'd understood that they'd been chapel-goers and if they'd called for anyone on their deathbeds, it would have been the Methodist minister.

Miles, she decided as she reached the gate of Buckthorn Farm, *I'll ask Miles.* She remembered that he'd hinted at something. She would ask him.

Her heart lifted at the thought of an excuse to see him.

Forty-Five

He was standing on the terrace when she walked to the manor later that week. He was looking out over the flat land, most of which he owned, apart from Buckthorn Farm's acres. But, she thought, even those would one day belong to his family.

He turned and saw her walking towards him. 'Charlotte – how lovely. Just in time for afternoon tea when Georgie gets home from school. Brewster has just gone to fetch him.' He laughed. 'I think Georgie is the most popular boy in the school when my motor car turns up. Brewster says he can hardly drive sometimes for the number of excitable boys squashed into the vehicle. I'm not sure it's entirely safe, but there you are. Thank goodness for quiet country roads!'

Charlotte laughed. 'I think your motor car is one of the few round here, so I shouldn't worry.'

'Can you stay for tea?'

'I'd love to, but first, before Georgie gets home, there's something I want to ask you. Did you know that the Reverend Iveson is leaving?'

Miles raised his eyebrows. 'No, I didn't. Why? I thought that business with your father was all sorted out after I wrote to the bishop.'

She nodded. 'I don't think it's because of that particular letter my father sent to the bishop.' She frowned. 'There's something else troubling the vicar, but I think

336

it has something to do with my father. Indirectly. He said it was a deathbed confession that is troubling him. He wouldn't – couldn't – tell me more, of course, and I respect that, but I've been thinking . . .'

'And?'

'The only person I can think of who's died in the last year or so and who I know asked to see Mr Iveson and who also had a connection with my father is old Harry Warren.'

'Aaah.' Miles let out a deep breath as if, suddenly, everything had become clear. 'Charlotte, my dear . . .' He put his arm about her shoulders and led her down the stone steps towards a garden seat set in the rose garden just below the terrace.

She trembled at his nearness. They sat down side by side and he took her hands in his. 'My dear, I began to suspect some – shall we say, skulduggery – when you came home and confided in me that you'd met your mother whom you'd been led to believe was dead all these years.' His tone hardened at the cruelty of such an act. Cruelty, not only to the child Charlotte had been then, but to the mother, too. 'The mystery of your mother's supposed grave in the churchyard and why Harry Warren demanded to be buried beside her. Why he'd bought the plot next to her in – in readiness?'

Charlotte bit her lip and lowered her gaze. 'I wondered about that myself. I – I thought perhaps there'd been something between them. Between my mother and Harry. An affair, perhaps. And that was why my father was so bitter. My mother's never said anything, but then, perhaps she wouldn't confess to such a thing. Not even to me. That's why – for a while – I didn't want to know. But now . . .'

Miles squeezed her hands gently. 'I don't think it

was anything like that at all. What I think happened –
and I don't believe even Joe knows this – was that
your mother did leave your father, just as she told you,
because of his cruelty to her. But her leaving happened
at the same time – by sheer happy coincidence from
your father's point of view – as Harry's wife died.'

Charlotte gasped and stared at him, her mind working feverishly. 'You – you mean it's old Mrs Warren
who's buried in that grave?'

'I think so, yes.'

'But – but how could they do that? I mean, the vicar
would know. And the undertakers. They'd all have
known. They must have done.'

'I expect so. But your father has always got his own
way, hasn't he? By fair means or foul, he manipulates
people. Bribes them, threatens them. Who was the vicar
here then?'

Charlotte frowned. 'I can hardly remember. An old
man, I think. I can't remember his name now. He –
he left soon afterwards . . .' Her voice faded away as
she began to realize that the incredible picture Miles
was painting was perhaps possible. Even probable. It all
seemed to fit.

'So, you think Harry was – was *involved* – and that's
what he wanted to confide in the vicar before he died
so that Mr Iveson would understand why he insisted
on being buried next to my mother's – well, what we
thought was my mother's – grave?'

Miles nodded. 'And that knowledge is hanging heavily on poor Mr Iveson's conscience, so much so that
he can't bear to stay here with the daily reminder. The
grave isn't far from the path he treads every day from
the vicarage to the church. Poor fellow, he can't betray

the confidences of a dying man. And apart from that, I'm sure he wouldn't want to upset Joe and his family.'

'They know nothing, I'm sure, because when Harry died they couldn't understand why he'd bought that particular plot and—'

'Father – Father! Oh, Miss Charlotte!'

They both turned to see Georgie scampering down the steps. Miles released her and Charlotte felt a sense of loss. Her hands – and her heart – were suddenly chilled.

'By the way,' Miles whispered with a chuckle, 'now that both his brothers are away, Georgie feels himself "second in command", so he's calling me "Father" now, and no longer the childish name of "Papa".'

'What a shame,' Charlotte murmured, before she had stopped to think. 'They grow up so quickly, don't they?'

'Yes,' Miles said with a wistful tone. 'That's just what I feel, too.'

But they could say no more, for the young boy was hopping up and down in front of them. 'Come and play, Miss Charlotte. Tommy has come to tea. And Sammy Barker too. We'll have a party.'

And indeed they did. It was a merry, impromptu tea party, all the more enjoyable because it was unexpected. Almost, Charlotte thought, letting her imagination and her longing run riot, like a proper family; a mother, father and three little boys . . .

Afterwards, they played a noisy game of football on the lawn and when it was time for the boys to leave, Miles walked down the lane with her towards Buckthorn Farm.

'What do you think we should do?' she asked, coming back to the topic of their earlier conversation.

'I think Joe should know. He thinks his poor mother is buried in Lincoln.'

'Yes,' Charlotte agreed. 'And that's another thing. Joe told me that when their mother died, his father wouldn't let any of the family go to Lincoln with him to see her buried – ostensibly with her family.'

'I expect that was all a charade. I don't think there ever was a burial in Lincoln. The funeral director must have been in on the secret, provided an empty coffin and, well, just acted as if they were going to the city. For one thing,' Miles went on, 'I doubt someone like Harry Warren could have afforded to pay for his wife to be buried so far away. Think of the cost. Don't you have to pay something to each parish the coffin passes through or something?'

'I've no idea.'

They walked in silence for a while until Charlotte said, 'Yes, I think you're right. We should tell Joe.'

'Want me to come with you?'

'Please,' she said without hesitation. She didn't really need him there. She knew the family so well that she could talk to them about anything. But it was another excuse to be with him again.

'We'll go tomorrow afternoon. I'll pick you up in the motor car. About two?'

'Well, that certainly solves a mystery, Mr Thornton,' Joe said, running his hand through his hair. 'Dun't it, Peg?'

They were sitting in the huge kitchen at Purslane Farm, surrounded by an appetizing smell of freshly baked bread. Teacakes, scones and a sponge cake were laid out on the dresser top to cool. Peggy set out half a dozen scones, jam and fresh cream on the table and bade them help themselves as she poured out cups of tea and then sat down to join them.

'It does, Joe. We always wondered why he'd bought the plot next to your mother, Miss Charlotte.'

Charlotte had confided in Peggy and Joe that she'd met her mother. They'd been genuinely shocked and Peggy shook her head, saying yet again, 'I can't believe she's been alive all this time. And that wicked old man has kept you apart. Oh, begging your pardon, miss, I know he's your father, but . . .'

'Don't apologize, Peggy,' Charlotte said grimly.

'And you say Mary and Edward knew?'

Charlotte nodded.

'I reckon that shocks me more than anything else. That Mary's kept quiet all these years. Never told you . . .'

'Don't blame her, Peggy. He's threatened them. She did what she thought was right to protect me. In a way, I'm glad I didn't know, because if he'd found out she'd told me, he would have dismissed them both and then where would I have been?'

'I suppose so,' Peggy agreed reluctantly. 'But I don't think I could have carried such a burden all these years.'

'You,' Joe teased, 'keep secrets? That'd be a first.'

He was rewarded by a playful slap from his wife, but everyone smiled.

Joe was thoughtful. 'Do you reckon if we tell the vicar – unburden him, like – he'd stay?'

'I think it's better to let him go,' Miles said. 'Like we said, it's a constant reminder for the poor chap whilst he's here. And you knowing might embarrass him even further.'

Joe was looking straight at Charlotte. 'But do *you* mind him going, miss?'

'Me?' Charlotte was startled.

Miles frowned. 'Why should Miss Charlotte mind?'

Joe and Peggy exchanged a smile.

'Because,' Peggy said softly, 'we always thought Mr Iveson was sweet on our Miss Charlotte. And she'd make a lovely vicar's wife.'

'Did you indeed?' Miles murmured, so softly that only Charlotte, seated next to him heard.

On the way home Miles was quiet and withdrawn. As she alighted from the car, he gave her a cursory nod and drove away at once. Heavy hearted, Charlotte went into the house to find Mary in a state of panic and wringing her hands.

'Miss Charlotte, thank goodness you're home. Your aunt and uncle are here. And there's such a row going on. Your father's so angry. He's shouting—'

'Oh no! She – she hasn't told him, has she?'

Forty-Six

Flinging open the door of the sitting room, Charlotte stopped to take in the scene before her.

Her father was standing behind his chair, but hanging on to it for support. Euphemia stood before him, her head thrown back, her bosom heaving with righteous indignation. Percy, meanwhile, had withdrawn as far as the front window, keeping out of the argument as much as he was allowed.

'Aunt Euphemia . . .' Charlotte moved forward, trying to ignore the raging row, but her father, purple in the face, shook his free fist at her. 'Keep out of this, girl. Go to your room. This minute.'

She ignored his order and went to his side. Gently, she said, 'Father, sit down. You're distressing yourself.'

His whole body was shaking, his eyes bulging, his face puce.

'Please, do sit down,' she urged him again. As his handhold slipped, he fell against her and she manoeuvred him into his chair. Then she turned to face her aunt.

'Please, Aunt, this is not good for him . . .' She stopped, appalled as she saw the expression on her aunt's face. It was no longer the kindly, smiling face of the generous woman. Euphemia's face was twisted in fury with an expression so like her brother's that Charlotte was deeply shocked. She moved towards her to beg her, too, 'Please, Aunt, don't distress yourself. I don't know what this is about, but—'

'It's about you, my dear. You – and your *mother*.'

Startled, Charlotte gasped. 'Please – don't. I beg you – ' She lowered her voice to an urgent whisper. 'You haven't told him, have you? You haven't told him that—'

Behind them, Charlotte heard a strange gurgling sound and turned to see her father slumped in the chair, his eyes staring, his mouth gagging open.

'Now look what you've done.'

'Me? I had nothing to do with it. He's an evil, deceitful man, who turned our father against Percy and me. He doesn't like to see anyone happy. Not even his own daughter.'

Charlotte was bending over him. 'Father – Father – ' She was hardly listening to what her aunt was saying. But instinctively, she turned to Percy for help. 'Uncle, please fetch Edward.'

'Where will I find him?'

'In the kitchen.'

'Where's that?'

'You stay here. I'll go.'

But she'd hardly turned towards the door before it opened and Edward hurried into the room. He must have been hovering in the hall, listening to the quarrel.

'The doctor, Edward. We need the doctor. At once. Get Eddie to go for him. And ask Mary to come.'

After Edward had gone, she said, 'Do you think we should move him? Get him upstairs into bed?'

Euphemia's mouth twisted. 'No, leave him be. Let him die where he is. It's no more than he deserves.'

'Euphemia . . .' At this, even the taciturn Percy protested. 'That's rather harsh, my dear.'

Charlotte's mouth hardened. 'I think you'd better leave, Aunt, if you please.'

'Oh, I'm going.' Euphemia was smiling now, but it was a hard, embittered smile. Beckoning imperiously to Percy, she flounced out of the room, her parting words shocking Charlotte. 'I've done what I came to do.'

'He's had a stroke,' the doctor pronounced. 'A bad one. The next few days will be critical.'

'Should he go to hospital?'

'Moving him might do more damage than letting him stay here.' He looked at her sharply. 'Can you afford a private nurse to live in for a week or so?'

'Of course. Anything.'

Dr Markham touched her cheek gently. 'You're a good girl, Charlotte,' he murmured. 'Not many daughters would be so caring after the way you've been treated.'

'He's still my father,' she said softly.

'And you,' the doctor insisted, 'are a remarkable young woman.' He cleared his throat and said more briskly, 'I'll make arrangements. She'll arrive by tonight.'

'She'll have to have my bed, Mary. I'll sleep on the truckle bed. We can screen off one end of the room.'

For the rest of the day, until early evening when the nurse arrived, Charlotte sat by her father's bedside. There was little she could do for him. She had no nursing knowledge and was afraid of doing more harm than good. She didn't even sit holding his hand. He was asleep or unconscious – she wasn't sure which. But her touch was not what her father would have wanted, she thought wryly.

345

Whilst she sat in the stillness of the sick room, her thoughts wandered over the years and all the events that had occurred in her life. Some, she'd learned so recently, were not what she'd thought they'd been at the time. Like the death of her mother. How could her father have been so vindictive, so vengeful? And how on earth had he managed to get others to join in his deception? Bribery, she thought, or threats. In the case of Harry Warren, she supposed, it had probably been a mixture of the two. A threat that he'd be dismissed if he didn't carry out Osbert's wishes and, at the same time, a promise that he and his family would always have work and a home if he went along with his employer's devious schemes. But, even so, Charlotte could not comprehend Harry agreeing to his wife being buried in someone else's grave, with no stone to mark her final resting place and nowhere for his family to visit and cherish her memory.

And the vicar? How could any man of the cloth agree to such a terrible deception? The vicar at that time had been an old man. Charlotte remembered him vaguely. Perhaps her father had had some hold over him, too, or he'd promised him a comfortable old age in return for his complicity. She sighed. Osbert Crawford was a difficult and complex man with a streak of cruelty. But at this moment she felt desperately sorry for him. Despite his treatment of her, his lack of love, his hatred almost, because she'd been born a girl and not the son he craved, she felt only pity for him. He'd wasted his whole life yearning for something that could not be – was never going to be after he'd treated his young wife so abominably that she'd been forced to flee for her life.

She didn't blame her mother. Not any more. She wanted – needed – to believe in her. To believe that the reason she'd abandoned her small daughter had been

346

forced upon her. Staying would have endangered her sanity, perhaps even her life. But the last few hours, Charlotte realized, had sadly disillusioned her about her aunt.

Euphemia was little better than her brother. Charlotte suspected that her actions – on the surface, kind and caring – had been for one reason and one reason only. To wreak revenge on the brother who had tried to rule her life and had succeeded in turning their father against her. Deep down, she was as embittered and vengeful as he was. Now Charlotte was sure this was the reason Euphemia had come back to Buckthorn Farm, had pretended affection for her niece, and had reunited her with her mother. It had all been for her own ends. Had she taken Alice in all those years earlier just to spite Osbert? Charlotte wondered, but realized she would probably never know the answer to that. She sighed. At least, her mother had seemed contented. She hoped it was the truth.

Nurse Montgomery – soon nicknamed 'Monty' – was in her early thirties. She was round-faced with a jollity that belied a fearsome, protective attitude towards her patient. Charlotte was relieved to hand over the responsibility to the capable woman, remarking only, 'Please let me know if there's anything you want.'

'I most certainly will, Miss Crawford, of that you can be sure.'

Thankfully, Charlotte escaped back to her office.

Nurse Monty took charge, requesting that the truckle bed be moved into Osbert's large bedroom.

'I need to be able to listen for him in the night,' she explained.

'I'm so sorry we haven't another proper bed; perhaps—' Charlotte began, but the nurse waved aside her apologies. 'I've slept on worse, believe you me.'

On the fourth day after his stroke, Osbert was roused out of unconsciousness. There was some paralysis, one side of his face was dragged down and he could not speak, but he could make angry signs that he wanted to write. Nurse Montgomery called for Charlotte to bring a pad and a pen to his bedside and with his unaffected hand he wrote in shaky, but quite legible handwriting, two words: Philip Baxter.

Deciphering it, the nurse asked, 'Philip Baxter? Who's he?'

'It's two people,' Charlotte explained. 'Mr Baxter is his solicitor and Philip is Philip Thornton.'

The nurse eyed her patient, lying back against the pillows, quite exhausted by the effort. 'Then I think,' she said quietly, 'you'd better send for them both.'

'I'll send for the solicitor, but Philip's away at school –'

Her father waved his good arm angrily and made gurgling noises.

'I think he wants you to send for him,' the nurse interpreted.

Charlotte shrugged. 'I can only ask his father.'

She left the room with Osbert shaking his fist at her.

'I'll send Brewster to fetch him.' Miles glanced at Charlotte, trying to read her expression. 'If that's what you want me to do?'

When she nodded, he said, 'Then I'll write a note to the headmaster explaining the situation.'

The solicitor arrived that same afternoon and Philip

was home by nightfall. The following morning the solicitor visited again, bringing Philip with him. They were closeted with Osbert for over an hour and a half, before summoning the nurse and Edward into the room.

When they all emerged, Mr Baxter looked grim and somewhat shell-shocked, Charlotte fancied, whilst Philip was smiling smugly.

'Mr Baxter . . . ?' Charlotte began, but the man merely rammed his hat on to his head, gave her a curt nod, and hurried out of the front door. Meanwhile, Philip stood in the centre of the hall looking around him.

'There'll have to be some changes made,' he muttered before he followed the solicitor from the house, leaving Charlotte staring after them.

'He's really done it, hasn't he? He's made his will and – and he's left Buckthorn Farm to Philip Thornton. Just like he threatened he would do.'

Forty-Seven

Charlotte was devastated. Until it was actually in writing, signed, sealed and witnessed, a tiny part of her had still clung to the hope that leaving Buckthorn Farm to Philip had been just another of her father's threats. He enjoyed playing with people's lives, manipulating them.

But now it was done. After her father's death, Buckthorn Farm would no longer belong to a member of the Crawford family.

Contrary to everyone's expectations – including his own – Osbert did not die. Slowly, he began to recover. He would never regain the full use of one arm but his speech returned, though he slurred his words and became angry and frustrated if people couldn't understand him.

'I really thought we were getting rid of the old bugger at last,' Edward muttered to his wife.

'Huh! Him? He'll live to be a hundred and twenty – just to spite us all. It's that lass I feel sorry for. She's trapped now for good an' all. And for what? To hand over the farm to that – that good for nothing when the old man does die.'

Life settled back into much the same routine that had existed before Euphemia's arrival. Just as before, Osbert never mentioned her and whether or not he'd known that Charlotte had learned the truth about her mother, it wasn't spoken of between them. But just now and

350

again Charlotte caught a wary look in her father's eyes. Whenever that happened, he would turn his head away, avoiding her gaze.

At the end of six weeks, just before Christmas, Nurse Montgomery declared that she was no longer needed and Dr Markham agreed. 'Edward and Mary can manage him between them. He's regained enough use in his limbs not to be helpless. He just needs a little assistance now and again.' Then the kindly doctor turned to Charlotte and asked, 'But what about you, my dear? I – er – ' He cleared his throat in embarrassment. 'I understand your father has not left you provided for in his will.'

Charlotte sighed. 'So it would seem.'

'Then it's high time you got on with the rest of *your* life, whatever you want that to be.'

She smiled thinly and promised, 'I'll think about it.'

But what could she do? Whilst she would keep in touch with them – and especially with her mother – she had no desire now to live with her aunt. She'd seen another side to the woman and life under her roof, Charlotte was sure, would be little different to the one she had now. Euphemia would be every bit as domineering as her brother. She wondered why her mother had stayed with them all these years? But perhaps the answer was very simple. She had nowhere else to go.

So Charlotte made her decision. However bleak and dismal her future seemed, she would stay with her father. She would do her duty and continue to run Buckthorn Farm.

She wrote carefully worded letters to her mother and to her aunt, making no direct reference to Euphemia's recent visit and the catastrophe it had caused. She merely thanked her aunt for her kind offer of a home, but stated that her duty lay with her father. She hoped that they would allow her to visit them, maybe staying a few days so that she might get to know her mother. To her mother, whom she didn't blame in any way for Euphemia's outburst, she expressed affection and a hope that they might meet often. She posted the letters and bravely faced her bleak future; a future devoted to caring for a man who didn't deserve her sacrifice. Her decision had not been made out of fear of him – she was no longer afraid of his anger – but because of her own sense of duty and loyalty.

'Honour thy father and thy mother,' was her faith's teaching. The good book said nothing about 'only if they should deserve it'.

So Charlotte settled her mind to the future, taking delight in her work. She loved Buckthorn Farm and – for the time being at least – it was still hers in all but name. She revelled in her continuing involvement with the Sunday school, for she loved the children. All of them – even the naughty ones!

And she counted the hours till she might see Miles again.

'So, another Christmas is upon us,' Miles said as they walked along the sand, leading their horses.

Their 'chance' encounters were not so much by accident now. At least, not on Charlotte's side. She knew when Miles was likely to be riding Midnight along the beach.

'I do hope you'll be able to join us at some time over the festive period. Philip and Ben will be home and – ' he paused and smiled, 'Felix is coming to stay with us over Christmas. As you might remember, he has no immediate family and life, even in the hustle and bustle of London, can be very lonely at such times.'

'How lovely!' she said and her pleasure was genuine. She'd liked the flamboyant artist.

She felt Miles's glance upon her as he added quietly, 'And he's asked specifically if you will be with us.'

'Has he?' She looked at him. 'How kind.'

'I don't think it's kindness, my dear. He likes your company.' Very softly, so quietly that she wasn't sure whether she had heard aright, he added, 'As do we all.'

Charlotte was invited to the manor to dine with the family and Felix on Boxing Day.

'Come and see all my presents,' Georgie greeted her excitedly, dragging her up the stairs to the playroom. 'I've got a train set. A Hornby clockwork one. Ben's setting it all up for me. It's got enough track to run all the way round the room. And carriages and even little people.' He flung open the door with a flourish. 'Look!'

For the next hour Charlotte knelt on the floor, playing happily with the two boys. Philip poked his head round the door once, sneered at the childish games and disappeared – much to Charlotte's relief.

At dinner, she was seated next to Felix, who kept them all entranced with his tales of the artistic world in the city. 'I'm opening a gallery soon. It's something I've always wanted to do.' He smiled archly at Charlotte. 'And whilst most of the paintings displayed will be my own,' he laughed heartily, 'that's the whole idea, of course, I shall also be on the lookout for other artists, especially unknown ones whom I can nurture.' He turned to Charlotte. 'Now, my dear, can I persuade you to show me some of your work?'

Charlotte blushed and shook her head. 'It's only a – a hobby with me. I'm not very good.' She hesitated, remembering her father's cruel destruction of nearly all her work. 'And besides, there aren't many paintings to see.'

'I'd like the chance to judge that for myself,' Felix said softly as he touched her hand.

At the end of the table Miles cleared his throat. 'Shall we adjourn to the drawing room, if everyone's ready? And Georgie – I think it's time you went to bed.'

The boy climbed down from his seat. 'Please, may Charlotte read me a story?'

'Well . . .' Miles glanced at her, a question in his eyes. 'If she doesn't mind.'

'Of course I don't mind.' She rose at once, glad to escape from Philip's sneering face.

'Now, don't be away too long,' Felix said, catching hold of her hand and raising it to his lips. 'Don't let that adorable little scamp monopolize you. There are others who want to enjoy your company, you know.'

To her relief when she returned downstairs, having tucked Georgie into his bed and kissed him 'goodnight', Philip had disappeared. Soon Ben excused himself and went to bed leaving only Miles, Felix and Charlotte in front of the blazing log fire. The rest of the evening was spent pleasantly enough, with Miles in the armchair beside the fire and Felix sitting beside her on the sofa. Charlotte couldn't remember a time when she had enjoyed herself so much and when at last she said she really must go home, Felix rose and gallantly kissed her on both cheeks.

'I hope we meet again very soon. I can't stay for New Year this time, though Miles has asked me; I must get back. My gallery has its grand opening in two weeks' time and there's so much to do.' His eyes sparkled suddenly. 'Now, why don't you come down to London for the opening? You could stay with me.' He turned to Miles, but almost as an afterthought. 'And you too, my dear friend.'

'Well . . .' Miles began hesitantly, but Charlotte said at once, 'I'd love to, but I'm sorry, it's really not possible. Though thank you for the kind invitation.'

Felix gave an exaggerated sigh and kissed her hand again.

'I'll see you to the motor,' Miles said abruptly. 'Brewster will drive you home.'

'There's no need,' Charlotte protested. 'I can easily—'

'I wouldn't dream of allowing you to walk anywhere so late at night and in the dark,' he said stiffly as he opened the front door and ushered her down the steps to the waiting vehicle.

He held out his hand to help her climb in and then he closed the door. 'Good night, Charlotte.' He turned away abruptly and as the motor car drew away, Charlotte was left staring at his back as he ran lightly back up the steps and into the house.

'Now,' she murmured to herself, 'what on earth has got into him?'

She wrinkled her forehead, trying to think whether she had said anything untoward, but for the life of her she couldn't think that she had said or done anything which could have offended Miles.

Forty-Eight

On the morning after New Year's Day 1928, Charlotte was surprised to see Miles ride into the yard at Buckthorn Farm, dismount, and stride to the back door.

'A happy new year to you all,' he said, removing his hat and ducking his head as he stepped into the kitchen. His gaze sought Charlotte. 'Ah, I was wondering if you would come for a ride on the beach – that is, if you're not too busy?'

'You go, Miss Charlotte,' Mary said at once before Charlotte had time to reply. 'The fresh air will do you good.' Mary turned to Miles. 'Her father was troublesome in the night, sir. Restless and – demanding. She's not had much sleep herself.'

'Oh – well . . .' Miles hesitated.

'No – no – a gallop on the beach'll blow all the cobwebs away. She can rest this afternoon.'

'It seems your question's been answered for me.' Charlotte laughed. 'Give me five minutes.' She turned and ran from the room to change into her riding habit.

'A cup of tea while you're waiting, sir?' Mary said.

They reached the beach and rode to the water's edge where the receding tide had left the sand firm enough for them to urge their mounts into a gallop. When they

356

slowed again they dismounted and walked side by side, leading their horses.

'Charlotte – there's something I want to say to you, but – but it's difficult.'

'Then the best way is just to say it outright.' She smiled up at him, completely unaware of the bombshell that was about to fall.

'Very well, then.' He paused and seemed to be gathering his courage. 'I would like to offer you my hand in marriage. I have been thinking about it for some time and—'

He got no further. Charlotte whirled round to face him, her temper roused by what she saw as an offer out of humiliating pity. 'Offer me your hand in marriage? How dare you? Is this still to do with Philip and his inheritance? Are you afraid that I will somehow find a way to contest my father's will when the time comes?'

He was staring at her, open-mouthed, shocked and – if she'd stopped for a moment to see – hurt.

'Charlotte, how can you even think – ? Oh dear, I haven't expressed myself very well. I—'

'You most certainly have not,' she snapped. She turned away from him and, gathering the reins in her hands, flung herself up on to her horse.

Looking down at him, she said sarcastically, 'I thank you for the great honour you have bestowed upon me, but I regret I must decline your offer.'

She turned and rode away. When she realized that he was making no attempt to follow her, she allowed the tears to flow. Tears of frustration and humiliation, but, above all, heartbreak. More than anything else in the world, she wanted to marry Miles Thornton for now she knew she loved him with all her heart.

But not like that; not because he felt sorry for her or because he wanted to further safeguard his son's inheritance. Even though Osbert had made a will in the boy's favour, he was perfectly capable of making another that nullified the first. By marrying her, Miles would ensure that Buckthorn Farm came into the Thornton family one way or another. But Charlotte was not going to allow herself to be used.

Oh no, not like that.

It wasn't until the following Sunday that she saw any of the Thornton family again. Since her father's illness, Charlotte attended Matins with just Mary. Her father was not well enough to go to church and Edward stayed with him. Now she and Mary sat together in the front pew.

She heard the Thorntons, all four of them, enter the church and felt them take their places in the pew on the opposite side of the aisle. She heard Georgie whispering. Then, suddenly, he was squeezing into the pew beside her, his hand creeping into hers.

'Father says will you come back to luncheon with me after Sunday school? He says to tell you he's sorry and he wants to talk to you again.'

She glanced down to see the young boy looking up at her with such an appeal in his blue eyes that her heart melted. She might be angry with his father, but there was no reason to take it out on Georgie. Miles had certainly chosen his ambassador well. She could not refuse 'her golden boy'.

'What is Papa – I mean, Father' – for a brief moment, George's new-found 'grown up' status deserted him – 'sorry about?'

She smiled down at him. 'Oh, something and nothing. Grown-up silliness. Don't you worry about it, darling.'

'But will you come? He's been grumpy all week. Ever since the day after New Year. Like "a bear with a sore head", Ben says.'

Charlotte stifled the laughter that bubbled up inside her. 'Yes,' she managed to say as the vicar appeared from the vestry to begin the service. 'I'll come.'

She sighed inwardly. Of course, she should have refused the invitation, but she wasn't strong enough to fight the overwhelming desire to be with him.

Luncheon at the manor was difficult. Charlotte wished that the ebullient Felix was still there to lighten the tension and take command of the stilted conversation. Even Georgie seemed unusually quiet. Philip excused himself from the table as soon as he could and as the meal came to an end, Miles said, 'Ben, will you amuse Georgie for a while? I want to talk to Charlotte.'

'But, Father—' Georgie began to protest, but Miles held up his hand to silence the boy. Then he rose and led the way to his study, Charlotte following in his wake, her heart thumping.

As the door closed, they both began to speak at once. 'Miles – I'm sorry—'

'Charlotte – I'm such a fool—'

She was standing on the hearthrug and he came to her and took her trembling hands in his. He looked down into her upturned face and said softly, 'Charlotte, I have grown fond of you. Very fond. Will you please – please consider becoming my wife?'

She gasped aloud – searching his face for any sign that this was all an act. She wanted to believe him,

359

yearned to believe him, but could she really trust him? She was so afraid of being hurt. Was her heart – which so longed to be loved by him – ruling her head? She fought for her reason to win. She half turned away from him so that they were both facing the portrait of his wife above the mantelpiece. She allowed her hands to stay resting in his, revelling in the strength and the warmth of his touch, as she looked up at the beautiful face of the woman in the painting.

'How – how can you say you want to marry me after loving someone as lovely as Louisa?'

She heard him sigh. 'You want me to be truthful?'

Turning to meet his gaze, she whispered, 'Always.'

Heavily, he said, 'I don't know.' Swiftly, he added, 'Oh, that sounds awful, insulting almost.'

'But it's the truth,' she said flatly. 'And it's the truth I want.'

He squeezed her hands. 'I know. And I understand, too, how difficult it must be for you to believe me. You've been held down for so long, belittled constantly by your father. Never allowed to – to meet anyone, so how are you to know when a man makes a declaration – ' he laughed wryly, 'and certainly such a clumsy one as I made the other day, that it's the truth? In addition to which Louisa's memory is still revered in this house. There are pictures of her everywhere. Philip remembers her well and will never entertain the idea of anyone taking her place. Ben has vague recollections of her and he's no doubt swayed by his elder brother. As for Georgie, well, of all of us, he's the only one who has no recollection of her. But he has been raised to know her.'

'And he carries the burden of thinking he caused her death.'

'I hope not. I've fought hard to explain that to him. No child should carry such guilt.'

'So – why?'

'I miss you when you're not here. I've gone down to the beach every morning, hoping to meet you – accidentally.'

She began to laugh, resting her head briefly against his shoulder.

'What?' he asked. 'Why are you laughing?'

'I have, too.'

'Have you? Have you really?' Now it was he who was uncertain, unable to believe what he hoped might be true. That she felt something for him too. He turned her to face him once more, his hands resting lightly on her shoulders.

'It's not the same feeling I had for Louisa, it's only fair to tell you that.'

Charlotte felt a coldness creep through her. But Miles was continuing, trying to be utterly honest with her so that there should be no secrets between them, no misunderstanding and, most of all, no misapprehension.

'You bring love and warmth and fun into the house when you're here. Georgie adores you and Ben, too, has started to talk about you and ask when you're to visit again.'

'And Philip?' she asked softly. 'How would Philip react to such news?'

Miles shrugged. 'Who's to know what my eldest son will do next? He's soon to go to university. He won't be here very much. And besides, it's my happiness and the two younger boys I'm thinking about. We're good friends, too, aren't we?'

'Yes, we are,' she said wistfully, 'but is that a strong

enough basis for marriage? One day the younger boys will be gone as well. What then?'

'It's not just for them. I get lonely. I want – and need – someone to share the rest of *my* life with. I care deeply about you, Charlotte. I want to look after you and make you happy. Do you think I could do that?'

Despite the fact that he had not once used the word 'love' when explaining his feelings for her, she could not lie to him. Her love for him, regardless of what he truly felt for her, would have to be enough. She loved him with every part of her being. If she were to refuse him now, she knew that there would never be another man whom she could love like she loved Miles. He'd said he was fond of her, he cared about her. He had become a good friend. It would have to be enough. She would put aside all foolish notions of a romantic, passionate lover. She knew that to be near him was all she ever wanted. All she would ever want.

'Yes – you could,' she whispered, but even now she had to be honest. 'But – but could I make you happy?'

'Of *course* you could. Oh my dear, we'll build such a happy home for the boys and our children – if we're blessed with any of our own; a daughter, perhaps, to make our family perfect.'

She didn't know whether to laugh out loud or allow the tears that were so close to fall unchecked. She was filled with a strange mixture of emotions. She loved Miles so much that she was willing to devote the rest of her life to him, but she was still unsure just why he wanted to marry her.

Was it, she couldn't help thinking, because he yearned for a daughter, just as, ironically, her father had craved a son? She could not, would not, ask him. She was honest enough to acknowledge that she might not like the answer.

'So, Miss Charlotte Crawford, will you marry me?'

'Yes, Mr Thornton, I will.'

Suddenly, he picked her up and swung her round. 'You've made me the happiest man alive.' Then, lowering her to the ground, he enfolded her in his arms and kissed her.

Forty-Nine

'Come, let's go and find the boys. We must tell them at once.'

'No – wait. This is going too fast.'

He laughed down at her. 'Not changing your mind already, are you?'

'Of course not, but – but there's so much to discuss. My father, Buckthorn Farm . . .'

'My dear, Mary and Edward will continue to care for your father. You can ride over every day, if you wish, to see him – run the farm, whatever you want to do. But at night – ' he touched her face with a gentle finger – 'you will come home to me.'

'But I should be here all the time, helping you. Running this house – being a dutiful wife.'

Now Miles threw back his head and laughed aloud. 'I don't want a "dutiful" wife. I want a soulmate, a friend and' – he kissed her again – 'a lover.'

Now Charlotte blushed and dipped her head.

'But you're right,' he went on. 'I should speak to your father first – ask his permission.'

Now it was Charlotte who laughed. 'His permission? I am twenty-seven. We don't need his permission.'

'No – but I'd like to ask him anyway. I want to see his face when he realizes that at long last his *daughter* is going to lead her own life.'

'Yes,' she said slowly. 'D'you know, I'd quite like to see that myself.'

'Then shall we go, hand in hand, like underage young lovers to seek his approval?'

Charlotte began to laugh and when Miles joined in, the sound carried out through the door and into the rest of the house. Hearing it, Georgie could contain his curiosity no longer and ran downstairs and into the study without pausing to knock, to find his father and Miss Charlotte in each other's arms.

A wide grin spread across his face. 'Are you two friends again, then?' he asked innocently.

They turned to look at him, then at each other as Miles said softly, 'You could say that, Georgie. We're definitely friends again.'

'Tell him,' Charlotte whispered. 'It's only fair.'

'Are you sure?'

When she nodded, he held out his hand to the boy, drawing him to them. 'Georgie, how would you like Charlotte to be your new mama?'

He gaped up at them for a moment and then he gave a whoop of delight and capered about the room, ending up with his arms round Charlotte, his head pressed into her waist. 'How wonderful! Oh, I must tell the others.'

'No – Georgie, let me . . .' Miles began, but the boy was gone, running from the room and shouting at the top of his voice. 'Ben – Philip – Father's going to marry Charlotte.'

'Oh dear,' Miles said.

' "Oh dear" indeed,' Charlotte murmured. 'I don't think that's the best way Philip should hear the news, do you?'

'Brace yourself, my dear,' Miles said, taking her hand

as they heard the clatter of footsteps coming down the stairs and heading across the hall towards the study.

Georgie arrived back in the room first, dragging Ben by the hand.

'Is it true?' Ben asked.

'Yes,' Miles said and Charlotte was overcome when Ben smiled, moved towards them to shake his father's hand. Then, blushing a little, he kissed Charlotte on both cheeks. 'I'm so pleased for both of you.'

'You – you don't mind?' she asked tentatively.

'Lord, no,' Ben said. 'I don't know why he didn't ask you months ago. We all love you—'

'You speak for yourself,' an angry voice interrupted and they all looked round to see Philip standing in the doorway, leaning nonchalantly against the doorframe, his arms folded. 'There's no need to marry her now, Father. The old man's made his will and everything will be mine when he dies – which can't be long now. And there'll be nothing she can do about it. I was there when he signed it. So, you don't have to marry her, you see. My inheritance is quite safe now.'

Miles took a step towards him. 'How dare you speak to me like that?' he raged. 'And in front of Charlotte, too. I've asked her to marry me because I want to. I *want* her to be my wife. There's no other reason. It has nothing to do with your blasted inheritance.'

As he took in his father's words, Philip's twisted spitefully. 'So,' he snarled, 'you wouldn't agree to marry her to protect my inheritance, but now you're going to put that all at risk. Don't you see, Father – ' suddenly, his tone was pleading, 'if you have a child – a son – he'll change his will again. He'll want his *grandson* to inherit, now, won't he?'

'So? What if he did?' He turned briefly to Charlotte to say, 'Forgive me, my dear . . .' Then back again to his son. 'What's so special about Buckthorn Farm? A few acres, a house, that's all?'

'But it'll be mine.' Philip thumped his own chest. 'All mine. And something I won't have to *share*.' He swept out his arm towards his two brothers and then turned about and stalked away.

Mildly, Ben, the quiet one of the brothers, said, 'You know, he never was very good at sharing his toys.'

'I suppose two out of three isn't too bad,' Miles said as he drove Charlotte to Buckthorn Farm. 'But how do you think your father's going to take the news?'

'Goodness knows,' she answered dryly. 'Or anyone else, for that matter.' She glanced at him. 'There are going to be a lot of raised eyebrows, you know.'

Miles chuckled. 'How delightful!' He took his hand from the steering wheel and reached across to grip hers. 'But everyone will be so pleased for you, my dear. Everyone loves you.'

She smiled weakly. Everyone except you, she thought.

They entered by the front door of Buckthorn Farm and went straight to the sitting room.

'Mr – Thornton,' Osbert slurred. 'How – nice. Fetch some tea, girl.'

'That would be nice, Mr Crawford, but first I have something to ask you. I'd like to ask you for the hand of your daughter in marriage.'

Slowly, Osbert raised his head, squinting up at the

tall man standing in front of him. Charlotte found she was holding her breath. Not that his answer mattered. She was of age and she was going to marry Miles anyway, whatever her father said. She'd already decided that. Whatever Miles's real feelings for her were, it didn't matter. Not to her. She wanted to marry the man *she* loved, no matter what. No, the reason she was apprehensive was because she'd no wish to distress her father and bring on another stroke.

'And you'll give – me a – grandson?'

Miles looked aghast for a second, but then he nodded. 'If we're blessed,' he murmured. 'A grandson – or a grand*daughter*.'

'Huh!' Osbert growled. 'Don't want any more girls in this family.' He frowned now at Charlotte. 'Aye, you can take her, and you're welcome. And you, girl, do something useful for once. Give me a grandson.'

As they left the room, Miles heaved a sigh of relief. 'Well, that was easier than I thought. I'd assumed he'd be reluctant to let you go.'

Charlotte laughed. 'Let me go? He can't wait to get rid of me. I wouldn't be surprised if he doesn't suggest Philip coming to live here with him.' She bit back the words she'd been about to blurt out; that her father had once suggested that Philip should change his surname to 'Crawford'.

'They'd be welcome to each other.'

'You don't mean that?'

'No – no, I don't suppose I do. But, just sometimes, my eldest son irritates me almost beyond endurance.'

'Well, as long as it's only "almost",' she teased. 'Now, let's go and tell Mary.'

The devoted Mary burst into noisy tears, but they were tears of joy. 'Oh Miss Charlotte – Mr Thornton, sir. What wonderful news! Edward – Edward, d'you hear? Our little Charlotte's going to be married.'

Edward nodded and smiled and shook Miles's hand. And there were tears in his eyes, too. ''Tis the best news ever, miss.'

'There's just one thing – will you stay here with Father? I mean, if you'd rather not – ' She paused and glanced up at Miles for support.

'If you'd rather leave,' he said, 'then we'll employ someone else to take care of him.'

Husband and wife glanced at each other. 'No, no,' Edward said. 'We know his little ways. We'll stay.'

' "Better the devil you know",' Mary said and then added hurriedly, 'begging your pardon, miss.'

'I'll see that you both get a rise in your wages,' Charlotte promised. 'You'll be taking on more responsibility.'

'That'd be very kind of you, miss. We'll need to put a little by for our old age,' Mary said.

'You see,' Edward said tentatively, 'we'd always believed we'd have a home here with you, miss, when you inherited the farm. But since we know that Master Philip will one day be the new owner, well, our future's a bit uncertain.'

'I think I can speak for my future wife,' Miles smiled, 'as well as for myself when I tell you that you need have no fears on that score. We shall find a home for you somewhere on the Ravensfleet Estate, you can be sure of that. Though I hope that won't be for many years yet.'

'Thank you, sir.' Mary, overcome with gratitude, kissed a startled Miles on both cheeks.

As they left the house again, Miles murmured, 'What good people they are.'

369

'I don't know what would have become of me if it hadn't been for them.'

He squeezed her hand. 'Then I have every reason to be grateful to them. And now, my dear, we have a wedding to plan.'

Fifty

Charlotte wrote to her mother and her aunt with the news. She didn't want an estrangement between herself and her aunt, but she was now a little wary of her. She was careful what she said or wrote. Despite her outward display of affection, Euphemia had the same vengeful streak in her that her brother had. It was in their genes. Charlotte fervently hoped she hadn't inherited that same flaw. She felt she must be more like her gentle mother, who'd run away from the cruelty. And yet Charlotte was now finding that there was a spark of defiance in her that surprised her. Until recently she'd never questioned her life, never compared it to the lives of others and found her own lacking. But now she did. She'd been treated abominably by her father and she owed him nothing. Yet her innate goodness demanded that she should still see that he was cared for and comfortable.

She received an enthusiastic letter back from Euphemia:

You must come and stay a few days with us. We'd love to have you. And we can go shopping in Lincoln for your wedding finery. Your uncle is insisting that he should pay for your dress and accessories. And your mother would so love to help you choose. Don't deny her that little pleasure, Charlotte, I beg you . . .

'Shall you go?' Miles asked when she showed him the letter.

'Yes, I think I will.'

'I'm thinking of asking Felix to be my best man.'

Charlotte looked at him in surprise. 'I thought you would ask Philip.'

'I did,' Miles said shortly. 'And he refused.'

'Ah.'

'In fact – I'm sorry to say it – he's refusing to attend the wedding.'

'Miles,' Charlotte cried, 'I don't want to be the cause of trouble in your family.'

'You're not, my dear. If anything's causing a rift it's your father's ridiculous actions. Philip's getting above himself. At eighteen he sees himself as a future land-owner.'

Charlotte shrugged. 'Well, he will be. You can't deny that.'

'No – but it's not good for a boy of his age to know it.'

She was silent for a moment before she suggested, 'What about Ben being your best man?'

Miles stared at her for a moment. 'I – I hadn't thought of Ben. I'd considered him too young.'

Charlotte smiled. 'Your quiet son has more maturity than some young men twice his age. If you'd like one of your sons by your side, then I think you should ask Ben. Of course, Georgie . . .' She broke off as they both began to smile at the mere thought of the boy. That was what Georgie did to people; he made them smile just thinking about him.

'Georgie would do it like a shot, but I *do* think he is a little young at seven, don't you?'

'I suppose so,' she said fondly. 'But he'd certainly liven up the proceedings as your best man.'

'Mind you, I'd forget to be nervous if I had him to worry about.'

'Nervous? You're not going to be nervous, are you?'

Miles laughed. 'I don't think so. I shall just worry you might have changed your mind and won't turn up.'

'Oh, I'll not change my mind,' she said firmly and then asked softly, 'Will you?'

'Never!' he said and gently raised her hand to his lips and kissed her fingers.

The wedding was fixed for the Saturday after Easter, so that Miles's sons would be still at home for the holidays.

Charlotte enjoyed a few days in Lincoln with her aunt and uncle and – more importantly – with her mother. Euphemia was nothing if not generous with Percy's money but he only smiled benignly and admired all their purchases. Euphemia swept Charlotte and her mother into the city's largest store, leading them from department to department and demanding the attention of the head saleswoman in each. Her aunt suggested the very latest fashion for the wedding dress, but Charlotte was adamant.

'I don't like the modern shorter dresses, Aunt. I'd like a traditional Edwardian style and a hat trimmed with yards of tulle rather than a veil.'

Euphemia beamed. 'Of course, my dear, you shall have exactly what you want. And have you decided on a bridesmaid?'

'Ah, now, that caused me a bit of a problem. I don't

have any close friends of my own age.' Euphemia and Alice glanced at each other, realizing what a lonely life Charlotte had led. 'Mary and Peggy felt they were too old, so I've asked Lily to be my matron of honour.' She smiled. 'She was thrilled and our local dressmaker is making her a dress in pastel blue.'

Euphemia gave an exaggerated sigh but, for once, said nothing.

Once the wedding dress, hat, shoes, gloves and underwear had been bought, Euphemia led the way to the hairdresser. 'And this time, my dear, I really think you should have your hair cut into a fashionable bob.'

'No, Aunt.' Once again, Charlotte gently stood up to her aunt. 'I think my hairstyle should match the style of my dress. I've become quite adept at putting my hair up now, though I would like the hairdresser to show me a style befitting a bride.'

'I agree,' Alice put in quietly.

This time Euphemia capitulated gracefully. 'I'm no match for both of you.'

But when the hairdresser had shown Charlotte how to put her long dark hair up in a profusion of curls and waves, even Euphemia had to admit that it suited her to perfection.

'Darling, you look absolutely beautiful,' Alice said with joyful tears. 'Do you think you'll be able to do it on your wedding day?'

'I'll get Peggy to help me. We can have a few practice sessions beforehand.'

They returned home tired but elated. 'I can't thank you enough, Uncle . . .' Charlotte began, but Percy waved her aside, smiling benevolently. 'Think nothing of it, dear girl. It's our pleasure. And to see you mother so happy too . . .'

'Ah, now, that's another thing,' her aunt said. 'We intend to come to your wedding, Charlotte. *All* of us.'

'Euphemia, dear, I don't think—' Alice began, but her sister-in-law was adamant. 'You have been denied access to your only child all these years, Alice. But you are going to be there on her wedding day.'

'Everyone thinks she's – she's dead. Just like I did. I told you, there's a grave in the churchyard with her name on the headstone.'

'Well, we're coming and, whatever happens, your father will deserve whatever's coming to him.'

'I would love to go,' Alice said, and suddenly there was a surprising note of firmness in her tone, 'but I will only go if I can be incognito. I will wear a hat with a veil and no one will know who I am. Now you're to promise me, Euphemia.'

Euphemia wriggled her shoulders but, for once, was obliged to say, 'Oh very well, then.'

'Miles, I don't know what to do. It could cause my father another serious stroke. If my mother turns up the whole village will know of his deception. I fully intend to put matters right about the gravestone once he's – he's gone. It won't matter then. It can't hurt him, but for her to come back now . . .'

Miles chewed his lip thoughtfully. 'It is a bit of a dilemma. But you say your mother's going to wear a veil. Will anyone recognize her?'

'I don't know,' Charlotte wailed. Her joy in her wedding day was already being spoiled.

Miles put his arms round her. 'Have you told your mother and aunt about the gravestone?'

She nodded and told him of Euphemia's response.

'Your aunt's certainly vicious towards your father, isn't she?'

'Yes – it goes back to their youth. Her father was against her marrying Percy and I think my father fuelled the quarrel. My grandfather evidently cast her off when she defied him. But my father's as bad – worse, if anything, than she is. He – he calls her the most dreadful names.' Colour rose in her cheeks as she recalled the distressing scenes she'd witnessed between her father and his sister.

'Do you want your mother to be at your wedding?'

'Oh yes, yes. She's the innocent in all this. She's gentle and doesn't want to cause trouble. It's Aunt Euphemia who's so vitriolic against my father.'

He put his arms round her and she leaned against his shoulder, revelling in his strength and his support. No longer was she so alone. She'd always had Mary and Edward, of course, and they'd been wonderful, but they'd never been able to help her with important decisions. Even if she'd asked their advice, they'd always said primly, 'It's not our place to say, Miss Charlotte.'

But now she had Miles.

'Why don't you sound your father out on his plans for the day? Is he to give you away?'

She raised her head to look up at him. 'I don't know. I'd never really thought about it. I'd just presumed he would.'

'Talk to him.'

'I will.'

Charlotte was trembling as she stood before Osbert.

'Father – you will give me away on my wedding day, won't you?'

He frowned. 'It depends,' he growled.

'On what?'

'On how you're going to be dressed. If you're going to deck yourself out like some trollop, then I have no intention of being disgraced. I shall not be there.'

Charlotte lifted her chin defiantly. 'I've already bought my wedding dress.'

He glowered at her. 'And I suppose *she* went with you? Helped you choose?'

'If you mean my aunt, then yes. She did.'

He glared at her, and she could read the question in his eyes. Did he guess that her mother had been there too? But the words remained unspoken.

'So,' she said at last. 'What am I to do? Do you wish me to show you what I shall be wearing and then you can make up your mind?'

His eyes narrowed. 'You're getting very uppity, miss. Just because Thornton's come to his senses and decided to protect his son's inheritance, there's no need to forget your duty to your father.'

'I won't. I'll always make sure you're cared for. I promise you that.' Then, boldly she added, 'Philip's afraid that if I do have a child – a boy – you will change your will.'

Osbert's eyes gleamed. 'I might. We'll have to see about that, won't we?' He gave a humourless laugh. 'So – he doesn't want you to have a son – and I do. What about Thornton? Does he want another boy?'

'Oh no,' Charlotte threw back over her shoulder as she left the room with, for probably the first time in the whole of her life, the last word. 'He wants a daughter.'

Fifty-One

'You are not wearing *that*!'

Her father thumped his stick on the floor with his good hand. Then he lunged out at the dress she was holding up for his inspection, trying to hook it out of her grasp and throw it towards the fire. Charlotte stepped backwards just in time.

'You hussy – you whore! Just like your – your aunt.'

For a moment she thought he'd been going to say 'mother'. With an outward calm she was not feeling inside, she said, 'This is the dress I shall be wearing on my wedding day, Father. So – do I take it that you will not be attending?'

He glared at her. 'You dishonour me. You bring shame to my name.'

'I'm sorry you feel that way,' she said with a quiet dignity. 'But very soon I'll no longer bear the name of Crawford, will I?'

He glared at her and was silent for several moments whilst she waited, her heart pounding nervously. Then he raised his head and said slowly, 'But I'll be there. I won't let folks say *I* didn't do my duty. But you'll make a laughing stock of yourself.'

'So, he's coming to the wedding, is he?' Miles said when she told him what had passed between her and her father.

'He says so. But I wouldn't put it past him to cry off at the last minute. And then who would I get to give me away?'

'There's your uncle or Edward – or even Felix. He'd step in if he was needed, I know, now that Ben's agreed to be my best man.' He paused and then, smiling mischievously, added, 'So – what is so dreadful about this dress?'

Charlotte laughed and tapped him playfully on the nose. 'Now, now, you know I'm not going to tell you anything about my dress. It's unlucky.'

'What does Mary think of it?'

Charlotte's eyes were suddenly dreamy. 'She thinks it's lovely.'

'And your aunt and mother helped you choose it – so what are you worrying about?' He put his arms round her. 'I'm sure it'll be wonderful.'

'I'll have to write and tell them that Father's going to be at the wedding.'

'By all means warn them, but let your mother make up her own mind. From what you've told me about her, I'm sure she'll do nothing that would embarrass you or spoil your day.'

Charlotte looked up at him with troubled eyes. 'Yes – but what might my aunt do?'

Charlotte's wedding day dawned fine and sunny, with a light breeze. She was incredibly nervous and Mary could do nothing to calm her anxieties. But it had nothing to do with her future husband or even his family. For once, not even Philip's spite could overshadow her happiness. Her only anxiety was her own relatives and what they might – or might not – do.

Mary went ahead, whilst Edward drove Charlotte and her father to the church in a flower-bedecked carriage that Miles had hired especially.

'Such nonsense,' Osbert growled as Edward almost lifted him into the vehicle. 'A waste of money. I hope you're not expecting me to pay for all this.'

'No, Father. Miles is paying for everything. The reception is in a marquee in the garden at the manor.'

'And your fripperies?' he sneered. 'Am I expected to pay for you to dress like a whore? And where are your spectacles?'

'No, Father. You're not paying for anything.' She bit back the words to tell him that her uncle had paid for her wedding finery and her going-away outfit; indeed, all her trousseau, even down to the half-dozen fine lace handkerchiefs. As for the question about her spectacles, she chose to ignore it.

As the carriage jerked and they set off towards the church, he grumbled, 'And I suppose you are going away on *honeymoon* for weeks on end.'

'Just one week, Father. We're only going to London.'

'That den of iniquity. What is the man thinking of? I'm beginning to have doubts about letting you marry him. It's not too late, we can still turn back.' He raised his voice. 'Edward—'

'I have no intention of turning back, Father. Drive on, Edward,' she commanded and her heart was singing as Edward slapped the reins to quicken the pace towards a new beginning with the love of her life.

The church was full to overflowing. Several people couldn't even get into the body of the church and crowded into the porch, jostling each other to hear the couple make their vows. Smiling and nodding, they made way for the bride, her father and Edward.

A gasp rippled amongst them as Charlotte lifted her head and smiled at them.

'Miss Charlotte, you look lovely,' someone called out.

The same surprise ran through the whole of the congregation, when Charlotte and her father made their slow progress up the aisle.

She caught some of the whispers. 'Why, she's lovely.' 'Just look at her.' 'Who'd have thought it?'

And when Miles turned to watch his bride coming towards him, she saw a brief look of amazement in his eyes, which he was unable to hide. He held out his hand and she took it, in that moment placing all her trust and her future happiness in his hands.

'Doesn't she look pretty?' Georgie's voice piped up from the second pew. Laughter rippled through the congregation and someone – she was sure it was Jackson Warren – called, 'More than that, Master Georgie. She's beautiful.'

Miles, his gaze never leaving her face, raised her hand to his lips and whispered, 'Indeed you are, my dear.'

She turned briefly to glance at Georgie and to her surprise saw both Ben and Felix sitting beside him. Then who – ? She leaned forward a little to look beyond Miles and saw, for the first time, that it was Philip standing next to him. The young man was staring straight ahead, stony faced, and Charlotte knew he was only there because he hadn't wanted his younger brother to usurp his rightful place. But at least, she thought, his presence will have made Miles happy.

She smiled up at Miles as they both turned towards the vicar who'd replaced Cuthbert Iveson. He was a much older man, with a benign smile and twinkling eyes. Her father would not be able to manipulate this man, Charlotte thought, as he began to speak in a deep resonant voice that carried down the church and even out through the door so that all might hear.

The service went ahead without any interruptions or hitches and at last they were walking back down the aisle between row upon row of beaming faces accompanied not only by the 'Wedding March', but also by a storm of clapping and cheering and shouts of 'Good luck' and 'God bless you'.

'See how everyone loves you?' Miles murmured.

She smiled up at him but the one question she longed to ask remained unspoken. But do *you* love me?

Just as they were about to step out of the church, Charlotte noticed a woman sitting in the far corner, half hidden behind a pillar and wearing a wide-brimmed hat with a veil over her face.

Alice Crawford had come to her daughter's wedding.

'Of course you're coming to the reception.' Euphemia's raised voice could be heard ringing through the church-yard as the guests and onlookers watched the couple emerge from the porch. Miles and Charlotte paused for photographs to be taken by the man who kept disappearing beneath the black cloth covering the huge box camera set up on a tripod between the graves.

'Smile,' he burbled.

'No one's recognized you,' Euphemia said. 'Just keep away from *him*.'

Mary hurried up to Charlotte. 'Your aunt's talking to – to the woman who was sitting at the back of the church. Is it – is it who I think it is?'

Charlotte nodded and glanced anxiously across to where her aunt and uncle were standing talking to the heavily veiled woman. She was about to turn towards Miles to seek his help, when another voice rose above the rest. 'Are we going to stand about here all day, taking ridiculous photographs?' Osbert rasped. 'Philip, my boy, your arm, if you please.'

Philip moved to his side. 'It seems,' Osbert said, his tone heavy with sarcasm, 'that I shall no longer have my daughter to rely on.' He sniffed. 'Not that she ever was much use. Now, shall you and I go back to Buckthorn Farm? Mary will make us a meal.'

Before Philip could answer, Miles cut in, 'Philip will be coming back to the manor for the reception. He agreed to be my best man, so he must fulfil his duties for the rest of the day. And Mary and Edward are our guests.' Mildly, he added, 'And I'd have thought you'd wish to be there – as father of the bride.'

Osbert glowered. He could not return to the farm on his own and Mary was busy throwing confetti and enjoying a rare day of freedom.

'Seems I have no choice,' Osbert grumbled. 'That girl! Such a lot of fuss. I hope your father is going to keep her in line, Philip. She'll get above herself, given half a chance.'

'Mm,' Philip said, his eyes narrowing. 'Well, we'll just have to see that doesn't happen, won't we?'

And then a rare thing happened; Osbert Crawford actually smiled.

Miles had let it be known that anyone and everyone was welcome at the manor. Mrs Beddows had been baking for weeks and extra help had been employed from Ravensfleet so that there was enough food to feed an army. The guests mingled freely and happily on the sunlit lawn, but one woman kept herself in the shadow of the trees at the end of the garden. Only Mary approached her, taking her a drink and some food on a plate.

Charlotte watched from a distance, but did not dare go to her mother for fear Osbert's eagle eyes would see and guess just who the stranger was. She spent the afternoon on tenterhooks, not enjoying her wedding day as she should have done.

It was almost over and Charlotte began to breathe more easily. A few guests were already drifting away and the afternoon was growing cooler.

Euphemia was standing before her. 'Well, my dear, it's time we were making our way home. We have a car waiting and your mother flatly refuses to come indoors. It's getting chilly now, so—'

'What's that?'

So intent had she been on saying goodbye to her guests that Charlotte hadn't seen her father standing close behind her. Her heart missed a beat as she saw Euphemia's eyes widen as if in surprise, but Charlotte had the uncomfortable feeling that her aunt had known all along that Osbert was in earshot. Maybe she'd even engineered it.

'Oh, Osbert, my dear brother. I didn't see you there. We're just about to leave. Now how about a kiss for your sister? Isn't it time we let bygones be bygones?'

But Osbert held himself aloof, glaring at her with hatred in his eyes. Through clenched teeth, his eyes boring into hers, he asked his sister, 'Who is that woman?'

Euphemia, her eyes sparkling for a fight, stepped

closer, but Charlotte caught her arm, 'Please, Aunt, no . . .'

But Euphemia was not to be outdone. She shook off Charlotte's hand, her eyes narrowing as she said slowly, 'Don't you recognize your own wife?'

Osbert reeled and might have fallen had it not been for his arm still through Philip's. The young man steadied him, but glanced, mystified, at Charlotte for an explanation.

Charlotte looked around her wildly. Miles – where was Miles? She saw him talking to Joe and Peggy Warren. She hurried across the grass. 'Miles – oh please, Miles, come quickly. My aunt . . .'

'My dear, whatever's the matter?'

She caught hold of his hand. 'The woman down there – under the trees – is my mother, and Aunt Euphemia has just told my father . . .'

Leaving Joe and Peggy staring open-mouthed after them, Miles hurried back with Charlotte towards her father and aunt, still locked in a battle of wills. 'Leave it to me, my dear.' Raising his voice, Miles greeted them heartily, as if knowing nothing of the contretemps. 'Mrs Bell – just leaving. And you, Mr Crawford. Philip, would you please accompany Mr Crawford to Buckthorn Farm? Brewster will drive you and I'll see that Mary and Edward know you've gone home.'

With a smooth, but authoritative air, Miles shook hands with them both and also with Percy, who'd ambled across the grass. 'I'm so glad you could come. Let me see you to your car?'

'But—' Euphemia began.

'Come along, my dear.' Percy, catching on very quickly, took hold of his wife's arm and, with surprising determination, led her away.

But Euphemia was not to be outdone. As Percy led her to the driveway at the side of the lawn and towards their waiting car, she called out in a loud, imperious voice, deliberately so that everyone would hear.

'Alice – come, my dear, we are ordered home.'

As the last guest departed down the driveway, Charlotte said, 'Thank you, Miles. Your diplomacy avoided an ugly scene.'

'I think I missed my vocation,' he chuckled, putting his arm round her. 'Now, forget all about it, my dear. No harm done.'

But Charlotte wasn't so sure. Soon, the whole district would hear the gossip and would be speculating on how Alice Crawford came to be still alive when she was supposed to be buried in the churchyard.

'Before we leave, there's just something I want to show you,' Miles said.

Charlotte had changed from her wedding gown into her going-away outfit. Their suitcases were packed and loaded into the car and Miles was to drive them as far as Grantham where they would stay the night in a hotel. The following day, leaving the car there, they would travel to London by train.

Taking her hand, he led her upstairs to the top floor and along the landing to a room at the far corner of the house.

'I've never been up here before,' Charlotte said.

'It's where the servants sleep but there's one room unoccupied and I just thought it would be ideal. It's a north-facing room, so there should be plenty of light from the big window. I've had it enlarged especially.'

Oh dear, she thought, he's decked out a nursery in pink. Oh dear . . .

But when he flung open the door, Charlotte gasped aloud. The whole room was fitted out as an artist's studio. There was everything there that she could possibly want and more; desk and chair, easels, drawing boards, canvases stacked against the wall, tubes of oil paints, watercolours, brushes of every size and shape, pencils, pens and inks, pastels, paper of all types and sizes in abundance and all manner of accessories that, at the moment, Charlotte had no idea exactly what they were for. She gazed around, her mouth open in wonder.

'It's my wedding gift to you, my dear. Felix had free rein. I don't think he's enjoyed himself so much in a long time. We didn't know what was your favourite medium to work in, so we just got everything we could think of. But if there's anything we've forgotten, just say the word.'

'Miles, I don't know what to say. This is wonderful.'

'I want you to be happy, my dear. And I know you love to paint. There's just one thing – Felix is demanding to see some of your work and now there's no excuse.'

'But I'm not very good . . .' she began.

'That's not what I've heard. Jackson Warren told me you'd painted some lovely pictures.'

Charlotte's face clouded as she remembered her father's cruel destruction of her work. But here she would be safe. Here she could paint and draw to her heart's content. They'd thought of everything. In one corner of the light, airy room there was a sofa and, close by, a small bookcase which Felix had filled with books on drawing and painting and the lives of some of the great painters.

There were tears in her eyes as she kissed him. 'It's the most wonderful wedding present. I never dreamed . . .'

He chuckled as he pulled her close. 'I do, of course, have an ulterior motive.'

'What?'

'Whenever you're missing, I'll know exactly where to find you.'

Fifty-Two

Charlotte was happy – happier than she'd ever been in her life or ever dared hope to be. Ben and Georgie accepted and welcomed her wholeheartedly. Only Philip was still prickly, but even he seemed to mellow a little after the incident over Louisa's portrait.

On the afternoon of their return home from honeymoon, Georgie flew across the hall, slipping and sliding on the polished floor as he ran to greet them.

'Papa, Charlotte . . .' He threw himself against them in turn, forgetting in the excitement of the moment that he was supposed to be quite grown up now. Ben smiled quietly from the staircase.

Philip appeared on the landing. He leaned over the banister. 'And what,' his voice rang out, 'do you mean by leaving instructions for Mother's portraits to be removed from the dining room and even from your study, Father? I suppose *she*'s demanded it, has she?'

Charlotte gasped and turned wide eyes on her new husband. 'You shouldn't have done that, Miles. I'd never ask such a thing.'

Miles ignored her. Instead, he raised angry eyes to Philip. 'We'll talk about it later.'

'No,' Charlotte said sharply. 'We'll talk about it now. Philip, please come down.'

Sulkily, the young man descended the stairs.

'Now,' she said, more gently, 'what is all this about?'

Georgie said nothing, but she felt his hand creep into hers.

'Philip?' Charlotte prompted. 'Please tell me.'

'Father left instructions that whilst you were on – whilst you were away, Wilkins should remove the paintings of our mother from view.' His lip curled. 'I suppose he thought it would upset you being constantly reminded of how beautiful his first wife was and how much he loved her.'

'Philip!' Miles thundered, but Charlotte put her hand on his arm and said softly, 'It's all right, Miles.' Turning back to Philip and including Ben and Georgie too, she said gently, 'I wouldn't dream of allowing the portraits of your mother to be removed. They will be put back at once and there they will stay.'

Philip blinked, wrong-footed for a moment. But then he smiled sarcastically. 'Another of your little schemes to ingratiate yourself into the family, is it? Making out you're not trying to take her place?'

Charlotte shook her head. 'I'm not.' But she could see he did not believe her. 'No one can take another's place. We're all individuals and loved, in different ways, perhaps, for ourselves, for who we are.'

Philip laughed, but without humour. 'And you really think my father loves you like he loved my mother?'

'Philip!' Miles began again and took a step towards his son, but Charlotte held him back and answered the boy quietly, 'No, Philip, I expect no such thing. Your father has been very honest with me about his reasons for asking me to marry him.' Her tone was firmer as she added, 'But those reasons, my dear, are private between us and no concern of yours.'

Philip laughed again. 'Oh, but I think they are. I

think they have everything to do with me. *And my inheritance.*'

Now Miles shook himself free of Charlotte's restraining hand and stepped towards his son. Through gritted teeth, he demanded an apology.

Philip stood his ground. 'See what she's done, Father? For the first time in my life, I'm going to disobey you. Already, she's coming between us. She'll break up our family. You'll see.' He glanced towards Charlotte now. 'I will not apologize, but I will say one thing. Whatever your ulterior motive is – and I'm sure you have one – I'm grateful for you allowing the portraits to be put back where they belong. I do thank you for that. And now I'm going back to school.'

As he turned to go upstairs, he passed Ben standing on the bottom step.

'You know, Phil, I never thought I'd say it because – until recently – I've always admired you and looked up to you. But you're an idiot – you have been ever since Mr Crawford promised to make you his heir. It's gone to your head and turned you into someone I don't like very much. Charlotte is a good person. I like her and so does Georgie and if she makes Father happy, then you should be glad. Glad for them both.'

It was the longest speech any of them had ever heard the quiet Ben make and they all stared at him. Georgie clapped his hands and began to skip around the hall, chanting, 'Philip's an idiot! Phil-ip's an id-i-ot.'

'Stop that, Georgie,' Charlotte said sharply and held out her hand to him. 'That's not nice.'

The little boy stopped and came meekly back to her. 'Sorry, Charlotte.'

She stroked his hair and smiled down at him and he

knew himself forgiven. As for Philip, he stared at Ben for a long moment and then turned and ran up the stairs, two at a time.

It had spoiled their homecoming, but Ben and Georgie made her so welcome, that Philip's cruel jibes, if not forgotten, were soothed. And once both Philip and Ben had gone back to school, Charlotte had her little golden boy all to herself.

Over the following weeks and months, life at the manor slipped into a routine that seemed to suit them all. Philip was away at school and, when he was at home, Charlotte took refuge in her studio. She studied the instructional books that Felix had left her and her work improved – even to her own critical eye. She experimented with all the different mediums that Miles had so generously bought for her. But watercolour and oils were her favourites. She grew bolder and painted larger pictures, stacking them against the walls or on the top shelf.

But she was still too shy to show her work to anyone and certainly not brave enough to hang her pictures on a wall.

At Christmas Felix visited them and now he was adamant.

'You mean to say, my darling Charlotte,' he said throwing out his arm in his usual flamboyant gesture, 'that I am to be denied seeing the fruits of all my labour? I, who designed and equipped your studio?' His eyes were twinkling merrily at her. He wanted to see her work, wanted to know if it was just a daubing of colours on to paper or canvas or whether this adorable creature had real talent.

He traced a finger down her cheek. 'My dear girl,

you have blossomed. Marriage suits you so and if your paintings are half as beautiful as their creator, then they should be hanging in every gallery in the land.'

'Oh, Felix.' Charlotte laughed, loving his teasing but never taking it seriously. 'Very well, then, but on two conditions.'

'Name them,' he said kissing her hand.

'Firstly, Miles must come too.'

'At last,' Miles said, joining in the fun and throwing his hands in the air in delight.

'And me,' Georgie piped up. 'I want to see your paintings too.' He beamed. 'You can paint me, Charlotte.'

She laughed. 'Do you think you could sit still for long enough?' And they all laughed, even Georgie.

It had been agreed that the boys should not call her Mama or Mother after Philip's outburst on their arrival home. 'I could never replace your mother,' she'd told them gently.

'You certainly could not,' Philip had muttered, but she'd chosen to ignore him.

'And I'd never want to try, so, I'd like you to call me Charlotte. All right?'

Georgie had flung his arms about her waist and Ben had nodded shyly. Only Philip had given a sniff that sounded suspiciously like disapproval. But then, she supposed, Philip would disapprove of anything she did. She was glad, at this moment, when they were insisting on seeing her work, that he was out riding.

'And the second condition?' Felix prompted.

'That you are entirely honest with me. Give me constructive criticism. I've studied all the books you've given me, but I could use some practical advice.'

'I promise I will tell you truthfully what I think,'

Felix said solemnly. He linked his arm through hers as they mounted the stairs side by side, Miles, Ben and Georgie following.

Her heart was racing as she opened the door and ushered them inside. It was the first time anyone had been into her studio. They all, even Georgie, respected her privacy.

'I've had a go at everything,' she began shyly, 'but I find I still like watercolour the best, though oil painting is now a close second. I can't seem to get to grips with pastels.' She laughed. 'I always seem to end up smudging my picture. I like pencil drawing, but I find pen and ink difficult and too – too—' She paused, searching for the word.

'Tedious?' Felix offered. 'I do, too.' He began to wander around the room, pausing in front of the canvases leaning against the wall to complete their drying process. A process that with oils took some time.

'That's the street in Ravensfleet,' Georgie cried. 'That's my school.'

'And that's the manor,' Ben pointed.

'And the beach where we go riding with the town's pier in the background,' Miles put in.

Felix was silent and Charlotte waited anxiously, surprised how much his approval meant to her. Still he said nothing, standing before each one, considering it, and then moving on to the next.

'And your watercolours?' Felix asked when he'd pondered over each and every one of her oil paintings.

She reached the stack of paintings from the top shelf of the bookcase and, standing a sensible distance from him, she held up each one, the paper trembling a little in her nervous fingers. Now no one made any comment, copying Felix's way of perusal. Laying the last one down, she looked at him, her heart thumping. 'Well?' she whispered, unable to wait a moment longer. 'Tell me the worst. I've wasted your time and all Miles's money.'

Felix stared at her for a long moment, his face expressionless. Then suddenly, he beamed and held out his arm to her. 'My darling girl, your paintings are wonderful – magnificent. They are good enough to hang in a gallery.'

'Felix,' she said, somewhere between laughing and crying, 'I asked you to be honest.'

'I am – I am. Would I' – he smote his chest with his fist – 'lie about *art*?'

'I –' she hesitated, searching his face, trying to see if he was teasing her, being kind to her feeble efforts.

Miles moved to her side and put his arm round her shoulders, then Georgie ran to her and hugged her waist. Ben was smiling and nodding.

'Your paintings are amazing, my dear,' Miles said. 'I'd never imagined how good you really are. To think that all this time . . .' He stopped, realizing that he was in danger of criticizing her father – something he'd vowed to himself he would never do.

'All this time,' Felix declared happily, 'she has been learning and practising and improving. My dear, there are one or two things I could help you with, but these paintings – almost all of them – are good enough to sell now. If you wanted to sell them, that is?'

'She can't sell them,' Georgie said. 'We'll hang them up here. We've plenty of room. Charlotte,' he looked up at her, 'may I have the one with my school on in my bedroom? Please?'

'Of course you can,' Charlotte laughed nervously, still overcome by Felix's praise.

'You must advise us on mounts and frames,' Miles said, giving her shoulders a quick squeeze and then moving away to discuss how best to show off Charlotte's work.

'It depends on the pictures themselves, of course, but also where you want to hang them,' Felix advised. 'Not everyone would agree with me, but my taste is that, if you're hanging say four or five together on a wall, they should all have the same mounts and frames. And the subjects should complement each other – perhaps have some sort of theme.'

'Yes, I see . . .'

Their conversation went on whilst Georgie dashed from one to another of the paintings, choosing his favourites.

Ben came to stand beside her.

'I don't quite believe this,' she murmured.

'Well, you'd better,' Ben said quietly. 'Old Felix wouldn't lie to you. And even we non-experts can see how good they are.' He paused and then asked, 'Have you ever tried portraits?'

She turned to meet his gaze. 'Why do you ask?'

He shrugged. 'Well, even though photography's all the rage these days, people still like their portraits painted. It's a status thing. I bet you could make a lot of money, like Felix says. If you wanted. Felix is a portrait painter.' It was a long speech for Ben, but he still hadn't quite finished. 'And – and I was thinking – it would be nice if you could do a portrait of Father. We've been on at him for years to have one done. We wanted him to commission Felix, but he said because he'd become a friend since then he didn't want to put Felix in a difficult position as regards a fee.'

Softly, she said, 'As a companion to one of your mother's?'

'Well – ' He hesitated, anxious not to hurt her feelings. 'Felix did the ones of mother. That's how we met him. I think he was going to do one of Father too, at that time, but then – but then Mother died and – and Father lost heart.'

She squeezed his hand and whispered, 'I'll show you something.' She led him to the far side of the room where, from behind a stack of new canvases, she pulled out a picture. With her back to the others, she showed him the painting she had done of Miles.

Ben gasped aloud. He glanced up at her and then back to the picture. 'Oh Charlotte, it's brilliant. Your others are good – very good – but this – this is fantastic.' Now, reluctantly, he dragged his gaze from the picture. Shaking his head slowly, not understanding, he said, 'Why have you hidden it?'

'I didn't know whether your father . . .'

'You mean he doesn't *know*? He didn't sit for you to do this?'

She shook her head.

He touched her hand. 'Please show it to the others. You *must*.'

'Well, if you think . . .'

'I don't think – I know. It's truly wonderful. Let me show them – please.'

'All right.'

'Sure?' Ben was gentle. He was not one to persuade someone into something they really didn't want to do.

She laughed nervously, 'No, I'm not, but if you think so, then – '

She thrust the portrait towards him and he took it, carrying it carefully to the centre of the room.

'I say, chaps, just look at this.'

They turned with one accord and Charlotte, still standing in the far corner, almost as if she was hiding, watched their reactions.

Georgie clapped his hands in glee. 'You *can* do people. Oh paint me, Charlotte. Please, please, please paint me.'

Felix threw out his arms. 'Ah, the masterpiece. *Magnifique!* Such care has gone into it. A work of love.'

But Charlotte was watching Miles's face. And then, slowly, he looked up and smiled. 'It's marvellous, my dear.'

And her happiness was complete.

Well, almost. There was one more thing she would dearly love to do for this man she loved so very much. And that was to give him what he desired most: a daughter.

Fifty-Three

But it seemed it was not to be.

As time passed and the family settled down into their new routine, there was no sign of Charlotte becoming pregnant and eventually they ceased to speak about it, but it lay between them like an unanswered prayer.

Apart from that one sadness, they were content. Miles was happy to play the country squire and to leave the running of the estate to his foreman, though more and more he sought Charlotte's opinion. She still ran Buckthorn Farm and saw that her father was well cared for and that Mary and Edward had all they needed. Osbert had improved sufficiently for Nurse Montgomery finally to depart, but she had promised to come back if there were any problems.

The community seemed shielded from the economic devastation that troubled the rest of the country during the early years of the nineteen thirties. Joe and Peggy flourished at Purslane Farm and whilst Jackson continued to enjoy his bachelor state and had a string of girlfriends all eager to lead him to the altar, he resolutely resisted. John, meanwhile, quietly married his long-time sweetheart. They rented a small cottage in Ravensfleet, and John continued to help his father and brother run the farm. Eddie and Lily, having moved into the Warrens' old cottage on Buckthorn Farm with Alfie, added to their family with another son and a daughter.

'They can breed like rabbits, but it seems you're barren, girl,' Osbert goaded Charlotte crudely. 'I hope you're doing your duty by your husband. I want a grandson.'

At such times, Charlotte would silently turn her back on him and walk out of Buckthorn Farm to her home, where there were no recriminations. Miles never once broached the subject, though secretly Charlotte consulted the doctor to see if it was her fault. Dr Markham declared her fit and healthy and told her not to worry.

'Sometimes conception doesn't happen, my dear, because you want it too much. You're too tense. Just relax and enjoy your life. You're happy, aren't you?'

'Very. I've never known such happiness,' she confided. 'But I know Miles so wants a daughter.'

'A daughter, eh? Well, well,' he murmured, knowing full well the humiliations that had been heaped on Charlotte's head all her life for being a girl. 'Life's strange, my dear, isn't it?'

In time, Philip gained a place at university to study law and after qualifying found work in London. Ben attended agricultural college and at the end of the course he came home to help run the estate. His career was mapped out for him and it seemed he was happy to follow it, gaining a quiet confidence in his own abilities and his future.

As for Georgie, all he wanted to do was to learn to fly aeroplanes and the RAF seemed to be the best place he could do that.

'Cranwell, Father,' he said as he neared his eighteenth birthday. 'That's where I want to be.'

But Miles had frowned. 'I'm not so sure, Georgie.

There are storm clouds gathering in Europe, I fear. And if there's a war, the RAF would be in the front line.'

Georgie only grinned. 'Then I'll be a fighter pilot.'

He'd not altered at all. Of course, he'd grown and was now tall and handsome with fair, curling hair and a strong, lithe body, and seemed always to have a permanent grin on his face. But he was still the same mischievous, lovable scamp he'd always been.

'Georgie's never-failing good humour can get a little wearing,' Philip would remark loftily on his rare visits home. 'Is he ever going to grow up?'

Privately, Charlotte hoped Georgie would never change. She couldn't help him being her favourite, though she would never have voiced such a thing. She treated all three boys fairly and only Miles was aware that her eyes lit up and her mouth curved into a smile when Georgie entered the room or even when his name was mentioned.

Nothing could dissuade the young man from applying to join the RAF and though they did nothing to try to stop him, both Miles and Charlotte felt their hearts sinking with fear when he waved the letter of acceptance, dancing a jig around the breakfast table.

Miles reached across the corner of the table and covered Charlotte's hand where it trembled on the white cloth. 'He'll not be far away. Cranwell's still in Lincolnshire. And Ben's home now.'

He did not mention Philip, sensitive as ever to the fact that his eldest son and his young wife had an uneasy relationship. Though it was never talked about, it was sometimes like watching two fighting cocks, skirting each other warily. He dreaded the day when one might push the other too far and there would be a flurry of feathers.

Charlotte continued her painting and Felix would visit every so often and bear away several canvases and watercolours, sending her what she regarded as a ridiculously large cheque when he sold them in his London gallery.

The only thing that she remained adamant about was refusing all attempts to encourage her to advertise her talents as a portrait painter. Those she confined to the people around her whom she loved, presenting them, rather shyly, with a work of art they would cherish.

She visited her mother, aunt and uncle in Lincoln regularly, often taking Miles with her, but her mother steadfastly refused to come to Ravensfleet.

'As long as I can see you from time to time and hear from you by letter, that is all I ask,' Alice declared. And for once, even Euphemia could not move her.

'They've quite a stubborn streak,' Miles laughingly commiserated with Charlotte's aunt. 'For such seemingly docile creatures, they can dig their heels in at times. I cannot get Charlotte to paint portraits by commission. She'd be in great demand, I know she would.'

Euphemia had smiled at him archly. 'The only thing she wants to do is to make you happy, dear boy.'

He'd smiled readily, even though there was the longing for a daughter that never left him. 'Oh, she does.'

'And you make her supremely happy,' she'd patted his arm, 'I never thought to see the dear girl so contented.'

Euphemia had not alluded to the 'patter of tiny feet' making their idyll complete. Her own childlessness made her sensitive to the feelings of both Miles and Charlotte.

Fifty-Four

At a few minutes past eleven on the morning of Sunday, 3 September 1939, the whole family at the manor sat in Miles's study, clustered around the wireless set listening to Mr Chamberlain's solemn pronouncement that the country was now at war with Germany. Electricity and even the telephone had come to the manor in recent years, though not to Buckthorn Farm. Osbert Crawford resolutely refused to have 'such newfangled nonsense' installed.

Miles switched off the set and sighed heavily. Charlotte's eyes widened with fear, but Georgie, having driven over from Cranwell for the day, rubbed his hands together gleefully. 'Now we can get at 'em. Hitler's been allowed to get away with far too much already.'

Philip, home from London, paced the floor. 'I suppose I shall have to enlist.' He glanced at his father. 'Do my bit.'

'You needn't. You could wait until you're called up. And even then, with your job, you might be able to apply for a dispensation.'

Philip gave a wry laugh. 'I doubt it, Father. Everyone's going to be too busy to be needing lawyers.'

Miles glanced at Ben. 'You'll be all right, son. The list of reserved occupations includes farmers.'

Ben stared back at him and seemed to straighten his shoulders. With quiet determination, he said, 'But

I don't want to do that, Father. I shall volunteer for the army.'

Georgie clapped him on the back. 'Good for you, old boy.' He grinned at Philip. 'Now, Phil, you just need to join the navy and we'll have all three services covered.'

Charlotte moved to stand beside Miles's chair and rest her hand on his shoulder. Softly, she whispered, 'You won't have to go, will you?'

'No, my love, not this time. Though . . .'

Fear clutched her heart. 'What?' she demanded swiftly.

'I think we should do something to help the war effort.'

'What?' she asked again.

Miles twisted his head to look up at her. 'Take in evacuees. They're coming in droves from the big cities. It started three days ago.'

For a moment, she stared at him, then smiled. 'Of course. What a brilliant idea, Miles. We've heaps of room here.'

'Right,' Miles heaved himself to his feet, 'no time like the present. I'll go and see the billeting officer in Ravens-fleet this very minute.' He turned briefly and touched Charlotte's cheek. 'Do us good,' he smiled, though the smile did not quite reach his eyes. 'To have something else to think about other than these three reprobates.'

The house felt very empty with only Ben still at home. Philip had returned to his law firm in London and Georgie, fairly bouncing with excitement, had headed straight back to camp leaving only Ben to carry on the work of Home Farm and the estate.

'What about the Warren boys?' Charlotte asked Miles. 'Do you think they'll go?'

'Shouldn't think so for a minute. They'll be in a reserved occupation for sure. Besides – ' he chuckled – 'I think you're forgetting just how old those "boys" are now?'

Charlotte thought for a moment, then smiled. 'Heavens, yes, I suppose I am. And I'm forgetting how old I am, too.' For a moment, her eyes were bleak. There was still no sign of a baby and the clock was ticking . . .

Breaking into her thoughts, Miles added, 'Apart from Thomas. How old is he now?'

'Twenty,' Charlotte whispered.

Of all the Warren family, Thomas was the only one who'd decided he didn't want to work on Purslane Farm. He'd turned out to be the brightest one in the family and was in the middle of a university degree studying medicine.

'I'd've thought he'd be a good bet to be granted a dispensation, if he applies. But I don't really know, Charlotte,' Miles said. Then his face brightened. 'Mr Tomkins – he's the billeting officer for Ravensfleet – telephoned this morning. He has an evacuee for us.' His smile broadened. 'A little girl.'

Charlotte forced her thoughts back to the present moment. 'How lovely. How old is she? Where is she from? When is she coming?'

'Whoa, whoa there.' He took her hands in his. 'She arrived three days ago with the party of children from London.'

'Three days!' Charlotte was puzzled. 'So why hasn't she been found a billet – a home with someone – before now?'

'Er – well,' Miles was hesitant. 'She did. In a way.'

'Then why – ?'

'She was sent back because she's – she's – difficult.'

'Difficult? How d'you mean?'

'She had head lice when she arrived. A lot of the children did, but this little girl was unlucky enough to be placed with two spinster sisters in Ravensfleet who just threw up their hands in horror and dispatched her back into Mr Tomkins's care. He and his wife have done their best, but he says she's very wilful and has tantrums. They can't get her to wash and they certainly haven't been able to deal with the lice.'

Charlotte's eyes softened. 'Poor little scrap. Sent away from her home. She must be so lonely and afraid. Oh Miles, let's fetch her. Now. Let's go this minute.'

Miles hugged her swiftly. 'I knew you'd say that. I'll get the car . . .'

As they walked up the front path of Mr Tomkins's neat cottage, they could already hear the high-pitched screaming from inside. Charlotte and Miles glanced at each other.

'Poor mite,' Charlotte murmured. 'She only needs a little love and care, I'm sure . . .'

As Mr Tomkins opened the front door to their third loud knock, Charlotte thought she'd never seen the usually calm, mild-mannered man look so harassed.

'Thank goodness you've come, but I'm not sure I'm doing you any favours . . .'

He was interrupted by a whirlwind of blond hair, wiry limbs and a face like thunder, pushing past him and then between Miles and Charlotte. The child ran down the path, flung open the gate and started off along the road.

'I ain't stayin' here no longer,' she shouted over her shoulder. 'I'm going 'ome. I'd sooner face old 'Itler's bombs than stay here anuvver minute.'

'I'll go after her,' Miles said grinning from ear to ear, completely unfazed by the child's tantrum. 'You talk to Mr Tomkins, dear.'

He set off after the girl, his long strides soon shortening the distance between them, for the child had slowed to a walking pace, though she still marched towards the railway station with a grim, determined set to her jaw.

Mr Tomkins smoothed his hand through his thinning hair and ran his forefinger round the inside of his collar as if it was restricting his neck. 'Do come in, Mrs Thornton. Mabel's just clearing up the mess. The child threw her breakfast on the floor. Dear me, I've never seen such a temper in a child. Perhaps we'd better let her go back.'

'No,' Charlotte said swiftly. 'We can't do that. We can't send her back into danger, if it's going to be as bad as they say.'

'Mm,' Mr Tomkins murmured. 'I suppose you're right, but the expected onslaught doesn't seem to be happening.'

'Not yet,' Charlotte said quietly, her thoughts drifting to Georgie. Resolutely, she turned them back to the little waif, sent far away from her home to strangers. 'But we can't take that risk.'

'Charlotte.' Mrs Tomkins came into the room. She and Charlotte were a similar age and had known each other from childhood even though Charlotte had never been allowed to make friends.

'Mabel.' Charlotte greeted her warmly and held out both her hands. 'Don't worry. We'll take her home. Do our best.'

Mabel grimaced. 'I wish you luck, because I think you're going to need it.'

'Where do you think they've gone?' Charlotte said, stepping to the front window and peering out through the lace curtains.

'She said she was going home, but she's not taken her belongings.' Mabel sniffed. 'Mind you, they're hardly worth taking. She's only got the clothes she's wearing and they've seen better days. Poor little lass. The only other thing she brought besides her gas mask was a moth-eaten old teddy.'

'And she's gone without it?'

Mabel nodded.

Charlotte's eyes gleamed as an idea formed in her mind. 'What's his name?'

'Her name, you mean? Jenny Mercer.'

Charlotte laughed. 'No – I meant the teddy bear's, actually.'

Mabel shrugged. 'I've no idea.'

'No matter,' Charlotte murmured, heading for the front door. Leaving the cottage, she headed down the path and out into the road. In the distance she could see that Miles had caught up with the wilful little girl. They were at the corner and were standing facing each other. Or rather, Miles was squatting so as to bring his face level with Jenny's.

Charlotte bit her lip, hesitating, unsure whether she should interfere. Perhaps Miles was doing a better job on his own. She walked slowly towards them. Then she saw Jenny turn swiftly away and begin to cross the road. Miles caught hold of the child's arm and a high-pitched scream rent the air. Charlotte quickened her pace.

The girl was wriggling and kicking out at Miles's shins, but he held her fast. 'You'll get run over, love. Calm down. I'm not going to hurt you. But you must look where you're going.'

He glanced helplessly at Charlotte but still kept a firm grip on the squirming little body.

'Jenny,' Charlotte began. 'If you're going back to London, haven't you forgotten a couple of things?'

For a moment, Jenny's efforts to break free stopped and she stared up at Charlotte.

'What?'

'For one thing, you must take your gas mask and for another – what about Teddy? You surely weren't going to leave him, were you?'

The young girl became perfectly still.

'If you promise me not to run into the road without looking both ways,' Miles said, 'I'll let go.'

Jenny nodded and Miles released his grip, though he remained standing close by – just in case.

'His name's Bert,' Jenny muttered and took a step – albeit a reluctant one – back towards the cottage. 'I'd better get him. And me gas mask.'

'And what about the train fare? Have you any money?'

As the child blinked and looked up at her, Charlotte saw that she had the bluest eyes she had ever seen.

'Don't need no money. We come on the train an' didn't 'ave ter pay.'

'I think that was special, because the train was bringing you all to the country. But if you choose to go back without the others, you'll have to pay.'

The girl looked suddenly even smaller, lost and

afraid. Her lower lip trembled and she ducked her head, but not before Charlotte had seen the tears welling in her lovely eyes. Now Charlotte squatted down in front of her. 'Tell you what, how about you come home with us for a day or two? If you really don't like it, then we'll pay for your train fare back home.'

The girl's head jerked up. 'Promise?'

'Well, I don't think your mum'll want you to go back to the city when she's sent you here to be safe, but if you're really so unhappy, then—'

'Don't think mi mum'd be bothered. She's got a fancy man an' I was in the way.'

'Oh – oh, I see,' Charlotte murmured, but she didn't really. She knew nothing about this child's background but it sounded as if she'd been sent to the country with the other evacuees more to get her out of the way than for her safety.

Charlotte stood up, smiled down at Jenny and held out her hand. 'You come with us, Jenny. Give us a try, eh? Maybe you'd like to stay with us for a little while and then we'll see, eh?'

The child looked up at her, staring straight into Charlotte's eyes. Then she nodded. 'All right, missis. I'll give it a go, but if I don't like it . . .'

'Then I promise we'll take you back to London ourselves and talk to your mum. All right?'

Again the little girl nodded and put her grubby paw into Charlotte's outstretched hand.

Above her head Charlotte and Miles exchanged a smile.

Fifty-Five

Georgie arrived home on a seventy-two-hour pass. The first sounds he heard on entering the front door were high-pitched screams and a great deal of splashing water emanating from the first-floor bathroom.

'What on earth's going on?' he laughed, dumping his kit bag in the hall and greeting his father, who emerged from the sanctuary of his study.

Miles smiled wryly. 'It's our new houseguest. An evacuee from London. She's got nits or head lice or something. She's not taking kindly to the treatment Charlotte is meting out. I'm keeping out of the way.' He chuckled. 'Playing the good guy when all the screaming's over.'

'You might be waiting a while, by the sound of it.' Georgie began to take the stairs, two at a time with his long athletic legs. Miles called after him, 'I'd change out of your uniform first, Georgie. It might be rather wet in there.'

'I will.'

Minutes later, Georgie was knocking on the bathroom door and opening it to a wall of noise and a wave of water sloshing across the linoleum towards him.

'Need any help, Charlotte?' he shouted above the din.

'Georgie! What a lovely surprise.'

At the sound of the man's voice, the child, fighting Charlotte's every attempt to wash her hair, was suddenly still and quiet. The silence was as deafening as the noise had been a moment before.

Georgie stepped through the water and squatted down in front of the girl and held out his hand. 'Hello, I'm Georgie. I'm very pleased to meet you.'

The child stared at him with her brilliant blue eyes. 'Would you like me to dry your hair for you, while Charlotte clears up all this mess?'

Jenny considered for a long moment, her face tear-streaked and sullen. Then, suddenly, she smiled and it was like the sun coming out from behind the darkest storm cloud. She nodded.

Charlotte wrapped the huge white towel round her skinny wet body and handed her over to Georgie with an inward sigh of relief.

'Take her to the nursery. Kitty's been busy all morning cleaning it and lighting a fire in there. It should be cosy by now.'

Georgie lifted the little girl up into his arms and carried her from the bathroom, leaving Charlotte to mop up the tidal wave and set the bathroom to rights. Not for the first time, Charlotte marvelled at how Georgie's charm worked such wonders.

A little later, when order had been restored to a still rather damp bathroom, Charlotte went along to the nursery. Miles was hovering on the landing.

'Do you think they're all right? I can't hear anything. The silence is almost worse than the noise.'

'Oh Miles, you should have seen her smile at Georgie.' She laughed and shook her head in wonderment. 'That boy never ceases to amaze me. He can charm the birds out of the trees.'

Miles chuckled. 'He always could.'

Charlotte smiled fondly. 'I remember.'

They listened outside the door for a moment before opening it quietly and peering round it. Georgie was sitting on the hearthrug, with the child curled against him, her head on his chest, whilst he read to her one of his own favourite books from childhood – *The Wind in the Willows*.

'Just look at her hair,' Miles whispered. 'What pretty blond curls she's got, now it's clean.' Charlotte glanced at him but his gaze was fastened on Jenny.

'Blond hair and blue eyes – what a little stunner,' he murmured.

'And she has the prettiest dimples in her cheeks when she smiles,' Charlotte whispered back.

He turned to her, dragging his gaze reluctantly away from the little girl for a moment. 'She smiled? She actually smiled?'

Charlotte chuckled softly. 'Oh yes – but only at Georgie.'

'That figures!'

They watched for a few moments longer before Georgie became aware of their presence. He grinned and beckoned them in.

'We're reading,' he informed them unnecessarily.

'So we see,' Miles murmured, his eyes still drinking in the sight of the clean, sweet-smelling child, leaning against Georgie and sucking her thumb. Her eyes drooped with tiredness.

'I think it's time she went to bed,' Charlotte said quietly, torn between not wanting to spoil the tranquillity, but conscious of her duty as a surrogate mother.

'Right, little one,' Georgie said, moving her gently from his lap and standing up. 'Time for beddibyes.'

Charlotte held her breath, expecting an outburst, but none came. When he picked her up, Jenny wound her arms round Georgie's neck and laid her head against his shoulder. She was almost asleep already.

'Poor little scrap,' Miles murmured, touching her curls gently as Georgie carried her out of the nursery and into the bedroom next door to it. He tucked her into bed, promising, 'Charlotte and Miles are right next door and I'm just down the corridor. If you want anything, you only have to shout and we'll come running. All right?'

'Mm.' There was a pause before she murmured, 'Bert?'

Georgie looked round at Charlotte and Miles standing in the doorway. 'What'd she say?'

'Of course. It's her teddy. Now where – ?' Charlotte hurried into the room and towards the bundle of Jenny's few belongings, fishing out the shabby teddy bear.

'Here he is – hiding amongst your clothes.' She tucked him in beside the child and then bent to kiss her forehead. 'Night, night, sleep tight, mind the—' Then she stopped.

Any reference to bugs was not the most appropriate thing to say to the little girl, she realized just in time. She bit her lip and exchanged a rueful smile with Miles.

They left a night light burning on the mantelpiece in case Jenny should wake in the darkness and be frightened. And then, sure that she was already sound asleep, the three crept out of the room, leaving the door ajar.

Georgie led the way downstairs and into the dining room, where Wilkins hovered anxiously. Dinner had already been held back almost an hour.

'Now,' Georgie demanded. 'I want to hear all about her and how she comes to be here.'

*

Over the three days Georgie was at home, Jenny never left his side. She followed him about the house like a little shadow, her teddy clutched in her arms, her thumb in her mouth. But there was one thing that even Georgie could not persuade her to do, which was to go outside.

'Wouldn't you like to see the animals? We've got pigs and chickens and one or two horses in the stables,' Georgie coaxed her. 'Maybe, my dad would get you a little pony and you could learn to ride.'

Jenny shook her curls vehemently. 'Don't like it.'

'What? A pony?'

'No, outside.'

'What do you mean?'

'It's too big.'

Georgie glanced helplessly at Charlotte and Miles, who shrugged, completely at a loss, too.

'What's too big, darling?' Now Charlotte knelt in front of her. 'A horse, d'you mean? We won't make you go on one if you don't want to.'

The girl blinked up at her. 'It's too big,' she repeated.

'What's too big, Jenny?' Miles asked gently. 'Try to tell us.'

'Outside. The sky. It's – frightening. There's no houses an' buildings.'

The three adults exchanged mystified glances, then suddenly Georgie's face cleared. 'I think I understand. She's used to living in the city with buildings all around her. The open flat land and the skies here must look huge to her, when you think about it. Is that it, Jenny love?'

The girl nodded, her shining curls bobbing. 'It's too big.'

'We understand, but there's nothing to be afraid of. Come.' Miles held out his hand, realizing that somehow he and Charlotte must prise her away from Georgie. He had to return to camp the following day. Miles foresaw trouble when the young man had to leave Jenny. 'We'll take it in easy stages. Come to the window and look out. Georgie, you go outside and wave to her. In fact, get one of the lads to bring one of the smaller horses on to the lawn so she can see it.'

The rest of the morning was spent gently coaxing the child outside and by lunchtime she was happily kicking a football backwards and forwards to Georgie on the front lawn.

'I bet she'd love the beach. Digging sandcastles and paddling.'

'Oh, one step at a time, I think, Miles. Besides, aren't they putting rolls and rolls of barbed wire along the beach now and building concrete pill boxes all along the coast?'

'Yes,' Miles said grimly. 'Soon we won't be able to go to the beach. What a shame!'

'Perhaps they'll leave a little space for holidaymakers in Lynthorpe. We could take her there.'

'Holidaymakers?' Miles's tone was doubtful. 'Do you think we'll get any next summer?'

But that was a question Charlotte could not answer.

Fifty-Six

'I'm not going without saying a proper goodbye to her.' Georgie was adamant.

'She'll likely scream the place down,' Charlotte warned.

'That'd be better than me sneaking off without her knowing. I'll explain it carefully. Tell her I'll get home again as soon as I can and that she's to let you or Miles carry on reading *The Wind in the Willows*.'

'He's right, darling.' Miles put his arm round her shoulder. 'We've got to be honest with her. I bet half these poor kids weren't told what was happening to them. They were just shoved on a train and waved off by tearful mothers, not even knowing where they were going or how long for. Georgie's right. We've got to be truthful with her.'

But Charlotte was right about one thing. There were tears – and plenty. A proper tantrum, where Jenny lay on the floor of the hall, screaming and kicking out at anyone who tried to get near her.

At last, the only thing Georgie could do was to say firmly above all the noise, 'I've got to go now, Jen. Won't you come and wave me off?'

But the screams only increased.

Georgie stood up, looking harassed. He hated leaving the child like this, but he'd no option. He had to go.

'I'll try to get home again as soon as I can, even if it's only for a few hours. In the meantime – good luck!'

Shaking his father's hand and kissing Charlotte's cheek, he ran down the front steps to the waiting pony and trap which they were already making more use of in an effort to save petrol.

'There are going to be shortages,' Miles had warned her. 'Just like in the last lot.'

Now, as they stood helplessly watching the writhing little body on their hall floor, shortages, rationing and all the coming privations they were sure they were going to feel, were nothing in comparison to this sad little girl so far from home.

Eventually, the sobs subsided and Miles, instead of being cross, merely held out his hand and said, 'Shall we go and see if we can find Ben and help feed the chickens? It's about time they were having their tea. Perhaps we could help feed the pigs too.'

Jenny stood up, scrubbed away her tears with the back of her hand, and marched towards the front door, Bert's legs dangling from her arms. Miles winked at Charlotte and followed the child.

The following weeks were not easy, but gradually Jenny seemed to be settling down. The first time they took her to morning service, Osbert Crawford descended from the pony and trap and stood looking down at the child standing between Miles and Charlotte.

'What on earth have you got there?'

'Father – this is Jenny Mercer. She's come to stay with us for a while.'

'An evacuee?' Osbert snorted. 'A *girl*? Couldn't you

have got a boy? At least a boy would have been useful about the farm.'

'We wanted a little girl,' Miles said firmly, putting his hand on Jenny's shoulder.

'Huh! What use is a girl?' Osbert eyed the child and sniffed.

The little girl returned his frown steadily and then, to Charlotte's secret delight, Jenny stuck out her tongue at Osbert, turned and marched ahead of them all into the church.

'The cheeky little urchin,' Osbert growled. 'I'd horse-whip her if she was mine.'

'Then thank goodness she isn't,' Miles said sharply and followed Jenny inside.

Osbert hobbled after them, but Charlotte was obliged to wait outside for a few moments longer – until she had controlled a fit of the giggles.

There were still tantrums, tears and a stubborn, scowling face when something didn't suit her, and Jenny flatly refused to go to the local school.

'I don't like the other kids. The ones what live 'ere, I mean. They call us "vaccies".'

'Do they, indeed?' Miles said grimly. 'Then I shall have a word with the teacher.'

'Nah, don't do that, mister. It'd only make it worse. Kids don't like telltale-tits.'

Miles couldn't bring himself to make her go, but the child's non-attendance bothered Mr Tomkins.

'It's our responsibility,' he told Miles anxiously on one of his weekly visits to check on Jenny's progress. 'She must go. Unless, of course . . .' He hesitated.

'Unless what, Mr Tomkins?' Miles prompted.

'Er, well, I wouldn't dream of suggesting such a thing in normal circumstances. Funds won't run to it . . .'

'Out with it, man.'

Diffidently, as if he expected to be sent packing with the proverbial flea in his ear, Mr Tomkins said, 'Unless you could arrange for her to receive her schooling at home.'

But Miles's face brightened. 'Of course. What a good idea. And perhaps there's more we could do here. I've heard tell that the school is so overcrowded with the influx of all the evacuee children that some of the pupils are only going for half a day. Is that true?'

'I – believe so.'

Miles beamed.

'We've plenty of rooms here not being used. We could – with the help and approval of the Education Authority – set up classes here. That way, Jenny would have some playmates and all the children would get their proper schooling.'

'It *sounds* like a good idea,' the man agreed. He was thoughtful for a few moments before saying, with a degree of increased interest, 'Let me make some enquiries and I'll get back to you.'

Events moved swiftly; the authorities were only too pleased to accept any help they could get, especially if it came from a reliable and well-organized source.

'There'll be inspectors calling. You understand that?' Mr Tomkins said earnestly, trying to make sure that Miles and Charlotte knew just what they were taking on.

'I wouldn't want it any other way,' Miles reassured him. 'And we'll do everything in our power to comply with whatever they want.'

So before long, the manor was overrun with noisy children running riot in the grounds and clattering through the hall to the dining room, which had been turned into a schoolroom. Mrs Beddows was in her element, cooking nourishing meals – only Wilkins wore a perpetually worried expression, but even he at last began to feel that he was 'doing his bit' to help the war effort and stopped feeling so guilty that he was too old to volunteer.

As for Miles and Charlotte – they revelled in every minute of it. Miles couldn't wait for lessons to end when he could round up all the children – about a dozen of them, locals and evacuees, plus Jenny of course. Then he'd lead them out on to the front lawn to referee a rowdy game of football. Charlotte timed her visits to Buckthorn Farm when the children were at their lessons so that she could be on hand to bathe a grazed knee or to play with those who wanted a quieter pastime, or just read a story aloud to a group.

Jenny seemed to settle in a little better. The tantrums grew less frequent and she began to smile more than she frowned. But her most often asked question was not, as they might have expected, 'When am I going home?', but 'When's Georgie coming home again?'

Christmas that year was strange – as if everyone was waiting for something to happen. Several of the evacuees who'd arrived at the beginning of September returned home when the expected air raids did not happen.

But no one sent for Jenny.

The whole family was home for the festivities, but it was Georgie whom Jenny monopolized.

'She doesn't give him a minute's peace,' Philip muttered, adamantly refusing to join in a game of charades.

'Oh come on, Phil, old chap. Lighten up.' Georgie laughed. 'The poor little scrap's miles from her home – her family. Come down off that high horse, just for once, eh?'

'Mm.' Philip frowned and regarded the little girl for a moment, before giving an exaggerated sigh and throwing down his newspaper. 'Very well, but only because it's you asking, Georgie. This family's never been able to refuse its golden-headed little cherub anything, now, has it?'

It was a merry Christmas, despite the thought at the back of everyone's mind that the waiting for the war to begin in earnest could not last for ever. Early in April the 'phoney war' came to an abrupt end when Hitler invaded Denmark and Norway. Then, at the beginning of June, news filtered through of the evacuation of the British Expeditionary Force from Dunkirk.

Now, it seemed, Britain stood alone and only the RAF could protect its shores and its people.

Charlotte felt a cold terror creep around her heart.

One Saturday morning in June when there were no lessons and no other children came to play, Jenny went missing.

Miles was beside himself. 'Where can she be? Oh Charlotte, she wouldn't try to go to the beach, would she?'

'She doesn't know the way, does she?'

'I've taken her a few times. She might.'

Charlotte thought for a moment and then shook her head. 'I don't think she'd go on her own. She's still a little nervous of the great outdoors and you said she found the vastness of the sea scary at first.'

'But Georgie takes her every time he comes home. She's not so frightened now. She just might have thought she'd go on her own. We must get everyone searching. And I mean everyone. Wilkins, Brewster, Cook, Kitty and all the men on the farm. Let's send word to Eddie, too—'

'Calm down, Miles. Let's not panic. We haven't even searched the whole house yet.'

'D'you think she'd go into the town? Try to get on a train home?'

Charlotte shook her head then gave a thin smile. She was as worried as Miles, but she was trying not to show it. 'If she has gone there, it's more likely she's looking for Georgie coming home.'

Miles's face brightened. 'Maybe she has. I'll get Brewster to drive into—'

'Wait a minute, Miles. Let's search here first. She'll come to no harm. Not in Ravensfleet.'

'You're right. Of course you are. But, Charlotte, I couldn't bear it if something's happened to her.'

Charlotte touched his arm and said softly, 'I know, I know.'

The child had wound her way into both their hearts, but Miles was besotted with her. Little Jenny was fast becoming the daughter he'd always longed for. But Charlotte was fearful for this man she loved so very much. Jenny wasn't theirs. Never could be theirs. She had a mother back in London who, one day, would want her daughter home again.

Despite, Jenny's offhand remarks about her mother's 'fancy man' and feeling that she was in the way, Charlotte could not understand any mother not wanting her child close by.

And yet, a niggling little voice reminded her, didn't your own mother run away and leave you? Not all mothers are the kind Charlotte knew she would be, she told herself.

She dragged her thoughts back to the present anxiety. With greater calmness than she was feeling inside, she said, 'Let's do this in an organized way. Not running around in circles like headless chickens.'

'You're right. I know you're right, but . . .' Miles ran his hand through his hair again.

'We'll search the house first, from top to bottom. Everywhere – every nook and cranny and then, if we haven't found her, we'll extend the search outside and rope everybody in.'

Miles nodded. 'Where shall we start?'

'Down here and work our way upstairs.'

'I've already looked in her bedroom and the playroom. She's not there.'

At that moment, Wilkins appeared in the hallway carrying a tray and Miles dispatched him at once to ask Mrs Beddows and the housemaid to join in searching the house.

After only a few minutes, whilst they were still searching the first floor bedrooms, they heard the maid, Kitty, calling from the top landing.

'Sir – madam, she's up here.'

Miles galloped up the stairs with the agility of a man half his age, with Charlotte running up behind him as fast as she could.

Kitty was waiting for them at the top, her eyes anxious.

'Is she all right?' Miles asked urgently. 'Where is she?'

'She's fine, sir, but – but it's madam's studio. Such a mess she's made. There's paint everywhere.'

'Oh no,' Miles breathed as he turned to Charlotte. 'Please, my dear, don't be angry. Whatever she's done, I'll get it all cleaned up, I promise.'

Charlotte linked her arm through her husband's and smiled up at him. 'Let's go and see, shall we?'

The sight that met their eyes took their breath away and they both stood in the doorway, their eyes roaming round the scene of devastation. Charlotte had not had time to paint recently, with all the extra work the children brought, and she hadn't been into her studio for almost a fortnight. The damage that Jenny had wrought had not been done in one day, nor even two or three. She must have been creeping up here for quite a while. The linoleum floor was splattered with paint and there were splashes on the white wall. She'd even used one of the walls to paint a childish picture on, when she'd run out of paper.

Pieces of paper, all covered with daubs of paint, littered the floor and Charlotte's precious canvases had been used, too. Open tubes of oil paints and watercolours oozed on to the desk and the table by the window and dirty brushes, caked with dried paint, were strewn around.

'Oh Jenny,' Miles began, sadly, but Charlotte squeezed his arm quickly and whispered, 'Don't, Miles, don't chastise her.'

The girl was standing in front of Charlotte's easel,

wearing the white smock which Charlotte herself used to protect her clothes.

That's why we've never seen paint on her clothes, Charlotte thought. I'd never have guessed. There've been no telltale signs. But there were plenty now. The child's fingers were sticky with blue oil paint and she had a streak of the same colour down her cheek. With a loaded brush poised in front of a canvas on the easel, she glanced up at them standing by the door and grinned.

'Hello, I'm painting a picture for Georgie.'

Charlotte took a deep breath and, leaving Miles standing by the door gazing helplessly at the carnage, she crossed the room. Smiling, she said, 'How nice, darling. May I see?'

She stood beside the child and together they scrutinized the canvas. Cerulean blue streaked the top part of the picture with the darker cobalt blue below it. Beneath that was yellow ochre.

'Why, it's the beach,' Charlotte said, and was rewarded by a beaming smile from the artist.

'I want some green for that spiky grass, but I can't remember what to mix.'

'Blue and yellow. Here, let me show you.'

Charlotte reached for her palette and, heads bent together over the board, she showed Jenny how to mix the different greens to represent the grasses and bushes that grew on the sandhills.

'I'll – er – um – leave you to it, then, shall I?' Miles said uncertainly.

Charlotte glanced up and winked broadly. 'We'll be fine.'

As he closed the door softly behind him, he heard Jenny's high-pitched voice say, 'I'm sorry if I've made a mess, Charlotte, but it is such fun, isn't it?'

And at once, he knew what he would buy the little girl for Christmas. Perhaps he could turn a corner of the playroom into her own little studio so that she wouldn't invade Charlotte's domain again.

He would talk to Charlotte later, he promised himself.

Fifty-Seven

A week later, Georgie managed to get home on a short leave. Charlotte met him in the hall before Jenny could reach him.

'She's painted you a picture,' she warned him, forbearing to tell of the disastrous consequences of the child's efforts. 'Miles got it framed. It's of the beach, so be sure to recognize what it is. Actually,' Charlotte put her head on one side and smiled, 'for her age, it's really quite good.'

Georgie hugged her close, holding her for what seemed like a long moment. Charlotte pulled back and looked up into his eyes. His smile was still there, but to her sharp, observant eye it looked forced. The brightness, the sparkle of mischief that had always been in his blue eyes, was gone.

'My dear – what is it?' she whispered.

He smiled ruefully. 'There's no hiding anything from you, is there?'

'Nor your father. Not where his boys are concerned.' She linked her arm through his and led him towards the stairs. 'Come up to my studio. No one will bother us there. We can snatch a few minutes alone. The children are still at their lessons. But keep your voice down. If Jenny hears you . . .' As they began to mount the stairs, she asked, 'Are you hungry? I could ask Wilkins to bring a tray up.'

'A whisky would be nice.'

Whisky, she thought, suddenly very concerned. It was two in the afternoon. But she made no comment, except to say, 'You go on up. I'll just find Wilkins.'

She joined him in her studio; he was sitting on the wide window seat staring down at the garden below.

'How's it all going, then?' he wanted to know. 'With all these kids?'

She had the distinct feeling that he was leaping in first, before she could ask him awkward questions.

Charlotte crossed the room which was once more neat and reasonably tidy for an artist's studio. Little trace of Jenny's first experiments remained, but one corner of the room had now been set out for the child. A little table with paints, brushes and paper of her own, kept her confined to her 'painting room' as she called it. When Miles had suggested setting something up for her in the playroom, Charlotte herself had said she could share her studio. 'Keep all the mess in one place,' she'd said smiling.

'Fine,' Charlotte said now in answer to Georgie's question as she took a seat beside him. 'We have a nice teacher who comes in every day. A young woman whose fiancé is in the army. They have lessons and then play out in the garden, if it's fine, before going home. Miles loves those sessions. He never misses them. And then he takes some of the ones who live the farthest away home in the farm cart. And *they* love that!'

'It sounds idyllic,' Georgie murmured wistfully.

'Not really. A lot of the evacuees are still homesick. But we're doing our best.'

'And Jenny? What about her?'

'She's settling in better now, though it's taken a while. We still get the odd tantrum, but Miles spends a lot of time with her.'

429

Georgie smiled pensively. 'The daughter he never had, eh?'

Charlotte couldn't answer. Her throat was too full of tears. Though it was never spoken of, never referred to, except by her father almost every time he saw her, Charlotte still lamented the lack of their own child in their lives.

She turned her thoughts away from her own sadness and said softly, 'So, my darling, how are things with you?'

He took a moment to answer. 'You'll have been following the news.' It was a statement rather than a question. 'You know all about Dunkirk. And I expect you have heard about Mr Churchill's speech that the Battle of France is over and – and the Battle of Britain is about to begin. Everyone's getting jittery about a possible invasion. We're not – we're not exactly at our strongest at the moment, Charlotte. It has to be said. Though I wouldn't say it to just anyone.' He looked across at her and held her gaze. Softly, he said, 'The RAF chaps are in for a pretty tough time. We're the only ones to defend our shores at the moment. You – you understand what I'm saying, don't you?'

Wordlessly, she nodded.

'If – if anything happens to me, look after Dad, won't you?'

Huskily, she murmured, 'Of course. You know I will.' But silently she thought, *But who will look after me if I lose my golden boy?*

Georgie forced a smile, held out his hand to her and, with his glass of whisky in the other, said, 'And now, let's go and find that little scamp.'

*

Jenny positively glowed at Georgie's unstinting praise of the picture she had painted just for him. 'I must hang it up in my room at once, alongside Charlotte's.'

Later that day, the four of them stood back to admire Jenny's painting of the beach hanging beside the painting Charlotte had done years earlier of the village school. It had hung on Georgie's bedroom wall ever since.

Miles put his arm round Charlotte's shoulder and, glancing down at her, winked. 'Do you know, my dear, I think you have a rival for your talent. You'll have to watch out. Felix will be coming to take Jenny's pictures back to London.'

Solemnly – and quite seriously – Charlotte said, 'There's real talent there, if only it can be nurtured.'

'Then we must make sure it is,' Miles said softly.

Their words passed over the child's head. She was still basking in Georgie's approval.

There was a tap on the bedroom door and Wilkins's face appeared.

'Excuse me, sir – madam. Master Philip has arrived home.'

'How lovely,' Charlotte said, injecting what she hoped was as much pleasure as she had genuinely felt at Georgie's arrival. But Jenny made no such effort. Her smile disappeared to be replaced by a glower.

Noticing, Georgie took her hand. 'Come along, let's go and greet him. And Ben will be home soon too. Then we can all have a lovely family dinner, because you're part of our family now, aren't you, Jen?'

The child looked up at him, smiling, and with adoration in her eyes.

Watching them, Miles felt his heart turn over.

*

Ben was later arriving home from his work than normal. Charlotte had to hold dinner back by half an hour, much to Mrs Beddows's consternation. He came into the room solemn faced and avoiding his father's eyes.

Charlotte's heart leapt in her breast. Something was wrong – she could see it in his manner and written on his face.

And so could Miles. 'What is it, son? Bad news?'

Several young men from the district – though no one close as yet – had been reported killed or missing since Dunkirk. Miles feared the worst.

'Let's have dinner.' Ben smiled thinly. 'I'm sure Mrs Beddows is in a flap already.'

'Tell us now,' Charlotte said. 'Another few minutes won't matter.'

Ben sighed. 'I'm sorry – I know you think I shouldn't, but – but I've volunteered for the army.' Now he met his father's gaze. 'I know I could probably get out of it, but I can't sit around here whilst others are – are going. My conscience won't let me.'

Charlotte gasped and sat down suddenly, her hand to her breast, her eyes wide and fearful. 'Oh, Ben, no.'

She felt Philip's eyes on her, his mouth twisting in a sardonic smile. He moved and put his arm about his brother's shoulders, but his gaze was on Charlotte's face.

No one else in the room had spoken. Miles and Georgie seemed to have been turned to stone by Ben's announcement. Jenny, wide-eyed, stood watching them all.

'I wonder,' Philip drawled, 'if I shall get the same reaction. As it happens, I've volunteered too. The army. That's what I've come home to tell you all.' Now he smacked Ben on the back. 'You've rather stolen my thunder, old boy.'

With a supreme effort, Charlotte jumped to her feet and clasped her hands, staring at them both. 'Why? Why? How could you do this to us? Isn't it enough that Georgie—?' she stopped, realizing that she was in danger of betraying the very emotions she fought so hard to keep hidden.

'Ah yes,' Philip said softly. 'Georgie.'

That was all he said, but no one in the room, except perhaps Jenny, misunderstood the meaning behind his words.

It was Georgie who broke the tension. He crossed the room in a few strides to slap his brothers on the back. 'Congratulations. Old Hitler doesn't stand a snowball in hell's chance with all three Thornton boys after him.'

Charlotte moved to Miles's side. She looked up into his face. He was grey with sadness and his strong shoulders seemed to sag. It seemed to her that he had aged ten years in a matter of seconds. But, true to his nature, he said no word of censure. He merely stretched out his hand – a hand that trembled a little – to congratulate his boys. And to wish them well.

But only Charlotte knew the dreadful fear that was in his heart, for it took root in her own and she knew she'd never know another moment's peace until this war was over.

Fifty-Eight

Osbert had plenty to say about Philip's foolish action.

'What on earth is he thinking of?' He thumped his stick angrily. 'Send him to see me,' he demanded imperiously. 'I'll talk some sense into him.'

'It's done now, Father,' Charlotte said heavily. 'And I don't think it can be undone.'

'We'll see about that,' Osbert growled.

But even Osbert Crawford was no match for His Majesty's Services and so now there was only Jenny left at home to brighten their day and take their minds off their boys. But thoughts of them were never very far away.

'How many more are going to go?' Charlotte worried.

'Too many.' Miles paused then, trying to turn their thoughts to other matters, although everything they discussed seemed to be connected to the war in one way or another. 'Tommy Warren has gone. Had you heard? The army, I think.'

'How's he managed that?' Charlotte asked in surprise. 'Surely he's classed as being in a reserved occupation, isn't he?'

Miles shrugged. 'Well, Ben was, too, but he managed it. I don't quite know what they've done.' Then he asked, 'What about the workers on Buckthorn Farm? Are you coping?'

Charlotte sighed. 'At the moment, yes, but I think Eddie is beginning to feel frustrated that he can't go.'

'Tell him there are countless soldiers who would give their eye teeth to swap places with him. He's doing a valuable job and shouldn't feel guilty.'

Charlotte nodded. 'I will.'

'It's a pity Ben and Tommy couldn't see it that way,' he muttered, frowning. Then he sighed, trying to bring his thoughts back to the hole in the workforce that Ben's departure would leave. 'We've got land army girls coming to Home Farm. I'll see if Joe needs anyone. What about one or two for Buckthorn Farm?'

'Mm, I'll talk it over with Eddie.'

Georgie made the most of his leave. No one else except Charlotte seemed to notice the haunted look deep in his eyes. If they did, they said nothing. Like Georgie himself, everyone put on a brave face and laughed and joked as if all was right with the world instead of acknowledging that perhaps their country was facing its darkest hour.

Georgie spent most of his time with Jenny, teaching her to ride the second-hand bicycle that Miles had bought for her, even sitting her in the saddle on a docile pony and leading her along the quiet lanes. He took her to the seashore to see if the samphire was ready for picking.

'We'll take some home,' he told her, 'and Mrs Beddows will show you how to cook it.' He laughed. 'She's quite the expert since Charlotte first showed me where to pick it and . . .' There was a catch in his voice as he remembered his happy childhood. As Georgie had no memories of his own mother, Charlotte had filled that void for him at least. And he knew she looked upon him as her own son, her special boy. He realized now, how desperately worried both she and his father must be about him. And now his two brothers had joined up too.

He stood up suddenly and glanced around. 'Come on, Jen,' he said, holding out his hand. 'Time to go home, the tide's coming in.'

When they arrived back at the manor, it was to find that an urgent message awaited him. All leave had been cancelled and Georgie had to return to camp immediately.

As he bade everyone farewell in the hallway, he shook his father's hand, clapped his two brothers on the back and picked Jenny up and swung her round. But he saved his special bear hug for Charlotte, whispering close to her ear, 'Look after yourself, dearest Charlotte.'

And then he was gone, running down the steps, his kit bag bumping against his legs, out to where Brewster waited to drive him to the station.

Over the following weeks, the war news was no better. Britain now fought on alone and, as Mr Churchill had called it, the Battle of Britain was being fought by the RAF over the south of England. And whilst Georgie was in the thick of the fighting, Philip and Ben completed their basic training and awaited a posting.

They both came home on a week's leave and Charlotte tried to make their time at home very special. She planned their favourite meals – as far as rations would allow – and made a determined effort to heal the rift between herself and Philip. But she couldn't prevent Georgie being never far from her thoughts. Ben went back to the life he loved – working on Home Farm – whilst he waited, but Philip didn't want to involve himself in anything. He whiled away the days reading or just sitting staring into space, preferring to be alone rather than in company.

Jenny stood in front of him as he sat on the terrace one sunny August morning reading the newspaper. She regarded him solemnly for several moments before Philip became aware of her silent presence. He frowned over the top of the paper. 'What d'you want?'

'Georgie's not here.'

'No-o,' Philip said carefully. The child was stating the obvious, he thought, so why – ?

'And Charlotte's gone to see that grumpy old man.'

'Ye-es.'

'And the mister's busy, so – '

'So?'

'Will you read to me?' She held out the book. 'It's the one Georgie gived me.'

'Did he now?' He could see the battered copy of *The Wind in the Willows* in the child's hands. It had always been a favourite – one he remembered his mother reading to him . . .

Before he knew quite how it was happening, Jenny had tweaked the newspaper from his grasp and dropped it on the floor. Then she handed him the book and clambered on to his knee.

'We've got to Chapter Eight where Mr Toad's just been put in a dinjun.'

'A dungeon,' Philip said mildly.

'That's what I said – a dinjun.' With Bert clutched under one arm, she put her thumb in her mouth, curled up on his lap and, resting her head against his shoulder, waited for him to begin.

Half an hour later, that was how Charlotte, returning from Buckthorn Farm, found them.

'He was reading to her,' she told an incredulous Miles. 'There she was, sitting on his knee, and he was reading to her. *And* doing all the funny voices just like Georgie does.'

'Well, I never,' Miles murmured. 'You know, Philip hasn't always had this – this prickly side to his nature. When he was young –' He stopped, afraid he would cause Charlotte pain, but she finished his sentence for him.

'When his mother was alive, you mean?'

Slowly, Miles nodded.

For the remaining days of his leave, Jenny monopolized Philip.

'Georgie's not here,' she told him candidly, 'so you'll have to do.'

Hearing it, Charlotte held her breath, expecting a bad-tempered outburst from her stepson. But to her amazement, Philip only laughed. 'Well, I suppose it's no bad thing to be second-in-command. So, Jenny, what do you want to do today?'

Charlotte turned away, shaking her head in wonderment. I must be dreaming, she thought.

Charlotte's thoughts were never far away from her beloved Georgie in his Hurricane. And though they tried not to speak of it too often, Miles's preoccupied air told her that his thoughts, too, were often in the skies over the Channel. Philip and Ben had both gone and there was only Jenny to take their minds off their worries.

Charlotte went as often as she could to Lincoln to see

her mother, aunt and uncle, but still there was no evading the talk of war that seemed to dominate everyone's thoughts. As she arrived home from one such visit in early September, Miles greeted her. He was distraught.

Seeing his ravaged face, Charlotte's knew in an instant that it was the news she'd dreaded the most.

Georgie.

He held opened the front door as she climbed the steps on trembling legs. She reached out to him. 'What is it?'

'The worst possible.' His voice was deep and thick with emotion. 'Georgie's missing. One of his pals telephoned. He was seen going down over the coast of France. There is a chance – a slim one – but . . .'

Charlotte was dying inside. Her 'golden boy' lost. Missing – presumed killed. That was the heartbreaking official wording they would receive in a day or so.

'Perhaps . . .' she began, clinging to any vestige of hope, but the bleak, defeated look in Miles's eyes told her she was clutching at straws.

'Don't tell Jenny,' he pleaded hoarsely. 'It'll break her heart. She idolizes him.'

Her throat too full of tears to speak, Charlotte nodded as Miles turned away towards his study. She let him go, aware that he needed some time alone. Slowly she climbed the stairs towards her studio to seek her own solitary consolation. But it was not to be found; Jenny sat in her own little corner daubing a piece of paper with yellow ochre and dots of green.

'I'm painting another picture for Georgie,' she said brightly. 'He'll be home again soon. That's samphire, that is. We picked it together – me an' Georgie.'

Charlotte had never known what it felt like to have her heart broken.

But in that moment, she knew.

'Where is she? I can't find her.'

Miles burst into the morning room where Charlotte was patiently darning a sock. Make do and mend was the order of the day now.

She raised her eyes, pausing in her work but not flying into a panic straight away. 'Isn't she outside with the others?'

'No. They're clamouring to be taken home. Miss Parker too.'

Miss Parker was the teacher who came every day to the manor.

Charlotte rose with an outward calm she wasn't feeling inside. 'You take them all home and I'll mount a search party.'

'Easier said than done,' he muttered, but turned away to do as she suggested.

'Be careful,' she called after him, knowing he would drive like the wind, taking the corners in the narrows lanes far too fast in his haste to get back.

This time Jenny was not in the studio, nor in any other part of the house.

'Where can she be?' Charlotte worried, biting the edge of her thumb as she hovered in the hall, uncertain what to do next. 'Where might she go?'

But she couldn't answer her own question. Jenny was still a little afraid of the great outdoors unless there was someone else with her.

'If only you were here, Georgie,' she murmured sadly, 'she wouldn't have gone missing. She'd be stuck to your side like a limpet.'

Miles burst in through the front door.

'They've told her,' he blurted out. 'Those little buggers have told her. About Georgie. That's why she's run off.'

Charlotte gasped and her eyes widened. 'Oh, how could they?'

He ran his hand through his hair and took a deep breath. 'I suppose we shouldn't blame them. The whole village knows. The kids are bound to pick it up and – and they don't understand . . .'

'But where's she *gone*? I've looked everywhere I can think of.'

'Where did Georgie take her? Where did they go together?'

'The shore!' Charlotte gasped. 'Last time he was home, he took her to the seashore.'

Fifty-Nine

Within minutes they were both on horseback riding towards the sea, neither of them daring to voice their fears. Jenny didn't understand the ways of the sea, its tides and treacherous currents and creeks. She wouldn't know what to do if the water came swirling in around her . . .

They galloped down the long lane towards the sea bank. Pausing at the top of the rise, they scanned the beach.

'The tide's coming in,' Charlotte cried.

'Samphire? Where's the samphire.'

'Yes, yes. They collected samphire. She was painting a picture. This way.'

Leaving their horses, Charlotte led the way carefully across the marshy ground to where the samphire grew.

'There – over there. I thought I saw something . . .' Miles pointed. 'No – I'm imagining it.'

They walked on, scanning the marsh and the creeks around them. And with every second the incoming tide was coming closer and closer. After a few moments Miles shouted again. 'There! There, Charlotte. I did see something.'

Charlotte too had caught a movement a short distance in front of them – something white and fluttering in the breeze.

'Look!' She pointed excitedly. 'She *is* here. There's a peg with a piece of white rag tied to it.'

Miles frowned, then he remembered. 'You – you think Georgie told her what you told us all those years ago? So she could find her way back?'

'I'm sure of it.'

They quickened their pace towards the peg and its makeshift flag.

'There's another – and another,' Charlotte cried.

Just then, a figure bobbed up, stretching up to glance around her, watching the tide and the encroaching water.

'There she is,' Miles breathed. 'Thank God.'

'Don't be angry with her, Miles. Please. If she's just been told about Georgie . . .'

Jenny had seen them and was standing perfectly still watching them approach, a look of fear on her face. She knew she was in trouble.

'My, you've collected a lot. Mrs Beddows will be pleased.' Miles smiled down at her, reining in his instinct to either shake her roundly or clutch her to him in a thankful embrace. Instead, keeping his tone level and calm, he went on, 'But the tide's coming in now, love. Time we were heading back. Come on. We've got the horses on the sea bank. You can ride in front of me.'

They walked back the way they had come, collecting the pegs and pieces of cloth as they went. Miles hoisted her up on to the horse's saddle and then swung himself up behind her. She was still clutching the bag of wet samphire she'd collected.

'I was all right, mister. Honest. Georgie told me to watch out for the water comin' an' how to set the pegs. I wouldn't have drownded. Georgie . . .' Her voice broke and her head dropped. Miles held her close feeling the thin little body racked with sobs.

Beside them, Charlotte rode in silence, her throat full of tears, remembering how she'd taught Georgie about the tides and how to mark the path back across the marsh.

And he'd passed the knowledge on to little Jenny. Georgie had kept her safe even though he'd not survived.

Late one afternoon in October, when Charlotte and Miles were having tea in the morning room, the door was flung open with a crash and Jenny leapt on to the end of the sofa.

'There's an 'orrible noise an' banging,' Jenny wailed. 'I don't like it.'

Miles got up and went to the window, whilst Jenny scrambled along the sofa and snuggled up to Charlotte. 'I don't like it,' she muttered again and put her thumb in her mouth.

'It's only the sirens,' Charlotte said, thankful that they were far enough away from Lynthorpe for them to be no louder than they already were.

'And planes,' she heard Miles mutter. 'There are planes almost overhead.'

Jenny gave a scream and buried her head against Charlotte as more dull thuds sounded in the distance. 'It's 'Itler. He's comin'.'

Intrigued rather than frightened, Charlotte tried to untangle herself from the child, but Jenny held on tightly.

'What's happening?' Charlotte asked.

In a low voice, Miles said, 'They're dropping bombs. On Lynthorpe.'

'Don't like it,' came Jenny's muffled voice. 'And Bert don't like it neither.'

The banging ceased and soon the 'All Clear' sounded.

'There, there, it's all over now,' Charlotte comforted Jenny.

It was over for that day but, a month later, several incendiaries fell in a field belonging to one of Miles's tenant farmers. No one was hurt but the incident was to bring Miles and Charlotte more heartache than they could ever have imagined.

'I want 'er back 'ome with me, where she belongs, an' there ain't nuffin' you can do to stop me.'

Miles and Charlotte stood on the driveway facing the stranger, helpless in the face of her anger. Jenny clung to Miles's hand and made no move towards the woman, whom Charlotte presumed to be her mother.

'I ain't coming,' Jenny blurted out and pointed a trembling finger at the tall, thin man lounging against the motor car, smoking a cigarette. He was thin faced and handsome, Charlotte supposed, in a flash kind of way. She fought back a rising bubble of laughter. The man reminded her of Max Miller, the outrageous comedian, whom they'd seen once at the theatre and heard often on the radio. This man sported a thin, neatly trimmed moustache and was dressed in a flamboyant check suit. Loud, Miles would have called it. 'Not if *he*'s still there.' Jenny spat out the final words.

Charlotte saw the flash of anger in the man's face and he pushed himself upright, jabbing towards Jenny with his cigarette.

'Now look here, young 'un, I've been good to you,

I have.' The man smirked. 'And even better to yer ma, so don't you go bad-mouthing me to these nice people.'

Jenny cowered behind Miles, her boldness deserting her suddenly.

'Mrs Mercer . . .' Miles released himself from Jenny's grasp and strode towards the woman, holding out his hand in welcome. 'Shall we go inside and have a cup of tea and maybe something to eat? I'm sure you must be—'

'We gotta get goin' if we've to be back before the blackout,' the woman said. 'It's a long way to London.'

Keeping the smile firmly fixed on his face, Miles glanced towards the man and spread out his hands. 'You could both stay here tonight. You're more than welcome.'

'Nah thanks, guv'nor,' the man answered again. 'Like the little lady ses, we've got to get back. I've got mi business to think of.' He winked broadly at Miles. 'Know what I mean.'

Miles didn't, but he could make a shrewd guess: black market 'business'.

'I'm staying here,' Jenny's shrill voice piped up. 'I ain't going back wiv 'em.' She turned to Miles. 'I'm all right here, ain't I?'

'Of course you are, Jenny.' He held out his hand to her. 'But let's go inside and talk it over.'

'Well —' the woman hesitated and glanced at the man. 'Just a cuppa while she gets her things together.'

They turned towards the house, all except Jenny. She tore her hand from Miles's grasp and began to run across the grass towards the little gate leading to the lane to Buckthorn Farm.

''Ere, come back, our Jen. Don't you want to come

home with your ma?' the woman called after her, but Jenny kept on running.

Inwardly, Charlotte smiled. She guessed exactly where the child was heading. Buckthorn Farm. But she wasn't worried. Mary would look after her. And, later, when the couple had gone, Charlotte would fetch her back. But meanwhile, she would play the perfect hostess.

When they'd had tea, Charlotte offered, 'Would you like to see Jenny's bedroom? To see for yourself how well we're looking after her? Won't you leave her with us a while longer, Mrs Mercer? She'll be so much safer here.'

'No, I want her home. She's been away a whole year now, an' I don't want no one sayin' I'm a bad mother, sending my child to live wiv strangers.'

'I'm sure no one would think that,' Miles said smoothly, carefully avoiding Charlotte's glance lest his face should give him away. 'In fact, quite the contrary. You've shown remarkable unselfishness in sending your daughter to safety. You are to be commended.'

The woman stared at him, clearly not understanding if she was being insulted or complimented. She sniffed. 'Well, that's as may be, but we want her home now, don't we, Arfer?'

Arthur shrugged. 'Whatever you say, Dot.' Again he winked at Miles. 'Just like to keep the little ladies happy, don't we, guv'nor?'

Miles beamed at him, recognizing an ally, albeit for very different reasons. The man didn't want Jenny back with them any more than Miles wanted to let her go.

But Dot was the little girl's mother and she was adamant. 'All the other kids is back now. Jen's the only one in our street not back home and folks is talking.'

She nodded towards Arthur. ''Specially now Arfer's moved in. But we're getting married, ain't we, Arfer? And we want her back. We want to be a family.' She smiled archly. 'You never know, there might be a little brother or sister for 'er one day.'

Miles was amused by the flash of sheer terror which flitted across the man's face, but Arthur hid it manfully and forced a thin smile. 'Yer never know yer luck,' he murmured.

'So,' Dot said, standing up, 'if you can let me have her things, missis, we'll be on our way. Arfer, go an' call 'er. She can't be far away.' She shuddered dramatically. 'She'll not like all them open spaces we drove through to get here, I know.'

'*I* don't know where she'll be. Look, Dot, she don't want to come home. It's obvious. Why don't you—?'

'Shut up, Arfer. She's comin' back with us and that's final.' She turned back to Miles. 'You'd best find her, mister, 'cos I ain't going back without her.' Dot sat down again, a stubborn look on her face.

'She could be anywhere –'

'Then you aren't looking after 'er very well if you let her run wild like this.'

'We don't – I mean –' Miles was floundering and Charlotte stepped in.

'Jenny will be quite safe,' she said calmly, pushing aside the memory of their own panic when the girl had gone missing. 'She knows the area well now, and—'

'Well, you'd best find 'er, missis,' Dot said again. ''Cos I'm staying here till you do.'

Charlotte caught sight of Miles's face and her heart turned over with love for him. They were going to lose Jenny and he was devastated. They were no match for this determined woman, who was, after all, the girl's mother. Miles sighed heavily and turned away. 'I'll send out a search party,' he murmured.

'I'll go,' Charlotte said at once and hurried out of the room before anyone could stop her. 'I'll organize it.'

The November afternoon was turning to dusk and there was still no sign of Jenny.

'Dot, we'll have to go,' Arthur insisted at last. 'We'll be all night getting home now. Have to go slow, y'know,' he winked at Miles, 'in the blackout.'

Miles nodded absently. He rather thought the man would break the blackout regulations, put his car lights on full beam, and drive like the wind.

'Oh, all right. Have it your way.' Dot stood up and wagged her finger at both Miles and Charlotte. 'But I want her home. I'm going to the authorities when I get back.'

Miles's face was bleak. But, at least, for the moment, Jenny would be staying.

Sixty

Charlotte found Jenny in the place that had been her own childhood hideaway; the hayloft at Buckthorn Farm. The girl had fallen asleep, nestled in the dry hay. Charlotte sat beside her, gazing out of the small, square window until Jenny roused herself, rubbed her eyes and sat up.

'Have they gone?'

'Yes – for the moment. But your mother wants you home, darling.'

Jenny's lower lip trembled. 'But I don't want to go. I like it here. Don't you want me any more?'

Charlotte put her arm round Jenny's shoulders. Her voice was husky and not quite steady as she said, 'Miles and I would like you to stay for ever, and that's the truth, but your mum loves you. She wants you to go home.'

The girl was silent for a long time before she said in a small voice, 'Are they coming back to get me, then?'

Charlotte sighed. 'Your mother said she would be going to the authorities when she got home. Darling – if she does – there'll be nothing we can do.'

'I could hide here again. They wouldn't find me.'

Charlotte was silent. She didn't tell her that she'd told the searchers not to go into the hayloft at Buckthorn Farm. She'd guessed that was where the girl would be. She'd deliberately prevented them from finding Jenny. She sighed inwardly. She knew the girl would have to go back to London sooner or later, but at least she'd won them a little time. Time in which they could all get used to the idea.

Especially Miles, though she doubted he would ever come to terms with letting Jenny go.

Christmas was always going to be difficult. It was their first since the awful news that Georgie had been posted missing and now it was likely that very soon Jenny would have to leave them. There'd been no word yet from Dot, but they all knew it was only a matter of time. Even if she'd changed her mind and decided to let her daughter stay in the country, once the war ended the little girl would have to go home.

'I don't suppose,' Miles murmured one night as they lay in each other's arms, 'that they'd let us adopt her?'

Charlotte sighed. 'I don't think so. The mother seemed – well – possessive. It didn't seem like real affection to me, more like a status symbol. That she wanted to appear a good mother in front of her neighbours. I got the impression that was why she wanted Jenny home. Because all the other children in the street were back.'

'Mm. She said as much, didn't she?'

There was a pause before Charlotte said, 'Maybe Dot latched on to what you said and has gone back lording it over everyone about how she had been selfless in allowing Jenny to stay with us.'

'Perhaps,' he murmured, sounding doubtful.

Philip arrived home on Christmas Eve. 'I'm one of the lucky ones,' he told them, dropping his kit bag and a pile of gifts on to the floor of the hall. 'I've got five

451

whole days.' His face sobered as he took a deep breath, 'But it's likely I'll be posted abroad soon after Christmas, so . . .'

He forced a bright smile and, before either Miles or Charlotte could make any comment, added, 'We're going to make it a good one, especially for little Jen.' Seeing their subdued faces, he glanced from one to the other. 'What? What is it?'

Charlotte sighed and moved to kiss his cheek, whilst Miles held out his hand to shake his son's. Drawing Philip into the morning room whilst Charlotte sent for tea, he told Philip about Dot Mercer's visit.

'I doubt we'll be able to hold out for ever. She was very determined and – ' he sighed heavily – 'she's the girl's mother.'

'Then let's do our best to make it a memorable Christmas for her.' Philip glanced at Charlotte as he added softly, 'It's what Georgie would have wanted us to do.'

To everyone's amazement, Philip was the 'life and soul' of Christmas. Ben hadn't been able to get leave, so it was Philip who took Jenny out that afternoon to collect holly and ivy to decorate the house. Then in the evening he commandeered everyone into helping with the decorating of the Christmas tree in the hall. And just before Jenny's bedtime, he suggested she should ask Mrs Beddows for a mince pie for Father Christmas and a carrot for his reindeers.

'We'll put them near the tree in the hall. He'll be sure to find them there.'

'Whatever made you think of doing that?' Charlotte asked. 'What a lovely idea.'

'One of the lads at camp was talking about his kids and it's what they do.' For a brief moment, his eyes were haunted. 'Poor feller. He was posted abroad last week. He'll not get home for Christmas.'

Just after midnight, Philip dressed up in a red dressing gown and cotton wool beard and crept into Jenny's bedroom with an armful of presents to fill the pillowcase that the excited little girl had hung on the end of her bed. And he was up at six o'clock the following morning, grinning from car to ear as Jenny woke the whole household with her cries of 'He's been! He's been! *And* 'ee's eaten the mince pie.'

'Who'd have thought it?' Miles murmured as they watched Philip kneeling on the bedroom floor helping Jenny open her presents. 'It's as if—'

He stopped, not wanting to bring sadness to the moment, but Charlotte added softly, 'Yes, it's as if Georgie's here, isn't it? That's just what he'd've been doing.'

Christmas Day and Boxing Day passed all too quickly with noisy games and such a wonderful array of food that Charlotte wondered if Mrs Beddows had links to the black market.

Miles threw back his head and laughed. 'I don't think so, my dear, though I wouldn't put it past Brewster. No, Charlotte, she's been holding secret meetings with Mary and Peggy for weeks.' He chuckled as he added, 'She's become a real country woman and revels in learning your ways.'

Charlotte was about to ask him if he had any regrets about moving to the country all those years ago, but at that moment, Jenny grabbed his hand and pulled him into a game of hide and seek through the rambling house.

'You too, Charlotte,' she insisted. And neither of them could refuse – even if they'd wanted to.

As he left on the morning after Boxing Day, Philip put his arms round Charlotte's waist. 'Charlotte, thank you for a lovely Christmas.'

'Thank *you*, Philip. You – you've been wonderful.' She kissed him and then, drawing back a little, murmured, 'Please, take care of yourself.'

For a brief moment, the same haunted look she had seen in Georgie's eyes was in Philip's. 'I'll try,' he said huskily and turned away abruptly.

He swung Jenny high into the air, making her squeal with delight, before setting her down again and shaking his father's hand.

And then he, too, was gone.

There were two serious air raids over Lynthorpe during January and February 1941, killing at least two residents. Soon after news of this had spread, the moment they'd all dreaded came when they saw Mr Tomkins riding up the drive on his bicycle.

Jenny ran and, for once, Miles and Charlotte let her go, preparing to face Mr Tomkins together. He dismounted from his bicycle, leaned it against the pillar at the foot of the steps, and climbed to the front door. Miles opened it.

'I'm sorry,' Mr Tomkins said at once as he stepped inside. 'The girl's mother's demanding we send Jenny back. She heard about the air raids here. One of the other evacuee children who comes from the same neighbourhood as Jenny wrote home and Dot got to hear about it. She's saying the girl's no safer here now than she would be in London. Her argument is that at least they've got the Underground to shelter in.' He sighed. 'And – in a way – you've got to agree with her. We've nothing like that here. Even an Anderson isn't quite the same, is it?'

Grim faced, Miles nodded. 'Then I shall take her home myself.'

'Oh, I don't know—' Mr Tomkins began, but whatever he'd been going to say was cut short by Miles saying firmly, 'That's the only way I'll let her go. I want to know she's going to be all right. If she isn't,' he glared at the inoffensive man who was only trying to do the duty that had been imposed upon him, 'then I shall bring her back here and no one – no one – will be able to stop me.'

This time, even Jenny was helpless in the face of her mother's demands. Backed by the authorities now, Dot held the trump card. She was the child's mother.

'She's better off back where she belongs,' was Osbert's only comment, but he was alone in his thinking. Everyone else in the district had taken the little girl to their hearts and they were all sorry to see her go.

Miles and Charlotte organized a farewell party for her. Since many of the children had returned home, lessons at the manor had ceased. The school now had room for the few evacuees still left, Jenny amongst them. But Charlotte invited all the children who'd had lessons at the manor, together with those in Jenny's class at school. Miss Parker, the Warrens and Mary and Edward came too, but Osbert refused to attend. 'Such a fuss over a grubby little city urchin.'

Mary and Mrs Beddows had combined their resources and made as many treats as rations would allow for the children. All the guests played rowdy games on the lawn, led by Miles and, at the end of the afternoon, as they waved everyone 'goodbye', Jenny slipped her hand into his.

'That was a lovely party. I just wish Georgie'd been here.'

Charlotte felt a lump in her throat and tears prickle her eyes. When Miles did not answer the child, she knew he was feeling just the same as she was.

How she missed Georgie every minute of every day. And now they were to lose the child who'd brought sunshine into their lives and helped to ease the pain of their loss.

'Do you want me to come too?' Charlotte asked the following morning – the day that Jenny had to return home. By poignant coincidence, the date was 1 March and would have been Georgie's twenty-first birthday.

Miles shook his head and Charlotte felt hurt. He didn't want her with him, she thought. Didn't want – or need – her support. But his next words lessened her pain, though only a little.

'I want to spare you having to leave her with – with *them*,' he said bitterly. 'I'm not even sure I'm going to be able to do it.'

'Then let me—'

'No, Charlotte,' he snapped. 'I have to do this.'

He turned away from her and Charlotte watched him go with tears in her eyes, feeling rejected yet again.

Jenny clung to her when the time for parting came and sobbed noisily. Charlotte could no longer hold back the tears that flooded down her face. Perhaps, after all, Miles was right. She wasn't able to hide her distress now and leaving the girl in London would be even worse.

'Promise you'll write to us, Jenny.'

Against Charlotte's shoulder, which was already wet with her tears, the girl nodded.

Charlotte watched them go until they were out of sight, then she turned and headed for her studio, but even here she could find no comfort. Not today. Jenny's childish paintings littered the floor and Charlotte couldn't bring herself to tidy them away. As for painting herself, which usually gave her such solace, she hadn't even the heart for that.

She retraced her steps downstairs and, putting on a warm coat and sturdy boots, she went out for a walk. She headed towards the sea bank, where she sat down and allowed the tears to flow for Georgie, for Jenny and even for herself because she couldn't give her beloved Miles what he most desired, a daughter. And now he'd lost the closest thing he'd ever had to that.

He'd lost the little girl who'd found her way into both their hearts.

Miles telephoned that evening to say that he couldn't get home that night and would stay in the city.

'Was it – bad?' she asked tentatively, not wanting to rub salt in the raw wound, but needing to know.

'Worse than you could possibly imagine,' he said tartly and rang off quickly.

The following day Charlotte waited restlessly for Miles's return, watching the driveway from the window of his study. She wanted to greet him the moment he returned. Her heart leapt as she saw movement at the end of the driveway. But it was not Miles returning.

It was a telegraph boy riding solemnly towards the house.

Sixty-One

The telegram was addressed to Miles. Charlotte bit her lip, fingering it, not knowing what to do. She was frightened to open it and yet afraid not to do so.

At her elbow, Wilkins said, 'The master would want you to open it, madam, I'm sure.'

Charlotte took a deep breath and slit open the thin, folded sheet. She read the words with growing dread.

'. . . *Regret to inform you Philip Thornton seriously wounded . . .*' There followed a telephone number for further information.

'It's Master Philip. He – he's been wounded.'

'Do you wish me to obtain the number for you, madam?' Wilkins prompted gently.

Charlotte bit her lip. 'No – no. I'll wait for Mr Thornton. He – he should be the one to telephone.'

'Of course, madam. Would you like me to get Brewster to drive you to the station? Perhaps you'd like to meet the train?'

But again Charlotte shook her head. She couldn't bear to give Miles yet more bad news in such a public place. 'No – no. It'd be best for him to get home first.'

'Very good, madam.'

She had to wait another two hours before she saw Miles walking up the driveway. She went to the front door and waited for him to reach her. She had the telegram in her hand and he knew at once that it bore bad news.

He gained the top step and leaned wearily against the door jamb. 'Which one is it this time?'

'It's Philip – he's been badly wounded. There's a number to ring.'

With a supreme effort, Miles pushed himself upright and walked, shoulders hunched, towards the study. Charlotte followed him, watching him with worried eyes as he sank into the chair behind the desk, reached for the telephone and motioned to her to hand him the telegram.

Wilkins entered the study quietly and set down a tray with sandwiches and tea. Charlotte nodded her thanks and the manservant left the room, closing the door discreetly behind him.

When, after what seemed an age, Miles replaced the receiver, he sat a moment with his head in his hands. At last he raised his eyes, bloodshot with weariness, to look up at her.

'He's in hospital, but there's nothing they can do for him except try to alleviate the pain as much as they can. He's very badly shot up and—' He buried his face in his hands and his huge shoulders shook.

Charlotte hurried round the desk and put her arms about him. He turned and buried his face in her neck, weeping unashamedly.

A little later, when he was calmer, they drank the tea though the sandwiches lay untouched. 'I'll hire a special ambulance, and a nurse – that one you had for your father, if she can come. We'll bring him home. He – he'd want to be here, I know.'

Charlotte wasn't so sure, but she said nothing as

Miles went on. 'I'll get the best doctors, the best surgeons. Surely, there's something that can be done.'

Still Charlotte remained silent. She doubted the medical people would allow Philip to be moved if he was so seriously injured. But she was wrong. Desperate for beds, the hospital was only too glad to release Philip into his father's care.

On the afternoon that he was carried into the manor and up the stairs to his bedroom, the sight of the young man's ashen face shocked Charlotte. Later, when Nurse Monty gave her permission and they were allowed to see him, some colour had returned to his cheeks, but he was thin and obviously in dreadful pain in spite of the morphine the nurse had administered. He reached out his arms to them both and they each took one of his hands and sat on either side of the bed.

'I'm – so – sorry.' It was an effort to speak and at once Charlotte shushed him and bade him rest. 'You'll soon be stronger. Now you're home.'

He smiled thinly. 'Dear Charlotte,' he whispered, 'ever the optimist, but I'm sorry to say that this time' – he managed a wry smile – 'I'm not pretending.'

Tears filled her eyes as she squeezed his hand gently, but she could find no words.

Philip closed his eyes and slept, but they remained sitting beside him until the nurse shooed them away. They left him reluctantly, knowing that every moment with him was precious.

'I suppose,' Miles said carefully as they sat together in the growing dusk, the first time they had found a little peace in the flurry of the last few days, 'we should let your father come to see him. Does he know yet?'

Charlotte shook her head. 'I haven't told him. What with Jenny going and – and then hearing about

460

Philip . . .' Her voice trailed away. There was silence between them until at last she said tentatively, 'You – you've never told me about Jenny and – and how things were.'

Miles sighed and ran his hand through his hair. 'It was awful. They live in a dirty, dilapidated back street. Kids were playing in the roadway, kicking a tin can about. Oh Charlotte, I wanted to gather them *all* up and bring them home – every last one of them.'

'And Jenny? Was she – all right when you left?'

Miles shrugged. 'I suppose so. Her mother certainly seemed to have made an effort. She'd got her some clothes – not new, but I wouldn't blame the woman for that. Times are really tough for them down there, what with all the Blitz damage and the rationing. But even Arthur had bought her some toys. And, surprisingly, a few books, too. Mind you,' Miles allowed himself a wry grin, ' "bought" might not be quite the right word for how he came by them.'

'I hope they'll let her draw and paint. I let her take a set of paints and brushes with her. And some of my paper, though she insisted on leaving her paintings here, all except one of the beach – like the one she – she did for Georgie.' Charlotte stopped. The tears were choking her. So much sadness. First losing Georgie and then Jenny being forced to leave them and now Philip, for whom there was little hope. They would have to stand helplessly by and watch him die. The best they could do was try to keep him out of pain and to be beside him until . . .

Breaking the long silence at last, Miles said, 'I think you should ask Philip if he wants to see your father and then let Osbert know. After all, he – might want to change his will.'

'I don't want him to do that,' Charlotte said at once. 'It would seem very cruel to Philip. No – no, I don't want that.'

Miles touched her face gently. 'My dear, dear Charlotte. Always putting others before yourself.'

If only, she thought, I really was his 'dear, dear Charlotte'.

Miraculously, over the next few days, Philip seemed to grow a little stronger. His appetite improved though he still ate like a bird. He was drowsy, yet his nights were restless and filled with nightmares.

'That's the side effect of the morphine,' Nurse Monty told them. 'But without it . . .'

Miles asked Dr Bennet, the young doctor who had replaced Dr Markham, to arrange for a specialist to visit. 'Surely there's something they could do?'

Dr Bennet eyed Miles shrewdly. 'You're right to want to explore every avenue. It's only natural, and I will see that we get the very best to give their opinion, but I should warn you against holding out much hope. Philip himself knows the score. I've talked to him. His injuries are such that his organs are failing, Mr Thornton. With your love and care he'll live a few weeks – maybe even months – but they can't give him new kidneys, liver and a whole string of intestines. My dear fellow, I'm being blunt, but I'm not one to give out false hope to anyone. If folk can't take the truth from me, then they'd better find themselves another doctor.' He paused and then said soberly, 'To be honest, Mr Thornton, I don't know how he's survived this long. Sheer willpower, I shouldn't wonder. I think he just wanted to get home – to be with you all for the short time he has left. Anyway, I'll get in touch with my colleagues. You shall have a second opinion. A third and fourth, if you wish.'

The young doctor was certainly from the same mould as his predecessor and well liked by his patients for it. He had a similar bluff, no-nonsense manner, yet he was kindly and caring, too. And he was as good as his word; two consultants came to the manor to examine Philip, a week after each other, but could not give any better a diagnosis than Dr Bennet had done.

'No more, Father. I've accepted the inevitable and so should you. And now,' Philip grinned weakly, 'you'd better let Mr Crawford come. I've a few things I want to say to him.'

Charlotte rode alone to Buckthorn Farm to break the news of Philip's dreadful injuries to her father.

At first Osbert ranted and raved and accused Miles of not trying hard enough to find medical attention for the boy. 'There must be someone somewhere who could do something.'

'Dr Bennet—'

'Bah – what does he know? He's still wet behind the ears.'

'We could ask Dr Markham, if you—'

'That country yokel. I never did like him.'

Charlotte sighed. 'We've had the best – the very best – specialists visit, but sadly they all say the same. There's nothing that can be done.'

'I'll see the boy myself. I'll rouse him. He'll make the effort for me.'

'You'll do no such thing, Father,' Charlotte snapped. 'I won't allow you to upset him.'

Osbert glared at her. '*You* won't allow it. Who do you think *you* are, all of a sudden? Just because Thornton married you, you think you're someone now, don't you? Well, you're nobody, miss, let me tell you.' He shook his fist in her face. 'You can't even give me a grandson!'

It was a cruel jibe, but Charlotte stood her ground. Her father no longer had the power to rule her life or to hurt her with his barbs. Life was dealing her the bitterest of blows: Georgie was lost, Jenny was gone, and Philip was facing death. Osbert's cruelty in the face of all that was nothing.

Of Ben, she dared not even think. If anything were to happen to Ben, too, then . . . She blocked the thought and dragged her mind back to the present. Taking a deep breath, she said, 'You'll come on condition you don't upset him – or not at all.'

Of course her father came to the manor, as Charlotte had known he would. She'd no wish to stay in the room with them, but she asked the nurse to stay within earshot. 'If you hear anything you're not happy with, please send him packing. And if you have any trouble, Mr Thornton is in his study. He'll be there until he knows my father has left. Just in case. If you need me, I'll be in my studio.'

Monty nodded and smiled. 'I think I can handle Mr Crawford. I've had plenty of practice, remember?'

The two women smiled at each other before Charlotte gave the nurse a brief nod and went upstairs to shut herself away at the top of the house. She was no longer frightened of her father as she had once been, but she was wary of him.

But the visit passed off peacefully and Charlotte was not even aware that Osbert had left until Kitty came to fetch her. 'Mr Crawford's gone, ma'am, and Master Philip is asking for you.'

'Oh dear, is he – ?'

'Nothing's wrong, ma'am. He's fine – well, as fine as the poor man can be, but he says he wants to talk to you.'

As soon as she sat down at the side of Philip's bed, he said, 'I'm sorry, Charlotte, I tried my damnedest, but he's a stubborn old goat, isn't he? I tried to get him to agree to change his will leaving Buckthorn Farm to you, but he refused.'

'Philip, I don't need the farm. Not now. You should write a letter making *your* wishes clear.'

'Once I'm gone,' he murmured, seeming to ignore her remark, 'he might reconsider.'

Charlotte said nothing. She believed her father would bequeath his farm to anyone he could think of, just so long as it wasn't his daughter. But she said nothing.

'I wanted you to have it, Charlotte. I owe you such a lot.'

She was startled. 'Me?'

'Yes, you. It was thanks to you I ever got up out of this bed and walked again. But for you, I might have been here all this time.'

Charlotte's tears flowed. 'Perhaps it'd have been better if you had been. At least, you'd have been safe.'

'But I'd've had no life. No life at all. Thanks to you, I qualified, had a few years as a lawyer, which I loved . . .' Then he grinned cheekily. 'Had a few girls, and I've fought for my country. No, Charlotte,' he squeezed her hand, 'I don't regret a moment. In fact, I'm grateful you gave me that chance. That I'm to die now, well, I'm not the only one. There are thousands of families mourning their sons. I just hope old Ben keeps himself safe . . .'

With those last words, he drifted into sleep.

It seemed that Philip's prayers for his brother were answered. News came in a long letter from Ben himself the very next morning that he'd been awarded the George Cross and was also being promoted:

> *I've been with a bomb disposal unit for some time now. I didn't tell you, because I knew you'd both worry. Anyway, I was wounded in the leg as the result of an incident. It's not serious, but it means I can't continue in bomb disposal. I'm being allowed to stay in the army. They seem to think I'll be useful training new recruits!*

'What did he do?' Charlotte asked.

Miles continued to scan the thin sheets of paper. 'He doesn't say. That's typical of Ben, isn't it? But it must have been something incredibly courageous.'

'If he's to train recruits, will he be safe?' Charlotte hardly dared to voice the question.

Miles nodded cautiously. 'Relatively safe, I hope.' They stared at each other, appalled to think of the danger Ben had been in every day and they hadn't even known.

When they told Philip the news, he smiled. 'Good old Ben. Who'd've thought that the quiet one of the three of us would be decorated? Rather appropriate, don't you think, the *George* Cross? Old Georgie would have been tickled pink.'

The thought brought tears to Charlotte's eyes; a mixture of pride and heartache.

She sat beside Philip's bedside talking when he woke or keeping silent whilst he slept. But as long as he clutched her hand and, quite literally, held her there, she stayed.

'Charlotte?' He woke suddenly, his eyes wide.

'Yes, dear. I'm here.'

He let out a long sigh and she felt him squeeze her hand. 'Can I ask you something?'

'Of course.'

'I don't want to hurt your feelings, but . . .' He stopped and Charlotte leaned closer, finishing his sentence softly. 'You'd like the portrait of your mother to hang on the wall opposite your bed, so you can see her?'

Slowly, he turned his head to look at her. 'How – how did you know?'

'I just felt that you'd like it.'

'And – and you don't mind?'

'Of course I don't.' She bit her lip and then added hesitantly, 'And would – would you like one of Georgie beside it?'

'You've painted one?'

Charlotte nodded. 'After that first one of your father, I've painted you all as you've grown.'

'Ben?'

'Yes, Ben too.'

'And – and me? Surely you haven't painted me?'

Now she laughed aloud. 'Of course I have. Why wouldn't I?'

'Because – oh, just because . . .'

Now it was Charlotte who squeezed his hand gently.

Sixty-Two

'Will you pose for me in your uniform and your medal?' Charlotte asked Ben when he came home on compassionate leave to visit Philip.

'I couldn't. I'd be far too embarrassed.'

'Then may I at least see your uniform and the medal and will you tell me how you'd wear it? Please, Ben.' Her voice dropped. 'It's for Philip.'

Ben smiled sadly. 'You're a crafty little minx, Charlotte Thornton. You know I can't refuse if you put it like that.'

Charlotte widened her gaze innocently. 'But it's the truth. He wants one of all of us. Even me.' She pulled a face. 'Though I'm not very happy about doing a self-portrait.'

'Then get Father to ask Felix to do one of you. I bet he would.'

Charlotte stared at him, not sure if he meant Felix would paint one or his father would ask his friend.

'Er – well – yes,' she murmured.

Ben agreed to sit for her and they spent a few companionable hours in her studio, talking when the mood was right or in comfortable silence whilst she worked. When the portrait was finished, they all assembled in Philip's room to hang the new picture beside those of Louisa, Miles and Georgie.

Philip pulled himself up in the bed, wincing as he did

so. 'That's wonderful, Charlotte. What a handsome fellow you are, Ben. I'm proud of you, old boy.' His voice shook a little. Then he cleared his throat and said with greater firmness, 'But there are still at least two people missing. You, Charlotte. I must have all of you. And Jenny? What about little Jenny? She was part of this family for a while.'

'I've got one of her – in fact, two or three. You could have a look at them and choose which you like best. And,' Charlotte added shyly, 'I've done another of your father recently. Would you like to see that too?'

'Aha, an updated version with my grey hair and wrinkles, I expect.' Miles laughed.

Half an hour later, two more pictures had been hung on the wall opposite the end of Philip's bed.

'There still isn't one of you, Charlotte,' Philip said.

She turned to him, forcing a teasing laughter into her voice. 'Now, what would you want a picture of me for? I'm here every day. All the time. In fact, you hardly get a minute's peace from me.'

Philip closed his eyes with a sigh, but there was a smile on his lips as he said, 'Father, talk to her, will you? I want all of you there. And can you fix a light so that it shines on them. You see, in the night, when I'm awake . . .' He drifted off to sleep, but they knew what he meant. He spent many long, wakeful and uncomfortable hours in the night. He'd insisted – no, demanded – that none of the family should sit with him and lose their sleep, so only the nurse ever kept him company during the lonely hours of darkness. But if he could see his family, feel them close by, especially Georgie and even Jenny, then it would bring him comfort.

'Have you really never done a self-portrait?' Ben asked Charlotte softly.

As Charlotte shook her head, Miles put his arm about her shoulders. 'She's far too modest, and I doubt she'd do herself justice if she did. I'll get in touch with old Felix. Perhaps he'd come for a weekend and do one of you. He could use your studio. I'm sure he'd do it as a special favour.'

'There's someone else . . .'

They all turned towards the bed as Philip, rousing himself momentarily, murmured, 'Alfie. I want to see Alfie.'

'What do you think he meant?' Charlotte asked as the three of them went back downstairs, leaving Philip to rest. 'Does he want us to fetch Alfie here – in person – or does he mean he wants me to do a painting of him?' Since the birth of his son, Philip had had little to do with either Alfie or Lily.

'I don't know,' Miles said. 'Could you do one? A painting of Alfie?'

'Yes.' Charlotte was confident. 'I see him often enough and besides, I can always make an excuse to visit their cottage if I need to.' Eddie, Lily and their growing family still lived in the Warrens' former home.

'I think he meant both,' Ben put in quietly. 'I think he wants a painting, yes, but I also think he wants to see Alfie in person.' He paused and then asked, 'Do you think they've told the boy the truth? How old is he now, by the way?'

Charlotte shook her head slowly. 'He'll be fourteen at the end of June and, no, I don't know they have told him. Lily told me not so long ago they keep putting it off because they find it difficult. But still, there might be a way.'

'*Now* what is that pretty head of yours scheming?' Miles smiled.

Charlotte tapped him on the nose. 'Never you mind.' She turned to Ben. 'Could you find out from Philip if you're right? It might be better coming from you.'

Ben nodded. 'I'll go back up. Sit with him until he wakes and bring the conversation round.' He looked at his father. 'May I tell him you'll get in touch with Felix? That would be a way to open up the topic again.'

'Of course. I'll telephone him at once.'

A little later, Miles sought out Charlotte. 'He's coming at the weekend. He'll be glad to get away, he says. London had a dreadful bombing raid last night and his gallery was badly damaged. I was lucky to get through on the telephone . . .' Fear haunted his eyes. 'Oh Charlotte, I do hope little Jenny is all right.'

Felix came the very next weekend, arriving in a flurry and throwing his arm round each one of them in turn, his beaming smile only sobering when he stood beside Philip's bed and looked down upon the broken body of the fine young man he'd known. Then he turned to the paintings on the wall, studying each one.

'Ah, she has such talent, your stepmother,' he murmured. 'Such a waste.'

Philip lifted his head. 'A waste? What d'you mean?'

'All those years when she was young she was denied the chance to learn and flourish. It's a miracle she paints as well as she does. But then, no amount of learning replaces genuine inborn talent. But if only she could have studied with the best . . .'

'Could she still?'

Felix gave a hearty laugh and turned to look at him.

'My dear, dear boy, Charlotte would never leave your father to go to study in London or anywhere else. She's devoted to him. "Besotted" might be a better word.'

'You mean – you mean she really loves him?'

'Oh my goodness, yes. Haven't you seen it in her eyes? At the mere mention of his name, her eyes light up and when they're together, her gaze follows him around the room.'

'Really.' He lay back as Felix came and sat down beside the bed. 'And my father? Does he love her?'

'Ah,' Felix sighed. 'Now that is a little more difficult to say. He loves her, yes, but I'm not sure it's in quite the same way.' His glance turned slowly to rest on the portrait of Louisa Thornton. 'There's always the memory of your mother, you see.'

'Poor Charlotte,' Philip murmured, and as he drifted into sleep once more, he heard Felix say, 'Poor Charlotte indeed. The only thing she wants out of life is to make your father happy and to give him his heart's desire. And even that is denied her.'

Sixty-Three

Felix promised to stay until the paintings were completed, working each day with Charlotte in her studio.

'At last,' he cried as he entered the room on the first morning. 'I am to be allowed to work in the room I created. What joy!'

Smiling, Charlotte sat at her own easel to work on the portrait she'd already begun of Alfie.

Ben, with his usual gentle tact, had found out that Philip did want Alfie to visit. Going to the cottage, Charlotte had learned that, no, Alfie had still not yet been told the truth as to the identity of his biological father. Instead, both Eddie and Lily, who'd no wish to keep a dying man from seeing his son, generously agreed that Alfie should visit the manor on the pretext of sitting for Mrs Thornton.

'I'm running out of subjects,' she told the boy, crossing her fingers behind her back at the half-lie.

'Thought you'd prefer to do our Lizzie. She's much prettier.'

'Well, maybe I will, when she's older, but I want to start with you.'

The boy visited the manor each day for a week and whilst he posed for Charlotte, she, in turn, was being painted by Felix. Though Alfie was a little in awe of the artist from London at the start, Felix soon charmed the boy and the sessions in the studio were full of laughter and teasing.

On the fourth day, Felix played his part in the scheme. Late in the afternoon when the natural light was fading, he threw down his brush and cried, 'Enough! Work is over for the day. Come, Charlotte, you must stop, too, and let this poor boy ease his aching muscles.'

Charlotte set aside her brushes and stood up, stretching her back.

'But before you go, dear boy,' Felix said, putting his arm about Alfie's shoulder, 'I want to show you just how good the portrait of you is going to be. She's painted pictures of all the family. They're hanging in Philip's room.'

The boy stopped. 'I can't go in there, mister. Me mam said he's very ill.'

'He'll be pleased to see you,' Felix insisted. 'He gets few visitors and a new face will brighten his day. You're a big lad now,' Felix added softly. 'Living on a farm, you understand about life and death. And you understand about the war too, don't you?'

'Well, I know what's happening, but I don't understand *why*.'

'Nor do a lot of us, dear boy, but we must all try to do our bit. And if your bit is to brave seeing an injured soldier and to bring him what comfort you can, then you'll do it, now won't you?'

Alfie was thoughtful for a moment, as if plucking up courage. When he nodded, Charlotte let out a sigh of relief and smiled at Felix, thanking him with her eyes.

'Come along, then, dear boy, you really must see these magnificent portraits and afterwards, well, perhaps you could have a word with Philip.'

So it became a routine that each day when work on

their pictures was over, Alfie would go to Philip's room and spend half an hour with him.

'Me mam's sent her best wishes,' Charlotte heard Alfie say as she closed the door quietly and left them alone. To her joy, the boy continued to visit Philip even after he was no longer required to sit for Charlotte.

'Charlotte! Charlotte! Come quickly!' Miles's voice resounded from the hallway, reaching to every corner of the house. Even in the studio, they heard him.

Charlotte's heart skipped a beat and then began to thud painfully. Her eyes wide, she exchanged a frightened glance with Felix. Oh no, not more bad news.

She ran downstairs, whilst Felix hovered anxiously on the landing. At the foot of the stairs, Miles was waving a piece of paper and smiling jubilantly. 'He's alive! Georgie's alive!'

Charlotte cried out with joy and launched herself from the third step into his outstretched arms. He swung her round, laughing and shouting, 'He's alive. Georgie's alive.'

The household staff, hearing the commotion came running. Mrs Beddows and Kitty from the kitchen and even Wilkins, always sedate and controlled, was flustered momentarily, beaming his relief and delight at the news. On the landing, Felix closed his eyes in thankfulness. How good it was to see his dear friends receive good news for once.

'Champagne, Wilkins. For everyone. And bring a bottle to Philip's room. We must tell him at once.'

They mounted the stairs, hand in hand. At the top, Felix tried awkwardly to embrace them both at once, his eyes shining with tears.

Philip was sleeping fitfully. His face was flushed and his eyes dark with pain.

'Do you think we should tell him?' Charlotte whispered as the three of them tiptoed into his room.

'I—'

'Tell me what?' Philip asked, his eyes fluttering open.

Miles couldn't contain his excitement, his relief, any longer. He moved to the side of the bed and put his hand gently on Philip's shoulder. His voice husky with emotion, he said, 'Georgie is alive.'

Philip closed his eyes on a long sigh and whispered a heartfelt, 'Thank God.'

There was a gentle tap on the door and Wilkins entered the room carrying a tray and beaming. 'The staff send their congratulations, sir. This is wonderful news.'

Philip opened his eyes and, wincing a little, pulled himself up in the bed. 'Tell everyone to come to my room, Wilkins. Let's have a real celebration.'

A while later, everyone gathered in Philip's bedroom to drink champagne. Mrs Beddows and Kitty giggled at the unexpected treat and the bubbles tickling their noses. When things had calmed down a little and the staff had returned to their duties, leaving the four of them alone again, Charlotte asked, 'Where is he? Is he coming home?'

Miles's face sobered suddenly. He shook his head. 'Maybe we shouldn't be celebrating so soon, but I was so overjoyed to hear he's alive when – when . . .'

Charlotte moved to his side and linked her arm through his. 'Of course we should celebrate. It's wonderful news. The very best. But – where is he?'

'In a prisoner of war camp.'

Charlotte stared at him. 'But – but is he all right? I mean, is he safe?'

Miles pulled a face. 'I don't expect conditions will be ideal, but he's probably safer there than flying a fighter plane.'

Charlotte was thoughtful. 'Can we write to him? Send food parcels?'

'I don't know. I'll get in touch with the authorities. The Red Cross, perhaps.'

'Is it a German POW camp?' Philip asked.

'I believe it's a place called Colditz.'

Philip raised his head, stared at his father for a moment, and then began to laugh.

Mystified, Miles and Charlotte glanced at each other and then looked at Philip questioningly.

'Dad, that's the safest place in Germany at the moment. It's a castle where they send unruly prisoners. All the escapees end up in Colditz Castle. Good old Georgie, he must have been giving the Germans a right run-around to end up there.'

'You mean, he's been trying to escape, Phil?' Miles asked.

'Several times, probably. It's the place they send POWs who *keep* trying to escape. Good old Georgie.' Philip raised his glass again. 'Give 'em hell, little brother.'

'I must go to London,' Miles said suddenly the following morning at breakfast.

Felix and Charlotte exchanged a puzzled glance.

'To see the authorities, you mean? About Georgie?'

'Well, perhaps, but I want to tell Jenny myself. She adored Georgie. I want her to know that he's alive.'

'Of course.' Charlotte smiled. 'Would you like me to come with you?'

477

'If you'd like to. But what about old Felix here? He's our guest . . .'

'Goodness, don't worry about me, my dears. I still have a lot of work to do on my painting. I shall be quite happy. And I'll keep Philip company too, when he's feeling up to it. No, no, you two go. And take my key. You can stay at my flat overnight, if you have to. Travelling is abominable just now.'

'We must take some food for Jenny's family,' Charlotte said, getting up from the table. 'I'll go and see Mrs Beddows.'

As Felix had predicted, their journey was fraught with delays and the carriages were packed with troops. But everyone was good-humoured and the soldiers readily gave up a seat for Charlotte.

At last they arrived in the city and it was already mid-afternoon by the time the taxi cab dropped them off at the end of the street where Miles knew Jenny lived.

'Bombing's not so bad now, mate,' the friendly taxi driver told them as he handed Miles his change. 'But you'll see for yourself how bad we had it in the Blitz. Let's hope it don't all start up again. It's like this all over the city.'

He nodded down the street where Jenny lived. 'You can see for yourself. That happened earlier this month. They reckon there was a hundred thousand bombs dropped on poor ol' London in one night. Poor devils down this street got it bad. Direct hit on those houses in the middle of the street.'

'What?' Miles's face paled and he turned around to look. 'Oh no – no!'

The taxi driver was pulling away from the kerb, leaving them standing on the uneven pavement.

Sensing Miles's anxiety, Charlotte linked her arm through his. 'Let's go and see before we start to panic.'

'But – but their house is in the centre of the row. Oh Charlotte . . .' His voice was hoarse with unshed tears.

They walked down the rubble-strewn street, appalled to see huge piles of debris where once a house – someone's home – had been.

Suddenly Miles stopped in front of a mound of bricks and shattered glass. A door lay drunkenly on its side and amongst the rubbish they could see torn curtains, a table, a broken chair, and even shattered pots and dented pans.

'Is it – is it *their* house?' Charlotte whispered.

'I – I don't know. I can't quite get my bearings. I only came that one time and Jenny led me here, so . . . There were children playing in the street.'

But today there were no children anywhere.

'It's number fifteen,' Charlotte ventured. 'That's where we've been writing.'

'Ah, yes, of course, then . . . ?' He glanced around and saw a woman climbing over the rubble further down the street. 'Let's ask her. She might know.'

They picked their way carefully towards the stranger, who was bending over, picking up bricks and discarding them, obviously trying to uncover some of her precious possessions – anything that she could salvage.

'Excuse me . . .'

The woman looked up at the sound of Miles's voice. She didn't smile and Charlotte was shocked by the look of defeat and hopelessness in her eyes.

'I'm sorry to intrude,' Miles said gently, 'but we're looking for number fifteen.'

The woman's face was grim as she pointed to the

ground beneath her feet. 'This is it. I lived at number seventeen – right next door.' She scrambled over the rubble towards them. Miles held out his hand to help her step down on to the pavement.

'Ta, mister.' On firm ground, she glanced from one to the other. 'You want to know what happened?'

Charlotte nodded.

'Took a direct hit, our houses did. Mine and Dot's. Well, what was Dot's. Rest of the street – ' she glanced behind her and waved her arm – 'damaged, o' course, but most of 'em's still standing. Still, we was lucky in a way. No one was killed in this street.'

Charlotte's heart lifted. 'So – where are they? Where's Jenny and her mother?'

The woman shrugged. 'Gawd knows. Done a moonlight weeks back. Just after Jenny came back from the country.' She glanced at them, searching their faces keenly. 'Are you the folks the little lass stayed wiv?'

When Charlotte nodded, the woman actually smiled, though it was a sad, wistful smile. 'Eh, fancy that. She never stopped talking about you. About the fields and the beach and how you let her paint pretty pictures. She loved it up there wiv you, she did.' Her face clouded. 'But Dot got a bee in her bonnet that we were thinking she was a bad mother 'cos all the other kids'd come home and hers hadn't. Silly cow,' she added with feeling. 'If my lads'd had a nice place with you, I'd've left 'em there till all this bloody lot's over. Hadn't got the sense she was born with, Dot 'adn't. And then she buggers off without a word of goodbye, an' we've lived next door to one another for ten years or more.' She shook her head. 'I blame that feller she took up with. A right spiv, if you ask me. I reckon the law was on his tail and that's why they 'opped it.'

'I should have fought harder to keep Jenny,' Miles murmured heavily. 'But Dot was the girl's mother and—'

'I know,' the woman said with feeling. 'More's the pity. Oh dear – there I go again. Dot was all right in her way, but she was a selfish cow. Everything always had to be what *she* wanted. Even that Arfer had to dance to 'er tune. She should've left the little lass with you. Jen was happy wiv you.'

Miles smiled feebly and said huskily, 'Thank you for that.'

'Have – have you any idea where they've gone?' Charlotte asked.

Again, the woman shook her head. 'Nah, an' if she's still with that Arfer, then I don't want to know. Tried to get my son involved with 'is black market racket, he did. I gave him a clip round the ear.' She laughed and her whole face was suddenly younger and free of worry for a brief moment. 'My son, I mean. Not Arfer, though for two pins I'd have given him a fourpenny one, an' all.'

Charlotte held out the basket of food they'd brought. 'We brought this for Jenny and her mother, but please, we'd like you to have it.'

'That's very kind of you, an' I ain't too proud to say "yes". Not just now, I ain't.'

'Come,' Charlotte said softly to Miles. 'We'd better go.'

'I'm sorry I can't offer you a cup of tea. I would, but . . .' The woman gestured towards her flattened house.

Miles roused himself. 'Have you somewhere to go? I mean, you and your family could come to us if—'

'Now that's real generous of you, mister. I 'preciate

that, I really do. But we'll be all right. We'll tough it out now. Can't last much longer. 'Sides, I need to be here when my old man comes home on leave. An' we've got a good shelter to go to. The Underground. We have a sing-song down there most nights. An' to be honest wiv you, the bombing's not been so bad just lately. Mebbe ol' 'Itler's realized he can't beat us Londoners.'

On that note, they said goodbye and made their way back to the station.

'Do you want to stay at Felix's flat, Miles?' Charlotte asked as they walked, clinging to each other for comfort and support.

'No. It was good of him to offer it, but I just want to get home. If there's a train, I want to get home. Oh Charlotte, where can she be? How can we find her?'

Sixty-Four

'You look a little pale this morning, my dear,' Felix said as they sat together working on the final stages of their two paintings. 'Is the strain getting too much for you?'

It had been a week since they'd returned from London and since then, Miles had shut himself away in his study, hardly eating, hardly speaking and not sleeping well, either. He'd spent hours on the telephone and written countless letters to anyone who might be able to help them locate Jenny. Charlotte often woke in the night to find the place beside her in bed empty. When she crept downstairs, she would find him sitting at his desk, staring at one of the pictures Charlotte had painted of the little girl and which Miles had insisted should hang in his study.

'Will we ever see her again?' he asked repeatedly, but Charlotte was unable to give him a hopeful answer. All she could say was, 'Perhaps we should be grateful they'd left that street. If not . . .' She left the words unsaid, but even the thought that Jenny was still alive somewhere in the world didn't seem to bring Miles any comfort. He wanted the little girl who'd become like the longed-for daughter here at the manor, safe and well with him. 'I'll never stop looking for her, Charlotte,' he vowed. 'Never.'

Nightly, as she said her prayers as she always had, Charlotte asked, 'Please, Dear Lord, bring him comfort.

He has borne so much sadness, please – if there's any way – let me help him.'

Now, in answer to Felix's question, Charlotte laid aside her brush and sighed. 'Maybe. I've been feeling unwell for a few days, but please, don't say anything to Miles, will you? I'm so worried about him. First, the wonderful news about Georgie, and then finding Jenny had gone and we can't find out where she is. It's too much of a see-saw of emotions for anyone to bear. Even for someone as strong as Miles. He's just devastated. And, of course, poor Philip . . .'

'My dear girl, Miles has a right to know if you're feeling under the weather. He'd want you to see the doctor.'

'I'm sure it's nothing. I don't want to cause him more worry.'

'I know, I know,' Felix said gently. 'But you should look after yourself, too. Please, go and see the doctor. For me, eh? If it's nothing, then you needn't even tell Miles, but you should go.'

Charlotte smiled at him, trying to quell the queasiness in her stomach. 'I will.'

'Then I'll make sure you do.' He winked broadly at her. 'We'll take a little ride in the pony and trap tomorrow morning by way of the surgery in Ravens-fleet.'

When she walked out of Dr Bennet's surgery, Charlotte was in a daze.

Felix could not read the expression on her face. There was something, he could tell, but wisely he asked no questions. Whatever it was, Miles should be the first person she told. They drove home in unaccustomed silence. Even the ebullient Felix could think of nothing to say except the question uppermost in his mind. And that he could not ask.

When she climbed carefully down from the trap, she smiled her thanks and walked slowly up the steps into the house. Felix watched her go with a heavy heart. Sighing, he took the pony and trap round the side of the house to the stable yard, where he whiled away the time petting the horses and talking to the stable lads.

'You know, I've never painted a horse. Perhaps I should try,' he murmured, trying to keep his thoughts away from what was happening in Miles's study at that very moment.

Charlotte opened the door to her husband's study very quietly and, for a few moments, stood watching him seated at his desk. His head was bent over the papers he was reading, his brow creased in concentration. She was pleased to see that at least he was starting to take an interest in something again other than his letters about Jenny. But she wasn't sure just how he would take her news.

Becoming aware of her presence he looked up and began to smile. But then his smile faded. He rose slowly.

'What is it, my dear? Is something wrong? Is it Philip?'

He came swiftly round the end of the desk towards her, holding out his hands.

Charlotte shook her head and said huskily, 'No, no. He was fine when I left.'

She closed the door quietly and then put her hands

into his. She stood looking up at him, drinking in every detail of his face – the face that had become so very dear to her.

'Left?' Miles frowned. 'I didn't know you'd gone out. Where've you been?'

'I – I've been into Ravensfleet to see Dr Bennet.'

'Dr—? My dear, are you ill?'

Tears welled in her eyes and spilled down her cheeks, but she was laughing. 'No – no. I'm gloriously, wonderfully well. Oh Miles, I'm – we're – going to have a baby!'

He stared at her, dumbstruck for a moment. Then he whispered hoarsely, 'Pregnant? You're – you're pregnant?'

'Yes – isn't it wonderful?'

But it didn't look as if he shared her joy. She felt his hands holding hers begin to tremble and he was biting down hard on his lower lip.

'Aren't you pleased? It's what we've wanted.' She paused and added uncertainly, 'Isn't it?'

It was certainly what she'd always wanted but now, watching the fleeting emotions on his face, she wasn't so sure about Miles. 'Yes – yes – of course it is, but—'

Her heart seemed to turn over in her breast. 'But – what?'

He drew her into his arms and buried his face against her neck. 'Oh, Charlotte – I'm so afraid. I couldn't bear it if anything happened to you, my love.'

She nestled against him, revelling in his tender words, words and emotions she'd never dared to hope to hear from his lips. She understood why he was afraid for her. He'd lost Louisa through childbirth and he was fearful of it happening again.

'I'll be all right,' she said softly. 'I'm fit and healthy and strong.'

He drew back a little and traced the line of her cheek with a gentle finger. 'But – but you're too old to be having a baby.'

Charlotte chuckled and her eyes sparkled. 'Evidently Mother Nature thinks otherwise.'

'But it could be – dangerous.'

She hugged him. 'Please don't worry so. Don't spoil it, Miles.'

'That's the last thing I want to do, but I'm afraid I can't promise to stop worrying.'

She took his hand. 'Let's go and tell Philip – and Felix. He took me into Ravensfleet but of course I said nothing on the way home. The poor man was bursting to ask questions, I could see. But he didn't.'

Miles began to smile. 'That's not like Felix.'

'No.' Charlotte laughed. 'He showed remarkable restraint.'

They began to climb the stairs, hand in hand, but halfway up Charlotte stopped and turned to face Miles. 'You do think we should tell Philip, don't you? I mean, he – he won't mind, will he?'

Miles reassured her. 'Philip has changed from the resentful young man he was, though I'm sad that it has taken a war and the prospect of death to do it.'

They entered the room together to find him sitting up in bed reading, looking the best he had done since arriving home. He looked up and smiled. 'What's this? A state visit?'

'You could say that,' Miles said as they sat down on either side of the bed. 'Charlotte has some news for you.'

'The portraits are finished? When can I see them? How long will they take to dry enough to hang?'

'They're nearly ready, but drying thoroughly will take a while, though Felix thinks we can frame them and hang them, if we're very careful.'

'But that's not what she wanted to tell you,' Miles chipped in.

Philip turned enquiring eyes towards Charlotte, who blushed. 'I – we're going to have a baby.'

She held her breath whilst Philip stared at her and then, to her enormous relief, his face broke into a wide grin. 'That's the best possible news I've heard since we heard Georgie was alive. But there's just one thing, Charlotte.'

'What's that?'

'It's got to be a girl!'

The three of them burst out laughing.

Sixty-Five

Over the next few weeks, Philip joked, 'I'm hanging on until your baby's born, Charlotte, and maybe even until old Georgie gives the enemy the slip and comes home.'

'I do hope he won't do anything silly.'

'He might try to escape again – if you call that "silly". Perhaps he'll just turn up on the doorstep one morning.' He chuckled at the thought.

Charlotte sighed. 'I just want him to be safe. It's all I wanted for all of you.'

'I know, I know,' he said softly. 'If he'd just hang on a while longer, I don't think the end will be long coming now.'

Charlotte glanced at him. She knew he was referring to the end of the war, but no doubt he was also thinking of his own end, too. Could he do as he wished and hang on until Georgie came home or until her child was born in six months' time?

The weeks passed and to her infinite sadness, Charlotte began to see a steady decline in Philip's condition. The doctor visited every other day and at Miles's insistence, he kept an eye on Charlotte too.

'She's fit and healthy and remarkably strong,' she heard Dr Bennet say as she showed the doctor into Miles's study after his visit to Philip's room and after

489

having had a chat with her. 'I wish I was as happy about all my mothers-to-be as I am about Charlotte. All that farm work when she was a young lass, I expect,' he added dryly as Charlotte smiled and turned to leave the room. A newcomer to the district, he'd learned about Mrs Thornton's early life at Buckthorn Farm.

She was pulling the door to, when she caught Miles's words. 'I wanted a word with you in private, Doctor. About Charlotte's confinement.'

Outside the door, Charlotte bent closer, holding her breath and feeling guilty at eavesdropping, and yet . . .

'I want you to know my feelings now, whilst I'm rational and not faced with – with an unbearable decision.'

'I understand,' she heard Dr Bennet's calm tones. 'If there should be complications, you mean?' He'd heard that the cause of Miles's first wife's death had been childbirth and he could understand the man's natural anxiety. Especially, given Charlotte's age.

'I want you to know that if there's a choice to be made, then Charlotte's life is to be saved. I – she means everything to me. Everything. I couldn't bear to lose her.'

Charlotte almost gasped aloud and clapped her hand over her mouth to stifle the sound. She'd never thought to hear such words of love and devotion and sacrifice, yes sacrifice. For at their next words she knew for sure.

'You'd forfeit the life of the child in favour of the mother?'

'Yes, I would.'

Softly, the doctor asked, 'Even if it's a girl?' He seemed to know everything and Charlotte realized that Dr Markham must have told the young doctor all about the patients he was taking on.

There was not the slightest hesitation before Miles replied firmly, 'Even if it's a girl.'

Her heart soared. Now she could believe that Miles loved her, truly loved her, as she'd longed for him to do.

'Madam . . .' Kitty's face appeared round the door of the sitting room one November morning.

Charlotte laid aside the tiny white coat she was knitting, giving it one last, fond touch before she looked up with a smile to say, 'Yes, Kitty, what is it?'

Before she had finished forming the question she could see from the girl's face, that something was wrong.

'It's Mr Philip, ma'am. He – he's asking for you – and the master.'

Charlotte rose at once and hurried as fast as her bulk would allow her to out of the room. As she began to pull herself up the stairs, she asked, 'Where is the master?'

'Out riding, ma'am. He's been gone about half an hour.'

'Send someone to find him. Tell them to go to the beach at Lynthorpe. That's his favourite ride.' She paused at the top of the stairs. 'Is he bad, Kitty?'

The girl nodded. 'Nurse is with him. She's telephoned for the doctor, ma'am.'

Charlotte nodded, unable to speak for the tears stinging her eyes. She blinked and pulled in a deep breath. She mustn't cry, she told herself firmly. She must be strong for Philip – and for Miles.

When she entered the bedroom, the sight of him shocked her. He was obviously in great pain. His face was grey, his cheeks hollow and the suffering in his eyes was unbearable. Sweat glistened on his forehead. Nurse Monty stood at the side of the bed, gently wiping his face. She looked up as Charlotte came into the room. Her solemn expression and her dark eyes told Charlotte that the end was very near.

Philip tried to smile and he held out a trembling hand. 'Sit beside me, Charlotte,' he gasped, his breathing laboured. 'Hold my hand.'

Discreetly, the nurse moved to the other side of the room, where she could not overhear their whispered words, but was still near enough if she was needed.

'Try to rest, my dear,' Charlotte said gently, wiping his forehead with the flannel Nurse Monty had passed to her. 'Save your strength.'

Philip closed his eyes but he opened them again to say, 'No – no. There's no time. There are things I need to say to you. Especially to you, Charlotte.' He paused, summoning up the strength to carry on. 'I haven't always been kind to you and I'm so sorry.'

'Don't, Philip. None of that matters. It never did.'

'It – matters to me. I was a conceited oaf and I'm ashamed. Say you forgive me?'

'Philip – there's nothing to—'

'Please – say it. I need you to say it.'

'Of course, I forgive you with all my heart.'

'I wasn't lovable like Georgie or even our quiet Ben. I was prickly and difficult and – and openly hostile to you, wasn't I?'

'I understood. You were the one who could remember your mother the best. It hurt you to see someone else in what you thought was her place. But I never presumed to do that, Philip. No one could ever replace Louisa in your father's heart or in yours. Certainly not me.'

'You've done a damned good job,' he rasped with some of his old spirit. 'You've come close. We all adore you, Charlotte, you must know that.' She felt him squeeze her hand. 'Even me – in the end.'

She felt the tears welling again and fought to hide them. Behind her, the door opened and Miles came into the room, still in his riding habit. He strode to the other side of the bed, pulled up a chair, and sat down.

'Hello – Papa.' Philip's use of the name the boys had used in their childhood threatened to be Miles's undoing. But, like Charlotte, he took a deep breath and managed to say gently, 'Son.'

'This is it, then,' Philip whispered. 'I'm so sorry I can't wait to see my little sister and – and to see old Georgie come home.'

'The doctor's on his way. He'll—'

'Papa – he can't work miracles. Let's face it – I need you both to help me face it.'

Miles and Charlotte exchanged a grief-stricken glance.

'Charlotte,' Philip said, 'I want to ask you something. Will you – if your baby's a girl – will you call her Louisa?'

'Philip, you can't ask—' Miles began, but Charlotte held up her hand.

'Of course I will,' she promised. 'I'd be proud to.'

Philip let out a deep sigh and closed his eyes. For a moment, they both thought he'd slipped away, but then his eyes fluttered open again. 'I've written a letter to your father asking him to make my son, Alfie, his heir. I don't know if he will, but I hope you don't mind, Charlotte. By rights, of course, he should leave the farm to you.'

'No – no – you did the right thing.'

'But—'

'No "buts", Philip.' She stroked his forehead. 'If it is left to me, I'll see Alfie gets it.'

'You will?'

'Of course I will.'

'But it should come to you and then, one day, to your daughter.'

'You're so sure it's going to be a girl, then?'

'Oh yes. It – it has to be – for – for Papa . . .'

They were to be the last words he ever said. His voice faded away and he slept. Though they sat beside him for the remainder of the day, he did not wake again and as darkness fell, Philip died peacefully in his own bed with his father and Charlotte beside him.

Ben came home for the funeral, resplendent in his uniform and wearing the George Cross on his chest. Philip was laid to rest in the village churchyard beneath the shade of a beech tree.

'He's free of pain now,' Miles said, trying to comfort them all. As they turned to leave they saw Eddie, Lily and Alfie standing a respectful distance away. Miles went across to them. 'Thank you for coming. It would have meant a lot to Philip.'

Lily bobbed a little curtsy and said. 'I've told him, sir. Alfie knows the truth now.'

Miles nodded and smiled at the boy who was dry-eyed but solemn-faced. He looked up into Miles's face and said, 'Eddie's me dad, sir, but I'm glad I got to know Mr Philip.'

Eddie put his arm round the boy's shoulder. 'I'll always look after him, sir. You can be sure of that.

I've never made no difference between him and me own bairns, an' I never will.'

'I know that, Eddie. But if you – any of you – need help at any time, you only have to ask.' He smiled and held out his hand to shake the boy's hand. 'After all, I am your grandfather.'

For a moment the boy looked startled and then he grinned. 'By heck, Dad, I've got a toff for a grandad.'

They all laughed and it didn't seem at all irreverent or unfeeling, Charlotte thought. It was the way Philip – the Philip of the last few months – would have wanted it.

That night, Miles drew Charlotte into his study,

'There's something I want to show you.'

He settled her in a chair beside his own at the desk and reached down a large old-fashioned bible from the bookshelf. He laid it reverently on the desk and opened it up at the flyleaf. On the page that should have been blank was a handwritten list of the births, marriages and deaths of the Thornton family going back several generations.

'Oh.' Charlotte smiled. 'How lovely. I'd heard of this being done in a family bible, but I've never seen one. Miles, do tell me about them all.'

They sat together with Miles's arm round her shoulders, their heads bent close as Miles pointed to each name in turn.

'It begins with the birth of my great-great-grandfather, then his marriage and the births of his two children.'

'Is that his handwriting, do you think?'

'I'm not sure. I suspect it was a later generation who

began the list, starting with names and dates as far back as he knew. See, the writing doesn't change until my own father wrote his marriage date and the birth dates of my brother, Christopher, and me.'

Charlotte looked up at him in surprise. 'A brother? You have a brother.'

Miles shook his head. 'No, not any more. He was killed in 1915 at Ypres in the Great War. See, here's his death date.'

Charlotte read the dates and felt the sadness behind the written words. 'The war to end all wars', they'd called the carnage of those years and yet now it was happening again.

'I think,' Miles said, bringing her thoughts back to earlier generations, 'it was my grandfather who started writing it all in this bible.' He pointed to the name Josiah halfway down the page. 'He would know his own father, Joseph, and he was old enough by the time his grandfather, Luke Thornton, died in 1835 to have known him too. He'd have been eleven. But look, Charlotte, this is what I wanted to show you – every generation – it's all boys. Luke had Joseph and Marmaduke, who never married because he died at twenty. Joseph had only one child, Josiah, and although Josiah had three children, again they were all boys; my father, Philip, and my uncles, Richard and Henry.'

'He only lived a few days,' Charlotte murmured pointing to Henry's name. 'How sad.'

'And it's even more sad that no one ever spoke of him. It wasn't the thing, you know, in those days to speak of the dead.'

Charlotte rested her head against his shoulder and whispered. 'We'll always talk about Philip. We'll keep his memory alive.'

Miles reached for his pen to write the last heartbreaking entry of Philip's death below that recording Louisa's death, but for a moment he hesitated. 'You see, I couldn't bring myself to enter Georgie's death. Not until we knew for certain. And now I'm so glad I didn't.'

Still he hesitated to begin writing. 'I wonder if I ought to write in the entry of Alfie's birth. I mean, he is Philip's son.' A small, wistful smile played on his mouth. 'But these austere gentlemen would never have entered an illegitimate child into the family bible, now, would they?'

'Darling,' Charlotte said softly, 'it's your bible now. You must write in it what you want to. Everyone around here knows Alfie is Philip's son. Even Alfie knows now. So, if you want to include him, you should.'

'Another son,' he murmured as he began to write with honesty.

Alfred, the illegitimate son of Philip Thornton and Lily Warren, born 30 June 1927.

Beneath that he wrote the details of Philip's death, adding, *As a result of his wounds.*

When the ink was dry he closed the book and turned to Charlotte. He touched her face gently. There was no need for words, not any more. Despite his sadness at the loss of his son, which they'd known for some time was inevitable, his overriding anxiety now was for the safe delivery of Charlotte's baby.

She could see his overwhelming love for her in his eyes and, now, she had no more doubts. Miles truly loved her.

She smiled and kissed him. 'And the next entry, my darling, will be a much happier one.'

He held her close and she felt his tears wet against her neck.

Sixty-Six

With cruel irony, only a week after Philip's death, Charlotte felt the first labour pangs. If only he'd lived another few days Philip would have seen her child born. But it was not to be.

Knowing that his wife's confinement could not be long away, Miles had asked the nurse to stay on another few weeks. Nurse Monty had beamed. 'I'd be delighted,' she'd said. 'I am a qualified midwife, too. My last appointment before coming here was to a Mrs Marshall in Lincoln, who had twins. Both born healthy, but a handful for a young mother.'

So Nurse Monty was on hand when Charlotte appeared out of her studio late one morning, clutching her stomach. 'Oh – oh. Miles – *Miles* . . .' she called and everyone came running.

Nurse Monty took charge with her customary calmness and organization. Charlotte was soon in the room on the first floor that had been set aside for the birth and where everything had been ready for weeks.

'Shall I call the doctor?' Miles hovered anxiously outside the door.

'There's no need for him to come yet,' Nurse Monty said, forbearing to say that she could manage to bring a child into the world without the aid of any man, doctor or not. She was aware of the circumstances within this household, however, and was sympathetic. The poor man had lost one wife through childbirth and the present Mrs Thornton was forty-one and this was her first baby. There could be complications. Nurse Monty was confident of her own capabilities, but she was no fool. The nearest hospital was several miles away and the doctor might be out on a home visit anywhere over a widespread area if called at the last minute. No, better to be safe than sorry, was Nurse Monty's maxim. So she added comfortingly, 'But it would be wise to let him know that Mrs Thornton has gone into labour, though we are in the early stages at the moment.'

But even the knowledgeable nurse was caught unawares by the speed with which Charlotte's labour progressed. Nurse Monty had expected a long, protracted labour, but within an hour, the contractions were coming closely together. Unable to leave her patient, Nurse Monty sent Kitty with an urgent message for the master, who was pacing the hall below. 'Send for the doctor at once.'

'Sir – sir – ' Kitty flew down the stairs almost tripping in her haste. 'Nurse says can you send for the doctor.'

Miles stopped in his pacing and stared up at the girl, terror in his eyes.

''Tis all right, sir. Nothing wrong, but babby is coming quicker than Nurse thought.'

Miles ran to the front door and dragged it open, then he stopped and heaved a sigh of relief. Dr Markham was climbing down from his pony and trap outside.

'Bennet's on holiday,' he said, mounting the steps. 'I'm acting as locum, so I thought I'd just look in. How is she?'

Miles felt relief flood through him. 'Further on than expected.'

'Ah, good – good. That's excellent.'

'Is it?'

'Of course, my dear fellow. Much less tiring than a protracted labour,' Dr Markham said, patting Miles's shoulder and then heading swiftly to the stairs. 'We'll keep you posted, Miles. Try not to worry.'

As Miles watched him go up the stairs, he muttered, 'You might as well ask me not to breathe.'

Only two hours later, Miles was allowed into the bedroom to find his wife sitting up in bed, red cheeked with her recent efforts but smiling happily. The child lay sleeping in the crib beside her bed. Miles took Charlotte in his arms and kissed her tenderly.

'Thank you, my darling,' he whispered.

Wrapped in each other's arms, they wept tears of joy and then giggled helplessly like two naughty children when they thought of what Osbert's reaction to their news would be.

Very late that night, when the house was quiet, Miles Thornton lifted down the heavy bible and laid it on his desk. He opened it at the flyleaf and read again the entries, written in different hands down the years.

He took up his pen and began to write with a proud flourish.

On Friday, 5 December 1941, to Miles and Charlotte Thornton, the precious gift of a daughter, Louisa Alice.

He sat back and reread the words, cherishing the moment.

'A daughter,' he murmured aloud, his voice husky with emotion. He imagined he was telling all the people listed on the page, generation after generation of sons. Somewhere, somehow, he hoped they were listening.

'I have a *daughter*.'

The Tulip Girl

For all my family and friends, with love

Acknowledgements

The glorious tulip fields of Spalding and district were the inspiration for this novel, although the story is entirely fictitious. I am very grateful to Mr Reg Dobbs, OBE, author of *Bulbs in Britain – A Century of Growing*, for his kind interest and help and the loan of photographs to help with the cover design.

Aspects of Spalding – 1790–1930 and *Aspects of Spalding – People and Places* by Norman Leveritt and Michael J. Elsden were a wonderful source of general information.

My very special thanks to Mr Robert Molson, who generously gave his time to introduce me to the area and to share his memories with me.

My love and thanks as always to my family and friends, especially those who read and helped edit the script in the early stages; my sister and brother-in-law, Robena and Fred Hill; my brother and sister-in-law, David and Una Dickinson; my friends, Pauline Griggs and Linda and Terry Allaway.

Prologue

APRIL 1959

'No, please. Don't shoot.'

Trembling, Maddie stretched out her hand towards the man holding the gun. Beyond him, through the barn's open door, she could see the tulips, row upon row like a multicoloured rainbow, dazzling in the warm sunlight. She had planted those fields with her own bare hands. Was everything she loved, everything she had worked for, striven for, now to be blown away in a moment's madness?

Here in the barn it was cool and dim. They stood facing each other, the four of them. Maddie, the two men and the boy.

'Please,' she whispered, begging as she had never begged in her life. 'Please, let the boy go?'

'Why should I?' His tone was harsh and cruel, so different from the voice she knew so well. Or thought she had known. 'If it weren't for him and . . .' The barrel of the shotgun wavered slightly and then swung sharply away from pointing at Maddie and the boy towards the other man, standing so still and silent in the shadows. 'You!'

There was such venom in his voice, a bitter hatred that had been festering for eleven long years.

A shadow appeared in the barn doorway. A woman's shadow. Maddie's eyes widened and she gave a little gasp of fear. Then she touched the boy standing near her on his shoulder, giving him a tiny push. 'Go,' she breathed. 'Go to her.'

1

She saw him glance at the two men, who seemed, now, only aware of each other.

'Go on,' she urged.

The boy took a step, his gaze still on the men. Then he ran. The barrel swung again, following the small figure hurtling towards the door.

As she saw the man's finger move towards the trigger, Maddie lunged forward, her hand outstretched to push the barrel aside and spoil his aim.

'No!' Maddie cried but the deafening blast drowned her scream. Lead shot splattered against the wall of the barn and in the doorway a figure fell, sprawling in the dirt.

Before Maddie's eyes, the rainbow field of tulips beyond seemed to turn blood red . . .

One

'What's her name?'

'Madeleine March.'

'Far too fancy . . .' Harriet Trowbridge sniffed her disapproval.

'We call her Maddie,' the matron said hastily.

'Plain little scrap of a thing, isn't she? I imagined she'd be . . . Are you sure she's the one?'

'Oh yes. Abandoned outside the gate in 1932. No one's ever come to see her so there's no family that we know of and I don't think anyone's going to come looking her for now after fourteen years, do you? That's what you were looking for, isn't it?'

'It is, yes. But she doesn't look old enough.' Harriet shot a disbelieving look at the matron. 'She only looks about twelve. And a small twelve, at that.'

Mrs Potter began to bridle. 'I hope you're not doubting my word, Mrs Trowbridge?'

'No,' the woman murmured, her thoughtful gaze still on the girl standing before them. 'But now I see her, I don't know if she'll manage the work.'

'She's strong.' The matron now cast an anxious look at her visitor. 'And – and biddable.' There was only the merest hint of hesitation in Mrs Potter's voice. She wasn't above lying through her teeth if it meant seeing this particular child gone from her orphanage. Mrs Trowbridge

3

seemed Heaven-sent, though anyone less angel-like would have been hard to find.

She was tall and bony-thin and dressed from head to foot in black. A felt hat was pulled down low over her forehead and the well-worn coat fell almost to her ankles, covering thick lisle stockings and stout, good-quality lace-up shoes. Her features were sharp. Her nose was straight and thin and her mouth seemed permanently pursed. Her grey eyes were bright and missed nothing, but there was no warmth in them, no humour, no kindliness.

'I should need to see her birth certificate. I presume she has one?'

Mrs Potter sighed. 'Well, yes. But it won't tell you much. Even the actual date of her birth is a guess. She was brought here on the twenty-fifth of March 1932 and we reckoned her to be no more than a week or two old – a month at the most – so that's the date we used.'

The surname was now obvious, but Harriet asked, 'Whatever possessed you to give her the name of Madeleine?'

'We didn't,' Mrs Potter snapped, trying valiantly to hold on to her patience. 'It was scribbled on a bit of paper and pinned to the blanket she was wrapped in.' The matron shook her head sadly, expressing a sudden pity for the child, whom, though she had been the bane of the woman's life for the past fourteen years, Mrs Potter could still not wholly dislike. 'Poor little mite hadn't any clothes. She was completely naked, 'cept for the blanket.'

Years earlier when Alice Potter had come to work at the Mayfield Home as a young widow, she had lavished upon the poor, motherless mites all the affection she would have given to her own children had she been so blessed. It was only the passing years and the responsibility of the post she now held that had made her often brusque and

4

insensitive. Still, at times, her maternal instinct surfaced and she would promise herself that she would be kinder, more affectionate towards the unfortunate waifs and strays in her charge.

But her resolution faltered when dealing with the likes of Maddie March.

The girl stood facing them now in mutinous silence, scowling so fiercely that her eyebrows almost met above the bridge of her tiny nose. Her teeth were clenched so tightly that they squeaked against each other and her mouth pouted ominously. The girl was thin and pale, but her blue eyes glittered with a rebellion that Matron and all the staff could not quite quell whatever dire punishment they inflicted upon her. Her short, straight hair was fair and could have been pretty but it was badly cut, hacked at by a harassed Mrs Potter with no time to spare for pandering to vanity. Washed only once a week by being plunged beneath the bathwater and soaped with carbolic, it was dull and lifeless. The girl wore a shapeless grey gymslip, tied around the waist with a girdle, a white blouse, knee-length grey socks and lace-up shoes.

Arriving back at the orphanage from the village school that took all the local children from five to fourteen, except those who transferred to the High School in the nearby town, Maddie had been told to report to Mrs Potter's room at once. She had not even been given time to change into her navy dress, her 'Sunday Best' that was only worn to Church or on very special occasions; Christmas Day, New Year's Day or when Sir Peter Mayfield, the Chairman of the Board of Governors, visited.

Maddie eyed today's visitor who was taking in every aspect of her appearance. Boldly, the girl returned the woman's critical stare, but resisted the urge to stick out her tongue.

5

The two women continued talking as if Maddie were not present.

'March 'thirty-two, you say?' For a moment, Harriet Trowbridge seemed almost as if she were thinking back and remembering what life had been like then. 'So,' she added slowly, 'she is old enough to leave school.'

The matron nodded vigorously. 'Oh yes, she's only kept going to school because . . .' Mrs Potter cleared her throat and altered what she had been going to say. 'I mean, until a position could be found for her.' It wouldn't do for this woman to know that already Maddie had been turned down for two jobs during the three weeks since her fourteenth birthday let alone the four prospective foster homes who had, over the years, sent her back to the orphanage, the last one after only two days.

Harriet sniffed. 'Right, I'll take her, then. When can you have her ready?'

'Oh, right away . . .' Then, lest she should appear too eager to rid herself of the girl, Mrs Potter added hastily, 'To save you the trouble of coming back for her, ma'am.'

The woman nodded and seated herself in a chair. 'Very well, but be quick about it. I don't like being away from the farm for long.'

Maddie felt Matron's hand gripping her shoulder and propelling her from the room. 'This is your lucky day, Maddie March.' And mine, Mrs Potter was thinking. 'Get your things together. You're leaving. And this time, m'girl, there's no coming back here if you don't suit, so just you mind you . . .'

'Leaving?' Maddie tried to stand still but the stout woman was no match for her and she was pulled across the hall and up the stairs towards the long dormitory. 'Where'm I going?'

'You're going to work on a farm. Be a milkmaid or summat. You'll like that.'

Maddie tried to imagine what it would be like, but failed. She had seen little beyond the high walls of the Mayfield Home for Orphan Girls except on the walk through the village in crocodile fashion with the other fourteen girls to school or to the church. There was the occasional trip on the bus to the nearest town of Wellandon, but even then there was no freedom to wander the streets and gaze in shop windows.

Apart from one or two, who at the age of eleven went on the bus to the Girls' High School in the town, all the girls from the Home attended the local village school until they reached the lawful leaving age. But no one else there wore uniform – only the Mayfield girls. Immediately, they were different, set apart.

So, for nine years, Maddie had marched to and from the school in Eastmere's village centre. Through rain and snow or beneath boiling sun. In winter, her hands were blue with cold for she had no gloves. In summer, she sweated in the gymslip and blouse they wore all the year round. Only the High School girls were provided with their school's regulation gingham summer dress.

But on Sunday, everything changed. Sunday was Maddie's favourite day of the week. No school and hardly any chores about the Home that all the girls had to take turns to do. No weeding in the vegetable garden or peeling potatoes. No helping to wash up twenty sets of plates, cups, saucers, knives, forks and spoons for the girls and the live-in staff after tea when the day workers had gone home. No washing in the laundry that was Maddie's Saturday morning chore with her hands becoming red and wrinkled in the hot water or her fingers trapped by the mangle if she wasn't quick enough feeding in the sheets. On a Sunday, there was only helping the younger girls to make their beds and clean their shoes for Church.

It was all thanks to the local vicar who served on the Board of Governors. He had insisted that the girls should strictly observe the Lord's Day. True, they had to attend Matins and Evensong and go to Sunday School, winter and summer, and the only book they were allowed to read on the Sabbath was the Bible, but for Maddie it was a day of blissful idleness.

Only on a Sunday could she dawdle to look over the hedges at the fields of waving corn or cows grazing in the meadows or pause to gaze into the window of Mrs Grange's village shop. And only on a Sunday had she seen whole families together, mothers and fathers with their daughters dressed in pretty frocks and sons in white shirts and ties and short, neatly-creased trousers. Or older, spotty-faced youths in their first pair of long trousers sporting, like a badge declaring their entry into manhood, an occasional tiny tuft of cotton wool on their chins where they'd tried their first attempts at shaving. Boys who, unseen by their parents and Mrs Potter, gave a cheeky wink to the girls from the Home.

Maddie had lost count of the times she had been reprimanded for smiling saucily back at them.

Oh yes, thought Maddie, only on a Sunday had she ever really seen the outside world. Suddenly, she quickened her pace and ran up the stairs ahead of Mrs Potter, who was puffing already.

Maddie March was leaving the orphanage. She was going out into the great, big world. Her heart beat faster and her eyes sparkled with excitement.

Wherever it was she was going, it couldn't possibly be worse than this place.

Two

'You don't mean we're going in that thing?'

Maddie would not have admitted it in a month of precious Sundays, but the huge black and white horse, standing patiently on the drive and harnessed to a farm cart, frightened her.

'Huh! Not good enough for you, eh, Miss Hoity-Toity?' Harriet sniffed. 'If it's good enough to deliver milk around the village every morning, it's good enough for the likes of you to ride in, girl. We can't afford a fancy pony and trap.'

Maddie glanced behind her at the faces pressed against every window on the three floors of the towering Victorian building.

Word had gone round. 'Maddie March is leaving. Come and see her go?'

'Whatever for? She'll be back in a day or so. No one can put up with her.'

'She won't be coming back this time. I heard Mrs Potter say so. She's too old now.'

'Not – not coming back?' Tears filled a small girl's eyes. 'Not never?'

Jenny Wren, so foolishly named by the over-sentimental Deputy Matron on duty when the child had been found abandoned outside the gates, ran in search of Maddie.

'Don't go, Maddie. Don't leave me. What'll I do without you?'

'You'll be all right. The others'll look after you.'

9

The child hiccupped miserably. 'They won't. They tease me. Only you ever stick up for me, Maddie.'

It was true. The scrawny child, who always managed to look unkempt no matter how ever much they scrubbed her, brushed her hair or tidied her clothes, was the butt of cruel bullying. Only Maddie, feisty and spirited, was ever on her side.

Jenny and Maddie had a lot in common. They were both thin and small for their age. Both had blonde hair and blue eyes and both had been abandoned outside the orphanage, Jenny as a newborn baby. But there the similarity ended, for Jenny was timid and weak, a born victim. Yet Maddie had loved her like a younger sister and had tried to protect her.

'I'm sorry, honest I am,' Maddie said, reaching out and touching the other girl's pale cheek. And she was, for she knew what Jenny's life would be like once she, Maddie, was gone. 'Mebbe in September when you're fourteen, they'll find you a job an' all.'

The younger girl sniffled hopelessly. 'Who'd want me?'

To that, Maddie had no answer.

Now, as she glanced back at the other girls, she grinned and stepped boldly towards the horse. As she stood beneath him, he lowered his massive head and nuzzled her shoulder leaving a wet patch on her grey coat.

'What's his name?'

'Rajah.'

Maddie reached up and patted his white nose and, without consciously thinking about it, she made a soft crooning noise in her throat. Then, her fear of the animal overcome, she looked up again at the windows and gave a royal wave to the watchers. But only to Jenny, standing at the top of the steps, did she blow a kiss. 'Chin up, Jen. I'll write to you.'

'Promise?' came the quavering voice.

'Cross me heart.' Maddie made the sign over where she presumed her heart to be.

'Come along. We're wasting time.' Harriet was climbing up on to the front of the cart. 'Put your box in the back and sit up here beside me.'

Mrs Potter herself helped Maddie lift the wooden box containing all her worldly possessions into the back of the cart. 'Now you be a good girl this time,' she hissed. 'I don't want you turning up on my doorstep again. You hear?'

'Not a chance, Mrs Potter,' Maddie grinned impishly. 'You won't see me again.'

'Let's hope not,' the matron answered tartly. 'You've put more grey hairs in my head, Maddie March, than all the other girls put together over the twenty years I've been here.'

If she was expecting the girl to feel contrition then Mrs Potter was wasting her time, for Maddie's grin only widened as she climbed up to sit beside Harriet. As the woman slapped the reins, the horse plodded forward and the cart scrunched down the gravel driveway away from the imposing square building that had been the only home Maddie had ever known. But the young girl did not even glance back once.

Nothing could dim her excitement at leaving, not Jenny's tears nor the silent, ramrod-stiff Mrs Trowbridge driving the farm cart with surprising expertise. Not even the rain that began to fall steadily as they drove away could dampen Maddie's spirits.

The village of Eastmere lay amidst the flat, fertile land of south Lincolnshire, three miles east of Wellandon, a thriving market town clustered along the banks of the River Welland. But it was not towards the town that

11

Harriet Trowbridge drove the horse and cart but along a lane leading out of the village southwards into the open countryside.

On the outskirts, they passed the gateway leading into Mayfield Park, the home of Sir Peter. Reminded of that tall, severe gentleman, whose every edict had ruled her life so far, Maddie asked inquisitively, 'Haven't you got a motor car?'

Sir Peter had a motor car with huge bulbous wings and when he drew up outside the Home, the girls would line the windows to watch, wishing they could have a ride in it. But not one of them – not even Maddie March – had ever dared to ask.

The woman beside her sniffed. 'Aye, sheeted down in the barn where it's been for the last six years or more. No petrol, y'see. Because of the War.'

'But the War's over now.'

Confined to the orphanage she might have been, yet even Maddie knew that much about the outside world. But only, she had to admit, because the evacuees with their strange speech no longer lined the lane to school, jeering at the crocodile of orphan girls and even throwing clods of earth at them.

'Barstards! They're a lot of little barstards, who ain't got no muvvers and farvers.'

And then had come the day they would never forget, the day that Mrs Potter had been obliged, by Sir Peter himself no less, to allow the girls to join in the VE Day party on the Village Green.

Oh, Maddie would never forget that day. A boy had kissed her on VE Day. She could almost still taste the sticky jam he had left on her upper lip.

'Aye, the War might be over for some, girl, but we're still feeling the pinch. Mind you . . .' the woman's tone mollified a little, 'we've been luckier than most, living on a farm.'

'What's it like, living on a farm?'

'A lot of hard work for everyone. As you will soon find out.'

Harriet flicked the reins and the horse clopped smartly along the lane, its silky cream mane and fetlocks rippling in the breeze. It didn't seem to mind the wet, Maddie mused, so I won't either. But she screwed up her eyes and pressed her lips together as the rain stung her face. She could see nothing of the surrounding countryside, shrouded in grey mist, and she had no idea where they were going or how long it would take to get there.

But they had travelled less than a mile when Maddie found herself clinging to the side of the cart as the horse, sensing home, turned sharply into a farmyard.

'Are we here? Is this it?'

The woman made no reply but climbed down. Maddie followed suit and then looked about her. In front of her was a square farmhouse surrounded by sheds and barns and wall-enclosed yards. As Maddie tried to take in her new surroundings, a black and white dog came rushing towards them, jumping up and barking furiously.

'Down!' Harriet thundered. The dog dropped to its belly, ceased its racket and gave a whine of surrender.

Maddie glanced admiringly at the woman. 'Isn't he good?'

'He's a working dog. Been trained to be obedient. Let's hope you have too, girl.'

She led the way into the house by the back door and, following, Maddie found herself in a wash-house. Along the wall near the door hung coats and capes and beneath them a line of boots and shoes.

'Come along, look sharp.' Harriet had paused in the

doorway leading further into the house to beckon her. Maddie's curious glance darted about her, still trying to take in the clutter; a brick built copper with wash tubs and dolly pegs and a mangle close by, a heap of coal boarded off in the far corner, two bicycles and a step ladder leaning drunkenly against the wall.

She followed the woman into the kitchen that smelled, not of stale cabbage water like the huge kitchen at the Home, but of freshly baked bread. Then stepping into the living room, Maddie saw that a fire burned brightly in the gleaming black-leaded range, to one side of which was an alcove lined with shelves of books. Directly opposite her, the window looked out on to a square of garden.

'Come along, I'll show you your bedroom. Bring your things.'

Carefully, Maddie skirted the table, covered with a green velvet cloth, and went towards the door Harriet was opening in the far corner of the room.

At the top of the steep, dark staircase they turned to the left into a narrow landing that ran the width of the house. Doors led off on either side and the woman pointed to the first door to the left and said, 'This is my room and you, girl, will be in this one opposite. So I can keep my eye on you.' She waved her hand further down the landing. 'There's a bathroom of sorts next to your room, but it's open to the landing. Further on, down that step there, is the master's room and the boys' bedroom opposite.'

The 'master' and – and 'boys'! Maddie blinked.

Harriet opened the door to the right into a small bedroom and jabbed Maddie on the shoulder. 'Just put your things in there for now. You can put them away later.'

Maddie stepped onto the peg rug at the side of the bed and looked around the room. The single bed, tight against the wall, was covered with a bright patchwork quilt and in the corner beside the tiny window was a marble wash-stand with a pink flowered ewer and bowl on it. Beneath the window was a chest of drawers.

'You'll wash in here of a morning. You can bring the water up each night. I don't want you running into the boys in your nightgown. They use the bathroom, but you'll only have use of it once a week to bath and wash your hair. I'll mind the menfolk stay out of the way then. There's no inside lavvy. Turn left outside the back door and it's on the corner of the house, opposite the water tank. Now, come along, there's work to do.'

By the time the men came into the house at six o'clock for their tea, Maddie felt like a little ragamuffin. She had swept the floor and shaken the peg rug from the hearth in the living room, dusted the furniture and cleaned the windows and now her face was smudged with grime and her apron looked as if she'd been crawling all over the coal heap.

'Hey, what have we here?' a cheerful voice spoke behind her. 'You had her up the chimney to sweep it, Mrs T?'

Still on her knees sweeping the hearth, Maddie turned around to find that the tall young man who had spoken had squatted down on his haunches to bring his face level with her own. She found herself gazing into the softest brown eyes she had ever seen. Kind, they were, and yet at the same time they sparkled with mischief. His face was tanned and his jaw square and when he smiled, she saw that his white teeth were even and perfect. Unruly curls, so black that they shone and glistened, fell onto his forehead.

Maddie swept the back of her hand across her brow and, unwittingly, left another streak of dust.

The young man chuckled. He leant towards her and

said softly, 'Go into the kitchen and wash your face and hands, else Mrs T won't let you to the table.'

'But I – I haven't finished yet,' Maddie said, flustered and blushing beneath the dirt on her face.

'It'll still be there in the morning, young'un.' He touched her shoulder, giving her a gentle push. 'Go on. She's setting the table now. You'd best hurry.' He nodded towards the kitchen where Maddie could hear the clatter of pots.

Giving one last swift polish to the fender with her duster, Maddie picked up all the cleaning materials and scuttled out of the living room into the kitchen. Stowing the polish and dusters in the cupboard under the sink as she had been told, she removed her hessian apron and bundled it under there too. Then she turned on the tap over the deep sink that was not, close to, so white as she had imagined. Tiny cracks, brown stained, gave its surface a mottled, dirty look. The ice-cold water spluttered into her hands. Maddie took the soap and nail brush from the dish on the draining board and scrubbed and scrubbed until her hands were red and raw, but clean. Then she sluiced her face with the cold water and smoothed back her short hair behind her ears.

She was moving hesitantly away from the sink when the door leading into the kitchen flew open, almost knocking her over.

'Sorry, lass. I didn't hurt you, did I?'

'No, no, mester. Just made me jump, that's all.' Maddie looked up into the man's face and found that it was an older version of the young man's she had met a few minutes earlier. Though his dark hair was liberally streaked with grey and his handsome face was weather-beaten and deeply lined, the brown eyes still twinkled and the smile was as gentle.

'You must be thc little lass from the orphanage?'

Maddie nodded. 'Yes, sir.' She smoothed her hands down her gymslip and smiled at him.

He looked her up and down, assessing but not unkindly. 'The work's hard, lass,' he said, doubtfully.

'I'm stronger than I look, mester.'

'Aye well,' he smiled. 'Mebbe you'll grow. We'll have to feed you up a bit, won't we?'

He gestured towards the living room. 'In you go. Tea'll be ready. I've to change me boots and wash me hands and then I'll be in. Go and sit down, lass. I won't be a minute.'

A joint of boiled bacon sat in front of where the master would sit at the head of the table, a carving knife and fork set on either side. In the centre of the table was a selection of pickled onions and home-made chutney and a large freshly baked crusty loaf with yellow butter in a dish.

'You sit here, girl,' Harriet pointed to a chair beside her, setting down a plate of buttered slices of plum bread for afters. 'And speak when you're spoken to and not afore. You've a mite too much to say for yourself, to my mind.' She frowned down at Maddie. 'You're only on trial here, you know. I can still send you back if you don't suit.'

Across the table the young man winked broadly at her. Maddie smiled back but managed to kcep her mouth firmly closed.

Three

There was a fifth person sitting at the table. A boy not much older than she was, Maddie guessed. He was very thin, so thin that his wrist bone protruded and his long fingers looked as bony as a skeleton's. Although his face and hands were lightly tanned from working out of doors, under the open-necked shirt Maddie could see a 'V' of pale skin. His mousey-coloured straight hair fell forward almost covering one eye. Every so often he flicked it back with a toss of his head. His grey eyes were large behind round, steel-framed spectacles. Maddie noticed that he kept looking at her from beneath the flop of hair, glancing up swiftly and then away again. She smiled at him but her attention was drawn back again and again to the taller, good-looking young man who came to sit beside him and directly opposite her and whose broad shoulders seemed twice as wide as the younger boy's.

The master came and sat down at the head of the table and they all bowed their heads while he murmured a short prayer in a soft, deep voice. Then he took up the carving knife and fork and began to carve the meat.

'Don't give the girl too much. I don't want her leaving any,' Harriet said.

The man glanced at Maddie, smiling. 'You can always come back for more if you can manage it.'

'Thank you, Mr Trowbridge,' Maddie said politely and was surprised when the young man opposite her threw back his head with a gust of laughter whilst the younger boy sniggered behind his hand. The master was amused, but beside her Maddie heard the woman's sniff of annoyance.

'I think we'd better introduce ourselves properly,' the man said. 'My name's Frank Brackenbury and the young rascal sitting opposite you is my son, Michael. Mrs Trowbridge you know already and this . . .' he indicated the young man sitting on his immediate left, 'is her son, Nicholas, but more usually called Nick.' He chuckled as he leant forward to say in a loud whisper, 'Much to his mother's disgust.'

So where, Maddie wondered at once, was Mrs Brackenbury? What had happened to her? And what about Nick's father?

'We don't know your name, young'un,' Michael said, interrupting her thoughts.

'Madeleine March.'

'She's called Maddie,' Harriet said at once. 'We don't want her getting fancy ideas about herself. If I had my way, she'd be plain Jane.'

Maddie felt the eyes of all three men upon her and a flush of embarrassment crept up her cheeks. No one spoke and the girl knew that, despite their kindness to her already, Mrs Trowbridge's veiled reference to her plainness could not be refuted.

Maddie lay on the soft feather bed watching the clouds scudding across the bright face of the moon. She was tired, yet sleep would not claim her. So much had happened in just a few hours. This morning she had woken up at the Home to the familiar sounds in the long dormitory: girls chattering, jostling each other to get to the washroom and then Jenny appearing like a wraith at the side of the bed.

'Walk to school with me, Maddie?' It was the same every morning.

''Course I will,' Maddie responded, patient as always, swinging her feet out of bed to touch the cold linoleum. Then the younger girl was smiling, skipping away happily to get washed and dressed, safe in the knowledge that her protector would be with her.

But tomorrow morning, Maddie thought now as her heavy eyelids began to close and the moon became a blurred, distorted shape, poor Jenny Wren would be on her own at school.

Maddie slept fitfully, waking every so often bathed in sweat to fling off the covers, only to wake again feeling cold. It's this bed, she thought. It's lovely and soft, but it's too hot. When she could stand it no longer, she got out and pulled the soft feather bed away leaving only the lumpy, hard flock mattress beneath it. She was about to climb back in when the door to her room flew open and the light was switched on, flooding the room and causing Maddie to screw up her eyes against it. Harriet, in a long white nightdress, her grey hair straggling down to her shoulders, stood in the doorway.

'What on earth is all the noise, girl? And what is this doing on the floor?' The woman pointed at the feather mattress heaped beside the bed.

'It was too hot,' Maddie declared. 'So I took it off.'

'Well!' Harriet was flabbergasted. 'Well, I never did. You ungrateful little chit.' The woman bent and, picking it up, said, 'We take the feather beds off in May and put them back in November, but if that's how you feel, you can do without it. Just one thing, me girl, don't come

20

running to me in the middle of winter when you're cold in bed of a night.'

Suddenly remembering the nights of shivering in the cold dormitory, when ice formed even on the inside of the windows, Maddie realized that such a bed would be a luxury. She lunged forward and grasped the feather mattress, trying to tug it from the woman's hands.

'Leave it here in my room, if it's mine.'

Their faces only inches apart, the girl and the older woman glared at each other. 'It isn't yours,' Harriet insisted. 'At least, it won't be if you carry on like this. You'll be back in that orphanage where you belong.'

'Is something wrong? Is she all right?' The deep voice spoke from the doorway, making them both jump.

'Oh, Mr Frank. I'm sorry you was disturbed.'

'Is she all right?' the man repeated, his glance going beyond Harriet to the girl.

'She complaining she's too hot,' the woman's tone expressed anger at the girl's daring, but the man was smiling.

'I'm not surprised. It's a warm night. I was too.' He nodded towards the offending bag of feathers. 'But I shouldn't take it right away, Harriet. This time of year the nights can turn just as cold again. Let her keep it in her room and she can do what she likes.'

The woman thrust the mattress away from her, pushing it towards Maddie and almost knocking her backwards onto the bed. 'Whatever you say, Mr Frank. Now . . .' She turned back to the girl. 'If you'd be so kind as to get into bed, then maybe the rest of us could get some sleep.'

The light was switched off and the door closed firmly, leaving Maddie in darkness.

The mester had been kind, Maddie thought as she

climbed back into bed, but in sticking up for her he had shown Mrs Trowbridge up. The woman would not forgive her for that.

Tonight, Maddie knew, she had made an enemy of Harriet Trowbridge.

Four

The banging on her bedroom door woke Maddie with a start before it was even light.

'Jenny . . .?' she said aloud and then remembered where she was.

'Come along, girl. Get up,' the woman's voice came from the other side of the door. 'There's work to do.'

Maddie groaned. 'It's the middle of the night.' But she pushed back the covers and scrambled out of bed.

Washing in cold water in the ewer was no hardship for the girl raised in an orphanage where the use of hot, or even warm, water was thought to be pampering the children.

'A little hardship is character building,' had been Sir Peter's edict, though Maddie doubted he, in his mansion, had ever washed in cold water in his life.

Maddie had only ever seen Sir Peter's house once. In the spring of 1943 there had been a garden party in the grounds to raise funds for the War effort. The girls from the Mayfield Home, which Sir Peter's own father had founded during the 1890s, had been marched, two by two, through the village to the home of their benefactor. Arriving at the entrance where once massive wrought-iron gates had hung, the children had found they still had a long walk through parkland before they came in sight of the house. Maddie remembered how weary Jenny had been. Then they had been required to stand in the sun on their best behaviour and smile politely whilst the smartly dressed ladies told them how lucky they were to have someone like Sir Peter with their best interests at heart.

That had been the day, she thought with a shudder, that they had seen the Hanging Tree.

There were several of the village children at Mayfield Park that day with their parents. Steven Smith, whom Maddie was obliged to sit near in school, had soon sought her out.

'It's the Mad March Hare.' He tweaked her hair and then stepped back sharply before she had time to lash out at him. 'What you doing here? Didn't think they'd let you out of the madhouse to come.'

Jenny shrank behind Maddie, clinging to the back of her skirt and peeping round the older girl to watch him. But Maddie grinned at him. 'Hello, Stinky. Didn't think they'd let a smelly little beggar like you come here, either.'

He drew himself up to his full height – an inch taller than Maddie. 'My dad shoes all Sir Peter's horses, so there.' Steven's father was the village blacksmith and the boy's clothes always reeked of the forge and the smell of singeing hoof. It was not an unpleasant smell, but Maddie used it to go one better on the nickname he had given her.

'Bet you've never seen the Hanging Tree,' he said.

From behind her came a little squeak of terror from Jenny. But Maddie said, 'The what?'

The boy moved closer dropping his voice to a scary whisper. 'There's a tree in the woods here where a feller hanged himself a few years back. Want to see it?'

Maddie felt Jenny's fingers on her skirt clutching tighter.

''Course we do,' Maddie said boldly, ignoring the whimper behind her. 'Oh no, Maddie, no.'

'Come on then.' The boy turned and began to walk,

hands thrust into the pockets of his short trousers and with a swagger in his step, towards the woods.

With a quick glance around her to make sure that Mrs Potter was not watching, Maddie prised Jenny's clinging fingers from her skirt and whispered. 'You stay here, if you don't want to come.'

'No, no. Don't leave me.' The small child seemed uncertain as to which would be the worse fate. Being left alone amongst all these strangers or following Stinky Smith into the dark unknown of the woods.

Taking her hand, Maddie said, 'Come on, then.'

Entering the cool dimness, their feet squelched on the mulch of several autumns' leaves. The breeze rustled through the trees overhead and birds rose from the top-most boughs at the arrival of the three intruders.

'Come on,' shouted their guide, his voice echoing eerily. 'It's this way.'

They came to a small clearing and at the edge Maddie stopped and gasped aloud. 'Oh how pretty it is. Just look, Jen, at all these flowers.'

The whole clearing was a carpet of wild bluebells, yet in the centre was a heart-shaped bed of yellow tulips edged with a border of forget-me-nots.

Steven pointed to the golden flowers. 'Them's been planted.'

'Who did it?'

The boy shrugged. 'Dunno. Someone belonging to the feller who hanged himself, I s'pect.' He moved towards a tree at the side of the clearing and put his hand flat against the trunk, tilting his head back to look up into the branches. 'This is where he did it.'

Maddie moved closer, but Jenny hovered on the edge of the clearing hopping from foot to foot. 'Maddie, I want the lav.'

Maddie stood beneath the tree as Steven pointed upwards. 'See them marks on that branch. That's where he tied the rope.'

'Maddie . . .' came Jenny's wail. 'I gotta go. Now!'

'Bob down behind those bushes then,' Maddie murmured, her gaze still on the tree.

'I daresunt. There might be – be . . .'

Steven turned, grinning wickedly. 'Think a bird'll peck ya bum?'

Maddie gave the boy a shove on his shoulder. 'Don't tease her. She's only little and we haven't ever been in a wood before.'

His eyes widened. 'Never been in a wood. Blimey. They don't let you out of that place much, do they?' But now there was a note of sympathy in his tone instead of mockery. For the village lad who had been allowed to roam the fields and lanes at will, never to have been able to walk in a wood before reaching the age of eleven seemed like being locked away in prison.

'Wait there,' Maddie instructed as she turned and went back to Jenny to lead her behind the nearby bushes. Moments later the two girls emerged, the younger one pulling up her knickers as, this time, she walked alongside Maddie right up to the tree.

'Who was he, then?' Maddie asked, once more squinting up into the branches. 'And why did he do it?'

Now he had more of an audience the boy ran his tongue around his lips and grinned. With a sly glance at Jenny he said, 'John Cuppleditch, they called him. He was a groom for Sir Peter and there was a – a scandal, yes, that's what me mam called it – a scandal . . .' He savoured the word. '. . . About him and Sir Peter's daughter, Miss Amelia.'

'What about them?' Maddie demanded.

26

'Me mam ses it was all round the village at the time. He was already married, see, and him and his wife had a little babby, an' all. Everyone reckoned him and Amelia Mayfield was going to run away together, but Sir Peter locked her up in the house and wouldn't let her see him no more. But . . .' The boy, young though he was and maybe not even understanding fully the meaning behind the words, was relishing repeating the village gossip. 'He came back at night to try to see her and Sir Peter chased him off the estate with his twelve bore.'

'You're making it all up.'

'No, I'm not. He did hang himself from that tree because Sir Peter threw his whole family, even his mam and dad and his little brothers and sisters as well, out of their cottage.'

'How could he do that?'

''Cos he owned the cottage where they lived. His dad was head groom, see. So he got the sack an' all. They was all living rough for a while in the woods, me mam said.'

'What happened to them?'

Steven shrugged. 'Dunno, but him . . .' The boy was warming to his gruesome tale. 'He comes back here one night, throws a rope over that branch, ties a loop round his neck and then climbed up and jumped off.'

The two girls shuddered and instinctively moved closer to each other.

'It was two days before they found him.' Steven leaned closer, whispering, 'His face was all bloated and black and he was just swinging here, the branch creaking in the wind . . .' He made a rasping noise in his throat, trying to imitate the sound.

Jenny squeaked and buried her face against Maddie, who put her arm about the girl. 'Come on, we're going.

27

Mrs Potter'll miss us.' As she began to lead Jenny from the clearing, she glanced at the boy and grinned. 'I tell you what, Stinky. You tell a good story.'

The boy swaggered as he followed them, saying, 'T'aint no story. It's all true.'

'Yeah,' Maddie said sarcastically, but she was smiling as she said it. All the same, as they left the clearing and plunged back into the gloom beneath the trees, she glanced back to take a last look at the heart-shaped bed of tulips, shining golden in a ray of sunlight that streamed in through the trees.

Maybe, she thought, his sweetheart, Amelia Mayfield, had planted the flowers near where her love had died.

Maddie was still thinking of her little friend, Jenny, as she went down the stairs and presented herself to Harriet in the kitchen.

'There you are at last, girl,' was the housekeeper's greeting. Maddie felt her glance assessing her.

'Why are you dressed in your gymslip and blouse? You aren't going to school any more, y'know.'

Maddie felt an angry flush creep up her face. Her eyes glittered and her mouth tightened. 'I haven't any more clothes. Only me Sunday best and I'm not wearing that to work in.'

The 'out of school' skirt and jumper that she had worn at the Home had been far too small for her and almost worn out.

'You can't possibly take these with you,' Mrs Potter had declared, holding up the jumper, shrunken and matted from constant washing in water that was far too hot. 'What'll they think?' she had muttered, shoving the offending garments into the rag-bag. So all Maddie had been

28

able to bring with her was her school uniform and the navy dress.

Neither of them had heard Frank Brackenbury approach until, from the doorway between the kitchen and the living room, he said, 'Then we'll have to get you some suitable work clothes, lass, won't we?'

Maddie spun round and gave him a beaming smile. Politely, she said, 'That would be very kind of you, Mr Brackenbury.'

'Mrs Trowbridge can take you into the town tomorrow. It's market day.' He lifted his head slightly and looked beyond Maddie. 'You wouldn't mind going for once, Harriet, would you? You needn't stay long.' Without waiting for an answer he looked down again at Maddie. He chuckled and his dark eyes twinkled. 'And Mr Brackenbury is such a mouthful. Call me "Mr Frank" like everyone else does.'

Behind her, the woman said nothing, but Maddie heard her sniff of disapproval. The girl stood waiting, unsure what she was supposed to do. Without even glancing at Maddie again, Harriet, her mouth tight, moved between the pantry and the cooker where a huge black frying pan of bacon, fried bread and eggs sizzled.

As if sensing her uncertainty, Frank said, 'Do you want her to help you, Harriet?'

'No, she'll only get under me feet. She'd best start learning what she's come for. The milking.'

'Right you are, then.' Again he looked down at Maddie and frowned thoughtfully. 'We'll have to find you summat to wear for today, lass. Them clothes aren't suitable for the cowshed. Come on, let's have a look-see what we can find.'

He led the way into the wash-house and searched amongst the clothes hanging from the line of pegs.

'Ah,' he said with sudden satisfaction. 'Here we are. I thought I remembered seeing these still here . . .' From the peg the man pulled a pair of khaki dungarees and held them out towards Maddie. 'The Land Army girls we had in the War used to wear these. They'll be a bit big for you, but you can tuck them into your boots. There's a pair of rubber boots here that should fit you. An old pair of Nick's. Oh, and there's a pair of socks here too. They'll keep you warm and help to fill the boots a bit.' He smiled at her as he held out the trousers and set the boots on the floor in front of her.

Maddie took the pair of trousers with the bib and cross-over braces and pulled them on, tucking her gymslip inside them.

'Now, roll the legs up to your ankles and then put the socks on over them . . .' the man suggested, holding out his hand to steady her as she thrust her feet into the boots.

'There now,' he said, surveying her. 'Not bad. Not bad at all. A bit big on you, but you'll do. You'll need a jacket, though.' Again he searched. 'This'll do. It'll swamp you, but it'll be warm.' He held it out for her and she slipped her arms into it. 'Right. Now we'd best be on our way or my poor beast'll be bursting their udders.'

As they stepped into the yard, Frank gave a piercing whistle and the black and white dog came racing round a corner to hurl itself against him. Then the excited animal bounded towards Maddie, jumping up at her.

'He won't hurt you,' Frank said swiftly. 'He's only young and a bit boisterous, that's all.'

Maddie laughed as the dog leapt even higher and she felt his tongue against her cheek. 'He's lovely. What's his name?'

'Ben.'

At the sound of his master's voice, Ben paused to look

round enquiringly, but hearing no further command, he carried on leaping and bounding around the young stranger.

Maddie summoned up her sternest voice, pointed to the ground and said firmly, 'Down, Ben.'

The dog gave a bark but then dropped to the ground, looking up at her with soulful brown eyes.

'Well, I never did,' Frank Brackenbury laughed. 'You've certainly got a way with him, young'un. Are you any good with cows?'

Maddie smiled up at him. 'I don't know, mester. I've never tried.'

'Well, lass, now's your chance.'

They walked down the lane, side by side, Frank with easy strides, Maddie clumping along in her oversized boots, trying desperately to keep pace with him. Ben ran ahead, pausing every so often to investigate an intriguing smell in the hedgerow.

It was a bright April morning, sharp, but promising warmth later in the day.

'Where are we going?' Maddie asked.

'To fetch the cows in for milking.'

Ahead of them she saw a meadow where six or seven cows stood herded together near the gate. Two stood close to the gate, their great heads over the top of it looking up the lane.

'They're bigger than I thought,' Maddie murmured, 'close to.' But still she went forward, undaunted, to try to pat the nose of the nearest beast, but it stepped backwards.

She felt the man watching her and turned to meet his gaze. He smiled and gave a little nod. 'I'm glad to see you're not frightened of them, lass.' He chuckled, a low

31

sound seeming to come from deep inside him. 'But they're a bit wary of you, 'til they get used to you. One of the Land Army girls was frightened to death of them. I never did get to teach her how to milk all the time she was here.'

He opened the gate and the cows meandered into the lane, turning towards the farm.

Maddie laughed, her voice clear and ringing in the early morning air. 'They know the way.'

''Course they do. They travel the same bit of road night and morning. They should do by now.'

Maddie glanced back into the field and saw, at the far end near a hedge, two cows still grazing contentedly.

'What about those two?'

Frank's smile broadened. 'Lazy pair. We'll have to fetch them.'

Maddie looked back towards the lane where the small herd were wandering towards the farmyard with Ben, now wholly committed to his task, barking at their heels.

'Do they go into the cowshed all by themselves then?'

'More or less,' he answered, as they began to walk across the grass towards the two dawdlers. 'But Michael and Nick are there finishing off the first lot.'

'The first lot?' The girl was surprised. 'You mean you've more than just these?'

'Oh yes. We've fifteen milkers and then some beast for beef.'

'Goodness.'

'We supply all the village with milk and even Mayfield Park.'

'Sir Peter?'

The man glanced at her. 'Aye, his household and all the folks who live on his estate.' He waved his arm to encompass all the land around them. 'This is all his. We only rent it to farm, y'see.'

'Oh.' Maddie was silent. Then she blurted out suddenly, 'He owned the orphanage, too.' She looked at the man walking beside her and, with a maturity far exceeding her years, added quietly, 'It seems Sir Peter Mayfield rules a lot of people's lives.'

'Aye,' Frank nodded. 'Aye, you could say that lass. He's a local magistrate an' all. He certainly rules the lives of anyone who dares to be brought up in front of him.' He gave a wry laugh and the young girl wondered fleetingly if he had ever had cause to stand in the dock in front of Sir Peter. She glanced at him again, doubting her own thoughts. Mr Frank seemed a kindly, God-fearing man. She couldn't imagine him ever doing anything against the law.

They reached the cows who raised their heads, chewing sorrowfully.

'I don't think they want to be milked,' Maddie laughed.

'They're not so bothered as some of the others.' He pointed to their udders. 'Their milk yield's declining now. See?'

Maddie looked and saw that their udders were not so swollen as some of those already on their way to the farmyard.

'We only milk them once a day now. Just in a morning.' He slapped the nearest one on the rump and slowly it began to move reluctantly towards the gate, still chewing as it went.

Maddie was about to follow when she suddenly caught sight of a flash of colour from beyond the hedge. Standing on tiptoes, she peered over into the next field and what she saw made her gasp with amazement and delight.

'Oh! Oh look. Just look,' she exclaimed, quite forgetting that the man with her must have seen the sight many times and be quite used to it.

Beyond the hedge stretched a field of tulips. They were planted in blocks of six rows and each block was a different colour, from pastel pink through red and yellow to dark purple, rippling and swaying in the early morning breeze.

'Isn't that the most beautiful sight you've ever seen?' the young girl murmured, enraptured and enthralled. 'It's like a rainbow. Except,' she added, 'that it's straight.'

He came and stood beside her. 'Well, you'd best enjoy it, lass, 'cos they don't last long. They'll be cutting the heads off soon.'

Maddie turned wide eyes to look up at him. 'Why?'

'They grow them for the bulbs, you see, and part of making the bulbs mature is to remove just the heads so that a lot of the goodness from the plant goes back into the bulb and makes it grow bigger.'

'It's a shame, though,' Maddie said, understanding the need but bemoaning the destruction of the pretty flowers.

Reluctantly, she turned to follow him back down the field, dragging her gaze away from the multicoloured carpet of flowers that stretched into the distance as far as she could see.

Then she skipped after the farmer, filled with a sudden happiness such as she had never felt before.

Five

'Now, you'll have to sit close up, 'cos you're only little.'
Michael was laughing down at her but his teasing was not
cruel. 'We'll start you on Betsy. She's a soft old thing and
she'll stand good as gold whilst you milk her, won't you,
old girl?'

The cow, tethered to the wall, flicked her tail but
munched contentedly on the hay in the heck level with her
nose.

'Sit on this little stool, put your head against her belly
and reach underneath. Then, very gently, squeeze her teats.
Like this, see.' The young man squatted down and Maddie
watched as he squeezed and pulled and the milk squirted
into the bucket beneath.

He stood up again. 'Right, now you have a go.'

A shadow appeared in the doorway and Maddie looked
up to see Nick carrying two empty buckets and moving
towards the next stall. 'She'll never manage it,' he said.
'She'll have to kneel underneath Betsy to reach her udders.'

'Tek no notice of him,' Michael grinned good naturedly.
'He's only jealous 'cos he'd like to be the one teaching
you, 'stead of me.'

Nick gave a wry snort and then nodded towards
Maddie. 'You want to watch him. He's a bugger with the
girls.'

Now Michael frowned. 'Less of that sort of language in
front of her.'

Nick smirked and tugged his forelock in mock obedience. 'Right you are, sir. Sorry, I'm sure, sir.'

Maddie sat down on the low, three-legged stool and rested her forehead against the cow.

'I think you'd do better if you rest your cheek against her with your shoulder sort of almost underneath,' Michael advised. 'You might be able to reach a bit further that way.'

'But I can't see what I'm doing then.'

Michael chuckled and winked. 'You'll have to feel your way, love.'

As Maddie giggled at his cheeky remark, she heard Nick clash the buckets together and Betsy moved restlessly at the sudden noise, jerking her back leg sideways and pushing Maddie off the stool so that she fell backwards onto the cobbled floor of the cowshed.

'Now look what you've done,' Michael shouted at Nick as he stooped to offer a helping hand to her.

'What's going on?' Frank stood in the doorway and then, as he glanced from his son towards the figure of Nick making his way along the line of tethered cows to the far end of the cowshed, he gave a quick, irritated shake of his head. 'Oh, you two at it again, are you? Give it a rest, Michael, and show this lass what to do.'

'I was doing,' Michael muttered. 'If others'd leave us alone.'

But Maddie noticed that he kept his voice so low that his father could not hear his words. Only she, close to him, heard.

'Now the milking's done, Nick,' Frank said, 'we'll show Maddie around. Where we're standing, lass, is the crewyard and besides the cowshed . . .' Frank gestured towards the buildings on two sides of the yard, 'there's Rajah's stable in the corner and then pigsties down that side. We've only two pigs just now. Then, in that far corner, is the boiler house. We use it in winter to heat the hen-house. That's that long building over yonder.' He pointed beyond the yard. 'Come on, I'll show you my battery house, but you must never . . .' for a moment his expression was stern, 'go inside it. I'm only just teaching Michael how it all works.' His expression lightened a little. 'I've promised Nick that I'll show him too, when he's older.' Now Frank smiled. 'But even he's banned at the moment.'

Frank led the way towards the lean-to barn at the side of the house. From his trouser pocket he pulled out a bunch of keys on the end of a long chain attached to his braces and inserted a key into the Yale lock.

'You stand there,' he said firmly. 'Both of you.'

As he stepped into the dark interior and switched on a light, Maddie and Nick leant against the door jambs, peering inside.

'This is a Lister engine,' Frank explained. 'It drives this generator that's linked to these batteries.'

The engine and the generator were set on a concrete plinth in the centre of the barn, but close by, set against one wall, was a wooden rack holding three rows of glass containers with lead plates suspended in each one and with cables running between them.

'These are full of sulphuric acid,' Frank warned. 'And the current is what they call direct current. Very danger-ous.' His face was serious. 'It might kill a person if they touched the bare wires and the acid would burn if you got any on you. So promise me, lass, you won't ever come in here on your own. You'll hear us start up the generator about once a week to charge up the batteries, but as long as you do as I say, there's nothing to worry about. And this . . .' He was pointing to one side of the rack of batteries now. 'Is the control panel.'

It seemed to Maddie to be a confusing array of dials and switches. 'What's it all do, Mr Frank?' she asked, mystified, yet intrigued.

'It generates the electricity that feeds the house and all the lighting.'

He switched off the light and stepped out of the barn, closing the door carefully behind him and checking that it was locked. 'See these?' He pointed to cables running above them from the corner of the barn across the yard to the hen-house and the buildings around the crewyard. 'They're connected to lights in all the buildings.'

'It's very clever,' Maddie said with genuine admiration.

'Well, we're too far out for mains electricity. A lot of farms out in the countryside have their own system. It's not so unusual.' Frank smiled down at her, touched by her ingenuous praise. 'Now, let's show you the front garden and then, except for the rest of the fields, you've about seen it all. I'm sure Mrs Trowbridge will have our breakfast waiting. I bet you're hungry, lass, aren't you?'

It took a week for Maddie to learn how to milk properly and, even then, she was much slower than the experienced Michael and even the younger Nick. Between milking, she was expected to help in the dairy, churning the butter, and in the house helping Harriet, who was, Maddie had now learned, the housekeeper. She and her son were treated like members of Frank's own family and Maddie's mistake had been a natural one to make. To outsiders, Harriet had all the appearance of being the farmer's wife. Only those within the walls of the farmhouse knew that Frank Brackenbury and Harriet Trowbridge went to their own bedrooms each night and, as far as the young girl was aware, stayed there.

Michael, Maddie learned, was in charge of the milk round. After milking each morning he would set off with the horse and cart and with three or four milk churns on the back.

'You'll have to come with me one day, young'un,' he told Maddie. 'I could do with some help some mornings. All this traipsing up and down folks' paths to fetch their milkcans and then all the way back to the door to deliver it.' He sniffed. 'Time was when they'd come out to the cart and fetch it themselves. Folks is getting lazier I reckon.' He winked at her. 'I blame the War.'

Maddie laughed. 'I've heard that before. Mrs Potter was always saying it.'

'Who's Mrs Potter?'

'The matron at the Home.'

The young man's face sobered and there was pity in his dark brown eyes. 'Were you happy there?'

Maddie shrugged her thin shoulders. 'Dunno,' and added wisely, 'it was all I'd ever known really . . .' She paused, omitting to tell him of her brief times of trial in foster homes. 'I've never known anything different.'

'Are you happy here?'

Her smile broadened in genuine pleasure so that he smiled too. 'Oh yes.'

'So you don't miss your old home, then?'

Now a tiny cloud shadowed her face. 'There's only one person I miss. My friend, Jenny.'

'Who's Jenny?'

Maddie told him. 'I promised to write, but – but I haven't had the chance.' She hesitated, not wanting to sound ungrateful.

He grinned. 'We've kept you too busy, you mean?'

'It's not that. It's . . .' She stopped.

'Go on,' he prompted.

'I – I haven't any writing paper and envelopes or – or a stamp,' she blurted out.

'Ah,' was all he said as he turned away, but the following day, when Michael returned from his milk round he handed her a brown paper bag.

'There,' he said, smiling down at her, his brown eyes teasing, 'now you've no excuse not to write to your little friend.'

Opening the bag, Maddie found a pad of writing paper, a packet of matching envelopes, six postage stamps and even a fountain pen and a bottle of blue ink.

'Oh thank you, thank you,' she said gazing up at him, her eyes filling with tears.

Maddie March had never known such kindness.

As the young man nodded, winked and then turned to stride away across the yard, Maddie watched him go, adoration in her blue eyes.

Six

'I meant you to buy new clothes for the girl, Harriet. Not someone else's cast-offs from Mother Topham's market stall. She'll look like a ragamuffin.'

'That's just what she is.' Harriet's voice was shrill. 'A wilful little ragamuffin bastard that nobody wants.'

'Harriet!' Frank was shocked. 'I never thought to hear such words pass your lips.' Now there was sarcasm in his tone. 'And you, a good Christian woman. Besides, how can you say that about her? She's only been here five minutes and I certainly haven't seen any sign of wilfulness. Have you?'

'You didn't see that matron at the orphanage, Frank Brackenbury. Couldn't wait to get rid of Miss Madeleine March. Why, she even helped load the girl's box on to the cart herself. Oh, I could tell all right. I dare bet you – and as you've just pointed out I'm a good Christian woman who doesn't believe in gambling and the like – but I dare bet you a week of my wages that girl has been in and out of that orphanage to different folks and been sent back a dozen times. Well, I'll tell you summat, Frank. She'd better mind her P's and Q's with me, else I'll be sending her back an' all.'

Maddie hadn't meant to overhear the quarrel. She had come into the wash-house by the back door and was removing her boots when she heard the raised voices from beyond the kitchen door. Now she stood immobile, not

41

knowing what to do. She certainly didn't want to go into the kitchen and if she went outside again, they might hear the door open and close this time and know that she had been eavesdropping.

'I never liked the idea of having a girl here, anyway. It's not right with two young lads in the household. Who knows what might happen. I can't keep me eye on the little madam all day.'

Maddie frowned. Why, then, if she didn't want her here, had Mrs Trowbridge been the one to come to the Home to pick her?

'I just thought a girl would be more use to you, Harriet,' Frank was saying, 'in the Dairy and helping with the housework. You seemed quite keen on the idea when I first suggested it and it was you proposed approaching the Orphanage, if I remember. I thought you wanted to give some poor lass a proper home.'

'Huh! That wasn't me reason.'

'Then what was?'

'Oh I – er – well . . .' For a moment, even to Maddie listening beyond the door, the woman seemed flustered. 'I thought she'd be less trouble if there are no parents to come banging on the door making sure we're not working her too many hours or making her do work that's too heavy for a girl.'

Maddie heard Frank's gasp. 'I'd never do that anyway, Harriet. You know that.'

'Mebbe so,' the woman said tartly as if she did not agree. 'But we'll have no trouble from Mrs Potter, I can tell you that. Pleased to be rid of the little baggage, she was.'

'I don't know what you've got against the little lass. She's a bit slow with the milking, I'll grant you, but she's careful and gentle with the cows.'

'She's a wilful little tyke. Mebbe you don't see it, Mr Frank, but I tell you she'll likely bring trouble on this house 'afore she's done.' She paused and then added ominously, 'There's bad blood in her veins, you mark my words.'

'I'm sure Maddie is quite safe in my household.' There was a slight emphasis on the word 'my', but Harriet did not agree.

'Well, I can vouch for my Nicholas, but I can't say the same about your lad. He's a one for the girls if the village gossip is to be believed. And if she leads him on . . .'

'He's just a normal seventeen-year-old.'

'Are you implying that my son isn't?'

Frank's voice was heavy now, tired of the argument. 'No, no, of course I'm not. He's only fifteen. Plenty of time for him to . . .'

'I wouldn't mind him meeting a nice girl. Of course I wouldn't.' Her tone implied the opposite. 'But he'll not be mixing with the village girls, I can tell you that. Oh no. If I let him even think of getting married some day, she'd have to be from a decent family. A girl who knows just who her parents are.'

'I think you might find, Harriet, that you have no say in the matter.'

'Oho, won't I, indeed?'

'The Victorian age has gone, my dear. And young men not much older than our sons have just been through another dreadful war. Do you really think they are going to allow their parents to dictate to them how they should run their lives? We haven't made a very good job of this century so far, now have we? We're not even halfway through it and yet we have allowed the flower of our youth to be decimated by two disastrous World Wars. No, Harriet, we owe it to those that are left to allow them to forge their own future out of the ruins we have left them. I don't envy them their task.'

'I don't know what you're talking about, Mr Frank,' Harriet said impatiently. 'You talk as if the War were our fault.'

'Well, wasn't it?'

'Of course it wasn't. It was the Government's. Besides, what did you expect them to do? Let that Hitler walk all over us?'

'It was our generation's fault, Harriet. That's what I meant.'

'Oh, you're getting too deep for me and changing the subject. We were talking about that little madam and the trouble she could cause living here. I still don't know why you wanted a girl here in the first place. But, that said, she's not worth spending a lot on. She might not be here long.'

The argument had come full circle and when there was no reply from Frank now, Maddie was terrified that the door would open and she would be discovered.

Suddenly, she had an idea.

She crept forward and opened the back door. Then she slammed it as if she had just come in. Then, humming the tune of her favourite hymn, 'Rock of Ages', she stamped her feet on the mat and clomped across the floor towards the coat pegs. She heard the kitchen door open behind her and plastered a smile on her face in readiness.

The smile became genuine when she saw who it was.

'We've finished the milking, Mr Frank. I reckon I'm getting the hang of it now.' She giggled at her own pun. 'Michael's gone on the milk round and Nick and Ben are taking the cows back to the meadow.'

'Good lass,' the man said kindly though Maddie, knowing what had just taken place, could still see the anger in his eyes even though he was trying to hide it behind a smile. 'Come and get your breakfast and then I'll show you what I want you to do in the Dairy. It's time you started learning that side of things now.'

Divested of her outdoor clothing, Maddie stepped into the kitchen to see the housekeeper standing at the stove vigorously stirring a pan of porridge, her back rigid with righteous indignation.

Maddie had never witnessed a row like that before. Not between two adults, who, though employer and house-keeper, seemed to be on almost an equal footing. She had seen the staff at the orphanage in trouble with Mrs Potter, but they, like the children in her charge, had been obliged to just stand there and take it. She had even, once or twice, heard the younger members of staff threatened with the dreaded cupboard under the stairs, the 'prison' as the children called it, where Matron locked them in the spider-ridden dark for the slightest wrong-doing.

But Harriet Trowbridge, it seemed, did not have to stand there and take it, not even from her employer, and whilst the quarrel had ceased now, Maddie knew instinctively that the animosity between the farmer and his housekeeper was far from over.

And she was the cause of it.

'I've got another little present for you, young 'un.'

'For me?' Maddie's blue eyes widened in genuine surprise and delight.

'Er – yes.' Michael seemed doubtful now and strangely unwilling to hand over the small package. 'I hope you won't take this the wrong way?'

'Why should I?'

'Well . . .' He paused and she saw that he was glancing at her hair. Self-consciously, she touched it.

'I thought . . .' he went on haltingly. 'I mean, you don't seem to have any proper shampoo. You use soap to wash your hair, don't you?'

Maddie nodded.

'Well, see – proper shampoo would make your hair shine. You've got pretty hair. At least . . .' He faltered again and his voice fell away.

Maddie smiled at him warmly. 'Thanks,' she said, reaching out for the brown paper package. 'I'll try it on Friday night when I'm allowed to use the bathroom.'

He grinned back. 'And you're not offended?'

''Course not.'

The first time Maddie used the shampoo, she used far too much and lather spilled out over the washbasin and onto the linoleum. But after she had rinsed and rinsed the soapiness away her hair squeaked with cleanliness.

As she stood up and towelled her hair vigorously, she jumped as Harriet spoke from the opening on to the landing. 'You're running far too much water, girl. And just look at that mess on the floor.'

Maddie was incensed as she felt the woman's glance lingering on her nakedness.

'Go away,' Maddie said. 'You're not allowed up here either. Leave me alone.'

Harriet's face twisted into a sneer. 'And what do you think you've to hide, miss? Just get on with your bath and don't use much water now. There's others need hot water after you and there'll be none left.'

If she hadn't known that it would be Michael who

wanted to take a bath later, Maddie would have run and run the hot water all away to spite the woman. But knowing the two boys followed after her, she did as she was bade and only used six inches, the regulation depth that had so been instilled in them all in the orphanage.

Later, as she towelled her hair dry, she could tell the difference even after using the shampoo only the once. It felt clean and silky. In the privacy of her bedroom she picked up the pair of scissors she had found in the kitchen drawer and had earlier smuggled up to her room. Combing the hair forwards onto her face, she carefully snipped and combed and snipped again until she had a fringe and wisps of hair drawn forward onto her cheek. In her thin face her blue eyes looked enormous and now, with the blonde hair framing her face, she looked like a little elf.

'Why,' Maddie whispered to herself, marvelling at her own reflection though without a trace of conceit. 'I look almost pretty.'

She got into bed and turned out the light to lay in the semi-darkness listening to the sounds from the bathroom beyond her bedroom wall.

She could hear Michael warbling and splashing.

Smiling, Maddie fell asleep.

Seven

'You know that field of tulips just beyond where your cows are, Mr Frank?'

Seated at the breakfast table Maddie spoke about the sight that had intrigued her ever since the morning she had first seen the field. Each time she fetched the cows, she would stand for a few moments just drinking in the beautiful sight.

'Stop your chatter and get on with your breakfast,' came Harriet's harsh voice.

Maddie saw Frank glance towards the housekeeper. He said nothing but brought his gaze round to Maddie and said quietly, 'Aye, lass, what about it?'

Early that morning she had seen a line of women moving amongst the blooms. 'They were cutting them this morning. Not leaving any long stalks on the flowers like you do to put in a vase, but cutting just the heads off.'

'Aye well, lass, they have to. Like I told you, they're running a business.'

'They use some as cut flowers, though,' Michael put in.

'That's true. They pack and send a lot away, but there's a market stall in town that's loaded with flowers this time of the year.'

'Oh, I'd love to see it.'

The man's smile broadened. 'Well, it's market day tomorrow and I was going to go myself to look at some beast. You can come with me, if you like.'

'It's the Spring Fair as well, isn't it, Dad?' Michael said. 'There'll be roundabouts and swings, won't there?'

'You're right, Michael. I expect it'll be in the Black Swan Yard and the field behind it.' Frank glanced round the table, now including everyone. 'I tell you what, we'll all go. Make an outing of it and have lunch at the White Hart.'

'Great,' was Michael's reply but Maddie saw Nick look towards his mother.

'Not me, Mr Frank,' she said sharply and then added, 'but thank you for the invitation.'

'Oh come along, Harriet,' Frank coaxed. 'You can't avoid going into the town for ever. Besides, you went not long ago when you got those clothes for Maddie.'

A glance passed between them and Maddie, anxious not to give away the fact that she had overheard their quarrel about the clothes, stared down at her plate.

Harriet too averted her eyes from Frank's gaze now, hesitating before admitting, 'No, I didn't. I got Mrs Grange from the corner shop in the village to get them for me.'

Frank was nodding slowly. 'Ah yes, Mrs Grange.' He picked up a forkful of bacon and chewed it slowly, his thoughtful gaze still on his housekeeper.

'Besides,' she was saying, 'who's to see to things here if we all go off gallivanting?' Her mouth was tight with disapproval. 'And what about your milk round, Michael?'

'I'll tell everyone on my round this morning that their milk will be a little late tomorrow. I'll come back from town once we've had this posh lunch and do the round in the afternoon.'

'Folks won't like that.'

'We'll see to everything before we go,' Frank said. 'And I'd really like you to come with us, Harriet.' His grin was boyish and he looked, for a moment, nearer the age of his own son. 'I'll even try to get the car going. If I can scrounge a drop of petrol, we'll travel in style. I'll have a look at it after breakfast.'

'We'll help you, Dad. Won't we, Nick? I'll only have time for a quick look with you now before I have to get off on my round, but I'll help this afternoon.'

Now the younger boy smiled but avoided looking at his mother. Maddie had no such qualms and watched the housekeeper's face. It was obvious that the woman was struggling to overcome some kind of fear that only Frank seemed to understand. To Maddie's amazement, she saw the tightness around Harriet's mouth slacken as she put her head on one side with an almost coy expression. 'Well, in that case, Mr Frank, yes, Nicholas and I would be delighted to go.' Turning to her son, she added, 'Now, you help Mr Frank by doing some of his jobs if he's going to be busy with the motor car. You can start by cleaning out the hen-house. And you can feed the pigs.'

Nick's mouth was suddenly sulky as he muttered, 'Yes, Mam.'

They rose from the table, Frank and Michael chatting animatedly about the motor. Outside, Maddie touched Nick's arm. 'I'll do the hen-house, if you want to go with Mr Frank and Michael.'

The pale grey eyes behind the spectacles blinked. 'Would you really?'

''Course I will. What do I know about cars and engines and things?' She grinned. 'But I have learnt how to muck out.'

A flush crept up the boy's face as he said, so quietly she hardly heard the words, 'I never thought you'd do something like that for me. If you're really sure, I would like to go an' watch. I like engines. Anything mechanical.'

'What about the pigs?'

'I'll do them later.'

It was the longest conversation she had had with Nick. She smiled at him. 'Go on, then. Go and stick your head under the car bonnet with Mr Frank.'

The hardened layers of chicken dirt were more difficult to scrape up than she had imagined, but once she had dug down to the concrete floor of the building and could get the sharp edge of the spade beneath the layers, it was easier. She was actually singing to herself when she heard Harriet's voice behind her.

'What are you doing? I told Nicholas to do this job. You should be in the Dairy.'

Maddie felt herself trapped. She knew if she told the housekeeper where Nick was, he would be in trouble.

Cheerfully, she said, 'There's nothing much to do in the Dairy, Mrs T, so I thought I'd help Nick.'

'Don't answer me back. There's always work in the Dairy, girl. And my name's Mrs Trowbridge to you.'

She moved into the dimness of the building treading carefully across the slippery floor and came close to Maddie. Gripping the girl's arm, she leant towards her. 'I know your little game, miss. Flirting with young Michael and even fluttering your eyelashes at Mr Frank. Don't think I don't know. Well, if I had my way, you'd be back at that Home quicker than you came.'

'You picked me,' Maddie shot back. Harriet blinked, shocked by the girl's effrontery.

'You cheeky little madam. I wish I'd left you where you were.' She thrust her face even closer. 'If you really want to know, girl, I didn't so much "pick" you as you was the only one available. The matron said that the other two who were school-leaving age had already got fixed up with

51

jobs.' Her grip on Maddie's arm tightened. 'That should have warned me, shouldn't it? Nobody else wanted you.'

'No, you didn't. You picked me purposely,' Maddie flashed back, now so angry that she forgot caution. ' "Are you sure she's the one," you said.'

For a moment, Harriet looked perplexed, almost guilty, as if she had been caught out. 'How . . .?' she began, but Maddie interrupted, unable to stop the words bursting form her mouth. 'I know exactly why you picked me. You thought I'd got no family. I heard you ask Mrs Potter if I'd got anyone belonging me and when she said "no", you thought no one would ever come looking for me. You thought you could work me to death and no one would know – or – or care.' Her voice threatened to quaver, but she carried on defiantly. 'Well, I have got family, so there. And one day they'll come looking for me . . .'

'Oh no they won't . . .' Harriet began, her eyes sparkling with malice, but whatever she had been about to say ended in a cry of alarm, as, hurt and humiliated, Maddie twisted herself free of the woman's grip so suddenly that Harriet was thrown off-balance. She tottered backwards, dropping the basket, half-filled with eggs. Her arms flailed helplessly as she sat down heavily in the dirt that Maddie had just scraped into a pile. For a moment, Maddie had the overwhelming urge to laugh, but as the woman groaned and screwed up her face in pain, the girl's mirth died.

She held out her hand to help. 'I'm sorry, Mrs T – Mrs Trowbridge. I didn't mean . . .'

'You – you little hussy. Wait 'til I tell Mr Frank about this.' Ignoring Maddie's hand, the woman struggled to regain her feet. 'Just look at all that waste.' She pointed to the eggs smashed on the floor, their yellow yolks oozing across the wet dirt. Already hens were running to peck at the raw egg. 'Get it cleaned up quickly. You'll have the hens breaking their own eggs to eat them next, once they get a taste.'

'What do you mean . . .?' Maddie began, but the woman's voice rose.

'Get it cleaned up, I tell you. Get this finished and then get the rest of the eggs collected.'

She turned and limped away, holding her right buttock.

Maddie no longer felt the desire to laugh. Now she was in real trouble.

'Send her back. She's useless. Good for nothing. She's trouble with a capital T.'

'Harriet, she's only a little lass. How can she be expected to do everything right just yet? Besides, what actually happened in there?'

Maddie waited, holding her breath. This time she was not eavesdropping on the quarrel between Frank and his housekeeper. This time she was right in the middle of it.

'She pushed me over.'

'No, I didn't. You'd got hold of my arm and I pulled myself free and you fell over.'

The woman glared at her. 'You pushed me. Said I was walking on your clean floor.' Harriet's mouth twisted into a sneer. 'Clean floor. I ask you, Mr Frank. Clean floor in a hen-house?'

Maddie gasped and felt her face flush with anger. 'That's a lie. I never said that.'

'Oh, calling me a liar now, are you? It's you that's the little liar.' Harriet turned to Frank. 'See how red her face is. Are you going to take her word against mine?'

Helplessly, Frank glanced from one to the other.

Maddie had always hated deceit of any kind. She'd

hated it in the Home when girls had taken one another's belongings and then lied their way out of trouble. She'd once sat on a girl until she'd confessed to taking Jenny's hairslide.

Through gritted teeth Maddie said now, 'I never tell lies.'

'Send her back, Mr Frank. Back where she belongs.'

For a moment he closed his eyes, sighed heavily and shook his head, irritated by the whole incident. Then he looked down at Maddie. 'I really don't want to have to do that, so try to be a good lass, eh?' His tone was gentle, almost sad, and then he reached out and touched her hair in a gesture of tender affection.

And that was Maddie's undoing.

She gave a little sob, turned and fled from the kitchen, through the wash-house and out of the back door.

Then she ran and ran. Out of the yard, down the lane to the meadow where the cows grazed, not stopping until she had run the full length of it and come to a halt at the hedge overlooking the field of flowers.

Now breathless, her crying was coming in huge, wracking sobs. The pretty blooms were all gone, only the headless stalks and the green leaves were left.

Gone too, was Maddie's feeling of security.

If Harriet Trowbridge could lie about a silly thing like that today, then there was no telling to what lengths she would go to get rid of Maddie. But what hurt the girl the most was that Frank had believed his housekeeper.

He had not believed Maddie.

Eight

'Are you getting ready then? We'll be going in half an hour.'

Maddie, watching Michael standing before the mirror over the mantelpiece to tie his tie, said, 'I didn't think I'd be going. Not now.'

It was almost eight o'clock the following morning. Everyone had risen early to finish the milking and have breakfast so that they could arrive at the market as early as possible, but nothing more had been said about Maddie going.

Michael came and leant on his hands on the table. 'That's all forgotten, young'un. Go and get ready. Look sharp.'

Still Maddie did not move. 'Hadn't you better ask Mr Frank?' Her voice was husky with the tears she was trying to hold back.

Since the previous morning, Maddie had been awaiting her punishment. For the first time since coming to Few Farm, Maddie felt as if she was back at the Home. It was just the same as Mrs Potter had done when Maddie had, to the matron's mind, misbehaved. Hour after hour had been allowed to tick by whilst Maddie pondered upon the inevitable punishment. What would it be this time? Extra chores, like scrubbing the tiles of the kitchen floor until her hands were red raw and her knees ached. Or would it be the cane? Maddie would imagine the thin cane whistling through the air behind her before it struck her bare bottom.

She shifted uncomfortably in the chair now under Michael's gaze, already feeling the anticipated pain. She guessed it would be Mrs Trowbridge who would administer the strokes and she knew that the housekeeper would relish each and every weal that appeared on Maddie's skin.

Or maybe she would be shut in a cupboard somewhere, though offhand she couldn't think of one here that resembled the one under the stairs at the Home . . .

She would have stood any one of these punishments without a murmur, Maddie thought, if only they would let her go with them to the market today. But she knew that Harriet Trowbridge would guess that the very worst punishment she could inflict upon Maddie would be to leave her at home.

Maddie bit her lip as she looked up at Michael. 'Mrs T won't want me to come.'

Michael straightened up. 'Well then, I'll take you. We'll go on our own, just you and me. But hurry up, 'cos if we've got to walk all the way to town, we'd best be off now.'

Maddie swallowed and her heart began to thump with excitement. 'D'you mean it? Really?'

He was grinning at her now. ''Course I do. Go on.'

Ten minutes later she was back downstairs, face scrubbed, hair brushed and dress changed, though the latter still caused her anguish. The yellow cotton dress, one of the second-hand garments from the market stall, hung shapelessly on her thin frame, the hem too long and uneven. And her stout, lace-up brown shoes were too heavy for a fine early summer day. But Michael smiled down at her and winked.

'Pretty as a tulip,' he said kindly, but she knew he couldn't mean it. 'Come on, then.'

As they were leaving by the back door, they collided with Frank coming in.

'Hello, you two. All ready?'

'We thought we'd go on our own, Dad,' Michael said quietly. 'Leave more room in the car.'

Frank glanced shrewdly from one to the other. 'Well, that's all right, but I was looking forward to us all going together. Won't you come with us?' He glanced from one to the other and then Maddie felt Michael's gaze upon her. He was trying to shield her, but it was up to her to tell the truth. Hadn't she said, so vehemently, that she never told lies. Well, neither would she let someone else even bend the truth to help her.

Squarely she faced Frank. 'I didn't think I'd be allowed to go. Not after what happened yesterday. So Michael said he – he'd . . .' She shot a glance at the older boy, hoping she wasn't about to get him into trouble with his father. 'He'd take me.'

'Oh Maddie.' To her surprise, Frank's voice was sorrowful rather than angry. His expression told her that maybe he guessed what had been in her mind, perhaps even imagined the harsh discipline she had endured already in her young life. 'You're not at the Home now, love. We're not going to punish you like that. If you do something wrong, well, we'll tell you about it at the time.' He moved closer to her and put his arm about her shoulders, looking down into her upturned face. 'We might get a bit cross now and again, but once it's over, that's it. See?'

Wordlessly, Maddie nodded. She couldn't speak for the lump in her throat, not caused by misery now, but by this man's kindness. She was even prepared to forgive him for seeming not to believe her the previous day.

'So,' he was saying, 'shall we all go together?'

Maddie looked at Michael, who smiled and nodded.

'Yes, please,' Maddie said in a small voice.

He gave her shoulder a quick squeeze and said, 'Good. Now, I'd better go and make myself look respectable.'

Harriet made a great play of limping across the yard to the motor car and easing herself into the front passenger seat beside Frank. Maddie, squashed between Michael and Nick in the back seat, said nothing.

'All set?' Frank asked as all the doors were slammed shut. 'Here we go. Come on, Bertha, old girl. I hope you haven't forgotten how to do it after all this time.'

With a grating of gears and a couple of kangaroo hops, they were out of the gate and gaining speed down the lane.

'I don't think it's Bertha that's forgotten, Dad,' Michael shouted. 'I reckon it's you that's forgotten how to drive her.'

'You could be right, son. Hang on to your hat, Harriet, I'm about to take you round this next corner on two wheels.'

Harriet gave a little shriek of alarm and clutched at her black hat whilst in the back seat the three youngsters held onto each other and thrust their hands across their mouths to stifle their laughter.

The cattle market was held in a wide street. There were no pens for the animals, like in the sheep market, and the beast just stood, quite patiently, in the open, cobbled street in clusters of four, five or six with only a drover to tend them.

Brought up in an all-female establishment, Maddie had never seen so many men together in one place in her life.

'Where have they all come from?' she asked, gazing around her in wide-eyed amazement.

'All over Lincolnshire,' Michael said. 'They even come from Nottingham, Leicester and Cambridgeshire.'

'Really?' She couldn't take her eyes off them. Some were dressed in farmers' workaday clothes, jackets, caps and stout boots, but some were smartly dressed in checked jackets and plus-fours. There were even one or two elderly gentlemen who wore black suits and bowler hats.

Maddie was fascinated by the sounds, the sights and even the smells. She breathed in the whole atmosphere, revelling in being a part of it, relishing the feeling of belonging. She watched the beast being paraded around before interested buyers and listened, open-mouthed, to the auctioneer rattling off the bids so quickly that she could scarcely follow him.

'Mind you don't nod your head, young'un, else you might find yourself the proud owner of half a dozen cows,' Michael teased.

Maddie laughed, but the next time the auctioneer's glance went around the crowd, she stood rigidly still, even holding her breath.

'Maddie! Maddie!'

She knew the voice even before she saw the small figure darting amongst the crowd, pushing her way through to reach her.

'Jen. Oh Jen.' The two girls flew into each other's arms.

'I've missed you so much,' the young girl was crying now, tears running down her face as she hugged her friend. 'It's awful there without you.'

'Did you get my letter?'

'Yes, yes.' She pulled back and looked up into Maddie's face, smiling now through her tears. 'It's the first letter I've ever had in me whole life.'

Maddie giggled. 'It's the first time I've ever been able to write one. But what are you doing here? In town?'

'Mrs Potter brought me. She's over there. I had an interview with someone who grows flowers, but I don't think I'll get the job. I'm too little to stand at the bench to pack them into the boxes, the man said.' She pulled a face. 'I don't think she's very pleased with me.'

'So, what's new?' Maddie grinned and they hugged each other again until Frank cleared his throat and said, 'Aren't you going to introduce us to your friend, Maddie?'

The girls pulled apart and Maddie, with the habit of years, pulled Jenny's coat straight and smoothed back her wayward hair. Then she bent and pulled up the girl's socks that were wrinkled about her ankles, as she said, 'I'm sorry, Mr Frank. This is my friend, Jenny, from the Home.'

Jenny smiled shyly as each member of the household from Few Farm acknowledged her in their different ways. Frank stepped forward and shook her hand, Michael flashed her his engaging grin whilst Nick smiled shyly from behind his spectacles. Only Harriet gave a curt, unsmiling nod, though her glance took in the child's appearance from head to toe. Maddie heard her sniff of disapproval when Frank said, 'Would you like to join us, Jenny? We were just going to have lunch at the White Hart.'

Jenny glanced over her shoulder. 'I'd love to, Mr Brackenbury. But I daren't. Mrs Potter . . .'

'Well now . . .' Frank held out his hand, 'let's you and me go and find this Mrs Potter and ask her if the Brackenbury family might have the pleasure of your company for lunch. How would that be, eh?'

'Ooh yes, please.'

It was the earnest 'please' that touched Frank's heart. He cleared his throat quickly and said firmly, 'Come on, then.'

They set off through the crowd together, the broad-shouldered farmer and the little girl who, though almost fourteen looked only eleven or twelve years old. Behind them, Maddie followed, intrigued to see Mrs Potter's face when confronted by a request that one of her charges, not to mention the infamous Maddie March too, should be asked out to lunch with a gentleman and his family. She turned briefly to tell Michael that she'd be back in a minute or two, but found, to her surprise, that not only he but Harriet and Nick were following in her wake.

This'll be good, the girl thought and smiled.

'Good morning, Mrs Potter.' Moments later Frank was raising his hat to the startled matron.

There was suspicion in her eyes as she eyed the man before her, then, ignoring his greeting, she hissed at the child, 'Get back where you belong, girl, and don't let me catch you darting off again. Ain't I told you about talking to strange men?'

Maddie stifled her laughter at the indignant look on Frank's face. 'My name,' he said stiffly, 'is Frank Bracken-bury and I believe you know this young lady?'

He moved aside to reveal Maddie, and the others, standing behind him.

Mrs Potter's eyes narrowed. 'Indeed I do.' She sniffed and, seeing Harriet too, she nodded. 'I suppose you want to bring her back to me, eh? Well, there's no place for her now. She's too old to come back to the Home. You'll have to fend for yourself, Maddie March.' She turned back to face Frank. 'I'm sorry, sir, if she's caused you bother, but I can't say I'm surprised.'

'On the contrary, Mrs Potter, we are delighted to have

Maddie live with us.' He paused and then added quietly, as if unable to resist doing so, 'I wouldn't send her back to your orphanage if I was to go bankrupt tomorrow.'

Mrs Potter had the grace to flush in embarrassment and, flustered, to say, 'Oh well, sir, I am pleased to hear it. Perhaps all my efforts were worthwhile in the end.'

With a hint of sarcasm, Frank said, 'Maybe so, Mrs Potter, maybe so.' He cleared his throat and said, 'What I came to ask you was would you allow young Jenny here to have lunch with us? I will bring her back to the Home later, if that would be convenient. In fact,' he added, as if he had just thought about it, 'she could go home with us and I would bring her back to you at whatever time you say later this evening.'

'Oh well, now, sir, I don't know about that.' Mrs Potter's mouth pursed primly. 'We don't normally let any of our girls go out with strangers.' But then she appeared to be calculating swiftly in her mind, the girl was coming up to school-leaving age. That very morning she had been turned down for one job. Maybe if Mr Brackenbury was pleased with one of her orphans then . . .? Mrs Potter smiled. 'But, of course, in your case, sir, since I know Mrs Trowbridge and you have already taken Maddie March, then I don't see any problem.'

She turned now and prodded the young girl on the shoulder. 'You just mind you behave yourself, miss.'

'Yes, Matron,' Jenny said in her meek voice and slipped her hand into Maddie's.

As they moved away from Mrs Potter, Jenny began to skip and chatter. Her excited, piping voice rose above the hubbub around them. 'Guess what happened last week? Mr Theo Mayfield came to the Home to visit. You know, Sir Peter's son. We was all called together and he told us that he's been appointed to the Board of – of – what is it they call them, Maddie?'

'Governors.'

'That's it. To the Board of Governors. He's ever so nice, Maddie. Ever so friendly and handsome. Fair curly hair, he's got. I always used to be a bit frightened of Sir Peter, but I don't think I will be of Mr Theo. I wish you could see him, Maddie.'

After they had walked all round the market again and Frank and Michael had stood before two cows for sale, pondering whether to make a bid and then deciding against it, Frank turned and said, 'It's too early for dinner yet, but I could murder a cuppa. How about the rest of you?'

'I could do with a sit down, Mr Frank. I can't stand on me feet any longer.'

Frank's eyes twinkled. 'You should have worn your comfortable shoes, Harriet, not your "Sunday-go-to-meeting" pair that pinch your toes.' He turned to the younger members of the party. 'You coming, or do you want to go off by yourselves?'

'We'll go and have a look at the fair, Dad.'

'Don't leave these two young lassies on their own, will you now?'

''Course not,' Michael said, almost indignantly.

'Right then. We'll come and find you there.'

As Frank and Harriet moved away, Michael said, 'Come on, I'll buy us all an ice cream each.'

Now that his mother was out of earshot, Nick was not to be outdone. 'Fancy a ride on the roundabout?' he said to Maddie. 'I'll treat you.'

Maddie grinned. 'You're on. What about you, Jen?' But the younger girl hung back. 'I daresunt. You go, Maddie. I'll just stand and watch.'

'We'll watch 'em and laugh at 'em when they fall off, shall we, young'un?' Michael said to Jenny and put his arm casually about her shoulders.

Maddie was startled by a sudden strange feeling that stabbed at her. She had never felt this way before, but when she looked at Michael with his arm around Jenny and saw him smiling down at her, she felt such resentment towards Jenny that it frightened her. And he'd called her 'young'un' too, the nickname that Maddie had thought was only for her.

Nine

The fair had come to Wellandon, as Frank had said, to the field behind the Black Swan a short distance from the cattle market. Fairground organ music greeted them as they drew near and they could hear the merry laughter and the shrieks from young girls as the handsome, dark-haired young man in charge of the roundabout sent it faster and faster. There were swing boats, dodgem cars, a waltzer, a helter-skelter and even a big wheel, as well as all manner of stalls; hoopla, a coconut shy and a shooting gallery. There was even a gypsy fortune teller in a small striped tent with an elaborate sign that said 'Madam Pallengro, Palmist and Clairvoyant'.

'Come on, Nick,' Maddie said deliberately, 'we'll show 'em.'

'Let's go on the Galloping Horses,' Nick said and held out his hand for her to climb up onto one of the white-painted horses whilst he climbed onto the one next to her. The ride, when it began, not only went round but also up and down and Maddie had not expected the peculiar feeling in her stomach. 'When it goes down,' she shouted to Nick above the hubbub, 'my tummy feels as if I've left it up there and then I meet it coming down as I'm going back up.'

Nick laughed and pretended to be galloping his charger. Faster and faster the music played and faster and faster the world spun around, so that soon the faces of those watching became a whirling blur to Maddie. She began to feel slightly sick and was thankful when the ride slowed and the earth began to regain its rightful shape.

'You all right?' Nick said as he held up his hand to help her slide down from the horse. 'You look a bit green.'

'Don't you dare tell them,' she muttered.

'They're round the other side. Let's go over there,' Nick suggested, 'make out we haven't seen them. Just till you've recovered.'

'Thanks,' Maddie said gratefully and followed Nick towards a shooting gallery, willing her legs to stop feeling quite so wobbly.

'There you are,' came Michael's voice.

Nick turned. 'Couldn't see you,' he lied glibly. 'We thought you and Jen had gone off together.'

'Not 'til I've challenged you to a shooting match. I might just stand a chance of beating you while you're still dizzy from that roundabout.' He turned to the two girls. 'Nick's a crack shot. Much better than I am.'

'Only 'cos I always get the job of going out to shoot rabbits in the fields or rats when the outside buildings get overrun with them,' Nick muttered, but Maddie could see that he flushed at Michael's compliment.

As they approached the shooting gallery, Nick's grin widened. 'It's a tube shooter. Ah well, you've no chance now, Michael Brackenbury.'

'What's a tube shooter?' Maddie asked.

'The guns are fired through a tube at the target,' Michael pointed. 'Look.'

On the side of a gaily painted wagon she saw that there were two guns mounted on stands, each pointing down a long metal tube which passed right through the wagon and out the other side.

'It looks like a gypsy caravan,' Maddie said and

Michael laughed. 'It is – in a way. The chap who owns the gallery lives in the wagon. I saw inside it last year and those tubes run right under his bed.'

'However do they move it all?'

'Like everything else on the fairground, it all comes to pieces and then he packs it all on the top of his wagon and off he goes. I like to come and watch them taking everything down. Talk about "a fine art". Everyone knows exactly what he's got to do. It's a sight to see, I can tell you.'

Maddie glanced at Nick, who was already moving towards the man collecting the money. She didn't think she had ever seen him looking so animated, so clearly enjoying himself. When he was smiling happily, he looked a different person to the sullen boy going about his work on the farm under his mother's watchful eye.

'Go on, Nick,' she called above the organ music coming from the roundabout, so loud that it dominated the whole fairground and even echoed into the surrounding streets. 'Win me a prize.'

He glanced back over his shoulder at her, a look of incredulous delight on his face. 'Right. I will.'

'Don't worry, Jen,' Michael said. 'I'll win one for you.'

Jenny, with a daub of vanilla ice cream on the end of her nose, smiled shyly up at him.

The girls stood side by side and watched the two boys take up their positions, covering their ears a moment later at the resounding bang, bang, bang from each one.

'They sound like real guns,' Maddie said when they came back.

'They are,' Michael said. 'With real live ammunition.' He smiled. 'So don't go standing near the end of those tubes – just in case!'

The man was coming towards them with the two

cardboard targets in his hand. 'The one on the left . . .' He glanced from Michael to Nick, who said, 'That's mine.'

'Well, young feller. Bull's eyes every time.' He grinned, showing worn, brown-stained teeth. 'I'll have to give you a prize.'

'What about me?' Michael asked.

The man slapped the target playfully against Michael's chest. 'You, son, will have to go away and practise harder. Way off the bull, you were. Every time.'

'Let the lady choose what she wants,' Nick said and Maddie followed the man to his wagon.

Sitting on top of a box, resplendent in a blue silk gown edged with lace, was the prettiest doll Maddie had ever seen. Her eyes widened when she saw it and she didn't even need to speak for the man to reach up for it and then place it in her arms.

'Oh, isn't it beautiful?' Jenny breathed when Maddie returned to them.

'Sorry, Jen, I'll . . .' Michael began, but at that moment they heard Frank's voice behind them.

'There you are. We've been looking all over for you. Come along now, we'd better go and get that lunch else there'll be none left.'

In the dim interior of the White Hart, Frank said, 'Now, you young ones sit at that table together and we'll sit over here in this quiet corner. All right, Harriet?'

As Maddie slid into the bench seat, she noticed the look of concern on Frank's face as he held out a spindle-backed chair for his housekeeper. Harriet looked pale and her eyes darted nervously about her. She kept the brim of her felt hat pulled low over her forehead and sat with her back to the other diners.

Maddie shrugged and turned her attention to Jenny, who slid onto the seat beside her, her wide eyes drinking in all the sights around her.

Jenny reached out and squeezed her friend's hand. 'This is fun, isn't it?'

Maddie nodded as she sat the doll between them and watched as Jenny touched the frilled skirt gently, almost reverently, with her small fingers. 'Isn't she lovely?' Maddie heard her murmur, more to herself than to anyone else.

Then she looked up and smiled around her, nodding across to where Frank and Harriet sat. 'Isn't Mr Brackenbury kind?'

Michael squeezed himself into the seat opposite Maddie and Nick perched beside him. He seemed almost as ill-at-ease as his mother and kept glancing furtively over his shoulder towards her.

'What about me?' Michael teased, hearing Jenny's remark. 'Aren't I kind too?'

Jenny blushed. 'Oh yes, you're all very kind. But I mean, him offering for me to join you for dinner. He doesn't even know me.'

'If you're a friend of our Maddie's, then that's good enough for us,' Michael said and winked at Maddie. She felt a warm glow suffuse her and felt sure now that Michael was only being friendly towards Jenny for her sake. He was not pushing her out in favour of a new and prettier little face.

She glanced at her friend. In the short time since Maddie had left the Home, Jenny seemed to have grown and filled out a little. Today, no doubt in honour of the interview with a prospective employer, she had on her Sunday best navy dress and a short blue jacket. Her hair, though clean, lacked the shine that Maddie's now had. How Maddie

longed to give her friend some of the precious shampoo
that Michael had bought for her. Then Jenny's, too, would
be a shining golden halo. And hers would be curly,
whereas Maddie's was straight.

As if reading her thoughts, Jenny turned to her and
said, 'Your hair's ever so pretty, Maddie. I like it cut short
around your face. And it shines so now.'

Maddie glanced across the table at Michael. 'That's
because I can now wash it in some lovely shampoo instead
of that awful carbolic, Jen.'

The younger girl's eyes were envious as her glance
roamed over Maddie's hair. 'I wonder if mine would shine
like that?' she murmured.

The young waitress was standing at the end of their
table, notepad in hand. Michael ordered for them all and
as the waitress left them again, Jenny stared at Michael
and Nick, glancing from one to the other. 'Are you
brothers? You don't look much alike.'

'No, we're not related but Nick and his mother have
lived with us since we were both babies. We're like
brothers, though, aren't we, mate?'

Suddenly, Nick grinned and Maddie marvelled once
more at how different he looked. Gone in an instant was
the sulky mouth, the resentful look in his eyes. 'Yeah,' he
agreed, 'we even fall out like brothers.'

Michael laughed. 'That's very true.'

Maddie opened her mouth to ask what had happened
to Michael's mother and to Nick's father but before she
could speak, Jenny leant against Maddie's shoulder and
said, 'Me and Maddie always say we're sisters. Don't we?'

Feeling guilty now about her earlier feelings of jealousy,
Maddie nodded.

'Of course, we're not,' Jenny went on. 'We know we're

not, but we like to think we are. Maddie always stuck up for me. The others tease me, you know. Me being small.'

'I know what that's like,' Nick said suddenly, but Maddie noticed that he glanced swiftly towards his mother before he spoke and he kept his voice low. 'The kids at the village school used to tease me and Mam sent me to another school. I had to travel miles on a bus all on my own to get there.' He paused as the remembered pain flitted across his eyes. 'I didn't like it there much either.'

'So that's why you never came to our school,' Maddie said. 'I wondered why I couldn't remember either of you. Did you go to the same school as Nick, Michael?'

'Part of the time.'

'He went to the Grammar School here in town. He's clever, is our Michael.' Once more, there was a tiny hint of resentment in Nick's tone, but Michael laughed it off easily. 'Oh, an absolute genius, that's me. I must say I use a lot of French on my milk round.'

'Did you learn French?' Jenny was round-eyed with admiration.

'Well, they tried to teach me it,' Michael said, 'but I don't think I learnt a lot.'

'He could have gone to university if he'd worked harder and stayed on,' Nick contradicted.

Michael pulled a face as if in embarrassment but, at that moment, their meals arrived and the subject was dropped as the hungry foursome picked up their knives and forks.

'Oh I couldn't eat another thing.' Jenny leant back in her seat and placed her hand over her stomach. 'I'm full right up to busting.'

71

'Me too,' Maddie said.

'Yes, not bad. Not bad at all,' Michael remarked and, raising his voice, he called across to his father and Harriet. 'Not up to your mark, Mrs T, but not bad at all.'

'Oh, go on with you, Mr Michael,' but Maddie could see that the housekeeper, flushed with the drink that Frank had bought for her, was flattered by Michael's remark.

As they stood up to leave, Maddie noticed that as Frank went to pay the bill, Harriet, with head lowered, scuttled towards the door and out into the street. As they followed her, Maddie whispered to Nick, 'Doesn't your mother like crowds?'

'Eh?' His grey eyes were owlish behind the lenses of his spectacles. 'Oh – er – no. She doesn't really like coming into town. Likes to keep herself to herself. Says the towns-folk are a lot of nosey parkers.'

'And do you?'

'Do I what?'

'Like to keep yourself to yourself?'

He shrugged and for the first time she heard the bitter-ness in his tone that this time was most definitely directed at his mother. 'I ain't had much choice one way or the other.' There was a significant pause before he added, 'Yet.'

Maddie grinned at him, confident that, given another year or so, he would stand up to his mother and be as rebellious as she would be in his shoes.

As Frank and Harriet joined them and they were about to cross the street towards the cattle market once more, a large black motor car drove slowly towards them, the market day shoppers parting, like the Red Sea, to let it pass.

'That's Sir Peter's car,' Maddie said, immediately recog-nising the vehicle she had seen parked outside the Home on many occasions.

They stood on the pavement for the car to pass by but as it drew alongside them, Harriet suddenly stepped off the kerb and stared in at the windscreen.

'Harriet!' Frank cried in alarm. He grasped her arm and pulled her away from the moving vehicle, steadying her as she tripped against the kerb. 'Whatever are you doing? You could have been knocked over.'

But her gaze was still on the black car moving on beyond them now. Maddie, too, stared after the car and saw, through the rear window, the pale face of a young woman. Long blonde hair curled onto her shoulders, though her eyes were shaded by the brim of her hat. The car moved on and the image became blurred.

'Good Lord!' Frank exclaimed. 'That must be Miss Amelia. You don't often see her out. I . . .' Frank stopped whatever he had been going to say and looked anxiously towards Harriet.

But Harriet Trowbridge did not appear to have heard a word he said. She was staring after the car, transfixed as if she had seen a ghost.

Ten

'Are you sure you're all right, Harriet?'

'Yes, yes, I'm fine, Mr Frank. I – wasn't thinking, I'm sorry. My mind was on other things.'

'Well, you must be more careful, my dear. There's getting to be more traffic about now than we've been used to.'

'I don't like the town. You know I don't. I didn't even see the car.'

Maddie glanced at Harriet. Why, the woman had been staring straight at it. She looked at Frank and saw the puzzled expression on his face. Maddie could see that even he, this time, did not quite believe Harriet.

'In that case,' he said slowly, 'you'd better take my arm, Harriet.'

Maddie watched as he held out his crooked arm towards his housekeeper and she, with a sudden smile of satisfaction, put her hand through it.

'Now, are you sure you're all right?'

'Oh yes, Mr Frank. I'm fine. It – just shook me up a little.'

'I want to have another look at those beast in the cattle market and then I think it's time we went home.'

'I'm just popping into that shop over there,' Michael said. 'I shan't be a minute. I'll catch you up.' Whistling, he sauntered across the street, his hands in his pockets, his cap set at a jaunty angle.

Maddie's gaze followed him until she felt Jenny suddenly clutch her arm. 'Look, there's that gypsy from the fair talking to that woman. She's holding her hand and looking at her palm. I bet she's telling her fortune. Oh Maddie, let's have our fortune told.'

'I haven't any money,' Maddie whispered.

'Oh.' The girl's face was crestfallen. 'Neither have I but I thought you would have. Now you're working.'

'Ssh,' Maddie said, 'I don't want . . .'

'What is it, love? What is it you want? Here . . .' Frank was pulling coins from the depths of his pockets.

'No, no, mester. I'm sorry. I didn't mean . . .' Jenny was flustered with embarrassment now.

'I know you didn't, love. I should have thought to give Maddie some spending money before we set out.' He caught hold of Maddie's hand, held it palm upwards and tipped the coins into it.

'Don't you go frittering good money away on such things.' Harriet had overheard the younger girl's suggestion. 'A lot of nonsense. Fortune telling.'

Frank glanced towards the darked-haired woman dressed in colourful gypsy costume.

Michael, rejoining them, asked, 'What's going on?'

Frank turned to his son. 'The girls would like to have their fortune told. Harriet doesn't approve, but I should like to know whether I'm going to become a millionaire.'

Michael laughed and slapped his father on the back. 'No chance, Dad, you'll still be fetching the cows in for milking when you're a hundred.'

But they all moved towards the Romany woman, who smiled a welcome. Only Harriet Trowbridge seemed reluctant, though she still stood with her arm through Frank's, close enough to listen to what was being said but not close enough to be involved. She doesn't want to miss anything, Maddie thought shrewdly.

'You stand by me, Nicholas. I won't have you taking part in such nonsense.'

Scowling, Nick obeyed his mother. So much for rebellion, Maddie thought wryly.

The Romany was much younger than she expected. In Maddie's imagination all gypsies were old and wrinkled, but this one's face was unlined, her black hair as shiny as a raven's feathers and her dark violet eyes were bright and knowing. Her flowing skirt and shawl were patterned with vivid, colourful scrolls and gold bracelets jangled on her wrists.

'Isn't she lovely?' Jenny whispered.

'Yes, yes, she is,' Maddie agreed, admiring the vibrance that was not just in the young woman's clothes but in her eyes too.

'How much for all of us?' Frank asked.

The woman smiled, showing even teeth, brilliantly white against her olive skin. She named a sum and Frank dug deep into his pocket. She took his hand into her own and studied his palm. With long fingers she traced the lines.

'You work hard. On the land?'

Frank nodded and Maddie heard Harriet sniff. 'Should've thought that was obvious to anyone.'

Maddie saw the Romany woman flash a quick, hooded glance at Harriet. 'You have a son . . .'

Harriet's muttering came again. 'That's obvious too, considering he's standing right beside him and looks the spitting image of him.'

'One son,' the gypsy said firmly. 'And she . . .' Now she looked fully at Harriet. 'Is not your wife.' She turned her brilliant smile upon Frank, 'Your housekeeper, maybe?'

'Why, yes. Yes, she is.'

'And that . . .' the gypsy pointed to Nick, 'is her son, but not yours.'

'Yes, yes. That's right.'

'That doesn't take a lot of guess work,' Harriet was scathing now, as if she feared Frank was getting drawn into believing the woman's powers.

Frank ignored his housekeeper. 'Go on, love,' he urged the fortune teller.

'You are a kind man, but that generosity of spirit is going to lead you to make a great sacrifice to save a loved one. Yet that sacrifice will bring you both happiness and sadness, too. A mixed blessing.'

Gently she closed Frank's fingers over his palm and looked deeply into his face. 'You will not see it as a sacrifice,' she said gently.

'Huh,' came Harriet's mutter again. 'Such nonsense.'

The woman turned to Michael. She studied his palm for several moments, until Michael grinned and said casually, 'Go on, tell me I'm going to die young and all the girls for miles around will weep at my grave.'

The gypsy did not smile but looked up to meet his gaze. 'No, you are not going to die the hero. But you are going far away, and though your heart will remain here, you will not return home. Not for many years. Maybe never.'

''Course he's going away,' Harriet said. 'His National Service is coming up next year when he's eighteen.'

Next the Romany turned to Maddie and Jenny and stood looking at them both, from one to the other and back again, before she picked up Maddie's hand.

'You are going to be very successful. Everything you touch will turn to gold. You will have a child . . .' She paused and frowned. 'You will know great love but also deep heartache. Joy and sorrow in equal measure.'

She turned away abruptly, as if not wanting to say more. She took Jenny's hand then and studied it but let it drop and, turning away without even looking into the young girl's face, she said, with almost a sharpness in her tone, 'You are too young. I do not read the palms of children.'

'But I'm only a few months younger than Maddie.' Jenny was disappointed. 'You read hers.'

The gypsy turned once more and regarded them thoughtfully. Quietly, she said, 'There are sometimes things it is better not to say. I'm sorry.'

Now she looked towards Harriet and Nick. She made no attempt to take their hands, to do a proper reading. Instead, she pointed towards them. 'You have great bitterness in your hearts. Both of you – mother and son. It will cause destruction.'

With that, she turned quickly away and walked back towards the fairground.

'Well!' Harriet was indignant. 'If ever there was a waste of good money, Mr Frank, then that was it. I'm surprised at you.'

But Frank was staring after the gypsy, lost in thought.

Back home, Michael insisted on showing Jenny all round the farm. As Maddie began to follow them out of the back door she heard the housekeeper's voice. 'You can help me set the tea, girl. And then you'd better get set into the milking.'

Harriet put her white apron around her waist, twisting the ties to form a bow behind her back with an angry movement. 'All this gallivanting. I don't know,' she muttered. 'And work here not getting done.'

Maddie cast a disappointed look across the yard to see

Michael waving his arms, gesturing towards the barn, the crewyard and the hen-house, whilst Jenny trotted beside him. Sighing, she went into the kitchen to help set the table for tea.

Later, as they were finishing the meal, Jenny said, 'Can I stay and watch you milk the cows?'

Frank glanced at the clock above the mantelpiece. 'Well, I did promise to have you back home before dark, but you've time enough to see the start and then Michael can run you home in the car.'

Jenny's eyes widened. 'Can you drive?'

Michael nodded and his father went on, 'Everyone on a farm ought to be able to drive. Nick can too, but he's not old enough yet to drive on the road.' He glanced towards Harriet and smiled, 'The only person I haven't been able to persuade to get behind the wheel is Mrs Trowbridge.'

'Shall you teach Maddie when she's old enough?'

'Oh yes,' Frank said, and Maddie felt a warm glow, but her growing confidence in belonging somewhere at last was cut short as she heard Harriet's familiar sniff followed by the words, 'That's if she's here that long.'

Eleven

'You go with Michael to take Jenny home,' Frank said, as dusk crept across the fields. 'Nick and I can manage the rest and Ben can take the cows back to the field.'

Maddie straightened up and carefully moved the bucket of milk. 'If you're sure, Mr Frank?' Then she turned towards the boy. 'Thanks, Nick.'

For a moment he looked a little sullen at being left out of the car ride, but then he smiled, perhaps remembering, Maddie thought, her offer to clean out the hen-house so that he could tinker with the car's engine – a kind gesture that had almost resulted in her missing the day out all together. His next words confirmed it.

'We're quits now, then.'

Maddie grinned and nodded and then hurried to change out of her Wellingtons.

In the yard, Jenny was playing with Ben, throwing a stick for the excited young dog to fetch and carry back to her. 'Isn't he lovely, Maddie? I wish there was a dog at the Home.'

'Maybe there'll be a dog where you go to live when you leave there.'

The girl's face sobered. 'I reckon the only job I'll get is at the Home. Peggy, one of the kitchen maids, is leaving to get married. Mrs Potter did say that if she can't fix me up, she'll give me a try.'

'Oh no,' Maddie cried. 'Don't stay there all your life,

Jen. Get out. Do anything rather than stay locked up in that place.'

'I would, but nobody else seems to want me.'

'You'll find something.' Maddie put her arm around the younger girl's thin shoulders and hoped she sounded more convincing than she actually felt. 'I'm sure you will. Why, look at me. Mrs Potter thought nobody would ever take me off her hands.'

Jenny smiled. 'Yes, you've been lucky. They're so kind to you. That Mrs Trowbridge is a bit sharp, but I expect that's just her way.'

Not for the first time in their young lives, Maddie marvelled at Jenny's placid nature, at her acceptance of what life handed her. Despite being abandoned by her mother and not even knowing who she was, despite living under the strict regime of the Home, despite being small, being picked on and teased by the majority of the other girls, little Jenny Wren rarely said an unkind word about anyone. It was as if she thought it was she who was at fault and deserved the treatment she received.

'Don't make excuses for her, Jen. She's a bad tempered old beezum . . .' Jenny giggled as Maddie grinned herself and added, 'But meeting Michael has made up for anything she can throw at me. I can handle her. What was it Brer Rabbit used to say?'

The two girls, who had often sat huddled together to read their favourite stories, now repeated the words together. ' "Born and bred in a briar patch, Brer Fox. Born and bred in a briar patch." '

Jenny was thoughtful. 'I know what you mean, but Mrs Potter does have a nice side to her. I'm not sure that Mrs Trowbridge has. She seems – well – spiteful, somehow.'

Maddie stared at her friend. To most people Jenny

81

Wren appeared to be childish for her age and weak, but every now and again she surprised even Maddie with her shrewd observations.

'You've hit the nail on the head, Jen. That's just what she is. Spiteful.'

Jen sighed. 'Like some of the girls at the Home. And I've got to go back to them.'

Maddie hugged her. 'Not for much longer. You'll get a job and get out of there. You'll see.'

'Come on then, you two,' Michael was calling. 'It'll be dark soon and I don't want someone waving a big stick at me when I pull up outside the Home.'

The two girls sat in the back of the car, laughing and chattering, the doll between them, but as the car drew nearer and nearer to the Mayfield Home, Jenny fell silent, her face pale, the joy dying in her eyes.

'Oh Maddie,' she said flinging herself against her. 'I've had such a lovely day. I don't want to go back.'

Maddie hugged her. 'Come on, Jen, chin up. It'll not be for long. Look . . .' She picked up the doll and put it into Jenny's arms. 'You take her.'

'Oh no, no, the others'll take her off me.'

'No they won't. Stand up to 'em, if they do.'

'I – I can't. You know I can't.' The whimper was back in the girl's voice.

Maddie grinned. 'Then let me know and I'll come back and sort them out. I won't let anyone take her off you. You keep her to remember the day.'

'Oh I don't need anything to remind me of today,' Jenny breathed and she was smiling again, if a little tremulously. But she hugged the doll to her. 'Thank you, Maddie. I'm going to call her Miss Amelia after that pretty lady we saw in the back of Sir Peter's car today.'

When Michael drew the car to a halt outside the front

door, there was no one in sight. He got out of the car and held open the door for Jenny to clamber out.

'I hope you don't get into trouble. We're a bit later than we should have been.'

'It'll have been worth it even if I do,' Jenny smiled up at him.

As Maddie watched, Michael drew a small parcel from his jacket pocket. 'Here, I'm sorry I couldn't win a doll for you, but I got you this to make up for it a bit.'

Jenny pulled in a breath of surprise. 'For me? Oh thank you, thank you.'

'You don't even know what it is yet. You might not like it.'

'Oh I will. I will like it – whatever it is,' the girl said fervently, clutching the brown paper bag to her chest along with the doll. Then she turned and bent her head to look into the car once more. ''Bye, Maddie.'

''Bye, Jen.' Now, Maddie had to force a smile on to her mouth. 'See you soon.'

As she ran up the steps and reached the top, Jenny turned to wave before disappearing behind the heavy front door.

'Come and sit in the front with me, now,' Michael said as he climbed in behind the wheel.

She did as he suggested but she did not look at him or speak to him. They had travelled about half the distance between the Home and Few Farm when he said, 'What's the matter?'

'Nothing.'

'Yes, there is. Are you sad to see her go back to – that place?'

'Yes.' She was, but it was not the reason she was sitting so silently beside him.

'She'll soon be able to leave, won't she?'

'September.'

'Well then?'

Maddie said nothing.

'It's more than that, isn't it?'

Still she did not reply.

'Ah. I know. You didn't like me giving her a present.'

'Of course I didn't mind that,' she answered quickly. Too quickly.

He took one hand from the steering wheel and reached out to touch her hand, squeezing it for a brief moment. His touch was warm and sent a shiver through her whole being. 'I only gave the poor kid a bottle of shampoo. Like I got for you.'

That was just it, Maddie thought. Like you got for me. She swallowed the lump in her throat and felt angry with herself. How can you be so selfish? she told herself sternly. And over poor little Jen too.

'That was kind of you,' she said and hoped he didn't notice the tremble in her voice. 'She'll love it – as long as the other girls don't take it off her.'

'Oh. I never thought of that. Will they really do that? Does that sort of thing happen a lot when you live in – in a Home?'

'Yes, but mostly only to someone like Jen. It never happened to me.'

Now Michael threw back his head and laughed aloud. 'I bet it didn't.'

As they pulled into the yard at Few Farm, even Maddie was smiling again.

Just before supper, Maddie thanked Frank for the day.

'You're very welcome, love.' He smiled gently. 'I don't think your little friend wanted to go home.'

'She didn't. She – she . . .' Maddie hesitated, for once in her life not wanting to appear pushy. 'She said she wished she could stay here for ever.'

Frank's eyes clouded. 'She was a nice little thing,' he murmured, 'but we haven't the work for another lass. And she's even smaller than you.' Now his eyes twinkled with merriment. 'I must admit, Maddie, that when you first came, I didn't think you'd be up to the work. But you have proved me wrong, lass. And, for once,' he added comically, 'I am pleased to have been wrong.' He shook his head. 'But yon little lass, well . . .' He paused leaving the unspoken words hanging between them.

Now Maddie had to be honest, but there was a note of disappointment in her voice that the man could not miss. 'No, she wouldn't be strong enough, Mr Frank.'

'Well, you invite her to come here to visit whenever you've time off, love. She'll always be welcome.'

Maddie's eyes shone. 'Oh thank you, Mr Frank. Thank you.'

At that moment Harriet's shrill tones came from the kitchen. 'Where are you, girl? I need a hand.'

Maddie grinned at her employer and turned away to help lay the table for supper.

'Reckon you two smell it,' Maddie said when Michael and Nick appeared as the last dish was placed on the table.

''Course we do.' Michael leant over the table and sniffed appreciatively. 'Rabbit pie. My favourite. And that pastry looks a treat, Mrs T. There's nobody can make pastry like Mrs T.' Michael nodded towards Maddie. 'You'll have to get her to teach you how to make it.'

Maddie watched as Frank at the head of the table served the pie, cutting through the flaky pastry with a sharp knife. Then with a spoon he lifted out the portions of pinkish-brown meat and the rich, tasty gravy.

'Leg all right for you, Maddie?'

She blinked. 'I – er – I've never eaten rabbit before, Mr Frank.'

'Ah. Then I'll give you a tiny piece to try and if you like it, you can have another helping.'

The plates were passed down the table for Harriet to put the potatoes on. Trying to blot out the vision of the cute fluffy little animal that the meat on her plate had once been, Maddie put a piece in her mouth. To her surprise it was sweet-tasting and different from anything she had tried before.

'Do you like it?' Michael asked and when Maddie nodded he reached across, lifted her plate and held it out towards his father. 'Give her a bit more now, Dad.'

For a while, there was a silence around the table whilst they all ate. Then, thinking she might learn more by feigning ignorance, Maddie said, 'Who was the lady in the back of Sir Peter's car? Miss Amelia, did you say her name was?'

Four pairs of eyes regarded her, but no one spoke.

Frank glanced away, down at his plate again and said nothing.

'Mr Theo was sitting in the front with Sir Peter,' Michael said. 'I did see that, but I didn't notice anyone else.' He turned to Maddie. 'Mr Theo's his son, but I expect you know that.'

Maddie nodded. 'There was a lady sitting in the back. A pretty lady,' she went on. 'With long blonde hair and . . .'

'It was her, wasn't it?' Harriet's voice was harsh and she was staring down the table at Frank.

'Aye. It was,' Frank, though reluctant, was obliged to agree. 'It's many a long year since she was seen in the town.'

'But who is she?' Maddie persisted.

Down the table, Frank and Harriet looked at each other for what seemed to Maddie, waiting impatiently for an answer to her question, an age.

'The lady was Sir Peter's daughter,' Frank murmured, but his gaze was still on Harriet's face. 'Miss Amelia Mayfield.'

Harriet sniffed. 'I'm surprised at him. Bringing her out in public.'

Frank sighed. 'Oh Harriet. It was all a long time ago now. The poor girl can't be locked away for ever.'

'I thought she'd gone a bit . . .' Harriet tapped her temple with her forefinger.

'Who could blame her if she had?' Frank murmured.

'Well, she brought it on herself, didn't she?'

'I suppose so, but . . .'

'Is she the one who planted the flowers in the woods?' Maddie began. 'Is she the one whose sweetheart . . .?'

Harriet reached out across the corner of the table and gripped Maddie's wrist so tightly that the girl cried out in pain. 'Get on with your supper, girl, and speak when you're spoken to and not afore.'

Maddie couldn't sleep. The events of the day were buzzing around her brain. She was reliving the excitement of it all. The bustle of the market place, the strange and yet exciting atmosphere in the pub and then, the touch of Michael's hand on hers in the darkness of the car.

Her heart thumped loudly at the memory and every nerve twitched and jumped so that sleep seemed impossible. But as tiredness eventually overcame her and she drifted into sleep, Maddie's dreams were disturbed by the memory of that sweet, sorrowful face looking back at her from the window of the car. Then the image became distorted and Miss Amelia's face became Jenny standing at the top of the steps at the Home, clutching the doll and Michael's gift, tears running down her face as she waved goodbye.

Twelve

'If you're going to be late up just because you've had a day out, then I'll mind you don't have another.'

'I'm sorry, Mrs Trowbridge. I couldn't get off to sleep.'

'Too much excitement. Well, get on then, girl, now you are up.'

Maddie raced to the field and up the slope to round up the cows. This morning the bulb field, bereft of all its magnificent colour, did not distress her so since she had seen for herself the previous day that people were able to buy at least some of the pretty flowers to take home. She had stood in front of the colourful stall in the market marvelling at the vibrant colours, red, yellow, pink and purple, and although she could understand now the necessity for their removal – it was a matter of business – she still thought it a shame that some way could not be found to make use of the discarded flower heads that she could see heaped in the corner of the field.

This morning she watched the workers in the tulip field, wishing, for a moment, that she was one of them instead of having to milk smelly cows twice a day.

'There you are,' was Frank's greeting as she herded the cows into the yard. 'Overslept a bit, did we?'

'Sorry,' she began, but he held up his hand. 'No matter, love, we're only just ready for these anyway. You take the ones we've milked back to the other field and we'll see to these few.'

Prompted by his words, Maddie said, 'Why's it called Few Farm?'

'Eh? Oh that.' Frank chuckled. 'Someone with a sense of humour, I suppose. Way back. Afore we ever came here.'

Michael, shooing the beast from the cowshed and into the yard joined in. 'A few acres, Maddie. A few cows, a few pigs and a few hens. And . . .' he added pointedly, glancing at his father with a cheeky look. 'Far too few workers to cope with all the work.'

Maddie laughed aloud, the sound ringing through the sharp morning air. 'Come on then, Daisy,' she slapped the rump of the nearest cow. 'I'll take you a few yards down the lane back to your field.'

Maddie felt a surge of happiness run through her. She loved it here. Already she loved Mr Frank and Michael. Her heart beat a little faster. Well, every time she even thought about Michael she got a strange trembly feeling in her legs and when she saw him, there was a funny sort of fluttering just below her ribs.

If only, she thought, Mrs Trowbridge and Nick were a little more friendly, life would be just perfect. Although, she had to admit, that once away from his mother, Nick was so much nicer.

The following Saturday morning, Michael said, 'Would you like to ask your little friend to come to tea this afternoon?'

'Oh yes, please,' Maddie said, but then her face clouded. 'Would Mrs Trowbridge mind?'

'Not if I ask her,' he said, grinning, and Maddie giggled. Michael had even the strait-laced Mrs T wrapped around his little finger.

'But how can I let Jenny know? It's too late to post a letter to her.'

'Ring her up.'

'Ring her. On a telephone you mean?'

'Well, we haven't got bush-telegraph, young'un. There's a phone box in the village. Come with me on the round this morning and we can ring her from there.'

Perched up on the front of the milk cart beside him, Maddie smiled up at him.

'I can't believe Mrs Trowbridge has let me come with you. Whatever did you say to her and how did you get Nick to do the dairy work?'

Michael winked at her and tapped the side of his nose. 'I have my methods, young'un.'

He paused and as she was still looking up at him expectantly, he said, 'I just reminded him about the day of the hen-house and how you had taken all the blame upon yourself.'

'Oh.'

'Oh, indeed.' His voice was grim now, though still gentle towards her. 'Are you used to taking the blame for what others do?'

Before she answered, Maddie thought back. It was not so very long ago and yet it seemed an age away. Slowly, she said, 'Yes, I suppose I did sometimes.' She smiled, remembering. 'Usually for Jen. Always for Jen. But I would never tell tales, see. Not about anyone. So I sometimes took the blame for others too.'

'I thought as much,' Michael muttered and then added firmly, 'Well, in our house, you need never take the blame if it isn't your fault. You hear me?'

A warm glow spread through her and there was a catch in her voice as she said, 'Yes, Michael. I hear you.'

They drove for a while without speaking but the silence

between them was comfortable, although Maddie was acutely aware of his arm brushing hers every now and again.

At last Michael said, 'First call is Mayfield Hall.'

Maddie glanced sideways at him. 'Shall we see her?'

'Who?'

'The pretty lady we saw in the back of the car yesterday. In Wellandown.'

'Oh. Miss Amelia. Shouldn't think so. I've been coming here for three years now – more if you count all the times I helped me Dad out even when I was still at school – and that's the first time I've ever set eyes on her.'

'Really?'

Michael nodded and his face was solemn as he added, 'Kept hidden away, she is, poor thing. She's . . .' he hesitated and stumbled over the words. 'Well, I don't quite know how to put it without sounding unkind.'

Maddie remembered Mrs Trowbridge's action the previous night when talking about Miss Amelia. She had no intention of repeating the housekeeper's unfeeling gesture, so she murmured, 'I know what you mean.' There was a pause before Maddie said, 'Perhaps she's getting better. Perhaps that's why she had a ride out in the car yesterday.'

'Maybe. I rather think,' Michael said slowly, 'that Mr Theo might have had something to do with that. He's a nice chap, Mr Theo. Now, I do meet him sometimes when I come to the Hall. He goes riding early most mornings and because we have to go round to the back door, I often see him going to the stables. Mind you, he's away a lot. At university, I think. Doing a law degree, somebody said.' Michael grinned down at her, his eyes twinkling. 'He's a very handsome chap. I shall have to keep my eye on you, else he might be running off with you, young'un.'

He was teasing her, she knew he was teasing her, but it

was a nice kind of affectionate teasing. What she couldn't say to him was that however handsome Mr Theo Mayfield might be, he didn't stand a chance with her. Not whilst Michael Brackenbury was around.

But as they drove up the long driveway and round to the back of the imposing house with its arched windows that always reminded Maddie of the windows in a church, they saw no one except the kitchen maid who answered the door to take in the milk.

Leaving Mayfield Park, they reached the outskirts of the village and Michael pulled the cart to a halt outside the first house and said, 'You run to the door and get Grannie Barnes's can.'

Not sure exactly what he meant, Maddie skipped up the uneven flagged path. As she raised her hand to knock at the door, it opened and a wizened old woman appeared. Her toothless mouth sank in and her white hair was drawn back from her face, but the brown eyes were sharp and knowing.

'So you're the little lass young Michael's been telling us about, are you?' She thrust a white enamel milk can towards Maddie. 'Well, let's see if you can fetch me milk without spillin' it, eh?'

Dutifully, Maddie trotted back to the cart, waited whilst Michael filled the can and then carried it carefully back to the old woman.

Taking it from her, she put the coins into the girl's hand, nodded and taking a step back, said, 'Ta, see you again.'

Maddie smiled. 'Thank you, Mrs Barnes. Good morning.'

After half a dozen such stops, Michael said, 'D'you know, I could do with you coming on the round every day. We're getting done in half the time.'

Maddie beamed, feeling again the fluttering beneath her ribs.

At the phone box, Michael showed her how to make the call.

'I think you'd better do it. Mrs Potter won't believe me.' She pulled a wry face, remembering the hen-house again and Harriet. 'Nobody ever seems to believe me.'

For a moment, squashed together in the red phone box, Michael looked down into her face. Softly, he said, 'I'll always believe you, Maddie.' It was the first time she could remember him using her name instead of his nick-name for her. 'I don't reckon you could tell a lie if you tried.'

She felt hot all over and suddenly tongue-tied. He was so close that she could feel his breath warm upon her face, smell the earthiness of him, see that the dark eyelashes fringing his brown eyes curled slightly. His skin was smooth and weather-beaten and there was a faint growth of dark stubble on his jaw. His black hair was covered with a checked cap, but tendrils escaped from beneath it and curled into his neck.

'Right,' he said, breaking the spell that had enveloped them both for a moment. He picked up the receiver and whispered, 'D'you reckon I can sound like me Dad?'

The tension broken, Maddie giggled. 'You look like him, so maybe you can.'

Moments later after dialling, feeding coins into the slot and pressing button A, Michael said, 'May I speak to the matron please?'

'Mrs Potter,' Maddie hissed.

There was a long wait and Maddie heard the pips and watched Michael frantically feed in another coin.

'Ah, yes. Hello, Mrs Potter. This is Mr Brackenbury of Few Farm . . .' Maddie stuffed her hand into her mouth to stifle her laughter. How neatly Michael was avoiding telling a deliberate lie.

'We so enjoyed having Jenny Wren with us last week, we would like to invite her to tea this afternoon.'

There was a pause, then Michael said, 'Right . . . Yes . . . Yes . . . That will be fine. Three o'clock, then. Thank you. Goodbye.'

He replaced the receiver in its cradle and Maddie clutched at his arm. 'What did she say? Is it all right? Can she come?'

''Course she can. We're to fetch her at three o'clock.'

'Oh.' Maddie's face fell. 'But have you asked your dad? I mean, will he let you drive the car again?'

'Probably not. We haven't a lot of petrol to spare, but we'll fetch her, Maddie. You and me. In the cart.'

Excitement surged, yet she dare not be too hopeful even yet. 'And – and what about taking her back?' Michael usually went out with his mates on a Saturday night.

Michael shrugged. 'Either Dad or I'll take her.'

And now Maddie's pleasure knew no bounds. Michael was going to stay at home all afternoon and maybe the evening too. He couldn't be planning to go out or else he wouldn't be offering to take Jenny back to the Home later.

Would he?

Thirteen

The four young people stood in the yard at Few Farm.

'So,' Michael began. 'What are we going to do?'

Nick scuffed the ground with the toe of his boot, hands thrust deep into his trouser pockets. 'What is there to do?'

'Well, we can go into the village to the pub later . . .'

'They're too young,' Nick countered and, glancing at Jenny, added, 'and they look it.'

'We could go into town.'

'I've no money. Have you?'

'A bit,' Michael said, but then looked around at the other three as if to say, but not for all of us.

'Looks like a walk then,' Maddie said cheerfully. 'Let's show Jen all the animals and . . .'

'Huh, I spend all day with them. I aren't spending me time off with them,' Nick muttered.

'What do you want to do then?'

He shrugged. 'I don't know.'

'We'll go for a walk in the woods. How about that?' Michael suggested.

Maddie brightened. 'Oh yes.'

There was a sly, devious look on Nick's face as he said, 'We'll show you the Hanging Tree.'

Jenny gasped in alarm. 'Oh no, Maddie, I don't want to go there. I don't like it. It's – it's creepy.'

Maddie tucked her arm through her friend's. 'It's all right. There's nothing can hurt you.' She was intrigued.

Now she had glimpsed Amelia Mayfield, the girl over whom a young man had killed himself, she wanted to visit the tree again. To think that he had died for love touched Maddie's heart. Maybe Amelia had been the one to plant all the golden tulips and forget-me-nots in his memory. 'We'll see if those pretty flowers are still there.'

'Maybe Jenny's right to be frightened,' Nick's voice dropped a tone, like a storyteller telling ghostly tales around the fire at night. 'It's an evil place. It's a crime to take your own life, y'know. Maybe he still haunts the clearing . . .'

'Stop trying to frighten them, Nick,' Michael said. 'And you should feel sorry for the poor chap who was desperate enough to do that. And poor Miss Amelia. She's never been right since. Her father keeps her a virtual prisoner in that great house of his. How would you like that, eh?'

Nick glared at him resentfully. 'I know how she feels,' he muttered.

'Don't talk daft. It's up to you to cut loose from your mother's apron strings. Come on, Maddie. You and me'll go. These two can do what they like.'

They walked through the village and out towards the woods on the edge of Mayfield Park, Michael and Maddie forging eagerly ahead, Nick following slouching along, hands thrust deep into his pockets and scuffing stones on the road with the toe of his boot. Some distance behind them all, Jenny hung back reluctantly.

Beneath the shadowy trees, Michael and Maddie walked close together.

'I love it here,' he said softly. 'It's so quiet and peaceful.'

Maddie lifted her face up, closed her eyes for a second and breathed in deeply, savouring the musty smells of dead and rotting leaves mingling with the scent of the new growth of blooms. 'So do I.'

She felt Michael take her hand and they walked on, Maddie's heart beating faster, until they came to the clearing.

'Oh, they're still here. No one's picked them,' Maddie said, delighted to see the heart-shaped bed of yellow tulips. But the pretty blooms were dying now, drooping forlornly, lonely and neglected.

'I suppose only Miss Amelia would pick them.'

'Did she plant them?' Maddie asked.

Michael shrugged. 'No one knows for certain, but that's what everybody thinks.'

Nick came to stand beside them.

'Where's Jen? You haven't left her alone? She'll be frightened,' Maddie asked.

Nick glanced over his shoulder. 'She's coming.' His smile was sly. 'She dun't like it here, does she? I wonder why?'

'She's sensitive,' Maddie stuck up for her friend. 'She feels things. She's easily frightened.'

'I'll go and look for her then,' Nick said and turned back to disappear amongst the trees the way they had come.

'Thanks,' Maddie called after him, grateful for his offer so that she could stay with Michael.

He released her hand and put his arm about her shoulders, pulling her closer, holding her against him. 'I'm glad you've come to live with us, Maddie,' he murmured against her hair and she felt the familiar churning just below her ribs.

'Oh Michael . . .' She turned towards him and lifted her face to look up at him. In the dimness of the wood, she could hardly see his features but she could feel his breath warm on her face. He was bending towards her, his mouth coming towards her own.

Suddenly, there was a shriek of terror and Jenny thrust her way through the bushes, her hair awry, her dress torn, tears running down her face.

'He's here. The man who 'anged hissen.' She flung herself forward against Maddie, wrapping her arms around the older girl and clinging to her.

'It's all right. It's all right,' Maddie soothed her at once and then more firmly said, 'Now, don't be silly. There's no such things as ghosts . . .'

At that moment the breeze rustled through the leaves overhead and an eerie wailing sound seemed to come from the tree.

Jenny screamed again and buried her face against Maddie.

Angrily, Michael said, 'That's no ghost. That's human and I know who it is.'

He ran across the clearing, skirting the bed of tulips and disappeared behind the tree.

'Michael . . .' Maddie called, suddenly afraid herself. What had seemed such a peaceful, even if poignant, place had now become fearful and threatening.

They heard a scuffling in the undergrowth, saw a bush shake and then from behind the Hanging Tree itself, Michael appeared dragging a wriggling Nick by the scruff of his neck.

'This is your ghost, Jen. Just Nick playing cruel tricks. Now, say you're sorry for frightening her.' He gave the younger boy a little shake. 'Go on.'

'I'm sorry, Jenny. I was only having a bit of fun.'

Jenny lifted her face from Maddie's shoulder to look at him. 'It's all right.' She scrubbed away her tears. 'I shouldn't be such a scaredy cat.'

'Come on,' Maddie said. 'We'll go back now.'

To her surprise as they all turned to leave the clearing

and make their way back through the woods, she saw Jenny fall into step beside Nick, glancing up at him with a shy smile.

'Just look at that,' she said to Michael. 'Would you believe it after what he's just done?'

Michael laughed. 'There's no accounting for taste.'

Fourteen

'I've told you never to go near that place,' Harriet Trow-bridge raged at her son.

'Don't tell of him, Maddie,' Jenny had pleaded as they entered the farmyard. 'He didn't mean it. He was only playing. It was my fault for being so silly.'

But there was no way they could hide Jenny's torn dress nor the steak of tears on her face and Harriet missed nothing. 'Whatever is Mrs Potter going to say if you go back to the Home in that state?' She sniffed. 'I don't think you'd better come here again if you can't behave yourself, child.'

Jenny's chin quivered with disappointment.

'We were just playing, Mrs Trowbridge,' Maddie was anxious as ever not to tell lies, but not wanting to tell tales on Nick either. She doubted the housekeeper would believe anything said against her precious son anyway. 'And Jenny caught her dress on a prickly bush.'

'You shouldn't be going into the woods anyway. Don't you know better than to go into places like that and with two young lads? No better than you should be.' Her glance went between the two girls. 'But then I suppose it's to be expected. Bad blood in the pair of you.'

'Aw, come on Mrs T,' Michael smiled engagingly and put his arm about the woman's shoulders. 'Don't be so hard on them. They'll come to no harm with us. You trust us, don't you?'

101

Harriet glanced sideways at him. 'Now, none of your smooth talk with me, young Michael. You might charm all the young lassies, but not me. As for trusting you, well, my Nicholas, certainly. But as for you . . .'

To Maddie's amazement the woman actually smiled as she tapped Michael playfully on the end of his nose. 'I wouldn't trust you no further than I could throw you.'

'Aw, Mrs T, I'm wounded. How can you say such a thing about me?'

'Go on with you. You'd better get this child tidied up and take her home.'

Mrs Potter was even more direct. 'That's the last time I let you out on a visit, miss. Just look at you.' She thrust her face close to Jenny's whilst both Maddie and Michael looked on helplessly. 'I hope you haven't been doing anything you shouldn't have.' Then she glanced up at Maddie. 'I might have known you'd have been behind all this. Well, Maddie March, you've seen the last of your little friend while she's in my care, let me tell you.'

'Mrs Potter . . .' Michael began, but the Matron held up her hand. 'Don't you start, neither. I've had enough of this pair to last me a lifetime. I thought I'd got shot of you . . .' she jabbed her finger towards Maddie. 'But you're still bringing trouble to me door. And as for you, young feller, you want to watch her. She's a bad'un.'

As the heavy door closed behind them and they climbed back into the cart, Michael let out a sigh of relief. 'What a dragon! How on earth did you stick living there?'

Settling herself beside him, Maddie said in a small voice, 'We've no choice, have we?'

On the drive home they were both silent. Maddie was saddened to think she would not see Jenny again for several months, probably not until she was fourteen and Mrs Potter had found someone to take her. She doubted Mrs Potter would even deliver letters to Jenny if Maddie wrote to her.

Once or twice she glanced sideways at Michael who seemed lost in his own thoughts, his mouth pursed in a hard line.

As he manoeuvred the cart in through the yard gate, he put his arm briefly around her shoulders and gave her a quick squeeze. 'Don't worry, young'un, this is your home now. We'll look after you. But I am sorry about poor little Jenny.'

Tears prickled Maddie's eyes and she felt a lump in her throat at his kindness. Trying to smile she said, 'We'll just have to wait until September. That's all.'

'Oh well,' Michael said cheerfully. 'That's not long.'

Maddie said nothing but she was thinking it's an awful long time if you're living in the Mayfield Orphanage under Mrs Potter's rule.

'Why did you give Jenny that doll? She told me you'd given it to her. I got it for you. You'd no right.' Nick's expression was a mixture of hurt and anger.

Swiftly Maddie said, 'I'm sorry, Nick. But that night when we took her back to the Home, she looked so lost and lonely and I felt so lucky being able to live here with all of you. I just – well, I . . .'

She fell silent but Nick was making no effort to understand her generous gesture. Instead, he said again morosely, 'It was for you. I wanted you to have it. I thought you liked it.'

'I did. I do, but Jen's like my little sister and I – I thought you'd understand and not mind. I am sorry, Nick.'

He was unforgiving. As he turned away, he flung the words back at her over his shoulder. 'I bet you wouldn't have parted with the doll if Michael had given it to you.'

Maddie opened her mouth to say, Of course I would, but the words were not spoken for even as they came automatically to her lips, she knew them to be untrue. And even to save Nick's feelings, Maddie could not lie.

He was right. Had Michael won the lovely doll for her she would not have given it away to anyone. Not even to little Jenny Wren.

Towards the end of August, Michael asked her, 'Would you like to come to the village hop with me on Saturday night?'

Over the past few weeks Maddie had felt that she and Michael were getting closer and closer. He would touch her hand, wink at her as he passed her in the yard and touch her foot with his own toe beneath the table at mealtimes.

And now he was asking her out. Properly.

Thinking of the pretty summer dress hanging in her wardrobe that Harriet had grudgingly bought for her on Frank's instructions, Maddie beamed and, a little breathlessly, said, 'I'd love to. Thanks.' Then her face sobered. 'But I can't dance.'

'No problem.' Nothing ever seemed a problem to Michael. 'Place gets so crowded, you can't dance the proper steps anyway. I tell you what, though,' he added as a sudden thought struck him. 'We'll get the gramophone going in the front room. I've got some Glen Miller records and I'll show you a few dance steps before we go. Besides,' he added with a mock leer and moved closer to her, 'it'll be a good excuse to hold you close.'

He put his arm about her waist and began to hum softly.

Nick's shadow appeared in the cow-house doorway. 'Your dad's waiting for you by the tractor to help him cut Five Acre Field.'

Michael pulled a comical face and whispered, 'Trust him to spoil our fun.' Louder he said, 'Right then. I'll see you later, young'un, for your first dancing lesson.'

As he left the crewyard, whistling, Nick sidled closer. 'You don't want to take any notice of him, y'know. He's got a string of girls in the village.'

Maddie faced him. She didn't want to fall out with Nick. It was bad enough having his mother forever sniping at her and finding every little fault with her whenever she could. She didn't need another enemy, but nor was she going to let him get away with trying to spoil everything.

'Michael's asked me to the village dance on Saturday night.'

'Huh!' Nick's voice was scathing. 'Well, he might take you, but once you're there you'll find yourself trampled in the rush. The girls are potty over him.'

'You jealous?' The question was out of her mouth before she could stop it.

Nick's mouth curled. 'Of him? Nah, not likely. He's heading for a fall, that one. Me Mam says he'll bring trouble to us all. She doesn't believe in all that nonsense, you know, that fortune telling at the fair a while back, but she did say she thought the gypsy had got it right about Michael.'

Maddie stared at him. 'Maybe,' she said thoughtfully, remembering what the dark-eyed Romany woman had said about them all and about Nick and his mother in particular. 'Maybe she got a lot more things right than we know.'

'Oh aye. You reckon you're going to end up a million-aire then, do you? Everything you touch will turn to gold. Is that it?'

Maddie turned away. 'I've work to do in the Dairy. I'd better get on with it. The only thing I'm going to turn into gold is the cream into butter.'

Suddenly, Nick smiled and Maddie noticed how swiftly he swung from one mood to another. He was so much nicer when he smiled and his pale grey eyes, huge behind his glasses, wrinkled with laughter. 'Well, if you look at it that way, I suppose she could have been right.'

Now Maddie laughed. 'It's the only way to look at it. I can't imagine me, a waif and stray with no real family and no proper name, ever coming into a fortune of real gold, now can you?'

The promised dancing lesson did not happen that night.

The tractor, old and temperamental, took twice as long to cut the corn in Five Acre Field.

'I reckon that tractor's about had its day. I'll have to think about getting another before harvest next year,' Frank said when he and Michael returned home after ten in the evening, looking exhausted.

When Harriet decreed, 'Supper and bed for the pair of you,' neither of them had the strength left to argue.

As he passed Maddie's chair on his way upstairs, Michael put his hand on her shoulder. 'I'm sorry, young'un. Maybe tomorrow night, eh?'

But the next night was the same; too late and too tired.

'I told you so,' Nick said. 'Makes all sorts of promises he's no intention of keeping.'

Maddie shot Nick a vitriolic glance, but said nothing.

On Friday night, Michael came into the kitchen where

Maddie was standing at the sink washing up the supper dishes.

'Come into the front room when you've finished. We'd better have that dancing lesson.'

Maddie hurried through the rest of her work and was soon scurrying through to the front room.

'Are we allowed in here?' she asked peering round the door. 'Mrs Trowbridge is looking daggers already.'

Michael had pushed back the huge leather settee and the armchairs from the centre of the room.

'Never mind Mrs T.' He wound up the gramophone and placed a record on the turntable. 'What are you standing there for? Come on in.' He paused whilst he bent over the gramophone, lifted up the head and gently placed the needle on the edge of the record. As the strains of 'In the Mood' filled the room, Michael straightened up and held out his arms to her. Maddie moved towards him and felt his arm go around her waist and his left hand take hold of her right. Her legs felt weak with love for him.

Though holding her, he stood a little apart from her, teaching her the steps. Their heads were close together as they both looked down at their feet.

'Don't worry too much,' he told her. 'Just get the feel of the music. The rhythm. Like this, see?' He swayed in time to the beat of the music and, watching his feet, Maddie copied him.

'That's great!' he said. 'I reckon you're a natural.'

They heard the door open and glanced up to see Nick watching them, hands thrust deep into his pockets as usual.

'Want to join the dancing class?' Michael shouted above the music.

For a moment there was a look of longing on the younger boy's face, rather like a child outside a sweet-shop

107

window with his nose pressed to the pane but with no money in his pocket to buy anything. 'Mam ses it's time Maddie was in bed.'

The music slowed to a growl as the gramophone wound down and Michael let go of Maddie and hurried across to turn the handle vigorously.

'Go on.' Looking at Nick, Michael nodded his head towards Maddie. 'You two have a dance. You can come with us tomorrow night, Nick, if you like.'

Maddie opened her mouth to say, Oh no, I just want it to be the two of us, Michael, when she saw the pleasure leap into Nick's eyes. Suddenly, she felt an affinity with the boy. She knew what it was to be the odd one out. The one outside always looking in. Mistakenly, she had thought he couldn't possibly be lonely, not living here. He was part of a family; he had a proper home. But now she saw that with a joyless mother, living in a house that was not theirs and with the handsome, ever-cheerful Michael who was like a brother, but not a brother, Nick was perhaps even more lost and lonely than she had been. At least she had always known exactly what she was. He was like a piece of a jigsaw puzzle that belonged to the picture, but somehow just didn't quite fit.

So Maddie smiled and beckoned him towards the middle of the room. 'Come on, then. If we dance, Michael can watch and tell us what we're doing wrong.'

Half an hour later, the three of them were helpless with laughter, dancing round in a circle, their arms entwined across each other's shoulders like Russian dancers. They didn't hear the door open again until Harriet's strident voice made them all jump and spring guiltily apart.

'Nicholas! What on earth do you think you are doing? Get to bed at once. And as for you, girl, you can pack your bags and leave. Right now.'

Maddie blanched at the threat, but stood her ground. 'You can't sack me. Only Mr Frank can do that.'

The woman stepped closer to her. 'I hired you. I can fire you.'

Maddie bit her lip. The first bit was true, so maybe she could.

'Now, now, Mrs T,' Michael began, moving towards her and attempting to put his arm around the house-keeper's shoulders. But she shrugged him off.

'Don't you "Mrs T" me. You and your flannel. You might think you can charm all the village girls and this one here too. But it dun't work on me.'

'But I take the blame, Mrs T. It was all my fault. I'm taking Maddie to the dance tomorrow night and she can't . . .'

'Oh no, you're not. You're most certainly not.'

Michael sighed and glanced towards Maddie. 'You'd better go to bed, young'un. We'll talk about it in the morning.'

'In the morning,' Harriet declared as she turned and marched out of the room, 'she'll be gone.'

Fifteen

Maddie hardly slept. She was torn between memories of being in Michael's arms and the final threat from Mrs Trowbridge hanging over her.

Could Michael really like her? she asked the darkness. She knew she had changed since she had first come to Few Farm. Good food and fresh air had made her grow and fill out in all the right places. Lying in her narrow bed, she ran her hands down her body, feeling the soft mound of her breasts, the tautness of her stomach and the growing pubic hair. She wished it were Michael's hands caressing her and at the mere thought a thrill of excitement gripped her, tingled in her groin.

She gave a groan as she turned on her side and squeezed her eyes tightly shut. By the morning, she might well be gone from the farm. Maybe she would never see Michael again.

'She's going nowhere, Harriet. And if you'll take my advice, you'll let the three of them go to the village dance tonight. What harm can it do, for Heaven's sake? They're young. They all work hard. These two lads – aye, your Nick as well – do men's work. At the end of the week, they deserve a bit of fun. And the lass does too. Heaven knows, she must have had precious little of it in her life so far.'

The quarrel was going on right in front of her as Maddie stood waiting for her fate to be decided. There was no escape. She couldn't turn and leave the room. She was forced to stand there, listening to it all. And yet they seemed to have forgotten her presence.

'Fun? Fun, you say? Life's not meant to be fun. When have I ever had any fun?'

'Harriet,' Frank's tone was softer, 'you must have been in love once. When you married . . .'

Harriet's face was purple and to Maddie's horror, she actually shook her fist in Frank's face. 'Don't you even speak his name in my hearing. Not after what he did to me.'

'My dear, you're letting the bitterness eat you up. And it's destroying Nick's life too. You can't keep him locked up here with you for ever.'

'He's got *his* blood in his veins. Bad blood. I've got to save him from himself.'

'He's a boy. Just a boy. Let him go with them tonight, eh?'

Harriet turned away. 'You do what you like with your own son, Mr Frank, and with the girl. I wash my hands of her. If she brings trouble to your door, don't look to me for help. As for Nicholas, he's my son and he'll do as I say.'

She marched from the room and they heard her banging pans onto the stove in the kitchen. Frank turned to Maddie. 'Run along, lass, and help with the milking. I'll be out in a minute.'

'Yes, Mr Frank.' She turned and scuttled through the kitchen and the wash-house and out of the back door. She was not to be sent away. She could stay here – with Michael. But her relationship with Mrs Trowbridge was getting worse by the minute.

She was subdued the rest of the day, concentrating on

111

not doing anything silly, working hard and anxious not to make any mistakes.

It was strange now, she thought, trying to understand her own feelings. She had never cared before about trying to please anyone. At the Home, she had invariably been in bother and had, quite justly her honest nature reminded her, deserved the title of troublemaker. Whatever dire punishment had been threatened and usually inflicted upon her had never deterred her. Madeleine March had gone her own way to the despair of Mrs Potter and the admiration of her peers.

But now she felt vulnerable. Now she didn't want to be sent away from Few Farm in disgrace. She wanted to stay here, close to Michael, and it was her feelings for him, she realized, that made her defenceless. Loving someone made you weak, she thought. Perhaps that was what it was like to be part of a family. You behaved yourself because you didn't want to hurt or upset those you loved. You didn't want to give them cause to be angry with you because you would then be hurt in turn by their anger.

Maddie sighed. It was all very complicated. Having feelings made life complicated. It had been much easier at the Home where no one had cared for her and she hadn't cared for anyone, she thought. Except little Jenny, of course.

Less complicated it might have been, she thought, as she caught sight of Michael drawing the milk cart into the yard, but she wouldn't go back to the Home in a million years. And as he saw her, waved, jumped down from the cart and came towards her with long, loping strides, her heart gave a lurch.

Not even for a million pounds, would she go back.

*

'If I had my way, girl, you'd be back to that orphanage before your feet could touch the ground.'

For one unguarded moment, Maddie was rash enough to answer back. 'Well, it ain't up to you, is it? Mr Frank's the boss around here. Not you.'

'Why you . . .'

They were standing in the bathroom, open to the landing, where Maddie had been washing her hair in the washbasin there in readiness for her night out with Michael. Now she stood, rubbing it dry with a towel. Soon, the soft shining blonde hair framed her face and her blue eyes met Harriet's resentful expression squarely.

The woman was staring at her and now it was not with rage, but something else. Some sort of emotion that Maddie could not put a name to.

'What's the matter?' Maddie asked.

The woman jumped, startled out of her own reverie. 'Eh? What? Oh – er . . .' Then she seemed to recover herself and she stepped closer and thrust her face close to Maddie's. 'Bad blood. You've bad blood in you, girl, that's what. I can see it in you by just looking at you.'

She turned away and Maddie heard the door of the housekeeper's bedroom slam.

Maddie blinked and shook her head. 'Funny woman,' she muttered. 'Seems obsessed with "bad blood" in everybody.' She had even said it of her own son.

Suddenly, for all his moody ways, Maddie felt acutely sorry for young Nick Trowbridge.

They heard the music and laughter from the village hall even before they reached it. Maddie clung to Michael's arm, suddenly unaccountably nervous.

'I don't know if I dare go in.'

Michael strained to see her through the darkness. 'Not scared, young'un, are you? Not you, surely?'

'Well, I am a bit. You won't leave me and go off with other girls, will you? I expect there'll be some here who knew me at school.' She pulled a wry face. 'The village girls never liked us. Some of their parents didn't like them mixing with the likes of us from the Home.'

Michael's face was a study. 'You're kidding me.'

Maddie pursed her mouth. 'I only wish I was.'

'Well then,' he tucked her hand firmly into his arm, 'tonight, we'll show 'em. You just stick with me.'

To Maddie's surprise, he was as good as his word, he did not leave her for a moment the whole evening. In the lull between the dancing he paraded her around the room as if showing her off to everyone and Maddie was secretly thrilled when more than one local girl cast furious glances in her direction. Only one dared to approach and, winding her arms about Michael's neck, said, 'I hope you're saving the last waltz for me, Michael Brackenbury, and seeing me safely home *as usual*.' The emphasis on the final two words was not lost on Maddie.

Gently Michael unfastened the girl's hold around his neck. 'Not tonight, Susan. I've to look after Maddie.'

Susan turned huge, innocent eyes upon Maddie. But in their depths the look was not so guileless. 'She'll be fine, won't you? All the boys are panting to dance with her. Let her have a bit of fun.'

'I don't want to dance with anyone else, thanks,' Maddie said quickly, returning the girl's stare, which was rapidly turning frosty. Now there was not even the pretence of friendliness. 'I'm with Michael.'

With the merest hint of emphasis on the word 'I', Maddie staked her claim.

The girl glanced back at Michael, who made no effort to contradict Maddie, so Susan shrugged. 'Have it your own way then.' And she flounced away, heels tapping angrily on the floor, her full skirt bouncing as she walked.

'Oops, I think I've upset her,' Maddie said, not in the least contrite.

Michael laughed. 'Don't worry about it. Susan was getting far too possessive for my liking, anyway. Do her good.'

For a fleeting moment, Maddie wondered if he was using her to rid himself of Susan, but as he drew her into his arms for the lilting last waltz, she forgot all about the other girl and even about poor Nick left sulking at home, too afraid to rebel against his mother.

It was a beautiful evening, but already the sharpness of autumn was in the air. Leaving the village, they walked into the pitch blackness of the lane leading to the farm.

'I love the dark nights, don't you?' Michael said, pulling her closer.

Maddie thought about her life in the Home. Bedtime was an hour earlier in winter in a freezing dormitory where the whole night was punctuated by the sound of one or other of the girls coughing and sneezing with colds or flu. On winter mornings, the girls woke to find ice on the inside of the windows and had to run, shivering, to the washroom to wash in cold water.

No, she thought, she didn't like winter and doubted she ever would.

When she didn't answer, Michael said, 'It'll be Christmas before we know it. What do you want Father Christmas to bring you, eh?'

In the darkness, Maddie grinned. 'Just you.'

'Eh?' Close beside her, she felt him give a start. 'What do you mean – just me?'

'I'd like you for Christmas.'

'What?' Now he was laughing, joining in her fun. 'All done up in pretty paper and tied up with tinsel?'

'If you like. Then you'd be all mine and I could play with you all day.'

His arm tightened around her waist. 'Oh Maddie,' he whispered close to her ear. 'You're a little darling. Do you know that?'

She didn't answer, didn't know how to. Michael stopped and in the middle of the lane, beneath the bright stars and the fitful moon, he put his arms around her and held her close. She lifted her face and felt his mouth warm upon hers.

'Don't be frightened,' he murmured. 'I won't hurt you. I won't ever hurt you. You're my girl now and I'll always look after you. I promise. I love you, Maddie.'

As he said the magical words, words that had never before in the whole of her young life been said to her, Maddie let the love that was in her heart for him overflow.

'And I love you, Michael. I've loved you from that very first day when I was sweeping the hearth.'

He laughed softly, his breath warming her cold cheeks. 'You had a smut on your nose, did you know?'

They laughed softly together, even though there was no one out here in the darkness to hear them.

He kissed her again and then they walked on slowly, their arms entwined around each other. 'What about your dad? Will he mind?'

''Course not. He's very fond of you, you know. I can tell. Specially when he sticks up for you against Mrs T.'

'Is she – I mean – are they . . .?'

'Sharing the same bed?' he said bluntly.

'Well, yes.'

'Lord, no. Who'd want to make love to that sourpuss?'

There was silence between them. Maddie longed to ask what had happened to his own mother, but their newfound closeness was so new, so fragile, that she dared not risk breaking the beauty of the moment.

He must have read her mind, for he said, 'Me mam died when I was born and for a while me dad coped with the help of his sister, who came here for a few months, and then later with help from the village. That's one of the good things about village life, you know. They do rally round when someone's in trouble. Mind you, the down side is that everybody knows everybody else's business. But there you are, I suppose you can't have one without the other.'

She was silent as he went on. 'Anyway, when I was about two, dad heard that Mrs T's husband had died in tragic circumstances and she'd been left with a tiny baby. So he did his own bit of rallying and asked her if she'd like to come and be his housekeeper and look after me.'

'How did her husband die?'

'Dunno. I've never been told and if you even so much as mention the subject she goes off the deep end.'

'Does Nick know?'

'Shouldn't think so. Even he's not allowed to ask questions.'

'Not about his own father?' She was astounded. 'That seems unfair.'

'Mm.' Michael was thoughtful. 'I have wondered if there's some dark secret about it all. I mean, I wonder if he went off with some other woman or something. Maybe he's not even dead at all. There's no grave in the churchyard. I know, because I've looked.'

Maddie laughed. 'You nosy parker, you.'

'Well, you'd think if he'd just died, or even been killed, that she would talk to Nick about him. I mean me dad doesn't talk a lot about me mam, because it upsets him. But if ever I ask about her, he will tell me.'

They had arrived at the farmyard now and the house was in darkness.

'Let's go into the hay shed,' Michael whispered. 'We'll be lovely and warm in there.'

As Michael opened the rickety door, the squeaking noise it made sounded loud in the stillness.

'There – there aren't any rats in here, are there?' Maddie asked nervously. 'I don't like rats.'

'I didn't think you were scared of anything, young'un,' he teased and then, sensing that she really was afraid, he added swiftly, 'Don't worry. We do get them in here sometimes. Wherever there's animal feed, you'll always get Mr Rat and his family. But we keep a supply of poison and put some down regularly. Besides . . .' he paused as he laid his jacket on the hay for her and then put his arms around her. 'I'm here to look after you.'

They snuggled down together, side by side. He kissed her and held her close and whilst her knowledge of kissing and petting was non-existent, Maddie found herself responding with a naturalness that surprised her. Even shocked her a little. Perhaps, after all, a little corner of her mind whispered, you have got bad blood in you, just like Mrs Potter and Mrs Trowbridge said.

But then Michael was kissing her with such ardour that every other thought was swept from her mind.

Sixteen

'I know where you were last night.' Nick's tone was sly.

Maddie glanced at him, puzzled. Of course he knew where they had been. At the dance. What was he on about?

'So?'

'There was bits of hay all over our bedroom floor this morning. Just you wait till me mam goes up there. You'll be for it. She's not daft neither.'

Now Maddie hid her face against the cow's side, her fingers trembling as she gently squeezed the milk from the beast's udder. Oh no, she thought. How could Michael have been so thoughtless? She had been so careful to remove every trace of hay from her clothing when she had got to her room. She'd pushed it all into an old paper bag and had thrust it into the stove in the kitchen this morning.

'And you were very late in. I don't think Mr Frank was best pleased either.'

Maddie quailed inwardly. This was worse than ever. Even Michael could not stand up to his father. If he was angry with her then . . .

'Did he kiss you?'

Angry now, Maddie shot back, 'That's none of your business.'

Nick smirked. 'So he did. I thought so. Well, you're not the first. And you won't be the last.'

Maddie opened her mouth to retort, but then she

119

thought about the girl at the dance, remembering the intimate way she had spoken to Michael, the way she had looked at him.

Maddie swallowed. 'Are you trying to get me into trouble?' she said. 'Go away and let me get on with me work.'

Nick gave a wry, humourless laugh. 'I don't have to make trouble for you. You're doing a good job of that yourself. And as for "getting you into trouble", if you know what I mean . . .?' Again the smirk was back. 'Well, Michael'll do that for you, all right.'

'You're just jealous,' she snapped.

Nick laughed. 'I aren't jealous of a little trollop like you.' The name-calling sounded strange coming from the young boy's mouth and Maddie knew instinctively that the words were not his own, but his mother's. 'A little bastard that nobody wants.'

Maddie stood up and faced him. 'So why did she come to the Orphanage and pick a little bastard to come and work here, eh?'

'You know why,' Nick said nastily. 'Because you ain't no family to make trouble.'

'The old beezum!'

'Don't you call my mother names.'

'I'll call her what I like and I don't care if you do tell her, because one of these days, I'll tell her mesen.'

Maddie picked up the buckets and marched past him on her way to the Dairy, the stirrings of pity she had begun to feel for this boy gone in an instant.

She was still dreading coming face to face with Frank, but when they all sat down together at the dinner table, he was smiling and, to her astonishment, he actually winked at her and said, 'Enjoy yourself last night, little lady?'

Under the table she felt Michael's foot gently touch

hers, but she dared not risk a glance at him as she said, 'Yes, thank you, Mr Frank.'

Close beside her she heard Harriet's irritating sniff.

Towards the end of October as they were sitting down to supper one evening, Frank said, 'I'll be going to market this week, Michael. I've heard that old man Weatherall is giving up his farm and selling his stock.'

'You're not thinking of buying his cows, Dad, surely? He's a mucky farmer.'

'He used to be a very good farmer, son. But the last few years he's got too old and ill to manage his farm properly. He's no son to carry it on.' There was a note of pride in his voice and yet his tone was tinged with pity for the man who had not been so fortunate as Frank believed himself to be. 'I've heard tell he's giving up all together. His beast are up for sale this week.'

Michael shrugged. 'Never mind what he used to be, Dad. It's what his herd's like now that matters.'

'Well, it's worth a look anyway and they'll be going cheap.'

'Maybe so. But are they a good buy, Dad, or a bad buy?'

'We'll take a look, son. Just a look.'

At the beginning of November, three scrawny looking beast arrived at Few Farm.

'I tried to tell him,' Michael spread his hands as Maddie and Nick stood surveying Frank's purchase. 'But would he listen?'

'Think you know more about cattle than your dad?' Nick said.

Michael shot him a look. 'Well, if he's going to buy beast like these three, then yes, I reckon I do.'

'They'll be all right.' Frank was coming towards them. 'Once we've fattened them up a bit. Take them to the meadow, Maddie.'

'Don't you think we ought to keep them separate from our stock? Just for a few days at least?'

'No, Michael, I don't.' It was the first time Maddie could remember hearing Frank speak sharply to his son. Then he asked a similar question to the one Nick had asked a few moments earlier. 'Don't you trust my judgement?'

'Dad, it's not that, it's just . . .' Michael's voice petered away. 'Oh all right, then. Have it your way.'

'I will. They were a damned good price.'

'They would be,' Michael muttered, but he kept his voice so low now that only Maddie, standing close to him, heard.

'Which field do you want them in, Mr Frank?' Maddie asked quietly. Even with her limited knowledge, she, too, was worried by the sight of the cows. They looked neglected, as if they had not been fed properly for weeks.

Frank jerked his thumb in the direction of the field adjacent to the tulip field. 'South End Meadow, lass.'

'Right. Come on, Ben,' Maddie called and the dog bounded towards her, his pink tongue lolling, his eyes bright and eager. But the cows ignored his excited barking and just continued to stand in the centre of the yard, their heads lowered, not moving an inch.

'Come on, cush, cush,' Maddie said and slapped the nearest one on its rump. She recoiled in horror as she felt the animal's bones through its skin.

Frank was right about one thing, she thought, they certainly needed fattening up.

122

Slowly, almost painfully, the three cows lumbered out of the gate and, with Ben barking at their heels, turned to the left towards the meadow. Maddie looked up as a dark shadow passed over their heads, a flock of starlings wheeled and dived above her head. As she opened the gate and Ben cleverly guided the newcomers into the field to join the other beast, the birds swooped down into the field, some landing on the hind quarters of the cattle, others on the hedges and on the ground. Ben ran about, barking excitedly, so that some of the birds, startled, rose into the air once more. But those perching on the cows' backs, were more daring and cocked their heads to one side to look down upon the dog with cheeky conceit.

Maddie laughed. 'Come on, Ben. Leave them alone. They can't do any harm.' She closed the gate and whistled to the dog, who obeyed her reluctantly. All the way down the lane towards the farm, Ben kept stopping, his tongue hanging out, and glancing back towards the impudent starlings.

It was a week later when, in the mist of early morning, Maddie went to South End Meadow to fetch the cows for milking and she found one of Mr Weatherall's cows lying dead in the middle of the field.

Seventeen

'I told you not to buy old man Weatherall's bloody rubbish.' Michael was blazing as they stood over the dead beast.

'Watch your tongue, boy. I won't have that sort of language.'

'Oh, you won't, won't you? Well, it's enough to make a saint swear and I'm no saint. Who knows what it's died of. It could have brought anything on to our farm that'll infect our whole herd.'

'Do you think I haven't the sense to examine beast thoroughly before I buy? Give me some credit. They were undernourished, I grant you, but that was all.' Even Frank's voice rose to a roar now. 'There was nothing wrong with them.'

Michael thrust his head forward and shouted, 'Well, there is now.'

For a moment they glared at each other and Maddie noticed that Michael clenched and unclenched his hands, but he kept them firmly by his side. Suddenly, the anger seemed to drain out of Frank and his shoulders sagged. He took off his cap, ran his hand through his hair and then replaced his cap.

'What's done's done,' he muttered. 'Let's have a look at it before . . .' His voice petered away as they both squatted down, one on either side of the beast, whilst Maddie stood near the animal's head and watched.

'Mr Frank,' she began tentatively. 'Its tongue's hanging out of its mouth and it looks all sore, sort of blistered.'

'What?'

She pointed and Frank moved to look at the animal's mouth. Michael was looking at the feet.

'There's sores and blisters here too, Dad.' His voice was flat now, sorrowful.

Maddie felt sudden fear as she watched father and son stare at each other, horror on their faces.

'Oh no, lad, not that. Oh please, not that,' Frank whispered hoarsely.

Soberly, Michael said, 'I'm sorry, Dad, but I think it is. It's foot and mouth.'

Frank stood up but his gaze was still on the cow lying at his feet. He drew the back of his hand across his forehead. 'Let's look at the rest of them.'

Rising too, Michael pointed across the field and said, 'Look at that one over there. It's got a trail of saliva hanging from its mouth. That's another sign, isn't it?'

Grimly, Frank agreed.

The three of them moved around the field inspecting the cattle.

'Mr Frank,' Maddie called. 'This one's lame. And – and it's not one of Mr Weatherall's. It's one of yours.'

Frank shook his head and stood in the middle of the field looking for all the world as if he were lost.

Michael and Maddie walked back to him.

'We've got it right enough,' Frank said as they drew near to him.

'What do we do, Dad?'

'We'll have to inform the local vet or the police – or both. Come on, let's go back to the house.'

As they walked down the lane, Maddie slipped her hand into Michael's and gave it a comforting squeeze, not

125

caring, for once, if his father saw them. Michael gripped her hand in return and, even though no words were spoken, she could feel his despair.

When they reached the farmyard, Michael put his head round the cowshed door and called, 'Nick, come into the house a minute.'

The boy appeared. 'Why? Where's the cows? Everything's ready.'

Michael, already walking towards the back door of the house, merely beckoned him. Shrugging, Nick followed.

Inside, Frank sat down at the table, resting his arms on it. 'Get us a cup of tea, lass, would you?' and Maddie, glad to have something to do, picked up the teapot.

Michael, too, sat down at the table, opposite his father. Once more the two exchanged sober glances.

'What is it? What's the matter?' Nick began as his mother came into the room from upstairs. She blinked as she saw everyone sitting there at the time when the milking should be in full swing. Her startled glance came to rest on Frank and she stood very still, waiting to hear the answer to Nick's question.

'One of Weatherall's cows is dead,' Frank began and glanced again at his son as he added heavily, 'and it's got blisters in its mouth and on its feet.'

Harriet gave a cry and her hand fluttered to her mouth. 'Oh no, Frank.' In her agitation she quite forgot the 'Mr' but no one other than Maddie seemed to notice.

Quietly, Maddie placed a cup of tea in front of Frank and then pushed one towards Michael.

Frank spooned sugar into the liquid and stirred it, intent on his action. 'That's it, then. We're finished.'

'No, we're not.' Harriet's voice was shrill. She sat down at the end of the table and leaned towards Frank. 'Why don't you bury it and say nowt? You keep an eye on all the rest and if any of them get it, you can isolate them in the barn and treat them.'

Slowly Frank lifted his head as everyone turned to look at her.

'It's a notifiable disease, Mrs T,' Michael said. 'We can't do that.'

'Who's to know?' Harriet snapped at him, her gaze leaving Frank for a moment. 'We can isolate ourselves too. No one need leave the farm for a while. We've plenty of food . . .'

'We can't do that,' Michael repeated. 'And supposing we did, what about the milk round? People will soon know something was wrong when I don't turn up with their milk every morning and I can hardly supply the locals with milk from a herd that's got foot and mouth.'

'But it's treatable. I've heard of it being done. Way back in '23 there was a case where a big estate got it and they got permission to be isolated. They only lost two or three. If you tell the authorities, Mr Frank, they'll slaughter all your cattle, every last one, and the pigs too, and where's your living to come from then, eh? And they'll probably kill everyone's for several miles around. They'll close the market. You know they will. Think what hardship that'll cause.'

'There's not that many farmers with cattle around here, Mrs T, you know there aren't. It's not a cattle area, so . . .'

'So all the more reason to keep quiet about it. We can keep it contained.'

'That wasn't what I had been going to say,' Michael said.

'Do you want to see your father ruined?'

'Of course not, but . . .'

127

'So who's to know,' Harriet said again, and this time there was a veiled threat in her words, 'unless someone tells 'em?'

Frank stood up and leaned on his knuckles on the table. Looking at Harriet he said, 'I am not going to do anything against the law. We'll notify whoever we have to.' Then he looked towards his son. 'Michael's right. I've only myself to blame. I should have known better than to buy those beast of Weatherall's.'

'We can't be sure how they got it,' Michael said. His anger had died now and already he was prepared to be more understanding. 'I mean, they say it can be carried on the wind or brought by birds . . .'

'Oh!' Maddie could not stop the cry escaping her lips even though she clapped her hand to her mouth. Wide-eyed she stared from one to the other. Now everyone turned to look at her.

'What is it, love?' Frank asked.

Slowly she let her hand fall away from her mouth. 'Oh Mr Frank. The – the day Mr Weatherall's cows arrived and I took them to the field . . .'

'Yes, lass, what about it?'

'There – there was a huge flock of starlings landed in the field. Some even sat on the cows' backs. Ben was barking, trying to frighten them away, but – but . . .' She bit her lip. 'But I brought him away. I – I said they couldn't do any harm. Oh Mr Frank, I didn't know. Ben knew, but I didn't.'

There was a moment's silence and then Frank, even amidst the drama of the moment, actually laughed. He moved and put his arm around her shoulders.

'It's not your fault, love. How many times a day do you think birds land in the field or take a ride on a cow's back when we're not there to shoo them off?'

'I – don't know.'

'Exactly. We can't be there every minute of the day watching over them. If it has been carried by the birds, there's not a thing we could have done about it.'

'Really?' Maddie felt comforted but she still felt very guilty because she had not followed Ben's example and frightened the flock of starlings away.

Frank gave her a quick squeeze, then he sighed. 'Well, I'd better go and get it over with.'

'If you're going down to the phone box in the village, Dad, don't forget to disinfect your boots before you go. There's some in the barn, I'll get it for you.'

As the three menfolk left the house, Harriet stepped towards Maddie and gripped her arm. 'You! I might have known you'd have had a hand in all this. You've brought nothing but trouble to this house from the moment you stepped into it.'

Eighteen

All Frank's cattle and his two pigs had been slaughtered and their carcasses burnt. That day had been heartbreaking for everyone on Few Farm. Even the slaughterman who came to carry out the operation did so in silence, the sympathy on his face plain to see. Then the dead cattle were piled in the middle of South End Meadow. Michael stacked bales of straw, wood and old tyres around them and in amongst them and doused the whole lot in diesel. The fire burned for two days and at the end of it Michael and Nick had to dig a hole as deep as they could to bury the ashes and then fill it in again.

Since then, the family had been confined to the farm and hollows had been dug in the lane on the approaches to the farm and filled with disinfectant.

'It's like having the plague,' Michael muttered, leaning against the five-barred gate leading into the farmyard, which had been closed and padlocked. For several days after they had made the awful discovery, Nick had sat on top of the gate, Frank's shotgun across his knees as a warning to inquisitive sightseers. From time to time they had heard a bang as he took a pot-shot at birds flying over the farm.

'I don't know what good he thinks he's doing,' Michael had muttered.

Maddie had sighed. 'I think he's just taking his anger and frustration out on them.'

'Well, I think he's venting his anger in the wrong direction. He should shoot old man Weatherall!'

Maddie had said no more. She knew Michael didn't really mean what he said but the fact that the thought even came into his mind, never mind the words actually passing his lips, told her the depth of his bitterness.

Now Maddie climbed up and sat on the topmost bar of the gate. 'I bet you miss your milk round, don't you?'

'Yeah, I do. Funny, I always used to moan about having to get up so early seven days a week but now I can't go, I'd love to be out there on the cart meeting all the old dears bringing out their milk cans.'

'You will again,' Maddie said, touching his shoulder. 'Soon.'

'We could restock but Dad doesn't seem to have the heart now.'

'Well then, when the authorities give permission, you'll have to be the one to do it,' Maddie said determinedly.

Michael smiled up at her. It was the first time she had seen him smile since their dreadful discovery, but even now it was only fleeting as he added worriedly, 'I really don't know what to do. The infection thrives in the cold, you know, and I don't reckon even the regulations allow long enough to let the land get really clear of it.'

'But no one else round here has got it, have they?'

'Not that I've heard. The chap from the Ministry or the Council or wherever he was from, congratulated us on our prompt action and said we'd probably saved the whole area from an epidemic.'

They glanced at each other, remembering Harriet's suggestion.

They heard the splashing of water and Maddie narrowed her eyes to look down the lane. 'There's somebody coming.'

131

'Really? Can you see who it is?'

'It's Jenny!' Maddie cried in delight and was about to jump down into the lane when Michael caught hold of her.

'No. You mustn't. We mustn't go out of the yard. She can come to the gate, but she can't come in.'

'I'm sorry. I forgot,' Maddie said at once.

Michael remained standing with one arm around Maddie's waist, making no move to remove his hold on her.

'Maddie!' Jenny called and waved as she clumped along the lane in oversize Wellington boots. 'Are you all right? All of you?'

Panting a little, she stood a few feet from them and read the large notice saying 'FOOT AND MOUTH PRECAUTION – KEEP OUT'. Jen pulled a face but then gave a little nod, understanding at once that she must stay in the lane.

'Where's Nick? Is he all right?' Jenny's glance went beyond them to search the yard.

'He's about somewhere.' He raised his voice and bellowed, 'Nick? You there, Nick? Young lady to see you.'

But the yard was empty and silent and Michael made no effort to move away to find him.

'Never mind. I'll see him another time, maybe?' Jenny said. 'Do you want anything bringing from the village if you can't go out?'

'We're fine, Jenny,' Michael said, 'but it's lovely to see you.'

'I got permission to come,' Jenny said, proud of her own initiative. 'I asked at the police station and the man there said as long as I got some boots and was sure to wash them well in the disinfectant.' She gestured back towards the hollow through which she had just splashed. 'Mrs Grange lent me these boots.'

'Mrs Grange? Her at the corner shop in the village?' Michael said.

'That's right.' Jenny was beaming now. 'That's what I've come to tell you, Maddie. I've got a job there and – best of all – I live in.'

'Oh Jen. I'm so glad. Oh I want to hug you, but I mustn't.'

The younger girl's face clouded. 'Is it that bad? I mean, I can't catch it, can I?'

'Well, there is a human form of it, but it's usually harmless,' Michael said. 'It's more to prevent you carrying it on your clothes to other places, see?'

The girl nodded.

'Tell me more about Mrs Grange and how you got the job. Did Mrs Potter arrange it?'

Jenny looked happier than Maddie could ever remember having seen her. 'No, I got it for myself. She'd taken me to a few places. You remember about the flower packing?'

Maddie nodded.

'Well, there were one or two other places, but always I was too small, not old enough or not strong enough.' Jenny frowned. 'D'you know, Maddie, it was almost as if she was taking me for jobs where she really knew I hadn't a chance of getting them.'

'She probably did, Jen. I wouldn't put anything past Mrs Potter.'

'But why? I mean, she always wants to be rid of us all as soon as we're old enough.'

'Not everybody. She keeps her chosen few on as staff. She kept Peggy on, didn't she? And Winifred. And it looks to me as if she'd her eye on you for the vacancy as kitchen maid.'

'But I wasn't one of her chosen ones.'

Maddie grinned. 'Not when you were with me, you weren't. But maybe since I left . . .' She left the words unspoken but they both knew that it had always been Maddie who had been the ringleader, the troublemaker. Jenny, on her own, was biddable and docile. Just the sort that Mrs Potter liked for her skivvies.

'Well,' Jenny puffed out her chest. 'I thought about what you said and decided there was no way I was going to stay there, so after school instead of going straight home, I started asking round a bit in the village to see if there were any jobs going and, guess what?' She clapped her hands together. 'When I went into the corner shop and asked Mrs Grange if she knew of anyone who might be looking for someone she said, "Well, now, in't that funny,"' Jenny mimicked Mrs Grange's broad Lincolnshire dialect perfectly. '"I were just thinking I'd like to get mesen a lass to help in the shop, like."'

Maddie and Michael clutched at each other, laughing at Jenny's clowning. 'Anyway,' the girl went on in her normal voice. 'I went several times to chat to her and last week I told Mrs Potter and moved my things out of the Home and into a lovely little room all of my own in Mrs Grange's place above the shop. There's pretty curtains at the window and even a bit of carpet on the floor. A comfy bed and a chest of drawers for my things. Not that I've got many, but I've got Miss Amelia sitting on the top of the chest.'

Michael laughed. 'Miss Amelia?'

Jenny nodded. 'The doll that Nick won at the fair. Maddie gave it to me and I called it Miss Amelia because we'd seen her that day in the car. You remember?'

'Oh, yes. So we did.'

'What did Mrs Potter say?' Maddie asked.

Jenny pulled a comical face. 'She wasn't very pleased. Said why did I want to leave when she had a nice little job all sorted out for me in the kitchen?'

'And?'

'And what?'

'What did you tell her?'

'Oh, well, I daren't tell her the truth. I mean, I couldn't tell her that I didn't want to stay there all my life, could I?'

'I would have done.'

'Well, yes,' Jenny glanced down, 'but I didn't like to.'

'I expect you're too nice to hurt the old girl's feelings. Is that it, Jenny?' Michael said and Maddie glared down at him.

'I suppose you mean, I'm not "too nice" then?'

Michael looked up at her but before he could answer, Jenny blurted out, 'No, it's not that. I'm just too scared, that's all.'

'But you weren't too scared to get out and find yourself a job. Well done, little Jenny, I say,' Michael smiled at her.

Maddie pushed Michael's arm away and jumped down from the gate. 'We'd better go in. It's nearly tea-time. 'Bye, Jen. You'd better not come again, though. I'll see you when we're let out.'

Then she turned and marched across the yard without a backward glance.

She heard Jenny's plaintive voice. 'But Maddie, it'll soon be Christmas. I'll see you at Christmas, won't I?'

She did not turn nor answer her even though she could feel their eyes on her. Jenny's puzzled and hurt, and Michael . . . Well she dare not think about the way Michael might be looking at her.

135

Nineteen

Christmas was a miserable affair. Although they were no longer confined to the farm, they were still asked to take meticulous precautions and none of them seemed inclined to leave it. Not even Michael wanted to go into the village to the pub or to a dance.

'They'll only start asking questions,' he told Maddie. 'And I don't want to talk about it. We've got to look forward now and plan what we're going to do.'

'Yes, but what are we going to do? Your dad won't even talk about it.'

'Well, he'll have to soon because we can't survive on a couple of acres of wheat and a few hens' eggs.'

On Boxing Day morning, Maddie asked, 'Mr Frank, could I ask Jenny to tea today, please?'

'Of course you can, love.'

'Oh aye,' Harriet put in at once. 'Another mouth to feed when we've scarcely enough for ourselves.'

'I'll go and see her this afternoon,' Maddie said, as usual ignoring the housekeeper. She was anxious to make amends for the way she had treated Jenny the last time she saw her. Since the day she had stood outside the gate, Jenny – just as Maddie had told her – had not visited the farm again.

She loved Jenny dearly, she always had done, so why

was it, she asked herself, that the moment Michael was even just nice to the younger girl, did she feel this awful jealousy, so acutely that made her act unkindly towards Jenny? It wasn't Jenny's fault. She didn't play up to Michael or flirt with him. In fact, she always seemed a little in awe of him. So how could she, Maddie, be so horrible? Jenny was like a sister. Hadn't they always said so? So how . . .? Maddie sighed. Not ever having lived in a proper family, she did not know how real sisters carried on. Perhaps, sometimes, even real sisters were jealous of each other. Especially if one was pretty and vulnerable; the sort that men liked to protect. And she didn't blame Michael, not at all. He was just being kind to the young girl, she knew, probably for her sake too. He knew that Jenny was the closest Maddie had to real family and he wanted to make her welcome, so why . . .?

Maddie sighed and shook her head, angry with herself. 'Just don't do it any more,' she told herself sharply as she put on her coat and left the house to walk to the village.

It seemed a long time since she had been into Mrs Grange's corner shop. The bell clanged as she opened the door and she stepped into the fascinating world of the shop that sold everything from sweets in glass jars that lined one shelf, fruit drops and aniseed balls, through jars of Bovril, packets of Quaker Oats with the picture of a man in Quaker dress on the packet, tinned tongue and salmon and Heinz beans to packets of Lux soap flakes. In the centre of the counter in pride of place stood an ornate cash register showing that the last customer's purchases had cost one pound four shillings and eleven pence ha'penny. Sacks of potatoes stood on the floor and along one counter was a line of second-hand books. Mrs Grange ran a lending library at one penny a loan.

There was a movement in the room at the back of the

shop and Jenny appeared from behind the brown curtain across the doorway.

'Maddie, oh Maddie.' She rushed round the counter and flung herself against Maddie, who hugged her tightly.

'Now then, you're the little lass from Few Farm, aren't you?'

Maddie looked up to see a woman had now appeared from the back room, dressed in a navy-blue skirt, a floral striped blouse with a brooch at the neck and a cardigan. She was small and dumpy but she smiled in welcome, her eyes bright behind round spectacles. Strangely, it seemed to Maddie, she wore a navy-blue felt hat, even indoors.

'This is my friend Maddie, Mrs Grange.'

The woman shook her head sadly. 'Aw lass, I'm real sorry to hear the trouble poor Mr Brackenbury's had. And him such a good man, too.' She shook her head. 'It dun't seem fair.'

'Well, we've been "let out" now so he can start to get back to normal.'

The woman shook her head. 'Not so easy, lass, is it? We're lucky it didn't spread, though. No one else has got it as I've heard.' She chuckled. 'And I'd be the first to know.'

Maddie smiled as Mrs Grange chattered on. 'Everyone's very thankful that Mr Brackenbury was so honest. You know, telling the authorities straight away, like. Some farmers . . .', she tapped the side of her nose, 'might have been tempted to keep it quiet and treat them theirsens.' She nodded knowingly. 'It's been done 'afore.'

Maddie swallowed.

'But Frank Brackenbury's a good man. He's proved that and it's not the first time, let me tell you.' Mrs Grange wagged her finger at Maddie. 'Oh, there's a lot I could tell you about Frank Brackenbury, if I'd a mind.'

'You mean, he's had foot and mouth before?'

'No, no, lass, not that. I didn't mean that. I meant some of the things he's done in his time has shown what a good man he is. Oh yes, I could tell you a thing or two.'

Maddie almost bit off the end of her tongue to stop her demanding at once, What things? But she managed to curb her curiosity. No doubt, she told herself, Jenny would soon hear everything, living with the local mine of information and she would always tell her best friend.

The shop bell clanged again as a customer stepped in and as Mrs Grange moved to serve her, Jenny whispered, 'How are you all? How's Nick and Michael?'

'They're all right, but everyone's very fed up. Poor Mr Frank doesn't seem to have the heart to get going again. And nobody else, not even Michael, can do anything without his approval.'

'Oh dear. So you've not had a very good Christmas?'

Maddie pulled a face. 'Not really. What about you? What did you do yesterday?'

'Mrs Grange went to her sister's the other side of the village and took me with her. Wasn't that kind?'

'Is the shop open all day today?'

'No. Only for the morning. Just to let people get their milk. Now Michael can't deliver they're coming here for it.'

'So, are you doing anything this afternoon, then?'

Jenny shook her head.

'Would you like to come to the farm for tea?'

Jenny's eyes lit up. 'Ooh yes, please, Maddie. Will Nick be there too?'

Maddie laughed. 'What's all these questions about Nick? You sweet on him?'

The girl was blushing. ''Course not. He's just – well – shy, isn't he? Like me. I mean . . .' The colour in her face deepened. 'I mean, Michael's lovely. So good-looking and – and confident. But he'd never look at someone like me. Besides . . .' Now she smiled coyly at Maddie. 'You like him, don't you?'

'Ssh.' Maddie glanced around. 'Not so loud.'

Jenny's voice dropped to a whisper. 'Does he like you?'

Maddie shrugged. 'Well . . .'

'Yes, he does.' The young girl nudged her. 'I could see last time I came. He'd got his arm round you. And the way he looked at you. I wish Nick would look at me like that.'

Maddie grinned and returned the playful nudge. She felt better now. At least Jenny had not set her sights on Michael. As far as she was concerned, Jenny could have the moody Nick and welcome to him.

'I'll see what I can do for you.'

When Jenny arrived at the farm later that afternoon, she shyly handed out a quarter of Butter Drops to everyone.

'You shouldn't have done that, love,' Frank said. 'It's very kind of you.'

'It's kind of you to have me here.'

'You'd have done better to have brought us a quarter of tea or a bag of sugar,' Harriet said tartly.

'Oh I'm sorry. I could have done, Mrs Trowbridge. I'll bring some next time.'

'No need, love,' Frank put in swiftly. 'Mrs Trowbridge is only teasing, aren't you, Harriet?'

Maddie knew that the housekeeper never teased or joked but the look that Frank now gave her forced the woman to stretch a smile on her mouth and say, 'Of course, Mr Frank.'

But as she turned away, Maddie heard the familiar sniff.

Michael had already popped one of the round brown sweets into his mouth. 'Mmm, thank you, Jen.' He winked at her but Maddie saw that Jenny's eyes were on Nick. He flicked the hair out of his eyes and muttered, 'Thanks.' Then he smiled at her and seeing it, Maddie marvelled once again at the change in the boy's appearance.

'What shall we do 'til tea time? It's too cold to go out.'

'I'll beat you all at Ludo,' Michael offered.

Nick's smile widened to a grin. 'No, you won't. I beat you last time.'

He hurried to the sideboard to get out the coloured board and the tiddlywinks that acted as each person's marker.

'Where's the dice?'

'Should be in the box.'

'Oh yes, here it is.'

For the next hour, the four sat round the table playing Ludo, Nick becoming more and more animated as he began to win whilst Maddie and Michael, sitting close to each other, held hands beneath the table between their turns.

And then, when Jenny began to catch up to Nick who could not throw the final number he needed to win, the game became noisier and noisier until Harriet appeared in the doorway. 'That's enough. I can hear you out in the kitchen. You must be giving Mr Frank a headache.'

'They're all right, Harriet,' came Frank's voice from his deep armchair near the fire. 'Let them have a bit of fun. There's not been much in this house this Christmas.'

'Well, I want the table now, if we're to have any tea today.'

'Three more goes each, then,' Michael said, 'and the one who's got the most counters home has won.'

Ten minutes later Jenny was shouting gleefully, 'That's my last counter home. I've won, I've won.'

Harriet came to stand at the end of the table, waiting with the white cloth in her hands to spread it. 'I could do with some help in the kitchen now, girl,' she said to Maddie.

'Can I help?' Jenny offered.

'No, no. You're a guest,' Michael said before the house-keeper could answer. 'Come on, I'll show you the piano in the front room. We usually light the fire in there at Christmas and play games, but this year, well . . .'

He said no more. There was no need to say that this year the family had had to cut expenses wherever they could.

As Maddie moved between kitchen and living room laying the table, she heard the murmur of voices from the best room. Then she heard the tinkle of the piano as Michael demonstrated the sound of the instrument to their guest.

He's never once shown me the piano, Maddie thought. Was there, after all, some truth in what Nick said about Michael?

Swiftly, she tried to quell the rising resentment. Remember, she chided herself, Jen's your sister – or as good as. No more jealousy. Besides, it isn't Michael she likes, it's Nick.

But who, the little voice inside her would not be silenced, liked Jenny? Nick – or Michael?

Twenty

The first snowfall came on the sixth of January, but Jenny still plodded from the village out to the farm to tell them, 'Mrs Grange says her next allocation of Jaffa oranges will be coming soon. It'll be one pound per ration book.' Shyly, she slid a blue bag of sugar onto the table and glanced sideways at the housekeeper.

'That's very kind of you,' Harriet said as she picked it up. 'A lot more use than sweets.'

Frank shook his head as if despairing of Harriet ever giving gracious and heartfelt thanks. From his chair he held out his hand, inviting Jenny towards him. He seemed to do little nowadays except sit by the fire.

'Will you be getting some more cows soon, Mr Frank?' the girl asked as she sat on the hearthrug at his feet and held her cold hands out towards the glowing coals in the range.

'I don't know, lass. We haven't had clearance from the authorities yet. Three months, they reckon, before we can restock.' He sighed heavily. 'But I don't know even then.'

'What we need is a good hot spell,' Michael remarked. 'But by the look of it,' he nodded towards the window and the heavy grey clouds beyond, laden with the threat of more snow, 'we won't get that for a long time yet.'

At the beginning of February, the blizzards began in earnest. It began like fine white dust, floating through the air, outlining the trees and coating the ground in a fluffy white blanket. Then the flakes became bigger and came thick and fast until it was impossible to see more than a few feet ahead. Soon, hedges, lanes and roadways were lost and only the tallest trees stuck up out of the snow.

'We've no water,' Harriet announced. 'The pipes must be frozen.'

'Maybe it's frozen in the tank in the roof. And I doubt we'll be able to pump any more up out of the well,' Michael said whose job it was to keep the household supplied with water.

'And the snow's banked to the top of the back door,' Harriet complained. 'I can't even get out this morning.'

'We'll come dig you out, Mrs T, if you get stuck in a drift.'

'I don't know what you're so cheerful about, Master Michael. You'd do better to get a shovel and start clearing some of it.'

'Aye, aye, Cap'n.' Michael saluted her smartly and then seeing that the housekeeper was really frightened by the atrocious weather, he put his arm about her shoulders. 'Come on, Mrs T, we'll sort it out. Nick and I will clear the snow in the yard and . . .'

'Have you seen it out there?' her voice rose shrilly. 'We're going to be cut off. Trapped out here. With no water and no heat and soon, no food.'

'We'll have plenty of heat. There's still some coal in the shed and plenty of wood in the barn. And I'll start the generator up today. We'll be all right.'

It seemed strange to Maddie that it should be the young man comforting the older woman, but her heart warmed to Michael for his gentle understanding.

'We've no milk or butter. No bread.' Harriet was determined to be pessimistic.

'We've potatoes in the barn and eggs.'

'I found three of the hens dead yesterday morning. From the cold, I expect.'

'I'll check the boiler.' Again it was Michael taking the lead. 'But,' he was saying, a cheeky smile twitching at the corners of his mouth, 'we could always rig up a pen in the wash-house and bring them where it's warmer.'

'Bring them into the house?'

'Better that than they all die of the cold, Mrs T.'

'Oh Michael,' Frank sank down wearily into his chair in front of the fire, 'it's a good job you're here. I don't know what we'd do without you.'

Michael turned and winked at Maddie. 'Come on, young'un. You can help too, but don't fall into a snowdrift or we'll never find you.'

The hardest part was digging their way out of the back door, but once they had cleared the snow that had drifted and piled up against the door and they could close it behind them, they stood a moment to rest, their breath like steam in the cold air.

'We'll make a pathway to the barn and then the generator shed and the hen-house,' Michael decided.

'It's like pictures you see of the North Pole,' Maddie murmured, her glance scanning the countryside.

Nick leaned on his shovel. 'It looks completely different, doesn't it? It's changed the landscape. I mean, if you didn't know where the road was and the fields and dykes, you couldn't find them.'

'That's the dangerous bit,' Michael said. 'Going through the ice into a dyke or a drain. But at least I reckon we could dig our way as far as the village, if need be, without too much trouble.'

'I wonder,' Maddie murmured as she picked up her own shovel once more, 'how Jenny is?'

145

'She'll be all right,' Nick said. 'She's about the only one who is, surrounded by all that food in the shop.'

But Michael thought otherwise. 'Not for long, she won't be. It's the only place the villagers will be able to get to for a while. The roads to Wellandon will be blocked. Mrs Grange's shop will soon be sold out.'

'Do you think so?'

'I know so, so if we want to get stocked up with a few supplies, we'd better get digging!'

'Dad, if you don't come out and see to the batteries, we're going to be without electricity an' all. You ought to check the voltage and the specific gravity.'

Frank waved him away. 'You see to it, Michael. You know what to do now.'

'No, I don't. Not really. Come on, Dad. Please. And we could use a little help with the digging. Maddie's about dead on her feet.'

It was the third day since they had started trying to dig their way to the village shop and already it was looking like a hopeless task. Fresh falls of snow filled in the pathway they had made and the lane resembled a glacial ravine.

Frank raised his head and looked towards her.

'I'm all right,' Maddie tried to smile, but the weariness was swamping her in waves.

Frank levered himself out of his chair. 'What am I thinking of? Sitting here, feeling sorry for myself when this lass is almost passing out. Why did you let me sit here, Michael?' He went towards the kitchen, still muttering to himself.

Maddie almost laughed out loud at the comical look on

Michael's face. He said nothing but grinned at her and pointed to the chair his father had just vacated. 'Now it's your turn, young'un, to have a rest.' As she opened her mouth to protest, he added, 'Go on. Do as you're told, for once. And I'll ask Mrs T to bring you a hot drink with a drop of whisky in it. You're not to do another thing all day. You hear?'

Maddie nodded. She had not even the strength left to argue.

'Oh, it's so cold. I don't think I'll ever feel warm again,' Harriet was still grumbling. These days she wore a thick cardigan over her blouse, skirt and the ever-present paisley apron. She continually pushed her hands up the opposite sleeve, not caring if she stretched the garment out of shape in her efforts to beat the cold.

Even Maddie, hardened throughout her childhood to the Spartan conditions at the Home, huddled near the fire in the range and stayed up as late as she could, putting off for as long as possible going to her ice-cold bedroom.

'That's the last of the coal, Mrs T,' Michael said, setting the brass coal scuttle at the side of the range. 'We're down to whatever wood we can find now. There's not as much in the barn as I thought.'

'There's always the wood pile behind the barn,' Nick suggested.

'Oh aye,' Michael countered. 'Under six foot of snow. You volunteering to dig it out? No, I thought not. Besides, it'll be too wet to burn decently. It'd smoke us out.'

'Maybe we could bring some in and dry it out a bit,' Nick said, but his suggestion lacked enthusiasm. It was as if the cold had seeped into their bones and sapped them of

147

all strength and vigour. With long faces they all gazed at the fire, wondering just how much longer they would be able to enjoy its heat.

'I'd have a good bake-up tomorrow, if I could,' Harriet murmured, 'but I've already run out of flour.'

'At least we've still got electricity. I bet a lot of folks have got power cuts,' Michael said.

Frank cleared his throat. 'Er, I've been meaning to tell you. We're running very low on diesel. I won't be able to run the engine many more times.'

Now there was silence in the room as they all faced the prospect of being marooned amidst the frozen, wind-swept white landscape, totally isolated from the rest of civilization.

The following morning Michael said, 'I'm going to try to get to the village today. At least I'll get some news, even if there's no supplies to be had.'

'You'll never get there,' Nick said scathingly. 'It's impossible.'

Calmly, Michael said, 'I'm not going to try to *dig* my way there. I'm going to make myself a pair of skis.'

'Skis?'

Michael grinned. 'That's what I said. I know it's no good trying to wade through it, either. It's too deep, but if I get some long, narrow boards, the lightest I can find and strap them to my feet . . .'

'That won't work,' Nick said.

'Why not?' At once Maddie defended Michael's idea.

'Skis have to curve up a bit at the front, don't they? Otherwise they'll just dig into the snow. You'd be better with some flat boards on your feet, like snowshoes.'

Michael shook his head. 'Take too long. I'd have to plod along so slowly with those. I want something where I can glide over the surface of the snow.' He gestured with the flat of his hand.

'A strip of metal would be better,' Nick suggested, 'because you could bend the end up then.'

'You're right, Nick.'

There was silence whilst the three of them thought hard.

'Isn't there a sheet of metal in the hay shed?' Despite the gravity of their present situation, Maddie smiled at Michael. 'I've heard it rattling in the wind.'

'You can't use that,' Nick began, 'it's blocking up a hole . . .'

'Oh yes, I can. One more hole in that shed won't matter.'

For the rest of the day there was a lot of banging and not a little swearing whilst Michael cut and shaped a rough pair of skis.

'You'll need some poles,' Maddie joined in excitedly, now seeing Michael's idea really taking shape. 'I don't know what they call them, but you know . . .' She clenched her hands and held out her arms as if holding a skier's pole in each hand. 'And you need a round circle near the bottom, but leaving a spike at the end to drive into the snow. I've seen pictures.'

Michael was nodding. 'See what you can find for me, young'un.'

By the time they'd finished, it was too late for Michael to go but the following morning Maddie was standing near the gate, the snow piled up on either side of her, watching as Michael set off on his homemade skis towards the village.

'You will be careful?' she called after him anxiously. 'Mind the dykes.'

'Don't worry, young'un. I'll be back.'

But when dusk fell in the late afternoon and Michael had not returned, the whole household became anxious.

Twenty-One

'You two go to bed. Mr Frank and I will wait up for him.'

'I'm not going until Michael's safely home,' Maddie said, her steady gaze never leaving Harriet's face. She had to admit that even the housekeeper was agitated and her order to Maddie and Nick had lacked its usual vigour. Whatever Harriet felt about her, Maddie, there could be no doubt in anyone's mind that she was fond of Michael. Very fond. It showed in the way she kept glancing at the clock above the mantelpiece and going to the kitchen window every few minutes to press her face close to the cold glass and stare out into the black night, the only light from the moon shining on the snow.

'Maybe he's stopped in the village. With Mrs Grange and Jenny at the shop,' Frank put in, with a sound faith in Michael's common sense. 'Surely, wherever he is, he wouldn't be trying to get home again at this time of night?'

'Maybe he's stayed at Susan's.' Nick's remark sounded casual and Maddie might have accepted it as such if she hadn't noticed his quick, sly glance at her as he spoke.

But it was Harriet who voiced the sharp question. 'Susan? Who's Susan?'

'Oh . . .' Nick shrugged and said airily, 'Just one of his girlfriends in the village. Maybe that's why he went in the first place. All that talk about going for supplies was just that. Talk. I reckon he was missing his girlfriend.' He paused a moment and then added, with even more pointed emphasis on the plural, 'Or girlfriends.'

Maddie could not stop the words from bursting out. 'Michael wouldn't do that.' As three pairs of eyes turned to stare at her, she felt herself blushing but muttered again defiantly, 'Well, he wouldn't.'

'Of course he wouldn't, love,' Frank said. 'You're right. He wouldn't worry us this way. Not deliberately.'

Maddie saw Nick open his mouth to speak, but then he closed it again thinking better of whatever he had been going to say.

'I still think you young ones would be better in bed,' Harriet murmured again, as she moved once more to look out of the window.

'Let them stay if they want to.' Frank sighed heavily. 'Besides, there's nothing they have to get up early for in the morning, is there? Not now.'

'We should go out and look for him,' Maddie said.

Frank shook his head firmly. 'No. Not in the dark. It would be too dangerous. There's no point in all of us getting . . .' He stopped suddenly, biting back the words and looked at Maddie. Each saw the dread in the other's eyes.

Maddie took a deep breath. 'Mrs Trowbridge,' she called. 'Come and sit down by the fire. I'll make us all some cocoa . . .'

The woman came back into the room, her hands pushed up the sleeves of her cardigan, her shoulders hunched against the cold.

'We've no milk.'

'Then I'll heat some water and make us some Horlicks. At least Michael managed to get the tap running again yesterday.'

A few minutes later, as she was handing round the

hot drinks, Maddie thought she heard a noise. She froze, her hand holding the mug outstretched towards Harriet suspended in mid-air. 'Listen. Did you hear anything? I thought I heard a noise . . .'

Then they all heard Ben barking. She thrust the mug at Harriet and now ran herself to peer out of the window. With a joyous shout, she cried, 'He's here. He's back,' and pulled open the kitchen door. Ben, allowed to sleep in the wash-house since the blizzards had begun, was scratching at the back door. As Maddie opened it, a flurry of snow swirled into the wash-house and Michael, looking more like a snowman come to life, was standing on the threshold stamping his feet and trying to shake off the snow.

'Oh come in, come in, do!' Maddie tried to grasp hold of him and pull him inside. 'We've been worried sick. Where have you been? Are you all right?'

The others were crowding behind her now, all firing questions at him.

'We thought you'd got lost.'

'How could you worry us so?'

'Wait a minute, wait a minute . . .' Michael was still not stepping inside but tugging at something behind him.

'Get down, you silly dog,' he said, but it was said with affection as Ben leapt up at him, barking excitedly. 'Nick, give us a hand, will you? I'm dead beat.'

Then they saw that Michael was pulling a sledge behind him loaded with sacks covered with a tarpaulin.

They pulled it into the wash-house and finally closed the door against the cold night. Michael leant against it, panting heavily. 'I'm – sorry,' he gasped. 'I didn't think it would take me so long . . .'

Suddenly his legs buckled beneath him and he slid down into an ungainly sitting position, still with all his outdoor clothes on and covered with snow.

'Here, son, let us help you. You must be exhausted.' Frank, Harriet and Maddie were all reaching towards him now, pulling him up, helping him out of his heavy coat and boots and half-carrying, half-pushing him towards the fire in the living room.

Harriet, her own discomfort forgotten, bustled about her kitchen, heating soup and setting the kettle to boil.

Only Nick stood aloof, just watching.

Michael sat in his father's chair, leant back and closed his eyes. 'I'm sorry, Dad. I didn't mean to worry you. I got to the village and there's hardly anything left in the way of provisions. You should see poor Mrs Grange's shop. I've never seen it looking so bare. So, I pressed on to the town.'

'To Wellandon? You went all the way to Wellandon? In this lot?'

Michael nodded. 'I know. It was stupid of me, I suppose. But at least . . .' He raised his head now and grinned, even though there were dark shadows of exhaustion beneath his eyes. 'I got us a bag of coal, some flour, milk and butter for Mrs T and even – a gallon tin of diesel for the engine.'

Frank put his hand on his son's shoulder. 'Oh Michael . . .' But he could say no more, for his throat was choked with emotion.

'Here, out of the way, Mr Frank, let the boy have this soup . . .' Harriet was her old self once more. 'And you two . . .' She turned towards Maddie and Nick. 'Bed.'

For once Maddie said meekly, 'Yes, Mrs Trowbridge,' and turned away to do as she was told, so thankful to have Michael safely home again that at this moment she would have done anything at all that the housekeeper asked her.

As they went upstairs to their rooms, Nick muttered, 'I

154

still reckon he's been with that Susan in Eastmere. It wouldn't take him the whole day and half the night to get to Wellandon and back.'

As she opened her bedroom door, Maddie turned and glared at him before she slammed the door in his face.

The following morning over breakfast – later than usual now there was no milking to be done – Michael told them about his treacherous journey.

'I was fine going from here to Eastmere because I know the road so well, but it wasn't quite so easy from there to Wellandon.'

'Haven't they cleared the road at all?' Frank asked.

'They've tried, but as fast as they've cleared it another snowfall has blocked it again.' He grinned at Nick and Maddie. 'Just like when we tried to dig a way along our lane.'

'You did well to get all you did,' Harriet was smiling at him, her hero of the hour. She placed a plate of bacon, eggs, fried bread and sausage before him. 'That's the last of the eggs. The hens have stopped laying, but you've earned it.'

'How are things in the town? Are they running short of supplies?'

Michael, his mouth full, shook his head. 'Not really. There's talk of supplies being dropped by plane to outlying farms that are cut off if they put something out in the snow that will show up. We could try that if it goes on much longer.'

'Oh surely we'll have a thaw soon.'

Michael's face sobered. 'There's going to be even more trouble when we do. When this lot melts, the river's never going to cope with the volume of water.'

There was silence around the table until Frank said, 'There's going to be floods, you mean?'

As Michael nodded, Frank let out a low groan of final defeat.

When the thaw started, Michael's foreboding came true.

'What are we going to do? First, foot and mouth and now this. We're ruined.' Frank had taken to his chair by the range once more. He sat with his elbows on the chair arms and dropped his head into his hands.

Michael stood on the peg rug in front of him. 'Come on, Dad, don't give up. At least the water hasn't come into the house, nor even the outbuildings. We've not got it as bad as some poor folks, 'specially in the town. They've been sandbagging the banks of the river, but they're fighting a losing battle because some of the streets are lower than the river level. Their homes are in danger of being flooded, Dad. And south of the town, they say it's much worse.'

The area Michael referred to was low, flat fenland that regularly flooded when the swollen Welland overflowed its banks.

'I know. I know there's a lot worse off than us, but . . . Oh it's just – everything. I don't even think it'll be worth trying to plant crops, the land will be so water-logged.'

'We can get a new herd. Start again.'

Frank shook his head helplessly. 'What's the use?'

Michael glanced at Maddie and then back to his father. He tried again. 'Come on, Dad, surely you've received clearance from the authorities, haven't you?'

Frank's only reply was a disconsolate shrug.

'But there must be something in all that paperwork you've been getting to say we can restock by now?'

'I don't know, lad. I haven't had the heart to read it. Just – just the instructions for what we had to do to deal with the outbreak . . .' His husky voice petered out.

Frank Brackenbury was a broken man. His years of struggle to make a meagre living had ended in defeat. All because of a disease and now the worst winter he could remember. Something he couldn't have foreseen, couldn't deal with and didn't know how to fight.

'We'll have lost the milk round anyway after all this time. Once folks find they can get their milk elsewhere, they're not going to come back to us, are they? Not just out of loyalty.'

Michael forced a laugh. 'I'm sure all my old dears would be delighted to have their handsome milkman back again.'

But Frank could not even raise a smile.

'Well, if you don't want to restock with beast,' Michael was trying his best to be enthusiastic, 'how about we use all the land for crops of some sort? Plough up the meadows. What about extending our acreage of potatoes or caulis?'

The man shook his head. 'I don't know. I think we'd have to get Sir Peter's approval to do that. To change the use of his land. And I don't even know if there are any sort of regulations about growing foodstuff on land that has been infected with the foot and mouth.'

'We can find that out one way or the other.' Michael was refusing to be defeated.

Maddie closed her eyes for a moment against the distress on Frank's face, against the worry creasing Michael's handsome features. The picture that came suddenly into her mind's eye made her reel with the excitement of it. The sheer, blinding beauty and the simplicity of it made her heart miss a beat and then thud loudly in her chest. She swayed and reached out for the edge of the table to steady herself.

'Maddie. What is it? What's the matter?' Michael's voice was full of concern as he caught hold of her arm to steady her.

Her eyes flew open. 'Nothing. At least . . .' She moved to Frank's side and touched his shoulder. 'Mr Frank, I've got an idea.'

The man looked up slowly, but before he could speak Harriet's shrill voice sounded as she came into the room from the kitchen. It was obvious she had been listening to every word that had been said. 'You? Got an idea? And how do you think a chit of a girl like you is going to come up with an idea if a man like Mr Frank can't . . .?'

Maddie felt Frank watching her closely. She knew he could see the fire in her eyes, her lips parted as if bursting to tell her thoughts. His quiet voice stilled the house-keeper's tongue. 'Let's at least hear what the lass has to say, Harriet.'

Maddie took a deep breath. 'Why don't you grow tulips, Mr Frank? The land must be right, because Mr Randall's fields are right next to your meadow.' Again in her mind's eye was the rainbow field that she had so often stood to admire.

'Flowers!' Mrs Trowbridge spat dismissively. 'What would a man like Mr Frank, a farmer born and bred, want with flowers, girl?'

'No, wait a minute. She might have got something, Dad.' There was excitement in Michael's voice too now. 'There would be nothing to stop us using the ground for bulbs, surely?'

Maddie's smile widened. 'You don't eat tulips, Mr Frank. Surely, they wouldn't come under any restrictions, would they?'

Frank stared at her for so long, trance-like, until Maddie, feeling suddenly awkward, prompted, 'Mr Frank?'

He blinked and seemed startled from his reverie. 'No, no, I don't suppose so. I don't really see how there could be? And, yes, the soil would be suitable, I'm sure.'

'Mr Frank,' came Harriet's aggrieved voice. 'Surely you're not going along with this foolish idea? You're a farmer not a – a flower-grower.'

Michael turned his charm on the woman. 'Oh Mrs T, it's a marvellous idea. We'd be horticulturalists.'

'Oh very grand, I'm sure.' Harriet was not to be mollified, not even by Michael. 'And what do any of you know about growing flowers, might I ask?'

'Nothing – yet.' Michael's grin widened. 'But give us a couple of weeks and Maddie and I will know all about it.'

Even Frank was smiling gently now and some of the hopelessness had gone from his eyes. 'Oh the confidence of youth, Harriet. Isn't it wonderful?'

Harriet sniffed. 'Very misplaced, if you ask me. But since I don't seem to have any say in the matter, I'll say no more about it.' With that, she turned away back to the kitchen where they could hear her banging saucepans onto the cooker.

Father and son exchanged a smile and Michael said softly, 'Well, I don't believe that we'll hear "no more about it" for a minute, but . . .' Now he turned to Nick who had stood silently throughout. 'What do you reckon?'

The young boy pushed his fingers through his flop of hair and blinked behind his glasses. He glanced, just once, towards the kitchen door and then looked back at Michael. Softly, he said, 'I think it's the only thing we can do. Even if we do wait the time they tell us before we restock, who's to say the same thing won't happen again.

159

And to change it all to crops would take an awful lot of work.'

'It'll still take a lot of work to plough it up for bulbs.'

'Yes, but it won't matter if there's a few wild oats and other weeds amongst tulips, will it?' Nick argued. 'Whereas, if you've got a lot of rubbish growing amongst wheat and such, it can ruin your crops if you want to sell it for grain.'

'You're right, Nick. Yes.' Frank leant back in his chair and rested his head, seeming to really relax for the first time in weeks. 'Growing flowers won't be plain sailing. I've no doubt there'll be some sort of blight they can get, or greenfly, or something. But . . .' He turned his smile on Maddie. 'I think it's a wonderful idea and, if it works, we'll all have you to thank, lass.'

Maddie swallowed. 'And if it doesn't?'

'It will work. We'll make it work,' Michael said, putting his arm about her shoulders. 'Won't we?'

Maddie looked up into his deep brown eyes. 'Oh yes,' she whispered and, meaning far more than growing a few fields of flowers, she repeated, 'We'll make it work.'

Twenty-Two

The discussion continued whilst Harriet set the table for supper.

'Of course, I'll have to go and see Sir Peter and ask his permission,' Frank took his place and picked up the carving knife and fork. 'It is his land, after all.'

'What's in the tenancy agreement?' Michael asked.

Frank shrugged. 'Can't say I've ever read it.'

'You're not very good with paperwork, are you, Dad?'

Frank smiled, more life in his eyes than they had seen for weeks. 'The farm just passed from me Dad to me. Same terms, same rent, same everything. Of course, the rent goes up every so often, but that's to be expected. Other than that, Sir Peter's never interfered.'

'What I mean is, Dad, does it actually say that you have to inform the landlord of change of use of the land?'

'Dunno, but I think it's courteous anyway. Don't you?'

Michael sighed. 'I suppose so, yes. But I just don't want anything – or anyone – to stand in the way.' He paused and then grinned as he glanced across at Maddie. 'I know. We'll send Maddie. She can charm Sir Peter into agreeing.'

Maddie's fork was suspended halfway between her plate and her mouth as she gaped, horrified, at Michael. 'You're not serious?'

'Of course, he's not, love,' Frank said quickly. 'Besides, it's my place to go. I'm the legal tenant.'

'I am perfectly serious. It's Maddie's idea. Why shouldn't she take the credit?'

Frank smiled at her. 'Well, you could come with me, lass. Your enthusiasm is certainly infectious and if Sir Peter hears for himself all your ideas, then perhaps it would be useful for you to be there.'

Maddie laid down her fork. Suddenly, she could eat no more for the nervous fluttering in her stomach as Frank added, 'We'll go as soon as the weather improves.' She was being asked to face the man who for so long had ruled every aspect of her life. What she ate, how she was dressed, what school she attended. And yet she had never even spoken to him. Not one word. He probably didn't even know she existed. At least, not by name. To Sir Peter Mayfield she was just another orphan in the Home his family had benevolently set up for orphaned or unwanted children.

But by the time they were able to visit Mayfield Hall, when Maddie had washed her hair and put on the new red dress that the family had bought her for Christmas, she no longer felt nervous. She felt ready to do battle.

'There you are,' Michael greeted her, his brown eyes appraising her approvingly. 'You look like a flower yourself. Sir Peter won't be able to resist you. My little tulip girl.'

Maddie giggled and felt her cheeks glow.

'I wish I was coming with you.' He stepped a little closer and gently touched her chin with the tip of his finger.

'Why – why don't you?'

He shrugged. 'Oh, I think it's best if just Dad and you go. We don't want it to look like a mass attack.'

'You ready, lass?' Frank's voice came from the kitchen and Maddie said a swift goodbye to Michael and hurried outside.

Frank, too, was dressed in his best suit and it was he

who was looking very nervous now. As she climbed into the car beside him, he said, 'I'm glad you're coming with me lass. I don't mind admitting, I get all tongue tied.'

'Do you mean you want me to do some of the talking?'

'Well, only if I get sort of lost or – or dry up, like. You know what I mean?'

Maddie nodded and sat back in her seat to run over in her mind all the arguments to support what they wanted to do.

They did not speak again until they drew up outside the front door of Mayfield Hall.

'Should we go round the back, do you think? To the servants' entrance?' Frank murmured.

'Have you never been here before to see Sir Peter about anything?'

Frank pushed back his cap and scratched his head. 'No. I've never had the cause. Sir Peter's been to the farm now and again. On horseback. Even though he's got two cars, he still likes to ride around his estate on horseback, you know. But no, I've never been here. At least, not like this. To seek an interview with him.'

'Well,' Maddie said firmly, with a great deal more confidence than she was feeling inside at this moment. 'You're a respected tenant. A gentleman farmer. I think you have a right to enter by the front door, don't you?'

Frank leant his arms on the steering wheel and looked up at the imposing mansion towering above them. 'I suppose so.'

'You sound doubtful.'

'Well, a few weeks back, I'd have agreed with you. But I'm a farmer no longer. Not now.'

'Mr Frank,' Maddie touched his arm, 'you've had some rotten bad luck. But it's not your fault. No one can say it's your fault. Not even Sir Peter.'

163

Frank's expression was still doubtful. 'I keep going over and over it in my mind. How did it happen? Was it my fault because I bought those beast of Weatherall's? Or was it birds that brought the disease because two of our own started at the same time, didn't they? I lay awake at night going over it all. '

'And do you have any answers?'

Frank shook his head and his voice was hoarse with sadness as he whispered, 'No. No, lass, I don't.'

Her hand still on his arm, she said gently, 'Then why not put it all behind you and look to the future? It's happened and we can't alter it. But we can do something different.'

Frank turned his head to look at her and, with eyes that were so like her beloved Michael's, he smiled down at her. 'You know, lass, I've heard the saying "an old head on young shoulders" but I've never before met anyone it fitted. Not until you came into our lives. For a lass of fourteen, you've a very sensible head – and a pretty one – on those slim shoulders of yours.'

Now was not the time to remind him that she had just passed the date of her official birthday. She was fifteen now. Instead, Maddie squeezed his arm, taking his words as the compliment she was sure he meant them to be. 'Come on. Let's go and face the lion in his den.'

Twenty-Three

They were both standing facing Sir Peter across the wide desk in his book-lined study, like two naughty school children summoned to the headmaster's office.

Maddie had never before been this close to Sir Peter. Of course, she would have recognized the tall figure dressed in check tweeds, the loud, bluff voice, so used to issuing orders and so used to being obeyed. But never before had she been close enough to see that his round face had a florid complexion with tiny red veins like a railway network on his skin; that his over-large nose was almost purple and that his moustache was now almost white. His hair, too, was white and so thin and sparse that the pink of his scalp shone through it. But his blue eyes were surprisingly bright and very sharp and knowing.

'Well, Brackenbury,' he barked. 'What is it?'

Frank twisted his cap round and round between nervous fingers as he began, haltingly, to explain. 'Well, sir, you know how I'm placed now. My livelihood's all but gone.'

Maddie could see the strain on Frank's face as if he carried the whole burden of guilt for the disease that had stricken his cattle.

'I have to admit, sir, that I was about ready to give up.'

Sir Peter said nothing. He leant back in the chair, his penetrating gaze never leaving his tenant's face.

'But then,' Frank went on, 'this lass here had what we

165

think is a very good idea. But, out of courtesy, I thought it only right to come and – well – discuss it with you first.'

Still Sir Peter did not speak, but his gaze came to rest now on Maddie as Frank looked to her and said, 'You carry on, lass. You tell Sir Peter about your idea.'

The landowner's scrutiny was disconcerting. He had been such a powerful force in her life, albeit from a distance. His name had always been the ultimate threat held over all the girls at the orphanage that carried his family's name and still enjoyed his patronage. He was staring at her now and there was a strange look on his face that had nothing to do with the reason for their visit to his home. It was as if he half recognized her and was searching his memory to place where he had seen her before.

Maddie almost laughed aloud. Oh he'd seen her before all right, but only dressed in the clothes of his own orphanage waifs. Now, with her hair washed and cut to a soft, crowning glory, her young body firm and yet showing the curves of womanhood, she could understand the man not recognizing her.

Maddie took a deep breath. 'Mr Frank isn't sure whether the restrictions extend to crops, you know, edible crops, as well as cattle when the land's been infected, so I said, why don't we plant tulips? Even if the disease is still on the land, it surely won't harm tulips.'

Sir Peter sat forward suddenly and leant his arms on the desk, staring at her. 'Flowers? You want to plant flowers on my land?'

Maddie's heart sank at his words and she was sure that, beside her, Frank's did too. There was the same scathing note in his voice that had been in Harriet's when Maddie had first made the suggestion.

'What else can we do?'

Sir Peter spread his hands, palms upwards, as if the matter were simple. 'Wait until you can restock.'

Frank and Maddie exchanged a glance and then both faced the landlord again. The girl, young though she was, guessed that Frank found the admission he was being forced to make, degrading. 'I haven't enough put by, sir, to buy ten or fifteen beast all at once. And despite waiting the regulation period, if the disease is still on the land, the same thing could happen again.'

'Ah,' Sir Peter said shortly and leant back in his chair again. 'I see.' There was a silence in the room before he said, 'If I waive a year's rent, would that help?'

'Well, it would, sir, but . . .' Frank said no more but the meaning in the unspoken words was plain enough.

'Mm, well, I'll give the matter some thought, Brackenbury,' was all Sir Peter would promise before they were shown out and found themselves walking down the front steps to the car.

'Oh well, it was a good try, lass, but it's obvious he's not keen.'

'But he did say he'd think about it.'

Frank cast her a wry glance. 'I wouldn't like my life to depend on him saying "yes", though.'

Maddie pulled a comical face in return. 'Neither would I,' she was forced to admit.

'I can't believe it. You and your father before you have been farming his land for years and never a bad word between you and the landlord. You told me so yourself. So why can't he trust your judgement now?'

Maddie gaped at the housekeeper in astonishment. Harriet was incensed, but it was Frank who voiced Maddie's own thoughts. 'I thought you didn't agree with us anyway. I'm surprised you don't say "I told you so".'

'That's as maybe,' Harriet bridled. 'What I say in this house is one thing, but when it comes to an outsider disagreeing, that's different.'

Frank smiled gently. Harriet Trowbridge, it seemed, regarded the household as her own family. She would strongly disagree with them in private, but was prepared to present a united front to the world at large.

'He's no right to stop you if it's what you really want, Mr Frank,' she railed. 'If you really think it's a good idea . . .' Maddie felt the woman's resentful glance rest on her for a brief moment before she added, 'and it's what you want us to do, Mr Frank. Then that's what we'll do.'

'Oh Harriet,' Frank ran his hand through his hair. 'I don't know now. I really don't. If I go against him, he could give me notice.'

Harriet's mouth dropped open. 'He wouldn't do that. He wouldn't dare.'

'There's no "dare" about it. He owns the land, when all's done and said.'

In a voice so low that Frank did not hear, although Maddie's sharp ears caught her words, Harriet said, 'We'll see about that.'

As the woman turned away and went back to her kitchen, Maddie saw a strange gleam in Harriet's eyes.

Now what, she thought as she gazed after her, was the housekeeper up to?

The following morning Maddie was even more astonished to see Harriet putting on her black coat and felt hat.

She rarely left the farm, Maddie knew. Either Michael or Nick did any shopping they needed. She never went

168

into the nearby town nor even down to the village shop. She didn't even seem to have any family or friends who came to the farm to visit her. Her whole life was centred around Few Farm and Frank Brackenbury. Apart from her visit to the orphanage and that one trip into Wellandon at Frank's insistence, Maddie could not now recall ever seeing the housekeeper leave the farm.

So Maddie's mouth almost dropped open when the housekeeper came to stand close by her. 'Now, girl, just you keep quiet about me going out,' she said in a low voice, glancing furtively about her to be sure no one was either watching or listening. 'Not a word to Mr Frank, nor to Michael. You hear me?'

Maddie shrugged. 'Nothing to do with me, Mrs Trowbridge. Is there anything you want me to do for you while you're out?' And she added sadly, 'As I've no dairy work now.'

'You can start the bedrooms for me. But leave Mr Frank's. I'll see to that.'

Maddie hid her smile. Thursday was the day of the week when Harriet always 'did' the bedrooms. Not even an obviously necessary trip out could be allowed to interfere with her routine.

'Right you are, Mrs Trowbridge. Off you go and have a nice time.'

'Huh. I don't know about that,' was the housekeeper's sour reply as she opened the back door. Maddie, following her into the wash-house to collect cleaning materials, watched as Harriet paused on the threshold, glanced quickly around the yard making sure no one was about and then hurried towards the gate.

'What *is* she up to?' Maddie murmured.

*

The mystery was solved three days later when, on the Sunday morning, Theo Mayfield rode into the yard of Few Farm on horseback.

Dismounting, he tethered the horse to the gatepost. Maddie was in her bedroom changing her dress ready for Church in half an hour and saw him from the window as he walked towards the back door.

She hurried down the stairs calling, 'Mr Frank, Mr Frank. There's a gentleman coming across the yard. I think it's Mr Theo.'

'What?' Startled Frank leapt up from his chair by the fire, throwing down the Sunday newspaper he was reading and then hastily stopping to pick it up and fold it neatly. 'Go and let him in, Maddie. Bring him in here.' He stood before the mirror over the range to straighten his tie and smooth down his hair that had already been combed into neatness ready for Church. But the action betrayed his nervousness.

'Good day. Miss March, isn't it?' Theo Mayfield actually touched his riding hat with the end of his whip in a courteous gesture. 'Is Mr Brackenbury at home?'

'Yes, sir. Please come in.' She turned and led the way through the kitchen and into the living room where Frank was waiting anxiously.

'Won't you sit down, sir? Can I offer you a drink or . . .?'

'No, no, Mr Brackenbury.'

Maddie was swift to notice that, unlike Sir Peter, Theo gave Frank the courtesy title of 'Mister'. 'I can see that you and your household are about to leave for Church. I'll not delay you, but I felt I should ride across to tell you that my father is ill.'

Frank cleared his throat. 'I'm sorry to hear that, sir. Nothing serious, I hope.'

Theo's face was sober. 'I'm afraid it may be. He suffered a stroke the night before last and the next few days are critical.'

'Oh, I am sorry.'

'Thank you.' Theo nodded and was obviously touched by the older man's genuine concern. Maddie saw that the young man pulled in a deep breath as he went on. 'Fortunately, my father had mentioned to me your idea of turning your land into growing tulips.'

'Yes, sir,' Frank began doubtfully. 'But Sir Peter didn't seem very taken with the idea.'

'Well, I think it's a very good idea. I told him so and he did seem to be coming round to your way of thinking. So, as he's obviously going to be incapacitated for some time and I have come home to take up the reins of running the estate, I'm happy to tell you that I'm in full agreement with your proposal.'

'Are you sure, Mr Theo? I mean, I wouldn't want you to go against your father's wishes.'

'No, no. No more would I, but, as I said, we talked at length about it and I think he began to realize that there's very little else you can do in the circumstances. Although I think it was the visit from your housekeeper that clinched it for you.'

'My housekeeper? Harriet?' Frank's surprise was obvious.

'Why, yes. Didn't you know? She was closeted with my father in his study for almost an hour on Thursday morning.' The young man laughed and shrugged. 'I don't know what she said to him, but she was obviously very persuasive because afterwards he just said to me, "I think we'll let Brackenbury have his way." Besides,' Mr Theo added, and this was obviously his own belief, not that of his father, 'the land is perfect for it.'

'Well, I'm very grateful to you, sir, if you're really sure?'

'I am. I understand, also, that when he spoke to you my father offered to waive a year's rent?'

'He did, sir, but that was to give us time to restock.'

Theo smiled at the honesty of the man. 'Well, you'll still have to buy stock, only bulbs instead of beast. And it will be some time before you get your first harvest of blooms so we'll still stick to that offer.' His smile broadened. 'I'm sure my father would agree.'

Frank's weather-beaten complexion, was even more ruddy. 'That's very generous of you, sir.'

'There is just one more thing. You'll have to write to the authorities – the County War Agricultural Executive Committee.' He pulled a comical face. 'A mouthful, isn't it? They're called War Ag's for short. They came into being in the War to oversee food production, but I think they still have some powers as we've still got quite a lot of rationing. I think you'll have to get clearance from them, Mr Brackenbury.'

'Oh.' Frank scratched his head, clearly puzzled. 'Well, yes. Thank you, sir.'

Maddie could see that Theo had noticed Frank's dilemma. He didn't know how or where to start.

'Tell you what,' the younger man said. 'I'll make the initial contact for you. I know one of the chaps there. Philip Taylor. I'll have a word with him, if you like, and ask him to get in touch with you.'

Plainly relieved, Frank said, 'I'd be most grateful, sir. That would be very kind of you.'

Maddie found herself beaming at the young man, who had not only given them his approval but had made a practical and helpful offer too.

'And see Bill Randall,' Mr Theo went on. 'He's a good-hearted fellow and I'm sure he will give you all the advice

172

he can.' Theo held out his hand. 'Good luck, Mr Brackenbury, and please don't hesitate to let me know if there's
anything more I can do.'

'Thank you, sir. You've been most kind.'

Maddie felt the young man's glance linger on her for a
moment as he said softly, 'Good day to you, Miss March.'

She smiled and said, 'Goodbye, Mr Theo and – thank
you.'

Both Frank and Maddie followed the young man to the
door and watched him walk back across the yard to his
horse.

'Well, that's a surprise, isn't it?'

'It is, lass. But all I hope is that the lad won't get into
trouble when his father recovers and finds out what he's
agreed to.' He shook his head, mystified. 'And I still can't
understand why Harriet thought she could help.'

Maddie begrudged giving praise to the housekeeper, but
her innate honesty made her say, 'Well, she obviously did.'

'Yes, she must have done. But how?'

'I don't know, but it sounds,' Maddie said slowly, 'as if
you've no need to worry about Sir Peter being well enough
to object for some time.'

And though she was not, by nature, a vindictive person,
Maddie could not find it in her heart to be sorry for Sir
Peter Mayfield.

Twenty-Four

'So then what do we have to do, Mr Randall?'

The big man laughed, the sound seeming to come from deep within his rotund belly. 'By heck, mate, you're keen, I'll say that for you.'

Maddie chuckled. She had met Bill Randall only once before and his habit of calling everyone he met – male or female, young or old – 'mate' always amused her. But it was a friendly term and Maddie warmed to him.

His expression sobered now. 'And I'll give you all the help I can, because I was sorry to hear about what happened to Frank Brackenbury. Very sorry. He's a good man and dun't deserve to lose his livelihood in such a cruel way. So, mate, let's get down to brass tacks, shall us? Has Frank got approval from the War Ag's?'

Maddie nodded. 'Mr Taylor visited us the day before yesterday and told us what we can do. Mr Frank's got seventy-five acres altogether. We're to plough up the meadows and plant about ten acres of bulbs to start with, he said, and the rest to potatoes and vegetables for a while, or wheat if we want to. Then we should be able to increase our bulb production gradually as the regulations relax.'

Bill Randall raised his eyebrows. 'I don't know if you'll manage ten acres in your first year, mate. It's not a good time to be setting up, y'know.'

Maddie's heart plummeted as the man went on. 'Bulbs is very expensive still, since the War, see. We're still having to import a lot and not only are we restricted in how many acres we can grow, but we can't get hold of the bulbs easy.'

Maddie bit her lip and nodded, but the big man was still smiling at her. 'Tell you what, though, I'll have a word with a few of my mates and we'll see what we can do to help old Frank.'

'Oh thank you, Mr Randall.'

'And you could try the bulb auction. They hold one in the cattle market every Tuesday in Wellandon. But be careful, don't go paying too much. And another thing, you do know that bulbs become like another crop? You have to rotate them along with whatever else you grow?'

Maddie nodded. She wasn't quite sure what he meant but she would report faithfully back to Frank and Michael everything that Bill Randall said and they would understand.

'I was forced to cut my bulb production right back in the War, y'know,' he was saying, 'and they're still only letting me increase steadily. A lot of our production went to America.'

'Why?'

'Because of the War, their supplies from Holland were cut off.'

'Oh.' Maddie tried to show polite interest but she didn't really understand. She was far more interested in finding out how Few Farm could get started with its first few bulbs. Mr Randall's next words brought her further disappointment.

''Course, it's the wrong time of year for planting, but I'll tell you what could be a good idea for Frank. A greenhouse.' The man beamed as if he personally had solved all of Frank Brackenbury's problems.

'A greenhouse?'

'Yes. Forcing flowers to grow out of season, 'specially in time for Christmas. It got very popular in the Twenties, but, of course, even they had to turn their greenhouses over for food production in the War. Y'know, tomatoes and such. But that way, you can get better prices. It's like everything else, mate. If you get a glut of flowers all ready at the same time, the price drops. But if you,' he winked down at her and tapped the side of his nose, 'can be the one to have flowers ready when no one else has. Well, then, you can up the price.'

'I see,' Maddie said slowly. 'At least, I think I do.'

With a willing listener, Bill Randall launched into the practicalities of forcing bulbs to bloom earlier than nature intended. 'It's hard work, lass. You pick out the biggest bulbs for forcing. They need to be in a cold store for a while and then you plant them in boxes outside in autumn. Keep them well watered and bring them into the heated greenhouses in batches, so that when they flower they'll do so at different times.'

Maddie smiled and nodded. 'I understand, so that you'll have a few trays ready for Christmas then a few at the beginning of January and so on?'

'You've got it, mate. That's the idea.'

'But wouldn't it be very expensive to build a big greenhouse?'

'Well now, it just so happens that I know where's one going for a song. Weatherall's old place. It's a bit dilapidated. The woodwork would need painting up and some of the glass needs replacing. But it could be taken down and moved to Frank's yard without a deal of trouble.'

Maddie pulled a face. 'I'm not sure how Mr Frank would react to hearing that it's from Mr Weatherall's.'

Mr Randall looked puzzled for a moment before he said, 'Oh aye, I was forgetting.'

Maddie tried to make a joke of it. 'He might think it'd carry some sort of disease that tulips get.'

The big man laughed. 'Well, I don't think a bit of timber and glass could do that. You won't be using his soil, now will you? You'd need to make your own foundations first and then just buy the wooden frame and the glass.'

'I'll see what he says.'

'Don't forget to tell Frank that he's got one thing in his favour.'

'What's that, Mr Randall?'

'His own electricity supply. He'll be able to run pipes from that boiler house of his to heat a greenhouse and control it with a pump . . .' The man beamed, 'Run by his electricity.'

Maddie's smile widened. 'I'll tell him, Mr Randall. And thank you for all your help.'

'Think nowt on it, mate, think nowt on it. I'm looking forward to the day when I can look over yon hedge and see your field of tulips.'

Frank, Michael and Nick listened intently to all that Maddie had to relate. Even Harriet, though she tried hard not to look as if she was taking any interest in the project, hovered within earshot.

When she came to the point of telling Frank just who owned the greenhouse that was 'going for a song', Maddie hesitated. But she need not have worried. Frank laughed wryly and said, 'Well, I reckon old man Weatherall owes me one, don't you? So now, we've just got to let Mr Theo know what we're doing and then . . .' Frank stood up and look around. 'We can get started.'

Michael gave his father a slap on the shoulder and then

177

turned and slapped Nick on the back, too. But he put his arms about Maddie's waist and picked her up and swung her round.

'My little Tulip Girl,' he said. 'It's going to happen, Maddie. We're going to make it happen. And it's all thanks to you.'

Maddie wound her arms about his neck and hugged him hard, the lump in her throat too big to let her speak.

Then, over his shoulder she caught sight of the venomous look in Harriet's eyes and the joyous moment was spoilt.

They ended up with not one, but two greenhouses.

As Frank and his near neighbours, and even the village folk and the townsfolk too, counted up the cost of the winter's blizzards and began to try to restore some sort of normality to their lives, Mr Theo called again at Few Farm. He arrived one blustery late April day when the noise of Mr Randall's concrete mixer filled the yard.

Michael, stripped to his sleeveless vest, shovelled gravel, sand and cement and tipped water into the rotating drum whilst Nick barrowed each mix to where Maddie and Frank waited. For a week they had dug out an oblong shape approximately eight inches deep to the length and breadth of Mr Weatherall's greenhouse for the foundations. They had put wooden boards all around the inside of the oblong – shuttering, Frank told Maddie – and now Nick tipped barrow load after barrow load of concrete mix into the hole for Frank to spread with a spade.

'Right, lass, now we have to tamp it,' Frank said and then, one at each end, they picked up a long wooden board and smoothed out the concrete with the edge of it, level with the top of the shuttering. The lumpy gravel sank into

178

the mixture and the top was skimmed with the wet cement and left to dry into a smooth surface.

It was as the last load was tipped in that Maddie jumped to hear Mr Theo's voice just behind her. She had not seen him arrive nor heard him above the noise of the mixer.

'I'm sorry,' he said at once as she turned around swiftly, her lips parted in a startled gasp.

'I didn't hear you,' she shouted above the clatter, but at that moment Michael turned the engine off and the noise died away. He came towards them and Maddie noticed that the two young men smiled at each other.

'Mr Theo. It's good to see you. Sorry I can't shake hands.' He spread his hands to show their dirty state. Theo laughed and stepped back a pace, but it was obvious that his action was only in jest.

'How are you, Michael?'

'We're fine, thank you.' He nodded down at the foundations. 'This is for a greenhouse.'

'A greenhouse?' Theo's glance appraised the size of the proposed structure. He watched as Frank and Maddie bent to their task to level out the last of the concrete.

Standing up and easing his aching back, Frank said, 'We've picked one up from old Weatherall's place, sir. We've already taken it down and brought it here in sections. We've even managed to salvage most of the glass too.'

'The woodwork needs painting, of course,' Michael put in, 'but it'll be a good start for us.'

Theo's eyes were still upon the wet cement and he tapped his lips with the tip of his riding crop, deep in thought. Then he glanced around him assessing where they had positioned the greenhouse alongside the hen-house, next to the crewyard.

179

'You didn't think of taking that old barn down, then, and building it there?'

'Well, sir,' Frank was hesitant. 'I didn't like to without your permission.'

'This is nearer the boiler house, sir,' Michael pointed to the corner building in the crewyard where the boiler house was situated. 'It'll be easy to run the pipes from there to the greenhouse to heat it. Like we do the hen-house.'

'Mm.' Theo's attention turned to the barn. He walked slowly towards it and stood looking up at it. Then he turned and wandered across towards the crewyard and the hen-house and even walked round the rear of the buildings. While he was gone from their sight for a few moments, Michael glanced at his father and asked in a low voice, 'What's he up to?'

Frank shrugged, 'I don't know,' and then they both turned to face Theo as he emerged from the nettles and thistles at the back of the hen-house. Still saying nothing, he walked past them once more and went towards the house, looking over the gate leading into the fenced garden at the front of the house.

'I just wondered,' he said, as he came back to them once more, 'if you wanted another greenhouse. We've got one that we're taking down, but it's a lean-to. It was on the outside of a walled garden. Never used. Allowed to fall into ruin and it's become an eyesore. I've instructed Talbot . . .' Theo referred to the Head Gardener at Mayfield Park, 'to take it down. If you can do anything with it, Mr Brackenbury, you're very welcome to it. But you'd need a suitable wall to put it against. There's no point in putting it behind there.' He gestured towards the hen-house. 'It wouldn't get enough sun. The best place . . .' he pointed with his crop, 'appears to be the house wall overlooking your garden. It would catch all the sun there. The greenhouse isn't worth very much, so I wouldn't charge you anything. Talbot was just going to scrap it. And whilst we're on the subject,' again he pointed with his riding crop, 'if you should want to, for any reason, you have my permission to take down the barn. And another thing . . .' Even yet, Theo wasn't finished, 'How about covering in the whole of the crewyard?'

'What?' Frank's mouth almost dropped open.

Theo smiled. 'Yes, I know it would be a huge building. But that's exactly what you're going to need. I suggest you leave the outbuildings just as they are . . .' He pointed with his whip. 'You'll need all sorts of places – a cold store, ordinary storage, cool and airy, for bulbs for replanting in the fields . . .'

Maddie was listening intently, soaking up the knowledge.

'. . . And,' Theo went on. 'Plenty of space for packing cut flowers, cleaning and grading bulbs and so on . . .' His keen eye was running over the whole area. 'Yes, the more I think about it, the better I like it.'

'I'm sorry, but I couldn't . . .' Frank began but Michael cut in. 'Oh Dad, it's a marvellous idea.'

'I know. I know it is, but . . .'

Theo held up his hand. 'Of course all the costs would be met by the estate, Mr Brackenbury. I would never expect a tenant to undertake such an expense. After all, to my mind, it'll improve the value of the property.' He gave them all a broad wink. 'Well, at least that'll be my argument when I have to justify the expense to my father.'

'Well . . .' Frank seemed almost overcome with emotion. 'That's very kind of you, sir. We'd certainly be able to make very good use of a big barn like that, and yes, we'd like to come and take a look at the greenhouse, if we may?'

'Of course. Any time.' Maddie felt his glance come to rest on her as he said again, softly, 'Any time.'

'We'll come over tomorrow afternoon, Mr Theo,' Michael said as he moved to stand beside Maddie.

She noticed Theo's glance move from her to Michael and then back again and she knew that he had sensed that there was something between her and Michael.

Theo gave a nod and touched his riding hat. 'See you tomorrow, then.' He turned away and walked back to his horse tethered at the gate.

'He's a nice young man,' Frank said. 'And generous too. A mite more generous than his father.'

Maddie turned in surprise. For one who had had it drilled into her the whole of her life that she owed everything to the kind benevolence of Sir Peter, it came as a shock to hear that he was not universally regarded as being so. It was only now that she was outside the walls of the Home and she could see how other people lived and conducted their lives that she could begin to make any sort of comparison.

Her thoughts were interrupted as Ben came bounding across the yard and paddled straight across the newly smoothed concrete.

'Oh Ben!'

'You bad dog!'

'Get away, animal.'

Poor Ben, thoroughly chastened though not understanding what he had done that was so dreadful, ran away into the lane whilst, laughing now, Frank and Maddie once more picked up the tamping board to smooth out his paw marks.

*

Later that night, when supper was over and everyone was about to go to bed, Michael said, 'Come on, Maddie, we'd better go and look if anyone else has decided to leave their mark on our handiwork.'

They stepped out into the clear night and walked across the yard. Michael slipped his arm around her shoulders. 'I've being trying to think of a way to get you to myself for a few minutes. And now I have the perfect excuse.'

Maddie giggled and put her arm about his waist. As they stood looking down at the concrete foundations, Michael moved to one corner and touched it with his finger. 'As I hoped, it's not quite dry yet. Still soft enough to leave a mark.'

'As you hoped? Oh you mean, we've got to stand guard all night?'

'No, I didn't mean that, although that's a very good idea, my little Tulip.' His lowered his voice to teasing wickedness. 'Are you game?'

Maddie stifled her laughter that sounded so loud in the night air.

'Come here,' Michael whispered. She stepped towards him and squatted down beside him.

He shone his torch on to the wet cement. 'Press your hand into it. Right here, in the corner.'

'But your Dad . . .?'

'He won't mind. He was annoyed at Ben, of course, because he went prancing about all over it. But just here, no one will notice it when the building's finished because it'll be under all the trays of bulbs, won't it? Let's leave our mark, Tulip. Yours and mine.'

The idea appealed to her. The imprint of their hands set in concrete, side by side for ever.

'All right then.' She rolled up her sleeve and placed her right hand flat on the soft cement, pressing until it squelched through her fingers. 'It's setting already, isn't it?'

Carefully she lifted her hand away to see that she had left a perfect impression.

'Now you,' she whispered.

Michael's hand hovered over her mark as he turned his left hand to the position he wanted and pressed it down. When he lifted his hand away, she saw that his imprint had overlapped hers a little so that it looked as if their two smallest fingers were entwined.

'Hold the torch for me,' he said as he pulled a screwdriver from his pocket. With the sharp end he drew in the cement the shape of a long-stemmed tulip curving around their two hand imprints. Underneath he wrote the year – 1947.

'There. Now that's there for our children and our grandchildren and even for their children to see.'

'Oh Michael.'

He leant towards her and in the cold night air, his lips were warm upon hers. 'Come on,' he murmured, 'we'd better go in, else I'll want to take you into the hay shed again.'

'Well,' she said boldly, 'why don't we?'

He stood up. 'Little hussy!' But he was laughing softly as he said it. 'My father warned me about girls like you.'

Maddie rose too and faced him in the darkness. But she was not laughing. She was very serious as she said, 'Did he? Did he really?'

He put his arm about her shoulder and began to lead her back towards the house. 'Yes, he did. He said, "One day, a lovely girl will come along and steal your heart and you'll have eyes for no one else after that." And do you know something, my darling little Tulip Girl?'

'No,' she whispered, hardly daring to breathe in case she woke and found she was dreaming. 'What?'

'He's right. I haven't. I haven't eyes for anyone else in the world now except you.'

Twenty-Five

'Do you know,' Michael said one evening at supper, 'I've just realized something.'

The summer had passed in a blur of hard work. They all still rose as early as they always had done and worked until the light faded in the evening. Some nights, Maddie almost fell asleep at the supper table. Then she would climb the stairs to fall into bed and wake the next morning feeling as if she hadn't been there five minutes. But once out in the yard or the fields, the thought of field after field of glorious tulips the following April spurred her on and her weariness would disappear. They harnessed Rajah to plough up the meadows. There were so many stones and roots that had to be picked out by hand that Maddie felt she would never stand upright again.

But all of them were working happily together. Frank seemed to have taken on a new lease of life and Nick looked healthier than Maddie had ever known him. His skin became tanned in the hot summer of that year and his rather mousey-coloured hair was streaked blond by the sun. Even his mother lost some of her sourness and brought their dinners out to the field where they sat under the shade of a tree to eat cheese and pickle with soft, crusty bread followed by her freshly-baked apple pasties.

'Why does food always taste so much nicer out of

doors?' Michael would say, and then gallantly add, 'not that yours doesn't taste wonderful wherever we eat it, Mrs T.'

'Oh, you and your flattery, Michael Brackenbury.'

And in the warm, soft nights Michael and Maddie would sometimes sneak out to the fields again, their arms about each other to stand together and dream of their golden future.

And now it was September and the greenhouses were both ready for the very first bulbs and the ground in the field too, was prepared.

'What's that, son?' Frank wanted to know in response to Michael's statement. Even though the anxiety was sometimes still in his eyes as to whether this venture would work, most of the time he worked so hard now that he had neither time nor energy left to worry. Whatever happened, it wouldn't be for the want of trying. Everyone in the household was doing their bit towards making it work.

'Maddie's been here almost eighteen months and she's never had a birthday.' Michael's own birthday was on the seventh of September in a few days' time.

'I haven't really got one,' she said glancing at Harriet and remembering vividly standing beneath her scrutiny whilst she and Mrs Potter discussed her. 'Only the date the Home gave me.'

'I don't understand,' Michael said.

'I was abandoned outside the door of the Home in March so they just gave me that date as my birthday. They thought I was about a month old.'

She heard Harriet's familiar sniff. 'That's why she's got such a fancy name,' the housekeeper put in, talking again about her as if she was not present, 'Madeleine indeed.'

There was a silence around the table, then Maddie said, 'Jen was left outside the door too. In the September and they thought she was newborn, so her birthday's the tenth of this month.'

Michael's smile widened. 'We'll have a party then, on the tenth. For Jenny, me and a rather late one for you, Maddie. What about it, Dad?'

Maddie saw Frank glance at Harriet, but before he could speak, Maddie cut in, 'No, it'd be too much work and we're all far too busy.' Then she added hastily as she smiled her thanks across the table, 'But it's very kind of you to think of it.'

'I don't see why we couldn't do something,' Frank said. 'What do you say, Harriet?'

Maddie almost laughed aloud as she saw the housekeeper's dilemma. Her glance went from Michael to Maddie and back again. How she would love to throw a party for her favourite's birthday, but if Maddie and the other little waif and stray were to be linked, then enthusiasm for the idea stuck in Harriet's throat.

Tight-lipped, Harriet said at last, 'Whatever you say, Mr Frank. But might I suggest it would be better on your birthday, Michael, as it's a Sunday.'

'All right, then. I was only thinking of having it on little Jen's birthday. Make it special for her, you know.'

Maddie, powerless to stop it, felt the sudden thrust of jealousy once more, despite her vow to quell it. She swallowed and forced herself to say, 'Can I help you, Mrs Trowbridge?'

Rising from her chair and beginning to gather the dishes together, Harriet said, 'I'm sure I can manage a few jellies and blancmanges without your interference, thank you.'

As fragile as a gossamer dandelion in seed, the house-keeper's good humour was blown away in a few seconds.

Beside her, Maddie heard Frank's sigh.

It was like the Christmas they should have enjoyed and birthday celebrations all rolled into one. Jenny arrived mid-afternoon on the following Sunday, her face pink with excitement. Shyly, she handed out the gifts she had brought, not only a tie for Michael and soaps for Maddie, but a small box of chocolates as a 'thank you' to Harriet and three white men's handkerchiefs for Frank, but also – and Maddie shrewdly guessed most important of all – she had brought a present for Nick, too.

'It's not my birthday 'til next month,' he said as he took it, but Maddie could see the pleasure in his eyes, his cheeks creasing in a wide smile. 'What is it?'

'Open it and see.'

Nick pulled off the wrapping paper. 'Oh! Oh!' His face was pink with delighted surprise. 'Thank you, Jen. It's great.'

'I'm sorry it's not new, but it is in good condition.'

'Yes, yes, it's hardly been used. It's great,' he said as he opened the book on engines and lovingly turned the pages.

'Maddie told me once how you like car engines and things.'

'Fancy you remembering that,' he murmured. Already the giver of the gift was rapidly losing his attention. But Jenny was quite content to sit and watch him poring over the book she had brought him. It was thanks enough for her.

*

They had a wonderful party. Even Harriet seemed to unbend a little when Frank kept refilling her glass with elderflower wine.

'You'll have me tipsy, Mr Frank,' she actually giggled protestingly, but Maddie noticed that she still held out her glass for more.

As yet another game of blind man's buff ended, Frank glanced at the clock. 'Nine o'clock already. I hate to break up the jollifications, but I think we'd better see Jenny back home.'

Maddie saw her glance hopefully at Nick. A walk in the moonlight with him would be the perfect end of a perfect day for Jenny. But Nick had already picked up his book and settled himself in the depths of an armchair.

'We'll walk you home,' Michael said. 'Me and Maddie.'

Maddie held her breath, waiting for Harriet's disapproval, but the housekeeper was lying back in her armchair, her gaze intent on the swirling pale liquid in her glass, a small smile on her mouth.

'Off you go then, else Mrs Grange will be locking you out.'

Goodbyes and thank yous were said all round and then they were out in the night air that already had the hint of autumn in it.

Maddie positioned herself between the other two and linked arms.

'It was nice to have a bit of fun,' Michael said, 'because from now on, it's going to be work, work and more work.'

Maddie laughed. 'It's been like that for months.'

'I know, but it'll get worse.'

'Or better,' Maddie said, 'depending on how you look

at it. We'll be even busier when the flowers and bulbs are ready for picking.'

'I could come and help when Mrs Grange doesn't need me,' Jenny offered.

'You're on,' Michael said, 'come next spring, we'll need all the help we can get.'

They saw Jenny safely to the back door of the shop and then Michael and Maddie retraced their steps down the lane. They walked side by side, not touching, until they left the outskirts of the village and Maddie felt Michael reach for her hand. They walked along, not speaking, just content to be together, hand in hand, until they came almost to the farm gateway. Behind the shelter of the hedge and hidden from the farmhouse, Michael stopped in the middle of the lane and took her in his arms.

'Oh Maddie, how long I've had to wait for you to grow up and there I was not even realizing you'd had another birthday.'

Maddie buried her face against his neck, winding her arms about him. She could feel the beat of his heart even through his clothes. It matched the beat of her own. He was kissing her face, her forehead, the tip of her nose and then his lips sought her mouth. 'Oh Maddie,' he murmured against her lips. 'I want you so.'

'Come on,' he said at last, taking her hand. They crept into the yard and without protest she allowed him to lead her to the hay shed. He began to kiss her in earnest, pressing her down into the soft hay. Then his fingers were searching beneath her clothing and she quivered as his cold hand found the warmth of her breast.

'Maddie, oh Maddie,' he breathed and then they were lost in the wonder of discovery of each other. Lost to time and place. Lost to sense and reason.

As Michael lay on top of her and gently, lovingly, made her his own, the whole world exploded into golden light. It was like a summer's day and they were lying amidst a rainbow field of tulips, the sun bright and warm and shining down benignly upon their love.

Twenty-Six

The work was even harder than any of them had imagined and what they would have done without Bill Randall's practical help and advice, Maddie could not think. Not only had he already lent them his concrete mixer and his wooden-framed plough to prepare the ground, but he obtained their very first supply of bulbs.

The day after the party, Bill's old truck rattled into the yard at Few Farm. Climbing down from the driver's seat he called out cheerfully to Maddie. 'I thought you might be able to make use of this little lot, mate.'

When she went to the back of the truck and saw pallet after pallet stacked high and every one filled with bulbs, her mouth dropped open.

'It's not easy for someone just starting,' Bill said, 'but I've spoken to one or two mates and we're all chipping in with some stock for you.'

Maddie felt a lump in her throat. Funny, she thought, I only want to cry when someone does something so unexpected and so kind for me.

'It's very good of you,' Maddie said, her eyes sparkling.

'There's different varieties but I've put labels on them, mate, to show you which is which. There's Clara Butt, that's a pretty pink, Inglescombe Yellow and Bartigon Red. Then there's Rose Copland, another pink, and William Copland, that's purple. Now,' he pointed to three trays, each marked with a black cross. 'These have been in my cold store since

193

the beginning of August. They're the ones for forcing in your greenhouse and they ought to be planted now in boxes, like I told you, ready to bring into your glasshouse at the right time. They're different colours, an' all.'

'Our very own rainbow,' Maddie murmured.

'Eh? What did you say, mate?'

She smiled at him. 'Oh nothing, Mr Randall. Thank you so much for all these. What do we owe you?'

'Don't worry your pretty head about that just now, mate. We'll wait for our money. We know Frank of old. He'll pay us when he can. We all know that. Oh, and I've brought you these.' He picked up a small cardboard box. 'A few very special bulbs just for you. They're called Keizerskroon and they're red with yellow edges. Very pretty, they are.'

Now the tears spilled over and Maddie wiped them away hastily and smiled up at the big man. 'I don't know how to begin to thank you, Mr Randall.'

He put his hand on her shoulder. 'Think nowt on it, mate. Think nowt on it.'

But Maddie thought a great deal of it.

'By heck, we're going to be busy planting this lot,' Frank said, scratching his head when he saw the bulbs, but Maddie only grinned. Already in her mind's eye she could see the waving tulips in full bloom.

'Then we'd best get cracking.'

'Well, yes, I agree. But what do we actually have to do?'

'Mr Randall said there's only enough here to plant a few acres for our first year, but because we've already got Mr Taylor's say-so, we can increase the acreage as soon as we can.'

'Maybe Mr Theo could help us,' Michael put in.

'Oh, I don't like to ask him,' Frank shook his head. 'He's been so good already.'

'We'll send Maddie,' Michael laughed, winking at her. 'I think he's a bit sweet on our Maddie.'

'We've enough to be going on with here, at the moment,' Maddie said, though she was laughing along with Michael, not even thinking that his suggestion might be serious. 'And the rest of the land we can use for potatoes or caulis.'

'Ah well, now I do know about growing them, but I have to admit, lass, I'm a bit lost with these flowers.'

'We need to start planting now,' Maddie told him. 'Mr Randall says the usual way is to plant them in rows, leaving every seventh row empty.'

'Why?' Nick asked suddenly. He had been standing listening to the conversation but until this moment had not joined in.

'To walk along for hoeing the weeds out and later for the picking.'

Frank and Michael nodded.

'What about the greenhouses? Do we plant some in there?'

Maddie shook her head. 'No. You only bring them into the greenhouse roughly a month before you want them to flower, though the time depends a bit on the different varieties. Take the Rose Copland, say you want that to flower say for Christmas, then you'd bring it into the greenhouse a month before.'

'What about the temperature?' Frank asked. 'We'll have to mind to get that right, won't we?'

'For the first week you keep it very moderate and then increase it to about sixty-five degrees.'

'Sounds easy,' Michael said, 'but I wonder if it's going to be.'

195

'We'll make it work,' Maddie said and she saw Frank and Michael exchange a smile.

'But what do we do with them 'til then?' Nick asked. 'Just leave them like this?'

'No. We plant them out first . . .'

'In the field? You mean we have to plant them out and then dig them all up again to bring in? That sounds like a lot of unnecessary work . . .'

'No, no. We put them in boxes. Look, like this one. Mr Randall brought a couple to start us off. He couldn't spare any more so we'll have to get some more from somewhere.' Maddie pointed to a wooden box approximately twenty-four inches by fifteen. 'You put them in these, well spaced, and then cover them thinly with soil and bring them into the glasshouse at the right time.'

There was a silence as the menfolk took it all in.

'Where do we put them until then?'

'In the field but I should think as near to the yard as possible. After all, we've got to carry them to the glass-houses, haven't we? How about in a row along the hedge side?'

'Sounds sensible,' Michael murmured.

Frank glanced at Nick. 'How's the trench coming along for the pipes from the boiler house to the first glasshouse?'

'All right. I should get it finished today.'

'I'll go into Wellandon to see a chap I know about the heating pipes,' Frank said. 'And I'll see about some more boxes, love.'

'And we'll get started with the planting, shall we, Maddie?' Michael said. 'I'll go and harness Rajah.'

*

The following morning when they were all seated at the breakfast table, Frank said, 'You know, it's not going to be an easy task to monitor the temperature in the glass-houses. I've been thinking about it and, Nick, since you like dealing with engines and mechanical things, how about I teach you all about the battery house and the boiler house and between us we'll look after the heating system for the greenhouses. Maybe we can think about a pump, like Bill Randall suggested.'

'And a thermostat,' Nick joined in and Maddie noticed the sudden spark in his eyes. Frank nodded and jerked his thumb over his shoulder towards the greenhouse that Mr Theo had given them. It had been built on to the side of the house and now covered the window of the living room. 'In fact, I'd like to know what you think about this greenhouse. How do you think we should heat it? I was wondering about running pipes from the boiler in the kitchen.'

'What? Dig up my floors?' Harriet said indignantly.

'No. We'd come through the wall from the kitchen there,' Frank pointed to the corner near the ceiling. 'And run them along just under the ceiling and out there . . .' Now he pointed to the corner near the outer wall. '. . . and into the greenhouse. What do you think, Nick? Of course, you'd still have to help with the field work, but what do you say to learning how to handle that side of things?'

Maddie didn't think she had ever seen such pleasure light the young boy's face. But before he could answer, his mother cut in, 'I don't want Nicholas meddling with anything dangerous, Mr Frank. You've always kept the boys out of your battery house.'

Frank sighed but this time he looked at Harriet down the length of the table. 'They're hardly boys now, Harriet,

197

either of them. And I've already shown Michael quite a lot about how things work. Nick's sixteen in a week or so and if his interest lies in the direction of things mechanical, then it's up to us to help him learn all he can. After all, maybe he won't want to stay at Few Farm all his life . . .'

'He'll do as I tell him,' she snapped and Maddie glanced at Nick in sympathy. No wonder he always seemed to have a sulky twist to this mouth. To Maddie's surprise there was a sudden flash in the boy's eyes as he turned to his mother.

'Mr Frank won't let me get into any danger and I'll always do exactly as he tells me.' Without waiting for her answer, Nick turned towards Frank. 'I'd like that very much, Mr Frank. Thank you.'

Harriet said no more but her face turned red with a rage she could hardly suppress.

'Good old Nick,' Michael said later as they snatched a few brief precious moments. 'I never thought I'd see him stand up to her like that.'

'Where's he gone now? I saw him going out of the gate after breakfast.'

'He's taken Dad's gun on a walk around the fields.'

'Why?'

'Rabbits. They'll nibble anything and everything if we don't keep them down.'

'I'm surprised his mother lets him have hold of a dangerous thing like a gun.'

Michael winked at her and put his finger to his lips. 'She doesn't know, so not a word. All right?'

Maddie nodded.

Michael sighed and kissed her forehead briefly, 'Well, we'd better get on with the work. Come on, Tulip.'

The autumn passed in a haze of hard work and loving Michael. Their times together were brief and snatched but all the more precious and exciting. Then came the day they were all waiting for – the first of the trays to bloom in the glasshouse. It was Nick, out early in the morning two days before Christmas Eve to check the temperature, who came rushing into the house.

'Come and look. Quick!'

'What is it? What's the matter?' Maddie cried, but he had raced off again without further explanation.

'Oh, don't say . . .' Michael was already out of the door, following him, whilst Maddie, still struggling to pull on her Wellingtons, shouted, 'Wait for me. Michael, wait.'

When she arrived at the door of the first greenhouse it was to see Michael and Nick just standing drinking in the sight of a tray of pink tulips that had burst into flower. Silently, Michael held out his hand to her and she moved slowly towards him, taking his hand but her gaze was on the beautiful flowers.

'We've done it,' he whispered and his voice was hoarse. 'We've really done it. Isn't that the loveliest sight?'

Maddie nodded, unable to speak. Since she had first seen the heart-shaped bed of golden tulips deep in the woods and then Mr Randall's rainbow field, as she always called it, she had dreamt of such a moment. True, it was only one tray of the flowers, but Maddie could not have felt prouder if it had been fifty acres.

And one day, she vowed, it would be.

Whilst Nick had been put in charge of the heating and Maddie had undertaken the day-to-day care of the bulbs, Michael had been the one to organize the selling of the blooms once they were ready. Already he had a buyer waiting in London and transport would be by train from Wellandon Station.

'Right,' he said now, breaking their trance. 'I'll get the boxes and we'll get these packed now. Then I'll take them to the station for the night train.'

'If they're not going until tonight, Michael,' Maddie said, thoughtfully, 'I think we should leave picking them until as late as possible. Mr Randall said we should pick early in the morning or late at night. I know that's right for the fields, but I suppose the same applies to the blooms in here.' She glanced at him. 'Doesn't it?'

Michael wrinkled his forehead. 'Well, I would have thought that now they're just coming out they don't want to be left much longer in the heat. We don't want them too far out, do we?'

Maddie bit her lip worriedly. 'No, I suppose not.'

'I don't think just the rest of today will hurt.' Nick shrugged his shoulders. 'Let's face it, we're going to have to learn by our own mistakes a bit at first, aren't we? I mean Bill Randall can't tell us everything. We've got to stand on our own feet.'

Maddie and Michael exchanged an amused glance. Nick was right, they had to agree, but such a statement coming from the boy whose mother ruled his every waking moment made them want to laugh.

'You've got a point there,' Michael put his hand on Nick's shoulder. 'So what do we do? Pick 'em and pack 'em now or wait 'til tonight?'

'Pick half of them now and the other half tonight and let's see for ourselves if it makes any difference,' Nick suggested.

Michael laughed. 'You're full of bright ideas this morning. That's exactly what we'll do, but we must get them to the station by six o'clock at the latest. At tulip time, you know, Wellandon handles hundreds of boxes every night. Before the War it was thousands and the number is building up again as more and more flower growers are turning away from food production as soon as they're allowed. Of course, there won't be that many this time of the year, but I don't want ours to get left aside in favour of the regular growers.' He bit his lip. 'I think I'll drive into town this morning, just to make sure that everything's all right for this first consignment. After that, it should be plain sailing.'

Through the day, Maddie picked all the flowers that were ready, laying them carefully in the wooden boxes in neat bunches. 'I'm coming with you,' she informed Michael as she helped him load the boxes into the boot of Frank's car. 'I want to see this first lot on their way for myself.'

'Don't you trust me with your precious tulips?'

She grinned at him, 'Of course I don't. You might decide to give them away to all your girlfriends in the village.'

Michael's dark eyes sparkled with fun. 'And when have I had time to see any girlfriends the last few weeks? Besides . . .' Now the look in his eyes was serious. 'The only girl I want is right here with me all the time.'

He reached out and grasped her hand, squeezing it tightly. 'Come on, let's go and sell your flowers.'

'Our flowers,' she corrected him as she climbed into the passenger's seat beside him. 'Everyone deserves the credit. Even . . .' she smiled impishly at him, 'even Mrs Trowbridge.'

'Oho,' Michael laughed. 'Now it really hurt you to say that, didn't it?'

Maddie said no more; she didn't need to.

*

It was dusk when they returned to the farm.

'Well, Tulip, that's the first safely away and we're still living up to our name,' Michael said as he got out of the car and stood in the yard.

'Eh?'

'Few Farm. Only now it's a few 'taties, a few caulis and a few tulips.'

'Oh you!' Laughing Maddie pushed Michael on the shoulder and, playfully, he caught hold of her hands, pulling her close to him, his dark brown eyes looking down into hers. The longing flared between them and suddenly the smile faded from Michael's eyes. She felt as if the breath had been knocked from her body as she looked up at him, her lips slightly apart. For a brief moment they were lost in a world of their own until Harriet's voice from the back doorway made them both jump and spring apart.

'Your supper's ready.'

When Maddie turned to walk towards the housekeeper, it was to see the look of pure hatred on the woman's face. For some time Harriet must have suspected that there was something between her favourite and the orphan girl she had brought into the house.

Now she had seen it for herself and knew for certain.

Twenty-Seven

It was in the January, when the blooms in the glasshouse were at their most delicate stage, that Maddie began to feel unwell.

Carrying another heavy tray in from the field to the second glasshouse, she felt suddenly dizzy and before she realized what was happening she had dropped the box and was pitching forward, the ground coming up to meet her.

'Maddie! Maddie, what is it?'

She heard Frank's anxious shout from behind her. She was trying to rise as he reached her.

'Have you hurt yourself, love? I shouldn't be letting you carry these heavy boxes. I ought to have got Michael or Nick to do it.'

'I – I'm all right, Mr Frank. Please. I must have tripped . . .' She bit her lip, not wanting to tell him a deliberate lie yet determined not to admit that she had been feeling queasy for the past week now. She couldn't be ill. Not now when there was so much work to do.

'You look a bit pale, love. You've been overdoing it. We shouldn't let you work so hard.'

Slowly Maddie got to her knees and then, carefully, she stood up. Frank held her arm, supporting her. 'We've all been working hard, Mr Frank.' She made herself smile at him, even though the waves of dizziness were still washing over her.

Frank nodded and looked down at her. 'We have. But

you, harder than any of us.' Gently, he added, 'You didn't need to prove yourself to us, you know. We wouldn't have blamed you even if your idea hadn't worked.' Then he smiled broadly. 'But it is doing, lass, I know it is. You should be feeling very proud of yourself.'

Maddie swallowed the bile that threatened to rise into her throat. 'We all should, Mr Frank,' she insisted, but nevertheless she was very touched by his words.

She took a few deep breaths and began to feel a little better. Together they knelt down and gathered the spilt bulbs back into the box.

'I just hope I haven't harmed these. They damage very easily, don't they?'

'Mm,' Frank agreed. 'I sometimes wonder if we shouldn't have daffs as well. They're a bit hardier. But I don't know.'

'Maybe we could. In time.'

He chuckled. 'You had thought about it, then?'

'Oh yes, I'd thought about it.'

Now Frank laughed louder. 'I thought you might have.'

They stood up together as he lifted the tray from the ground. 'Now, young lady, I'm carrying this into the greenhouse for you and you're not to carry any more heavy boxes today. And you get an early night. You hear me?'

Maddie managed to smile and say, 'Yes, Mr Frank.'

'You little slut!' The bedroom door was flung open so violently, it struck the bed behind it and ricocheted, shuddering.

Maddie, spittle running from her mouth where she had been retching into the bowl, raised bleary eyes to see Harriet towering over her.

'You're in the family way, aren't you?'

Horrified, Maddie straightened up and reached for the towel to wipe her mouth. 'What – what do you mean?'

'I've heard you. Every morning this week you've had your head over that bowl there. You've got morning sickness, girl. And last night when Mr Frank said you'd fallen in the field and looked as if you were going to pass out, then I was sure.'

Maddie gasped, her eyes widening. 'No. Oh, no.'

'Oh yes,' the housekeeper said grimly. 'Well, we'll see what Mr Frank has to say about this little lot, shall we?'

Maddie reached out and grasped the woman's arm. 'Please don't tell him, Mrs Trowbridge.'

Maddie didn't think she had ever seen such malice in anyone's eyes. Such venom, such glee. 'I can't *wait* to tell him.'

'Look, I know you want me gone from here. So, all right, you win. I'll go away but not until we've got all the cropping done at the end of April, and maybe the lifting in June. Then I'll go. But please don't tell Mr Frank. I mean – I mean you don't want to cause him any more worry, do you?' She was babbling now in her anxiety. 'He's just getting back on his feet. The flowers from the glasshouses made good money in London at Christmas and New Year and they're still selling well. But there's a lot of work. I can't possibly go yet.'

Harriet's face was a sneer. 'How do you think you're going to hide it, eh? You'll start to show before then. Don't you know anything about having babies?'

Maddie didn't answer. No, she knew nothing or she would have already guessed. Instead, she said, 'Then I'll go before I start to – to show. Mr Frank needn't know. No one need know.' Casting about frantically for another reason, she added, 'And you don't want him blaming you for not having kept a better eye on me.'

'Blame me!' She was indignant. 'I'm not the one to blame. He was too soft with you from the start. Letting you go to the village dances and round on the milk cart with young Michael. And then giving way to your ridiculous scheme to grow flowers.' She almost spat the next question. 'Whose brat is it, anyway?'

Maddie gasped aloud. 'It's Michael's.'

'Huh! I don't believe that for a minute. It's some village lad's, I don't doubt.'

'It is Michael's. It is.' Maddie was almost in tears at the injustice of the woman. How could she believe that it could possibly be anyone else's?

'I love Michael. I wouldn't let anyone else . . .' she hesitated and then added, 'touch me.'

Harriet's lips were a thin, unforgiving line. 'You dirty, foul-mouthed little trollop. Well, if it is his, you've led him on. I don't blame him. I blame you. You're out on your ear now, that's for certain. Because I'll not stand by and see you pull a fine young man like Master Michael down into the gutter alongside you, saddling him with your little bastard.'

She pulled her arm from Maddie's grasp and turned to leave the room. The girl sank down onto the bed and groaned. She knew what Harriet had said was true. She had no reason to doubt the older woman's knowledge and during the past week she had wondered why what she had first thought was a bilious attack was going on so long. It had struck her as very odd. Now she knew why.

That the housekeeper would take great delight in telling the rest of the household, Maddie had no doubt, so she dragged herself up again and dressed.

Better face the music, she told herself.

Halfway down the stairs, she heard the raised voices. Frank's and then Michael's.

'How could you? A young girl in our care, Michael. And she's still under age. You could go to prison for this, never mind the trouble you've brought on her and shame upon this house.'

As Maddie opened the door leading from the stairs into the living room, she saw that Michael and his father were standing on the hearth rug in front of the fire, staring at each other. His face white, Michael said, 'What do you mean, under age?'

'She's only fifteen, for God's sake.'

'No. Oh no. She can't be. She's sixteen. Surely, she's sixteen?' He was casting about frantically. 'She had a birthday. She told us so. We had a party. She's got to be sixteen.'

'She was fourteen when she came here,' Harriet put in. 'So now she's fifteen.'

'Fourteen?' Michael's voice was a strangled whisper of disbelief. 'How could she have left school at fourteen? I was fifteen when I left. So was Nick.'

Frank ran his hand through his hair. 'You stayed on a little longer because you were at a Grammar School and Harriet wanted Nick to stay on a little longer too. The statutory school-leaving age has only gone up to fifteen this last year.'

'I didn't know, Dad. I swear I didn't. I thought she was sixteen. I never touched her until after that party. And I wouldn't have done so yet, if – if . . .'

His voice trailed away and he looked so desperate and almost afraid that Maddie longed to run to him, put her arms about him and tell him that she would take all the blame. She wouldn't let anything dreadful happen to him. But she remained quite still just inside the door, watching and listening.

Then she heard Michael pull in a deep, shuddering breath. 'I'll take care of her, Dad. I'll . . .'

'And how are you going to do that? The farm is barely supporting us now. With another mouth to feed and without Maddie able to work, how do you think we're going to manage? And changing to growing blasted flowers. I wish I'd never listened to her now. In fact, I wish to God . . .'

Frank became aware of Maddie standing, ashen-faced, in the doorway. He glanced at her and then looked away, running his hand distractedly through his thinning hair yet again. Harriet, standing at the end of the table, her arms folded beneath her bosom, watched the scene unfolding before her, a gleam of satisfaction in her eyes.

Nick was sitting at the table, his eyes downcast on his cereal bowl, though he was not eating. Only Michael came to her. He put his arms about her and his voice was gentle now as he said, 'Oh Maddie. I'm sorry. Why didn't you tell me?'

'I . . .' At his kindness, Maddie felt the tears spill over as she laid her cheek against his chest. 'I didn't know.'

Now he held her at arm's length and looked down at her. 'What do you mean, you didn't know?'

Blinking through her tears, she stammered, 'I didn't understand why I was being sick in the morning.'

'You mean you haven't seen a doctor?'

Maddie shook her head.

'Oh well, then . . .' Instantly there was relief in his voice. 'Maybe you aren't.'

'But Mrs Trowbridge . . .' she began.

Now his tone was bitter. 'Oh aye, we all know that our dear housekeeper would do almost anything to get you sent away.' He looked over his shoulder, his eyes narrowing as he looked towards Harriet and speaking directly to her now. 'But what I can't understand is why you brought Maddie here in the first place.'

'Her sort should be punished. They bring misery to good folk around them with their devious, scheming ways. And I was right, wasn't I? She's brought trouble on this house, just like I said she would.'

'So why?' Michael persisted. He had let go of Maddie and was moving back towards Harriet now. 'Why did you bring her here?'

'That's my business,' she snapped.

'Let's not go into all that now,' Frank said wearily. 'We've got to think what's the best thing to do.'

Harriet rounded on him. 'Whatever do you mean? There's only one thing to do. Throw her out. Out on the streets where the little slut belongs.'

'Harriet, no one is going to be thrown out. My son is as much to blame as Maddie.'

'Oh no. No, no, no,' Harriet screamed at him. 'I won't have you blaming Michael. He's not to blame. It's her. She led him on. It could be anybody's. Any one of the village lads. She's always running to the village to see that Jenny. How do we know what she gets up to when she's away from here?'

Very slowly and deliberately, Frank said, 'Maddie stays here.' There was a moment's silence in the room before he added with a heavy sadness, 'It is Michael who must go away.'

Now it was Maddie who cried, 'No, oh no.'

Frank came towards her and though he didn't touch

her and his eyes were shadowed with sorrow, there was understanding in his tone. 'Look, it'd be better if he went away. At least, for a while.'

'See how you've broken up this family.' Harriet's spiteful tone would not be silenced.

For the first time in her life, Maddie's resolve crumbled. Tears poured down her cheeks and she flung herself against Frank, begging, pleading hysterically. 'Please, oh please, Mr Frank, don't send him away. I'd sooner you sent me away. Not Michael.'

'Let her live in the woods,' Harriet said. 'That's where her sort belong.'

Frank turned and glared at her. 'If you don't shut up, Harriet, it will be you leaving this house.' The woman stared back, but, for the moment, she said no more.

Frank stroked Maddie's hair. 'There, there, love. Don't get so upset. It's not good for the child. You must think of the bairn, now, you know. After all . . .' Gently he released her limpet hold on him and looked down into her face. 'It is my grandchild.'

Fresh tears welled and she buried her face against him. 'Oh Mr Frank, I'm sorry. I'm so sorry.'

The argument wrangled on for several days. Michael did not want to go.

'I don't want to leave you, Maddie. Dad's right. It is my fault just as much as yours. You'll be sixteen very soon. In March. I can't understand why we can't get married then.'

Bending over the tray of budding tulips, she asked in a small voice, 'Do you really want to marry me, Michael, or are you just saying it now because – because of . . .?'

Standing beside her in the warm greenhouse, he

210

answered quickly, 'Of course I want to marry you. It's just a bit sooner than we'd thought, isn't it? That's all.'

They'd never talked of marriage before, so even though she wanted to believe him with all her heart, Maddie couldn't quite believe, deep inside her, that he wasn't just saying it now because of the coming child. What was the phrase – a shotgun wedding? Well, no one was holding a shotgun to Michael's head. He had no need to marry her.

They worked on in silence. 'I think,' Maddie said. 'Your dad's worried that with me having no family, the authorities might start asking too many questions, about my age and that.'

'I just don't know how you're going to manage all the work, if I do go away like Dad suggests, that's all.'

'I know.'

The silence between them grew longer. There was nothing left to say – it had all been said – and there seemed no way round the problem.

Michael straightened up and eased his back. 'You go into the house, Maddie. You look so tired and there are dark shadows under your eyes. I don't like to see you looking like that.'

'But . . .'

'No "buts",' he said firmly. He stepped in front of her and put his hands on her shoulders. He looked down into her upturned face. 'Oh Tulip, I wouldn't have hurt you for the world, but I think it would be best if I did go.'

'No, please, Michael. Please don't leave me.' She clung to him again, desperately, not caring now who saw them.

Gently he disentangled himself from her clinging arms, but held her hands between his own. 'I must. But I will come back. I promise you faithfully, I will come back.'

Tears blurred her vision as she pulled away from him and stumbled blindly out of the greenhouse, quite forgetting in her misery to open and close the door carefully so that she did not cause a sudden rush of cold air, uncaring, for once, about her precious flowers.

She did not go into the house. She could not face Frank's worried expression nor the glee in Harriet's eyes. Instead she went out of the gate, into the lane and turned towards the village, but halfway along she took the fork in the road that led to the woods belonging to Mayfield Park. She met no one and was thankful. Sobbing, she ran on and on until she came to the edge of the trees. Gasping for breath she leant against a trunk for a moment but then plunged into the leafy shadows. Mindless of the briars scratching her legs and tearing at her clothes, she crashed her way through the undergrowth until she came to the clearing.

The bed of tulips that grew year after year without, so far as Maddie knew, any tending showed nothing now of the colourful display that would be there in three months' time. Now the ground was cold and hard and bare.

Maddie flung herself down where the golden flowers would bloom, digging her fingers into the ground. She rested her head on her arm and cried until exhaustion overtook her.

She didn't see a figure amongst the trees, who stood uncertainly, watching her weep.

Twenty-Eight

'But where can she be?'

'I thought she'd come into the house. She was looking so tired,' Michael, facing his father, spread his hands. 'I told her to come in and I'd finish off in the greenhouse.'

'What time was that?'

'Just after two.'

Frank turned to Harriet. 'Did she come in?'

The woman shrugged. 'Not that I saw.'

'Nick? Have you seen her?'

'No, Mr Frank. And I've looked all round the out-houses. Even . . .' He cast a sly look towards Michael. 'Even the hay shed.'

'She might have gone to see Jenny, Dad,' Michael suggested.

'That's a thought. I'll go . . .'

'No, I'll go. I can be there in five minutes on my bike.'

Half an hour later Michael returned with a breathless Jenny, who had run all the way alongside him.

'What's wrong?' Her eyes were wide and fearful.

'Hasn't she told you?' Harriet feigned surprise. 'I thought you'd have been the first to know. I thought you were like sisters.'

'Told me what?' Poor Jenny's glance was going from one to the other, her voice frantic now. 'Tell me? What's happened to her?'

Harriet bent and thrust her face close to the girl's. 'She's got herself pregnant, that's what.'

The words were said harshly, without a vestige of feeling or understanding and the woman smiled maliciously as Jenny's open mouth formed a horrified, 'Oh no.' But at least Jenny didn't need to ask who was the father of Maddie's child, for her glance went straight to Michael.

Frank's deep voice intervened. 'Do you know where she might have gone, love?'

'She was very upset when she left me,' Michael said. 'I – I'd just told her that I thought it best if I did go away for a while . . .' His voice trailed away.

'We thought she might have come to you?' Frank went on, but as Jenny shook her head, he asked, 'Do you think she would go back to the Home?'

Now the shake of her head was vehement. 'She rather die than go back there . . .' And then realizing what she'd said, the girl clapped her hand over her mouth with a little squeak and tears filled her eyes.

Frank put his arm around her shoulders. 'Don't worry, love. We'll find her.'

Maddie roused to the sound of soft and gentle singing, like the crooning of a lullaby. She blinked, rubbed her eyes and sat up and then she blinked again, this time in surprise. Sitting on the opposite side of the tulip bed was a woman. A pretty woman with long, curling fair hair. She wasn't looking at Maddie but at the ground, her fingers gently pull out a stray dead weed and then patting the earth as if she were willing the blooms to sprout up under her touch. Maddie held her breath, not wanting to break the spell of the pale winter sunlight shining through the trees on to the woman's hair, casting a golden halo around her head. She

214

looked up and Maddie stared straight into her blue eyes. Slowly, Maddie let out her breath, yet, still, she dare not speak even though the singing had now faded away. The woman's eyes were looking at her and yet they didn't really seem to be seeing her. There was a vacant look in them. No, Maddie decided, that wasn't quite fair. It was more a dreamy expression, as if the woman were lost in a world of her own; an imaginary world that, to her, was far more real than life around her.

Softly, hesitantly, for she had the feeling that the stranger would shy away like a frightened doe if alarmed, Maddie said, 'Hello.'

The woman stared at her and now her eyes seemed to focus properly on Maddie's face. She smiled but did not answer and then she bent her head again, her gaze once more upon the ground.

Suddenly, Maddie realized who this woman was. She had seen her once before. Only the once, peering out the rear window of a motor car as it passed them by in the market place. This was Amelia Mayfield.

'They are beautiful, aren't they, in the spring?' Maddie said gently. 'Did you plant them?'

The vacant look was back as Amelia's shoulders lifted fractionally. A light breeze rustled through the trees and the sunlight faded. Maddie shivered, but the woman seemed impervious to the sudden change. Softly, deep in her throat the crooning began again.

Maddie was fascinated by her and although she knew she ought to be getting back to the farm, somehow she could not bring herself to rise and walk away from Amelia.

She looked, Maddie thought, to be in her mid-thirties and yet her manner and actions were those of a child. An innocent, lost child. Poor Amelia. So it was true what they said about her, that her tragic love affair had affected her mind and that she was kept hidden away in Mayfield Park for her own protection.

Should she be out here, then, Maddie wondered, alone in the woods? Was she allowed out this far alone? She was still debating what she should do when she heard a voice calling and the sound of someone crashing their way through the undergrowth.

'Amelia? Are you there, dear? Amelia? It's Theo. Don't be afraid. It's only Theo.'

Maddie watched as Amelia took not a scrap of notice. It was as if she didn't even hear her brother calling. She just carried on singing and smiling to herself.

Without making a sudden movement that might startle her, Maddie stood up and tiptoed to the edge of the clearing.

'Mr Theo,' she called. 'We're here.'

For a moment the sounds of movement through the trees ceased and then, beginning again, came towards her.

'Miss March!' He said, catching sight of her but immediately his concerned glance went beyond her to his sister sitting on the ground. At the sight of her, Maddie saw him relax visibly. Then his glance came back to her and she saw him frown as he took in her dishevelled appearance and her tear-stained face.

'Miss March, are you all right? Is there – anything I can do?'

Maddie summoned a brave smile. 'Thank you, Mr Theo, but I'll be fine now. I – I must be going, but . . .' She glanced back over her shoulder towards Amelia. 'I didn't like to leave her here alone.'

'Thank you.' So briefly, that later she was to wonder if she had imagined it, he reached out and touched her hand.

'I – must go.' She turned away from him but at the edge

of the clearing she paused and looked back towards the woman still sitting on the grass. Then her glance took in the tree where the desperate young man had taken his own life. Love made you weak and vulnerable, Maddie thought. She had never shed so many tears in her life as she had during these past few days. Strangely, though she could not have explained why, she felt stronger now. Perhaps it was seeing the poor, lost creature, still mourning her beloved, that made Maddie, in that moment, determined to face whatever blows life inflicted upon her. Never, never, she vowed, would she allow anyone to have such power over her that she ended up like Amelia Mayfield.

'They're all out looking for you,' was Harriet's greeting. 'Running around like headless chickens over a little trollop like you that don't deserve it. But there, that's men's stupidity for you.'

With a quiet dignity, Maddie said, 'I'm sorry if I've caused anyone concern.'

'Oh, you've caused concern, all right. You'd have done us all a favour if you had taken yourself off and never come back.'

Maddie returned the woman's look. 'Perhaps you're right, Mrs Trowbridge. Perhaps that's exactly what I should do, because if Michael does go – as he says he will – life's not going to be worth living in this house. Not for me. Is it? You'll see to that, I've no doubt.'

She turned and went out of the back door again and walked to the gate. She saw Frank and Michael walking down the lane towards her and she waved. As they neared her she said, 'I'm sorry to have worried you, Mr Frank.'

He gave her a curt nod and said, 'Well, as long as you're all right. But don't do it again.' Without another word he went through the gate, across the yard and into the house.

Maddie's troubled eyes followed him. 'He's angry with me, isn't he?'

Michael put his arm about her shoulders and sighed. 'You had us worried, Maddie. Where were you?'

'I . . .' She hesitated, not wanting to tell him where she had been. He might read more into her actions than even she had meant. 'I went for a walk that's all. I needed to be on my own. To think. Michael . . .' She twisted to face him. 'It would be better if I went away. Right away. There's places for people like me.'

He touched her cheek with the tip of his finger, trying to brush away the dried salt of her tears. 'You've spent all your life in an institution. I won't let you go back into one. It's my fault as much as yours. More, really.' He put his arms around her and held her close. 'We'll work it out, Maddie. But you must be brave if the best thing is for me to go away . . .' His hold tightened, hugging her to him. 'Just for a while. Just until after your birthday. Then I'll come back and we can be married.'

'Are you really sure you want to? You're not just saying it?'

''Course I'm not. I love you, Maddie.' He laid his cheek against her hair. 'Don't ever think otherwise. Promise.'

Muffled against him, she said, 'Promise.'

The day Michael left, Maddie thought her heart would finally break.

They had not made love again since the discovery of her pregnancy, but now Maddie longed to be in his arms, to be loved just one more time before he went away but he had seemed distant, awkward with her.

'Come on,' he said now, taking her hand. 'Let's go for a walk. There's time before the train goes. I want to talk to you away from the house.'

They walked to the field and leant over the gate. 'In a couple of months or so, this will be your very own rainbow field framed in gold, Maddie.'

They had planted the bulbs in blocks of different colours, pink, red and purple. But more than any other colour, they had planted Maddie's favourite yellow.

'Hey,' he turned to look at her, grinning. It was the first time he had really smiled in ages. 'Remember what the gypsy said that day? Maybe that's what she meant. Everything you touch will turn to gold.'

Maddie picked the green mould from the top bar of the wooden gate with her fingernail. 'She also said, I'd have joy and sadness in equal measure. She was right about that, wasn't she?'

Tears threatened again.

'Don't cry, Tulip,' he said, putting his arm about her shoulders. 'I'll come back, I promise you. Then we'll get married and be a real family.' He turned to face her, tenderly cupped her face in his hands and gently kissed her mouth. 'Whatever happens, Maddie, always remember that I love you and that I will come back.'

They turned and walked back to the house, their arms wrapped around each other, not caring, for once, who saw them.

The moment of Michael's leaving was strained and awkward.

'I'll come with you to the station, son,' Frank said, but Michael shook his head.

'No, Dad. I'd sooner you didn't.' He nodded stiffly

towards Harriet. His easy, teasing manner towards her had disappeared completely now, but to Nick he said, 'I'm sorry the work is going to fall on you now.'

To Maddie's surprise, Nick smiled. 'S'all right. We'll manage.' And the two young men shook hands.

Michael stood a moment looking round at them all, as if committing their faces to memory, but his glance came back to rest on Maddie. 'I'll write,' was his last promise as he raised his hand and walked away across the yard and out of the gate.

Twenty-Nine

'Well, I hope you're satisfied with yourself. You've broken up this family good and proper. I suppose next you'll lose Mr Frank his farm all together with your fancy notions. Flowers, indeed. Whoever heard of a farmer growing flowers?'

'Shut up, shut up,' Maddie rounded on the woman. 'The fields are doing well. We've a lot of work ahead with the weeding and then the picking and you'd do better to support your beloved Mr Frank than finding fault.' Boldly, she moved closer to the housekeeper. 'Why don't you give him a bit of credit? If he hadn't wanted to do it, then he wouldn't have done, would he?'

Harriet's mouth was a sneer. 'Oh, you've a lot to learn about men, girl. They're weak, the lot of 'em. They always make a mess of things and leave us women to pick up the pieces. And then blame us for it happening in the first place. You caught him when he was down and not knowing which way to turn. And up you come with a fancy notion and he grasps at it, like a drowning man. And Michael, too. If he is the father of your child, and I for one don't believe he is, but if he is, then I expect you caught him when he wanted a bit of comfort.'

Maddie gasped as the tirade went on.

'And what's he done now but run away, leaving us to face all the gossip? Aye, and maybe a visit from the police an' all. And what'll they do to Mr Frank? They'll likely

221

think he's the father of your bastard and throw him in jail. Oh, I know about you. You've bad blood in you and bad blood will always out.'

'You know nothing about me. How can you?'

'Oh, I know what I know,' Harriet said smugly and began to turn away. Maddie caught hold of her arm.

'What do you mean, you know about me?'

'Let go of me this instant . . .' Before Maddie had time to loosen her hold, the woman raised her right hand and dealt the girl a vicious slap on her left cheek, then she gripped Maddie's shoulder so fiercely that her fingers dug into the girl's flesh. She bent forward, pushing her face close to Maddie's. 'Why don't you do us all a favour,' she hissed. 'And hang yourself from that tree in the woods?'

Shocked by the woman's venom, Maddie pulled herself away and ran out of the back door, across the yard and into the lane. She was shaking and her cheek stung. She couldn't go back to the field to help with the hoeing. Mr Frank would want to know what had happened and she didn't want to tell him. He probably wouldn't believe her anyway. He would never believe that the woman he had taken into his home when she had been destitute could say such a thing. Even Maddie could hardly believe it herself now. She knew Harriet hated her, but even she had not realized quite how malicious the woman was.

She found herself walking towards the village. She quickened her step. Jenny. I must see Jenny.

As she opened the shop door, Mrs Grange behind the counter and her one customer turned see who had come in.

Maddie's heart sank as she saw who the customer was.

'Well, well, look who it is?' Mrs Potter's voice was thick with sarcastic glee. 'I've just been hearing about you. Got yourself into trouble even quicker than I thought.'

Maddie, her jaw hardening, glanced at Mrs Grange, whose face turned pink. She lowered her head, hiding beneath the brim of the blue hat she always wore.

'I've come to see Jenny.' Maddie held her head high and returned Mrs Potter's stare.

'Well, now,' Mrs Potter folded her arms under her ample bosom. 'I don't know if we ought to let her see the likes of you. You might lead her into your bad ways. What do you say, Mrs Grange? I'm only thankful I got rid of you afore you brought shame on my orphanage.'

' 'T'isn't your orphanage. If it's anyone's, it's Sir Peter's.'

'He's ill now and Mr Theo might have been voted on to the Board, but he hasn't the say-so that his father had. Besides, I can twist that young man round my finger any time I want.' Mrs Potter turned to Mrs Grange, 'I shouldn't let her see young Jenny, if I were you.'

Anger flooded through Maddie. She was back on familiar ground, facing the woman she had never been afraid of because she didn't care a jot what Mrs Potter thought about her or what she could do to her.

'I will see Jenny. Just try and stop me . . .' And before either Mrs Grange or Mrs Potter could even move, Maddie was around the counter and through the brown curtain into the rear of the shop.

'Jen? You here, Jenny?'

There was the sound of footsteps on the stairs and a door opened and she was there.

'Maddie! Oh Maddie!' Jenny's excited squeak left Maddie in no doubt as to the girl's pleasure at seeing her. They hugged each other and both began to speak at once and then laughed together. Then Maddie's face sobered as she held the girl at arm's length and said quietly so that the two women in the shop could not hear, 'I wish you hadn't told Mrs Grange about me. The whole village will know now.'

Jenny's eyes widened. 'I didn't, Maddie. I haven't said a word to anyone. Really, I haven't.'

Maddie stared into her eyes and saw the truth there. 'I'm sorry, I couldn't think . . .' Then she stopped. Of course. Harriet Trowbridge. Although the woman rarely left the farm, the only place she did visit occasionally was the village shop. In fact, she was quite friendly with Mrs Grange who often did shopping in Wellandon for the housekeeper from Few Farm. Hadn't it been she who had bought those dreadful second-hand clothes from the market stall? Maddie reminded herself. No doubt, she thought wryly, she had been instructed by Harriet to buy the dreariest, most shapeless clothes she could find.

'Oh well,' she sighed. 'It was bound to get out eventually, but, you see, because I'm not sixteen 'til next month, Michael could get into dreadful trouble. He could be arrested.'

'But he's gone away now, hasn't he?'

Was there nothing the village shop didn't know? Maddie wondered. She nodded.

'Well, then, that's all right. Isn't it?'

'I don't know,' Maddie said heavily. 'If everyone knows now, then sooner or later the local bobby's going to hear of it, isn't he?' She almost added, And I know someone who'll probably make sure he does.

'Oh Maddie, don't worry. It'll be all right,' Jenny smiled. 'Just think how lucky you are. You're going to have a little baby to love. A baby all of your very own.' Then, as other thoughts crowded in, her first delight faded.

'You are all right? I mean, they're not throwing you out at the farm?'

Maddie shook her head. 'No, but now Michael's gone, it's awful. Mr Frank hardly speaks and Mrs Trowbridge only opens her mouth to be nasty. She's vicious, that woman.' Maddie wrinkled her brow thoughtfully. 'I know she doesn't like me, but I can't understand what I've done to deserve such hatred.'

'What about Nick?' Jenny blushed even as she said his name. 'He's not nasty to you, is he?'

'No. Funnily enough he's been nicer ever since Michael went. But he's under his mother's thumb. What she says, goes, as far as he's concerned.'

Jenny was thoughtful. 'I don't see quite why everyone's so worried. You'll be sixteen by the time the baby's born, won't you?'

'Yes, but I wasn't when – when it happened. You know?'

They all knew the facts of life. It had been explained to them by Mrs Potter who had left the girls in her charge feeling that the whole business was not only distasteful, but sinful too, even within marriage, let alone outside it.

Jenny hugged her again. 'Don't worry, Maddie. As long as you can stay at the farm, it'll be all right.'

'If only I knew where he's gone. What he's doing. If he's all right. I can't sleep at night for thinking about him.' Maddie gulped back the tears that threatened.

'He'll write soon. When he's got settled somewhere,' Jenny comforted. 'And then, when you've had the baby, Michael can come home and you'll be so happy.'

As Maddie rested her cheek against her little friend's hair and closed her eyes, she sent up a silent prayer that Jenny might be right.

But somewhere, deep inside her, she dared not even hope that she would be. The words of the gypsy came back to her: 'joy and sorrow in equal measure'. Well, she had known the joy, had touched the heights of ecstasy with Michael. Even through the days and weeks of the foot and mouth disaster and struggling against the harsh winter, even through all that, his love had given her faith in the future. Their future. Together.

Maddie's very soul shuddered as she realized that though the hell of the last few weeks had been dreadful, it did not equal the heaven she had known. If the prophecy were true, then Maddie March would have to face a great deal more anguish yet.

No letter came from Michael in the first week.

'He'll be busy getting settled in,' Frank said and added, unable to keep the anxiety out of his tone. 'Wherever he is.'

Nor during the second week and by the third week the disappointment was showing in Frank's eyes too.

Maddie plunged herself into work, trying to stave off the sickness that still gripped her each morning and the ache in her heart.

'Don't worry,' Nick said as they worked side by side. 'He'll get in touch as soon as he can.'

Maddie tried to smile. 'You've been awfully good since Michael went.'

It was true. Nick went out earlier than normal every morning, returning at breakfast with the mail in his hand, his grey eyes sympathetic when, each day, there was still no word.

'You know,' Maddie said slowly, 'I could understand

it, in a way, him not writing to me. But I would have thought he'd've written to his dad.'

She saw Nick glance at her and then away again.

'What? What is it?'

He gave an exaggerated sigh. 'Maddie, I know you're – well – in love with him, I s'pose . . .'

'Of course I am.' She was hot with indignation. 'How can you even think I'd have – that I'd have . . .' she pointed to her own stomach, 'done anything with him if I hadn't been?'

Nick was shaking his head sadly. 'Oh Maddie, I tried to tell you, but you wouldn't listen.'

'What?' There was a sudden icy feeling creeping round her heart.

'You're not the first, you know.'

She was silent a moment, remembering the girl at the dance. Flatly, she said, 'I didn't think for one moment that I was.'

'I mean – you're not the first he's got pregnant.'

'*What!*' Now she was shocked and hurt. She felt as if Nick had thrust a knife into her heart. Instinctively protective, she crossed her arms over her stomach. 'Who? When?' she demanded.

Nick shrugged. 'Brenda somebody. She had a babby last year and the gossip in the village said it was Michael's.'

'Oh, gossip. Is that all? I mean, did the girl come here? Did her parents tell his dad?'

Nick shrugged. 'How should I know?'

'You seem to know plenty,' she said tartly.

'Maddie . . .' His tone was reproachful. 'I'm only telling you for your own good. I don't like to see you getting hurt.'

She frowned. She hated it when anyone said something

227

was for her own good. It had been one of Mrs Potter's favourite phrases.

'Tell you what,' Nick was smiling now, 'soon as we hear where he is, I'll go and see him for you. Put your mind at rest, like.'

Maddie was thoughtful. 'Well, I could go.'

'No, no,' Nick said swiftly. 'That wouldn't be a good idea. If anyone guessed, it could get him into trouble. A lot of trouble. No, it'd be better if I went.'

'Or his dad. His dad could go.'

'I think Mr Frank is too upset with him at the moment.'

Maddie sighed. 'I suppose you're right. But there doesn't seem to be much chance of anyone being able to go to see him if we're not even going to hear where he is.'

Before Nick should see the tears welling in her eyes, Maddie turned and walked away. I won't cry, she told herself fiercely. Whatever happens, I'm not going to cry ever again.

Thirty

The following morning at breakfast they heard Nick's boots pounding across the yard even before he flung open the back door and almost fell into the kitchen.

'There's a letter.' He held out a torn and muddy envelope, the writing all smudged where the ink had run. 'I found it in the lane. The postman must have dropped it.' He held it out to Frank who took it and carefully unfolded the sheets of paper inside.

'Is it from Michael?' Maddie could no longer hold back her excitement.

Frank nodded. 'It's dated two weeks ago.'

Maddie's face was a picture of joy. 'There, I told you. He did write. That stupid postman. Just wait 'til I see him.'

Frank was reading the letter. 'It's very short,' he murmured. 'But he does give us an address. He's joined the Army.'

'He must be wondering why we've not written back.' She paused before she asked, unable to keep the longing from her tone, 'Is there a note for me?'

Frank looked up at her. 'Sorry, love. Not this time, but he says he'll write to you very soon.'

Maddie swallowed the lump in her throat and smiled bravely. 'Well, I just hope the postman doesn't drop that one in a puddle.' She looked at Nick. 'Thanks,' she said simply and rose from the table, leaving her breakfast untouched.

Later in the day Nick found her in the fields.

'Mr Frank ses I can go to see Michael.'

'What about your mother? Has she given her divine permission?'

'I wish you wouldn't be so hard on my mother. It's just her way, you know.'

Maddie said nothing.

'She's had a hard life.'

'Really?' She could not keep the sarcasm from her tone. Harriet Trowbridge's life didn't seem all that hard to Maddie.

'Yes. After my father died, she had nowhere to go. No other family. Mr Frank took her in as his housekeeper.'

Maddie nodded. 'What happened to your father?'

'I'm not sure. He died. She never talks about him and I never ask. It always upsets her.'

'Well, I'd want to know, if I was you. I'd ask her.'

There was a pause before he asked quietly, 'Do you ever wonder about your own parents?'

''Course I do. But there's not a lot of point in trying to find out anything. I was dumped outside the orphanage, that's all I know. Obviously, they didn't want me then and since no one's ever come looking for me, they still don't want me, even if they are out there somewhere.'

'We've got a lot in common, really, haven't we?'

'Have we? I don't see how. At least you've got a mother, even if she won't tell you much about your father.'

'And you're going to be a mother soon. But do you really think that your baby will ever have a father either?'

Angry tears smarted her eyes, but she would not allow them to fall. 'Of course it's got a father. Michael.'

Very softly, Nick said, 'But he's not here. Is he?'

They worked on in silence, until Maddie could hold back the question no longer. 'When are you going to see him, then?'

'Day after tomorrow.'

'Will you take a letter for me?'

'Of course, Maddie.' His tone was gentle now as she felt him touch her arm and turned to see that he was smiling. A wide, generous smile that lit his whole face. 'I only want you to be happy, Maddie. I wish you'd believe that.'

There was a sudden lump in her throat at his kindness. 'I do,' she said and bent her head over the growing bulbs.

'Is he all right? Where is he? Can I go and see him?'

The questions tumbled from Maddie's lips on Nick's return. He glanced at her and then quickly away again, almost as if he could not meet her eyes.

'What is it? What's wrong?'

'He – he thinks it best if you don't meet up. At least, not yet.'

'Did you give him my letter?'

''Course I did.'

'What did he say?'

'That he'll write to you soon.'

'Did you tell him about his letter to us getting lost? And that was why none of us had written to him?'

Nick nodded.

'And?'

'And what?'

231

'What did he say?' Maddie insisted. 'Tell me everything he said. Please, Nick.'

'He's doing his basic training. He says it's very hard and exhausting. After that, he'll get posted somewhere. Maybe abroad, even.'

'Abroad?' Maddie was horrified. 'But he'll get leave, won't he? He could come home on a visit, couldn't he?'

'Yes, he'll get leave, but he thinks it's best if he doesn't come home.'

'But he said, when I was sixteen, he'd marry me. Did he mention that?'

'He doesn't want the Army finding out about you being pregnant and underage. If he starts asking for leave to come home to get married when he's only just gone in, they might start asking awkward questions.'

Maddie turned away back to her work with mixed feelings. Michael was all right. Nick had seen him, but he had not brought back the loving messages Maddie longed to hear. No promise of marriage now, not even a suggested meeting nor a letter for her.

Maddie bit down hard on her lower lip. I won't cry, she told herself fiercely. I won't.

'He's not coming home, Mr Frank.'

'I know, love, I know.' His face was sorrowful, too, and Maddie again regretted the trouble she had brought to this kindly man's door. Yet she would never say she was sorry about the coming child. Michael's child. Her child. Their child. And one day they would be married. She knew they would.

'Maddie,' Frank was saying slowly. 'I've been thinking.'

She held her breath as fear flooded through her. He was going to send her away. He'd changed his mind about standing by her. It would be Mrs Trowbridge's fault. She'd gone on and on about it. About the shame and the trouble that Michael might be in. And Maddie was sure that it was she who had spread the gossip around the village. So now, Mr Frank wanted her gone.

'I . . .' Frank removed his cap, ran his fingers through his hair and then replaced the cap. 'I don't know how much Nick has told you about his visit to Michael.'

Maddie repeated, word for word, what Nick had said. When she had finished, Frank, much as Nick had done, glanced at her and then lowered his gaze.

'Maddie, love. Nick says that Michael isn't sure he should marry you now.'

'What? But he said he loves me.'

Frank reached out and touched her shoulder. 'I'm sure he does, but he's so young. You both are . . .'

Despite her promise to herself, her lower lip trembled and tears welled in her eyes. 'You're turning me out?'

'No, no,' Frank's denial was swift and obviously genuine. 'No, never think that, Maddie. Please.' He sighed deeply. 'Michael doesn't want to be tied down. Not yet. He has a chance to see a bit of the world now he's in the Army.'

'I don't believe you. Nick's said all this, hasn't he? I don't believe him.'

'It's what Michael told him. What Michael asked him to tell us.'

Maddie was silently fighting the tears.

Now Frank put his arm about her shoulders. 'We must think of you and the child and what is best for both of you.'

Michael marrying me would be the best thing for both of us, she wanted to shout, but still she could say nothing.

'Look, Maddie, there's something I want you to think

about. Very carefully. I . . .' He paused as if searching for the right words. Maddie looked up into his face and saw the concern for her in his eyes as he went on, 'I – I want you to think about marrying me.'

Maddie was speechless with shock. Marry Mr Frank? The thought appalled her. She liked him, loved him in the way she might love a father-figure, but marry him? When she loved Michael?

His arm about her tightened. 'We could be married as soon as you're sixteen and then, if the gossips want to say it's my child, well, all the better. Michael will be safe then. It'd be the best thing for everyone. So what do you say, love?'

Maddie tore herself away from him. 'No, no. Oh, I couldn't.' She turned and ran.

Thirty-One

'You scheming little hussy.'

For a moment Maddie thought Harriet was going to strike her again but then the housekeeper turned her attention to Frank. 'Have you taken leave of your senses? 'Course I know you're only doing it to save your son. And I can't blame you for that, I suppose. But I can't see why you think you have to go as far as marrying this little slut.'

Quietly, Frank said, 'She's carrying my grandchild.'

'Huh! And how sure of *that* can you be, eh?'

Frank glared at her. 'I'm sure.'

'Well, that's it then. We're leaving. Nicholas and I won't stay another minute in this house if she's to be mistress of it.' Her face twisted into a sneer. 'I hope you'll be very happy together, a cosy little twosome to manage all the work.' She jabbed her forefinger towards Maddie's stomach as she said, 'And how much longer do you think she's going to be any help?'

Frank ran his hands through his hair. Wearily, he said, 'Harriet, there's no need for you to go anywhere. Nothing's going to change around here.'

'Not change? Not change?' Harriet screamed at him. 'When she becomes Mrs Brackenbury and sleeps in your bed?'

'I want to protect Maddie and the child – and my son.' He glanced sympathetically at Maddie before adding, 'You've got to believe it, Maddie. Michael's not coming back. And in a way, I can't find it in mesen to blame him. Oh, I know he ought to stand by his responsibilities, but he's too young to be saddled with a wife and child. I'm only sorry, Maddie, that he's landed you with it all. That's why I want to try to help.'

Maddie's eyes blazed. 'Don't you say you're sorry about the bairn. Don't anyone say they're sorry. I'm not. I'm glad I'm having Michael's baby. And if he doesn't want me or his child, that's up to him. But I'll never be sorry. Never!'

The two looked at her in astonishment and then a small smile twitched at Frank's lips. 'I wish my son had your courage, lass. Really, I do.'

'Courage, me foot,' Harriet snarled. 'She's a scheming little hussy who's wormed her way in here and reckons she can end up running all this.' She swept her arm in a wide arc to encompass not just the house, but all the land around it. She leant closer to Maddie, 'Well, let me tell you, you little madam, Sir Peter'll not let a bastard orphan without a name be one of his tenants. And especially not *you.*'

'Harriet! That's enough.'

'Aye, it's enough all right. I've had enough, an' all.' She turned as if to leave there and then, but was stopped when Maddie said clearly, 'I'm certainly not trying to take Mr Frank's farm away from him. Although,' she couldn't help adding wickedly, 'I think Mr Theo might well grant me the tenancy.' She paused and then went on quietly, 'Besides, I haven't said I'll marry Mr Frank.'

The woman turned and, her eyes narrowing, said, 'Ah, but you will. It's all part of your plan, isn't it, girl? By heck, I rue the day I brought you here. Well, I've only mesen to blame. I know that. Not for the first time, do I wish you'd never been born. Aye, and I'm not the only one who wishes it an' all.'

'What do you mean?'

'Nothing. Nothing at all.' She turned away and went into the kitchen from where they heard the clattering of pans being banged about in temper.

Maddie looked at Frank, who shrugged helplessly.

'Will she go, d'you think?' she asked.

'I doubt it. Where would she go? No, Harriet'll not leave.' For a moment Maddie thought he sounded wistful, almost as if he were wishing she would. He sighed heavily and then looking at her steadily, he said quietly, 'Think about what I said, love. It'd be for the best. I'm sure of it.'

Maddie's sixteenth birthday came and went and still she would not agree to marry Frank. In April, she was able to stand at the end of the field and see that her dream had come true. Stretching before her was her 'rainbow' field. Pink and yellow, red and purple. She should have been elated, bursting with pride and joy. Yet her sweet success tasted like dust in her mouth, her dreams were in ashes for there was no Michael standing beside her, sharing what should have been the most wonderful moment of her whole life. Instead, the beautiful blooms, bright in the sunlight, mocked her unhappiness.

Surely, he had loved her as she had loved him and, deep in her heart, she knew she always would. Surely, his sweet words could not have been all lies and yet, as day after day went by and there was no word, no letter – nothing – even Maddie's faith in him faltered.

As she stood with her hands protectively over her stomach, looking out across the fields, she felt a tiny flutter beneath her ribs and knew it was the moment that her child had first moved. It lived and moved within her. It was a little piece of Michael that she would cherish for ever. He could never leave her completely because she had borne his child and those bonds could never quite be severed, not by anyone. Not even by Michael himself.

For the first time since his departure, Maddie smiled and lifted her head to the bright blue sky, feeling the breeze on her face. She had a home, she still had the support and gentle kindness of Frank and soon she would have a child to love and care for. For the first time in her life, she would have someone who truly belonged to her. She would have a family. But, a little voice told her, your child needs a father.

'Mr Frank, what do you say to the idea that this year – our first year – we sell as many of the flowers as we can? If we pick them at the moment they're just coming into flower, we should get the best of both worlds, shouldn't we?'

'How do you mean, love?'

'Well, we can sell the flowers and still get a fair amount of nourishment back into the bulb to build up our own store of bulbs for next year.'

'Not sell to the dry bulb market, you mean?'

'Not this year.'

'I thought you had to leave as much stem as possible,' Nick put in. 'Just take the head off. We can't do that if we're going to sell them as cut flowers, can we?'

'No, I know. But I thought we'd try to hit the middle of the road, just this year. What do you both think?'

Now she included them both and glanced from one to the other.

Frank and Nick exchanged a look and then Nick said, 'Well, I think it's a good idea.' He smiled across at Maddie, 'But then your ideas always are.'

Maddie laughed. 'Flatterer.' Then she turned to Frank, who nodded and said, 'I don't see why it shouldn't work. It might not be what Bill Randall would tell us we ought to do, but I'm willing to give it a try. We've got a good outlet for the blooms already in place that . . .' He stopped abruptly and glanced, embarrassed, at Maddie.

'It's all right,' she said quietly and reached out to touch his hand where it lay on the white table cloth. 'You can say his name, you know. The outlet that Michael set up.'

She saw sadness in his dark eyes, a sadness that reflected her own and once more she was filled with guilt at the sorrow she had brought upon this good man.

'Yes, yes,' he was saying swiftly now. 'And I was thinking that I ought to sell the car and buy a truck. It would be much more useful to take the boxes of flowers to the railway station,' Frank said. 'Besides, when do we have time to go out in a car now?'

'That is a good idea. And Mr Randall says we ought to think about turning the old cowshed into a cold store,' Maddie said. 'We can't keep asking him to store our bulbs for forcing in his cold store, can we?'

Theo had been as good as his promise. The crewyard had been covered over, though the smaller buildings – the cow-house, pigsties and Rajah's stable – had stayed as they always had been but were now enclosed within the huge, asbestos-covered barn. The area that had once been the walled yard was now a level concrete floor – a vast space for sorting and packing cut flowers and for grading bulbs. The original small buildings were ideal for storage.

'More expense,' Harriet muttered as she set mugs of cocoa on the supper table. 'You and your grand ideas.'

Frank ignored her grumbling and carried on the conversation as he carved the meat and handed out the plates. 'You find out all about it, love,' he said to Maddie, 'and we'll see.'

When the time came for the picking, Maddie found that when she bent to pick the blooms, the growing mound of her stomach got in the way. She tried squatting, rather that stooping, and found it was easier.

'You all right, Maddie?' Nick asked with concern.

'I'm fine,' she answered, trying to raise a bright smile.

He sighed. 'I wish I could take all the workload off you,' he said worriedly. 'But there just aren't enough hours in the day . . .'

'Nick, you're being wonderful the way you've helped since – since . . . Well, just lately. I am grateful.'

'I wish you'd see a doctor,' he blurted out, reddening a little at having to touch on a delicate matter. 'You haven't seen one at all, have you?'

Maddie shook her head. 'I daren't, Nick. A doctor would ask awkward questions. Besides, there's no doubt now that I am expecting, so I don't need it confirmed. And I'm healthy enough. I don't need any medical attention. So, why bother?'

'Well, I just thought . . .' His voice trailed away uncertainly.

She smiled at him. 'It's nice of you to be concerned. No, really, I mean it. And I would go – despite the embarrassing questions – if I thought there was anything wrong with me that might harm the baby.' Softly she added, 'I meant what I said. I am sorry for the trouble it's caused. More sorry that you will ever know that Michael has had to go away, but I will never, ever, be sorry about the baby.'

Nick was staring at her. Then, his face scarlet, he mumbled awkwardly, 'We'll look after you, Maddie. You and the baby.'

He turned away abruptly then and went to the far end of the field to start picking a fresh batch of dark red tulips.

Maddie watched him go, shaking her head. He was a strange boy, she thought, but he really did have a much nicer side to him. And these days she was seeing much more of it.

Thirty-Two

'Do you know what happened this afternoon?' Maddie told them as she served steaming potatoes at supper time. 'Some woman stopped her car in the lane and came to the gate to ask if we sold cut flowers. You know, by the bunch, straight out of the field.'

'Did you sell her some?' Nick asked.

'Well, no, because we've got an outlet, haven't we?'

'But only for our best blooms. They don't take the rubbish ones that have opened too far, now do they?'

'No, but it wouldn't be fair to sell her that sort either, would it?'

'Depends,' Nick said, cutting the slice of boiled ham and dipping it into the mustard on the side of his plate before popping it into his mouth. 'There's a big difference between the top-grade flowers we send to London and the absolute rubbish that is only fit to be thrown away. I mean, we can't physically get to every flower just at the perfect moment to pick it, can we? If you'd picked her the sort of flowers that we wouldn't send to the markets, but that still look pretty good and if you hadn't charged too much, I reckon she'd've been happy enough.'

'You know,' Frank said, entering the conversation for the first time. 'Nick might have a very good point there. I know some of the growers have buckets of flowers stood at their farm gates and sell to passers-by and I'll tell you something else that Bill Randall was telling me this morn-

ing. There's a local growers' association been formed . . .
Oh and by the way he reckons we should join, but what I
was going to say was that the members of this association
have set out a route all round the fields this year for
sightseers to follow. He says there's more and more folks
coming to the area every year to see the tulip fields.'

'I can believe that,' Maddie said. 'I saw a bus down our
lane this afternoon. I thought it must be a day trip gone
down the wrong road, but I wonder, now you've said
that.'

'There you are, then,' Nick smiled. 'It'd be a bus trip all
right, but it'd've come to see the tulips.'

They looked at each other around the table and then,
for some reason she couldn't quite explain the three of
them all looked in Harriet's direction.

'What? What are you looking at me for?'

'I was just thinking, Harriet, that you could have some
flowers here, outside the back door and sell to callers,
couldn't you?'

'Oho, not me, Mr Frank. I've enough to do with all the
cooking and the housework. Besides, I don't want
strangers traipsing up to the back door.'

'Well, it's true you do have enough work, Harriet,
because none of us have time to give you a helping hand.
I'm sorry, I shouldn't have suggested it.'

'I tell you what we could do,' Maddie said, feeling
excited and enthusiastic for the first time since the dreadful day that Michael had gone away. 'In fact, there's two
things we could do. One, we could have a trestle table
and flowers in buckets at the gateway into the field and
also,' she grinned triumphantly around the table, 'we
could sell them to Mrs Grange in the corner shop for her
to sell on.'

There was a silence before Nick, frowning slightly,

asked, 'Why should she want to sell them? Not many of the locals would buy flowers. Most of them grow them, if not in their fields, then at least in their own gardens.'

'Not for the locals,' Maddie said, 'for the sightseers. If they're coming here in their cars and even by the bus load, you can't tell me that a good few of them won't drop in at the corner shop to buy drinks or a snack. In fact, we ought to suggest it to Jen that she gets Mrs Grange to sell sandwiches and cups of tea. She might even open up a little tea shop.'

'Do you know,' Harriet said softly, surprising them all, 'that's something I would love to have done. Run a little tea shop.'

There was a silence before Frank said, 'Well, why don't you? You could do it here, if you like. We could . . .'

'No, oh no!' Harriet held up her hands, palms outwards as if fending him off. 'I didn't mean it. I couldn't do it. I couldn't mix with folk, now could I? Not now. Not after . . .' She broke off and stood up, beginning to pile the dirty plates together. 'I wasn't serious. I only meant that if things had been different, it's the sort of thing I could have done. But not now, as things turned out . . .' Maddie saw her look down the length of the table straight into Frank's eyes. 'I couldn't. Besides,' she added with definite finality, 'like I've just said, I haven't the time.'

'It's a shame,' Maddie said softly, her gaze on the woman's face. 'You're such a wonderful cook, it couldn't help but succeed.'

Harriet's eyes swivelled to look at Maddie, who met her gaze steadily. For a fleeting moment there was a genuine rapport between them. Harriet recognized that Maddie's words were sincere and briefly, oh so briefly, she was touched. But then she picked up the plates and turned away towards the kitchen and the moment was lost.

'Where are you going, all dressed up?'

Nick stood before her, smiling and playfully barring her way across the yard.

'I'm going to find Michael and talk to him myself.'

Anxiety crossed his features. 'Oh Maddie, don't do that. You'll only get hurt. Let me go again. Let me find him and talk to him. Tell him what Mr Frank has suggested.'

'I want to see him. I need to hear it from him myself. If it's really true that he no longer . . .' she swallowed painfully before struggling on, 'cares for me, then I must accept it and move on with my life. I'm ready to do that now, but first, I must find out if it's true.'

'Don't you believe me?' he asked, suddenly offended that she should doubt his word.

She hesitated a second before she made herself say, ''Course I do, but – but I thought if I could see him, talk to him again, he . . .' Her voice trailed away. The truth was, she didn't quite believe Nick. But she wouldn't have believed anyone who had told her the same news. She needed to hear it from Michael himself.

'Look, he'll have moved on from where he was. And we haven't heard any more from him, have we? We don't even know where he is now. Tell you what,' Nick went on swiftly as he saw Maddie's dejected look, 'as soon as we hear, I'll go and talk to him again and tell him what his dad's suggested. I don't reckon he'll like that. Not one bit. No more than I do. I don't think you should marry Mr Frank, tying yourself to an old man like him.' He reached out and touched her hand. 'I mean, even if Michael doesn't want to marry you, later on you might meet a young feller who wouldn't mind you having a babby already. Someone who – who really cares about you. Someone who just wants to look after you and make you happy.'

Maddie glanced at him doubtfully but said nothing, her mind returning to Michael. She sighed. 'If you think he'll not be there any more, then I suppose there isn't any use in me going. At least, not today.'

Now Nick took hold of her hand and said, with more authority in his tone than she had ever heard in his voice, 'Leave it to me, Maddie.'

It was two weeks before another letter arrived.

'He's written to me,' Nick told them waving an envelope, but not offering for any of them to read the letter. 'I was right. He's finished his basic training.' Nick pulled a face. 'Ses it's been hell. I'm going up to see him tomorrow. But it's miles away. Somewhere up in Yorkshire. I'll have to be away overnight.'

'That's all right, lad,' Frank said. 'I'll give you the money for the train fare. It's good of you to go. I'd go mesen, but him and me'd only fall out and it wouldn't look good. And Maddie certainly can't go.'

'I don't see why not,' Maddie muttered.

As ever, Harriet defended Michael. 'You stay away from the lad. You've caused enough trouble for him already. Fancy him having to leave his home and family all because of the likes of you.'

'He'd have been gone by now, anyway,' Frank said patiently. 'He'd have been called up for National Service.'

'Mebbe so. But he won't be able to come home on leave, will he? Not while she's still here.'

'If Maddie would only agree to marry me like I suggested, he could come home. The gossip will be turned on me then.'

'Aye, and have you thought what might happen to you? You're so wrapped up in helping everybody else, your son and even this little trollop here, that you haven't stopped to think what they might do to you. You'd never stand prison.'

'If that's going to happen, then I shall go away,' Maddie said determinedly.

The housekeeper rounded on her. 'You'd have done better to have packed your bags and gone long since, if you'd really thought anything about this family. And when your bastard's born, stick it in an orphanage. It's what they did to you, isn't it?'

Maddie stared at her for a moment. 'What do you mean "what they did"? Who do you mean by "they"?'

For a brief moment, Harriet was flustered. 'Well, somebody dumped you outside that orphanage, didn't they?'

'Yes,' Maddie said slowly, still staring at the woman. 'Yes, they did.'

For a fleeting moment it had sounded to Maddie as if Harriet Trowbridge knew just who had left her on the doorstep of the Mayfield Home.

Thirty-Three

When Nick left the following morning, his mother loaded him with food parcels for Michael. 'They'll not be feeding him like he's used to.'

And Maddie loaded him with messages. 'Tell him I need to see him. Tell him – tell him . . .' She hesitated. It was difficult to give this young man, who was still only little more than a boy, intimate messages to pass on. 'Tell him I love him. It doesn't matter if he doesn't want to marry me. I understand that. I'm not bothered, just so long as – so long as . . .' She faltered unable to ask directly if Michael still loved her.

Nick touched her hand. Gently, he said, 'Don't worry, Maddie. I'll talk to him and when I come back I'll tell you everything he said. Word for word.'

'Promise?'

'I promise.'

She watched him go, questioning why it was not she who was going. She despised what she considered weakness in herself. Once, she would have gone, whatever anyone said, yet now it was as if she dare not go, dare not face the truth she feared to hear.

Her hands covered her belly protectively. 'Love is making you weak,' she murmured to herself, wondering if the old fearless, Madeleine March who hadn't cared a fig for anyone – except Jenny – was gone for ever.

As Nick rounded the corner in the lane and disappeared

from view, she turned away but for the rest of the day her mind was not on her work. It was on a train heading north to see Michael.

The following day Nick returned late at night looking pale with tiredness.

'What did he say? Is he all right?'

'Let him get inside the door, girl.' Harriet took the overnight bag from her son's hand and led him to the table. 'Sit down, lad, and get something inside you. You look worn out.'

'It's them trains, Mam, great noisy things, pothering smoke. And then I had to walk two miles from the station to the camp and wait in a cold guard room for an hour 'til they'd let me see him.'

Maddie stood at the end of the table, watching him eat, biting back the tumult of questions.

Nick glanced up at her once or twice but then quickly down again at his plate as he wolfed his meal.

'Eat slowly, Nicholas,' his mother scolded. 'You'll get indigestion. You look as if you haven't eaten for two days.'

'I haven't,' he mumbled, his mouth full.

'What?'

'Only what you gave me, Mam.'

'But didn't you get breakfast this morning where you stayed?'

'No, they don't serve it in the railway station waiting room.'

Harriet gasped. 'You mean, that's where you slept? In the waiting room on the station?'

Nick nodded.

The housekeeper cast a resentful glance at Maddie as if to say, There, look what my son has had to suffer because of you. But Maddie was not concerned about Nick's few hours of discomfort, even if they had been on her behalf.

'What did he say?'

Frank came to her and put his arm about her shoulders. 'Come and sit by the fire, love, and when he's finished eating, Nick can bring his tea and sit with us and tell us what happened. Come along,' he urged finally as Maddie stiffened herself against his arm.

A few minutes later, they were all seated around the fire but Nick still avoided looking at Maddie. He cleared his throat and glanced uncomfortably at Frank.

'Michael said to tell you, Mr Frank, that he won't be coming back to the farm, not even when he's finished his National Service. He – he said to tell you that he's taken to the Army life. He intends to sign on as a regular.'

'What?' Frank was staggered, his mouth agape.

'He can't. He must come home,' Maddie cried.

'How can he possibly know if he likes the life yet? That's ridiculous. Are you sure that's what he meant, lad?'

The young man nodded. 'I pleaded with him, Mr Frank. I said just what you've said, but he was set on it.'

'I don't believe you,' Maddie whispered.

'Did you tell him what I had proposed?' Frank asked. 'About Maddie, I mean?'

Nick nodded.

'And?'

'He agrees it's the best idea for everyone.'

Maddie gasped and her insides trembled. 'No, no. I don't believe you,' she cried as her eyes stung with tears she would not allow to fall. 'He wouldn't agree to that. He couldn't . . .' Her voice fell away and there was silence in the room, the only sounds the flames crackling and hissing in the grate. But even before the warmth of the fire, Maddie shivered. She felt as if her heart were turning into ice.

'I'll have to go and have a chat with the vicar,' Frank said. 'I need to know what we have to do.'

Maddie glanced at him but said nothing. She didn't want this marriage. She really didn't. And yet since Michael's final rejection of her, it seemed the only way. At least in the eyes of the world her child would be legitimate. It would not carry the stigma of 'bastard' all its life. It was for this reason alone that Maddie had finally been persuaded to agree to the marriage.

'Although you're sixteen now,' Frank was saying, 'I think we still need parental consent, but because you haven't any parents . . .' His voice petered away as he frowned, thinking. 'I suppose Sir Peter is your guardian, in loco parentis, I think they call it.'

'What does that mean, when it's at home?' Harriet asked sarcastically.

'In place of her parents and I'm just assuming it's him because she lived at his orphanage.'

'I don't know,' Maddie said now. 'Mrs Potter always said that once we were school-leaving age, we were out and couldn't go back, so I don't see . . .'

'Don't argue with Mr Frank,' Harriet snapped. 'You want to think yourself lucky. Now he's having to go round telling folks, we can expect a visit from the police any day now, I shouldn't wonder. Want to see him carted off in handcuffs, do you?'

Maddie swallowed. For the sake of her child, she would marry its grandfather, though the lie she was being forced to live out went against her instinctive honesty.

'No one must ever know the child is Michael's,' Frank pleaded with the whole household. 'Beyond these four walls, the child is mine. I'm counting on you, Harriet, just as I'm counting on you both to stay here. You and Nick.'

Maddie watched the conflict visible on the woman's face. She was sure now that Harriet Trowbridge had harboured hopes of marrying Frank herself, but now these hopes were dashed for ever. Maddie held her breath, half-hoping that the woman would keep to her threat, pack her bags and leave.

But now Harriet and Frank were staring at one another, their gaze held by the past in which neither Maddie nor even Nick had any part.

'More secrets, eh Frank?' Harriet said softly.

'Aye, more secrets, my dear.'

Slowly, Harriet nodded.

'And Nick?' Frank persisted. 'He'll not say anything? Because I don't think he's in favour of this plan. I think, maybe, he thinks that when he's older . . .' Frank gestured towards Maddie.

Harriet's eyes widened in horror. 'What? You mean – he . . . With her? Oh no. Never.'

Frank put his head a little on one side and smiled as if he had just played his trump card.

Harriet was still struggling with the conflict raging within her. At last she said, 'Well, in that case, Mr Frank, there's nothing more I can say.' And both Frank and Maddie knew that to save her son from even thinking of marrying Madeleine March, Harriet Trowbridge would finally sacrifice her own hopes.

They were married in July after the main work of lifting the bulbs for storage through the summer had been done.

'You'd do better to make out you're older than you are. Put seventeen when you sign the register.'

'More lies, Mrs Trowbridge,' Maddie muttered.

'What's a lie, if it saves him from prison, eh?'

Maddie shuddered, but for the first time in her life she had to agree. Perhaps in such dire circumstances, a lie was justifiable.

'Besides,' Harriet went on. 'It's not really as if you are certain about your age, is it?'

'Mrs Potter said . . .'

'And what does Alice Potter know?'

Maddie stared at her. 'You know her?'

'What? Oh . . .' For a moment Harriet was flustered as if realizing she had said too much. 'Of course I know her. I met her when I brought you here. And . . .' she wagged her finger in Maddie's face, regaining her control now, 'I rue the day I did.'

'But you referred to her as Alice just now.'

'I did no such thing. I said Mrs Potter. Your hearing must be defective.'

'There's nothing wrong with my hearing. You said, "And what does Alice Potter know?" '

'I did no such thing. Don't argue with your elders and betters, girl.'

'Elder, maybe,' Maddie muttered. 'Better, certainly not.'

'What did you say?'

Maddie grinned at her. 'Nothing, Mrs Trowbridge,' she said innocently, thankful that if anyone had defective hearing, it was the housekeeper.

'Have you told the vicar my age?' Maddie asked Frank as they drove towards the church in his motor car. 'Because Mrs Trowbridge thinks I ought to say I'm seventeen.'

253

Frank glanced sideways at her. 'I wouldn't want you to lie. Not for me, Maddie, and not in church especially.'

'I've always been truthful,' Maddie said slowly, 'even if it got me into trouble. Somehow, I can't tell lies.' She paused and looked sideways at him. 'I wasn't lying that time about the hen-house, you know.'

Frank sighed. 'No, I know you weren't, love.' He paused and then haltingly said, 'There's things about Harriet you don't understand. Maybe one day, you will. But just trust me, Maddie, will you?'

She looked at him again, this time long and hard. His face was in profile to her as he kept his gaze firmly fixed on the road ahead. It was a good, honest face, she thought. A little troubled. In fact, a lot troubled. There were dark shadows beneath his brown eyes and he didn't seem to smile as much as he had when she had first come to the farm. Maddie felt a stab of guilt. She had been the cause of some of his anxiety, though she could hardly be blamed for the difficulties with the farm.

They did not speak again until he drew the car to a halt outside the church, switched off the engine and turned to face her.

'Before we go in, Maddie love, there's just something I want to say to you.' He licked his lips that were suddenly dry. 'We both know why we're doing this.'

Maddie nodded and determinedly swallowed the lump that rose in her throat as she thought of Michael.

It should be Michael standing beside me today. I should be about to become Mrs Michael Brackenbury, not Mrs Frank. But she said nothing. Michael didn't love her, or at least he didn't love her enough. She was on her own now. And she'd do whatever it took to protect her child. With a deep sigh for what might have been, Maddie knew she must face the future without Michael. In that moment, she locked away all memories of him, all thoughts of him and looked to the man at her side. The man who was willing to give her child a name. When it was born, it would bear the legitimate name of Brackenbury and even though there would perhaps be another lie to be told when she registered the child, at least it would have every right to that surname and Frank, legally, would be its father.

Frank was speaking again, haltingly with embarrassment. 'I want you to know that I don't expect you to be a wife to me. What I mean is, I shall make no demands upon you. The marriage will be in name only.'

Maddie looked at him then, full in the face. That good, kind and caring face that she was already very fond of. Suddenly, she smiled at him, 'Oh no, Frank,' she said, calling him by his Christian name for the first time without the title Mister in front of it. 'Oh no. If we are to be married, I shall be your wife in every way.'

For a moment he looked startled and then he too, smiled. He reached for her hand and raised it to his lips. His voice slightly husky, he said, 'Well, if you're sure, my dear.'

'I am,' Maddie said firmly and then added, 'Can I ask you something now?'

'Of course, love.'

'I – I don't want to pry . . .' Suddenly, she felt hesitant, but before she married Frank she wanted to know the answer to something that had been puzzling her ever since she had come to Few Farm. 'Or – or to bring up painful memories for you, but would you tell me what happened to your first wife and why you never talk about her?'

As Frank leaned back against the car seat and sighed heavily, Maddie said swiftly, 'Oh I'm sorry, I shouldn't have asked . . .'

'No, no, love. I can understand that it must seem a bit

odd to you.' He glanced at her and smiled gently. 'Specially for someone who probably longs to know about her own family.'

Maddie found it difficult to speak as the long buried yearning rushed to the surface. More than ever before, as she waited for the birth of her own child and now as she was about to enter into marriage, she missed the comfort of a mother, father and even of brothers and sisters.

'It must seem to you as if we don't want to talk about her,' Frank was saying softly, 'but nothing could be further from the truth. I loved Michael's mother dearly but she died at his birth. She's – she's buried here in this church-yard. In fact, if you like, when we've seen the vicar, I'll take you to see her grave.'

Maddie nodded and whispered, 'I'd like that.' There was a pause and then she asked, 'But why do you never talk about her? Why are there no photographs of her around the house?'

'There were at first. In every room and for the first year or so after her death I never stopped talking about her. My sister came to look after the baby and me at first. I think I must have driven her mad going on and on about Elizabeth and how happy we'd been. But she was very good. She never complained. I think she realized it was my way of coping.' He sighed. 'But my sister couldn't stay for ever. She had her own life. And it was when Harriet moved in as my housekeeper that things had to change. She'd had a very unhappy experience. I can't tell you about it, Maddie, because I gave my word to her years ago never to talk about it, but because she wanted the past buried, it was difficult for me to talk about mine. Gradually, I noticed she removed all the photographs of Elizabeth and the only one I have left is in my bedroom.' He turned to her. 'But I'll put that away now, if you . . .'

'No, no,' Maddie reassured him. 'Not on my account, please.'

'So,' Frank went on, 'the only time I could ever talk about Elizabeth was to Michael as he grew older.'

There was silence and although he said no more, the unspoken words hung in the air. *And now he's gone, there's no one I can share my memories with.*

Maddie leaned across and gently kissed Frank's weather-beaten cheek as she whispered, 'Well, you can talk to me about her, any time you like. In fact, I'd like you to.'

Again he raised her fingers to his lips as he murmured simply, 'Thank you, my dear.'

Thirty-Four

'I suppose I ought to go and see Michael again and tell him he has a son.'

Nick was standing at the end of the big double bed in the main bedroom that Maddie now shared with her husband and had done since the day of their marriage.

She smiled to herself when she remembered the look on Harriet Trowbridge's face when she had moved all her belongings, such as they were, from the tiny room along the landing into the master's bedroom. The woman had said nothing but the high colour on her cheeks, her tight mouth and eyes that sparkled suspiciously with tears of either disappointment or rage – Maddie could not have said which – spoke loudly her feelings.

'You needn't bother on my account,' Maddie said tartly now and brushed the downy head of her tiny infant with her lips. 'I don't care if he knows or not. John has a father.'

Nick jumped visibly and his eyes widened. 'You're – you're not calling him that, are you?'

Maddie blinked. 'Yes. Why shouldn't I?'

'Does – does me Mam know?'

'Nobody knows yet. I've only just decided. We said we'd leave the naming until we knew whether it was a boy or a girl. Well, now we know. And his name's John.'

'So – so Mr Frank doesn't know?'

'No.'

'Oh. Er – well, I think you'd better see what he ses.'

'Why. What's wrong with the name?'

'Nothing. But . . .'

'But what?'

Nick waved his hand and said, 'Oh nothing. See what Mr Frank ses.' He turned as if to leave when Maddie said, 'Nick, there is someone I'd be ever so grateful if you would tell.'

He turned back to look at her.

'Jenny. Would you go and see her for me, please? And ask her to visit?'

He pulled a face. 'All right. Just so long as she doesn't start following me about all over the place again.'

As Nick left the room, Maddie lay back against the pillows and closed her eyes. She felt elated, triumphant. She had her baby. A fine, healthy son. The birth had been surprisingly easy. All those old wives' tales about being in agony for days had not happened for Maddie. She hadn't even had time to wait for the midwife to arrive and Frank had delivered his own grandson.

The baby snuffled in his sleep and Maddie laid her cheek against his head. 'Oh John, part of me longs for your real daddy to see you. I'd love to see you in his arms and see the pride and joy in his eyes, just like it was in your grandad's when he handed you to me for the first time. But you're never going to know your real daddy, my darling boy. He – he doesn't want to know us any more. Either of us.'

In the privacy of the bedroom, Maddie allowed the tears to fall. Just this once, she told herself.

'You never miss a trick, do you, you little hussy, to humiliate me?'

Maddie was startled from a light sleep to find Harriet

bending over her. 'What – what on earth are you talking about?'

'It's not enough that you've taken the only man who's ever shown me any real kindness, but you have to stick the knife in and twist it, don't you? Wanting to call your little brat, John. Oh, but you're clever, I'll grant you that. Cleverer than even I'd given you credit for.'

Maddie blinked, feeling vulnerable and helpless under the woman's verbal attack that felt as if at any minute it might turn physical. Weak from the labour of her child's birth, relatively quick and easy though it had been, for the first time in her life, Maddie felt threatened.

'What are you talking about?' she asked in a voice that sounded far firmer than she felt.

'You know very well what I'm talking about.' She leaned closer and Maddie could feel the angry woman's spittle raining on her face. 'Oh I under-estimated you. That was my mistake. I thought I could get my revenge on you, but I was wrong. But . . .' the face came even closer so that their noses were almost touching, 'I aren't finished yet, girl.'

Suddenly, she straightened up, turned and left the room.

Maddie sank back against the pillows. 'Well,' she said aloud and glanced down at the cradle beside her where her son slept on, serenely undisturbed. 'What on earth was all that about?'

She heard Jenny's excited chatter on the landing even before the door opened and she was rushing headlong into the room. 'I came as soon as I could. Nick came to the shop to tell me. How are you? Where is he? Can I hold him? Ooh . . .' The last was a long-drawn-out sigh when she bent over the cradle. 'Isn't he just perfect?'

Maddie laughed. 'Well, I don't know about that. You might not think so if he woke you every three hours, even all through the night, demanding to be fed.'

'I wouldn't mind,' Jenny murmured, never once taking her gaze from the baby. 'When will he wake up? Can I hold him if he does?'

'Of course you can, but come and sit by me.' She patted the bed beside her and Jenny came reluctantly and perched on the edge, but still her glance was on the child.

'I'm sorry I missed your wedding,' Jenny said.

'Me too, but – well – in the circumstances it all had to be done very quietly.' She paused a moment before she said hesitantly, 'Jen, there's something I've got to ask you. A big favour.'

''Course. What is it?' Jenny was still only half listening. She was leaning away again, watching the baby and his every tiny movement.

'Jen, listen to me a minute. This is important.'

Jenny giggled. 'Sorry, Maddie, but I love babies. You know I do.'

Maddie remembered now how the only time she had ever seen Jenny really happy at the Home was when a baby had arrived. Sometimes she had been allowed to help in the nursery. Maddie had thought, at the time, that it was because it took her away from the other girls' teasing, but now she realized it was because Jenny had genuinely loved the little mites.

'What is it, Maddie?'

Maddie took a deep breath. This was very difficult for her. 'You know I never tell lies, that I always try to be truthful?'

Jenny nodded.

'Well, I have to ask you to help in a little – well – not exactly a lie but not quite telling the truth. Mr Frank wants

261

people to think that the baby's his. That way, if there's any trouble because I was underage when I conceived, it'll be him they'll come after not – not Michael.'

'Well, I can try,' Jenny's tone was doubtful, 'but I think everyone in the village knows it's Michael's and that's why he's gone away. Mrs Trowbridge saw to that. It was her that told Mrs Grange, 'cos I asked her and she said it was. I know Mrs Grange's a bit of a gossip, Maddie, but she's not malicious. Not like Mrs Trowbridge.'

So, Maddie thought, she had been right. She sighed. 'Oh,' she said flatly, 'so it's too late to kill the gossip then?'

''Fraid so, but I shouldn't worry about anyone coming after Mr Frank. If they'd been going to do that, they'd have done it by now. By the time the rumour did get round the village and probably PC Parsons got to hear of it, Michael was long gone.' She leant forward. 'Have you ever stopped to think that Mrs T might have deliberately spread the rumour once Michael was safely out the way so that Mr Frank wouldn't be blamed?'

Maddie stared at her. No, she hadn't thought of that. 'She wouldn't . . .' She began and then stopped. She had been going to say, 'She wouldn't do that to help me', but now that she thought about it, such an action was not to help her but to save Frank and that Harriet Trowbridge would most certainly have done.

Maddie closed her eyes and shook her head and lay back against the pillows. 'Oh, it's all too much. Maybe you're right. Maybe we should just let well alone.'

'What did you put on the birth certificate?'

Maddie pulled a face. 'Frank wanted me to put his name but when it came to it I couldn't. I explained it all to the Registrar and he said that in the circumstances it would be best left blank. If the real father isn't there to say

262

he's the father, then I couldn't put Michael's name on anyway.'

'Oh well,' Jenny patted her hand. 'At least he's got his mum's name on the certificate and the name Brackenbury that's really his. That's a lot more than you and me have got, Maddie.' She paused and then asked, very softly, 'Do you ever wish you did know who your real family are? Why – why they left you like they did?'

Realistically, Maddie said, 'Not really,' and added wryly, 'I might not like what I find out. Why, does it bother you?'

Jenny glanced down at the patchwork quilt covering the bed and traced her finger around the hexagon-shaped patterns. 'Yes,' she whispered. 'It does bother me. I have the strangest feeling sometimes that I ought to know, I mean, that I ought to be able to find out.' She looked up then, straight into Maddie's eyes. 'For both of us really. We're so alike. And it was funny how we were both left outside the same orphanage in the same way and only a few months apart. We might be related. We might even be sisters. Oh Maddie, I'd love to be your real sister.'

'Your head's full of romantic notions, Jenny Wren. Real life's not like that.' Her voice hardened. 'Look what's happened to me. I fell in love with Michael and I really thought he loved me in return. And what happens? Off he goes leaving me with a bairn. If it hadn't been for the goodness of his father, I'd be living in Mayfield Wood by now. No, Jen, don't get any romantic dreams of someone turning up to claim you as their long-lost daughter. We're the bastards of some trollop, just like Mrs Potter always said we were.' She paused and looked at the crestfallen face of her friend. She reached out and took her hands. Then she smiled, 'But I grant you, it is just possible we could be sisters. You were newborn when you were abandoned, but I wasn't. I was at least a month old, they thought, if not more. So shall we settle for that, eh?'

'Oh yes, Maddie. Yes.' Jenny wrapped her arms about Maddie and hugged her close almost squeezing the breath from her.

'How are you feeling, love?'

Frank came and sat on the side of the bed and took her hand in his.

Maddie had been asleep and now she roused herself, yawned and stretched and glanced immediately to the cradle at the side of the bed.

'You were both sound asleep. I didn't want to wake you, but I have to talk to you,' Frank whispered, his voice so low that she could hardly hear him.

'Don't tell me. The name.'

Frank nodded.

'Mrs T was up here a while ago, but I really couldn't understand what she was on about. She was talking in mysteries.'

There was such a look of deep distress in his eyes that Maddie said at once, 'Oh I'm sorry if the name means something to you I didn't know about.' Her mind was running riot. Perhaps it was the name of someone in his family he'd lost, perhaps . . .

'It's not me it upsets, but Harriet. Like I told you before, I'm not at liberty to explain everything to you. All I can tell you is that it was her husband's name. Nick's father's name.'

'I see,' Maddie said slowly, though even now she did not fully understand.

'It brings back tragic memories for her. She thought

264

you'd done it on purpose, but I've told her that's nonsense. How could you possibly have known her husband's name?' He paused. 'What did make you think of that name, Maddie?'

'I honestly don't know. I just like it, I suppose.'

'Well, it would be kinder if you could think of another name you like.'

'Of course,' she agreed readily.

Frank raised her hand to his lips in an old-fashioned courtly gesture. 'Thank you, my dear.'

'Is there a name you like, Frank?'

He smiled sadly, 'Well, the obvious one is Michael, isn't it?' Her face tightened and seeing it, he hurried on, 'But of course that's not a good idea for several reasons.' He thought for a moment and then said, 'What about Adam?'

'Adam.' Maddie repeated the name once or twice savouring the sound of it. 'Yes, I like it.' Her eyes clouded for a brief moment, feeling for a moment the acute loneliness of one without any blood relatives to call her own. 'I wonder what my own father's name was?' she murmured wistfully.

Moved, Frank took her into his arms. 'Don't, love. We're your family now.'

Maddie returned his hug, comforted by his kindness and yet her heart still ached for Michael.

Her face buried against Frank's shoulder, she screwed her eyes tightly shut as if trying to blot out the memory of his face. I won't think of him, she vowed. He's gone for ever. I won't even think of him again.

But she knew it was a vow she could not keep.

Thirty-Five

The first day that Maddie ventured downstairs, she was greeted with an ecstatic welcome from Ben. She made a huge fuss of the dog and then carefully introduced him to the wriggling, gurgling little baby in the pram.

'How do you think he's going to be with him, Frank?' Maddie asked quietly, as Ben stood looking into the pram, his nose resting on the side, his tongue lolling, his tail wagging.

'I think he'll be all right, but we should watch him at first.'

But it seemed that Ben, robbed of his four-legged charges, undertook to stand guard near the pram every time it was set outside in the front garden or the yard.

Fondling the animal often, Maddie would bury her face in his rough coat and whisper, 'He's little Michael, Ben. And you miss his daddy, as much as me, don't you?'

The dog, seeming to understand, would whine and try to lick her face in comfort.

Once Maddie was really up and about again, the household slipped into a routine, though it was an uneasy one. Harriet rarely spoke to Maddie, except when she was obliged to do so, but her manner towards Frank, instead of being resentful, seemed to Maddie to be even more fawning than before.

Though it irritated her, it did not really bother Maddie, but there was something that did worry her far more. She was anxious for the safety of her child. Soon she would have to return to the fields for, in another few weeks, it would be planting time again and it would not always be practical for her to take the baby with her. There was no alternative but to leave the child in the care of the housekeeper. I'd sooner leave him with Ben, Maddie thought to herself.

The first morning she returned to outdoor work, Maddie worked in the glasshouses, close to home and went into the house every hour to check on the child.

'I thought he might be hungry,' she made the excuse, which she hoped was a plausible one since she was still breast-feeding him.

'I can always give him a bottle,' Harriet said and sniffed. 'I haven't quite forgotten how to do it, you know.'

Maddie said nothing, but bent over the cradle, her anxious eyes examining him. But he was sleeping peacefully, his tiny fingers curled in repose.

As if sensing her unease, Harriet came to stand on the other side of the cradle. 'I do know how to look after a baby, you know. He'll be quite safe with me.'

Maddie raised her eyes slowly and the long look she gave the woman said it all. Not a word passed her lips, but she knew Harriet Trowbridge would be left in no doubt as to her suspicions.

As she left the house again, Maddie realized that the housekeeper now had a weapon more powerful than ever before; she could hurt Maddie through her child. The only thing – or rather person – who protected Maddie and her baby was Frank.

But the woman was so devious, Maddie thought. If there was a way to do something that would not point the finger of blame at her, then Harriet would do it.

Maddie sighed. Once more, her overwhelming love, this time for her child, had made her vulnerable.

Over the next few months, Maddie had to admit that her fears seemed groundless. Far from carrying on her resentment towards the child, Harriet was captivated by the little chap. It was not until Maddie overheard Harriet talking to Frank one evening that she began to understand a little perhaps why, even though her antagonism towards Maddie herself was still evident, Harriet was charmed by Maddie's son. Harriet obviously thought that Maddie was upstairs when in fact she was in the kitchen heating the baby's bottle that had now become necessary since her own milk was not so plentiful. So Harriet made no attempt to keep her voice low and her words carried clearly through the half-open door.

'Do you know, Frank, I can't bring myself to dislike the little fellow.'

'Why on earth should you, Harriet?'

'Because he's *hers*.'

Frank's heavy sigh was clearly audible. 'Oh Harriet, I don't understand why you're so against poor Maddie. After all, you brought her here from the orphanage. If you remember, it was you who was adamant we should have a girl from the Home. I wasn't so sure myself at the time.'

'I had my reasons.'

'What, exactly?'

'Well . . .' There was a brief pause and Maddie sensed that Harriet was floundering for a reply. 'Well, with an orphan you've no parents demanding this, that and the other. No one coming to see if they're working a few more hours than they should. Checking up. All this Welfare

State – huh! Hard work never hurt anyone. I don't hold with it, all this namby-pambying children today.'

'And was that the only reason?'

There was a pause before Maddie heard Harriet say sharply, 'You're too sharp by half, Frank Brackenbury.' Then her voice softened as she deliberately changed the subject. 'It's like having Nicholas little again and this time I can enjoy looking after the little man without all the worry I had then.'

Maddie heard the low murmur of Frank's voice but as the milk boiled up and threatened to spill over, she made a dash for the saucepan and could hear no more.

So Maddie returned to her work in the fields with a lighter heart and though she still did not entirely believe that Harriet would never bring her pain through her child, she did now think that the woman would not harm the baby boy.

'It's nice to have you back,' Nick said, as they planted row after row of bulbs alongside each other.

'It's nice to be back.'

'You have recovered quickly, haven't you? And you've got your slim figure back, except . . .' His voice faded away but Maddie had seen that his glance lingered on the fuller shape of her breasts.

Nick was only a few months older than herself and it was natural that he should start to be interested in girls. And since she was the nearest . . .

'Have you got a girlfriend, Nick?' she asked, keeping her tone light, teasing, but not unkind.

'Huh, who'd look at me? Besides, they wouldn't get further than the gate, now would they?'

'What about Jenny? She really likes you, you know?'

'Does she?' His tone was non-committal.

'Why don't you ask her out sometime? You could take her to the village dance or to the pictures.'

'I don't think . . .' he began and then he glanced up and stopped whatever he had been going to say. 'What's he doing here?' Now his tone was full of belligerence.

Maddie straightened up. 'Who?' she began and then, as she saw the rider on horseback picking his way carefully down the edge of the field, she said, 'Come to see what we're doing with his land, I expect.'

The rider had dismounted and was standing beside his horse holding the bridle and watching her as Maddie stepped carefully towards him along the single row left empty between the bulbs.

'Good afternoon, Mr Theo. Have you come to see how we're getting on?'

He smiled as he touched his riding hat with his whip. 'Good day to you. I trust I find you well?'

Closer now, Maddie looked into his eyes and saw that his enquiry held genuine concern. She wondered if he knew. At his next words, she was left in no doubt.

'I understand congratulations are in order.' His voice was soft and its tone still kindly, yet the smile was gone from his mouth and there was a strange look in the depths of his eyes. 'Both on your marriage and the recent birth of your son.'

'Thank you,' she said quietly.

'And the child? All is well with you both?'

'Thank you, yes.'

'Ah. Good, good.' He paused, shifting uneasily from one foot to the other. Then turning to other matters he became more at ease. 'I've brought you some good news.'

'Really?' Her heart lurched. Was it Michael? Had he

somehow got news of Michael? It was the first thing that sprang to her mind.

'Yes. I've just had word from the authorities that you can plant another two acres of bulbs this year and I'm sure it won't be long now before restrictions are lifted altogether.'

Despite the plummeting of her heart in disappointment, Maddie smiled, 'That is good news. Thank you.'

There was a pause as for a moment he held her gaze. Then he glanced over her shoulder and said, 'By the look on Nick's face, I'm keeping you from your work. I must go. Be sure to give my regards to – er – your husband.'

He gathered the reins in his hands and mounted. 'Good day to you . . .' There was the tiniest pause before he added, 'Mrs Brackenbury.' Then, once more, he guided his horse carefully along the side of the field towards the gate.

She stood watching him until she heard Nick's truculent voice behind her say, 'Are you going to help me plant the rest of these bulbs today or not?'

Thirty-Six

It was a bright warm autumn day when Maddie tucked baby Adam into the deep-bottomed black pram and wheeled him down the lane towards the village. She had promised to visit Jenny and Mrs Grange at the corner shop and today she had allowed herself the afternoon off to do just that.

She parked the pram outside and climbed the steps to push open the door. The loud clang of the doorbell made the two people standing behind the counter and their one customer look up.

'Oh Maddie.' She heard Jenny's cry at once as she came darting around the counter from her place and saw Mrs Grange nodding a welcome.

After the first greeting, Maddie glanced towards the young man standing near the counter, holding his hand out for his change from the old-fashioned till.

'Well, if it isn't Stinky Smith. Fancy seeing you.' Almost before the words were out of her mouth, she felt Jenny's sharp nudge in her ribs.

'Don't call him that any more, Maddie. He's got a nice job in town now, in an office, haven't you Sti . . . I mean, Steven?'

Maddie looked him up and down and had to admit at once that the name no longer suited him. Standing before her was a well-dressed young man in a suit, white shirt and tie with his once unruly hair slicked neatly back.

But the grin he gave her was as cheeky as ever. 'And I hear the name the Mad March Hare doesn't fit you now.' The grin widened. 'The mad bit might, of course, but I hear you've changed your name.'

Maddie was suddenly on the defensive, wondering what was coming next, but Stinky – or Steven – as she told herself she must now call him, seemed quite at ease. 'Where is the little fellow then? Outside is he? Come on, Ma, let's have a look-see.'

'Cheeky young imp, you are,' Mrs Grange laughed but came round the counter and passed through the door Steven held open for her. Puffing, she descended the three steep steps and bent over the pram.

'He's a lovely little chap. Hasn't he got a shock of dark hair? Get a lot of indigestion when you was carrying him, did you, love?'

'Not particularly,' Maddie laughed.

'Ah well,' Mrs Grange nodded sagely, 'they always say if you have it bad when you're carrying, the babby'll have a lot of hair.'

At that moment the child whimpered and wriggled.

'Bring him inside. I should like to have a hold of him.'

'Well, I'd best be on me way,' Steven said. 'See you, Jen. Don't forget. Sat'day night?'

Jenny turned a little pink. 'All right.'

Minutes later, they were sitting in Mrs Grange's back room and she had taken the child from Maddie. Cuddling him against her ample bosom, she rocked him gently to and fro.

'Now then, now then,' she crooned, 'let's have a proper look at you. Why, you are just like your daddy was when he was a babby. He was a handsome little chap an' all.'

Maddie frowned and then forced herself to laugh and

say, 'Oh Mrs Grange, you don't look old enough to remember Frank as a baby.'

The huge bosom heaved with laughter. 'I aren't, lovey. But I do remember Michael as a bairn.' Now she stared straight at Maddie as if defying her to deny the truth.

Maddie felt herself colouring and dropped her gaze. So what Jenny had told her had been true. It was too late to stem the gossip and, for once, the gossip had been the truth.

She heard Mrs Grange chuckle softly and say, 'Don't worry, lass. All the village know the truth and they know that Mr Frank has married you to save that young scally-wag's skin.' She laughed even louder as she added, 'Even the village bobby knows all about it, but he's not going to do owt when you and the bairn are being well cared for and that young scamp safely out of the way, now is he? He knows as well as the rest of us, that Mr Frank's not to blame.'

'I . . .' Maddie felt herself growing hotter by the minute.

'Mind you,' Mrs Grange went on. 'I must say I was surprised at young Michael going off like that. I had him made of sterner stuff than that. Oh, I know he flirted a bit with the village lasses and I don't doubt there's more than one around here fancied her chance with him, but I wouldn't have thought he would have deserted you the way he did. And I have to say it . . .'

And who would be able to stop you, Maddie thought, but she held her tongue between her teeth to stop the words from slipping out.

'We'd have thought better of him if he stayed and faced the music and stood by you.'

'I – it's not as simple as that,' Maddie blurted out, forced to speak about something she had vowed she never would again.

'No, lass, I don't suppose it is. Life ain't simple. It never was.' The woman was still rocking the baby in her arms, but now she was glancing from Maddie to Jenny and back again, a thoughtful look on her face. 'Are you sisters?' she asked bluntly.

Maddie and Jenny exchanged a glance and then, with a similar gesture, they both shrugged. 'We don't know who we are, really,' Maddie explained and added wryly, 'only that we were both not wanted 'cos we were dumped on the steps of the orphanage only a few months apart.'

'Were you really?' Mrs Grange said. 'Now, I'd call that more than a coincidence, wouldn't you?'

'Wh-what do you mean?' Jenny stammered.

The woman opened her mouth, but at that moment the shop door bell clanged loudly and Mrs Grange held out the child towards Maddie and levered herself up from her chair. 'No rest for the wicked,' she laughed as she waddled through into the shop.

They heard voices and were surprised when only seconds later Mrs Grange poked her head back around the curtain. 'It's Nick Trowbridge looking for you, lass. He ses can you go home. There's been an accident.'

Maddie's eyes widened. 'An accident? Who?'

Clasping the baby to her, Maddie hurried into the shop and around the counter. 'What's happened?' she demanded.

Nick was white-faced. 'It's Mr Frank. A fork's gone through his foot. He needs to go to the hospital.'

'Have you called a doctor or an ambulance?'

Nick ran his hand through his hair ruffling it and making it stand up on end so that he looked wild. 'No, no. I came to find you. I didn't know what to do.'

'Where is he?'

'In the field – where it happened.'

'What? You've just left him there? Alone?'

'I didn't know what to do.'

'Leave the bairn with us, lass, and you go,' Mrs Grange offered. 'He'll be all right.'

Maddie did not hesitate, but passed the child back into the woman's arms.

'There, there, my pretty,' Maddie heard her crooning to the gurgling child as she hurried out of the shop. 'You'll be all right with me and young Jenny here . . .'

'Come on,' Maddie urged Nick. 'We'd better run.'

By the time they reached the field, Maddie's legs were trembling and her breathing laboured. She hadn't realized, until put to the test, just how much the birth of her child had sapped her strength.

'Down here.' Nick led the way along the side of the field and then Maddie could see Frank lying on the ground.

Maddie took one look at the blood oozing out of the man's boot and seeping into the earth. 'Go back to the village phone box and phone the doctor,' she said swiftly to Nick. 'On second thoughts, you'd be quicker going to his house. It's only across the road from the phone box.'

Nick was off again at a run but Maddie called after him. 'Get Michael's bike from the barn. You'll be quicker.'

Then she knelt on the wet earth and gently touched the man's arm. 'Frank?'

He opened his eyes and groaned. 'Oh Maddie. Thank goodness you've come.' He reached up and gripped her hand. 'Can you – get me boot off, lass?'

'Do you think I should?'

Frank, biting his lower lip, nodded.

Carefully, Maddie loosened the laces and eased the boot from his foot. As she did so the blood flow seemed to increase until to Maddie's horror it was pumping from the wound.

'I don't think I should have done that. It's – it's made it worse. It's bleeding more.'

'No, no, it'll be all right. It'll wash the dirt out. Take the sock off an' all.'

The blood was vivid against his white skin and now she could see that there were two wounds where the fork had pierced his foot.

'I've been meaning to throw those old boots away. It serves me right for being such a penny-pincher. The fork wouldn't have gone through a decent pair of boots.'

Frank now levered himself up on to his elbow and looked down at his foot. 'I've a clean handkerchief in my pocket, lass. Get it out and bind it tightly round the foot now.'

Maddie did as he asked, but the thin cotton was soon soaked with blood.

'Press your fingers on top of the hanky over the worst wound, lass. That'll stem the flow a bit.' Again she did as he bid.

Frank tried to smile. 'You'd make a good nurse, lass.'

It seemed an age before Maddie lifted her head and saw Nick hurrying down the field, with the doctor, complete with medical bag, close behind him. But Maddie had the sense to keep the pressure on the wound until the doctor knelt beside her and took charge.

Only then, did Maddie stand up and stumble a little way down the field to retch into the hedge bottom.

'It's all your fault.' Harriet's tirade was scathing. 'I 'spect he was worrying over you and all the trouble you've brought. I wish I'd never brought you here. I shouldn't have let my own . . .' The woman stopped abruptly and contented herself with a malicious glare at Maddie.

'It was my fault,' Nick said agitatedly pacing the kitchen. 'I didn't look what I was doing. I was digging away along the row and then I stuck me fork to one side to bend down to pull some weeds out by the roots and I – I didn't realize . . . I mean I hadn't heard him come up beside me. I stuck the fork straight through his boot.'

Maddie stared at him. '*You* stuck the fork through his foot?'

Nick nodded miserably.

'I didn't see him, Maddie.'

'But – but . . .' She began and then fell silent. She couldn't understand how anyone could be that close and yet Nick had not seen, heard or even felt his presence.

'I didn't look round and it was windy and I'd got me scarf tied tight round me ears. I didn't hear him.'

Maddie sighed. 'Oh well, it can't be helped. Accidents happen.'

'And what if Mr Frank's wound goes septic? What if he gets lockjaw and dies? What then?' Harriet rounded on her son.

Maddie felt the colour drain from her face whilst Nick looked stricken with guilt.

'He – he won't,' she tried to declare stoutly, but even to her own ears, her tone lacked conviction. 'He won't,' she said again and then added uncertainly, 'will he?'

But Harriet only smiled nastily as if to say, 'We'll see. We'll see.'

Maddie turned away. Frank was safely in the local hospital and receiving the very best attention, but she must go back to fetch Adam from the shop. She could imagine that Mrs Grange and Jenny would be hard pressed to pacify a very hungry child by this time.

As she passed by the coat pegs in the wash-house, from the nearest one she caught sight of Nick's yellow scarf dangling there. She stopped and for a moment stood very still, thinking hard.

There was something wrong. Something about that scarf but, in her agitation, for the life of her she could not think what it was.

Thirty-Seven

Frank did not stay in hospital, although the doctor called regularly at Few Farm to check on the wound.

'We ought to tell Michael,' Maddie, though reluctant now ever to let his name pass her lips, felt obliged to make the suggestion.

'I'll go.' Nick's offer was swift.

Three pairs of eyes looked at him.

'There's no need for that,' Frank said quietly. 'I'm hardly at death's door.' He turned his head away and stared into the fire. Maddie felt the familiar pang of guilt for she could hear the regret in Frank's voice. He was missing his son.

'We could write to him,' she suggested.

Sharply, Nick said, 'We haven't an address.'

'So how do you propose to go to see him, if you don't know where he is?'

'I'll just go back to the camp he was at and they'll tell me where he is now.'

There was silence before Maddie, frowning, said, 'Well, can't we write to the Commanding Officer of the camp and ask him to forward a letter on? Surely they do that sort of thing?'

'It'd be easier if I went in person,' Nick insisted stubbornly. 'Then we'd know he'd got the message.'

'It really doesn't matter,' Frank murmured, but his tone denied his words. In his voice, Maddie could hear the longing to see his son. She bit down hard upon her lower lip. It was a longing that was echoed deep within her own heart, if only she allowed herself to admit it.

This time when Nick left to visit Michael, Maddie sent no letter, or messages. She could not even bring herself to wish Nick a 'safe journey' and for the next two days she threw herself into work, caring for her baby and planting in the fields.

She was not unhappy, she told herself over and over. How could she be? She had a beautiful baby boy, who was a delight and a joy to her. Through the kindness of Frank Brackenbury, she had his name, a home and she knew he was very fond of her. It was far more than she might have expected with her background. And yet, though she strove not to let her thoughts dwell on him, she could never forget Michael and what might have been, what could have been, she thought sadly.

But Maddie was not a girl to allow bitterness to fester and warp her nature, like Harriet had done. She had never held any resentment against her parents for abandoning her even though she had often been curious to know why. During her time in the Home, she had never been unduly worried about knowing what her roots were – not like it seemed to bother Jenny. Yet now that she had a child of her own, Maddie found that the urge to find out about her blood family was growing stronger. Out in the fields where the work, even though she loved it, was repetitive and monotonous, she had time to think. To keep her mind from wandering to what Nick might be doing and what Michael was saying to him, she focused her thoughts on all the clues – few though they were – about her birth. And Jenny. She could not disregard Jenny. Although, at first, their game of being sisters had been a pretence, merely a way of believing that they each belonged to someone, Maddie now had the strange and insistent feeling that they were, somehow, connected to each other.

Maddie went over all that she knew. She had been left at the Home in March 1932 and had been some weeks old, though no one had been prepared to state a definite number. Then in the September of the same year, a new-born baby had been abandoned outside the Home in a very similar way. Jenny had been very tiny, Maddie remembered one of the nurses at the Home once saying so. Perhaps she had even been born prematurely. That thought had not occurred to Maddie before now. Then, she had not known so much about giving birth.

They certainly looked alike. Their hair colour was the same, although Jenny's was curly. They both had blue eyes.

Then there had been the gypsy. Maddie wasn't quite sure whether she believed in anyone being able to foretell the future, but the dark-eyed Romany had been uncannily near the truth in some of the things she had said. And she had refused to read Jenny's hand. Was it really possible that she had seen something she knew she could not reveal?

Maddie shook her head. Mentally she was going round in circles. She was no nearer finding out the truth of her parentage, or Jenny's, than she ever had been.

She sighed, stood up and eased her back. Time to go and feed her son. At least he'll always know who his mother is, she vowed. If only . . .

Maddie clenched her jaw and marched along the furrow to the end of the field, firmly dismissing any thoughts of Michael from her mind.

*

'He says he won't ever come home again.'

Despite her determination to put him out of her mind, at Nick's words Maddie's legs threatened to give way beneath her. 'Not – not ever?'

Nick shook his head.

'But why? I mean – surely he wants to see his father, if – if not me and his son?'

Nick shrugged. 'What's the point? Now Mr Frank's married you and taken on Adam as his own son, what's the point in him coming back at all? Only cause more trouble. That's what he said.'

'I – see.' Maddie said slowly. But she didn't see at all. Not really. She could scarcely believe all that Nick was telling her. Surely Michael, the Michael she knew and loved, could not be so heartless towards his own father, even if his feelings towards her had changed.

'Did . . .' she licked her lips, 'did he mention me or – or Adam?'

Nick shook his head.

'But you told him he had a son? You told him his name?' Despite her resolve, she could not stop herself asking the questions.

'Of course I did,' Nick was defensive. 'That's partly what I went for, isn't it?'

'And he said – nothing?'

Again Nick shook his head and avoided her direct gaze.

'He didn't want to come home to see his father?' When Nick still did not reply, Maddie said again flatly, her last vestige of hope gone, 'I see.' And now she did. Michael wanted to sever all ties with her, his son and even with his father. The huge lump that rose in her throat threatened to choke her, but Maddie lifted her chin and said, 'Well then, if that's the way he wants it, we all know where we stand now, don't we?'

She turned away from Nick before he should see the tears in her eyes. She would never again allow anyone to see her shedding tears over Michael. Not ever, she vowed.

But Harriet would not let the matter rest. 'I would never have believed it of him,' she declared at the dinner table. 'I'd never have thought that he could be so callous and towards you of all people, Mr Frank. You did tell him about the accident, Nicholas, didn't you?'

'Yes, Mam.'

Maddie watched as Frank pushed the food around his plate, totally uninterested in eating. She sighed, but said nothing, feeling once more the heavy weight of guilt pressing upon her.

Thirty-Eight

'Why don't you ask Mrs Grange, Jen?'

The next time she and Jenny were alone together, Maddie brought up the subject of their births.

'I didn't know you were so interested. When I used to say I wished I knew who my mam and dad were, you always used to shut me up.'

Maddie looked down at the sleeping infant in her arms and stroked his blond hair gently. 'Did I? I'm sorry, Jen.'

The girl shrugged. ''S all right. I'd got you.'

They glanced at each other and smiled. They'd certainly shared all their lives together, just like real sisters.

Jenny nodded towards Adam and said shrewdly, 'I suppose having him has made you wonder more about your real family, has it?'

Maddie nodded.

'Well, I'll ask her.' She laughed. 'There's one thing certain.'

'What's that?'

'Mrs Grange will tell me everything she does know.'

The two girls laughed together.

'There's someone else you could ask, an' all. Stinky. Do you remember that day in the woods when we were kids? The day he took us to see the tree?'

'Will you please stop calling him Stinky?' Jenny said, with a firmness Maddie had never before heard in her tone. 'His name's Steven.'

'Oh-ho,' Maddie teased. 'This is getting serious. Jenny Wren, you're blushing.'

Accused of it, Jenny's face grew pinker.

'Are you going out together, then?'

'Well . . .' Jenny glanced at her coyly. 'We went to the pictures again last week.'

'So, is Nick out of favour now, then?'

Jenny shrugged. 'I like him. In fact, just between the two of us, I like him best, but he doesn't seem interested in me. I – I think it's you he likes.'

'Me? Don't be daft, Jen. His mother detests me.'

'Maybe so. But Nick doesn't.'

'Oh, I think you're wrong there,' but even as she spoke, her denial lacked conviction. 'Anyway,' she went on, 'why don't you bring Steven, to the farm? Maybe that way you could make Nick jealous.'

'I couldn't do that,' Jenny said primly. 'It wouldn't be fair on Steven.'

'Well, bring him anyway. I quite like old Stinky. He's certainly turned out a lot better than I thought he would.'

'Only if you promise to call him *Steven*.'

'All right, all right. I'll try. Really I will.'

'I won't have strangers coming here. Especially not from the village. Poking and prying into everybody else's business.'

'They're my friends, Mrs Trowbridge,' Maddie said quietly, but firmly. 'And they're coming for tea on Sunday.'

'Well, don't expect me to get it ready.'

'I won't.'

'I shall stay in my room. You can bring me my tea on a tray.'

'Yes, I'll do that. It'd be a pleasure.'

Harriet eyed Maddie suspiciously, not sure whether she had imagined the sarcasm.

'Have you asked your husband?'

'Yes, I have, and he's quite happy about it.'

Harriet sniffed but could say no more.

It was a merry little party that sat around the tea table the following Sunday. Steven, as Maddie kept reminding herself to call him, was excellent company. He laughed and joked with Nick, who, obviously relieved that Jenny had transferred her affections elsewhere, was kinder to the girl herself. Once or twice, Maddie saw Jenny glancing between the two young men, a slight frown creasing her smooth forehead, almost as if she were comparing the two.

I wonder who will win? Maddie thought to herself.

'Where do you work, Steven?' Frank asked. 'With your father?'

'No. Me elder brother's going to take on the smith.'

Frank smiled. 'Another Smith as our smith, then?'

It had always been a village joke that the blacksmith should be called Smith. Steven smiled. 'That's right, but there isn't enough business now for more than me Dad and our Ron. So I got mesen a stall on the market.'

'I thought you'd got a posh job in an office?' Maddie said.

Steven pulled a face. 'I had. But I left. I couldn't stand being cooped up inside all day and shuffling bits of paper about. It didn't seem like real work to me.'

'What do you sell?' Maddie asked.

'Anything and everything that'll make me a bob or two.'

Maddie laughed. 'Bunches of tulips for Christmas?' It

was the thing that was uppermost in her mind at the moment. The work in the greenhouses was progressing well and they were promised a bumper crop. She had already brought in the first trays to be ready in time for Christmas. But Maddie's worry was selling them at the right time and at a good price.

Last year Michael had dealt with all that and she wished now that she had learnt more about how he had made his contacts in the first place. They still had the ones he had found, but now, with their increased production, she needed more outlets.

'You're on,' Steven was saying. 'But I shan't be able to take all those two greenhouses will produce. But I presume you've got other outlets.'

'Just a couple, but we need more now.'

'Oh well, then, I'll see what I can find out for you.'

Later, washing up together in the kitchen, Maddie said, 'Well, Jen, did you ask him?'

'Ask who, what?'

'Did you ask Steven if he knew any more village gossip that might help us find out who we are?'

'Oh that. Oh yes, but he doesn't know anything about us.'

'What about Mrs Grange?'

Jenny frowned. 'Yes, I asked her, but do you know, it was most odd. She clammed up when I started asking her. Reckoned she knew nothing about any babies being left outside the Home.'

'But you didn't believe her?'

Jen shook her head. 'Knowing the village grapevine like I do now, no, I don't.'

'And you couldn't get her to tell you anything?'

'Not a word.'

There was silence, before Maddie said, 'So, we're no nearer finding out who we are, are we?'

'We could ask Mrs Potter.'

'I wouldn't ask her if she was the last person on this earth to ask,' Maddie said vehemently.

To this, Jenny made no answer.

Steven was as good as his word and by the time the blooms were ready, there were more buyers from London clamouring for their flowers than they could supply.

'I know we can't get rid of the little barn because we need that for storage and parking the truck under cover, but you know we could knock the hen-house down and put another greenhouse there for next year,' Nick suggested. 'We've only got a dozen hens or so now for eggs for ourselves and they could easily live in a much smaller shed. What do you say, Maddie?'

'I'll talk to Frank.'

Nick looked mutinous. 'Why do you always have to ask him? You know he's so soft with you that he'll go along with anything you say. Besides, I don't think he's very well. He's slowed up a lot lately. Haven't you noticed?'

To her dismay, Maddie realized that she had not. She had been so wrapped up in the care of her child and the work with the tulips. But now she thought about it, since autumn had turned into winter, he had spent more and more time huddled near the range in the living room.

Now, she would certainly talk to him.

Later that night in the darkness of their bedroom as they lay together, the child asleep in his cot at the end of their bed, Maddie put her hand out and touched Frank's shoulder.

'Mm?' He stirred at once. 'What is it, love? What's the matter?'

'I'm sorry. Were you asleep?'

'Not really.'

'Frank, are you feeling quite well? You've been looking a bit tired lately.'

'I'm fine, Maddie. I do get a bit of an ache still in my foot, but I don't say anything about it. I don't want to upset Nick. It was an accident.'

'But are you sure the work's not too much for you? We have been dreadfully busy.'

He turned towards her and she moved into his embrace. He kissed her gently. 'My darling girl, I'm touched that you should be so thoughtful. But I'm fine, honestly, although . . .'

'Yes,' Maddie prompted.

'Well, I must admit I've been feeling a bit under the weather. I've been having a bit of stomach trouble lately.' He chuckled, 'But I daren't say anything in case Harriet thinks I'm blaming her cooking.'

'Then you must go to the doctor. It can't be anything you've eaten, because Harriet is a good cook. I will say that for her.'

Softly, close to her ear, he said, 'Even though you can't find it in your heart to say anything else good about her?'

'It's hard to.'

She felt his breath sigh against her face. 'Oh Maddie, if only you knew. She deserves your pity more than your censure. She's had a very difficult and unhappy life. I wish I could tell you all about it, but it's not my secret and years ago, when she first came here, I promised her faithfully I would never tell another living soul. I can't break that promise, Maddie, not even to you.'

'I know, I know,' she said gently. 'Don't worry about it. Go to sleep, but in the morning, you, Frank Brackenbury, are going to the doctor.'

Thirty-Nine

'If I'm not better after Christmas, I'll see the doctor then. But I can't let him tell me I've to stop work all together. Not just now, can I?'

'If you think that is what he would say, Frank, then you certainly ought to see him.' Maddie smiled, trying to make light of it, but the anxiety never left her eyes. 'If you don't go, I'll call him here.'

Frank smiled. 'Aye, I know you would. But I promise you I'll go if I feel worse, all right?'

'We-ell,' she said slowly, watching his face, trying to decide just how much he was holding back from her. 'Just so long as you promise that you'll go after Christmas if you still don't feel really well by then.'

'All right,' he agreed and they left it at that.

In December they were all busy in the glasshouses and, to Maddie's relief, Frank did seem much better. He did not put in as many hours' work as she and Nick, but they could not have managed without his help.

'Have you spoken to Frank about another greenhouse?'

'Not yet, but I will after Christmas. Can you fetch another tray in, Nick? I'll clear this corner out . . .'

'See, we are getting short of space. We could do with another one,' he said, as he went out of the door, closing it carefully behind him.

I know, I know we could, Maddie answered him silently in her head. But where is the money to come from?

They were doing well, there was no doubt about that, but most of their bulb stock went back into the ground the following year and cut flowers alone would not support them.

Frank saw to all the financial side but, now and then, he did discuss it with her.

'We must start to pay Sir Peter rent again from January, you know,' he had told her only the week before. 'We've had our one year's grace.'

As she swept the corner clear of scattered earth, the figures ran through her mind. Then suddenly, she was motionless, staring down at the concrete floor. There, in the far corner, she saw the imprint of their hands – hers and Michael's – joined together for ever and surrounding them, his drawing of a tulip. She squatted down and, trembling a little, she laid her hand over Michael's imprint. His hand had touched this spot. She closed her eyes and felt the tears well behind her eyelids and sting her throat.

Then, with a swift, angry movement, she stood up and brushed the earth into the corner, covering the cruel reminder. How happy they had been that night. How . . .

I won't think about it, she told herself firmly. I won't even remember it's there.

But for the rest of the day the image of the two hands, their fingers entwined, was in her mind and disturbed her sleep that night.

On Boxing Day, Jenny came to visit, this year bringing Steven with her. She had delivered her presents to Few Farm on Christmas Eve, but Steven brought the biggest box of chocolates for the whole family that Maddie had ever seen.

'Come in, come in,' Maddie said as she opened the door, trying to smile. At once Jenny said, 'What is it? There's something wrong. I can see it in your face.'

Maddie gave a quick, rueful smile. 'Can't hide anything from you, Jenny Wren, can I?'

'No,' the girl said solemnly. 'But then we're sisters, aren't we?'

'Are you?' This was the first time Steven had heard them say it and now he glanced from one to the other. 'You are a bit alike, but I didn't know you really were . . .'

'We're not,' Maddie said at once. 'At least we don't know what we are, because we don't know anything about our backgrounds, do we?'

As Steven opened his mouth, Jenny forestalled him. 'Never mind about that now. Tell me what's wrong, Maddie. Is it Adam?'

'No, no,' Maddie said swiftly. 'It's Frank. He was very sick in the middle of the night. He says he must have overeaten and drunk too much.' She made a helpless gesture with her hand. 'And, yes, we did overdo it a bit yesterday. Mrs Trowbridge put on such a marvellous Christmas dinner it was hard to resist, but . . .'

'But,' Jenny took the words from her, 'you think it's more than that?'

'He's not been really fit for a few weeks, although he had seemed a little better just before Christmas.'

'It could be a stomach ulcer, you know,' Steven volunteered. 'My dad's got one and every so often he's as sick as a dog and then, when it settles down, he's all right for a bit. You should get him to see Dr Hanson, Maddie.'

'Oh, I will now, don't you worry. First thing tomorrow morning, he's down to that surgery. But come on in. He's downstairs, even though he's still feeling a bit fragile and he won't stop apologizing to us all.'

'Are you sure you want us to stay?' Jenny asked worriedly.

'Of course. He'd only be upset to think he'd spoilt the day.'

Jenny beamed. 'Right then. Now where's my little man? Where's Adam?'

'He can't find anything wrong,' Frank said on his return from the surgery the following morning. He sat down in the chair by the fire, exhausted even by the short trip to the village.

'I thought as much,' Harriet said. 'I suppose you . . .' she jabbed a finger towards Maddie, 'are trying to make out I'm poisoning him with my cooking.'

Maddie gasped. 'The thought never entered my head, Mrs Trowbridge. You're a wonderful cook.'

The woman glanced at Maddie but the words had been said so genuinely that even she could not doubt Maddie's sincerity. Not this time.

'You've been working too hard, Mr Frank,' Nick said, smiling down at the man and putting his hand on his shoulder. 'Now, don't you worry about a thing. Me and Maddie can cope with the work for the next few weeks. You just rest and get yourself better.'

Frank smiled and patted Nick's hand. 'You're a good lad, Nick. I don't know what we'd do without you both.' His glance took in the housekeeper, too, but then his worried eyes came back to Nick. 'Are you sure you can manage the battery house? You must be very careful in there, you know.'

'I'll be careful,' he promised and Maddie marvelled yet

again at Nick's confidence, which seemed to be growing daily. She went to the cradle placed by the window and picked up the child. She planted a swift kiss on his round cheek and then carried him to Frank. 'So the only thing you've got to do for a while is play with your . . .' she hesitated fractionally before adding, 'little boy.' She didn't want to say 'grandson' and she could never bring herself to call him Frank's son.

'Oh well, I can do that all right,' Frank said, smiling happily as he took the child onto his knee.

Adam, now almost five months old, gurgled up at the man Maddie knew he must be brought up to believe was his father.

Frank's condition worsened. Within two weeks he was too weak to get out of his bed. His skin looked yellow and was cold and clammy to Maddie's touch.

'I feel so weak and dizzy,' Frank moaned. 'I've never felt like this before in the whole of my life.'

Between them they nursed him and Maddie was grateful for Nick being there. He sat up with Frank through the night sometimes whilst Maddie moved back into the tiny bedroom she had once occupied, taking the cumbersome wooden cot with her, squeezing it in to stand between the narrow bed and the wall.

'You need your rest,' Nick told her. 'You've the baby to think of. I can snatch a couple of hours in the day if I need it. You can't.'

He carried tray after tray up the stairs with anything that his mother could think of to tempt Frank's appetite. But Harriet was distraught. 'I don't know what to do. Everything I give him seems to make him sick. Nicholas, has he eaten that soup you took up?'

'Yes, Mam, most of it. But I had to spoonfeed him. He hadn't the strength to sit up and take it himself.'

For the first time ever, Maddie felt sorry for Harriet. The woman was beside herself with anxiety and it showed not only in the way she fretted about Frank, but also her manner towards Maddie had, for the moment, changed dramatically.

'Maddie, send for the doctor. Please. He ought to take him to the hospital.'

'I don't think that's a good idea, Mam,' Nick said before Maddie could even reply. 'How can they look after him any better than us?'

'I think your mother's right. He needs medical and nursing care that we can't give him.' She turned to Harriet. 'I'll go to the village and ask the doctor to call as soon as he can.'

'Let me go,' Nick said at once. 'You've the child to care for.'

'No. I'll go, Nick. I can take Adam in his pram.'

'But I can be quicker on my bike.'

Quietly, Maddie said, 'No, Nick. I'm going myself.'

'Don't you trust me?' he blurted out, his face turning red.

She stared at him for several moments, before she asked slowly, 'Now why on earth should you think that?'

Nick gave an angry snort and blundered from the kitchen, slamming the back door behind him.

The doctor was just hurrying down the steps of his house towards his car when Maddie arrived.

'Doctor, Frank's much worse. He's so weak. Please, would you come and see him?'

The doctor glanced at his watch. 'I'm on my way to a

297

difficult confinement, a breech birth. I'll look in to see Frank on my way back.'

'Thank you, doctor. We'd be very grateful.'

As the doctor moved away in his car and she turned the pram towards home once more, a voice hailed her.

'Maddie, Maddie. Wait a minute.'

She glanced over her shoulder to see Steven Smith running towards her. 'How's things?' he said as he drew level and fell into step beside her. 'How's Mr Frank?'

'Not good, Stink – Steven.' She glanced at him, but he only grinned. Even in her anxiety the nickname she had always used came naturally. 'I've just seen Dr Hanson and asked him to call again.'

Steven nodded. 'Good.' There was a brief pause before he said, 'Is there anything you need a hand with? I don't have a market anywhere on a Monday. I know you must be missing Mr Frank's help.'

'Well, there is something. Could you take the boxes of flowers to the station tonight on your lorry? We've a couple of trays ready in the greenhouse and I'm going back home now to pick and pack them.'

'Of course I can. What time do you want me to come?'

'They've got to be there in time for the six o'clock train.'

'Right. I'll be there in good time, Maddie.'

There was a pause, but he still walked alongside her making no effort to leave her. Suddenly, he said, 'You calling to see Jen?'

'Yes, but I can't stay long. I must get back to pick those flowers.'

'I'll come along with you then.'

Again there was silence between them as they walked along until Maddie asked slyly, 'Are you and Jen going out together, then?'

Steven pulled a face. 'I wish we were. Oh, she'll come out with me. To the pictures and that, but, well . . .' He hesitated and Maddie noticed that his face had reddened slightly, so she finished his sentence for him.

'She doesn't seem as keen on you as you are on her?'

'That's about it.'

She wondered whether to tell him about Jenny's infatuation with Nick, but decided it would be kinder to say nothing. Instead she advised, 'You just carry on asking her out and being nice to her. I think you'll win her over in the end.'

'You think so?' He sounded so unsure, so unlike the Stinky Smith she thought she knew. He'd been a little imp at school, but she'd always been a match for his devilment and had never felt intimidated by him. Nor by anyone else, she thought with an inward smile, if it came to that. Yet now, obviously in love with Jenny Wren, Steven was diffident, almost shy.

How love changed people, Maddie thought wryly, thinking back to her own weaknesses where Michael, and now little Adam, were concerned.

She smiled up at Steven and, mentally crossing her fingers, said, 'I'm sure of it.'

As soon as Dr Hanson saw Frank, he said, 'He'll have to go to the hospital. I'll arrange it. Pack whatever he'll need and I'll send an ambulance.'

'No, I'll be fine,' Frank said weakly from the bed. 'I just need to rest. That's all.' They watched him as he tried to raise himself, but he could hardly lift his arm up, let alone push himself up to a sitting position.

The doctor's face was grim as he went downstairs and

faced the three of them in the living room. 'I think you would be wise to contact his son.'

Harriet's eyes widened and she let out a little cry and staggered, reaching out blindly for a chair to support her. At once Maddie was at her side and easing her down into Frank's chair by the fireside, where she lay back moaning, 'Oh no, no.'

Maddie said haltingly, 'We don't hear from Michael now. Only Nick has seen him since he left home. And the last news we had of him was that he would never . . .' She pulled in a deep breath. 'Come home again.'

The doctor's voice was gentle as he turned to Nick and said, 'Well, I think you should try to see Michael again and tell him that if he does not come home soon . . .' His voice deepened. 'He may never see his father again.'

Behind them, Harriet began to sob.

Forty

At just gone half past four, Steven's lorry drew into the yard. He climbed down, slammed the door and was calling out as he came across the yard, 'Maddie? Where are you?'

She poked her head out of the door of the big barn and shouted, 'Here. I'm in here. I haven't got the packing finished yet. Frank's had to go to the hospital.'

Steven nodded. 'I guessed as much. I've just passed the ambulance on its way to Wellandon. Here . . .' He picked up a bundle of raffia and moved to stand beside her. 'Let me help. A dozen to a bunch, is it?'

Maddie grinned at him. 'Baker's dozen.'

'Tut-tut.' Steven shook his head. 'And there I was thinking what a clever business woman you were. Just think how many you're giving away. For every twelve bunches, you're giving a whole bunch away.'

'Ah,' Maddie tapped the side of her nose. 'But they can't come back at me then and tell me one of the blooms was too far out or a stalk damaged. We did talk about it, me and Frank,' her voice shook a little, thinking about the man who had become so dear to her and who at this moment was being admitted to hospital. She should have gone with him. She should be at his side, but the flowers would not wait and they were their livelihood. She knew he would understand. 'But we decided,' she went on more strongly, 'that if we gave a little, we might not get any complaints.'

301

'And have you had any?'

'Complaints?' Despite her anxiety, she smiled at him. 'Not one.'

A shadow fell across the open doorway of the barn.

'Oh! Hello, I didn't know you were here.' Nick's tone was flat, devoid of any note of welcome.

'Come to lend a helping hand,' Steven grinned at him. 'Maddie asked me if I could take the boxes to the station.'

'There was no need. I take them.'

'You'll have enough to deal with here,' Maddie put in quickly. 'Now Frank's so ill.'

'How do you think I've been managing these last weeks and helping look after him?' There was a barely concealed sneer in Nick's tone now. 'It'll be easier now he is out of the way.'

'Nick . . .!' Maddie began but swiftly he added, 'You know what I mean. Now that he'll be well looked after, we can concentrate on the work. That's all I meant.'

Steven had his head down now, concentrating on tying the bunches and laying them carefully in the wooden boxes, but Maddie could see that there was a tightness to his mouth that had not been there before Nick's appearance.

'These boxes are returnable, aren't they?' Steven said, changing the subject.

'Yes. But sometimes we have a job to get them back.'

For a moment, he appeared to be deep in thought, then he said, 'I might be able to help you out a bit there . . .'

'I thought you might,' Nick said, sarcastically. 'Well, if you're taking over, I'll get on with the work in the battery house. Or do you want to have a go at that an' all?'

'Nick!' Maddie was suddenly angry, but before she could say more, Steven touched her wrist and said softly, 'Leave it, Maddie.'

302

'Steven, I'm so sorry,' she said, as Nick disappeared across the yard towards the battery house.

Steven shrugged. 'Funny lad, isn't he?'

Maddie sighed and said softly, 'Moody, I suppose you'd call it. But with a mother like he's got and the life she's made him lead, well . . .' She said no more, but knew that Steven understood her meaning.

Frank was in hospital for a week during which time they did all sorts of tests, yet still they could not put a name to the cause of his debilitating illness.

'I'm coming home tomorrow,' Frank told Maddie on the following Sunday afternoon.

'Have they said you can?'

'No,' he smiled at her and held up his hand as she began to protest. 'But I feel so much better and I hate being here. I'll be better at home.'

'Will they let you come?'

'How are they going to stop me?'

'Oh, Frank, you mustn't go against the doctor.'

'I won't, Maddie. But Dr Hanson will be in tomorrow morning. I'll have a word with him then. Just you bring my clothes tomorrow afternoon.'

'I heard Mr Brackenbury was ill. I came to see if you needed any help?'

Maddie gave a little gasp of surprise at the sound of his voice. Behind her, she had heard the greenhouse door open and gently close, but she had not looked up from picking the tulips.

'Oh, Mr Theo. I'm sorry, I thought it was Nick coming in.' She stepped towards him down the narrow aisle between the rows of trays on either side of the glasshouse, brushing the earth away from her fingers.

'No, please, don't let me stop you. I know how important it must be to crop the blooms at just the right time. We can talk as you work. That is . . .' he hesitated, 'if I won't be in your way?'

'Of course you won't. But I would like to get on. I've these to pack for Nick to take to the station and . . .' she smiled, 'time's already running out on me.'

'Then, please, do carry on, Maddie. I'm sorry – Mrs Brackenbury.'

Maddie laughed as she turned back to her task. 'Call me Maddie. Everyone does.'

'Thank you. Then you must call me Theo, without the Mister.'

She glanced briefly over her shoulder at him. 'I couldn't do that. It wouldn't be right.'

'Why ever not?' Then softly, he added, 'I'd really like you to.'

'Oh – well . . .' Maddie was unaccountably flustered. To consider calling Sir Peter's son by his Christian name in such a familiar manner was against all Mrs Potter's strict rules. And even though she was no longer under the woman's thumb, the upbringing was hard to leave behind. 'I'll try.'

Whilst Maddie worked, they talked. Theo wanted to know all about Frank's illness and what was being done. Then Maddie asked, 'How's your father?'

'Better, but not better, if you know what I mean. He's recovered from the stroke as far as he's going to.'

Maddie said nothing, but glanced at him enquiringly. She heard him sigh as he said, 'He's paralysed and there's little hope of further improvement.'

'I'm sorry,' she said with sincerity, although her pity

304

was more for the young man standing beside her than for Sir Peter.

'Yes,' Theo said quietly. 'He's not the . . .' He hesitated and Maddie had the feeling that he altered what he had been going to say. 'The man he was.'

There was a long silence now whilst he watched her work. It was not an uncomfortable silence between them yet Maddie felt obliged to break it. 'I'm sorry that Mr Frank hasn't sent you any rent yet. He means to start paying you again this month, with the New Year, but . . .'

Theo held up his hand. 'Please, Maddie, don't even mention it.' He smiled at her. 'To tell you the truth, I had forgotten all about it. Our estate bailiff sees to all that and it really hadn't crossed my mind again.'

'Well, we hadn't forgotten.'

'No, I know that. But don't worry about it just now. You've enough to cope with.' He stood idly slapping his riding crop against his legs as he watched her work. 'These flowers are lovely. You really have done well, Maddie.'

Maddie gathered together a dozen or so golden blooms and, turning, gave him a wide smile. 'Please, would you take these for your sister?'

Embarrassed, he held up his hand, 'No, no, really, I didn't mean . . .'

'I know you didn't,' she said softly. 'But please take them to her. I – I know how much she loves them.'

Their glances met and held and he gave a tiny nod, acknowledging that she understood far more than was being said between them.

'Thank you,' he said quietly, reaching out for them. There was no need for him to say more except, 'I'd better be getting along and not hinder you any longer. Give my regards to Mr Brackenbury.'

'He's hoping to come home tomorrow.'

'Then I'll call to see him next week. Goodbye for now, Maddie.'

'Goodbye, Mr Theo, and thank you.' Somehow she just couldn't bring herself to drop the 'Mr'.

'As I said,' he murmured softly. 'Don't mention it.'

As the sound of his horse's hooves down the lane died away, Nick came into the greenhouse. 'What did he want? Come to demand his rent?'

'Exactly the opposite,' Maddie said tightly. 'He'd forgotten all about it.'

'Oho, I bet!' Nick countered sarcastically and went out again, slamming the door so that the glass rattled.

'Mind the . . .' Maddie shouted after him, but already he was striding across the yard, too far away to hear, so that her voice fell away on the final word, '. . . plants.'

'Oh, it's good to be home.' Frank gave a deep sigh of satisfaction as he lowered himself into his chair.

'Well, I must say you look better, Mr Frank,' Harriet fluttered around him, bringing a rug for his knees and prodding the fire into blazing warmth.

'I feel it, Harriet, I'm thankful to say.'

'Have they said what it is?'

Frank shook his head. 'No. Some sort of gastroenteritis, they think.'

'Have they given you a special diet . . .?'

'Oh Mam,' came Nick's voice. 'Let the poor man get settled before you start firing questions at him.' He came and laid his hand on Frank's shoulder. 'It is good to have you back, but I'm sorry, I must go and start the generator or we'll have problems.'

Frank looked up, suddenly worried. 'Are you managing all right, Nick?'

Maddie saw the fleeting flash of resentment in Nick's eyes, but it was gone in an instant and she hoped that Frank had not noticed it.

'Of course I am,' he said and smiled so genuinely that Maddie had to admire his self-control. 'I had a good teacher.'

Maddie went out to the greenhouse, leaving Harriet to fuss around Frank. There were three more trays ready for cropping and packing.

'Will you be able to take these to the station this evening?' she asked Nick when he joined her in the greenhouse.

'Sure you don't want to ask Steven?'

She glanced at him but he was grinning at her and she smiled back. 'He was only trying to help and we were a bit pushed that day, Nick.'

'I know. And you're right.' He came and stood close to her and, to her surprise, he put his arm around her shoulders. For a moment, she stiffened under his touch. It was what Michael used to do and the memory hurt. Then she relaxed, relieved that Nick seemed prepared to accept outside help now and again.

Softly, so that Frank would not hear, for they were in the greenhouse attached to the house wall and both Frank and Harriet were only on the other side of the living-room window, Maddie said, 'We'll have to have some help come April. This year there'll be more to cope with than even the three of us can manage. And that's if Frank's fully recovered.'

'Oh, he'll be fine by then,' Nick said airily. 'But you're right. And to be honest, I'd sooner it was Jenny and Steven than complete strangers.'

307

There was silence between them for a moment, but still Nick did not remove his arm. 'Maddie,' he said slowly. 'I've been thinking that perhaps I should still go to see Michael. Like the doctor said.'

She looked at him, their faces close together. 'Why? He's so much better now. I – I don't think his life's in danger now.' When Nick made no reply, she added, 'Do you?'

He sighed before answering. 'I really don't know what to think. I just wondered if – if the hospital have found something that they're not telling us about.'

'They'd tell me, wouldn't they? As his wife?'

'You're very young, Maddie. Maybe they wouldn't tell you. Or me.'

'What about your mother then?'

She felt him shrug. 'She's not his next of kin. Besides, she didn't even go to visit him in hospital, did she? Actually, that did surprise me, you know. I thought she would have made the effort for Mr Frank.'

'But you think . . .' Maddie said slowly, beginning to see the reason behind his suggestion. 'That they would tell his son? They would tell Michael?'

'Yes, I do.'

She was thoughtful for some moments, though her hands were still busy picking the flowers. As she moved to reach over, Nick's arm fell away from her shoulders. His action had surprised her and although his touch had not really bothered her, when his arm was removed, she felt relieved.

'Maybe you're right,' she said at last. 'Maybe you should see him again and at least tell him everything that's happened. I suppose . . .' The words were difficult to say. 'It's only fair.'

'It's more than he deserves,' Nick muttered. 'But I'm thinking of Mr Frank more than – him.'

'Me too,' Maddie murmured, but in her heart she knew that was not strictly the truth.

There was no way that they could keep the reason for Nick's absence for two days a secret from Frank and although he objected at first, Maddie could see that his protests were only half-hearted.

'Now don't you go sleeping in station waiting rooms again. It's too cold this time of year,' his mother insisted, ladening him up with food parcels, not only for Michael this time but enough to sustain Nick for two days, too.

'No, I won't. I'll find somewhere I promise. No more, Mam,' he held up his hand as she tried to stuff yet another parcel into his rucksack. 'I'm biking to the station. I really can't carry another thing.'

Maddie walked with him to the gate. 'Tell him everything, Nick, won't you?'

'Don't worry, Maddie. I'll sort it out.'

And he was gone, wobbling down the road on his bicycle and whistling cheerfully.

Forty-One

That evening as Maddie was undressing Adam in front of the warm glow from the range, without warning the lights went.

Harriet, in the kitchen making cocoa, gave a cry of alarm. 'Oh, the milk! I can't see – wait a minute, there's a torch in the table drawer.'

Maddie sitting perfectly still until her eyes became accustomed to the dim light cast by the fire, heard Harriet scrabbling about. 'It's all right,' came her voice again. 'I've found the torch.'

Maddie finished undressing Adam and waited until Harriet came into the room, the light from the torch wavering in front of her.

'Will you be all right if I take the torch? I must go and see what's happened.'

'Don't you go out there. Mr Frank wouldn't want you anywhere near his battery house.'

'Mrs Trowbridge, I can't leave it. The pump will stop and the greenhouses will go cold. I'll go up and see Frank.'

Carrying Adam against her left hip, Maddie took the torch and climbed the stairs. Frank was in bed and, because he had already put out the light, he was unaware of any problem.

'Frank, I'm sorry to wake you . . .'

'Mm . . .?' came his sleepy voice. 'What is it, love?'

'The lights have all gone out. What do I do? Isn't there a lever in the battery house that I just put up a notch?'

'Don't you go in there, Maddie. Let me go.' He pushed back the bedclothes and began to get out of the bed.

'I can manage it, if you just tell me what to do.'

'No, no. I don't want you going in the battery house and besides,' he smiled at the child in her arms, 'that little chap is dropping to sleep in your arms. You put him to bed. I'll go and see to things out there. I can't understand it, though,' he added as he pulled on his trousers over his pyjamas and tapped his pocket to make sure he had his keys. He slipped his arms into his dressing gown and thrust his feet into his slippers. 'Nick had the engine running only yesterday. I can't think what's happened.'

He paused only to light the candle in its pink holder that always stood on the bedroom mantelpiece and then he took the torch from her hands. 'Can you manage with that light to put him to bed?'

'Yes, but . . .' He was moving quite strongly out of the bedroom. Maddie, torn between going with Frank, and seeing to her child, said, 'Are you sure you're all right, Frank?'

'Yes, yes, love. You see to Adam, bless him.' He came back and planted a kiss on the sleepy little boy's head. Then he looked at Maddie, his brown eyes twinkling, his cheeks, though a little thinner just lately, creasing into such a loving, caring smile, that she smiled back at him. Their glance held for a long moment before Frank turned away and headed for the stairs.

'The lights have come back on,' Harriet greeted Maddie a little time later when at last she came downstairs. Adam, though tired, had taken a long time to settle. 'But Mr Frank's not come back in.'

Maddie stared at her. 'Not come back in,' she repeated stupidly. 'But I thought when the lights came on again, he'd be back in. I just thought he'd stayed down here to have a hot drink . . .' Her voice faded away.

'He shouldn't have gone out there in the cold. Couldn't you have done it?'

'He wouldn't let me. But I'd better go out and see what's happening. Listen out for Adam if he starts to cry, won't you?'

Harriet's face positively beamed. 'Of course I will.' And though Maddie knew that Harriet would probably find an excuse to climb the stairs and bend over the cot, crooning softly to 'her little man', she had no choice but to go out to Frank.

Whatever could be wrong that was keeping him out in the cold battery house so long?

Maddie ran to the barn at the side of the house and pulled open the door. Thankfully, he had not closed it behind him, locking her out, for Maddie had no other key. Only Frank, and now Nick, had keys to the battery house. 'Frank, Frank, where are you?'

His torch lay on the floor casting an eerie beam of light . . .

Maddie's scream echoed around the rafters and a bird, perching in the eaves, flew off in fright. Frank was lying on the floor directly beneath the control panel, his mouth agape, his eyes wide and staring and she knew without even touching him that he was dead.

'Well, it looks like accidental death to me,' Dr Hanson said. 'It looks as if he's reached up to the panel and then fallen backwards and hit his head on this.' He pointed to the sharp corner of the concrete plinth on which stood the engine and the generator. 'Of course, he might even have had a heart attack. There'll have to be a post-mortem and an inquest, Maddie, but it should be quite straight-forward.' He looked up at the police constable standing solemnly in the doorway, notebook in hand. 'You agree?'

'Well, yes, but I was just looking at his hand, doctor. Looks odd to me. Do you think there could be a fault on that there thing?' Constable Parsons nodded towards the brown knob on the control panel.

'Well, get it checked, if you're not happy.'

The constable made a note in his book. 'Sad though, ain't it? I always thought what a clever chap Frank was to generate his own electricity.' Sorrowfully, he looked down at the twisted form lying on the ground. 'Shame if it turns out that's what's killed him.'

Maddie turned away and saw Harriet standing in the doorway. Woodenly, the housekeeper moved towards them, staring straight ahead, past Maddie, past the police-man. She stepped into the battery house and knelt down beside Frank. She leaned over him and stroked his fore-head, a low, keening sound coming from her throat.

From her apron pocket, she took a pair of scissors and, reverently, she cut a lock of his hair and held it in the palm of her hand. Then she straightened up and walked out of the barn without speaking to, or even glancing at, anyone.

PC Parsons closed the door and checked that it was locked. 'I'll get Frank moved for you, love. We don't want to think of him lying there all night, but after that, you mustn't come back in here and you mustn't let anyone else come in here either until I've had an expert check that there control panel. I just want to be sure what's happened here.'

'Of course,' Maddie nodded. 'Nick's away and neither me nor Mrs Trowbridge want to go back in there.' A sob caught at her throat and she stumbled away.

The following afternoon, as darkness closed in around the farm, Maddie stood at the gate, huddled in her warmest coat, yet still shivering, though more from the shock and the dreadful night and day she had just lived through than from the cold.

She heard him whistling first even before she saw the dim, wavering light of his bicycle lamp coming towards her. She wanted to run towards him, but her legs would not move and she was still standing there, like a statue, when he spotted her almost at the last minute. He wrenched on his brakes and the wheels slithered on the loose gravel as Nick brought the bike to a standstill.

Before she could speak, he said, 'Michael won't come. I told him how – how serious it is, but . . .' His glance at Maddie was apologetic. 'I did try, Maddie. Honestly, I did.'

'It's too late,' she said bluntly. 'Frank's dead.'

She was sorry she had broken the news so abruptly when she saw, even through the dark, Nick's face turn white and his lips part in a horrified gasp. He gulped before he stuttered, 'B – but he seemed so much better. He . . .'

'It wasn't the sickness. He's been killed. There was an accident. In the battery house. We don't quite know what happened . . .' Her voice trailed away and unshed tears filled her throat.

'Me Mam?' Nick asked hoarsely. 'How is she? Is she all right?'

'She's taking it very badly. She's sat at the kitchen table all day just staring into space.'

'Why aren't you with her, then? What are you doing out here?'

'I – I had to come out. Adam's in bed asleep and I came out to the greenhouse . . .'

'Oh aye. You'd still have to carry on working, wouldn't you, Maddie? Nothing's as important as your blasted tulips, is it? They still have to be picked, even on the day poor Mr Frank's died.'

He pushed hard down on the pedals and rode into the yard, leaving Maddie standing by the gate, staring after him.

'I'm sorry,' she said to Nick the following morning. 'I didn't mean to sound unfeeling. It's my way of dealing with it. To work hard. Keep busy. It's the only way I can cope. I'm going to miss him dreadfully. I owe him a lot.'

'You owe him everything,' Nick was not about to let her off lightly. 'Where would you be without him, eh? Out on the streets. You and the kid, both. That's where.'

For once, Maddie stifled the sharp retort that sprang to her lips. She did not say the words 'And by the sound of it, but for him, that's where you and your mam would have been an' all.' Instead, she said gently, 'You're right. But we all say things when we're upset.' She waited for him to apologize for what he had said, but Nick was silent.

Maddie sighed. 'I must get changed and go into town. To the hospital to – to collect his things. That's where they took him,' she added, explaining. She waited again, this time for him to say 'Do you want me to come with you?' But once more, Nick said nothing, only nodded.

Maddie squared her shoulders. Very well, she thought. I'll go on my own. In fact, I won't even ask them to look after the baby. I'll take Adam to Jenny and Mrs Grange.

A little later, as she was manoeuvring the pram out of the back door, Nick came to the kitchen door. 'You haven't talked the funeral arrangements over with me Mam. Don't you think you should?'

As the pram bounced over the threshold, Maddie looked back at him briefly. 'Of course I shall, but I can't do anything yet.'

'Why not?'

'Because there'll be a post-mortem and an inquest.'

The horrified look on his face startled her. His voice was a strangulated whisper as he asked, 'A post-mortem? What on earth for?'

Maddie shrugged. 'It's usual in sudden deaths.'

'But – but they know what killed him. You said the doctor said so himself.' There was a strange desperation in his tone. 'Why can't the doctor just sign the death certificate?'

Maddie shrugged. 'Maybe he will. I don't know.'

'They shouldn't be cutting poor old Frank about now. Why can't they let him rest in peace?'

The vivid picture of her husband's body being mutilated, however sensitively it was done, disturbed her, but to cover it she said brusquely, 'It'll hardly hurt him now, will it?'

He hesitated before saying, 'No, but it will destroy me Mam.'

'Actually, I think your mother would rather like to know what his mystery illness was. After all, that was what killed him, in a way.'

'I don't understand what you mean.'

'Like you say, perhaps he was careless because he

316

wasn't feeling well and, because of that, your mother seems to be blaming herself.'

'How can she?'

Again Maddie shrugged. 'Her cooking, I suppose.'

'What? You mean, she thinks her cooking made him sick? That's stupid.'

'Of course it is. I know that. But again, it's because she's so upset. She's not thinking clearly.'

Suddenly, she felt sorry for the distressed young man. He must have looked upon Frank as his father. She reached out and patted his arm. 'Don't worry. It'll be all right. I must go. You just look after your mam.'

After his harsh words earlier, she dared not ask him to do any work in the greenhouses.

'Of course we'll look after him,' Mrs Grange bustled round the counter, her hands outstretched already to pluck the child from his pram. 'I'm so sorry for your trouble, lass. Mr Frank was a good man. A kind man. Look how he took you into his home and looked after you.'

Maddie felt a lump in her throat and could only nod.

'And you're not the first, neither. There, there, my little man. My word, you grow every time I see you. He'll be walking afore you know it, Maddie.' She raised her voice. 'Jenny. You there, love? Adam's here.'

Maddie smiled faintly to find herself ignored.

Jenny appeared and hugged her. 'Oh Maddie, isn't it dreadful? Have – have you sent word to Michael?'

In her embrace, Maddie stiffened. 'There's not much point. Nick's just been to see him to tell him how desperately ill his father is – was. But he didn't want to know.'

'Oh, so that's why Steven saw Nick on his bike the other night, riding through the village?'

Maddie nodded. 'Yes, he only got back last night.'

'No, this was the night before last. Late, it was. Gone midnight.'

Maddie shook her head. 'No, it couldn't have been Nick. That was the night he was away, seeing Michael.'

'Steven must have got it wrong then,' Jenny shrugged and went on, 'and you say Michael didn't want to come home to see his father even though he was so ill.'

Maddie bit her lip to stop it trembling.

Jenny was appalled. 'That's terrible. But even so, I think Michael has a right to know what's happened now. After all, he's Mr Frank's heir, isn't he?'

'No,' Maddie shook her head. 'I am. And after me, Adam. He told me that he'd made a new Will and – and cut Michael out of it entirely.'

'Oh no,' Jenny breathed. 'I never realized he was so bitter.'

'I didn't, until he told me that. It was after Nick had been to see Michael several times and then the last time he went, I mean before this time, he came back with the message that Michael had no intention of ever coming home again. So . . .' She sighed heavily. 'He made a new Will.'

Jenny bit her lip. 'But I still think you should send word to Michael. Somehow. It's his *father*.'

The two girls stared at each other, both thinking the same thing. If we had only known our father, then we wouldn't treat him this way whatever family quarrel there had been.

'I must go,' Maddie said flatly. She raised her voice as she added, 'Thanks for looking after Adam, Mrs Grange.'

'It's a pleasure, love. Any time.' And she knew the woman meant it.

It was not until she was on the bus to Wellandon that

she remembered Mrs Grange's words. 'And you're not the first he's taken in, neither.'

'The doctor has signed the death certificate. The blow on the head when he fell killed him.'

'So,' Nick said slowly. 'It wasn't anything to do with the electricity then?'

Maddie shook her head. 'No, the expert they sent out said he couldn't find anything wrong on the control panel, or anywhere else for that matter.' She frowned as she murmured, 'So we still don't know what caused the lights to go out in the first place.'

To this, Nick said nothing. Instead he asked, 'So, what have they put as the cause of death?'

Maddie dropped the piece of paper onto the table. 'Read it for yourself. It's all in long medical words that I don't understand.' Still, she could not erase the dreadful picture from her mind of how she had found Frank. 'Where's your mother, Nick? I'd better talk to her.'

'You do what you like. You're his wife.'

Well, it wasn't taking very long for Harriet Trowbridge to get back to her normal, resentful self, Maddie thought wryly. 'But what would he have wanted? To be buried in the village churchyard?'

'Where else? He's lived here all his life. His wife's buried there.' There was a malicious gleam in her eyes as she said, 'I'm sure he'd want to be put next to her.'

Maddie ignored the intended slight. 'And the service? What sort of service would he want?'

'Well, he wouldn't have wanted a fuss, if that's what you mean.'

In a low voice, Maddie said, 'But he'd have wanted his son here, wouldn't he?'

To this, Harriet made no reply.

'I'm not going traipsing after him again,' Nick declared. 'It's a waste of time. He won't come. I'll write to the camp. At least I know where he is at the moment and the letter won't get passed from one camp to the next like I did when I went looking for him.'

'Is that what happened?'

'Oh, you don't know the half of it. You haven't asked, have you?'

'Nick, I'm sorry. I . . .'

Suddenly, he smiled the smile that lit up his whole face and he put his arm about her shoulders. 'No, I'm sorry, Maddie.'

Before she could stop herself, she felt herself stiffen under his touch, but she managed to smile at him and say, 'It's all right, Nick. We're all upset by what's happened. But we've got to stick together and help each other.'

'Oh Maddie,' he whispered close to her ear. 'You don't know how glad I am to hear you say that.'

Forty-Two

'I can't face it. I can't go.'

Harriet sat at the kitchen table in a flood of tears. 'I can't face all those prying eyes, all the gossip going on around me.'

Maddie looked down at the woman with a mixture of sympathy and exasperation. Why on earth couldn't she pull herself together and attend Frank's funeral?

She tried to keep her voice level as she said, 'If anyone's going to be gossiped about, I should think it'll be me, not you.'

'Oho, you don't know the village folk like I do. They've long memories and long knives.'

'We'll be with you. Nick and me. We won't leave you.'

'What about the baby? I'll stay here and look after the baby.'

'Mrs Grange is going to have Adam. She'll bring him to the church, but if he cries then she'll take him straight out.'

'See . . .' Fresh tears flowed. 'You don't even trust me to look after him now.'

Maddie sighed, but managed to hold on to her patience. 'I never thought for a moment that you wouldn't want to come to Frank's funeral. He'd want you there. You know he would.'

She sniffled miserably. 'Well, if you put it like that.'

'I do put it like that. Never mind the nosy parkers from

321

the village. What do they matter? Think what Frank would have wanted.'

It seemed the whole village was there when Frank was laid beside his first wife. Maddie read the headstone. 'In Loving Memory of Elizabeth, beloved wife of Frank Brackenbury, who died 1st October 1929, aged 23'. She would see that Frank had a similar headstone, Maddie promised silently. For she had loved him, she realized now. Oh, not in the same way as she had loved Michael. Never in the same way. She doubted she would ever love anyone else with that same overwhelming passion. But Frank had been a kind and gentle husband. She wished now that they could have spent many more years together.

As she turned away from the yawning hole, she saw Theo Mayfield standing amongst the throng of people. As the villagers began to move away, Maddie noticed that he did not move. He stood very still and, knowing he was watching her, she felt drawn to move towards him.

Nearing him, she held out her hand. 'It was kind of you to come today. Frank would have been very touched.'

She felt his warm grasp. 'Your hands are cold, Maddie. It's been an ordeal for you. Please allow me to take you home in my car.'

Swiftly, she shook her head. 'Oh no, no. It wouldn't do.'

He was smiling gently at her. 'You surprise me. I always thought you didn't mind flouting convention.'

She knew his words were not offensive so she smiled in return. 'No, I don't. I've done a bit of it already, haven't I?'

He nodded. 'Yes, and I admire you for it. And I'm

about to do a little "flouting" of my own, Maddie. I'm going to grant you the tenancy of Few Farm in your own name. How does that sound?'

Maddie gave a long sigh of relief and tears sprang to her eyes. 'Oh Mr Theo, I can't tell you how grateful I am.'

She felt the slight pressure on her hand, which he was still holding. 'It's not your gratitude I want, Maddie.' The words were so softly spoken that later she was not sure whether she had heard him correctly, for now he released her hand and gave a little bow. 'I must have a word with Mrs Trowbridge and her son. She seems very distressed.'

Maddie nodded and glanced back to where Harriet was having to be almost bodily supported by Nick. 'She is. But then, she's been his housekeeper for a long time and I think . . . Well, best just to say I think she had a high regard for him.'

Theo murmured, 'So they say,' before he added, with genuine sympathy, 'Poor Mrs Trowbridge.'

As he left her, Jenny, with Mrs Grange carrying Adam, came to her. Hovering just behind them was Steven. The girl, as always, flung her arms about her. 'Oh Maddie, Maddie. It's so awful.'

'I know, I know, love.' She hugged Jenny quickly and then reached out for her son, who was fretful and holding out his arms towards her.

'Poor little lamb,' Mrs Grange crooned as she handed him over. 'It's as if he knows something's wrong.'

'I'm sure he does,' Maddie said, holding him close to her and taking comfort from the warm little body next to her own. 'Now he's lost two daddies.'

The faces before her were solemn and their glances fell away as if they were embarrassed to meet her eyes.

'We must get home. Poor Mrs Trowbridge seems about

323

on the point of collapse. Thank you for coming . . .' Her glance included Steven. With more murmured words of condolence from them, Maddie moved away.

It was as she walked down the pathway, through the churchyard towards the gate that to her left in the farthest corner of the churchyard, she saw a tall, fair-haired figure standing with a bunch of flowers in her hands. The woman was looking down at just a patch of ground. There was no headstone, no visible grave, for the ground was overgrown with long grass and nettles.

Maddie stopped and though Adam wriggled in her arms and now kept up a constant grizzle of discomfort, for a moment she ignored him.

'Amelia Mayfield?' she murmured and screwed up her eyes to try to make out the figure more clearly. 'What on earth . . .?'

And then, without being told, Maddie knew. That must be where Amelia's lover was buried. In that far corner of the churchyard, most probably in unconsecrated ground, which was the usual resting place for suicides. Then she saw Theo walking towards his sister, saw him gently take the flowers from her hands and lay them on the ground at her feet. Then he put his arm about her shoulders and led her away to his car.

Tears blurred Maddie's vision and though she would not allow them to fall, her heart went out to the lonely, distressed figure of the woman who had mourned her lost love for so long.

As long as, deep in her heart, Maddie would mourn for hers.

'Making up to him, smiling at him and before poor Mr Frank was cold in his grave. I saw you.'

324

It hadn't taken Harriet long to resume her goading.

'Mam, give it a rest,' Nick frowned at his mother, standing up to her more boldly than Maddie could remember.

'Trying to get round him to give her the tenancy to this place, I shouldn't wonder. Oh, but you've another think coming, girl, if you think that's ever going to happen. My Nick has more right than you ever did—'

Bluntly, Maddie interrupted. 'It already has.'

'What? What do you mean?'

'It's already happened. Mr Theo told me at the funeral. He's going to draw up a new document, all legal, with me as the sole tenant.'

With that Maddie turned and left the house, but not before she had seen the look of pure hatred in Harriet's eyes.

But what disturbed her the most was to see that same look mirrored for a fleeting, unguarded moment, in Nick's eyes, too.

Forty-Three

'I suppose,' Harriet said, sitting down at the supper table, 'it would be too much to ask that you and Nicholas should have joint tenancy of the farm?'

'Oh, Mam,' he said at once. 'Don't spoil it for Maddie. It's a wonderful opportunity for her, especially with her background.'

Maddie glanced at him, stung to retort, but the words died on her lips as he added hastily, 'Well, you know what I mean. But you deserve it, Maddie. It was your idea and you've worked as hard as any of us. You have to admit, Mam, that her idea has worked.'

Maddie saw Harriet's glance and heard her sniff of disapproval, but now, she said nothing.

Nick was smiling broadly, his whole face alight, his eyes crinkling behind his glasses. There was not a trace of the bitter resentment Maddie thought she had seen earlier.

'No, you have the tenancy, Maddie,' he said and added, jokingly touching his forelock, 'but I would like to continue working for you, ma'am.'

Thankful for his change of heart, Maddie laughed. 'I couldn't manage without you, Nick.' Then, summoning up all her reserves of forgiveness and understanding, Maddie turned to Harriet and added, 'Nor you, Mrs Trowbridge.'

*

Theo Mayfield was as good as his word and he brought all the official papers to Few Farm himself for Maddie to sign. When everything was settled, he smiled at her and said, 'Now, you shall be the first to know my bit of news.'

Maddie's eyes widened. He must be getting married. And the thought came unbidden, Oh what a lucky girl whoever she was, to have Theo as her husband. So sure was she that this was what he was about to tell her, that it took a few moments for her to take in what he was actually saying.

'Although I've taken over the running of the estate since my father's illness, there is so little for me to do. The estate bailiff has been with us for years . . .' He pulled a comical face. 'To tell you the truth, Maddie, he knows more about running things than I do. So . . .' he was smiling so happily, his eyes dancing, 'I'm setting up my own solicitor's practice in Wellandon. You probably didn't know that I went to university to study law. I'd got my law degree and had even done the necessary practice with a law firm in Peterborough, but then my father fell ill and . . .' He spread his hands. 'Well, you know the rest. But this . . .' he indicated the papers she had just signed, 'is the first legal tenancy agreement I've drawn up as a fully-fledged solicitor. You, Maddie, are my first client.'

She rose from the table. 'Then I think we should drink to that, Mr Theo, even if it is only with Mrs Trowbridge's elderflower wine.'

She fetched glasses and the decanter from the sideboard. Pouring a little of the clear liquid into each glass she held hers up and looked at him. 'A toast to – to . . .' Then she laughed. 'Oh, I don't know the name of your firm.'

'It's to be a partnership. Mayfield and Crouch. Tom Crouch was with me at the firm in Peterborough. He's a great character and couldn't wait to come in with me.'

'Then here's to your success, Mr Theo. To Mayfield and Crouch.'

He echoed her words and then added, 'And to you, Maddie, as the new and legal tenant of Few Farm. Here's to you.'

They settled to a new routine, uneasily at first, but as the years passed and Maddie made no move to oust Harriet Trowbridge or her son from Few Farm, their lives together continued. Adam grew sturdy and strong and became the apple of Harriet's eye. It seemed as if, robbed of Frank to fuss over, the woman needed an outlet for her strange, doting affection. Maddie herself never expected – nor got – any kindness or even friendliness from the woman. What puzzled her, though, was why Harriet never lavished love on her own son. She was possessive towards Nick and still tried to rule his life, yet Maddie had never once seen her even touch him. She never kissed him, never hugged him nor even patted his shoulder. But now, she positively drooled over little Adam, until the growing child himself began to squirm away from her clinging hands and wet kisses. Maybe it was because, Maddie thought pensively, with each day Adam grew, heart-achingly, more and more like Michael.

Funny woman, Maddie would shake her head sometimes. But at least she had no fear now that the housekeeper would ever harm the child out of spite against his mother.

Towards the end of 1949, Nick was called up to do his National Service but arrived home after only the first week. 'I've failed me medical.'

'What?' Harriet's eyes, for once, had been wide with fear.

Nick had laughed and put his arm about her shoulders. 'It's all right, Mam. I'm not going to drop dead. But the doctor just said I wasn't A1 and it's enough to exempt me.'

'So, you mean you haven't got to go away at all?'

Nick's grin widened. 'That's about the size of it, Mam.'

'Well, thank goodness for that,' Harriet had said. But even then, Maddie remembered, she had not hugged her son, nor even made any further enquiries as to the details of his health problem. And Nick, she noticed, did not volunteer the information either.

Only she, Maddie, had said later, 'It's nothing serious, is it, Nick?'

'Oh no,' he had smiled, but for the moment no longer flicked back his hair. That had been cut to Army regulation shortness. 'No, I'm still fit enough to work, if that's what you're worried about.'

'Well, of course it is.' But she said the words playfully so that Nick would know that she was genuinely concerned about him.

Steven did go to do his National Service, but every leave he rushed home to be with Jenny.

'Why on earth don't you put that poor lad out of his misery and marry him?' Maddie said, exasperated. 'He absolutely adores you. Who'd have thought it? Stinky Smith in love.'

'Oh Maddie,' Jenny had smiled and, for once, had not reprimanded her friend for the use of the nickname. 'I do like him a lot. In a way, I love him, but . . .'

'But you're still hankering after Nick.'

Easy tears filling her eyes, Jenny nodded as she whispered, 'I've loved Nick from that first time I came to the farm. Can you remember?'

'Oh yes,' Maddie murmured, feeling guilty at the memory. 'And I thought you were after Michael.'

'Michael!' Jenny's eyes were large. 'Whatever made you think that?'

'He was kind to you. Bought you some shampoo. Just like he had for me. I – I thought he liked you. I was jealous.'

'You? Jealous of me? Oh Maddie, how could you even think he'd look at me when you were around? I could see even then how it was between you.' Her face sobered. 'How I wish it could have been different for you.'

They stared at each other. Softly, Maddie said, 'Me too.'

'For God's sake stop going on about *her*.'

They were working side by side in the field. Nick stood up suddenly, towering over Maddie who was bending down, carefully placing the bulbs in rows in the ground. 'I don't like her,' he said harshly. 'I never have. You can tell her so. Tell her to marry Steven Smith.'

Slowly, Maddie stood up and faced him, staring open-mouthed at his outburst. She had broached the subject, trying to sound him out once and for all so that she could help Jenny make up her mind. But she had not expected such a vehement, passionate denial. But at his next words, she began to understand.

'There's only one girl I've ever wanted. You. But you had to go and fall for Michael and all his smooth talk, didn't you? What chance did I have against him? And then, to make it worse, when he left you, you had to go and marry his dad. You couldn't wait, could you, for me to grow up? I'd have married you, Maddie, whatever me Mam said. I'd have loved you and looked after you. Aye, and Michael's bastard too. I'd have put up with him, too, if I could have had you.'

He flung the basket of bulbs on the ground so that they spilled out and rolled in all directions and stamped off, his boots leaving deep footprints in the soft earth.

Perplexed, Maddie stared after him.

For the rest of the day, Nick avoided her and Maddie was grateful. She needed to think. His outburst had shocked her. She had never thought, never dreamt for one moment, that Nick felt like that about her. But then, she reminded herself, she had been so wrapped up in Michael from the first moment she had set eyes on him that she had never given a thought to Nick. And after Michael had left, she was so devastated that she had allowed herself to be talked into marriage with Frank. Not that she regretted that, she told herself hastily. Frank had been a good man, a caring husband and father to Adam. But now Frank's protection was gone. And she must face the fact that Nick might believe she would turn to him now. Surely, she reasoned, he was only imagining his feelings for her. He hardly met any other girls, thanks to his mother. So it was only natural that the adolescent boy – who was now a man, she reminded herself sharply – had imagined himself fond of her. There was Jenny, of course, who had worn her heart so openly on her sleeve, but whom he had rejected. She sighed. Oh, why did life have to be so complicated?

Later, she told Jenny what had happened. 'I'm sorry if it hurts you, love, but you've got to know. Don't waste your life pining for him.'

Jenny sighed heavily. 'I suppose part of me knows that

already. But I didn't want to be unfair to Steven, sort of treating him as second best. You know?'

Maddie nodded, feeling a lump in her throat. For her, anyone and everyone would always be second best to Michael.

Jenny smiled tremulously and pulled in a deep breath. 'Well, I've a lot of thinking to do. Besides, we may be jumping the gun. Steven hasn't actually asked me yet.'

Now Maddie laughed. 'He will, oh he will, Jen. As sure as the sun will rise in the east tomorrow morning.'

The next time they met – over the supper table – Nick did not refer to his earlier outburst at all. Maddie was surprised, but relieved. Instead, he chattered on about the day's work and planned the following day's jobs with Maddie nodding approval. Mentally, she crossed her fingers that his earlier outpouring would not be repeated.

As the seasons came and went, the whole district around Wellandon flourished and became renowned for its bulb growing. From the first tentative idea, 'Tulip Week' grew just like the flowers themselves and stretched over three weekends. Every year more and more sightseers followed the planned route around the fields. A Tulip Queen, chosen from the young girls who worked in the industry, toured the fields on the three Sundays, dressed in a long gown with a velvet cape and a crown upon her head.

Six years after Few Farm had, in desperation, turned to horticulture, Nick was able to say, 'I've counted at least twenty buses down our lane today and as for the number of cars, well, I just lost count of those. And we've sold all the flowers that were on the stall at the field gate.'

332

'Really? That's brilliant. But they were the last of what we've got available to sell as cut flowers this year. We must knob the rest.'

Nick nodded agreement. 'I know and we ought to start that tomorrow.'

'We must,' Maddie said firmly. 'And this year, Adam is old enough to help.'

Suddenly, for no reason that she could think of, Nick said, 'Time that lad had a proper father again. When are you going to marry me, Maddie?'

His words startled her. From the day he had first told her of his feelings, he had never again mentioned them and as the months and years had passed, she had begun to believe that the boyish infatuation had withered.

Now, standing before her, was the man he had become. He still wore spectacles and his hair still flopped forward, to be flicked back every now and again with a quick toss of his head. But he had filled out. His shoulders were broader, his body lithe and strong and although he would never have the striking good looks of Michael, or even of Theo Mayfield, nevertheless, when he smiled, his face had a cheeky, boyish charm.

Maddie pulled in a deep breath and tried to make light of his question. Even she wasn't sure if it was even intended to be serious. 'Well, not this week, Nick. We're too busy.'

'Yes,' Nick said slowly, but now he was no longer smiling. 'That's what I thought you'd say.'

'I don't know how we'd have done it without you.' Maddie put her arms around Adam's shoulders, but her words included not only her son, but Jenny and Steven too. 'We've had a bumper crop this year and without you all helping to head and now lift them, I think we'd have lost some.'

It was a warm evening in June and the five of them were walking back towards the farmhouse, all hoping that Harriet had prepared what would for them amount to a harvest supper.

'The only thing that upsets me,' Steven said, 'is when we headed them back in April there was nothing we could do with the discarded heads. Just a huge mound of glorious colour dumped in the corner of the field. Such a waste.'

Maddie laughed. 'Can't you think of a way to make a bob or two out of them?'

'We-ell, I have got something in mind.'

'What?'

'Ah,' he tapped the side of his nose. 'Now you just wait and see. The Mad March Hare's not the only one who can come up with brilliant ideas, you know.'

'Go on then, Stinky,' she nudged him playfully. 'Prove it.'

'I will,' he promised, a serious note now beneath the banter. 'Oh, I will.'

Forty-Four

'Over my dead body.'

As Maddie came in the back door and took off her boots in the wash-house, she could hear Harriet's voice raised hysterically.

'You'll not marry that slut while there's breath in my body, Nicholas. It's bad enough that we have to live here under her sufferance . . .'

Maddie slipped her shoes on and opened the door into the kitchen. They were facing each other across the kitchen table and Harriet, in the midst of rolling out pastry, was shaking her rolling pin at Nick.

'What on earth's going on?' Maddie demanded and they both turned to look at her. Harriet lunged towards her, arm raised, and Maddie flinched beneath the expected blow and raised her arm to protect her head. But Nick moved quicker than either of them and grasped his mother to pull her away.

'No!' he shouted. 'You'll not lay a finger on Maddie. You hear me?'

Maddie was shocked by the stricken look on the woman's face and, despite the threat, she was moved to feel sorry for her. Now Harriet sagged against Nick in defeat and would have fallen to the floor if he had not held her upright, his arm about her waist. Her arms hung down limply now and the rolling pin clattered to the floor.

Nick almost dragged her into the living room and

pushed her roughly into a chair. Then he stood over her. He opened his mouth but at that moment they heard Adam's footsteps clattering down the stairs, his merry voice calling as he opened the door into the room. 'Mrs T, Mrs T, are you going to make gingerbread men for tea?'

Then he stopped abruptly when he saw that all was not as normal.

'What is it? Are you poorly, Mrs T?' He came to her and put his hand on her arm and smiled that same engaging smile that had once been Michael's. His brown eyes were full of a concern that was strangely adult in the eight – almost nine – year old. Harriet drew him to her and held him fiercely. For once, sensing her distress, he submitted to her embrace without protest. Above his head, Harriet regarded her own son with bitterness.

'At least,' she said, 'this little chap loves me.'

'There's no call to talk like that, Mam,' Nick was more composed now, but his tone was still tight with anger. 'Just calm yourself down and forget all about what I said. Besides . . .' he gave a quick, sideways glance at Maddie. 'Nothing's been settled yet.'

'And it'd better not be,' Harriet said and her resentful gaze was now turned upon Maddie.

'What's been happening?'

'Nothing. Nothing, Maddie. Leave it. It's best left.' And then, in a voice so low that his mother could not hear, he said, 'For now, at least.'

He turned and slammed his way out of the house before Maddie could make her feelings known. For once, she was in full agreement with Harriet. If what she thought had been said was true, then she too would have said, 'Over my dead body.'

*

'Maddie, Maddie. Where are you? I've got something to tell you.'

Jenny was calling out as soon as she stepped into the house and then the door into the kitchen was flung open. 'You'll never guess . . .' she began and then stopped short as she saw Maddie carefully placing a tiny candle on the cake she had been decorating.

'Oh Maddie, that's lovely,' Jenny said, closing the door and coming to stand beside the table. 'You know, I really can't believe that Adam is ten years old already. Don't the years fly by.'

Maddie stood back to admire her handiwork. 'There, what do you think to that?'

'He'll love it. However have you managed to make it in the shape of a train, even with wheels and a funnel? And then the carriages behind with three candles on each.'

'Oho, I can't take the credit for making it. That was Mrs Trowbridge.'

'I'd have thought she'd have wanted to put the finishing touches to it herself then. Where is she? Out?'

'Out? You've got to be joking. She never goes out. You know that.'

'Where is she, then?'

'Lying down.'

'Lying down? Mrs Trowbridge. Now you've got to be joking, Maddie.'

Maddie shook her head, a worried frown creasing her forehead. 'No, I wish I were. She's not been feeling too good lately. You know . . .' She looked up at Jenny and kept her voice low. 'It worries me a bit. It's just like poor Frank when he started to be ill.'

'Do you think you should have the water in the well checked?'

Maddie nodded. 'I'd thought about that, too. Yes, I will if it goes on.'

'What does Nick say?'

'Tells me not to fuss. Says she's getting on and she's bound to get ill now and again.'

'Getting on? How old is she?'

'Don't know exactly, but she must be getting on for fifty.'

'Fifty! That's not old, Maddie. Mrs Grange is sixty-five and won't even think of giving up the shop.' She giggled mischievously. 'I reckon she'll still be trying to serve her customers when they carry her out feet first.'

'Jenny!' Maddie laughed, pretending to be shocked, but secretly she was happy to see that 'poor, little Jenny Wren' had blossomed into a pretty young woman with a saucy sense of humour. No doubt Stinky Smith's influence had a lot to do with that.

'Talking of Nick,' Jenny was saying, carefully now. 'How does he treat Adam? I mean, would he make a good father to him?'

Maddie glared at her. 'Now, don't you start, Jen. I've no intention of marrying Nick, or anyone else for that matter.'

Jenny sighed. 'I don't want to see you spending the rest of your life alone.'

Jenny was the one person to whom she could say anything, confide the innermost secrets of her heart. Maddie sat down and faced her. 'Look, Jen,' she said quietly now and with more than a trace of sadness in her tone. 'I've only ever really loved one person in my life, apart from you and that's very different. I was fond of Frank, very fond. He was a lovely man and I miss him, but if I hadn't been so young and alone with no family of my own, then – then I probably wouldn't have married him.

But I'm not going to marry again unless I fall in love – really in love – with someone. And I don't feel that way about Nick. And I don't think I ever will.'

Jenny nodded and had a confidence of her own to share. 'Poor Nick. And do you know something, Maddie? That's how I do think of him now. As "poor Nick". I think when I first thought I loved him, it was because I felt so sorry for him. He seemed like me. So shy and lost. No friends. But now, with Steven, it's so different. He's always so cheerful and happy-go-lucky. Always full of ideas and plans.' She shook her head. 'Now, Nick just seems so moody and – to be honest, Maddie – a right misery.'

'Yes,' Maddie agreed quietly. 'But who can wonder at it?' She pointed to the ceiling and Jenny knew she was referring to Harriet, resting in her room above them. She echoed Jenny's words. 'Poor Nick.'

There was silence between them until Jenny said, 'And we're still no nearer finding out who we are, are we, Maddie? Maybe we have got family somewhere. Does it bother you?'

'Not really.' Maddie laughed wryly. 'I'm too busy to think about it much. But maybe . . .' Her tone sobered. 'I'd like to know if only for Adam's sake.'

'I know. I've been thinking more about it too, just lately. And the reason I have is all tied up with my news.'

'Oh Jen, I'm sorry. What is it you want to tell me?'

'Steven's asked me to marry him now he's "on his feet" as he puts it. And now I've realized who it is I really love,' her cheeks grew faintly pink, 'I've said "yes".'

'Oh darling,' Maddie jumped up and flung herself around the table to hug Jen. 'That's wonderful. When?'

'We're going to get engaged at Christmas and married next summer.'

'This is marvellous news. Do tell Steven how glad I am, won't you?'

'You can tell him yourself tonight. He's coming to Adam's birthday party this afternoon.'

'Double celebration then.'

Over the years Steven's gift as a salesman had made him one of the most popular market traders in the district. He now employed others to run his stalls on the various local markets whilst he delved into other areas where he could 'make a bob or two'.

That evening when at last an over-excited ten-year-old had finally been persuaded to go to bed, Maddie, Nick, Jenny and Steven toasted the news of their engagement. Even though she had made the effort to join in the party for her 'little man' who was now growing so fast that he would soon no longer fit the endearment, Harriet was still feeling unwell and had gone to bed too.

'There's something else to celebrate an' all,' Steven said, his grin wide. 'It's all settled. Next year there's to be a proper Tulip Parade with decorated floats and everything. We tried it this year, you know, with one lorry from a local firm to carry Miss Tulipland 1958 and a couple of decorated cars to follow, but next May we're hoping that more locals will take part and make a proper do of it. There's a chap coming over from Holland to help design the floats and show everyone how to build them. You'll have to send one in from Few Farm, you know, Maddie.'

'We wouldn't have time to be taking part in such nonsense,' Nick said sourly, before Maddie could speak. 'We've enough to do.'

'Oh, I don't know, Nick. It would be good publicity for us and fun too.' She turned to Steven. 'Do you know how to build a float?'

'Roughly. Ideally it ought to be designed around a

340

vehicle of some kind, so that it can be self-propelled and take part in a parade through the town centre. You make a metal frame – my brother can do that for you if you like – in the shape you want and then cover it with straw that's been stitched together to make a sort of straw matting. Then that's cut to shape too and last of all – and that can only be done at the very last minute – you pin on the tulip heads.'

'What, each one? Individually?' Jenny asked.

Steven nodded. 'Yes. With wire shaped like a huge hairpin. It's a lot of work but the result is worth all the effort.' He beamed with satisfaction as he added, 'And all those lovely flower heads being used instead of thrown away.'

They laughed together – all, Maddie noticed, except Nick.

Forty-Five

'Jen, do you think you could give us a hand with the flowers?'

April was upon them again and the workload facing Maddie was daunting. For once, even she felt unable to cope. 'Of all the times for it to happen, Mrs Trowbridge has to go and be ill again. I've the house to see to now and looking after her.' As the words came out of her mouth, they sounded unfeeling even to Maddie's own ears. 'Adam can help after school and at weekends and in the holidays, but Nick'll never manage everything on his own.'

Jenny raised her eyebrows, but seeing how harassed Maddie was, she made no comment and merely said, 'Of course I can. Do you want me to ask Steven too?'

'Would you? Oh thanks.'

'I'll have a word with Mrs Grange. I've some holiday due.'

'Some holiday that'll be,' Maddie said, apologetically.

Jenny smiled and murmured, 'Oh I don't mind.'

Smiling for the first time in days, Maddie hugged her. 'Oh, it's good to have a sister, even if we have only adopted each other.'

'I'm getting the doctor to your mother, Nick. She's getting worse instead of better. And what worries me is that she has all the same symptoms that Frank had. I'm going to talk to the doctor and ask him if he thinks it could be the water in the well. Maybe we ought to get it tested.'

Nick wrinkled his forehead. 'If it was the water, then we'd all be ill, wouldn't we?'

Maddie spread her hands helplessly. 'I don't know. I just don't know. Oh, I feel so ignorant about things like this.'

'You can't know everything, Maddie.'

'But I can find out. I'll ask the doctor how to go about it.'

Dr Battison gave her all the help she needed, but when the report on the well water came back, there was no problem.

'Crystal clear and a lot healthier than some of the water our townsfolk have to drink,' Dr Battison told her.

'So that's not it.'

'No,' Dr Battison agreed, but the way he said the word implied that he thought there was more they could do.

Maddie looked at him. 'What? What is it?'

The doctor was frowning and shaking his head. 'Her symptoms puzzle me. Of course they're similar to gastro-enteritis, but . . .' He sighed. 'There's something niggling me. Something's not quite right and I'm damned if I know . . .' He cut his own sentence short and appeared to be lost deep in thought.

'That's what Dr Hanson said about Frank,' Maddie murmured.

'What?' His tone was suddenly sharp with interest.

Dr Battison was new to the area. He had arrived the previous year to take over the country practice when Dr Hanson had retired. He was young, dynamic and go-ahead and whilst many in the village had yet to trust him completely – such had been their faith in the old doctor – Maddie had liked him at once. This was only the second time she had had cause to meet him, the first being when

343

she had taken Adam to the surgery to be told the boy had chicken pox.

'I said, that was what the doctor said about my husband when he was ill just before he died.'

The young man was frowning. 'But I understood that your husband was killed by an accidental fall in the barn where you have your electrical equipment?'

'He was. But he was very ill just before it happened. He'd been in hospital and they'd got him a lot better and sent him home. He had no more of the sickness but he was still very weak and – and . . .' She faltered a little, remembering once more her nightmarish discovery. 'He shouldn't really have gone out there. He should have left it all to Nick. But Nick was away for the night and the lights went out . . .' Her voice trailed away. It sounded, even to her own ears, such a pathetic reason for a man to lose his life.

But Dr Battison was not sitting in judgement. 'Tell me more about the illness he had before that happened.'

Without invitation, he sat down at the table and, following his lead, Maddie sat down opposite him.

'Well,' she began, wrinkling her brow, trying to remember exactly how it had been. 'His illness started just like Mrs Trowbridge's has done. Very slowly so that at first no one, not even the one who's ill, takes a lot of notice. She's been getting stomach trouble on and off for almost a year now and I remember the first time she had a bad attack because it was on Adam's tenth birthday last August. I remember thinking then that it was like Frank had been. I even said so to Jenny.'

'Jenny?'

'Jenny Wren at the corner shop. She lives with Mrs Grange.'

'Oh yes, I know. Go on.'

'Well, I can't tell you any more really.'

344

'Was the well water tested then?'

Maddie shook her head. 'No. Dr Hanson admitted Frank to hospital and they did some tests, but before the results were through, Frank came home. He'd been much better in the hospital, you see. The accident happened the next day and I suppose . . .' Again her voice faded away, but the doctor nodded understandingly and finished the sentence for her. 'It was no longer necessary to know the results, especially if none of the rest of the household were affected.' He looked at her sharply. 'You weren't, were you?'

Maddie shook her head. 'Not until now.'

Dr Battison was thoughtful, idly tracing a figure eight on the tablecloth with the tip of his forefinger. 'And now there's still only one member of the household ill?'

'You say the symptoms are like gastroenteritis?'

'Mm.'

She stared across the table at him. 'But you're not completely satisfied that it is that, are you?'

'No,' he said shortly and was silent for a moment, still thinking, before he said, 'I'm going to take her into hospital for observation and run some tests.'

'What sort of tests?'

Suddenly, he seemed evasive. 'Oh, the usual.' He stood up but now he was avoiding looking at her directly. 'Pack a few things for her and I'll arrange the ambulance for this afternoon.'

Maddie held the back door open for him. 'Goodbye, Doctor. Thank you for coming.'

He nodded briefly and she watched him as he crossed the yard. She had begun to close the door when she saw him stop and glance towards the huge barn. She saw him look back towards the house, but because the back door was now almost closed and she was watching him through

345

a tiny slit, she knew he could not see her. To him, it would seem as if she had shut the door and gone back into the house.

Dr Battison walked towards the door to the barn and disappeared inside it.

'Now, just what are you up to?' Maddie said aloud and then she realized. He was probably looking for Nick to talk to him about his mother. After all, Nick was her relative, not Maddie. She was about to pull the door open again and step out into the yard to tell him that his searching the barn was fruitless, that Nick was in the fields, when she heard Harriet's cries from upstairs. 'Maddie, oh Maddie. Come quickly.'

Clicking her tongue against her teeth in exasperation, Maddie closed the door and ran lightly up the stairs, 'I'm coming, Mrs Trowbridge, I'm coming.'

Harriet was hanging over the edge of the bed, retching into the chamber pot. Maddie put the palm of her hand against the woman's forehead, smoothing the grey hair out of the way. The skin felt clammy to her touch and when the exhausted woman lay back against the pillows once more, Maddie could see the perspiration glistening on her face, now drained of all its natural colour that had been replaced by a strange tinge of yellow.

'What – what did he say?' Harriet asked weakly.

Touching her hand, Maddie said gently, 'You're to go into hospital. I'm to pack a few things for you . . .'

'No, no, I don't want to go. I want to stay here. Nick can look after me, if I'm too much trouble to you.'

'Oh Mrs T,' Maddie said. Feeling guilty now because she had, at first, been irritated by the woman's illness, she used the pet name that Michael had always used. 'You're no trouble to me. But it's for the best. They'll find out what's wrong with you and . . .'

'I don't want to go.' Her voice was rising hysterically. 'I won't go. You just want to get rid of me so you can have this place to yourself.'

'That's not true. You know we can't manage without you. Any of us.'

Harriet was sobbing now. 'Oh little Adam. I shan't see him again.'

'Don't upset yourself, Mrs Trowbridge. We'll come to visit you and I'll bring Adam.'

She was reaching out, clasping Maddie's hand. 'You will? You promise?'

'Of course I do.'

She seemed to relax a little and later, as she and Nick watched the ambulance drive away down the lane carrying Harriet to the cottage hospital in the town, Maddie thought how sad it was that her thoughts in that moment of crisis had been not for her own son, but for Adam.

Not for the first time, did Maddie feel a stab of pity for Nick Trowbridge.

Forty-Six

'How is she?'

They were standing in the hospital corridor, the three of them, Maddie, Nick and Adam, too, looking, for once, solemn faced.

The sister shook her head. 'No change, I'm afraid,' then added with an encouraging smile, 'but it's early days yet.'

'Can we see her?' Nick asked.

'Of course. But only two at a time and I would ask you to stay no longer than half an hour. She is very weak.'

'Thank you,' Maddie began to move towards the ward at the end of the corridor.

'Excuse me asking . . .' Maddie turned back to look at her as the sister nodded towards the brown bag Maddie was carrying. 'Is that a change of clothing for her?'

'Well, yes, partly. A clean nightdress and hankies, but I've brought a few eggs and some pasties . . .'

The sister's mouth pursed and she shook her head again. 'I'll take the clothes, but I must ask you to take any food back home. Mrs Trowbridge is to have only the diet the doctor has prescribed for her. He gave strict instructions that she was to be allowed no food at all to be brought in to her.'

Nick tried a weak smile. 'Not even grapes?'

But the sister was unsmiling. 'Nothing. The doctor was most specific about it.'

'Well, I can understand that,' Maddie said at once.

348

'Obviously, it's all part of trying to find out what's causing her sickness.' She smiled. 'But you're welcome to the eggs, Sister, and the pasties, if you can make good use of them.'

She saw the woman hesitate and smooth the palms of her hands down her white apron. She ran her tongue around her lips before she said, almost reluctantly, 'Thank you, Mrs – er . . .'

'Brackenbury,' Maddie supplied.

'Mrs Brackenbury, but I'd better not.'

Adam was moving away down the corridor, anxious to find the woman who had always looked after him whilst Maddie was working. She was like a grandmother to him.

'You go,' Maddie said to Nick. 'You and Adam go in first and then send him out after ten minutes or so and I'll come in. You stay with your mother all the time we're allowed.'

Nick smiled ruefully. 'I'm sure she'd rather have Adam all the time than either of us.'

'Go on,' Maddie pushed his shoulder gently. 'Go on with you.'

When they arrived back at Few Farm after that first visit, they found Jenny pacing the yard.

'There you are. I was just about to give up and go home. Have you seen her? How is she?' Though she asked the usual question, Maddie could see at once that there was more than just her concern for Harriet troubling Jenny.

'Come on inside and I'll make us all a pot of tea.'

'Don't bother for me, I must start the generator up else we'll have no electricity by morning,' Nick said.

'Can I go to the village on me bike, Mam?' Adam asked. 'To see Donald?'

'Who's Donald?'

'Donald Fisher. He's just come to live in the village and started our school.'

'All right but be home by six o'clock. You hear?'

'Yes, Mam.'

'And change into your old trousers first. I don't want you ruining your best pair.'

'Yes, Mam,' they heard him shout as his feet pounded up the stairs.

Maddie smiled at Jenny. 'Looks like it's just you and me for tea, then.'

Jenny nodded and Maddie couldn't help noticing that the girl looked relieved.

The reason became obvious as soon as they sat down on either side of the kitchen table with cups of tea in front of them.

'I'm glad I've got you on your own,' Jenny began when Adam had gone hurtling out of the yard gate on his bicycle. 'There – there's something I've got to tell you.'

'Oh dear,' Maddie said lightly, trying to take some of the worried look from Jenny's face. 'Not expecting, are you?'

Jenny gasped and her mouth dropped open. 'No, I'm not,' she retorted indignantly.

'Well, don't make it sound as if it's the worst crime in the world,' Maddie said and could not keep the trace of bitterness from her tone as she added, 'I'm sure Steven wouldn't desert you.'

'No, I don't think he would,' Jenny replied quietly. 'But it's not that. It's – it's about you.'

'Me?'

'Yes. There's gossip in the village about – about Mrs Trowbridge's illness.'

Maddie shook her head, baffled. 'What about it?'

'That – that it's like Mr Frank had.'

'We know that.'

'They're saying that it could be that – I mean . . .'

'Oh for Heaven's sake, Jen, spit it out. Just what are the old busybodies saying?'

Now the words came out in a rush. 'That you're poisoning her. That you poisoned Mr Frank to get the farm and now you're trying to get rid of Mrs Trowbridge. Everybody knows the two of you have never got on.'

'I – am – *what*?' Maddie was horrified that anyone could even think such a thing, let alone voice it aloud.

'Maddie, I'm sorry. But I thought you ought to know . . .' Her voice trailed away into a whisper.

'Oh I ought to know, all right.' Maddie stood up as if she would confront the gossipmongers there and then. 'Who's saying these things, who's . . .?'

'Maddie, just sit down and listen, will you?'

Frowning, her mouth pouting, Maddie reluctantly lowered herself into the chair again. 'How do the village folk know we don't get on, unless someone's told them? Mrs Trowbridge doesn't mix with any of them and I've certainly never said anything.' She glared at Jenny, who said defensively, 'Well, it wasn't me. But there's several people who know. They've long memories, village folk, and it was common knowledge when you first came to the farm. Folk used to get their milk and eggs and butter from here then, don't forget.'

'Mrs Trowbridge has always said that.'

'What?'

'That the villagers have got long memories. Seems she was right.'

Jenny was frowning now. 'There's a lot more to it than

351

you and me know, Maddie. Even Mrs Grange keeps hinting at secrets and scandals from long ago, but she'll never really tell me what she's on about.'

'Have you asked her?'

'Not – not really.'

Grimly, Maddie said, 'Then maybe it's time you did.'

Forty-Seven

Because of Jenny's warning, it was not such a shock to Maddie when PC Parsons wobbled up the yard on his bicycle, dismounted and leant it against the wall of the house.

'You there, young Maddie?' He opened the back door and walked into the wash-house without waiting for an invitation.

He'd always called her that from her days at the Home. He wasn't the sort of man to alter his ways just because she was now twenty-seven and he close to retiring age.

'At the moment, I am,' she said, opening the kitchen door. 'Come away in. Cup of tea?'

He eyed her over the spectacles he wore, as he removed his helmet and tucked it under his arm. 'I don't think I will just now. Thank you.'

He manoeuvred his bulk around the kitchen table and followed her into the living room where he placed his helmet on the table and sat down.

Coming straight to the point, as was his way, he said, 'There's nasty rumours going around the village, lass, that you've not been as careful as you might have been with washing your hands after dealing with weedkiller and rat poison and such-like on the farm before you serve up the dinner.'

Maddie stared at him. A cheeky retort sprang to her lips, but although he had broached the subject in a half-comical way, his expression was very serious. This was not a laughing matter and she would serve herself no purpose by treating his visit in a jocular manner.

Holding his gaze, Maddie said calmly, 'I'm always very careful, Mr Parsons, about such things. And I very rarely touch the weedkiller or the rat poison. That's Nick's job.'

'You suggesting that it's Nicholas who is poisoning his mother?'

Now Maddie was getting angry, but she managed to keep her voice level as she said, 'I'm suggesting that neither of us is doing any such thing.'

'Well, someone is. The doctor's tests show that she has a high level of arsenic in her system.'

Maddie gasped and knew that the colour fled from her face. She was helpless to stop it as the policeman continued relentlessly. 'But you do have arsenic on the farm, don't you? Dr Battison saw it for himself in the barn.'

Speechless with shock now, Maddie's thoughts were reeling. This was a nightmare. An horrific dream. She would wake up any minute to hear Harriet banging on her bedroom door to wake her up. It had to be. It couldn't really be happening.

She was suddenly cold and shivering. It was all too terribly real.

'Mam, Mam . . .' Adam was bursting in through the back door. 'Donald's dad won't let him play with me any more. He ses . . .' The boy stopped short as he saw the policeman sitting at the table, then, his gaze still on PC Parsons, he sidled to his mother to stand beside her.

Maddie put her arms about him. She forced herself to speak, but her voice was a hoarse whisper as she said, 'Adam, go and find Nick for me, will you?'

The boy sped away, pleased, she guessed, to escape.

PC Parsons was nodding sagely. 'I expect that Donald's father's heard the rumours an' all.'

Maddie stared at him. 'Are you arresting me?' she asked bluntly.

'No,' he said, but before she could breathe a sigh of relief, he added, 'Not at the moment. But I would like you to come down to the station with me and make a full statement.'

'What on earth about? I've told you, I . . .'

'Well, to answer questions then. We want some answers, Mrs Brackenbury.'

Now Maddie knew real fear. It was the first time ever that the friendly PC Parsons had ever called her by her surname.

But PC Parsons was no longer being friendly.

In her wildest nightmares, Maddie had never thought to find herself in a prison cell. The tiny square room brought back the claustrophobia of the cupboard beneath the stairs that Mrs Potter had used as her own particular prison cell for wrongdoers. But in there Maddie had been able to hear the sounds of the other girls, of the household going about its routine. Everyone took their turn in the cupboard and everyone knew that soon they would be released.

But now, Maddie had no such reassurance. Here she could hear nothing of the world beyond the heavy door and the thick walls and had no idea what was to happen to her.

They had questioned her for four hours in the police station in Wellandon. Even PC Parson's police house in Eastmere had not been official enough. She had been arrested, cautioned and brought to the town in a police car, driven through the village for all to see. And when the questioning got them nowhere, they locked her in a cell where she spent a cold and sleepless night.

A cold-eyed detective sergeant interviewed her, walking around her whilst she sat at the table and a young detective constable, sitting opposite her, took notes.

'Why did you do it, Brackenbury?' Gone was any pretence at politeness. Now she was a suspected criminal.

'I didn't.'

'Thought you would inherit all his money and the tenancy of his farm?' He thrust his face close to hers. 'And you did, didn't you?'

Helpless against his reasoning, which, even to her ears, sounded plausible, Maddie was silent.

'And now you want to rid yourself of his housekeeper. You've never got on, the two of you, have you?'

'I haven't done anything,' she protested. 'Not to Frank nor to Mrs Trowbridge.'

He strolled around behind her, his closeness making every nerve in her body tingle. Slowly he came around to stand facing her, then he leant on his hands on the table, towering over her. 'How did you do it, eh? So that you didn't poison everyone in the household.'

'I didn't have anything to do with the meals before Mrs Trowbridge was taken ill.'

'But you have since, eh?'

'Well – yes.'

'So, it would have been quite easy for you to administer a first, small dose of arsenic, just enough to make her ill and then, when you took over the food preparation, you began to increase the dosage, eh? It would be easy then to put it into just her food, wouldn't it?'

'I didn't. I swear I didn't do anything to harm anyone.'

He ignored her protestations as if she had not spoken.

'Who's next, eh? Her son, Nicholas, or . . .' He leant menacingly closer and his voice dropped to a shocked whisper, acting as if he couldn't believe even her capable of such wickedness. '. . . .Your own son?'

Maddie gasped, staring at him. Now she began to tremble. What hope had she of proving her innocence if this man could believe she could do such a thing?

He straightened up now and resumed his pacing around her. Maddie wasn't sure which was the most unnerving.

'You say you didn't have anything to do with the preparation of food?'

'No. Mrs Trowbridge did all that.'

'Nothing at all?'

'No.'

Again he was in front of her and now he thumped both fists down onto the table so suddenly that Maddie almost leapt from her chair. 'You're lying! Do you mean to tell me that you never prepared anything that the people in that household ate or drank? You never so much as made a sandwich, or a pot of tea, or . . .' The menace in his tone was back. '. . . The cocoa at night?'

She opened her mouth to ask 'How did you know?' but without uttering a word she clamped her lips tightly together.

'Ah, *now* we've nothing to say, have we?' He jabbed his forefinger towards her. 'You put arsenic in the house-keeper's cocoa that you used to make every night for the whole family. And I dare bet that was the way you did it with Frank Brackenbury, too. And when we've exhumed his body, we'll prove it.'

He turned on his heel and left the interview room, leaving Maddie staring after him, open-mouthed and very afraid.

She was taken back to the cell and left alone for the

next two hours before being taken back to the interview room again. Here, there was always one constable or another in the room with her, but they never spoke to her. Even when someone brought her a cup of tea, they did not speak, even though she said, automatically, 'Thank you.'

Eventually, the door opened and Maddie stiffened, expecting the return of her ruthless inquisitor. Instead, it was another stranger to Maddie who now entered the room and sat down in front of her. He was dressed in plain clothes, like the previous one, but whereas the first detective had been thin and wiry, this one was very overweight. His jacket was undone and his shirt buttons strained as he moved, looking as if they would pop off at any moment. He had a round, florid face and he breathed noisily, but to Maddie's surprise he was smiling at her as he sat down on the opposite side of the table.

'My name's Detective Inspector Johnson and you're Maddie, aren't you?' As she nodded, he went on. 'Yes. Now let's see if we can clear this little matter up and we can all go home, eh?' He leant back in the chair and linked his fingers across his belly. 'My colleague a bit rough on you, was he? Well, he's only doing his job. But let's you and me see if we can sort this out, all nice and friendly like, shall we?'

Maddie felt herself begin to relax a little. At least she felt that she could talk to this one, that he would listen.

'Let's say you didn't do it deliberately. Let's say it's all been a terrible accident. Did you ever mix up weedkiller, Maddie?'

She shook her head. 'No. Nick always did that.'

'Nick?'

'Nicholas Trowbridge.'

'Ah yes, Nicholas. Mm.' DS Johnson regarded her steadily. 'We have a statement from Mr Trowbridge that says although it was normally his job, he had shown you how to do it. That true?'

'Well, yes. On a farm like ours, we have to be able to do each other's jobs, just in case one of us is ill . . .' Her voice trailed away. Every time she spoke it seemed as if she dug a deeper hole for herself. She felt as if, at any moment, the sides were going to cave in and she was going to be buried alive.

'So . . .' his tone was still deceptively mild, but she saw the sudden spark in his eyes. He had her now, he knew he had her trapped. 'You admit you know how to mix up weedkiller or maybe rat poison with a base of arsenic, which you keep on the farm? And you also admit that it was the custom for you to make the cocoa at night?'

In a small voice, Maddie could say nothing other than, 'Yes.'

Now he leant forward and rested his arms on the table. 'So, how do you think it looks to us, Maddie?'

A spark of resilience ignited inside her. Maddie faced him with surprising calm. 'It must look to you,' she said slowly, 'as if I'm guilty. I see that. But I'm not. I swear to you I have done nothing to harm anyone.'

Her gaze held his steadily and for a brief moment she saw the flicker of doubt in his eyes. Then slowly he stood up. 'You're a cool one, I'll say that for you.'

They were the last words she exchanged with anyone for twenty-four hours.

Forty-Eight

'Am I allowed to send a message to a friend?'

When a constable brought a meal into the cell, Maddie asked the question. During the time she had been left alone, she had been doing a lot of thinking. Though fear still clawed at her belly and the food they brought every few hours stuck in her throat, nevertheless, she was calmer now and able to think more rationally.

'What friend might that be?'

'Jenny Wren who works at the corner shop in Eastmere.'

The constable glanced over his shoulder as if unsure whether he should be even speaking to the prisoner, let alone doing favours for her. In a low voice, he said, 'She's already been in to the station three times, asking about you.'

Maddie gave a tremulous smile and relief and gratitude flooded through her. Jenny would never let her down.

'Please, when she comes again . . .' Maddie said, for she was sure she would. 'Could you ask her to look after Adam? That's my son. He's only ten. It's not fair on Nick that he should have to look after the boy. He'll have enough to do trying to keep things going on the farm.'

There was relief on the constable's face. 'Oh, that's all right. One of the things she said to tell you was that the lad was staying with her and Mrs – er – Grange, is it?'

Maddie nodded and breathed a sigh of thankfulness. 'Yes, Mrs Grange.'

As he turned to go, he even smiled at her. 'That's all right, then.'

'Yes, yes, it is. Thank you.'

It was not until the heavy door had clanged behind him and she was alone once more that Maddie realized she had not asked him what else it was that Jenny had said.

Maddie passed another night in the small, dark room, though this time she did sleep a little. The following morning shortly after breakfast, she was taken once more to the interview room and mentally she steeled herself for yet more questioning.

As she waited, with only the silent constable sitting in the far corner for company, she wondered which of her two interrogators it would be this time.

The door opened and the desk sergeant announced, 'A visitor for you. Your solicitor.'

Maddie looked up and began to say, 'But I haven't got a solicitor . . .' but the words remained unspoken as she gave a start of surprise as the man walked into the room.

'Mr Theo.'

He was smiling as he came and sat down opposite her, placing a folder of papers on the table beside him. But she could see the concern for her in his blue eyes. For the first time in a very long time, tears threatened to overwhelm her.

'Maddie.' His voice was gentle. 'How are you? Are they treating you well?'

She could not speak for the lump in her throat, so she nodded. The lump grew bigger as he reached across the space between them and took both her hands into his. The warmth of his touch filled her with a new hope. He had come to help her. She knew he could see the unshed tears welling in her eyes, as he patted her hands and said, 'There, there, we'll soon have you out of here. They can't hold you longer than another few hours without charging you and they haven't done that, have they?'

Maddie shook her head and her voice was husky with emotion as she said, 'I don't know what they've done, except ask me lots of questions and then not believe my answers.' She bit her lip and, unable to prevent the quaver in her voice, added, 'Mr Theo, do you believe me? You don't think I – I could poison anyone, do you?'

His reply was swift and genuine. 'Of course I don't. Why else do you think I'm here?'

For a moment she clung to his hands like a drowning person. 'I don't know, but I'm so glad you are. Thank you, Mr Theo.'

'For a start, Maddie, let's drop the Mister, shall we? From now on it's Theo. You did promise once before,' he added softly. 'Remember?' Without waiting for her agreement or otherwise he gently released her hold on him and opened the file lying on the table. 'Now, let's start at the beginning. Since they are involving Frank Brackenbury's death in their enquiries, we shall have to do so as well. When exactly did he fall ill and can you remember his symptoms?'

Maddie frowned, trying to dredge back in her memory. 'Adam was about five or six months' old because I remember asking him to look after him whilst I worked. That was before he got really bad, whilst he was still able to sit by the fire in the living room, you know.'

'No, go further back than that. The very first time you saw that there was something wrong.'

Now she remembered. 'It was Nick who remarked on

362

it first. He asked me if I'd noticed that Frank seemed to be slowing up in his work.'

'And had you?'

'No, not until Nick mentioned it. But then, I was always so busy what with Adam and trying to build up the new business . . .' And, she added privately, trying not to think about Michael.

'Mm. And then what happened?'

'Well, I asked Frank if he was feeling all right and he admitted that he had been feeling "a bit under the weather" as he called it. He said he still had a bit of pain in his leg.'

'His leg?'

'Yes, there'd been a bit of a mishap. Nick had accidentally speared Frank's foot with a fork.'

'And was that all that was wrong?'

'No, Frank said he'd been having a bit of stomach trouble . . .' She broke off as she met his steady gaze. Theo nodded and said quietly, 'Go on.'

'He made a – a joke and said he hadn't wanted to make a fuss in case Harriet – that's Mrs Trowbridge – thought that he was blaming her cooking.'

'And was he?'

Maddie shook her head, 'No, of course not. It was only said in fun. I know it was.'

'So then what happened?'

'Well, I made him go to the doctor, but he came back and said the doctor – Dr Hanson it was then – couldn't find anything wrong.'

'But he got worse?'

'Yes. Every day we could see him getting weaker although it was very gradual over quite a long time, but in the end he couldn't get up out of his bed. I called the doctor to the house then to see him. He . . .'

'Wait a minute, don't go so fast, Maddie. I want you to think back very carefully. Who prepared Frank's food or drink during that time? Who nursed him when he took to his bed?'

'Well, we all did. Of course Mrs Trowbridge cooked all the meals, just as she always did. But I made drinks and even Nick carried his meals up and sat with him throughout the night sometimes to let me get a bit of rest. He was ever so good . . .'

'Nick?'

'Yes, but . . .' Her eyes widened as she stared at him. 'Oh no, you don't think – you can't think . . .?'

Theo held up his hand, palm towards her, 'Maddie, I'm not thinking anything at the moment. I am just trying to establish what actually happened and the order of events to get things clear in my own mind. Now, go on.' He reached across the table again and gave her hand a quick squeeze. 'You're doing very well. You've got a wonderful memory.'

So Maddie went on with her story, remembering in detail all that had occurred leading up to Frank's death. She didn't consider herself to be clever or to have a particularly good memory. It was just that everything was so clear because it was not possible to forget that dreadful time. Sometimes, she wished she could have blotted out the whole thing. And now she was being asked to relive it again and, all the time, Theo made notes on a large, lined notepad. She told him everything right up to the time she had found Frank in the battery house and they had all believed that in his weakened state, he had been careless.

When she fell silent at last, Theo shuffled his papers together. 'Have the police asked you to sign anything?'

Maddie shook her head.

'Well, they might want you to make a formal statement

before they let you go. If they do, don't sign anything until I'm here. You understand.'

'Yes, Mr . . . Yes, Theo.'

As he stood up, she asked, 'Will they really let me go?'

Theo glanced at his watch. 'They'll have to, unless they're going to charge you, and I don't see how they can.' Her hopes soared only to be dashed at his next words. 'At least, not yet.'

'You mean – you think they will?'

Theo's face was sober. 'It depends what evidence they find. They'll no doubt be interviewing Dr Battison and, I'm afraid, they'll be searching the farm and taking away any kind of poisonous substances they find on the premises.' He glanced at her sympathetically. 'And then, of course, there's what the forensic team find in Frank's body.'

Maddie shuddered, seeing horrific pictures of poor Frank being disturbed from his resting place. It wasn't right and yet she'd have to let it happen if it was all that would prove her innocence. 'It's so awful,' she said aloud. 'Them digging him up.'

Theo sighed. 'It's the only course open to them – and us, I'm afraid. I've already asked at the hospital if by any chance the blood samples that were taken to do those tests on him when he was ill might have been kept. But, of course, they weren't, because at the time there were no suspicious circumstances surrounding his death. That was quite obviously an accident.'

'I suppose they'll be saying next that I tampered with something in there so that he got a shock and . . .' Maddie muttered.

'Don't worry about that. I can easily prove you know nothing about the workings of the electricity supply. You don't, do you?'

Maddie shook her head. There was a pause and then she asked, 'What do they need to test for poison in his body then? Blood samples?'

'Yes, or tissue or hair or . . .'

'Hair?' Maddie was staring at him.

'Yes, why?'

Excitedly, Maddie said, 'Mrs Trowbridge cut a lock of hair from poor Frank before they took him away. I saw her do it.'

'Did she, by Jove?' Theo too was looking excited and hopeful. 'Where is it?'

'It'll be in her bedroom. Nick could find it.'

He stood up. 'I'll go to the farm now and see him, Maddie. This just might save them the trouble of exhuming Frank's body.'

'And when they test the hair and there's nothing there, they'll let me go?'

'Oh, you won't have to wait as long as that. I'll have you out of here in the morning. What they'll probably do is release you on police bail to return to the police station in two or maybe three weeks. That depends on how long it takes them to make their enquiries. But, you must be prepared, my dear, that if they do find traces of arsenic, then . . .' Theo said no more and when he had left, Maddie felt even more lonely than she had before he had come.

Forty-Nine

Theo arrived again next morning and demanded her release and Maddie found herself outside the police station, blinking in the sunlight and pulling in great gulps of fresh air. But before she had time to savour her freedom, Theo was hustling her towards his car.

'Come on, Maddie, I don't want us to attract attention.' He almost pushed her into the back seat and got in beside her, slamming the door and ordering his chauffeur to drive off immediately.

'What do you mean?' she asked as the car reached the outskirts of the town and gathered speed.

Theo leant back against the plush upholstery and sighed. 'I'm sorry, Maddie, but the locals have you charged, tried and convicted already. They think you're guilty.'

'Everyone? Even – even Jenny?'

Theo managed to laugh. 'Oh not Jenny. Dear, loyal little Jenny. You'd be amazed what she's been up to on your behalf. It was she who came up to the Hall with the ever-faithful Steven in tow, to ask me to help you.'

'She did?'

'She most certainly did. Quite the little tigress in defence of her own, isn't she?'

Maddie stared at him. Jenny? A tigress? Loyal, yes, she'd known that. But a tigress? Now this was something new.

'You know, she intrigues me. In fact, you both do. But – er . . .' He hesitated before murmuring, 'But you for quite a different reason.' Then more briskly, he asked, 'Do you know anything at all about her background?'

Maddie shook her head. 'No. No more than I do about my own. But we've a lot in common. We were both abandoned outside the Mayfield Children's Home. Me at a month or so old – they were never quite sure just how old I was – but Jen was newborn.'

'Really? And when was this?'

'1932.'

She saw his eyebrows rise as, again, he said, 'Really?'

'Why?'

But now he seemed disinterested as he turned his gaze away from her. 'Oh nothing. I just wondered. Anyway . . .' He reached out and took her hand, 'I'm sorry, my dear, but I have to tell you that Nick couldn't find the lock of Frank's hair you mentioned, so they are still going to exhume the body. And besides, to be honest, I don't think they would have taken just that lock of hair as sufficient evidence, even if we had been able to find it.'

The brief hope that had sustained her through the past night, died.

They were passing through Eastmere now and Maddie became uncomfortably aware of the curious glances of the villagers. Some even took a step towards the car, bending to peer in through the windows as the vehicle slowed to a halt outside the village shop.

'You wait here in the car,' Theo said. 'I'll fetch Adam.'

'Isn't he at school?'

'No. We thought it best to keep him at home for a

while. He was getting taunted. Children can be very cruel to each other, can't they?'

Oh indeed they could, Maddie thought grimly, remembering the times when she had championed poor Jenny. And now, ironically, it was Jenny defending Maddie's son. Life had a peculiar way of coming full circle, Maddie thought.

Maddie jumped suddenly as an egg splattered against the car window beside her and she heard the jeering of three youths.

'Lock the car door, miss,' the chauffeur advised, 'until you see Mr Theo coming back.'

'Oi, you!' Startled again, Maddie glanced round but then she saw that the shout had come from Steven who had appeared in the shop doorway. She saw him jump down the three steps and run after the youths.

Maddie sat huddled miserably in the back seat feeling more of a prisoner now than she had in the cold, dark cell at the police station. Through the rear window she watched as Steven caught up with one of the lads, grabbed hold of him and shook him, shouting and shaking his fist into the lad's face. The boy – little older than Adam, she saw now – looked frightened out of his wits. His two mates had disappeared round a corner, leaving him to face the man's wrath alone.

At least someone's on my side, Maddie thought. And Stinky Smith of all people.

'Maddie, oh Maddie.' Jenny's smiling face was suddenly outside the car window and as Maddie released the lock on the door, she climbed in and sat close beside her, putting her arms around her and holding her close. 'Thank goodness, Mr Theo got you out of that dreadful place. How are you? Are you all right?'

Maddie avoided answering her question by asking another. 'How's Adam? Is he all right?'

'Sort of. He's upset that his so-called friends have all turned against him.'

'Oh Jen. Thank God for friends like you and – and Steven. What would I do without you?'

'Silly thing,' Jenny laughed. 'We're sisters. Remember?'

She looked over Jenny's shoulder and saw that Theo and Adam had appeared now at the top of the steps. With his hand resting protectively on the boy's shoulder, Theo seemed to be looking up and down the street before they emerged from the doorway. At the sight of her son, Maddie's heart turned over. She had been away for only a short time and yet it had seemed an eternity. As she looked into his eyes, she could see that it had left its mark on Adam too. The boy had grown up overnight, it seemed. And there was something else, too. More than ever, he was like his father.

She was never going to be allowed to try to forget Michael, she thought, for with her every day was a living, breathing reminder.

'Won't you stay here with us?' Jenny was urging her, bringing her thoughts back to the present.

'What? Oh no – no, thanks. I must get back to the farm. There's work to do.'

Jenny's eyes were still troubled. 'Do you really think you should go back there? I mean – Nick's still there.'

'Nick? Why shouldn't he be there?' Maddie searched her friend's face. 'You don't mean – oh you can't mean – that Nick thinks I'm guilty.'

'No, no, he doesn't, but . . .' Jenny turned away, ducked her head and got out of the car. 'Mr Theo, she wants to go back to the farm.'

Then Theo came to the car and, though he made no

effort to get in, he bent down and looked in at her. 'Don't you think it might be better for you to stay here? Mrs Grange is agreeable, if that's what's worrying you. Or you can come to the Hall if you prefer.'

'No, no, I must get home.'

'I don't like you being out there on your own. The feeling in the village is far worse than I had imagined. Jenny and Steven – and young Adam – have just been telling me.'

'Then it would be far worse to stay here,' Maddie argued reasonably. 'And I'd be putting innocent people – Mrs Grange and Jen – at risk too.'

Theo seemed to be struggling with some inner conflict.

'What?' Maddie asked. 'What is it?'

'Nothing,' he said swiftly, a little too swiftly to be convincing. It was as if he wanted to say something but didn't know whether he should do so. Eventually, he said, 'Well, at least let Adam stay here. Please, Maddie. We'll bring him to the farm to see you. Every day. I promise. But just let him stay here with them. At least – for the time being.'

Much as she wanted to be with her son, Maddie nodded. 'All right then, but just let him get into the car for a minute. Let me talk to him.'

Theo straightened up and beckoned to the boy.

'Oh darling,' Maddie put out her arms as he climbed in beside her. 'This is all a horrible mistake. You don't believe I did anything wrong, do you?'

'Oh Mam . . .' Suddenly he was grinning at her. 'Of course I don't. None of us do. Only the stupid villagers who don't know you.'

She hugged him to her. 'That's all right then. I can stand anything if only you believe in me.'

He put his arms around her waist and buried his face

against her shoulder. His voice was muffled as he asked, 'Are you sure you're going to be all right at the farm?'

'Of course, I am. Nick's there.'

Adam raised his head and as she looked down into his upturned face, Maddie shivered suddenly at the strange expression in the young boy's eyes.

Fifty

Nick came towards her with his arms outstretched as the car drew into the farmyard.

'Maddie! Thank goodness you're all right.' He was smiling happily, his face alight with relief. He hugged her to him and then held out his hand towards Theo. 'Mr Theo. How can we thank you enough for your help?'

To Maddie's surprise, Theo ignored Nick's outstretched hand and instead said curtly, 'It's not over yet. I should wait for the outcome of the post-mortem before you begin to celebrate.'

But Nick's smile stayed in place. 'What can they hope to find from that?' His tone was derisory. 'They'll find arsenic in his body, I don't doubt.'

Maddie felt a shiver of alarm as she glanced at the frown on Theo's face. 'Why do you say that?' he asked Nick sharply.

Nick shrugged. 'Stands to reason. It's in the ground all around here, isn't it? It's used in weedkillers, isn't it? More than likely the ground is sodden with it.'

Theo said nothing but his steely gaze never left Nick's face.

'May we you offer you a drink, sir?' Nick said.

'No, thank you. I must be on my way.' Now his glance lingered on Maddie. 'If you need anything, you know where to find me.'

With that, he gave a curt nod towards Nick and climbed

373

back into the car. Nick put his arm around her shoulders as they stood and watched the driver reverse down the track and into the lane.

'Phew. Thank goodness he's gone. Poking his nose in where it's not wanted.'

'Oh Nick, don't say that. He got me out of that awful place.'

'He got there first, I'll grant you. And with his position around here, they would listen to him. But don't think the rest of us weren't trying.' For a moment there was belligerence in his tone. 'We don't need his sort. I'll look after you, Maddie. It's just you and me now. We'll be all right together.'

Deliberately, she asked, 'How's your mother?'

'Much better. They're talking about her coming home the day after tomorrow.'

'What? Here?' With bitter sarcasm, she added, 'You mean they're actually going to let her come back here where I might try to poison her again?'

'Oh, I've explained all that to them at the hospital. I told them it was all a dreadful accident. Mam must have somehow been mixing up the weedkiller and then gone back to her baking. They seemed to believe me. Now, come on in. I've got a lovely meal ready for you to welcome you home. See, I knew they'd have to let you go. They can't prove a thing.'

They were walking towards the house as Maddie said thoughtfully, 'But your mother never touches the outside work. She never has anything to do with the weedkiller.' She stopped and stared at him. He had moved ahead of her a little before he turned to glance over his shoulder at her and said, 'I know that and you know that. But they don't.'

'That's not the point. How did your mother come to get arsenic in her system, then?'

Nick shrugged and spread his hands. 'Your guess is as good as mine.'

'You mean, you think I did it?'

''Course not.'

'Then how . . .?'

He came towards her again and put his arm about her shoulders and tried to draw her towards the house. 'I've told you. Somehow, it was a dreadful accident. Do stop worrying about it, Maddie. I've got you home and all to myself. I'll look after you. I won't ever let anyone take you away from me again.'

For the moment, Maddie allowed him to usher her into the house, through the wash-house and the kitchen and into the living room where, she had to admit, a wonderful spread awaited her.

'Oh Nick,' she was moved to say. 'You've done all this? For me?'

For the rest of the evening, Nick laughed and joked and kept the conversation away from what must have been at the back of both their minds. Maddie tried to respond, was grateful for his efforts in trying to take her mind off things, but she was worried for Adam and anxious about the impending post-mortem. As Theo had said, it wasn't over yet.

As he locked up for the night, Maddie was surprised to see Nick take the shotgun from its usual corner behind the door in the living room and place it on the kitchen table. 'Just in case we get any unwelcome visitors from the village,' he said, winking at her.

'Nick, you can't do that. Oh, don't let's cause any more trouble.'

375

'It's all right. It isn't loaded. It's only just to frighten them off. You go up to bed, Maddie. I think I'll stay down here and keep watch.'

'You're making it sound like a siege.'

'It may well be. You've never been on the receiving end of these folks' viciousness. But me and my mam have.'

'Whatever do you mean?'

'It's a long time ago now, but I tell you, you don't know 'em and what they can do. Not like I do.'

'But, Nick, you need your sleep. We've a lot of work to catch up on tomorrow.'

'I've kept up with it pretty well. And I can doze in the armchair. I'll be all right, honestly. You go up and get a nice bath. There's plenty of hot water. I've made sure of that for you.'

She knew she ought to thank him for all his efforts to welcome her home, to pamper her, but somehow the words stuck in her throat. There was something unsettling about his attitude. Something she could not quite put her finger on.

Maddie was thoughtful as she went up the steep stairs, wishing for once that there was a door to the bathroom with a good, sturdy lock.

She need not have worried. Nick remained downstairs whilst Maddie bathed and washed the smell of the police station cell from her hair, but once in the bedroom she had shared with Frank, she heard Nick's footsteps coming up the stairs and along the passageway, nearer and nearer.

She knew a sudden irrational fear as he tapped on the door and said in a soft voice, 'You all right, Maddie?'

Her voice sounded high-pitched even to her own ears as she said, 'Of course. Thank you, Nick. Good night.'

'Good night, Maddie. Sleep tight.'

As the sound of his footsteps moved away again, she let

out the breath she had been holding. She was imagining it all. The events of the previous two days had shattered her nerves and left her unable to think straight.

Nevertheless, for some reason she could not have explained, before she put out the light and climbed into her bed, she took the ladder-backed chair from beneath the window and lodged it beneath the door knob.

Fifty-One

The following morning – Saturday – Jenny and Steven brought Adam to the farm as they had promised. The boy rushed into his mother's arms, hugging her tightly around the waist. 'We've come to help you in the fields. Me and Jen, that is. Steven's got to go to Peterborough this afternoon to meet someone, but we can stay, Mam.'

'There's no need,' Nick interrupted, coming up behind her. 'Everything's under control.' He nodded towards Jenny and Steven. 'Me and Maddie can manage.'

Steven gave a hearty laugh that to Maddie's ears sounded forced. 'You mean you're going to pick that lot on your own? Just the three of you?' He nodded in the direction of the field where this year's crop was planted. Row upon row of tulip heads waved and danced in the breeze. Maddie's rainbow field of vibrant colour. Steven shrugged. 'Oh well, if you're sure.'

'We'll manage,' Nick said again.

'Are you staying to lunch?' Maddie asked Jenny and Steven.

'No, no,' Steven said, a little too quickly. 'I must get going if I'm to get to Peterborough for one.' He glanced at Jenny and Maddie saw them exchange a secretive smile.

'I'm staying all day,' Jenny said brightly. 'Until Steven gets back.' Then she looked at Nick as if daring him to defy her.

Maddie was astonished. She would never have believed

it of her little Jenny Wren. But what was it Theo had called her? A tigress. That was it. A tigress in defence of her own.

But Nick was not to be defeated easily. 'I really think you'd be helping Maddie most if you took Adam back to Mrs Grange's and kept him there. Out of harm's way.'

'Out of harm's way? What on earth are you talking about, Nick?' Jenny retorted. She put her head on one side and stared at him. Levelly, she asked, 'How can Adam possibly come to any harm here?'

'We might very well get a visit from some of the villagers. The ones,' Nick said pointedly, 'who think Maddie is guilty. Mr Frank was very popular around here. They might take it upon themselves to form a lynching mob.'

'Don't be silly, Nick. We're not living in the Wild West.'

'Huh, you don't know these folk like I do,' he muttered.

Quietly, but with a sureness Maddie had never heard before, Jenny said, 'Oh but I think I do, Nick. Yes, I think I know the village folk very well now. Probably a lot better than you, stuck out here at Few Farm.'

Churlishly, he said, 'Stay if you must, but I have to go into town this afternoon to see my mother and while I'm gone, I want Maddie to stay in the house and lock the doors.'

Suddenly, Maddie realized how she was allowing everyone else around her to make decisions for her. Of course, she had needed Theo's help – still did – but she was not going to allow Nick or anyone else to dictate to her what she could or could not do.

'I'll come with you to the hospital. I'm not going to barricade myself away here. I've nothing to feel guilty about.'

Jenny gave her another quick hug. 'That's the Maddie I know.'

She saw Adam glance quickly at Jenny and Maddie had the strange feeling that there was a kind of conspiracy between them, between the three of them, if it came to that: Jenny Steven – and Adam. 'Can't we all go, Mam? I'd like to see Mrs T.'

Without any further reference to Nick, Jenny said, 'Right, that's settled then. Off you go now, Steven, or you'll be late.' Again, a special look passed between them and for a foolish moment, Maddie felt excluded and so alone.

Then Jenny was tucking her arm through Maddie's and glancing over her shoulder, but Nick had moved away. 'It'll be all right,' she said in a low voice as they waved Steven off. 'I promise you, Maddie. Everything's going to be all right.' And then, obviously deliberately changing the subject, she said in her normal voice, 'Steven's brother has finished the metal frame for your float for the Parade. It's not long now, is it?'

Maddie sighed. 'Oh Jen, I really wanted to be a part of the first real Parade, but now . . .' She left the words hanging in the air. It was a question she could not – dare not – even try to answer.

Harriet was sitting up in the end bed when they entered the ward. It seemed to Maddie that there was a lot of whispering as they passed between the row of beds on either side, but she kept the smile fixed on her mouth and her eyes on Harriet.

'How are you feeling?' she asked at once as they drew near the end bed.

'Better, but it's no thanks to you, is it?'

Maddie's heart sank. So, they had told her. But her next words seemed to belie this. 'Sat here day after day with not a visit from either of you. Not even young Adam's been to see me. And me own son . . .' Her reproachful gaze rested on Nick now. 'You haven't been near me for three days.'

'We've – er – been a little busy, Mam.'

'Ah well, yes, of course work comes before anything or anyone else, doesn't it?' She sniffed. 'Always has done. Even when poor Frank was alive.'

Nick fetched a chair and placed it beside the bed for Maddie. As she sat down, he rested his hand briefly on her shoulder and Maddie saw at once the startled look in Harriet's eyes as her glance went from one to the other.

'We've had a spot of bother, Mam, but everything's going to be all right now.'

'What sort of bother?' Harriet's tone was sharp with fear. 'Not – not Adam? Nothing's happened to Adam, has it?'

'No, no. He's waiting outside with Jenny. They'll come in to see you in a few minutes.'

'What's she here for?'

The explanation came haltingly from Maddie's lips. 'Adam's been staying with her. At the shop. Just for a night or two.'

'Maybe that's just as well until I get home.' Harriet sniffed again. 'You two can't look after him properly, you're always too busy. What that lad would do without me, I don't know.'

Nick sat on the edge of the bed and took his mother's hands in his. 'Well, when you come home, we'll just be one happy family again, won't we?' He turned and winked at Maddie, who managed a weak smile. For once she was lost for words. Anything she might say to Harriet, even though the woman seemed ignorant of recent events, would have a hollow ring even to Maddie's own ears. She almost wished now that Harriet had been told the truth.

To deal with her anger would have been far easier. But to sit here, trying to make polite conversation and, worse, plans for an uncertain future was impossible.

Behind her the whispering went on. Well, the rest of the ward seemed to know something even if Harriet didn't, Maddie thought wryly. No doubt one of their visitors had come in with the choice bit of gossip but no one had had the nerve to tell Harriet Trowbridge.

'So, when are they letting you out?' Nick asked and Maddie shuddered at his choice of words.

'Monday morning. I thought it would be tomorrow, but the sister says the doctor must see me before they can discharge me.'

'Right-o,' Nick said cheerfully. 'I'll come and fetch you home in the truck. I'll ask the sister on the way out what time you're likely to be ready.'

They chatted spasmodically for another half an hour, but when the silences became longer than the periods of talk, Nick stood up. 'We'd better be going. Come along, Maddie . . .'

'You go, Nicholas,' Harriet said, 'I want a word with her. And then you can send Adam in for a minute.'

Nick frowned. 'What do you want to talk to Maddie about?'

'Never mind, just run along.'

Still, Maddie thought, she speaks to him like a little boy and she could sympathize with the scowl on Nick's face as he left the ward without another word to his mother.

'Now then, you,' Harriet began and Maddie's heart sank. So she did know after all. For a brief moment she closed her eyes and steeled herself against the expected onslaught. But in the next instance, her eyes flew open as Harriet said, 'Is there something going on between you and Nicholas, because there'd better not be?'

'What – what do you mean?' Now she was more than ever puzzled.

Harriet reached out and grasped Maddie's arm. Her grip, in view of her recent debilitating illness, was surprisingly strong. 'There can't ever be anything between you and Nicholas. You hear me, girl?'

'There isn't . . .' Maddie began, but she was shocked into silence at Harriet's next words.

'Because you're his half-sister.'

Fifty-Two

Maddie felt as if she had been punched just below the ribs. Her legs threatened to give way beneath her and her head began to swim.

'What – what did you say?'

'I said – you're half-brother and sister. You, girl, are the bastard of my husband and that little trollop at the Hall, Amelia Mayfield. But you're not to say a word to Nicholas. I don't want him knowing what bad blood he's got in his veins. You hear me, girl, not a word to him.'

Maddie's mind was in turmoil. It couldn't be true. The woman had gone mad. Her illness had turned her brain. She pulled herself free from Harriet's grasp and staggered the length of the ward, reeling like a drunkard, unheeding now that the eyes of all the other patients were watching her.

They were waiting for her in the corridor. His hands thrust deep into the pockets of his trousers, his forehead creased in a petulant frown, Nick asked, 'What was it she wanted?'

'I – er – oh – nothing, just – just, you know . . .' Maddie floundered.

'No, I don't know. That's just it. What's the matter? You've gone white. What's she been saying?'

Jenny was at her side in an instant. 'Sit down, Maddie. I'll get a nurse to get you a glass of water.'

Maddie swallowed and leant against Jenny. 'I'm all right.'

'What's she said?' Nick demanded again. 'Tell me or I'll go back and . . .'

'No, no,' Maddie said swiftly. 'Leave it, Nick. Please. It's nothing – nothing. Just . . .' She latched on to the first thing that came into her fuddled mind. 'She wants me to do some shopping for her. Women's things, you know?'

'Is that all?' His face cleared. 'Why didn't she say so then instead of making a big mystery out of it. I thought for a moment someone had told her about what's been going on.'

He tried to take hold of her arm, almost as if trying to prise her away from Jenny. Maddie flinched at his touch. 'Don't,' she said, before she thought to stop herself. As she saw the frown on his face once more, she made herself say, 'I'm fine, really. Come on. Let's get home.'

'Can't I see Mrs T?' Adam asked, casting a forlorn glance at the door leading into the ward.

'Just run in and have a quick word with her then,' Jenny said, taking the lead. 'But only a minute, mind.'

The boy sped away but by the time they had walked out of the hospital and towards where the truck was parked, he had caught them up. 'She ses the first thing she's going to do when she gets home is bake gingerbread men for tea.'

'You sure you're all right in there, Adam?' Jenny asked as she helped him climb into the open back of the truck. 'It must be a bit draughty.'

The boy grinned. 'I'm fine. I'm just glad it's not raining.' He looked towards Nick. 'Just don't go fast round the corners, Uncle Nick. I might get thrown out.'

Nick laughed, his face creasing into lines of laughter. 'Well, that's one way of getting rid of you.'

Despite the recent shock, Maddie thought, why can't Nick be like that all the time? Laughing and joking, he was so much nicer. But now, suddenly, she was seeing him through very different eyes.

Was she really her half-brother?

As they got out of the battered old truck in the yard of Few Farm, Jenny held out a hand to help Adam climb out. 'You're still with us then?'

He grinned cheekily at her. 'You don't get rid of me as easily as that.'

'Well, I hope not,' Maddie thought she heard Jenny murmur.

That night, after Jenny had gone back to the shop taking Adam with her, Nick locked all the doors and double-checked the windows.

'I think if the villagers had been going to do anything, they'd have done it by now,' Maddie remarked.

'Can't be too careful,' Nick said, laying the shot gun on the kitchen table again.

The following day, they laboured side by side in the fields. Maddie worked automatically for her mind was still reeling from Harriet's revelation. She had hardly slept, going over and over Harriet's bitter words.

Was she really Amelia Mayfield's daughter? Perhaps that explained why she had felt so drawn to the poor woman. Maddie drew her hand across her forehead with a sigh as another thought struck her. And if she was, then Theo was her uncle.

She stood quite still for a moment wondering why the realization did not bring her the expected pleasure. She admired and liked Theo. Very much. So why did the thought that she was related to him bring a strange stab of disappointment?

As dusk fell and they packed up for the day, Maddie turned back and stood gazing at the field of tulips, glowing bronze in the setting sun.

'Isn't that the most beautiful sight you've ever seen?' she murmured, a catch in her voice, but Nick was already too far away to hear. Tears blurred her vision. 'I don't want to lose it all,' she whispered, suddenly filled with dread at what the coming week might bring.

'You going to stand there all night?' came Nick's truculent voice from down the lane as he trudged towards the farm, carrying a hoe in one hand and in the other, the shotgun that, since the day of Maddie's release from police custody, he had carried everywhere with him. He had even, she had discovered afterwards, taken it in the back of the truck hidden beneath a pile of sacks when they had visited the hospital in Wellandon.

Maddie dragged her gaze away from the lovely view and turned to follow him, wondering how, on the one hand, there could be such peace and tranquillity and beauty whilst on the other, such tragedy and menace and ugliness were hanging over her

'Nick? Nick, where are you?'

Maddie stood in the middle of the yard. It was halfway through the Monday morning and still he had not left for the hospital. She had never thought that she would be anxious to see Harriet Trowbridge back home, but now she had a whole list of questions she needed to ask her. Whether she would be able to wheedle any answers out of the woman, was another matter, but Maddie was determined to try.

She heard a movement in the big barn. Nick was there, sweeping the floor. 'There you are. What time have you to go to the hospital to fetch your mother?'

'This afternoon,' Nick said, setting the brush against the wall and coming to stand in front of her. 'And you're to stay in the house while I'm gone. You hear?'

'Look, Nick, I'm very grateful for all that you've done. All that you're still doing, but stop ordering me about. There's a lot of work to do and I mean to get on with it. If any of the lads from the village do come here – and I don't think they will now – they're hardly likely to harm me, are they?'

'Oho, you don't know what they're capable of . . .'

'Just what are they capable of, Nick? Tell me, because I'd really like to know.'

They stood glaring at each other, but then the anger died in Nick's face. He put his hands on her shoulders.

'Oh Maddie, we were meant to be together, you and me. I've always known it.' His grip tightened and he pulled her towards him into his embrace. She put her palms flat against his chest and tried to push him away.

'Nick, don't . . .'

'It ought to be just the two of us here, Maddie. Just you and me working side by side, with no one else to interfere.'

'Don't be silly, Nick. Your mother's coming home this afternoon. And Adam . . .'

'She'll have to come here for a while. I know that, but we can get rid of her – somehow. We can get rid of them both and then it will be just the two of us.'

'No! What on earth are you saying?' Maddie wrenched herself free and, standing back from him, stared into his face.

There was a wild look in his eyes, a look of desperate longing for her. But it was not the look of love, but of

388

obsession; a jealous, self-centred obsession that sought to oust everyone else from Maddie's life.

'Nick,' she tried to keep her tone calm and placating, tried, desperately, to be understanding and kind. 'There can't be anything between us. You must know that . . .'

Nick laughed, but there was no humour in the sound. Now, to Maddie's ears there was only menace. He stepped towards her, his arms outstretched again, but she backed away.

'Maddie, Maddie, don't. I love you. I want to be with you always. Just the two of us. Don't you realize how I feel about you? How I've always felt about you?'

Maddie shook her head. 'No, no, Nick. I'm very fond of you. But I don't love you. And besides . . .'

Nick's features were contorted with rage. 'It's him, isn't it? I'll kill him if you . . .'

'Who? Who are you talking about?'

'Theo Mayfield.'

Now Maddie gave a nervous laugh. The idea was so preposterous that even amidst the drama of the moment, she could see the funny side. 'Don't be stupid, Nick. Mr Theo would never look at me.'

'Oh, but he does. He does look at you – *that way.*'

She stared at him, suddenly remembering all the occasions when Theo had smiled at her, touched her hand, paid her compliments and, yes, she had to admit it now, there had been more in his eyes that ordinary friendliness.

She swallowed and tried to laugh it off, but even to her own ears her laughter sounded hollow. 'Don't be silly. There's only one person I've ever really loved and he left me, didn't he?'

Nick's eyes narrowed and there was a devious look in them. 'You think so, eh?'

'What – what do you mean?'

'Nothing. He's gone and good riddance. And Theo Mayfield? Well, you're not the sort of girl he'd marry, are you? Oh, a quick tumble in the hay. Get you pregnant, yes. But his sort wouldn't marry you.'

How could he profess to love her and yet say such cruel things? Maddie thought. He doesn't even know what love is.

That's it, she thought with sudden, blinding clarity. That's it. Nick has never known what it is to be truly loved. Not by anyone. Not even by his own mother.

He was speaking again, dragging her back to the moment. 'But I'll marry you, Maddie. I've always wanted you . . .'

'Nick, please, you must listen. We can't – your mother . . .'

'Forget my mother, I've told you . . .'

'No, no, listen to me. You don't understand. The other day in the hospital, when she called me back. It – it wasn't what I told you.'

'What do you mean?'

'She – she told me something. Something about us. You and me.'

'Oh, I know she doesn't want us to . . .'

'It's not just that,' Maddie interrupted him. 'She has a reason. A very good reason, if what she said is true.'

There was silence in the huge barn now, only the sound of the rafters creaking and the breeze straying in through the open door to rustle a stray piece of raffia on the concrete floor.

Slowly Nick said, 'What did she say?'

'That I am the daughter of your father and – and Amelia Mayfield. That you and I are half-brother and sister.'

The silence in the barn lengthened and deepened as they stared at each other.

'I don't believe it,' Nick said hoarsely at last. 'It's another of her lies to stop us . . .'

At that moment there was the sound of a car pulling into the yard. Thankfully, Maddie turned and, before he could put out a hand to restrain her, she ran to the doorway.

Relief was in her voice as she said, 'It's Steven's car.'

She could see him behind the wheel and beside him, Jenny. Already, Adam was clambering out of the back and running towards her. 'Mam, Mam. This gentleman's come to see you. He says he knows you.'

Then Maddie saw the tall, dark-haired man unfolding himself from the back seat of the car.

The whole earth seemed to spin around her. Her vision blurred and her legs were suddenly weak. As if from a great distance, she heard a voice speak his name and realized it was her own. She stood staring at him, drinking in the sight of him. He had changed little in the eleven years since she had seen him. If anything, he was even more good-looking. His shoulders were broader, his skin tanned and healthy. There were a few lines around his eyes and tiny flecks of white at his temples, but there was a change. She could see it now as he came closer. It was in his eyes, those dark brown eyes that once had been full of laughter. Now, there was a sadness in their depths.

She wanted to run to him, to pummel his chest and cry out to him, 'Why? Why, did you leave me? Why did you never come back?' and then to clutch him to her, winding her arms around him and holding him so close that he could never go away again. But she could not move a muscle. She stood rooted to the spot staring at him and saying again just the one word.

'Michael!'

Fifty-Three

He was standing before her now, looking down into her upturned face, taking her hands into his. And his touch still had the long-forgotten magic. She wanted, oh how she wanted to hate him, to scream at him and call him all the vile names she could think of and yet here she was trembling at the sight of him, the love surging through her once more at the feel of him. She was aware of no one else in the world at this moment, not her son standing beside her looking up from one to the other, watching them, a broad smile on his face. Not Steven and Jenny standing beside the car, their arms around each other. She had even forgotten Nick, behind them somewhere in the barn. At this moment there was only Michael and Maddie in the whole world.

'Michael, oh Michael.' She said his name over and over again, breathing it, savouring it, revelling in the sound and shape of the word that she had refused for so long to let pass her lips.

'Maddie.' He whispered and the word was a loving caress. She looked into his eyes and still, even after all this time, she could see the love in them for her shining out.

And now she said it, voiced the question that had been a searing wound in her heart for almost eleven years. 'Why, Michael? Why?'

'I could ask you the same question, Maddie?'

'Me? Why me? I wasn't the one who went away and never came back. I wasn't the one who deserted you.'

'Deserted you?' The shock on his face was genuine. 'I never deserted you. It was you who said you never wanted to see me again, that you were marrying someone else.'

'Who told you that? Who . . .?' And then she stopped short and whispered the name at the same instant that Michael said, 'Nick.'

As realization began to trickle through her mind, she said flatly, 'Nick came back from visiting you to say that you no longer loved me. That you were joining the Army and never coming home again.'

Michael's face was grim. 'I think Nicholas Trowbridge has some explaining to do. Where is he?'

'Right here.' His voice came out of the shadows at the back of the barn.

They moved towards him, Maddie, already with the anger growing inside her, and Michael, still holding her hand. Adam, puzzlement in his face, followed them.

The three of them were already in the middle of the barn when Nick emerged from the shadows and they saw that he was holding the shotgun levelled towards them.

Maddie gasped and at once grasped Adam's shoulder and pushed him behind her. At the same moment she felt Michael's hand tighten on hers and he, too, gave a brief glance behind him to make sure that the boy was protected by them both.

'Take it easy, love,' he murmured to Maddie. 'Leave it to me.'

'Get away from her,' Nick said and when Michael made no move to leave Maddie's side, they both heard the click as the hammer was pulled back and the gun cocked. 'I said, get away from her.'

Still pointing the gun at them, Nick moved around them

so that he was a little nearer the door, cutting off any escape route.

'Move!'

Maddie gave Michael's hand a quick squeeze. 'You'd better do as he says. I don't think the gun's loaded, but . . .'

'Oh, it's loaded, Maddie. It has been all the time. I was ready for anything. The police or the villagers. Anybody. No one is going to take you away from me again. You hear? No one.'

'Nick,' she tried to keep her voice calm and level. 'Put the gun down. Let's talk about this. Please.'

'Get away from her.'

Michael sighed and, reluctantly, moved a short distance from Maddie and Adam.

'Over there, right away from her.'

Michael backed towards the side of the barn, his gaze fixed upon Nick as the barrel of the shotgun followed him, pointing at his chest.

'You shouldn't have come back, Michael. You've spoilt everything. Now I'm going to have to kill you.'

'No, please. Don't shoot.' Trembling, Maddie stretched out her hand towards Nick. The barrel swung and pointed at her now. 'Please,' she whispered, begging as she had never begged in her life. 'Please, at least let Adam go?'

'Why should I?' His tone was harsh and cruel, so different from the voice she knew so well. Or thought she had known. 'If it weren't for him and . . .' The barrel of the shotgun wavered slightly and then swung sharply away from pointing at Maddie and the boy towards Michael, standing so still and silent in the shadows. 'You!'

There was such venom in his voice, a bitter hatred that had been festering for eleven long years.

Behind him, a shadow appeared in the barn doorway. A woman's shadow.

'Maddie?' came Jenny's voice. 'What's going on? Are you all right?' Maddie's eyes widened and she gave a little gasp of fear. Then she touched Adam on his shoulder, giving him a tiny push. 'Go,' she breathed. 'Go to her.'

She saw him glance at the two men, who seemed, now, only aware of each other.

'Go on,' she urged.

Adam took a step, his gaze still on the men. Then he ran. The barrel swung again, following the small figure hurtling towards the open door and Jenny.

As she saw Nick's finger move towards the trigger, Maddie lunged forward, her hand outstretched to push the barrel aside and spoil his aim.

'No!' Maddie cried but the deafening blast drowned her scream. Lead shot splattered against the wall of the barn and in the doorway Jenny fell, sprawling in the dirt.

Heedless of the danger now, Maddie flung herself forwards. 'Jen, oh no. Jenny!'

She was only vaguely aware of Nick running past her out of the barn, of Steven running towards them and, as Nick passed him, Steven lunging at him, trying to grab him. But Nick pushed him away. She heard Michael's voice, close by her, shout, 'Let him go. He's dropped the gun.'

Then Steven was running forwards. 'Is she hurt? What about Adam?'

'I'm okay,' the boy said quickly and then the four of them were now bending over Jenny, afraid to touch her and yet ... Gently, Steven cradled her in his arms. They saw the blood oozing through her dress near her thigh. Her face was deathly pale and her eyes closed.

*

'Where do you think Nick's gone?'

Maddie was the first to ask the question two hours later when the four of them, Michael, Adam, Steven and herself had returned to the farm. Adam had escaped unscathed and Jenny's injuries were far less than they might have been.

'You saved Adam's life,' Michael told her huskily, 'and probably Jenny's too. If they'd caught the full blast of that shotgun . . .'

They had taken Jenny to the casualty department and had been reassured that she would recover quickly once the pellets had been removed from her leg and her hand.

'I really don't know,' Michael said now in answer to her question. 'And at this moment I don't care where he is. You and me, Maddie . . .' He took her hands. 'Have got a lot of talking to do. But first . . .' he turned and smiled at Adam and his voice was hoarse as he added, 'I want you to introduce me to my son.'

Maddie saw Adam's eyes widen and his mouth dropped open as he glanced from Michael to her and then back again.

'My dad. You're – you're my dad?' There was no mistaking the excitement and the joy in the boy's voice and all Michael and Maddie could do was to nod in unison for neither, at that moment, could speak.

Adam was grinning as he turned to Steven and said, 'Hey, Uncle Steve. This is my dad.'

'Yes, old son, I know.'

Maddie cleared her throat and said, 'I thought perhaps you'd told him.'

Steven shook his head. 'I daren't,' he said, comically. 'Jen threatened me with all sorts of dire punishments if I spoiled the moment for the three of you. And,' he added, glancing at each of them in turn, 'I see that she was right.

But now,' he added as he put his hand on Adam's shoulder, 'let's leave your mam and your dad to themselves for a bit, eh? And we know Jen's in good hands, so – what shall we do? Go fishing?'

Adam glanced at both Maddie and Michael, reluctant for a moment to leave, but then he smiled as he looked up at Steven and shook his head. 'I'd like to, but there's a lot of tulips need knobbing if we're to get a good crop of bulbs this year and build a float in time for the Parade.'

The adults glanced at one another and Steven winked at the other two as he said, 'Right you are, then. Lead the way . . .'

Michael watched them go, the man and the boy crossing the yard side by side. There was a catch in his voice as he said, 'Oh Maddie. My son. After all this time, I've found my son.'

He turned then and opened his arms to her and she went into them as if the years between had never happened.

Fifty-Four

Much later, Michael said, 'Now, we must talk.' They sat together, squeezed into the armchair at the side of the fire that had always been Frank's. 'Incidentally . . .' He patted the arm of the battered old chair fondly. 'Where's Dad?'

Stricken, Maddie stared at him. 'You mean, you don't know?'

'Know what?'

'Oh Michael.' Tears sprang to her eyes. Tears for Frank, tears for Michael and even for herself. 'He – he was taken ill ten years ago. Adam was about five months old . . .'

Realization was clouding Michael's face. 'You mean, he's dead?'

Haltingly, she told him about his father and they sat together in silence for several moments. She laid her cheek against Michael's hair, feeling his inner struggle to come to terms with the dreadful news. His father had been dead for ten years and he had not even known.

'Didn't you get Nick's letter?' she asked gently at last.

Michael shook his head.

'But Nick came to see you when he was very ill. To ask you to come home to see him.'

Michael's voice was hoarse as he said, 'No, he didn't. He only ever came to see me once. To tell me . . .' He reached up and traced the line of her face with a gentle finger. 'To tell me that you never wanted to see me again and that you were going to marry someone else for the sake of the baby. Until this morning, I didn't even know I had a son and I still don't know who – who your husband is. Is it Nick? Are you married to him?'

'Oh Michael,' she buried her face against his neck. 'This is awful. Awful.'

He put his arms tightly around her and held her close, burying his head against her hair. After a few moments, he raised his head. 'Tell me everything from the beginning, Maddie. Tell me your side from the day I went away. And then, I'll tell you mine.'

'Jenny and Steven didn't tell you anything then?'

Michael shook his head. 'No, apart from introducing me to Adam when I arrived this morning, they hustled me straight out here.'

'So they haven't even told you about – about the trouble I'm in?'

Again Michael shook his head.

'So why did you come back now?'

'Steven met me in Peterborough last Saturday. He told me you needed me, that you wanted to see me, but he wouldn't say why. But I didn't need to be told any more, Maddie. I've waited years to hear that you wanted to see me again. I couldn't get here fast enough, but I couldn't come back with him then. I had to go back to camp and explain to my Commanding Officer that I needed compassionate leave – urgently. '

'How did Steven find you? We've had no word from you for years.'

There was a strange look on his face as he said, 'I'm beginning to understand that, but all Steven did say was that he'd been to Mr Theo for advice and he was able to find out where I was stationed. I stayed in the Army after my National Service. I didn't know what else to do, since – since it seemed I was no longer welcome at home.'

Maddie groaned and closed her eyes at the eleven wasted years, but whispered, 'Oh thank God for Theo.'

Michael blinked and then asked, 'Theo, is it now?'

'He's been very kind to me. He – he's my solicitor. But for him, I'd still be in the cells at the police station.'

'The what!'

Sitting so close, she felt his muscles tighten.

Maddie sighed. 'Oh Michael. There's so much you don't know . . .' she looked at him sadly, 'and so much I don't know either.' Her face was filled with sorrow as she said, 'And when you've heard the whole story, you might want to get on the first train out of here again.'

'Never, my darling,' he reassured her huskily. 'Whatever it is, we're going to face it together.'

So she told him all that had happened since the day he had walked out of her life. She told him of her love for him, her hurt at his desertion and how she had buried all feelings for him so deep that she would hardly ever allow his name to pass her lips.

'So Adam knows nothing about me? And yet he seemed to take the news quite calmly just now.' There was a note of pleasure in Michael's tone as he added, 'He even seemed pleased.'

Now came the most difficult part of all. 'Well, I've never actually told him that Frank was his father. He was only little when he died, but he's been led to believe . . . Oh Michael, this is awfully hard . . .'

'Go on, Maddie.'

'It – it was your father I married.'

'Dad? You're joking?'

'No. He – he was very kind to me. He persuaded me that it was the best thing for the baby. And when Nick, after one of his supposed visits to you, said you never wanted to come home again and that you were signing on . . .'

Michael was silent trying to take in the enormity of the news he was hearing.

Maddie swallowed painfully but went on with her story, bringing him right up to date with the frightening events that were taking place now.

'You mean, they're digging poor Dad up?'

She nodded, unable to speak.

'My God! This is a nightmare.'

'I know. That's just how I feel. But it isn't, Michael. It's happening and there's nothing anyone can do to stop it.'

His face was grim. 'There must be. There must be something we can do . . .' His voice died away helplessly.

There was a silence between them before Michael took a deep breath and began to speak.

'Nick's deceived us both. He's played the go-between and yet lied to both sides. As I said, he only ever came to see me once, but I've written countless letters, sent cards at Christmas and on everyone's birthday. I even sent gifts at Christmas to the child I knew I must have, even though I didn't know whether it was a boy or a girl.'

'We never got any of them. We only ever knew about two letters. No wonder Nick always met the postman or went to the post office to collect the mail.'

'He's been very, very clever.'

Bitterly, Maddie said, 'Twisted, I'd say.'

'He must be in love with you himself, Maddie. That's the only explanation for all this, for everything he's done. He wants you for himself and he's tried to get rid of everyone else and . . .'

They were staring at each other now and then simultaneously they both cried, 'Nick.'

401

'It was him,' Michael said. 'He must have given Dad the arsenic and then, when they took him into hospital and started to do tests, he must have got scared and tried something else.'

'You – you mean, you think he caused the accident in the battery house?' Maddie was horrified to think that Nick could want to kill the man who had been like a father to him. 'But how could he have done it?'

Michael shook his head thoughtfully. 'I think he might somehow have caused a problem with the batteries.'

'But that wasn't what killed him. He fell backwards and hit his head. If Nick did plan it, he couldn't have been sure of that happening, could he?'

'No,' Michael agreed. 'But we've always been told how dangerous the battery house is. Dad instilled it into all of us. Maybe – maybe Nick *thought* it would kill him. It was just chance that, in a way, it did. But I still can't work out how he did it.'

Maddie bit her lip, frowning. 'There's something else I ought to remember, and I can't. It's – it's something about that night but I can't . . .'

Michael kissed her forehead and murmured, 'Don't worry, darling. Maybe it'll come back to you.' He sighed heavily. 'There's nothing going to make it come right, and yet . . .' His voice fell away as he murmured, 'I would like to know exactly what he did do.'

'And – and now? Do you really think he's been trying to poison his own mother?'

'I wouldn't put anything past him, not after what you've told me and what he tried to do today,' Michael said grimly. 'He could have killed Adam and Jenny, you know. By the way, where is Mrs T? Is she still in hospital?'

Maddie's eyes were wide as she gaped at him. Then, despite the sadness of the last hour or so and all the trauma they both knew they still had to face, she clapped her hand over mouth to silence the laughter that bubbled up inside her. 'Oh heck. I forgot all about her. She'll still be sitting there in her hat and coat waiting to be brought home.'

Fifty-Five

'There's something else,' Maddie said as they walked hand in hand out to the field where Steven and Adam were picking the heads from the tulips.

'Oh no,' Michael said. 'I really don't think I can handle any more.' He gave her a rueful smile as he said, 'Go on, then. My shoulders are broad enough.'

Indeed they were, Maddie thought, for a brief moment revelling in the strength of him that she needed so desperately at this moment, more than ever before.

'I think we ought to leave Mrs Trowbridge where she is for the moment, if the hospital can keep her. At least for another day, if we can.'

' 'Til we find Nick, you mean?'

'Well, that, yes,' Maddie agreed. 'But she said something very odd to me the last time I visited her. Nick put his arm round me when we were with her and she looked absolutely furious. I thought, like we've always known, that she doesn't want him to have a girlfriend or even friends of any sort, but it was more than that.'

'Go on.'

'She sent him out of the ward, said she wanted to speak to me alone. And do you know what she said?' They both stopped and turned to face each other, standing in the lane leading to the field. 'She said – she said that Nick is my half-brother.'

'Your what? How on earth does she make that out?'

'She said I was the bastard of her husband and Amelia Mayfield.'

Michael actually laughed aloud. 'Oh Maddie, this is getting dafter by the minute.'

But Maddie was not laughing. She said nothing and Michael's face sobered. He put his arm around her shoulders at the sight of her stricken face.

'Don't worry, darling. I'm back now and we'll sort everything out. I'm here to take care of you now. I'll look after you.'

They were the same words that Nick had used, but oh what a world of difference there was between the two people who uttered that same promise.

With Michael's arm around her, they walked on and came to stand at the end of the field, watching Adam and Steven moving steadily down the rows, carefully deheading the tulips. Field after field of blooms stretched far into the distance.

'You did it, my darling Tulip,' Michael said softly and at the sound of his loving nickname for her, Maddie's eyes filled with tears. The rainbow danced and blurred before her eyes, but now she allowed the tears to fall unashamedly and unchecked for they were tears of happiness. Michael was home, beside her once more, this time for ever.

They were all squeezed into Mrs Grange's tiny living room behind the shop, sitting around the table or in the two fireside chairs. Adam perched on the arm of one of them, leaning against his mother's shoulder. Even Theo was with them. He had arrived at Few Farm to tell Maddie the bad news, that the result of the post-mortem had revealed extensive amounts of arsenic in Frank's remains.

'It's no more than we expected, Mr Theo,' Michael had

said and went on to tell him swiftly of the day's cata-
strophic events, finishing by saying, 'We're just on our way
to Mrs Grange's – all of us . . .' he gestured not only
towards Maddie, but to Steven and Adam too. 'To see if
she can throw any light on the mystery for us. It might
help us to understand Nick a little better.'

'May I come along?' Theo had said. 'I think, with what
I've found out too, we may be able to piece things together.'

And so now they were sitting in the small room whilst
Mrs Grange bustled around with cups of tea and fancy
cakes. 'I'll just close the shop and then we won't be
disturbed,' she said. 'You are sure my little Jenny's going
to be all right, though? She's like a daughter to me, you
know.'

'She'll be fine, Mrs Grange. Honest,' Michael reassured
her.

'Oh Michael, it's so good to see you again. And I can't
think what Mrs Trowbridge will say when she knows
you've come home.'

'No,' Michael said quietly and glanced at Maddie.
'Neither can I.'

They waited, sipping their tea, whilst the woman scurried around her shop, locking the door and turning the
notice on the door to 'Closed', switching off the light and
emptying the till of its money. Returning to the room, she
dumped the cloth bag of notes and coins into a drawer in
the sideboard and took her place at the table, patting the
ever-present blue felt hat into place. 'Now then . . .' She
was smiling and seemed, Maddie thought, excited at the
prospect of being the centre of attention for the next few
minutes. 'How can I help you?'

Maddie saw Theo and Michael exchange a glance
before Michael took the lead and said, 'Mrs Grange, we

should be very grateful if you would tell us all you know about Mrs Trowbridge and Nick. About their past.'

The woman glanced at Theo, but when he smiled and nodded encouragement she took a deep breath and began. 'Well, it's all a long time ago now. Early Thirties it would be, Thirty-one or -two, something like that.'

They waited patiently, without interrupting her, whilst Mrs Grange dredged through her memory, reviving the old gossip of years ago.

'Harriet's name wasn't Trowbridge then, it was Cuppleditch.' She looked around the gathering triumphantly and was obviously disappointed when everyone stared at her blankly. 'She was Harriet Cuppleditch, married to John Cuppleditch?' Again there was silence whilst they waited for her explanation. But then as she opened her mouth to speak, Theo muttered, 'My God, you don't mean . . .?'

'I do,' Mrs Grange beamed. 'Him that hanged 'issen in your woods, Mr Theo.'

A ripple of movement went around the room as everyone shifted uneasily.

''Course it weren't your fault, Mr Theo,' Mrs Grange added hastily. 'You was only a bairn. The Cuppleditch family, John's parents that is,' she went on, 'all lived in one of Sir Peter's cottages. John's father, Matt, was Sir Peter's head groom and John, as soon as he left school, went to work with his dad in the stables. Harriet was a kitchen maid in the house. That's how they met. She lived in, of course, at the Hall. They did in them days. John married Harriet . . .' She paused and wrinkled her forehead. 'Come to think of it, I reckon Trowbridge was her maiden name. Yes, I'm sure it was. Anyway, they got married. They were too young, only eighteen or so and things didn't go right from the start. They moved in with

John's parents and there was already a big family of them. John was the eldest of five children, so at that time in their little cottage there'd have been mam, dad and four kids and then John and Harriet and their babby, Nick, when he was born . . .' she wagged her finger and smiled, 'only six months after they was wed, an' all. So it was a shotgun wedding.'

Maddie shuddered at the reference to a gun and put her arm around Adam. 'Well, about this time, Mr Theo, your sister, Miss Amelia, started to learn to ride and as young John was so good with the horses, they asked him to teach her.' She nodded at Theo. 'I bet your dad rued the day he'd had that bright idea.'

Theo said nothing but glanced down at his hand resting on the table, lines of sadness etched into his kind face.

'She was such a pretty little thing in those days, Miss Amelia. Always laughing and chattering. So friendly to everyone she met. She always made you feel you were her equal, you know what I mean?'

She did, Maddie thought, for Theo was just the same. He never played the lord and master like his father had done. He never tried to rule other people's lives. He just tried to help them. She felt a flush of embarrassment creep up her neck. The tale had to be told, Maddie knew, but she wished that Mrs Grange was not telling it with such glee.

'Well, as I say. She was so pretty, so lively, such fun and poor John's wife, Harriet, had turned into a real misery since she'd had the babby. Maybe if they'd had their own home, things would have been different. But who knows? Anyway, John and Amelia fell in love and when Sir Peter found out, he locked her away at the Hall. But it was too late. She was already expecting John's child.'

Maddie gasped aloud and knew now that the colour drained completely out of her face. Mrs Grange was looking at her now and nodding. 'That's what Harriet means. She thinks you're that child.'

Now Theo was leaning forward, his arms resting on the table. 'I never knew my sister had a child.'

Mrs Grange turned to look at him. 'You'd be too young to be told, Mr Theo. You were only about eight, if I remember rightly. Your father did everything he could to keep it secret. But in a village like this, there's not much that escapes us.' She tapped the side of her nose. 'But we know how to keep quiet when need be.'

Oh they'd have kept quiet all right, Maddie thought, with a sudden spurt of bitterness. They'd have gossiped and revelled in the juicy bit of scandal amongst themselves but the livelihood of most of the villagers depended on Sir Peter Mayfield. They'd have kept their counsel, all right. They'd have kept Sir Peter's family secret for him. Right until this very moment.

'And you mean to tell me that Amelia had a baby and she just dumped her outside the Orphanage?' Theo was quite defensive now. 'My sister would never have done such a thing.'

'Of course she wouldn't. But your father would and by the time the child was born, she was, well, a bit turned in her head, like. You see, John had hanged himself by then. She was grief-stricken and I expect they hustled the baby away and told her it was stillborn or summat.'

There was a murmur around the room.

Theo asked harshly, 'Why on earth did John hang himself?'

'When your father found out about them, he sacked both John's father, Matt, and John and turned the whole family, aye, Matt, his wife and all the bairns and John and his wife and child, out of the cottage. They lived rough in the woods for weeks and it was winter. February time, I reckon. Matt's wife was expecting another bairn . . .'

'Matt's wife?' Theo said. 'Don't you mean John's?'

But Mrs Grange was adamant. 'No, it were Matt's wife. I tell you there was a big family of them and you often get that, you know. A child can sometimes be older than its own aunt or uncle.'

Theo pulled a disbelieving face but said no more.

'Well, poor Matt's wife – Mary, I think they called her – gave birth there in the woods, in the freezing cold and she died. After that, John went haywire. Out of his mind with guilt. He was absolutely beside himself that not only had he been the cause of his whole family getting turned out of their home, but, indirectly, he'd caused his own mother's death. And, of course, he'd lost Amelia too. He just couldn't live with the burden of guilt, poor feller.'

There was silence before Maddie asked, 'What happened to the baby that was born in the woods?'

'Everyone thought it must have died, too, and been buried with the mother, because soon after, Matt left the district taking the older bairns with him, but there was no young babby with them when they left. Even I know that, because I saw them the day they went. He came into the shop, Matt did, to buy a bit of food, you know. I made him up a hamper, at me own expense, I did, 'cos I felt so sorry for the poor man.'

If she was expecting congratulations for her generosity, Mrs Grange was disappointed. Everyone in the room was far too shocked by what they were hearing to even think of it.

'But Mrs Trowbridge – I mean, Harriet Cuppleditch – stayed here?' Michael asked.

'Your dad took her in. A wonderful man was your

father, Michael. He'd lost your mam and he needed a housekeeper to look after him, and you, so he took Harriet and young Nick into his home and treated them like his own family.'

'So that's why Harriet would never mix with the village folk. She would only ever come as far as your shop.'

'Aye well, she knew I knew everything, but I'm no gossip.' She preened herself. 'I'm only telling you all this now because you asked me to.'

That was true, Maddie thought. The woman had made a few remarks over the years, hinted at the mystery, but she had never been guilty of rattling the skeletons in other people's cupboards.

But now she had her moment of glory and she was relishing it.

Theo glanced across the room towards Maddie, a thoughtful frown on his face. 'You say, Mrs Grange,' he said slowly, 'that Mrs Cuppleditch gave birth in February?'

'About then. I'm sure that's right. I know it wasn't long after Christmas.'

'And what year?'

'Like I said, Thirty-one or -two. Somewhere there.'

'I want you to be more precise than that, Mrs Grange, if you can. Please think back very carefully.'

There was silence as Mrs Grange tutted and huffed and puffed as if racking her brains. 'I know,' she said suddenly. 'It was about the same time as that little baby got kidnapped in America, 'cos I remember thinking . . .'

'You mean the Lindbergh baby?' Theo interrupted.

'Yes, that's it, because . . .'

'That was 1932. March 1932.' He gave a weak smile as if to apologize for seeming so clever. 'I had to swot up the case as part of my studies for my law exams,' he explained.

Maddie was staring at him. 'That's when I was left

outside the Home. That's why they called me Madeleine March. Because I was found in March and because – because the name Madeleine was written on a piece of paper and pinned to the blanket I was wrapped in. I heard Mrs Potter telling Mrs Trowbridge the day she came to . . .'

Suddenly it was all falling into place. There had always seemed something strange about the way Harriet, who never went out anywhere, had visited the orphanage to pick out a girl to work at Few Farm. Not *a* girl, Maddie realized now, but *the* girl. Again she remembered Harriet's words. 'Are you sure this is the one?' Harriet had, for some twisted reason of her own, sought out the child she believed had been born to her own husband's lover.

'But why?' Maddie asked and only realized she had voiced the question aloud when Michael said gently, 'Why what, love?'

'Oh, nothing. Go on, Theo. You were going to say something.'

'Well,' Theo said slowly, as if he too were thinking aloud. 'I've always been puzzled by you and Jenny.'

'Jenny?' Maddie was surprised.

'Mm. You see, there's a resemblance between you. People remark on it, don't they?'

Maddie nodded. 'We – we even called ourselves sisters at the Home and – and it was more than just because we had no family and wanted to belong to someone.'

'But you see,' Theo went on. 'Although you are a bit like each other, it's Jenny who always reminds me of my own sister.'

Now he stared straight at Maddie. 'I didn't know about my sister having a baby, but I do remember – very vividly – being told that she was very ill with an infectious disease and that I could not see her for several weeks. That was in the summer of 1932. And the reason I can remember it so clearly is because in the September I was hustled away to boarding school at eight years old and wasn't even allowed to say goodbye to Amelia. Now,' he added bitterly, 'I know why.'

'So you think,' Michael was leaning forward, 'that Jenny is your sister's child.'

'Yes. I do.'

'So. What about Maddie? Who is she?'

Now everyone's eyes turned to look at Maddie and she felt herself reddening under their scrutiny.

'I think she's the baby that everyone believed had died in the woods. I think she's Matt Cuppleditch's child.'

There was silence whilst everyone digested Theo's reasoning. They must all have found it plausible for not one of them raised any argument.

Michael reached out and took her hand in his. 'So somewhere, Maddie, my darling, you do have a family.'

'You're my family, you and Adam,' she said and began to say, 'I don't need . . .' But she stopped mid-sentence. She did need them. She wanted desperately to know the rest of her family. The realization surprised her. She had thought herself a loner, able to cope with life on her own, but suddenly she found herself longing to know the truth.

As if reading what was in her mind, Theo said gently, 'If we can find Matt Cuppleditch or his older children, they could confirm whether the baby did die or whether he left the child at the Home. But Maddie,' there was compassion in his eyes as he looked across the room at her, 'just remember how very difficult it must have been for him . . .'

She was shaking her head. 'Oh I don't blame him, don't think that. If anyone's to blame then it's . . .' She stopped, appalled at what she had been about to say.

'I know,' Theo said softly, his deep voice suddenly shaky with emotion. 'Don't think I condone the part my father must have played in all this.'

'You were only a bairn, Mr Theo,' Mrs Grange reached across the table and patted his arm. 'Only eight years old. No one can possibly blame you.'

'I know, Mrs Grange. But at least now I can try to put things right a little. With your agreement, Maddie, I'll try to find the Cuppleditch family and then we'll see, eh?'

She nodded, but then added in a whisper, 'But what about the other business, Theo? What about the forensic evidence they've just found?'

'I don't think you have anything to worry about that any more, Maddie, my dear. It's obvious now who did try to poison Frank and his own mother.'

'Nick?'

Soberly, Theo nodded. 'He was obviously in love with you, but that love became an obsession. A dangerous obsession.'

'What do you think he'll do? I mean after he ran away from the farm and we haven't seen him since? Where do you think he's gone?'

Theo sighed. 'There's no knowing what he might do. He knows now that he can never have you. Michael's return has shown him that.'

'Oh no! No!' Maddie's eyes were wide and her hand fluttered nervously to her mouth. 'Oh, he wouldn't, would he?'

'What? What are you thinking, Maddie?' Michael asked urgently as she turned tear-filled eyes towards him.

Her voice was a hoarse, terrified whisper as she said, 'His father, John Cuppleditch, couldn't have the girl he loved and look what he did.'

Fifty-Six

They found him hanging from the very same tree where, twenty-seven years earlier, his father had died.

The police took charge. It was they who cut his body down and gently carried him out of the wood to the waiting ambulance that took him away to the mortuary.

'How are we to tell his mother?' Maddie said, as she and Michael stood with their arms around each other watching the vehicle bounce away over the uneven ground until it reached the road.

'I think I had better do that, don't you?'

'I think you're the only one who can. You or Adam, but he's far too young to have to do that.'

'Are you going to tell Jenny?'

'Yes, yes. That'll be a mixture of sadness and joy, won't it? Poor Nick is dead and yet, we are pretty sure now that we are related. Not sisters, but aunt and niece.'

'You must tell her what Theo said, that once she knows the truth, he wants to take her to meet her mother, Amelia.'

'He's such a kind man, Michael. I don't know what I'd have done without him these past few weeks. Even over the years, if it comes to that.'

'Should I be jealous?'

Maddie had no such pretensions. She had not believed Nick's ravings. 'No. He's just a really kind person. I'm glad . . .' She stopped and only went on again, haltingly, when Michael prompted her. 'I was going to say, I'm glad he's running things now, but that sounds as if I'm glad Sir Peter is the way he is. Paralysed and unable to speak. But I wouldn't wish that on anyone.'

'I know. But Fate has a peculiar way of sorting things out sometimes. Maybe it's all for the best, eh?'

Jenny was ecstatic to think she was really related to Maddie.

'Now don't get your hopes up too much,' Maddie tried to warn her. 'Theo's got to trace the Cuppleditch family first and even then . . .'

'Oh we are, Maddie, I just know we are.' Sitting up in the hospital bed, her hand and leg swathed in bandages, nevertheless Jenny looked the happiest she had ever looked. 'I'll have to start calling you "Auntie Maddie".'

'There are two people waiting outside to see you,' Maddie teased her. 'Each with the biggest bouquet of flowers I have ever seen in my life. I reckon they're trying to vie with each other to outdo the other.'

Jenny's eyes widened. 'I suppose – I hope . . .' she said firmly, her eyes sparkling with love, 'that one is Stinky Smith.'

They giggled together like two schoolgirls. 'But,' Jenny went on. 'Who's the other one?'

'Your "Uncle Theo"!'

'How did she take it?'

Maddie, her task the easier one of the two, was anxious to know how Michael had fared having to tell Harriet about Nick.

'Surprisingly well, but I had a long talk with the sister

before I told her, just to make sure it was all right to do
so, you know, and they're going to keep her in for another
few days to make sure she doesn't have a bad reaction to
such awful news.'

Michael's face was grey with sadness. Maddie put her
arms around him. 'It must have been awful for you to
have to tell her that, especially the first time you saw her
after all this time.'

'That's what's worrying me, really. I'm just wondering
whether she really took it in about Nick. I mean, she was
so pleased to see me and then she was asking about Adam
and telling me all about him and what I'd missed by
staying away. As if it was my fault,' he added bitterly.

Horrified, Maddie said, 'You didn't tell her everything
Nick's done?'

''Course I didn't. It was bad enough what I did have to
tell her. Mind you, maybe she ought to be told some day.'

'We'll see,' Maddie said.

He glanced at her and then looked away again, an
anxious look in his dark eyes. 'Maddie, what are we going
to do about her?'

'Do about her? What do you mean, do about her?'

'Well, what's going to happen to her when she's fit
enough to come out of hospital?'

Maddie blinked at him, not understanding. 'Am I being
particularly thick or something? I thought she'd come back
here. This is her home, isn't it? You don't mean you don't
want her here, Michael?'

'No, no,' he said swiftly as relief flooded his face. 'But I
thought you might not. After all, she's never been very
nice to you, has she?'

Maddie smiled. '"Born and bred in a briar patch, Brer
Fox, born and bred in a briar patch."'

'Eh?'

She laughed. 'Oh never mind. You ask Jen sometime. She'll tell you what it means, to her and me anyway. But to get back to Mrs T. You're right. She's never liked me, but now I know why, I can understand. But she loves Adam. Don't ask me why, when he's my son, but she does. She's always loved him more than she loved her own flesh and blood. Maybe because he was *your* son. Even when I first came here, I could see that you were her favourite.'

'Poor Nick,' Michael murmured and shook his head sorrowfully.

Yes, it was poor Nick, she thought for even though he had robbed her of eleven years of her life and put her family through a frightening ordeal, she felt no bitterness towards him, no hatred or resentment. What she felt for the unhappy young man was an overwhelming pity.

'It's very sad when no one in the world loves you, not even your own mother.' There was such a wistful sadness in Maddie's voice that Michael put his arms around her and held her close.

'I love you, Maddie. I always have, from the first moment you came to the farm.'

She nestled against him, feeling safe and really loved now. For the first time in the whole of her life she knew she was loved and wanted by the man she had given her heart to. 'But I know what it feels like. Both Jen and me know just what it feels like.'

He stroked her hair. 'I know, I know. And I'm going to do my damnedest to find your family for you.'

She put her arms around him. 'You're my family. You and Adam. We're a real family now.'

He chuckled and she heard the sound deep in his chest. 'Well, we will be once I can drag you to the church and get a ring firmly on your finger, Mrs Brackenbury. Oh hell!'

He stopped and she lifted her head and looked into his eyes. 'What is it?'

He looked down at her. 'I've just thought. I hope there's no bar to me marrying my step-mother.'

They stared at each other and then simultaneously, they both burst into fits of laughter, leaning against each other.

'It's – it's not funny,' Maddie gasped.

'I know,' Michael spluttered. 'It's – it's deadly serious.' He fell back on the bed, his chest heaving as he fought to control his mirth – and failed.

Maddie flopped down beside him and soon the laughter subsided as they lay in each other's arms and found again the joy they had known so long ago.

Fifty-Seven

They brought Harriet home from the hospital three days later.

'Sit down by the fire, Mrs T,' Michael said, 'and . . .'

'Now stop fussing me, Michael. I'm quite fit again now. Just let me get back into my kitchen. Maddie's no time to be running about after me. The work's all fallen on her shoulders now.' For a moment the lines on her face drooped with sadness and, despite her protestations, she sat down heavily in the chair.

'You take it easy, Mrs Trowbridge. We can manage,' Maddie tried to keep her voice cheerful.

The woman looked at Michael and no one could have missed the hope and joy in her tone as she asked, 'You're staying? You've come home?'

Michael smiled and nodded. 'You're not going to get rid of me again, Mrs T, I'm afraid.'

She reached up and touched his face and said huskily, 'I never wanted it in the first place, lad.'

He held her hands and bent over her. 'I know, I know. But I'm back now – at least I will be once I've got myself out of the Army – and we're going to take care of you.' He glanced at Maddie to include her, to make sure that Harriet understood just how it was going to be. 'We're all going to take care of each other.'

'Where's my boy?' Harriet asked suddenly, giving both Maddie and Michael a shock. They exchanged a worried

420

glance but then at Harriet's next words they both breathed a sigh of relief. 'Where's Adam?'

'He'll be in later.'

Harriet nodded and, with a sigh of contentment lay back in the chair, and closed her eyes.

Michael gestured to Maddie and they were about to creep away, when she said, 'I'm sorry for what Nicholas did. I'm sorry he hurt the two of you the way he did.'

They turned and looked down at her, exchanged another glance and with mutual silent agreement sat down.

'Who told you?' Michael asked gently.

'I worked a lot of it out for myself. I've had a lot of time to think laid there in that hospital bed.' She sniffed. 'Uncomfortable beds they are. I'll be pleased to get back into me own tonight.'

Maddie hid her smile.

'And then,' Harriet went on, 'there was a lot of whispering in the ward. I heard snatches when they thought I was asleep. What's happened to Jenny? Something's happened to Jenny, hasn't it?'

'She's going to be fine. She was hurt, but she's going to be all right.'

'How? What did he do?'

'The gun went off. I don't think he meant . . .' Michael was trying to be kind, but Harriet said sharply, 'Gun? He had the gun?'

'He was trying to protect Maddie. He – he wanted Maddie himself.'

Harriet nodded. 'I guessed as much.' She looked at Maddie now. 'Did you want him?'

Maddie shook her head. 'No. I've never wanted anyone in my life except Michael.'

Harriet nodded. 'You shouldn't have married Mr Frank, you know.'

'No, I know that now. I'm sorry if . . .'

Harriet flapped her hand. 'Oh, I don't mean because of me. He'd have never married me.' She smiled sadly. 'I loved him, of course, but if he'd felt anything for me except pity, he'd have married me long before that, now wouldn't he?'

Michael and Maddie were silent for there was no answer they could give without wounding the woman further.

'I was as bad as you,' Harriet nodded towards Maddie. 'I should never have married John. Oh, I thought I was in love with him. He was me first boyfriend, but we were so young. And silly. When I found I was expecting, we got married. It was the only thing to do in them days or end up in a home for unmarried mothers.' She shuddered. 'I tried to be a good wife to him. I cooked, washed and cleaned for him. Bore him a son. All men want sons, don't they? So they say. And then how did he repay me? Seduced the daughter of his employer and got us all thrown out of our home. I didn't deserve that. None of us did.'

No, Maddie wanted to cry, but did you ever show him affection? Did you make him feel loved? Did you let him know that you needed him? Aloud, all she could say was, 'No, of course you didn't deserve that. I'm sorry.'

'But living with his folks, we never had a chance and the love died. Then, of course, when he fell for Miss Amelia . . .' She broke off and looked at Maddie again. 'I did come to the Home to pick you out, you know. I knew their baby had been abandoned outside the Home. One of the maids who worked at the Hall knew about it. I reckon the whole village knew, but nobody ever said a word. I was curious to see what his child was like. I wanted – I wanted . . .' For a moment she dropped her head down as she whispered, 'I wanted to take revenge on you. And then I even used you like a weapon over Sir Peter.'

'Sir Peter?' Now Maddie was mystified.

Harriet nodded. 'That time you and Mr Frank went to the Hall and he wouldn't give his permission to change the use of his land. I went to see him the next morning.'

So, Maddie thought, remembering now, Theo had been right.

'I – I threatened to tell all I knew about him leaving Amelia's child – his own grandchild – outside the orphanage.' She put her hand across her face now in shame. 'And the next day he had that stroke. I must have caused it.'

Now it was Maddie who reached out and took the wrinkled hand between her own. 'Don't, Mrs Trowbridge. Don't upset yourself. It's over now. All in the past.'

'No, no,' Harriet's voice was stronger. 'I must tell you. I want to talk about it. It's been like a weight all these years. Maybe if I'd told Nicholas the truth, talked to him about his father, been honest and open, then maybe all this would never have happened. I've got to take a share of the blame.'

'No, no . . .' Michael began, but she shook her head, denying him the right to excuse her.

'Poor Nicholas,' she said. 'I never wanted him in the first place and then I resented him because of what his father had done and I shouldn't have done that. It was cruel.' She sighed. 'And crueller still of me to love you, Michael, more than my own flesh and blood. But I couldn't help it. You were such a sunny-natured little boy and Nicholas was always so difficult. It was so easy to love you.'

And then Adam, too, because he had been Michael's son, Maddie thought, but she said nothing.

'Maybe if I'd shown Nicholas more affection . . .' Harriet sighed heavily and added, 'I can't turn the clock back, can I?' She patted Maddie's hand. 'But I can try to make it up to you.'

'Mrs Trowbridge, there's something you ought to know. We've – er – found out a bit more in the last few days. We've talked to Theo and, well . . .' Maddie faltered, not knowing if she could carry on. She looked to Michael for help.

Responding, he took over, saying gently, 'We believe that Maddie is not your husband's child, but his sister.'

'His sister?'

Michael nodded. 'There was a baby born in the woods, wasn't there, to John's mother?'

Harriet nodded. 'Yes. There was. I was there. I was there when poor Mary gave birth.' Harriet shuddered. 'You could hear her screams echoing through the trees. It was awful.'

'And she died, didn't she?' Michael prompted. 'Mary, did you say her name was?'

Harriet nodded. 'Yes, she died that same night. There in the woods, in the freezing cold.' She paused and then went on. 'After that, the villagers took pity on us all. Your father took me and Nicholas in and folk in the village looked after the rest of the family. I think they all felt guilty when they heard what had happened. All except Sir Peter, that is. He hadn't an ounce of pity in him, that man.'

'And the baby? Mary's baby?' Maddie asked softly.

Harriet glanced at her. 'She stayed with her father and later, I heard she had died, though I was surprised 'cos when she was born she was a lusty little thing, a real fighter, you know.' Harriet was staring at Maddie now as the realization crept into her mind and she murmured, 'A real little fighter, just like you.'

There was silence in the room, the only sound the singing of the kettle on the hob.

'We think,' Michael went on, 'that when the family left the village, they left the baby at the Home.'

Harriet nodded, though her gaze was still fastened on Maddie. 'To think that I helped deliver you, there in the darkness and the cold. I held you and tried to keep you warm against me. I even fed you from my own breast because I still had milk . . . And all this time I thought you'd died.'

Gently, Michael said, 'There's something else we must tell you.' He hesitated, unsure how Harriet would take the news. 'We believe that the other child, Amelia's baby, is – is Jenny.'

Harriet's gaze swivelled and fastened on Michael. 'Jenny?'

'Yes. Mr Theo says she resembles his sister, although there is a likeness between Maddie and Jenny. But there would be, wouldn't there? After all, they are aunt and niece.'

Harriet nodded slowly. 'Yes, yes, they would be. And you and me,' she turned again to look at Maddie. 'We're sisters-in-law, then, aren't we?'

Maddie nodded.

A smile twitched at the corner of Harriet's mouth. 'So, I picked the wrong one from the Home, then, did I?'

'Seems like it.'

'Serves me right,' and added with some of her familiar spirit, 'I shouldn't have been such a bitter, twisted old bat.'

'How – how shall you feel about Jenny now?' Maddie had to ask, had to know, for Jenny was a very important part of her life and always would be.

Harriet sighed and leant her head back against the chair. 'It's over now, all over. I don't feel that awful hatred any more. Just a terrible sadness. I shan't take it out on Jenny, I promise you.'

Impulsively, Maddie leant forward and kissed Harriet's pale cheek. 'Thank you, Mrs Trowbridge. Now, Michael and I must get some work done. We've a float to build for the Parade on Saturday. You sit and rest.'

'No, no.' Harriet heaved herself up. 'I've some ginger-bread men to make for Adam when he comes home. I promised. Besides, I can't wait to get back into me kitchen. I 'spect it's in a right mess.'

Maddie chuckled. She had never thought that she would be thankful to hear that the housekeeper had not lost all her grumbling ways.

'Right, we'll be off.'

'Dinner will be ready at twelve thirty and don't be late in.'

'No, Mrs Trowbridge.'

'I suppose,' Harriet said, 'now that we're sisters-in-law, you'd better call me "Harriet".'

Maddie grinned at her. 'I'd prefer "Mrs T".'

Harriet smiled, tremulously at first, but with a growing sureness. 'Mrs T, it is, then.'

They left her to return to her kitchen and her work of caring for the household. 'We must fetch Adam home,' Maddie said softly, closing the door between the kitchen and the wash-house, behind her. 'It'll help her to have him back here.'

Reaching up to lift a coat down from the pegs and searching for his Wellingtons, Michael said, 'The sooner the better. I can't wait to start getting to know my son.'

But Maddie was hardly listening, she was staring at the yellow scarf that Michael had just uncovered as he removed the coat from the peg. Nick's scarf.

'What is it, love? You look as if you've just seen a ghost.'

Maddie leant against the wall, her gaze still on the scarf. 'I – I feel as if I have. I've just remembered something else.'

'Oh, what you were trying to remember about the night Dad died?'

Maddie shook her head. 'No, no, not that. Something else. When he got injured with a fork.'

'Injured? You didn't tell me about that. What happened?'

Swiftly, Maddie recounted the events, ending up by saying, 'I remember Nick saying that he didn't hear Frank coming so close to him because he had his scarf tied tightly round his ears against the wind.' She stared at Michael now, her eyes wide. 'I was so upset at the time, it didn't register properly, but I do remember later looking at that scarf here on the peg, so he couldn't have been wearing it. Oh Michael, do you think he did that on purpose, too?'

'Wouldn't be at all surprised,' Michael said drily. 'And when I get time, I'm going to have a snoop around the battery house, just to see if I can piece together how he did that. Because I'm sure now that he did. What I can't understand is *how* he did it, if you say he was away for the night. He could have easily done something if he'd been here, but he had to be away, didn't he, to make it so that Frank had to be the one to go out?'

'Oh!' Maddie clapped her hand over her mouth. 'Now I've remembered. It was Jenny.'

'Jenny?'

'Yes, she said that Steven thought he'd seen Nick on his bicycle in the village that night and I said no, he must have been mistaken and it must have been the following night, the night Nick came back, that he'd seen him. But now . . .'

Grimly, Michael nodded. 'It's all starting to fit together now, Maddie. Come on, we're going to look around that barn right now.'

Fifty-Eight

It took them two hours of searching every nook and cranny in the battery house and then in the big barn; of feeling along dusty shelves, of sweeping cobwebs from every corner and scrabbling through rusty, neglected tools.

'What exactly am I looking for?' Maddie stood back, smudges of grime on her face.

'I'm not really sure, I . . .' Michael glanced at her and then came towards her, 'Oh Maddie, you look just like the day I first saw you.' Gently, he wiped away the smudge from her forehead and then kissed her.

Playfully, she smacked his arm. 'Now don't start that, else I'll take you into the hay shed again . . .'

Michael chuckled. 'I'm game if you are.'

They fell against each other, kissing and laughing until Maddie said breathlessly, 'Oh do stop. We must find whatever it is we're supposed to be looking for.'

'Yes. Right,' Michael said, firmly setting her away from him. 'Remind me later to carry on where I left off, though.'

'Oh I will. I certainly will,' she whispered and they smiled at each other.

It was when Michael tipped out the bin that held the corn for Harriet's hens that they both heard the chink of metal on the concrete floor. Squatting down, they delved beneath the pile of corn and unearthed a round brown knob, very similar to the knob on the control panel in the battery house. Michael picked it out and wiped away the dust. He stood up slowly, holding it in the centre of his outstretched palm. 'So, that's how he did it?'

'How? What is it?'

'A metal knob instead of a bakelite one. The minute Dad touched this, he would have got a nasty shock.'

'Would that account for the marks on his hand?'

'Probably. I think Nick hid somewhere . . .' He glanced about him towards the buildings on two sides of the big barn. 'In here somewhere, maybe. He'd've had to move the spring pointer off the studs to change the knob,' Michael murmured, thinking aloud. 'So then the lights would go out and he'd leave them off so that someone would come out. But how did he know it wouldn't be you?'

Maddie shook her head. 'Frank never taught me anything about the battery house.' She shuddered. 'But I nearly did come out that night. I didn't want Frank to come out in the cold and I wanted him to tell me what to do.'

'But Dad did come out,' Michael said softly, 'just as Nick hoped.'

'Then what?'

'Well, I think after the accident had happened, he switched the knobs back somehow, hiding this one deep in this bin. Mrs T would never have guessed what it was, even if she'd ever found it. Then I think he did leave and that's when Steven saw him cycling through the village.'

'You're – you're not going to tell Mrs T all this are you?'

Michael shook his head. 'No. There's no need. The poor woman's got enough to come to terms with. No, Maddie we'll keep this just between ourselves.'

For a moment he gripped the metal knob tightly in his hand and Maddie saw tears sparkle in his eyes. 'Poor Dad,' he said, brokenly.

Maddie went to him and they put their arms around one another, each remembering Frank Brackenbury in their own special way.

It was the day of the Tulip Parade and everyone at Few Farm was trying to put the recent nightmare behind them.

Nick had been buried quietly in the lonely corner of the churchyard near his father. Only his mother, Michael and Maddie were there to mourn him. Although Harriet had shed no tears, she had clung to Michael's arm and leant heavily against him throughout the short service conducted at the graveside. Maddie could understand the tumult of emotions the woman must be feeling. Her own feelings were chaotic; sadness for poor Nick and for Frank, who should still have been with them. Yet there was joy, too, in having Michael home and knowing he loved her. And then, there was Jenny. Her darling little Jenny Wren. They really were related after all. If only, Maddie had thought as the vicar's voice droned on, if only I could know the rest of my family . . .

Now, today, they all wanted the Tulip Parade to signify a new beginning. Maddie and Michael had worked through the night to finish their float for the Parade. Adam had been sent to bed, still protesting, at midnight but they had stayed in the big barn all night, pinning the tulip heads on to the straw matting.

'Who made the frame? It's very clever,' Michael asked, standing back to admire the shape of the huge tulip sitting on the open back of the farm truck. Even the cab was decorated with an archway of flowers above it in rows of different colours, like a rainbow of tulips in the sky.

'Steven's brother, Ron. He works as the blacksmith now. He's very clever with his hands. Must get it from his

431

dad.' She paused a moment, the head of a golden tulip resting in the palm of her hand. 'I wonder what I get from my family?'

'A way with animals, I shouldn't wonder. I'll never forget the way you handled Ben and waded in amongst the cows without batting an eyelid.' They smiled at each other, remembering. 'By the way what happened to poor old Ben?'

'He was so miserable after your dad died and with no real work to do since the cows had gone, we let him go to a farmer near Holbeach. It – it . . .' She hesitated again. 'It was Nick's idea.'

'Even wanted the poor old dog out of the way, eh?' There was silence before Michael went on, 'Yes, I reckon that's what you've got from your family. Their way with animals . . .' He grinned at her. 'To say nothing of a way with people, too. Your dad was head groom for Sir Peter and didn't Mrs Grange say that your brother was very good with them, too? That was how he came to teach Miss Amelia to ride?'

'Mm,' Maddie said absently, now scarcely listening. She had latched on to the words 'your brother' and now she said them aloud, savouring the sound of them. 'My brother.'

'What? What did you say, love?'

She smiled self-consciously, but there was no need to be shy with Michael. Never again would there be secrets or awkwardness between them. 'I was just trying out how it sounded. My brother. I've never been able to say it before.'

'Or dad. You've never said that either.'

'No,' she said wistfully. 'Do you think I'll ever get the chance?'

''Course you will. Trust Mr Theo. He'll find them. He said he would.'

Maddie smiled at the almost childlike faith Michael now had in Theo. Any charges against Maddie had been dropped as soon as Theo had explained to the police all that had happened. They were satisfied that the tragic young man who had taken his own life had also been guilty of administering arsenic to Frank, to his own mother and even allowing Maddie to stand accused of his crimes.

'Mr Theo's put adverts in this week's local papers already, hasn't he?'

'Yes, but they could be anywhere. My father could be dead. He'll be quite old by now, won't he?'

'Well, getting on a bit, yes. But that doesn't mean to say he's not still alive. How many other brothers and sisters did Mrs Grange say there were, apart from poor John?'

Maddie remembered exactly. 'Four besides me and John. But I don't know whether they were girls or boys. Maybe somewhere I really have got a sister.'

'Harriet would know.'

'Yes, I've thought about that. But I don't like to keep bringing the subject up. I don't want to upset her.'

'I shouldn't worry too much about that. She seems her old self again.' He grinned at Maddie. 'Ordering us all about, just like she always used to. I even heard her call you "girl" the other day.'

Maddie laughed. 'Yes, she did. But somehow, it doesn't have the same sting to it now. And,' she added pulling a comical face, 'at my advanced age, it's quite a compliment.'

'There,' Michael said as he popped the last tulip head into place. 'I think that's finished. What do you think?'

Maddie felt the lump in her throat. 'It's beautiful.'

'And all our own work,' Michael said proudly.

433

'With a bit of help from Stinky Smith and his brother,' Maddie reminded him.

'Oh yes. Who's going to be the Tulip Queen?'

'A young lass from the town.'

'It ought to be you,' Michael put his arm around her.

'I'm too old,' Maddie laughed and kissed him. 'But thanks for the compliment.' They stood admiring their handiwork. 'Who's going to drive it in the Parade? You?'

'No, I think we'll let Ron Smith drive it for us. He's earned it, don't you think? Besides,' he gave her waist a squeeze, 'I want to watch the Parade with you and Adam. I can't bear to be parted from you for as long as an hour,' he teased.

'Now you can stop all that canoodling,' came Harriet's voice behind them at that moment. 'Your breakfast's ready.'

They turned to find her standing in the doorway of the barn and went towards her, their arms still around each other. Michael put his free arm about the older woman and together they went into the house.

'Maddie! Maddie!'

They were standing watching the Parade, the four of them, when Maddie heard Jenny's voice calling her name and turned to see her pushing her way through the crowd.

Her hand was still bandaged and she was limping slightly, but Jenny was smiling happily.

'Are you all right?' Maddie said as she hugged her. 'Should you be out of hospital so soon?'

Jenny giggled. 'They couldn't keep me. They took all the bits of shot out and I badgered the doctor to let me out. But Steven and – and Theo . . .' she glanced back over her shoulder, 'have been so kind. They scarcely let me out of their sight. If Steven's not with me bullying me to take care, then Theo is. Oh Maddie, it's so wonderful to have a real family and what's even better is to know that we – you and me – are really related. Every morning when I wake up and remember, I still can't quite believe it.'

Maddie felt a swift stab of envy, but immediately felt guilty. She had her family. Michael and Adam, and even Harriet now, and still she had Jenny. She would have to be satisfied with that.

Jenny was interrupting her wandering thoughts. 'When the Parade's over, Theo wants us all to meet him at the White Hart for tea. Mrs Trowbridge as well.' Jenny leant closer to Maddie and whispered, 'Does she know about me?' When Maddie nodded, Jenny added, 'And how did she take it?'

'All right. She's changed.' Maddie grinned, 'Well, not *that* much, but she's coming to terms with the past. No more grudges.'

Jenny gave a sigh of relief. 'Thank goodness. Anyway, you'll come to the tea party then?'

There was an air of excitement about Jenny and Maddie wondered briefly if there was an announcement to be made about Steven and herself. Maybe, Maddie thought, they've finally set a date for their wedding.

'We'll be there,' Maddie promised. 'All of us.'

'Good. I must go. See you later . . .' And she disappeared into the crowd as quickly as she had come.

'It's going to grow and grow, this Parade, Maddie. Whoever thought it up, it's a brilliant idea.'

'Well, Steven was in on it from the first, but several people have all worked together to make it happen.'

'Only a few floats this year but, you watch, every year there'll be more and more.'

'Look, Mam. Here it comes. The first one's the Tulip

435

Queen.' Adam was pointing excitedly to the first float in the procession. The pretty girl in a long white dress and a tiara upon her head, sat at the centre of a huge flower with red petals, waving to the crowd as the float passed by. The following decorated lorry had a large crown fashioned out of metal and adorned with flower heads. After that came a car with a circle of flowers around it at bumper level, so wide that it doubled the width of the car.

'How on earth is he going to get that round corners?' Michael laughed.

Then came a tractor almost completely covered with red flowers and the lettering 'Join the YFC' picked out in golden tulip heads. The next float was their own from Few Farm, proudly driven by Ron Smith almost hidden beneath the profusion of flowers.

'Oh Mam, just look at that one.' The last float in the procession was perhaps the biggest of all; an enormous butterfly, the details of its wing markings picked out with different coloured tulips.

'Isn't that beautiful?' Maddie breathed. 'Steven was right, when he said there ought to be a better way than just dumping the discarded heads. What a lovely way to make use of them.'

'Now, next year,' Michael was laughing beside her, 'we'll build the biggest and the best float ever.'

Despite all the recent tragedy that had touched them all, a warm glow of happiness spread through Maddie's soul. Michael would be here, with her and Adam, next year and all the years to come.

Even if she never found out the truth about her family, she could be happy with that.

Fifty-Nine

As the last marching band passed them by, Michael said, 'Come along, we'd better go and find Jenny and Steven – and Mr Theo.'

He was waiting for them in the bar at the White Hart and came forward to greet them.

'I've hired a private room,' he told them. 'But before we go in . . .' He took Maddie's hand and looked down at her. 'I have a surprise for you, Maddie, but I thought I should, in fairness, warn you.' His glance went beyond her now to Harriet. 'And you, Mrs Trowbridge. I didn't want it to be a shock for you. For either of you.'

Puzzled, Harriet glanced at Michael, who put his face close to hers and whispered in her ear. For a moment the woman looked startled, but then she nodded. 'I'll be all right, Mr Theo. Maddie has a right to . . .'

Before she could say any more, Theo smiled and put his finger to his lips. 'Not another word, Mrs Trowbridge, or you'll spoil my fun.' He held out his arm to Maddie and said softly, 'Are you ready?'

Maddie gave a laugh that sounded strangely nervous. 'Well, I'm not quite sure what for, but yes.'

Michael, with Harriet on his arm and Adam bringing up the rear, followed behind them.

As he opened the door, she saw Steven first and then Jenny sitting beside Amelia Mayfield and holding her hand.

'Oh Theo. I'm so glad. How lovely to see them

437

together.' In a low voice she asked, 'Does your sister understand?'

Quietly, Theo said, 'I'm not sure, but we're hoping in time . . .'

'Oh thank you, thank you for doing this for Jenny . . .' Maddie began to say, but Theo was shaking his head. 'That's not the surprise, Maddie.'

She became aware then that there were three other people standing at the far side of the room. An old man, leaning on a stick, and a younger man and woman standing one on either side of him.

Maddie looked at them and when her glance came to rest on the woman, her mouth opened in a shocked gasp. She was older than Maddie, possibly by as much as ten years, but she had the same fair hair, the same blue eyes, and even the same saucy smile that lit up her eyes until they sparkled.

It could be me in a few years time, Maddie thought. And then she knew. This was her sister. It had to be.

Theo was leading her towards them and she was clinging to his arm, suddenly afraid that her legs were going to let her down.

The old man was staring at her and as she drew closer she could see that tears were coursing down his wrinkled cheeks, but still he never took his gaze away from her. And as she stood before him, she heard his whisper. 'Madeleine.'

The stick fell out of his grasp and clattered to the floor. The old man tottered and swiftly the two on either side of him caught hold of him and steadied him. But he seemed oblivious to his own frailty, for he was stretching out both his arms to Maddie.

She went into them, putting her own arms around his neck and murmuring, 'Dad, oh my daddy.'

'My baby, my baby!' He was weeping openly now against her neck and clutching her to him. 'I'm sorry. Forgive me. It broke my heart to leave you, but I couldn't take care of you. You might have died like my poor Mary. I didn't know what else to do. Forgive me. Forgive me.'

There was scarcely a dry eye in the room. Even Harriet was fishing in her handbag for her handkerchief.

And then as Maddie drew back and looked into Matt Cuppleditch's face, she held his hands between her own and said, 'It's all right. It's all right, really. There's nothing to forgive. I'm just so happy to have found you.' She looked to the two standing beside him. 'All of you.'

Then they were all laughing and crying together. Theo brought a chair for Matt and they clustered around him, all speaking at once.

'We saw the piece in the paper and showed it to Dad,' the woman began to explain. 'Then Roland . . .' she nodded towards the man, 'rang Mr Theo.'

'I wanted to come back for you, so many times,' the old man was murmuring, 'but I felt so ashamed of just leaving you there . . .'

'We're living near King's Lynn now. It's not far away . . .'

'He's talked so often about you. I'm Alison, by the way. Aren't we alike . . .?'

Her brother, Roland, was interrupting. 'There's two more of us, but they live in London. They're coming to see you as soon as they can. But they've families. You've more nephews and nieces, besides Jenny.' He smiled across at Jenny, anxious to include her.

'You know about Jenny?' Maddie asked and her new-found brother nodded. 'Mr Mayfield . . .'

'Theo, please,' Theo put in.

Roland smiled, 'Theo has explained everything.'

There was no bitterness, no recriminations, they were just so happy, all of them, to be reunited. The only difficult moment was when Maddie turned and drew Harriet forward. 'You remember Harriet, don't you?'

There was a silence in the room now as everyone watched and waited.

Matt looked up at her and then held out his hand. 'Of course we do. How are you, my dear?'

Harriet was overcome and unable to speak but she took the old man's outstretched hand and nodded vigorously. Relieved, everyone began to talk at once again.

It was all right. Everything was going to be all right.

To one side of the room, unseen by Maddie, Michael held out his hand to Theo. 'Thank you, Mr Theo, for all you've done for Maddie. Thank you for making her happiness complete.'

Theo took his hand and placed his other hand on Michael's shoulder. His voice was husky as he said, 'You're a lucky man, Michael Brackenbury. Take care of her, won't you?'

'Oh I will, Mr Theo. I will.'